THE BUTCHER'S BOY

and

NIGHTLIFE

THE BUTCHER'S BOY

and

NIGHTLIFE

Thomas Perry

Quercus

This omnibus edition published in 2009 by Quercus
The Butcher's Boy first published in Great Britain in 1982
Nightlife first published in Great Britain in 2007 by Quercus

21 Bloomsbury Square
London
WC1A 2NS

A CIP catalogue record for this book is available
from the British Library

ISBN 978 1 84916 096 4

Printed and bound in Great Britain by CPI Bookmarque, Croydon

10 9 8 7 6 5 4 3 2 1

THE BUTCHER'S BOY

INTRODUCTION

Michael Connelly

It used to be that the quickest way for me to descend into a creative depression would be for someone to approach me and identify him- or herself as a fan of my work, but to then add the dreadful line 'But your first one is still my favorite.'

It didn't matter if the approach was in person at a bookstore or on the street, or through the U.S. mail or the Internet. I always took it very badly, and the compliment would serve to make me question what I was doing. This of course was completely unknown to the cheerful giver of the supposed compliment, because I was always able to maintain a frozen smile or the distance of mail, electronic or otherwise.

There was a time when I would actually respond, hoping to dissuade the reader of his or her own words, saying things like 'That's impossible!' or 'You don't really mean that!' But I soon realized it wasn't impossible and they did really mean it.

And that is the source of the depression; that's the rub. Writing, whether you consider it a craft or an art or both, is something that should get better with practice. It stands to reason. Writing comes from experience, curiosity, and knowledge. In short, it comes from life. The writer must improve with age and experience and life. So too the writing. Therefore, if I were to accept the compliment of the reader, wouldn't I be accepting the decline of my work? As of this writing, I have published twelve novels. If my best work was my first, what am I doing here?

Well, I don't feel that way anymore. I don't get depressed. It took me a long time, but I understand something now. First novels are like first loves. They are moments of discovery and celebration of things hopefully to come. They are windows. They carry with them the long reach of promise. Now when readers tell me they still like my first novel the best, I can take the compliment. I don't argue. I smile and say thank you.

All of this leads me to say that *The Butcher's Boy* might be my favorite novel by Thomas Perry. I say *might* because I am not certain – the man has written several very fine novels. (And of course I don't want to be responsible for making the author depressed in case he has not made the same journey and come to the same conclusion I have.) And I say *might* because I know there is still much good stuff to come from this writer.

But in rereading *The Butcher's Boy* in order to prepare for the writing of this introduction, I was struck over and over by the assuredness of this work and by its long reach of promise. I was amazed by what Perry knew when he knew it. I see it in the prose, the pacing, the choices. It's taken me a long time to learn what the cornerstones of this craft are, and yet there they are at work in Perry's first outing. Hey, *sure* he has gotten better since. But he sure started out near the top floor of the building.

Over the years and the millions of words, I have come to learn that it is all about character and velocity.

A book is like a car. It pulls up to the curb and the passenger door swings open to the reader. The engine revs. Do you want a ride?

Once you get in, the car takes off, the door slamming shut and tire rubber burning in its wake. Behind the wheel the driver's got to be highly skilled, heavy on the pedal, and most of all, oh man, most of all, somebody you want to be with. He's got to drive near the edge of the cliff but never over. He's got to turn sharply just as you think you know where you are going. He's got to gun it on the final lap. And he's got to tell you the story all along the way.

If not, it is going to be a short ride.

I'm here to tell you that *The Butcher's Boy* is not the short ride. No matter whom you are cruising with in this story, you've got your hands braced on the dashboard. There is not a single throwaway character in this book. They are all real, they are all captivating. Perry approaches his people with a less-is-more philosophy, never confusing description with character, cutting all of that away and leaving only the telling details that open a window onto a true world.

This economy creates momentum. The story gathers speed and moves with an unalterable urgency. All characters, all action, relentlessly moving toward the same vanishing point on the horizon. They asked me to write a few pages here, but I think I could have covered it with one word: *relentless*. This book is a relentless journey in a car with no mirrors. No looking back.

This velocity is also created by the masterly intertwining of multiple narrative tracks. Perry came out of the gate with a narrative that would offer a great challenge to any writer. How do you bond the reader to a professional hit man? How do you get the reader to get in the car with a killer? Perry answered the call by creating a character who is meticulously detailed in all ways but his name. The telling details of life on the road and on the run connect him to us. His ingenuity and skills win the day.

Perry also balances the outlaw portrait with another strong character, that of the heretofore deskbound crime analyst Elizabeth Waring. She's unsteady in her new surroundings yet just as professional as her quarry. The juxtaposition of these two characters as they move separately but ultimately closer and closer is the gasoline that drives this car. It is rare that I have seen this pulled off successfully, and never with such success in a first novel.

Riding along all through this journey is Thomas Perry's command. The authenticity is on display on every page, in every paragraph. From how hot desert air feels on the skin in Las Vegas to how paperwork is shuffled in the Justice Department to how a hired killer slips into a locked hotel room to fulfill a contract, the author's skill in creating his world repeatedly awes the reader. Verisimilitude.

Every page is absolutely authentic, and that creates a velocity of its own.

Character, control, and momentum. Perry has pulled off a wonderful trifecta in this novel. It is a rare accomplishment. So unusual is a book like this that it reminds me of how its own character Elizabeth Waring viewed her search for an unnamed, unknown hit man.

It was like trying to capture an animal that was so small and rare and elusive that you sometimes doubted that it existed.

Well, Thomas Perry captures the rare animal with this book. It exists. There are no doubts.

When *The Butcher's Boy* was first published, twenty years ago, it received many accolades. Among them was the Edgar Award for best first novel. This award is bestowed by the Mystery Writers of America and is not taken lightly. I think the book you are about to read deserved that honor hands down.

Time now for you to start the story. The car is at the curb, waiting. The door is open and the engine is thrumming as high octane moves through its heart. Get in and ride.

MICHAEL CONNELLY is a former reporter for the *Los Angeles Times* and the author of eleven acclaimed Harry Bosch thrillers, the most recent being *Echo Park*, and several standalone bestsellers, including *The Lincoln Lawyer*.

ONE

The union meeting, thought Al Veasy, had gone as well as could be expected, all things considered. He had finally figured out why the retirement fund was in such trouble all the time, when everybody else in the whole country with anything to invest seemed to be making money. And he had explained what he knew, and the union members had understood it right away, because it wasn't anything surprising if you read the newspapers. The big unions had been getting caught in similar situations for years. Low-interest loans to Fieldston Growth Enterprises – hell of an impressive name, but zero return so far on almost five million dollars. If the company was as bad as it looked, there would be no more Fieldston than there was growth. Just a name and a fancy address. When the union started to apply pressure some lawyer nobody ever heard of would quietly file bankruptcy papers. Probably in New York or someplace where it would take weeks before the union here in Ventura, California, heard of it. Just a notice by certified mail to O'Connell, the president of the union local, informing him of the dissolution of Fieldston Growth Enterprises and the sale of its assets to cover debts. And O'Connell, the big dumb bastard, would bring it to Veasy for translation. 'Hey, Al,' he would say, 'take a look at this,' as though he already knew what it meant but felt it was his duty to let somebody else see the actual document. Not that it would do anybody any good by then.

Or now either. That was the trouble and always had been. Veasy could feel it as he walked away from the union hall, still wearing his clodhopper boots and a work shirt that the sweat had dried on hours ago. He could smell himself. The wise guys in their perfectly fitted three-piece suits and their Italian shoes always ended up with everything. The best the ordinary working man could hope for was sometimes to figure out how they'd done it, and then make one or two of them uncomfortable. Slow them down was what it amounted to. If it hadn't been Fieldston Growth Enterprises it would have been something else that sounded just as substantial and ended up just the same. The money gone and nobody, no person, who could be forced to give it back.

He kicked at a stone on the gravel parking lot. There probably wasn't even any point in going to the government about it. The courts and the bureaucrats and commissions. Veasy snorted. All of them made up of the same wise guys in the three-piece suits, so much alike you couldn't tell them from each other or from the crooks, except maybe the crooks were a little better at it, at getting money without working for it, and they smiled at you. The ones in the government didn't even have to smile at you, because they'd get their cut of it no matter what. But hell, what else could you do? You had to go through the motions. Sue Fieldston, just so it got on the record. A little machinists' union local in Ventura losing 70 percent of its pension fund to bad investments. It probably wouldn't even make the papers. But you had to try, even if all you could hope for was to make them a little more cautious next time, a little less greedy so they wouldn't try to take it all. And maybe make one or two of them sweat a little.

Veasy opened the door of his pickup truck and climbed in. He sat there for a minute, lit a cigarette, took a deep drag, and blew a puff out the window. 'Jesus,' he thought. 'Nine o'clock. I wonder if Sue kept dinner for me.' He looked at the lighted doorway of the union hall, where he could see the men filing out past the bulky shape of O'Connell, who was smiling and slapping somebody on the back. He would be saying something about how we don't know yet and that it's too early to panic. 'That's right, you big dumb bastard,' thought Veasy. 'Keep calm, and you'll never know what hit you.'

Veasy turned the key in the ignition and the whole world turned to fire and noise. The concussion threw O'Connell back against the clapboards of the union hall and disintegrated the front window. Then the parking lot was bathed in light as the billowing ball of flame tore up into the sky. Afterward a machinist named Lynley said pieces of the pickup truck went with it, but O'Connell said there wasn't anything to that. People always said things like that, especially when somebody actually got killed. Sure was a shame, though, and it was bad enough without making things up.

TWO

'Here's the daily gloom,' said Padgett, tossing the sheaf of computer printouts on Elizabeth's desk. 'Early today, and you're welcome to it.'

'Thanks,' said Elizabeth, not looking up from her calculations. She was still trying to figure out how that check had bounced. Even if the store had tried to cash it the next morning, the deposit should have been there at least twelve hours before. Eight fifteen, and the bank would open at nine thirty. She made a note to call. It was probably the post office, as usual. Anybody who couldn't deliver a piece of mail across town in two days ought to get into another business. They had sure delivered the notice of insufficient funds fast enough. One day.

Elizabeth put the checkbook and notice back in her purse and picked up the printout. 'All those years of school for this,' she thought. 'Reading computerized obituaries for the Department of Justice for a living, and lucky to get it.'

She started at the first sheet, going through the items one by one. 'De Vitto, L. G. Male. Caucasian. 46. Apparent suicide. Shotgun, 12 gauge. Toledo, Ohio. Code number 79-8475.' She marked the entry in pencil, maybe just because of the name that could mean Mafia, and maybe just because it was the first one, and the other prospects might be even less likely.

'Gale, D. R. Female. Caucasian. 34. Apparent murder. Revolver, .38. Suspects: Gale, P. G., 36; no prior arrests. Wichita, Kansas, code number 79-8476.' No, just the usual thing, thought Elizabeth. Family argument and one of them picks up a gun. She went on down the list, searching for the unusual, the one that might not be one of the same old things.

'Veasy, A. E. Male. Caucasian. 35. Apparent murder. Dynamite. Ventura, California. Code number 79-8477.' Dynamite? Murder by dynamite? Elizabeth marked this one. Maybe it wasn't anything for the Activity Report, but at least it wasn't the predictable, normal Friday night's random violence.

'Satterfield, R. J. Male. Afro-American. 26. Apparent murder/robbery. Revolver, .32. Washington, D.C. Code number 79-8478.' No.

'Davidson, B. L. Female. Caucasian. 23. Apparent murder/rape. Knife. Carmel, California. Code number 79-8479.' No again.

Down the printout she went, letting the sheets fall in front of her desk to re-form themselves into an accordion shape on the floor. Now and then she would make a check mark with her pencil beside an entry that didn't fall into the ten or twelve most common murder patterns. It was Monday, so she had to work fast to catch up. One thing Elizabeth had learned on this job was that a lot of people killed each other on weekends.

It was just after ten when she reached the final entry. 'Stapleton, R. D. Male. Caucasian. 41. Apparent murder. Revolver, .45. Suspects: Stapleton, A. E., 38; no prior arrests. Buffalo, New York. Code number 79-

102033.' Padgett, the senior analyst in charge of analyzing reports, would be on his morning break, she thought. The timing was always wrong, somehow. Whenever you got to the stage where you needed somebody it was either lunchtime or a break. She picked up the printout and carried it across the office to the glass-walled room where the computer operators worked.

She was surprised to see Padgett at his desk behind the glass, frowning over a report. She rapped on the glass and he got up to open the door for her without putting down the papers he was reading.

'I thought you would be on your break, Roger,' she said.

'Not today,' said Padgett. 'Must have been a big weekend. Four of our friends bought airline tickets in the last three days.' He always called them 'our friends,' as though the years of scanning lists for familiar names had prompted a kind of affection.

'All to the same place?'

'No,' he said. 'Two to Las Vegas, one to Phoenix, and one to Los Angeles.'

'It's probably the weather,' said Elizabeth. 'They don't like it any more than we do. You still have to scrape the snow off your car if it's a Rolls Royce.'

He looked impatient. 'Okay, love. What did you find?'

'Eight possibles. The numbers are marked. The rest are the usual weekend stuff – rapes, muggings, and arguments that went a little too far.'

'I'll have Mary get the details to you as soon as they're printed out. Give her fifteen minutes. Take a break or something.'

6

'Okay,' she said, and walked out again into the large outer office. She saw that Brayer, her section head, was just putting a few papers into a file, then throwing on his sport coat.

'On a break, Elizabeth?' he asked.

'Yes,' she said. 'Can't do anything until the computer spits out the day's possibles.'

'Come on,' said Brayer. 'I'll buy you a cup of coffee. I'm waiting on something myself.' They walked down the hall and into the employees' lounge. Brayer poured two cups of coffee while Elizabeth staked her claim on a table in the far corner of the room.

Brayer sat down, sighing. 'I sometimes get tired of this job. You never seem to get anything worthwhile, and you spend an awful lot of time analyzing data that doesn't form a pattern and wouldn't prove anything if it did. This morning I've been going over the field reports of last week's possibles. Nothing.'

Elizabeth said, 'Just what I needed – to hear my section chief talking like that on a Monday morning.'

'I guess it's the logical flaw that bothers me,' said Brayer. 'You and I are looking for a pattern that will lead us to a professional killer, a hit man. So we pick out everything that doesn't seem routine and normal. The point about professional killers is that they don't do things to draw attention to themselves. What did you get this morning, for instance?'

'A shotgun suicide. One where they tortured a man and then cut his throat. One where a man was poisoned in a hotel dining room, one where the brakes failed on a new car. And a dynamite murder, and—'

'There!' said Brayer. 'That's just what I was talking about. A dynamite murder. That's no hit man. It's a

7

mental defective who saw a hit man do that on television. What we ought to be looking at is the ones that don't look unusual. The ones where the coroner says it was a natural death.'

'You know why we don't,' said Elizabeth.

'Sure. Too many of them. Thousands every day. But that's where our man will be. And you wouldn't be able to tell whether it was a hit man or pneumonia. Dynamite, shotguns, knives, hell. You don't have to hire a professional for that. You can find some junkie in half an hour who could do that for a couple of hundred.'

'We help catch one now and then, you have to remember that.'

'Yes, we do. You're right. We're not just wasting time. But there has to be a better way to do it. As it is, we find what we find, not what we're looking for. We catch lunatics, axe murderers, people like that. Once every few years an old Mafia soldier who wants to come in from the cold and can tell us who did what to whom in 1953. It's okay, but it's not what we're after.'

'John, how many actual hit men do you suppose there are operating right now? The professionals we look for?'

'Oh, a hundred. Maybe two hundred if you count the semiretired and the novices who have the knack. That's in the world. Not too many, is it?'

'No, not many when you're trying to find them by analyzing statistics. From another point of view it's plenty. I'd better go call my bank while I've got a minute. They bounced my check unjustly.'

Brayer laughed. 'Typical woman,' he said. 'Mathematical genius who can't add up her checkbook.'

Elizabeth smiled her sweetest smile at him, the one that didn't show that her teeth were clenched. 'Thanks for the coffee. I'll have the activity report in an hour or two.' She got up and disappeared out the door of the lounge.

Brayer sat there alone, sipping the last half of his cup of coffee and feeling vaguely bereft. He liked to sit at a table with a pretty woman. That was about as far as he allowed it to go these days, he thought. It made him feel young.

'May I join you, or am I too ugly?' came a voice. Brayer looked up and saw Connors, the Organized Crime Division head, standing above him.

'You're perfect, Martin,' said Brayer. 'You being the boss, this being Monday, and you being ugly enough to fit right in. It's a pattern.'

'Thanks,' Connors said. 'How are things going?'

'Rotten, I'm afraid. Elizabeth went back to pick out the second-stage possibles, of which there are several. None very promising, but they all take time. The field reports from last week are all blanks except the one from Tulsa, which is three days late and is probably just as blank.'

'I almost hope so this morning,' said Connors. 'We've got just about every investigator in the field, and Padgett's airline reports say at least four of the people we keep an eye on bought tickets west this weekend.'

'Anything in it?'

'Probably the usual. Old men like warm weather. At least I do. And Roncone and Neroni have investments out there. Legitimate businesses, or at least they would

9

be if those two weren't in on them. But there's always a chance of a meeting.'

'Maybe we'll get lucky,' said Brayer without enthusiasm. 'Well, I think I'll go see if Tulsa phoned in. I'd like to close the books on last week before Elizabeth comes up with today's massacres.'

'How's she working out, anyway? It's been over a year.'

Brayer sat back down and spoke in a low voice. 'To tell you the truth, Martin, she's a real surprise. I think if I had to retire tomorrow, she'd be the one I'd pick to replace me.'

'Come on, John,' said Connors. 'She can't possibly know enough yet. There's a difference between being clever and pretty and running an analysis section. She hasn't even been in any field investigation yet.'

'But I think she's got the touch,' said Brayer. 'She's the only one in my section that's smarter than I am.'

THREE

Two this week, he thought. Too many. After the next one, a vacation. At least a month. The old lady in front of him stepped aside to count her change, so he moved forward. 'One way to Los Angeles, the three o'clock.'

'Five fifty,' said the weary ticket agent, running his hand over the bald spot on his head as though checking to be sure nothing had grown in there while he wasn't paying attention.

He paid the money and waited while the man filled in the ticket. It would be no problem. After something like Friday, a man buying a ticket on Saturday morning for someplace far away might have stuck. A man buying a ticket for Los Angeles on Monday afternoon was nothing. He wasn't leaving the vicinity of a crime. He was just leaving. This man behind the counter wouldn't remember him. Too many people in line buying the same ticket, as fast as he could write. Not even time to look at them all. Not the men, anyway.

He stepped aside and pocketed his ticket. The clock on the wall said 2:45. Almost time to board. Not much time to hang around the bus station and get stared at. No reason for anybody to remember having seen him, because they hadn't seen anybody in the first place. No chance they'd check on the motel either. He'd registered Friday afternoon three hours before the truck blew up, and the truck had been thirty miles away in Ventura. Another county. All clean and simple. From Los Angeles, you could take any kind of transport to anywhere. You practically had to set yourself on fire to attract a second glance in LA.

On Monday, February twelfth, at 2:43 p.m., a man not fat, not thin, not young, not old, not tall, not short, not dark, not light, bought a bus ticket for Los Angeles at the Santa Barbara bus station. He was one of twenty or thirty that afternoon that you couldn't have told from one another, but that didn't matter because nobody looked at any of them. If the police were looking for someone in the area, it wasn't on a bus coming toward Ventura on its way to Los Angeles.

Elizabeth studied the second set of printouts on the day's possibles. The man who had been killed by the shotgun had left a note that satisfied his family and the coroner. The death by torture was linked to a religious cult that had been under investigation for a year and a half. The brake failure was officially attributed to incorrect assembly at the factory in Japan. That left the man poisoned in the hotel dining room and the victim of the dynamite murder.

The autopsy report on the unlucky diner convinced Elizabeth that there wasn't much point in following up with an investigation. Chances were that he hadn't even ingested the poison on the premises. It was a combination of drugs, all used for treatment of hypertension, and taken this time with a large amount of alcohol. Elizabeth moved on to the last one.

12

Veasy, Albert Edward. Machinist for a small company in Ventura, California, called Precision Tooling. Not very promising, really. Professional killers were an expensive service, and that meant powerful enemies. Machinists in Ventura didn't usually have that kind of enemy. Sexual jealousy? That might introduce him to somebody he wouldn't otherwise meet – somebody whose name turned up on Activity Reports now and then. Thirty-five years old, married for ten years, three kids. Still possible. Have to check his social habits, if it came to that.

Elizabeth scanned the narrative for the disqualifier, the one element that would make it clear that this one too was normal, just another instance of someone being murdered by someone who had a reason to do it, someone who at least knew him.

She noticed the location of the crime. Outside the headquarters of the Brotherhood of Machinists, Local 602, where he had been for a meeting. Her breath caught – a union meeting. Maybe a particularly nasty strike, or the first sign that one of the West Coast families was moving in on the union. She made a note to check it, and also the ownership of Precision Tooling. Maybe that was dirty money. Well what the hell, she thought. Might as well get all of it. Find out what they made, whom they sold it to, and tax summaries. She'd been expecting a busy day anyway, and the other possibles had already dissolved.

She moved down to the summary of the lab report. Explosives detonated by the ignition of the car. She made a note to ask for a list of the dynamite thefts during the last few months in California. She read further. 'Explosive not dynamite, as earlier reported.

13

Explosive 200 pounds of fertilizer carried in the bed of the victim's pickup truck.' Elizabeth laughed involuntarily. Then she threw her pencil down, leaned back in her chair, and tore up her notes.

'What's up, Elizabeth?' asked Richardson, the analyst at the next desk. 'You find a funny murder?'

Elizabeth said, 'I can't help it. I think we've established today's pattern. My one possible blew himself up with a load of fertilizer. You should appreciate that. You're a connoisseur.'

Richardson chuckled. 'Let me see.' He came up and looked over her shoulder at the printout. 'Well, I guess it hit the fan this weekend,' he said. 'But that's a new one on me.'

'Me too,' said Elizabeth.

'How do you suppose it happened?'

'I don't know,' said Elizabeth. 'I've heard of sewers and septic tanks blowing up. I guess there's a lot of methane gas in animal waste.'

'Oh yeah,' said Richardson, suddenly pensive. 'I remember reading about some guy who was going to parlay his chicken ranch into an energy empire. But you know what this means, don't you?'

'No.'

'Brayer's a walking bomb. His pep talks at staff meetings could kill us.'

Elizabeth giggled. 'I knew I shouldn't have told you about this. I suppose I'll have to listen to a lot of infantile jokes now.'

'No, I think I got them all out of my system for the present,' said Richardson.

Elizabeth groaned. 'Go back to your desk, you creep.'

Richardson said, 'I'm going. But you know what?'

'What?'

'I'd have this one checked out.' Elizabeth made a face, but he held up his hand in the gesture he used to signal the return of the businesslike Richardson. 'Seriously,' he said.

'Checked out with whom?' asked Elizabeth, moving warily toward whatever absurdity he was anxious for her to elicit from him. 'And why?'

'I'm not sure who. I guess the bomb squad. Maybe even somebody over in the Agriculture Department. Maybe this sort of thing happens all the time. Who knows? I'm a city boy myself. But if it does we ought to know about it. We might be sending agents out into the field once a week to find out some farmer blew himself up with his manure spreader.'

Elizabeth studied his face, but he seemed serious. 'I don't know if you're joking or not, but what you're saying makes sense. It'll take a few minutes to clear this up, and I've got some time on my hands this afternoon.'

'Then do it,' he said. 'If only to cater to my curiosity.'

In the Los Angeles airport there are some people who stand on the moving walkway, letting the long belt carry them to the end of the corridor. Others walk forward on it, combining muscle and machinery into something over a dead run; and others, probably the biggest group, don't use the machinery at all. This group consists of people who have spent too much time sitting down and know they'll soon be sitting again for a few hours, or people who arrived at the airport an hour earlier than they needed to. Among them was a man not tall or short, not young or old, not light or dark, with a oneway ticket to Denver in his breast pocket. When the stewardess checks his boarding pass for the seat number a few minutes from now, she won't be able to decide whether he is on his way to one of the military bases in that area, or one of the ski resorts. And she certainly won't ask. After that she won't have time to notice. As soon as the lights go on she will be too busy to study faces. Once they are strapped in she will look mostly at their laps, where the trays and the drinks and the magazines will be.

The man at Treasury said, 'That one's not in our bailiwick, I'm afraid. Have you tried the FBI?'

'Not yet,' said Elizabeth. 'I'd hoped to get something on it today.'

The man chuckled. 'Oh, you've noticed. But I'll tell you what you can do. There's a guy over there who knows just about everything about explosives. Name's Hart. Agent Robert E. Hart. If you call him direct you'll avoid all the referral forms and runarounds. He's the one you'd get to in the end anyway. He's at extension 3023. Write down that name and number, because it'll come in handy every now and then. Agent Hart.'

'Thanks,' said Elizabeth. 'That'll save me a lot of time.'

Elizabeth dialed the FBI number and waited. The female voice on the other end seemed to come from the soul of a melting candy bar: 'Federal Bureau of Investigation.' Elizabeth retaliated, making her voice go soft and whispery. 'Extension 3023 please, dear.'

'That'll hold her,' thought Elizabeth.

'Whom would you like to speak with, ma'am?' said the voice, now suddenly businesslike and mechanical.

'Agent Hart,' said Elizabeth.

'I'll ring his office,' said the voice.

The line clicked and there was that sound that seemed as though a door had opened on a physically larger space. 'Hart,' said a man's voice.

Elizabeth wondered if she had missed the ring. 'This is Elizabeth Waring at Justice, Agent Hart. We have an explosives case and we need some information.'

'Who told you to call me?'

'Treasury.'

'Figures,' he said, without emotion. 'What do you want to know?'

'Anything you can tell me about fertilizer blowing up.'

'About what?'

'Fertilizer. Er . . . manure. You know, fertilizer.'

'Oh.' There was silence on Hart's end.

Elizabeth waited. Then she said, 'I assure you, Agent Hart, this isn't a—'

'I know,' he said. 'I was just thinking. What's the LEAA computer code designation?'

'Seven nine dash eight four seven seven.'

'I'll take a look at it and call you back. What's your extension?'

'Two one two one. But does that happen? Have you heard of it before?'

'I'm not sure what we're talking about yet,' said Hart. 'I'll call you back in a few minutes.' He hung up and Elizabeth said 'Good-bye' into a dead phone.

She looked up and saw Padgett dash by with a cup

17

of coffee in one hand and an open file in the other. Just then a loose sheet in the file peeled itself off in the breeze and wafted to the floor. He stopped and looked back at it in remorse.

'Got it,' said Elizabeth, and sprang up to retrieve it for him.

'Thanks,' said Padgett. 'Too many things at once.'

'Are your friends having a nice time out west?'

'Much better than I am,' he said. 'We've got to get a few investigators out there today before anything has a chance to happen, and I don't know where we're going to get them.'

'You mean it might be something?'

'Probably not,' he said, 'but you never know. You can't take a chance of missing another Apalachin just because somebody's got the damned flu and somebody else is at an airport that's fogged in.'

'How about holding the fort with technicians until the cavalry arrives? Locals even? Wiretaps and so on.'

'You know what that mess is these days,' said Padgett. 'And we don't even have probable cause. Just four men we can't even prove know each other taking winter vacations within a couple hundred miles of each other. Want to go in front of a judge with that one? I don't, and I've been there.'

'Well, good luck with it,' said Elizabeth, not knowing what else to say. The telephone on her desk rang, and she answered it with relief. 'Justice, Elizabeth Waring.'

'Hart here,' came the voice.

'Good,' said Elizabeth. 'What can you tell me?'

'It's pretty much what I figured,' he said. 'It's the fertilizer all right.'

'You mean manure blows up?' she asked, a little louder than she had intended. She looked up and noticed that Richardson was watching her with a smirk on his face.

'No,' Hart said. 'Fertilizer. The kind they make in factories and sell in stores. A couple of the nitrate fertilizers are chemically similar to dynamite. If you know how to detonate them you can use them the same way. They're cheaper and you don't have to have a license to use them. If you run out you can go down to the store and buy all you want.'

'That's incredible,' said Elizabeth. 'Do people know about this?'

'Sure,' said Hart. 'A lot of construction companies use fertilizer all the time. Been doing it for years.'

'Then my case is closed, I guess,' said Elizabeth. 'The poor man probably just blew himself up by accident. But somebody ought to sue whoever makes that fertilizer. It could happen to anybody.'

'No it couldn't,' said Hart. 'It doesn't blow up by accident. You have to use blasting caps and an electric charge. Theoretically the gasoline in Veasy's pickup truck is more dangerous than the fertilizer. More explosive power and easier to set off.'

'So you think it was murder?'

'Or suicide. I haven't seen enough to tell, really, but I don't think it's likely he bought a bag of fertilizer for his garden and it just went off. I suppose if he was carrying blasting caps or shotgun shells or something, and the conditions were right, maybe. But the report says he was just sitting in a parking lot, not jolting along a country road, and something would have to set off whatever served as the detonator.'

'So it is murder.'

'I don't know. But if this is a case you're interested in I wouldn't write it off yet. I'd at least find out what he was carrying around in the bed of his pickup, and whether he even bought any fertilizer.'

'Are you on this case too? What I mean is, is the FBI interested?'

'No. At least I don't think so. If the explosive had turned out to be dynamite we would have been. There you have a federal statute having to do with a traceable substance. But as it is, unless it somehow ties in with another case, I doubt there'll be anyone on it. Local jurisdiction, no reason for the FBI to take an interest.'

FOUR

'Gentlemen, we're running this country like a god-damned poker game. The average man sees that he has nothing and somebody else has everything. He doesn't make trouble because he's optimistic enough to think that after the next hand he'll have everything. Watch out for the day when he figures out that the chips aren't changing hands the way they used to. And when he finds out that it's because the fellow with the chips is playing by different rules, we'd better be ready with our bags packed. You talk about a tax revolt, hell, there'll be a real revolt. See you next session, if there is one.'

'It's the only game in town, Senator,' said the senator from Illinois, putting his arm on the old man's shoulder and walking with him out of the committee hearing room. 'Don't worry. We'll get a new tax bill passed next session. You put the fear of God into them.'

They were walking down the quiet private hallway that led back under the street to the Senate office building. No one was now within earshot. The old man continued, 'Hell, Billy. You're young yet. Boy senator from Illinois. But I may not even be alive next session. I'm seventy years old, you know. Six terms in the Senate. I'm not going to have a seventh, one way or the other, and when I go the chairmanship goes to—'

'I know, to Fairleigh. You watch seniority pretty closely if you don't have any yourself. But don't worry, Senator. Your tax bill is in the bag. Our esteemed colleagues aren't even dragging their feet anymore. Too much mail from home.'

'I hope you're right, Billy,' said the old man. 'But I'd have felt a lot better about it if we could have gotten it all out on the floor this session. You know, I got a letter today from a woman who makes fifteen thousand dollars a year after twenty years working as a secretary. Her husband makes twenty-five thousand, so the first dollar she makes is taxed at forty-three percent. No tax shelters for them. By the time you figure state taxes, social security, and sales taxes that woman is losing over half her income. Maybe eight thousand dollars. Of the fifty richest people in my state, not one of them pays eight thousand a year in taxes. A lot of them don't pay anything and never have. And the recent tax bills gave the rich the biggest subsidy yet. We've got to make some changes.'

'I know, Senator,' said the younger man, patting him on the shoulder. 'I've been with you on this since I got here. It's what got me elected. I said I'd try to work with you on income tax reforms that would help the average citizen, do whatever you wanted. They didn't vote for me, they voted for you.'

'That's bullshit. You got here because you were the best governor they'd had in twenty-five years. And you'll get re-elected because you're the best senator for the last thirty. If something happens to me before we get this bill passed I'm counting on you to ramrod it.

Remind a few people of what they promised us. You know who I mean.'

'Well, here's my office,' said the senator from Illinois. 'Don't worry. We'll both be here to remind them, and we probably won't have to. Most of them will get an earful while they're home for the break. I leave myself in two hours. First speaking date is tonight.'

'Oh, to be young again,' said the old man. 'See you in a few weeks, Billy.' The younger man watched the older senator walk down the hallway toward his office. The familiar blue suit was hanging from the old man's stooped shoulders, but the white head was still held erect. The Honorable McKinley R. Claremont, senior senator from the great state of Colorado. He wasn't fooling anybody with that frail elder-statesman routine. Anybody who was interested could check his schedule and see he had a press conference set for eight fifteen tonight in the Denver airport.

'You're sure about all this?' asked Brayer.

'Of course I'm sure,' said Elizabeth. 'I'm sure of the facts, that is. I'm not sure about what interpretation to hang on them, because there aren't enough of them. Veasy was carrying two hundred-pound sacks of nitrate fertilizer in his pickup truck. He must have bought them that day acccording to the Ventura police, because nobody saw them before that. Somebody apparently came along while he was in a union meeting and did something to the fertilizer so it would explode. And the FBI agent said that was perfectly possible for somebody who knew how.'

Brayer leaned back in his chair and tapped his pencil

23

absently on the glass desk top. He stared off into space. Finally he turned to her and said, 'I'm afraid I don't know what to make of it either, but it's sure not ordinary. Whoever did it was fast on his feet. He'd have to ad lib, if the fertilizer was only bought that day.'

'So what do we do now?' asked Elizabeth. 'Does it warrant an investigation or not?'

'I'm not sure I know what warrants an investigation these days. We're supposed to be keeping an eye on organized crime, not giving an Academy Award for the most imaginative performance by a murderer. Do you have any reason to believe this fellow Veasy might have had anything to do with the Mafia?'

'He didn't have a record, if that's what you mean, and his name didn't come up when I had Padgett run the Who's Who program on the computer. But who knows? Maybe he borrowed money, maybe he smuggled something for them – Ventura's got a harbor. Maybe anything. It could even have had something to do with the union. We just don't have anything to go on.'

'Except the fact that whoever snuffed him was clever about it.'

'Right,' said Elizabeth. 'Clever enough to be a professional?'

'I don't know. Maybe a world-class amateur, maybe a lunatic with beginner's luck. But there's always the chance it's the real thing. Lunatics and beginners usually spend some time planning. They're not up to working with what they find.'

'So you're going to dispatch an investigator?'

'I'm not sure yet. I'm not even sure if I have anybody

I can send right now. What was that FBI agent's name, again?'

'Hart. Robert E. Hart. Extension 3023. Why?'

'I'll see if I can con his boss into sending him. If he's as good as the Treasury man said and I haven't heard of him, he's young enough and new enough to be eligible for legwork.' He picked up the phone, then looked at her expectantly.

'You mean I have to leave?' she asked.

"Fraid so. It's hard to lie, cheat, and steal in front of an audience. Close the door on your way out.'

FIVE

Just one more before payday, and then a little vacation. Sometimes he wondered how long he would keep it up. At the beginning he'd thought five years was a long time, but now it had been six – no, almost seven, and still going strong. Living in motels and rent-by-the-week cottages could get to be pretty old after a month. It would be nice to be back in Tucson, where he could relax a little and get the old edge back. Eating in fast-food places and spending half your time traveling wasn't so good for your body. It had to catch up with you sooner or later.

Denver wasn't bad this time of year, though. Cold and clear. Later he'd take a walk down Colfax Avenue and see a movie. The plane wouldn't arrive until tonight, and the press conference would make the eleven o'clock news. For the first day or two the old guy'd be surrounded by reporters and hometown minor-league political hacks anyway. After that, when the rosy glow faded, there'd be time to work something out. Just a matter of seeing your best shot and taking it, like pool.

He turned off the television and walked to the dresser. He leaned over his suitcase and peered at the face in the mirror. A little tired from the plane ride is all.

No lines, nothing, he thought. It would be ten years yet before it was the kind of face people remembered.

Brayer opened the door of his office and beckoned to Elizabeth, who was sitting at her desk glancing at a newspaper. She brought it with her into Brayer's office.

'Get down to Disbursement and pick up your travel vouchers,' Brayer said. 'There's a plane at eight that'll get you to LA International by ten o'clock Pacific time, and a hop to Ventura that'll get you in by eleven.'

'Me?'

'Do you see anybody else?'

'But I'm an analyst, remember? Good old Elizabeth? I'm no investigator. I haven't been out of this office since—'

'You're going, Elizabeth,' he said. 'You've got the rating and the qualifications. Just because you haven't done it before doesn't mean you can't do it, or if it comes to that, that I can't order you to. I checked it with Martin Connors. So you're going.'

'So the FBI wouldn't do it?' she smiled slyly.

'Yes, they will. But they'll only guarantee to let us use Hart for two days. They can pull him back any time after five o'clock Wednesday afternoon. And they'll only send him if he's there to investigate explosions, not handle the whole case by himself. Now get down there to your friendly local travel agent in Disbursement so they have some chance of getting you both on that eight-o'clock plane.'

'I'm on my way,' she said, heading for the door. 'I hate snow anyway.'

'If you come back with a tan anywhere but on your

27

face I'll skin it off you and nail it to the wall,' said Brayer. 'You're not on a vacation, Waring.'

She stopped in the doorway and said, 'I thought the usual thing was the Death of a Thousand Cuts?'

'Get going,' he said. To himself he thought, Damn. The best I've got. Maybe the best data analyst outside the National Security Agency, off on a wild goose chase. The worst part was that he had needed to convince Connors to arrange it. He tried to remind himself there was no need to worry. The case and the timing could hardly be better for starting her in the field. It was the longest kind of long shot, complete with a trail that was already cold. She'd have little chance to put herself in harm's way before she was ready, getting in on armed surveillance or arrests. With four of the capos suddenly showing up in the West on the same day, it hadn't been hard to convince Connors that it was time to try Elizabeth in the field. The department really did need seasoned field investigators, and if she worked out, who could tell? A female with her brains out in the field – hell, it might make a difference some time. But, he thought, if Connors ever got around to reading the preliminary reports and saw the kind of case he'd sent two people out to investigate, Brayer would have some explaining to do. He consoled himself by planning what he'd say to Grosvenor, when and if he finally bothered to report in from Tulsa.

As Elizabeth stood in the elevator she was glad Brayer had said that about the suntan. California would be warm. It wouldn't do to show up wearing a heavy overcoat and wool skirts. It wasn't a vacation, as he'd said, but there was nothing in the rules that said you had to humiliate yourself in front of strangers, looking as though you'd arrived in California by walking over the North Pole. Besides, the bathing suit she had in mind didn't take up much room.

At the United Airlines desk there were two men. One sat drinking coffee, looking impatient, while the other did all the work. When Elizabeth reached the head of the line and handed the man her travel voucher, he nodded to the other and said, 'Miss Waring, Mr. Hart is here waiting for you.'

Hart dropped his cup in a basket and stepped around the desk to help her with the suitcase. 'Good to meet you,' he said, looking at the suitcase instead of at her.

'Same to you,' she said. For once she meant it. He was tall and thin with a kind of delicacy about his hands and a rather unruly shock of light brown hair that probably made him look younger than he was. He guided her away from the desk to a line of seats facing the loading gate like a man conducting a lady off a dance floor. This wasn't going to be so terrible after all.

When they were seated she noticed that he had somehow managed to pick a spot that looked as though it was in the middle of things, but wasn't close enough to anyone so they couldn't talk.

He said, 'Before I forget, are you carrying a weapon?'

'Yes,' she said. 'They admitted there wasn't any reason, but regulations say field investigators have to. Are you?'

'Yes,' he said. 'Same regulation. We'll have to board early so we don't attract too much attention when they wave us through the metal detectors.'

29

'I'm glad you came,' said Elizabeth, venturing onto the most dangerous ground first so she wouldn't have it in front of her later. 'What made the FBI decide to get involved?'

'Your Mr. Brayer. He asked for cooperation and the Bureau is being very cooperative these days. Ten years of bad press, all the political stuff, massive housecleaning after Hoover died – you can imagine. Brayer offered a fairly straightforward murder case with a chance of something bigger, and all he needed was two days of legwork.'

'So the Bureau jumped at it? I hope it's not a waste of your time,' said Elizabeth.

'No,' said Hart. 'The Bureau is re-establishing its usefulness, doing favors. So either way it's no loss to the organization. As for me,' he said, and Elizabeth could see he was going to step out on the tightrope, 'I've been on assignments that didn't pan out before, and none of them involved flying to Southern California with a pretty lady.'

Nicely managed, she thought, if a little clumsy. So he too liked to cover the hard part first. She rewarded him with the best smile she could risk. No sense in setting him up for some kind of embarrassment, but at least let him know we're friends.

The voice in the air said, 'United Flight 452 arriving at Gate 23,' and Hart looked at his ticket. 'That's us,' he said.

They sat in silence and watched the rest of the passengers filing in and getting settled. Then the door slammed with a pneumatic thump and the engines wound themselves up to a high whine and the plane began to taxi out away from the buildings into the night. At the end of the apron it spun around and faced into the wind, the engines screamed, and they shot down the runway into the sky.

Elizabeth said, 'You had your job long?'

'Four years, about,' said Hart. 'You?'

'Only a little over a year. It's interesting, though. What made you decide to work over there?'

'Came back from the service, went to an undistinguished law school where I earned an undistinguished record,' he smiled. 'Seemed like a good idea at the time. Either that or spend the next twenty years researching precedents and hoping to become a junior partner somewhere. This sounded like more fun.'

'Sounds familiar,' said Elizabeth.

'You too?'

'With variations. For me it was Business Administration, and the twenty years would have been spent doing market analyses,' said Elizabeth, and turned to look out the window. They were above the clouds now, and she wondered how long she could keep looking out there before he remembered that all she could see was the tip of the wing.

Movies were always a good way to spend those early hours of the evening in a strange town. A large crowd, a dark place, and a built-in etiquette that kept people from looking too closely at each other or starting a conversation. By the time the lights came up in the theater and he joined the file of people pouring out onto the sidewalk, he was hungry.

Years ago Eddie Mastrewski had told him always to forget he was using a cover. You should be whatever you pretended to be, all the time except when you were actually working. That way there were only a few hours a year when anything could happen to you. The rest of the time you really were an insurance salesman or a truck driver or a policeman, and you weren't in any more jeopardy than anybody else. If you slipped once your other life would go a long way toward saving your ass. Besides, it gave you something else to think about. Eddie was a butcher.

Of course that had all happened in the days before the trade got so busy. Nobody had that kind of time anymore. You were crazy if you passed up the kind of business you could get. It was easier now too. Everybody was a stranger, and everybody traveled. The only cover you needed was to look like the others and do what they did when they did it. Right now people were eating. He walked down Colfax looking for a restaurant that was crowded enough.

'Don't be a jackass, Carlson,' said the old man. 'If I'm in any danger it's not from some guy with a gun, it's from some big corporation afraid of a bill that would take away its tax advantage. Criminals don't give a good goddamn about tax reforms because they don't pay any taxes.'

'What I'm saying, Senator, is that things aren't that simple or predictable,' said Carlson, a man in his thirties who was so tastefully dressed and well groomed as to appear abnormal. 'You're a national figure now. Your picture is on the televison every night. The exact composition of your politics isn't what we're talking about. It's the visibility in the media. That alone makes you a target. If your picture happens to be on the screen at the moment some borderline case finally gets his big headache, you're going to need security.'

'Fine,' Claremont said. 'Get me some security, then. Meanwhile get the hell out of my way and let me do my job.'

'Right, Senator,' said Carlson, opening the door of the limousine for Claremont and climbing in after him, still talking. The black automobile moved away from the curb and into the traffic so quickly that it looked as though the two men had barely caught it in time.

The plane touched down at Los Angeles International and Elizabeth began to prepare herself for whatever came next. Five hours in the air after a full day of work, and now at least one more hour before she could be alone and take her shoes off. She wondered what she must look like by now, then put it out of her mind. She probably looked like a woman who had just worked a thirteen-hour day, she thought, and there wasn't a whole lot she could do to hide it.

Elizabeth went over the notes she had taken during the long flight. First stop in the morning would be the Ventura police. Hart would handle the postmortem on the remains of the truck and the lab reports and the interview with the technicians. Elizabeth would read through the full report and interview whoever had written it, then follow whatever leads looked promising.

As the no-smoking light flickered and the engine wound down she wrote an additional note on her pad: *bank records*. If Veasy had a business relationship with organized crime there would be something that didn't fit. He would have made some surprising deposits or some surprising withdrawals. Or if not, there would be a discrepancy between the bank accounts and the way he had lived – maybe a sign that he had a source of money that didn't pass through the accounts. She added *safe deposit box?* to her notes, then put the pad in her purse.

Elizabeth was glad to be able to move again. Airplane seats are small for a woman five feet five. She wondered what it must be like for Hart.

They joined the line of passengers moving past the stewardesses and out the door into the movable corridor that carried them to the terminal. Then they were in an airport lobby. Hart led her down another corridor to a second lobby, where there was a check-in desk for Golden West Airlines. He had a few words with the desk manager and then waited while the man picked up a telephone and turned his back. He hung up and said, 'You can board at nine fifty-five at Gate Forty-one, Mr. Hart. Your bags will be transferred automatically, of course.'

As Elizabeth and Hart wandered across the lobby, she checked the big wall clock: nine thirty. Not enough time to relax, too much time to wait comfortably in one of those blue plastic chairs. She was glad when Hart said, 'How about a drink while we're waiting?'

They sat in a dark corner of the bar with their backs to the wall. The traffic was fairly thin, so the waitress was there for their order immediately. She scurried off to get them their drinks. She was back so fast that they hadn't said anything to each other.

'I've been thinking about this case,' said Elizabeth. 'It's going to be a little bewildering.'

'They always are,' said Hart. 'This one is going to be

more than that. You'll be better off if you think of it as preliminary research instead of a case of its own.'

'What do you mean?'

'You're looking for professional touches. If you find any, that's about all you'll find, most likely. There's not much chance we'll make any arrests. If it's a professional there won't be anything to connect him with Veasy, and more likely than not we've never heard of him before. And this time there isn't even a case on record of anyone who works that way, so if it's a pattern this is the first of the series.'

'So I shouldn't get my hopes up,' said Elizabeth. 'I haven't.'

'Oh I don't know,' said Hart. 'Hope doesn't cost anything. But we've got very little this time. In a truck explosion like that there can't be any fingerprints. But there may be something connected with the method or the circumstances that'll be useful later.'

'I've got a few ideas to start with,' said Elizabeth. 'Maybe we'll get lucky.'

He nodded and sipped his drink. 'Maybe, if we're thorough and careful and don't make any mistakes ourselves. But the best thing to do as the start of it is to forget about looking for anything in particular. Just look and write down everything you see or hear. It may make sense to somebody a year from now.'

Elizabeth smiled to herself. He was a man all right – telling her not to get her hopes up, and then suggesting that it would all work out in a way that was too far off for anybody to predict. The endless replay of John Wayne handing the woman a pistol and saying ominously, 'Save the last bullet for yourself' before he

35

climbs over the stockade with a knife clenched in his teeth.

Elizabeth picked up her purse. 'Nine fifty. Time to go.'

He bolted the last inch of his Scotch, tossed some money on the table, and followed her out into the lobby. One more short flight, she thought, and then the chance for some rest.

He walked out of the restaurant and bought a *Denver Post* from the vending machine at the curb. Time to start doing some research on him. If they didn't publish his schedule, at least they might have a picture of him. You had to start somewhere. He remembered hearing a story about Dave Burton trying to collect on a next-door neighbor once. Probably not true, but you never knew. Things like that could happen if you weren't careful, and the big ones like this were worth taking a little extra time with. For that kind of money, why not? And this was the last one for awhile. Another one of Eddie Mastrewski's proverbs. Always take it slow when you're tired. The police can be dumb as gorillas, make a million mistakes, but at the end of it they still get paid and go home to watch television. You make one and you're dead. If the police don't get you the client will because he'll get scared.

Getting out had to be the simplest part this time. He'd thought of that part right away, as soon as he'd heard the timing. A charter flight to Las Vegas, booked in advance. There was some kind of rule about that. Charter flights had to be advance booking, so the police wouldn't look closely for fugitives there. If you

36

couldn't leave from another town, a charter flight wasn't bad.

Elizabeth held her exhaustion in abeyance while the little plane flew along the coast toward Ventura. At first she could see the incredible lighted expanse below her, stretching down the long valley to fade into a feeble fluttering like stars. Then the plane moved out across the coastal range and over the water, and there was only darkness and calm on her side of the cabin.

It seemed like only a few minutes before the little airplane began to descend. The Ventura airport wasn't much. They put a short wooden staircase next to the fuselage for people to step on, and there was an eager young man in a gold sportcoat that seemed to belong to an absent older brother to serve as spotter for the deplaning passengers. He smiled and hovered, his hands held out silently announcing his intention to catch any passenger who might begin to fall.

The night was calm and warm, like late spring. The airport reminded her of a small town bus station, but they managed to find a cab driver lounging out front who knew the Ocean Sands Motel, where Disbursement had made their reservations. She was pleasantly surprised to see the sprawling, vaguely Spanish stucco building half-buried in luxuriant, unfamiliar vegetation. She wondered at first if Disbursement had made a mistake, but then remembered that the economies were always inconsistent: the leather-bound notepads with the cheap, thin paper in the office told it all.

Hart took charge and registered for them. Elizabeth couldn't help wondering if it was just his faintly antiquated courtesy again, or if his experience of hotels was all of the sort where the woman didn't sign her own name. She didn't think about it for long, because as soon as the key to her room was in her hand she was on her way toward the cool, clean sheets. When she was lying there it occurred to her that she probably hadn't bothered to say good-night to him. She didn't think about that for long either.

He always made a point of staying away from women when he was traveling. It wasn't that any of the ones he was likely to meet would suddenly become suspicious and make inquiries to the police, or anything like that. It was just that it was too damned complicated. You had to make up something to tell them about yourself, maybe even make up a fake address and phone number, agree to be someplace at a particular time. Things like that took most of the fun out of it anyway, and added an element of danger.

So he walked more slowly to keep from catching up with the one ahead of him on the sidewalk. She was definitely trolling for someone – maybe him. He couldn't see her face, but her way of walking – her back arched slightly and her hips rolling a little as she strolled down Colfax Avenue – he had seen a thousand times. Women almost always walked fast when they were alone, especially on this kind of street. When they didn't, it was usually to say, I'm not going anywhere in particular and don't have anything to do: I've got all the time in the world. Another time, he thought as he watched her, his eyes moving irresistibly to the round, firm buttocks. A week from now it would be different.

She turned then and he knew that she was aware of him. She stopped to look in a store window, but he knew she was studying his reflection. He fixed his eyes in front of him and walked purposefully ahead at the same pace. As he passed her she began to walk again. If anyone else had seen it, it must have looked like an accident. A pretty lady window shopping, a man on his way to the parking ramp down the street to pick up his car. He heard her say, 'If you like it, maybe you should try it.' The voice was soft and confident at the same time, perfectly modulated to establish a kind of intimacy that said I know everything you feel and desire: I know you. He felt a wave of resentment well and pass over him at the violation, the casual assumption of knowledge like an assertion of possession.

He slowed and said, 'Excuse me?' feigning a look of surprise.

She smiled the satisfied-cat smile they always had, with the lips closed and the amused eyes. Then she said, 'If you're lonely, I'm not doing anything.'

In one part of his mind he was thinking she was extremely tempting – huge, bright blue eyes that seemed to peep out from behind a veil of heavy brown hair. In another part all the danger signals were reminding him that this was neither the time nor the place. To have anything to do with her now would put him in jeopardy: she was risking his life and he was angry about it. So he said, 'Oh, I'm sorry, Miss. I'm a married man.' He did his best to look flustered, to make her think she'd been wrong this time, to convince her that this time she'd picked a man who hadn't even seen her. And then he quickened his pace, behaving like a frightened businessman who wanted nothing more at the moment than to escape the place where he'd been embarrassed, but after thinking it over and smoothing out the rough edges, wouldn't be able to resist telling his wife and one or two close friends about it because he thought it magnified him: a real prostitute came up to me on the street and ... well, she offered herself to me. I couldn't believe it.

He turned off on a side street and kept going, moving along in his preoccupied businessman's stride. Then he turned again onto a narrow street that ran parallel with Colfax – almost an alley, really. It was darker, and on one side were the backs of stores and taverns and restaurants, nestled together and indistinguishable from one another with their steel fire doors and loading docks and navy-blue dumpsters piled with cardboard boxes.

The girl had put him into a bad mood, reminded him of how impatient he was for this trip to end so he could go back to Tucson and relax. It wasn't easy to live for days at a time without so much as talking to anybody, and for weeks without saying more than 'What's the soup of the day?'

He glanced at his watch. A little after ten. Time to head for the motel and read the paper while he waited for the eleven o'clock news. Then the watch disappeared in a flash of pain, and he was aware that he had heard the sound of whatever had crashed into his skull even while he felt it. But he was on the ground now and his left kneecap seemed to hurt too. Dimly he could see a rock the size of two fists beside him as he rolled in the gravel. He didn't have time to decide whether that was what hit him. He just scooped it in and had his arm cocked when he saw a human figure bending toward him for the next blow. With all of his strength he hurled it into the darkness where the face

40

must be, pushing off the ground with his right foot at the same time. There was a sickening thump as it hit, and a high, tentative half-scream that never got all the way out before the shape crumpled.

He was up and moving now, whirling around because the other one would be behind him. This time he wasn't quite fast enough. A blow across his back with something long like a club electrified him with pain and terror, and he wasn't sure he could move himself. But then something hit him in the face and he was on the ground again and the other one was winding up for a kick. He grabbed the stable leg with one hand, pulling the man off balance, and punched up into the groin with the other – a quick, hard jab. This time there was no cry of pain, only the sound of the air leaving the man's lungs. Then the man lay on the ground doubled up like a foetus, rocking and grunting.

He stood up and looked for the others, but no, there had only been two. Muggers, he thought. Jesus! He looked down at them. The first one was probably dead. He wondered what he should do about the other. He didn't have anything with him – not even a knife. He couldn't leave them this way. They had almost certainly gotten a good look before they'd done anything. He walked over the first one, picked up the bloody rock that lay by his head, and brought it down once, hard. Then he did the same to the other one. He dragged them by the ankles into the shadows behind the dumpster and moved away down the alley, limping from the pain in his left knee. His back was throbbing and he could feel a thin trickle of blood warming his right cheek, but he couldn't tell if it was his head or his face. The face worried him. Muggers. Jesus.

The Senator sat back in his chair and watched a commercial for new cars. There wasn't really anything in it about cars, but there was a small Japanese car there, and a lot of enthusiastic Americans cavorting around it, showing surprise and pleasure and amazement to a spirited musical score.

Then the news came on. Carlson went over and turned the volume up a little. Not enough so the Senator would have to take notice of the fact that Carlson knew he was old and probably didn't hear as well as he used to. Just enough to make explicit the view they shared, that commercials were a kind of atmospheric interference but the speech at the airport was the very essence of importance.

A newsman was saying, 'Congress ended its regular session today and began its mid-session break. We'll have footage of Senator McKinley Claremont's return to Denver. There was a brief flareup of fighting in the Middle East, an earthquake shook Central America, and New England is wracked in the worst snowstorm in twenty years. More about these and other stories in a moment.'

The Japanese car commercial came on again. 'It's the same commercial exactly,' said the Senator, peering at the screen in amazement as the enthusiastic Americans mugged and pantomimed their way through the song again. 'Carlson! When did they start doing that?'

'Doing what, Senator?'

'Playing the same damned commercial twice in a row?'

'Are they? I didn't notice,' said Carlson.

SIX

He moved as quickly as he could. There'd be plenty of time to baby the bumps and bruises later when there wasn't anybody to watch him do it, but now the important thing was to get back to the motel room and out of sight before anybody found the bodies. He made a quick inventory as he walked – there was a tear in the left knee of his pants, and the whole suit was dusty. With effort he brushed himself off. There was definitely blood on his face, but that was easily taken care of. He pulled out his handkerchief and brought it to his right cheek, but had to stifle a yelp at the pain.

'Damn,' he muttered, wishing vaguely that there was something more he could do to them. There was no question it would show: by morning there would be a bruise, and the swelling had already started. He just hoped there wouldn't be a scar. Maybe all the blood was coming from beyond the hairline. 'Damn!' he said again, under his breath. 'Stupid. Rocks and clubs, like animals. Baboons!'

Down the alley he could see the pool of light of the motel parking lot. He stopped to listen for a car coming his way, but there was nothing. He was surprised to see that he still had his newspaper. He didn't remember picking it up. But a wave of relief washed over him. He opened the paper as though he had been reading it since he parked his car down the alley. Then he took a deep breath and came around the corner of the motel, heading for the back stairway. He heard a door somewhere in the other wing slamming but he kept on going, trying hard not to limp. His ears picked up the sound of keys jangling and muffled voices, but he kept on going, gritting his teeth against the pain. Up the stairs he climbed, using the handrail to keep the weight off the leg. He swung around with the paper under his arm, keeping his left side to the light as long as he could, then pressing his face so close to the wall it almost touched while he unlocked the door.

He was inside, and breathing hard. He carefully stripped off his clothes, leaving them in a pile on the floor, then walked into the bathroom. The mirrored wall told him what he had feared. He stared at it, and what stared back at him was a thin, nondescript man in his early thirties who looked as if he'd walked away from an airplane crash. The right side of his face was already beginning to blacken and swell, and a thin trickle of blood was beginning to snake down from his temple. He watched it saturate the sideburn and then quickly curve down the cheek to the chin. As he leaned closer to search the face, the drop reached the point of his chin and fell, making a bright blotch in the sink. He carefully washed his face, then ran the water in the bathtub.

He sat on the edge of the tub and stared at his knee while he waited. A scrape, a cut with a little dirt in it maybe. He flexed the leg, studying the pain as though he were finetuning it. No cracks or chips, he thought. Just a scratch is all. But the face – he wasn't ready to

44

think about that yet. He padded out into the other room and turned on the television. The news was just coming on. He caught sight of himself in the other mirror, sitting naked on the bed. A small, whitish animal with a few tufts of hair. And hurt, too. As he watched, the injured face in the mirror contracted a little, seemed to clench and compress itself into a mask of despair. A sigh like a strangled squeak escaped from its throat. He said aloud to the face, 'You sorry little bastard.' And then the moment was gone. The people on the television screen seemed to be dancing around, celebrating something having to do with a little car parked behind them. He wished them all dead.

Then the newsman came on. He padded back into the bathroom to check the water. It was beginning to get deep enough now, so he turned the tap off and tested the temperature. Too hot: time enough to watch the news.

When he got back to the bed, Claremont and his aide were descending the ladder of the plane. It was pretty much what he'd pictured – a white-haired, stiff-necked old coot in a three-piece banker's suit of the sort you could hardly buy in a store anymore, followed closely by a neat, short-haired, milk-complexioned young man who appeared to be the prototype of a new doll.

He studied their moves as they approached the terminal. The Senator looked old and frail and a little tired. Then there was a different scene, at a podium bristling with microphones. He was saying, 'We're going to fight it through this time to the end. We've got key people from both parties working very hard in Washington and in their home districts.'

Claremont looked old and vulnerable all right. Too old to run or fight, probably too old to even make much noise. He had that sharp-eyed hawkface look that old people got sometimes, and his temples were marbled with blue veins. The picture changed and the newsman was talking about something having to do with some dark, intense little men in olive-drab fatigues. He switched off the television, went into the bathroom, and slowly settled himself into the hot tub. He studied the knee again, watching the tiny pink cloud swirl away from the cut like liquid smoke. Then he settled back, relaxing every muscle in his body. In a minute he would submerge his head and try to clean those wounds too. That would hurt but it had to be done. No sense getting an infection.

He tried to think the situation through. He couldn't travel with a face like that. People remembered things like black eyes and bruised faces. And in the morning they'd find the two bodies, and start looking for somebody who'd been in a fight. The first place they'd look would be in the hotels and motels around here, starting with the cheapest first. It would look like a gang fight, but not enough like one to keep them from checking out transients right away while they could still put their hands on them. He'd paid in cash for the room, three days in advance, like always. And then there was the charter flight for Las Vegas – paid in advance too. But that didn't leave until Thursday night. Too soon for the face to get back to normal, and too long to wait while the police looked for a man who'd been in a fight. So it had to be tonight. There was no other way. He had to be somewhere else before they knew what they were looking for. And then his mind stopped dead. There was still the Senator. How could he do the Senator and get out of Denver in one night with a face like that? He thought again about the two men in the alley. If only they hadn't picked him out, or picked that alley, or had thought of it another night. But there wasn't much he could do about it now. He started again from the beginning. How can I travel with a face like this?

McKinley Claremont sipped the last of his bourbon and watched the film of the Arab gun crew expertly loading and firing at a distant hillside. He wondered if it was stock footage, or if they were really getting that organized. In '67 he'd been to Egypt on a fact-finding tour and it hadn't been like that. After a couple of rounds, the ammunition they had with them had turned out to be the wrong size, so the crew he was with just sat down and started eating and drinking. Two hours later a captain told him they were waiting for the supply lines to get untangled, or for further orders, whichever happened first. Meanwhile they sat in the sun behind their useless cannon, waiting.

Carlson interrupted his thoughts. 'I'd say it came off very well, wouldn't you, Senator?'

'All right, I guess,' said the Senator. 'On television they don't get the chance to spell your name wrong, anyway.'

'Big day tomorrow,' said Carlson tactfully.

'Right,' said the old man. He set down his glass and raised himself slowly from his chair. 'Call me at eight and while we're having breakfast we'll try to figure out what's got to be done. That is, if we've got time for breakfast?'

'Yes sir,' said Carlson. 'First appointment isn't until ten.'

'Fine, see you in the morning then.'

'Good night, Senator,' said Carlson, already halfway out the door. 'My room is right next door if you need anything. Four oh eight.' The door shut.

Claremont shuffled over to the closet and brought out his pajamas. He tossed them on the bed and then took off his suit, carefully hanging it up so it wouldn't get wrinkled. If he didn't hate the idea of losing his privacy, he'd get a valet, he thought. Living out of a suitcase half of each year was bad enough. Then you had to decide whether to spend your time worrying about wrinkles or give up the few minutes of solitude you ever had.

He eased himself into the strange bed and tried out a couple of positions for comfort. Politics wasn't so bad for the young fellows, he thought. Trouble was, by the time you knew anything and had enough seniority to make anybody listen to it, you were too old. He peered through the darkness at his teeth soaking in the glass on the nightstand. Those things were older than some of the men in the House of Representatives. He chuckled to himself. Still plenty of bite to them, though.

He felt the water around him loosening the taut muscles and soaking some of the hurt out of him. He began to feel stronger. Now and then he would take a deep breath and lean back with his chin tucked into his chest to submerge his whole head. Then he would wait until his breath came back and do it again for as long as he could. Finally he sat up, took the soap between

48

his hands, worked it into a lather, then rubbed soap over his head and face. It was as though dozens of hornets were stinging his scalp, his cheek, his temple. He gasped to fill his lungs again and ducked under. Slowly the pain went away.

He waited a few seconds, then climbed out of the tub and began toweling himself off, gingerly. When he came to his knee he dried around it. No telling what germs there were on a hotel towel, and no sense leaving blood stains. He looked in the mirror again. This time the face didn't seem quite so bad, with the hair combed and no clot of blood on it. It was the cheek and the eye that'd give trouble, but with the right pair of sunglasses, maybe not so much, at least until tomorrow night.

He knew what he had to do now. There just wasn't any other way. As he dried himself he walked out into the bedroom. He picked up his watch from the dresser and put it on. Eleven thirty-nine. It would be a long night, no matter what. If only this had happened when he was working on something normal. He could call them and ask them to send somebody else, or even farm it out himself to someone he knew – Eddie Mastrewski had done that with him a couple of times. That reminded him of something Eddie had said, and it brought back the nervous anxiety: 'Never work when you're hurt, kid. If you don't feel good you won't think straight, either. And if people can see it they'll remember it. I don't mean major surgery either. I wouldn't work with a pimple.' Eddie was full of reasons not to work.

He put on clean clothes and carefully combed his wet hair. There was one consolation, he thought. If anybody saw him and he did get away, what they'd remember about him was the bumps and bruises, and they'd be gone in two weeks with any luck.

The whole thing would have to be changed now. He had planned to get a high-powered rifle with a scope, and get him through a window in his hotel. That was the way the crazies whose fantasies didn't include getting their pictures in the newspapers all did it. There wasn't time for that now, and he didn't have a gun, and – no use even thinking about it. He'd just have to live with the situation as it was.

He went to his suitcase and rummaged around for a few seconds, collecting some things. A pocket knife, a ballpoint pen, a clean handkerchief, a pair of sunglasses. He tried on the sunglasses and studied his reflection. It wasn't great, but it was something. He made a mental note to get a pair with bigger lenses, maybe the wraparound kind. Then he sat down to read the newspaper.

There was an article on the front page about the Senator's return. He studied it, but could find nothing that would tell him where the old man was staying tonight. He flipped through the paper until he came to a second article. This one had pictures of the old man and his aide getting out of a limousine in front of a building. Only part of the facade was visible, but it was a hotel, all right. They had said the old man had never lived in Denver. He had started out as a state assemblyman in Pueblo and still owned a place there. He studied the picture for clues. There was a doorman wearing one of those ridiculous comic-opera costumes, but no insignia on it, and nothing on the marble facade

50

of the building except a number. He smiled. That would do it. 1905.

He picked up the telephone book and leafed through it until he came to a page marked *Hospitals–Hotels*. There were dozens, but it didn't take him long. The Constellation Hotel. 1905 19th Street. He went through the rest of the list to see if there was another one with a 1905 number – he had been the victim of enough coincidences for one day – but there wasn't. So that was it. He studied the section carefully, looking for the hotel's ad. There wasn't any. So he turned to *Restaurants*. In a few seconds he'd found what he needed.

He got up and packed his suitcase, then tore his bed up a little. He set the key on the dresser, and looked around one last time to see if he'd left anything before he turned out the lights. He walked down the back stairs and through the alley. The cold made his knee stiffen up a little, but he was walking better now. A few blocks down there was another motel, and a telephone booth at the gas station across the street.

When he came to it, he called a cab company.

'I'd like a cab, please.'

'Where are you now?'

He read the sign across the street. 'The Wee Hours Motel on Colfax.'

'Where do you want to go?'

'The Pirate's Cove Restaurant on Alameda.' He'd almost said Alameda and 19th. Never work tired or hurt.

'Right. He'll be there in about five minutes.'

They always said five minutes, he thought. Now the suitcase. He couldn't ditch it here. The police might not recognize the rock as the weapon and go around to all the trash cans looking for something else. Never overestimate the police, count on them figuring out the obvious. He decided to hold on to the suitcase for the moment. The worst thing the cabdriver could think was that he was skipping out on a motel bill in the middle of the night.

He saw the cab pull up in front of the motel across the street. The driver was staring at the office window for his fare, so he didn't see the man with the suitcase until he was almost to the car. When he did he reached behind him, swung the back door open, and said, 'Pirate's Cove?'

'Yep, that's me.'

The cab was fitted with an oversized heater that blew a continuous rush of hot, impure air into the back seat. After the cold outside he figured he could tolerate it for a few minutes. He sat in the driver's blind spot.

The driver said, 'Hell, of a cold night, ain't it?' as he pulled away from the curb.

'Sure is. Glad you got here so quick.'

'Not much business this time of night. Mostly dedicated lushes who've lost their licenses. A few old folks out visiting each other. Now and then a whore or two.'

'Must be hard to break even.'

'Not too bad, really. When it gets slow we hang around the airport for the late flights. Nobody wants to call Aunt Mary to come pick them up at two a.m.'

'I guess not.'

They sat in silence for awhile. He could see one advantage to the late shift. Even on Colfax the traffic was light, and the cab was able to glide down the street catching each signal just at the moment when it turned green. He looked at his watch again. Just a little after midnight. He resented the way time was passing. He was going to need as much as he could get. At the Pirate's Cove he reached over the seat and gave the driver a bill. 'Ten cover it?' he said, facing downward away from the light.

'Sure,' said the driver. 'Thanks.' He'd tipped generously but not enough to be remembered.

''Night,' he said and quickly got out, heading toward the glass door of the restaurant. When he heard the cab pull away he bent down to tie his shoe until the car was too far away for the driver to see him. Then he straightened up and moved off down the street toward the Constellation Hotel.

It was seven stories, shaped like a cereal box. He went around the block to approach it from the rear. There was a parking ramp and a broad loading dock. To the left of the dock he could see that one part of the back wall was pierced with ventilators and fans with screens over them and a number of pipes – the kitchen. Just in front of it he noticed a small wooden stockade. He walked up to it, opened the gate, and looked inside. There were two large garbage dumpsters. He opened the first, and the smell of it nearly gagged him. He tried the other, and it seemed to be mostly cardboard boxes flattened to save space. He set the suitcase on top and closed the cover, then made his way to the back entrance of the parking ramp.

There was an elevator, so he entered it and studied the panel of buttons, then pushed *Lobby*, and waited. He hoped it wasn't too empty. The way he looked he

53

couldn't afford much company, but if he were alone it would be worse. When the doors opened he stepped out quickly, keeping his head down and moving across the lobby at a slight angle from the front desk toward the only doorway he could see. There were two young couples, well dressed, lounging in the oasis of furniture in the center of the room. One of the women had her shoes off and was rubbing her toes wearily. The man with her said something about a nightcap and she rolled her eyes in distaste.

He knew exactly what he was looking for, but had no way of knowing if the hypothesis were correct. As he came abreast of the front desk he quickly stared at the mailboxes. Room 406, unquestionably, he thought. He had to try it, anyway. The person most likely to have written messages pile up in his mailbox this late at night in a hotel would be the Senator. He kept on going out the front door to the street, then walked around to the parking ramp again and pushed the elevator button for the fourth floor. This would be the hard part.

When the door opened he was prepared to see a uniformed guard, but the corridor was empty. As he searched for 406, part of his mind was taking note of which rooms seemed to be occupied. He heard voices behind one door, the background music from a television show behind another. There were Do Not Disturb signs hanging from some of the doorknobs. He went past 406 and down the corridor to take a look at the other elevator and the stairway. He had to get out of here afterward.

At the end of the hallway there was a room where

the sign said, *Please Make Up the Room*. He wondered – it could just be somebody who'd reversed the sign by accident, meaning to leave the *Do Not Disturb* side out. He stopped and listened. There was no sound. He decided to chance it.

He took out his wallet and selected a credit card, then carefully slipped it into the door latch, easing the door open and waiting for the chain to catch. The door wasn't chained, so he moved inside and stood still, his back to the door, listening. He waited for his eyes to get used to the light, trying to sense whether there was anyone asleep in the bed. He crouched, trying to line up the surface of the bed with the dim glow of the window. When he succeeded he was sure. The silhouette of the bed was flat.

Quickly he walked to the window and out to the balcony. The Senator's balcony would be the fifth one over. He wondered if he could even do it now, tired and hurt and cold. He studied the row of identical, iron-railed balconies. Yes, he thought, that was the way in. They were far enough away from each other so a fat-ass architect would assume no one could make it from one to the other.

He went back into the room and closed the window. He looked around for something long enough to reach. There was a long, low table along one wall. He studied it – no, it was bolted down too securely, and it was too heavy to handle alone. Then he noticed the closet. It was a double closet, huge, for a hotel room. He looked inside and saw the shelf. Perfect, he thought. It was a good ten inches wide and eight or nine feet long. Thank God for good, substantial hotels. And it was screwed in, too. Working rapidly, he used his pocket-knife to take out the screws, then brought the shelf out with him to the balcony.

He stopped to take one last look at the layout of the room, memorizing the location, size, and shape of each piece of furniture. Then he slowly and carefully extended the board across the void between his balcony and the next one. It reached, the other end making a light tap on the railing as he set it down. He lifted his right leg up and got his knee on the board, then the other one. He winced with pain. He had forgotten that. It would be a long, hard crawl. The shelf bowed in the middle as he eased his weight onto it, but it seemed safe enough. Four floors below him he could see the little fence with the garbage dumpsters in it, a tiny square in the corner of the parking lot. He thought about falling all that way; lying there in the cold, smashed on the pavement. But then he was at the end of the board. He swung his legs down to the balcony and turned to pull the shelf behind him. One down, four to go.

One after another he took them, not thinking about the rest of it now, not thinking about anything but crossing the cold, empty space that separated him from the fifth balcony. And then he was there. He leaned the shelf against the wall, then thought better of it. There might be some vantage, from some other building, where somebody could see it. He laid it down flat on the balcony, then ran his hand along the edge of the sliding window to feel for the latch. There wasn't one on the outside. Another security feature, he thought. Then he went to the other end of the window and checked that, hopelessly.

He would have to take the chance of leaving a sign. He opened his knife and slipped the blade under the rubber molding a few inches below the level of the inside latch, then slowly brought it up. The glass shifted minutely. He smiled, and kept smiling even though it hurt. It was just as he'd hoped. The latch was secure, but the glass wasn't fitted tightly to the aluminum frame. Using a gentle, steady pressure of his finger tips, he slid the large pane as far as it would go away from the latch, then stuffed his handkerchief into the crack to hold it there. He studied his accomplishment. He had about an eighth of an inch to work with now. Using his knife as a pry, he bent the aluminum frame a little to gain a few more thousandths of an inch. Then he took the knife and pointed the blade up under the latch. The spring was strong, but he managed to lift the hook clear of the catch and slide the window free. He stopped for a moment with the window open a hair, and pressed the molding and frame back into shape. He whisked his handkerchief over the glass and the frame, just in case. They wouldn't put it in the papers, he thought, but they'd send somebody to do it even if they thought he died of old age.

He took out the ballpoint pen he'd brought with him and held it up out of the deep shadows. He took out the clear plastic refill and looked at it. To any other eye it looked like nothing, a refill that only had about a third of its ink left. But the last two thirds were a clear liquid, like water only thicker.

Touching the window with his handkerchief, he quietly slid it aside and slipped into the room, closing it behind him and moving away from the light. He stood there, silent and unmoving, studying the room. Claremont was sound asleep, his slow, regular breathing faintly audible.

Now to find just the right thing, he thought. A bottle of pills, maybe. Or a laxative. Old people make a big deal out of taking a shit. He saw a glass on the coffee table, so he went over and sniffed it – liquor. That wouldn't do now. He could feel the seconds slipping past him, seconds he needed. He moved into the bathroom straining his eyes to find something for his purpose, but no – it was too dark. He thought of just forgetting the whole thing and smothering him with a pillow, but that was too dangerous and chancy. The bed was next to the wall, and all the old bastard would have to do was pound it once or twice in the struggle and that would be that. Old or not, he could make noise. He came out of the bathroom and stared at the sleeping figure. There was nothing – only the bed, the nightstand with the lamp and the glass. The liquor would have been great if he'd managed to get here in time to help with the mixing, he thought, but not now. And then he realized it wasn't the same glass. The liquor glass was on the coffee table.

Slowly and carefully, he drifted over to the bed and stared at the nightstand. He had to look a little to the side to discern anything much in the darkness. He brought his face close to the glass and then almost laughed out loud. Of course, he thought. False teeth! He slowly reached over and poured the contents of the pen refill into the glass.

Then he drifted back out to the balcony and closed the sliding window behind him. In a few seconds he was already on the third balcony and putting down his portable bridge to the second. He looked down again, this time elated by the height, but he held himself in check. Always work slowly when you're tired, he reminded himself. He channeled his concentration into his work, moving along the shelf and then pulling it after him, setting it on the next balcony and easing himself onto it. And then he was there. He slipped back into the room and closed the window, this time letting it lock. Then he went to the closet and set the shelf back on its supports. For a second he considered just leaving it, but no. Later he'd regret it. He took out his knife and carefully replaced the screws. Then he forced himself to stand quietly for a moment. Did he have everything? Was anything out of place? He reached into his coat pocket and screwed his pen back together. Then he took a few deep breaths, listened, and stepped out into the hallway.

At the elevator he pressed the button for the parking garage. The doors sighed and opened immediately. That was a good sign, he thought. In all that time since he'd come up, nobody had used that elevator. He glanced at his watch. It was only one fifteen. And then he realized he was getting an erection. It struck him as funny, but he didn't dare laugh yet.

When the elevator doors opened again and he felt the cold night air he forgot about it. He moved across the parking ramp and out to the lot. At the fenced-in dumpsters he stopped and retrieved his suitcase, then kept on going. At the first public trash can he came to, he broke his pen in two and threw it in among the crumpled cups and napkins and bottles and cans. He moved again, nursing his injured knee into exactly the right pace for a man disappearing into the night.

The Senator stirred, then woke up. The room seemed awfully cold. The Constellation hadn't been the same since they'd remodeled it in 1972, he thought. It was those damned fancy windows and balconies and things. The workmanship just wasn't any good anymore. People didn't take pride in their work. But then he reminded himself that he was an old man, a cranky one at that, and it was probably just his bad circulation. He rolled over and composed himself to go back to sleep. 'A goose probably just walked over my grave.'

SEVEN

When the telephone rang it tore Elizabeth out of sleep, leaving her in an unknown place. After a second or two she remembered it was Ventura and a motel room, but it took four rings for her to see the telephone and one more to get her hand on it. The call was from Hart, who wanted her to be ready for breakfast in twenty minutes.

Elizabeth hung up and went to the nightstand for her watch. Seven o'clock exactly. Then she went off to the bathroom to brush her teeth and see about a shower. As she hurried through the morning rituals she tried to keep herself from becoming too excited. Even if there were a clue, something to go on, it would probably take months to follow it up, and by then the case would be common property. A hundred people in a dozen overlapping agencies would be involved. And there still wasn't any reason to believe she had finally crossed the trail of a genuine professional hit man or that he'd be of any use if they caught him. It was like trying to capture an animal that was so small and rare and elusive that you sometimes doubted that it existed, but if it did exist it would be capable of killing you. No, this was worse, because there wasn't any point in hunting it down unless you could keep it alive and teach it to talk.

When they walked into the foyer of the Ventura police station, a sergeant carrying a mug of coffee was crossing the floor toward a corridor of tiny offices. He veered toward them, giving a reassuring half-smile. 'Hi. Are you being taken care of?'

'Agent Hart, FBI, and Miss Waring, Justice Department, to see the chief,' said Hart, flashing his badge.

'Okay,' said the sergeant. 'This way, please.' He shot a look over his shoulder as he conducted them down the hallway. 'Chief know you're coming?' he asked.

'Yes,' said Hart.

Elizabeth said nothing, having reminded herself as they were coming up the steps that she'd learn more by listening and watching than by trying to take charge. But the fact that Hart had said FBI and Justice department hadn't been lost on her. Technically the FBI was just one of the divisions of the Department of Justice although that had been very easy to forget the few times she'd been inside the massive J. Edgar Hoover Building with its millions of files and hundreds of millions of fingerprint records and its museum. For the moment, anyway, she would leave Washington protocol for Washington.

The sergeant led them into one of the tiny offices, where an older version of himself sat behind a wooden desk, frowning over some papers as though he were translating them with difficulty from a foreign language. When he saw he had visitors he looked relieved. He turned the papers face down in a far corner of his desk and popped up, his hand held out. 'You must be agents Hart and Waring,' he said. 'I'm Bob Donaldson. Always happy to cooperate with the FBI.'

'Thank you,' said Elizabeth, forestalling the correction Hart would probably feel was necessary. 'As they probably told you on the phone, we're interested in the Veasy murder.'

'Well now, ma'am,' said the chief. 'We're still not absolutely and completely sure it was a murder yet. We're coming around to the hypothesis, but we aren't sure.'

'I'm sorry,' she said, smiling. 'I misspoke, calling it what we're looking for rather than what we're looking at.'

He seemed appeased. 'I've notified the homicide squad that you'd be here, and told them to be ready with the reports of the investigating officers and so on. Beyond that I thought we'd just wait and see, let you look around and pick out the leads you want to follow.'

'I'd like to take a look at the physical evidence, since that's what I do best,' said Hart. 'Miss Waring would like to study the reports. That way we can do two things at once.'

'Good idea,' said the chief, as though the idea struck him as revolutionary. 'Sergeant Edmunds, take Agent Hart to the lab, will you? Miss Waring, I'll show you the reports.' He took her elbow in a gentle but somehow weighty pressure, as though he were guiding a prisoner who wasn't quite dangerous enough to be handcuffed, and led her down the corridor.

There was nobody in the room marked *Homicide* when they got there, but Donaldson sat her at a table and gave her a stack of reports. 'I'll be back in a minute,' he said.

She heard his voice in the next office. 'Where the hell

are those guys? I told them these people were coming this morning.'

Another male voice said in a bored monotone, 'Out on a call. Found a Mexican lemon picker stabbed to death out on Telegraph Road about half an hour ago. Macaulay told me to let you know if you asked.'

'Oh,' came the chief's voice, now much quieter. Then there was a moment or two of silence. At last the chief said, 'Well, when they come back in tell Macaulay I want to see him.'

Elizabeth heard him returning from the other office. She looked up at him in the doorway and listened with an expression of interest while he recapitulated the substance of the conversation she'd just overheard. She wondered how he could not know the sound carried between the little cubicles, but apparently he didn't. Then he was gone and she was able to look over the reports in peace.

Until the instant of his death, Veasy hadn't been particularly noteworthy. He had a wife who'd been in his graduating class at Ventura High School, and three children born in the second, fourth, and fifth years of their marriage. They lived in a three-bedroom house in a tract which they'd been paying on for about eight years. Veasy was a machinist, making fairly good money working for Precision Tooling. The investigating officer had made a note at the bottom that his sources – the wife, the shop foreman, two fellow workers, and a neighbor – had not the slightest idea that Veasy had any enemies.

There was no indication that he owed anybody any money except the mortgage on his house. He didn't gamble except for an occasional poker game at the union hall and the beer frames in his weekly bowling league. He had never been arrested or had anything to do with known criminals. Elizabeth was more than disappointed. She was bored. The only thing about the man that made interesting reading was his death.

She turned to the interviews with the witnesses. The whole thing had been completely unexpected. The monthly meeting of Local 602 had adjourned, he had climbed into this truck and was blown up. That was all any of them seemed to know.

After an hour and a half of reading and study, Elizabeth had made only two notes: to interview Richard O'Connell, the union president, about the minutes of the meeting, and to request file checks of Precision Tooling and Local 602. The file checks would have to wait, because it would be lunchtime at Justice now. She went to one of the empty desks and dialed the extension at Precision Tooling that O'Connell had given the homicide man. Yes, O'Connell said, he could see her at ten thirty.

Elizabeth sat for a minute staring at the file. She got out her telephone credit card, deciding to take a chance that Padgett was still busy enough to be working through another lunch hour.

On the other end she heard Padgett's phone snatched up and his voice say, 'Justice Padgett' as though it were a title.

'Roger,' she said. 'I know you must be busy if you're answering phones at twelve thirty, but I need some background. I need a file check on a company in Ventura, California, called Precision Tooling, and on Machinists' Local 602.'

'All right, but what specifically?'

'I'm afraid I'll need the whole thing on both. Any indication that anything isn't aboveboard. History, assets, cast of characters, everything.'

'So you don't know what you're looking for.' He said it without emotion, as though he wasn't surprised.

'I'm afraid not, Roger,' said Elizabeth. 'I'm fishing.'

'I'll get somebody on it after lunch. Give them a couple of hours and call back.'

'Thanks, Roger. I'll do that. You're a love.'

'I'm that all right. But Elizabeth?'

'What?'

'Try to keep it within bounds. Fishing can get expensive.'

She put her notebook away and went down the hall to Donaldson's office. She found him still pondering the same sheaf of papers. 'Chief,' she said, 'I wonder if I could get a ride in a squad car. Agent Hart has the keys to our rented car, and I don't want to interrupt him.'

'A ride? Sure,' he said. He lifted his phone and said, 'I'm sending Miss Waring to you. Get her a car and driver. Right.'

The factory was a small, rectangular aluminum building surrounded by a chain-link fence with an open gate. The place seemed to be all metal. Even the sounds that came from it were metallic, the noise of metal machines cutting and grinding and shaving metal, heating, bending, cooling it.

When she entered the shop, a man working a lathe lifted his safety goggles and walked over to her. 'Are you Miss Waring?' he asked. He seemed to be about

66

fifty, balding, and with the massive forearms of a man who worked with his hands.

'Yes. Mr. O'Connell?'

'We can talk out in the yard where it's quiet.'

She followed him through the shop – where the whine of machinery was punctuated by an occasional ring of a hammer or the clank of chains – and out into a small asphalt square where there were a picnic table and benches. 'Is this where you eat lunch?' she asked.

'That's right,' said O'Connell, sitting down. 'Now what can I tell you?'

'Mr. Veasy's death was rather unusual, as you know, and so we're working with the Ventura police to find out whatever we can about it. If there's anything at all you think should go into the record, I can guarantee that it will.' She watched him for a moment, but he was just waiting for her to continue.

'I'd like to know what went on at the union hall that evening. Do you have the minutes of the meeting? I understand you're president.'

'There aren't any minutes of that meeting. We didn't vote on anything, so there wasn't much to write down,' said O'Connell.

'Do you remember what was said?'

'We were talking about the investment of the pension fund. How to get the best return for our money, how to keep it safe, you know. The usual things.' He looked at her through clear, empty gray eyes.

'Did Mr. Veasy say anything that you remember?'

'Al? Sure,' he said, beginning to smile as he remembered. 'He was a great talker all right. He was complaining about the quarterly statement from our

67

biggest investment. Said we weren't getting anything back for our money, that we were speculating instead of saving, and that we were gonna lose it.'

'Do you agree?'

'No,' he said. 'Not at all. A union has to do something or inflation will eat up the pension funds before anybody has a chance to use them. You have to put money into things that'll produce profits in the long run, even if nothing much happens the first year or two.'

'What investment bothered him?'

'Well,' said O'Connell, 'we have a lot tied up in an investment corporation called Fieldston Growth Enterprises.'

'Mutual funds?' Elizabeth wrote down the name.

'No. Land, mostly. Resorts, golf courses, retirement places. Al didn't like it one bit. Said he'd tried to find out about them and couldn't. There weren't any resorts or anything that they owned, so he panicked. They're new, so they haven't done any of that yet. But I've seen brochures with the designs and layouts, and it'll be big. I'm sorry Al couldn't live to see it.'

'What else happened that night? Did he argue with anybody?'

'No, not really. He and I went round a little about the pension fund, but it wasn't personal.'

'Did anything else seem to be on his mind? Was he depressed lately or nervous?'

'Al Veasy didn't commit suicide,' said O'Connell. 'His truck blew up is all. Must have been a leak in the fuel system. Could happen to anybody the way they make 'em now. If I was his wife I'd sue General Motors.'

'So it looked to you like just a tragic accident?'

'What else? Murder? What for?'

'I just have to cover all the possibilities, Mr. O'Connell.'

Elizabeth thanked him and walked back to the waiting police car. Both doors were open and the officer was leaning against the trunk gazing off down the road through his mirror-lens sunglasses. He was probably nice looking, she thought, but you'd have to get him out of uniform to tell. They always seemed to be covered with bits of metal. 'Where to?' he said.

'Twenty-seven twenty-four Grove Avenue.'

'Veasy's house?'

'That's right,' said Elizabeth. All the stops were routine, she thought – no way to break out of it, nobody new to ask.

The rest of Elizabeth's morning was just as unproductive. What she got from Mrs. Veasy was inarticulate grief. At least the investigating officers had managed to find out a little about the dead man's habits. But they did this kind of thing every day, and were probably pretty good at it – ignoring what people were trying to say – their theories, opinions about people and life and death – and listening for what they had to throw in to make it comprehensible to an outsider – specific information about the victim's habits, behavior, friends, and enemies.

Elizabeth was suddenly tired. She glanced at her watch and saw that it was almost noon. 'Let's go back to the station,' she said. The policeman drove with a special kind of authority, a tiny bit faster than anyone else on the straight, level highway, so the other cars would move aside to let them cruise by. She looked out on the rows of low suburban houses as they slid past, now and then surprised by a squat date palm or a row of towering eucalyptus trees. If it weren't for the plants this could be Indiana. Or Virginia, anyway. Just about anything seemed to grow here. But not on Grove Avenue. The houses were built so close together there wasn't even room for a decent lawn.

When they reached the station she asked to use the desk sergeant's telephone and called Padgett in Washington. 'Hi, Elizabeth,' he said. There was something odd about his voice, but she couldn't identify it. Amusement? Spite?

'Hi, Roger,' she said. 'What have you got for me?'

'Precision Tooling isn't going to help much. They're purer than Caesar's wife. Started in 1936 by a couple of master machinists who hired a few friends, then grew when the war came. Made airplane parts, patterns for drop-forged ship fittings, things like that. Been a minor defense subcontractor ever since.'

'Any chance of new stockholders? Unusual loans or anything?'

'Elizabeth, these people have been on our books for thirty-five years. They get a new clearance every time a contract comes up for renewal. If they moved the water cooler we'd know it. They're in perfect health.'

'Well, save the file for me anyway. What about the union?'

'Clean too, at least so far. They're part of the file, but we're still checking with the Department of Labor. All we know at the moment is there aren't any shady characters hanging around the factory; that was all Defense was interested in. Labor should know something.'

'When they answer ask them for information on the pension plan.'

'The what?'

'The union's pension fund. And oh, yes. I'm afraid I've got a new one. Fieldston Growth Enterprises. The union invested in it.'

'All right, but keep the fishing to a minimum, okay?'

'Sure, Roger. Whatever you say,' said Elizabeth, without conviction. 'I'll call you early tomorrow.'

'Wait a minute, Elizabeth,' said Padgett. 'Brayer wants to talk to you.' The irony was back in his voice.

Then Brayer's voice said, 'Elizabeth, have you heard the news about Senator Claremont?'

'No. What about him?'

'He died in his hotel room in Denver last night. It looks like a stroke or a heart attack, but the autopsy will take a while. There's going to be an investigation, so I'm taking you off what you're working on. I want you in Denver by late afternoon or early evening.'

Elizabeth couldn't help herself. She said, 'What for? It's crazy! I've been on this case exactly four hours, not to mention the fact that there's nothing for me to do in Denver when I get there.'

'No use arguing about it, you're going. It's orders from the Attorney General's office. We've got to send a field agent, and you're the closest one that I can spare today. This thing Roger's working on looks big, and everybody's tied up.'

'You trying to tell me the FBI doesn't have a field office in Denver?'

'Damn it, Elizabeth! I'm not going to stand here for the rest of the day justifying my decisions to you.

71

There are reasons, that's all. Now get moving.' He hung up, hard.

Elizabeth whispered to herself as she hung up the telephone, 'Yes, sir!' When she looked up, Hart was coming down the hall with the chief of police.

'Chief, thank you very much for your cooperation,' he said. 'We'll be in touch.' It was all very cordial, but there was an edge to his voice as though he were trying not to sound angry.

As they walked down the steps to their rented car he said, 'Was that your call from home?'

'Yes,' she said. 'Did you get one too?'

'Of course. A little while ago.' The anger was definite now.

'I don't understand it.'

'I do,' he said. 'Politics. Pure politics. They have to reassure the senators who vote on budgets that we take it seriously when one of them dies. Even if it's a heart attack.'

'But I'm not even a field investigator. I'm a data analyst.'

'Who cares? There's not going to be anything to investigate. We're just there for the roll call.'

'That still doesn't explain why they pulled us off an actual fresh murder when there must be thirty or forty teams closer to Denver who are better qualified than I am at least—'

'How do you know this was a murder?' he asked.

'Well it is, isn't it?' she said. 'Nothing else makes any sense at all. I was at Veasy's house this morning. They have a yard you could cover with a bedspread, and he was supposed to be carrying big sacks of fertilizer around in his pickup truck. What for? And the other

72

thing is that you're really angry and I don't think you would be unless you thought it was a murder too, so we can at least agree on that even if nobody else does. If you didn't think the case was important – that is, a murder – you wouldn't care if they took us off it.'

As she spoke, the words came faster and faster until Hart could hardly follow her. He took his eyes off the road for a second and saw Elizabeth was staring straight ahead with her brows knitted a little, which meant she had settled that part of it and was already launched into the next stage, whatever that might be, so before she got too far he'd better tell her. 'Do you want to know what I found this morning in the union hall parking lot?'

She turned to him again and smiled. 'Of course, Bob.' He wasn't sure if she was humoring him or not, but he went on.

'A few bits of wire and a fragment of the jacket of a blasting cap. Both charred. So I guess we know that much, anyway.'

'Yes,' said Elizabeth. 'That much is for certain. Now if only we didn't have to go on a side trip to Colorado. I wonder what it's like there this time of year.'

'Cold, clear. Now and then some snow.'

'Terrific,' she said. 'And all just so the Senate staff can look at a report in two months and see that two people from Washington were there.'

'Oh, I'm afraid it's worse than that, Elizabeth. They won't have to wait more than a day. There'll be reporters, photographers, probably national televsion. Senator Claremont was a very important man. That's the real reason why they sent us, I think. After tomorrow's newspapers whoever's there won't be of much use in undercover stuff, and we're home office.'

'Oh, God,' she said, and slumped back in the seat. She thought, wonderful. Elizabeth Waring on national news in her thin California clothes investigating a death by old age. On national television. While somewhere in Southern California there would be two clerks, both of them busy forgetting what the man looked like that bought the hundred-pound bags of fertilizer and blasting caps last Friday around supper time. Probably they'd be watching television. And what they'd see was . . . Elizabeth Waring. In Denver, Colorado, there, by her official presence alone to reassure ninety-nine men over sixty that there was no such thing as a death by old age.

EIGHT

By now most of it had probably happened, he thought. Just after daylight somebody would have gone through the alley and seen the two of them lying there. Around 7.30 or so whoever owned the car would have come out expecting to drive it to work. And the Senator – hard to say what time a senator would get up in the morning, but it would be before now. There was no question he was already dead.

It had been a long, cold night, he thought. It wasn't so bad now – almost a different world. But he was tired, and some of the aches and pains were beginning to feel as if they might be more than that. He went over it in his mind again. He had waited to get a couple of miles away before he'd even looked for a car to hotwire. He'd found a two-year-old Pontiac parked on the street and taken it north on Route 87 to Cheyenne, Wyoming. Cheyenne had been the only choice, really, and that worried him a little – only two hours of driving time from Denver. But he'd have a long lead before anybody noticed it, where he'd left it. He was proud of that one, and it cancelled out the fact that Cheyenne was too obvious. It takes someone a day or so to decide that a car in a parking lot attached to a housing complex not only doesn't belong to him, it doesn't belong to anyone else either. Then it takes a day for somebody to get up the nerve to complain about it. The walk to the airport had taken some more time, but at least it had been too dark for anyone to see him.

He had managed to get on the 7:00 a.m. flight from Cheyenne to Salt Lake City, and now he was on the noon plane to Las Vegas. He'd phoned in a reservation to Caesar's Palace from Brigham Young Airport. The warm, clean air of the plane was a foretaste of what would be waiting for him in Las Vegas. And then, he told himself, it would all be over. No more fear, no more cold, and a chance to rest and take care of his wounds. This had been the worst trip he'd ever made. A nightmare. But at least the worry was over now – that had been the worst – the hot, physical fear, and the other part that knew you were going too fast, probably making mistakes because you were scared. That was all over now. Right now there were probably policemen searching for one or two young men who looked as though they'd been in a fight, but if they were, they were looking in the poorer sections of Denver, Colorado. They might be looking for a stolen Pontiac Grand Prix, brown, with a white vinyl top. If they were, they probably weren't looking for it in an apartment complex in Cheyenne, Wyoming. None of these things had anything to do with the man who would be checking into Caesar's Palace this afternoon, limping a little, and wearing dark glasses that hid a few bruises and a cut or two. A man who had suffered for taking a chance on a ski slope that was beyond his capacity wouldn't raise much comment in Las Vegas.

The inexhaustible supply of people of that sort was what paid the rent.

The engines cut back and the blunt nose of the giant airplane seemed to run head on into a more solid medium, slowing and falling at once. Hart looked over at Elizabeth, who was peering out the window over the craggy formations of the Rockies, her forehead pressed against the glass. There was something special, almost intoxicating, about being close to a beautiful woman. There was a space around her, a few inches, that belonged to her and seemed to be permeated with her smell and sound. And something else, like an electrical charge, that seemed to tug you closer to her, but set off a warning signal that reminded you not to let yourself drift any closer, because in a moment you would touch, brush a sleeve or a shoulder against a soft arm, and then it would be too late. You could never relax inside the charged zone that belonged to a beautiful woman unless there was some kind of prior under-standing between you that made it all right to touch because you had touched before. He wondered if Elizabeth was aware of the tension too, sitting there thinking about it and wishing the plane would land so she wouldn't be forced to think about it anymore, wouldn't be held in enforced immobility while each of them hovered in suspension at the border of the other's personal space.

Beautiful women like this one were a special prob-lem. The big, almond-shaped green eyes, the tiny waist, the impossibly thin wrists and long, graceful fingers made her seem as though she belonged to a superior species, smaller and more delicate than ordinary mortals and yet quicker. The impression might have been of an insubstantial creature, but it wasn't that at all – what he felt was astonishment, almost as he might for a small antelope or an ocelot, an animal, a miraculous thing unconscious of what it was. He sensed in himself an overwhelming desire to touch, to verify that she was real and had the feel, the surface, and weight that his eyes told him she had.

She turned her face to him. 'I hope we can get through this quickly and get back to work.'

Hart said, 'Do you think the case is the real thing? I mean, we knew it was no accident, but we also know Veasy probably didn't buy the fertilizer himself. It seems to me the theory that it was a pro hinges on his being able to work with whatever he found.'

Elizabeth frowned. 'Yes, there is that. But we don't really know what we're looking for, so anything we find out is to the good. The fact that it took a day for the local police to come up with the theory that it was dynamite, and another day to figure out that it wasn't, and then it took another day for us to prove that the explosion was planned seems to me to show that whoever it was knew what he was doing.'

'But that doesn't make it much more likely that this is a case of the sort that your section would be interested in, does it?'

'No, but I've got a couple of other things I'm checking on. The method isn't what's worrying me right now. I'm satisfied that he's good enough at what he does. What's missing is a reason for anybody to hire him to do it. And I still think he was hired. There's nothing about Veasy to give me an excuse to believe it, but I do. People who just get mad at each other use guns or knives.'

The airplane whistled down to meet the runway, then thumped to a stop before taxiing to the terminal. Elizabeth and Hart sat still while other passengers filed out, then slipped into the queue when there was an opening. As soon as they were in the carpeted tube that stretched from the airplane to the terminal Elizabeth spotted the man. He wasn't obtrusive enough to come to the attention of the other passengers. He could have been an airline employee, but he wasn't. He stood there beside a wall ignoring everyone who went by him, looking straight at Elizabeth. She said to Hart, 'We're being met.'

'What?'

She leaned into him so her face was close to his ear and said, 'They've sent someone to meet us.'

Hart said, 'I see him. It's good. Maybe we'll get this over fast.'

They walked up to him and he said, 'Mr. Hart? Miss Waring? Come with me, please.' They followed him, and Elizabeth was surprised to see him open a side door at the end of the tube. Then they were in a small room with an entrance on the other side.

'Right on time,' said the man. 'I'm Pete Turnbull, FBI Denver.' He held out his hand for each of them to shake. Elizabeth studied him and decided he couldn't have been more than twenty-five, but was trying by means of his neat, banker's blue suit and the serious, competent look on his face to cross the line into the thirties. It made him look precocious, like an overeager junior executive.

'Good to meet you,' said Hart. 'What now?'

'I'll take you to the office, where they'll fill you in on the case. Give me your baggage tags and I'll arrange to have your suitcases catch up with you there.'

They handed him the tags, and he disappeared through the other door for a second, then reappeared, smiling. 'There's a car waiting,' he said, and they followed him out the door and down a corridor to the main lobby.

At the big swinging doors Elizabeth felt a gust of cold wind, so she wrapped her lightweight coat around herself tightly and plunged after Turnbull into the open air. In a second they had passed through it into the waiting car, which was parked in a loading zone with its motor running. Turnbull took the wheel and maneuvered them expertly into the circular drive and away.

'What can you tell us about it?' asked Elizabeth.

'The Senator?' said Turnbull. 'Not much, really. You'll get the full rundown. I'm not on it. What I know is he died this morning, early, and was found by his legislative assistant a short time later. That much is in the papers. The rest of it, if there is any more, they're keeping quiet for now.'

Elizabeth looked at Hart, who seemed to be deeper in thought than the case would warrant. Then he said, in a voice that was too casual for the expression on his face, 'Do you know if they've ordered an autopsy?'

'I haven't heard. I suppose they have, though. I know about five agents were put on this case today, and they're on overtime as of two hours ago, so they'd probably at least do that much.'

Hart's expression didn't change. He sat back in the seat and said nothing.

The federal office building was a relic of the era when politicans liked to remind themselves and their constituents that this was, after all, the US government. The building was huge, with lots of Corinthian columns that weren't there to support anything except the public's awe and reverence.

Elizabeth and Hart entered through the broad portal, expecting to see the place had been empty since five o'clock. It was true that the dozens of smoked-glass doors off the foyer seemed to be locked up for the night, but there were still people coming and going, and off to the left there were five men who were unmistakably reporters sitting on one of the massive oak benches.

At the far wall was a directory of offices. The FBI was on the second floor, so they walked up the marble staircase. Elizabeth identified what had been nagging at her since she'd seen the place. It was like the buildings in Washington, with everything on a scale larger than people. The railing was too thick for a human hand to grasp, the doorways were at least ten feet high, the benches in the foyer made the reporters look like lost children. It was as though someone had taken great pains to make it clear that this was an outpost of Washington, and by no means a minor one. When they reached the second floor there was no question where they should go next. The cavernous hallway was dark and empty except for a single lighted office at the end.

Inside the office there was a single desk where a receptionist sat during the day. Agent Turnbull ushered them through the outer office and opened the door to a small room with a long conference table, where three men in shirtsleeves were talking across open file folders. Behind her Hart said, 'Hello, we're Waring and Hart.' Elizabeth decided it sounded like a company that sold expensive clothes to British gentlemen.

The men stood up and shook hands while the one at the end of the table said, 'This is Bill Greenley. And Joe Mistretta. I'm Mike Lang. Have a seat, and we'll get you caught up. It won't take much time, because we don't know a whole lot yet. I think Bill can do it quickest.'

Greenley was a man in his middle thirties who sounded to Elizabeth to have spent some time testifying in courtrooms. He had seemed a little uncomfortable during the obligatory amenities, and now he launched into his recitation as though it had been prepared and rehearsed in advance. 'We've placed the time of death between 0630 and 0800 today. There was no one with the deceased at the time, but the Senator's legislative assistant, Mr. Carlson, came to meet him for breakfast at 0800 and found him dead. The preliminary report from the autopsy says the body temperature was eighty-six degrees at 1000 today, which would mean no more than four hours. Claremont was partially dressed at the time of death.' He added parenthetically, 'As though he were getting ready to go to breakfast. The preliminary report contained the observation that the cause of death was heart failure. Not damaged. Just stopped.' Greenley set aside the sheet of paper he'd been looking at and took up another.

'The secondary report indicates that the Senator's

blood contained traces of an unidentified toxic substance, which was probably introduced orally.' Greenley paused to look at Elizabeth and Hart as though he wanted to let his statement blossom in their minds before he pushed on to the next level. 'The toxic substance has been determined to be the probable cause of death.'

'Does it have any competition?' asked Hart.

'No,' said Greenley. 'No lumps, bruises, cuts, or signs of a struggle. Heart and circulation okay for his age, according to the coroner.'

'Have you got a lab analysis of the substances found in the room yet?'

'They're still working on it,' said Lang. 'But if you mean a simple overdose, I think not. Here's the list of the stuff they found. The only medicine was aspirin.' He handed a sheet from another file to Elizabeth, who held it so that Hart could read it too: 'Rolaids, one roll, unopened. Listerine mouthwash, four-ounce size. Polident, one box, seventeen. Aspirin, Ascriptin brand, one-hundred-tablet size. Empty glass, probably from alcoholic beverage. Glass for soaking false teeth. Deodorant, Mennen stick.'

For the first time, Elizabeth spoke. 'Who's actually in charge of the case? The Denver police?'

'Right,' said Lang. 'They knew we'd be interested, and so they called us in at the start. But at least for the moment it's theirs.'

'What are the ground rules?' asked Hart.

'As close to full cooperation as we can make it. Right now all we're doing is laboratory work, and they're doing the rest of it. We've agreed to share all information both ways. If somebody finds something that points away from Denver we take over that part of it.'

'What if it turns out to be murder?' said Elizabeth.

'The unidentified toxic substance is making that look like a possibility,' said Lang. 'I don't like it, but there's no use hiding from it, and that's why we asked for reinforcements this morning.' Elizabeth and Hart exchanged glances, but Lang continued. 'If that's what it is, we take full responsibility. Assassinating a senator is a federal crime.'

Elizabeth sat quietly and felt a wave of weariness come over her. Ventura seemed to be far behind her now, receding into some impassable distance composed of complications rather than mere time and space. For a while the Ventura case had begun to look hopeful, she thought. No, not hopeful, really, but so peculiar that there had to be something to it. She promised herself she wasn't going to forget about it. But now there was this. It would have to be gotten through somehow before she could start learning about her own killer. She was surprised to find herself thinking of him in those terms, but now that she had, she accepted it. That was what he was – her own. Her first.

'So what would you like us to do while we're waiting for the lab work?' asked Hart.

'That's one of the things we were trying to decide when you arrived. We've asked for everything Washington could send us on the Senator – friends, enemies, habits, even old news stories. It'll take time for them to dig it out, though, and it probably won't give us anything we didn't get from Claremont's assistant hours ago. The best we can do at the moment is probably to put together as much of the background as we can, and figure out what to do if that toxic substance turns out to be arsenic, say, or cyanide. It might be best if you just went to your hotel and got some rest. No use all of us sitting here.'

'Or maybe to the Senator's hotel,' said Hart. 'I suppose it's still being held pretty close by the local police. Would we step on their toes if we went over to take a look?'

'No,' said Lang. 'That's part of the deal. Joe, can you take them over? I'll call you if the lab work comes in.'

Hart and Mistretta waited at the doorway for Elizabeth to go first, but then Mistretta edged out in front, striding down the hallway and struggling into his coat. They followed him down the stairs and along an unfamiliar back corridor that opened on a parking lot with only about a dozen cars scattered at varying distances from the building, looking forlorn and stranded. A light snow had begun to fall.

As Mistretta turned out of the lot and drove down the side street toward the Constellation Hotel, Elizabeth said, 'Joe, where do you think this case will end up? Murder?'

'When you see the room you'll be able to make up your own mind, Elizabeth,' said Mistretta. 'But I won't hedge, because an hour from now you'll have reached the same conclusion anyway. The door was locked from inside, the window was locked from inside, there is no reason to believe anybody saw the Senator from midnight until 8:00 a.m. I think before the night is over we'll have a lab report that the toxic substance was some kind of poison you can buy over the counter. And I think tomorrow by noon we'll have a confidential report from the Senator's doctors at Bethesda Naval Medical Center saying he had terminal cancer, or an even more confidential report that he was being blackmailed, or something of that sort. Because whatever happened to him, the chances are pretty good that he did it to himself. And if I have to make an early call, I'll go with the odds every time.'

Elizabeth thought about this for a few seconds, and then Mistretta added, 'And it was poison.'

'So?' she asked. 'Unusual, I'll admit, but it happens.'

'True,' he said. 'But it's hard to find a poison that doesn't leave the victim feeling pretty awful for an hour or two before he dies. And if he doesn't expect to feel that way he picks up a phone and calls somebody.'

The hotel room looked as though it had been the scene of some unusually messy kind of mechanical failure. Every smooth surface was covered with a thin film of greasy black dust. The bedclothes were churned into a pile at the foot of the bed. On the rug in the center of the floor was the chalked silhouette of a human form, caught in an attitude suggesting a grotesque dance.

Elizabeth found an empty spot in the room and stood, looking around without touching anything. It was hard to imagine what the place had been like when it was occupied by living people. The police had apparently looked at everything, dusted the whole room for fingerprints, taken everything that was movable back to the laboratory for study.

Her trained mind shifted into its analytical mode and concentrated on the elements before her. The

86

absent cups and glasses were taken care of; the body; Claremont's luggage. She looked into the closet. His clothes were gone too. All that was left, really, were the four walls and furniture, covered with fingerprint dust. She walked to the bathroom. The U-shaped trap was gone from beneath the sink; the drainpipe ended abruptly a foot below the fixture. Even the toilet had been tampered with: the tank cover was on the floor covered with the ubiquitous black dust.

'This isn't doing me much good,' said Elizabeth. 'It doesn't look like a hotel room anymore.'

'I know what you mean,' said Mistretta. 'If there ever was anything to find in here, it'll turn up in the lab reports. The forensics people were in here for six hours. It looks like they've covered everything.'

'Do you mind if we try something else?'

'Why not?' said Mistretta. 'Until the final autopsy report comes in, anything's as good as anything else.'

'Then I'd like to see another room like this one. The best thing would be an empty one on this corridor,' said Elizabeth.

'Good idea,' said Hart. He had been silent the whole time, walking around the room making notes on a pocket pad, tearing off sheets, and stuffing them into his pockets.

'Take your pick,' said Mistretta. 'They've closed off the whole floor for the time being. They're all empty.'

They tried the next room, but it was torn up too.

'The assistant's room?' asked Hart.

'Right,' said Mistretta, who closed the door and led them to the next one.

Inside, Elizabeth's imagination felt comfortable again. The room was designed to be exactly the same

87

as the Senator's, but it still had that peculiar air of suspension that hotel rooms seemed to have, as though somebody had been there so recently that if you turned your head quickly some relic or remnant of their personal lives would be visible for an instant. She walked around the room, opening drawers, peering into the closet, finally, focusing her attention on the bathroom. Everything gleamed with a precarious expectancy that made her want to open the seals and move things around, like walking on fresh snow. But her mind moved for her, counting and calculating and remembering.

When she returned to the bedroom Hart was kneeling in the open doorway scrutinizing the locks. He said, to nobody in particular, 'Not much to stop anybody if the deadbolt wasn't in.'

Mistretta said, 'No good. The assistant says their bags were with them from the time they left the airport, and they didn't go out after they got here. When he left the Senator threw the bolt. In the morning they had to call the maintenance man with an electromagnetic gizmo to open it up. That didn't work either because the fit was too tight, so they drilled it.'

Elizabeth wondered why she hadn't seen that, but apparently Hart hadn't either. It wasn't much comfort, she realized, as she walked to the window.

Mistretta saw her fiddling with the latch and said, 'That's been checked too. There's a little wear on the molding, but the lock is working perfectly. No prints on the inside handle, and no handle on the outside.'

Elizabeth went out onto the balcony. It was really night now and an icy wind clutched at her hair and the skirt of her coat. She looked around at the identical balconies, beside her and above and below. No, it was probably too farfetched. Four floors below her was the parking lot, where the cars were only shiny-colored rectangles with no depth to them. Somebody who wanted to kill a senator could do it in a thousand ways that didn't involve swinging on a rope that high up in the cold. Might as well ask, anyway.

Elizabeth came in and shut the window. The air in the room seemed unnaturally still and quiet and warm. 'What about the balcony?' she asked. 'Any way to tell if anyone was on it?'

'Not much point to it, since the lock would have kept him in the cold anyway,' said Mistretta, 'but they checked it. There wasn't anything much. No prints on the railings, no rope marks, nothing on the glass except the usual smudges and a couple of spots where the maid had given it a quick swipe with a dustrag.'

Elizabeth said, 'Wait a minute. Let's go take a look.'

Mistretta shrugged and followed her back to the Senator's room. Hart appeared to be unaware of them; he was now in the bathroom, kneeling beside the bathtub and studying the drain.

Elizabeth went directly to the Senator's window, walked out to the balcony, and looked back into the lighted room. There was a thin film of dust over the whole surface of the glass, dappled with lighter dots where fingers had touched it. But in two places about two and a half feet apart, there were clean spots, where someone had brushed a cloth in a circular motion. She came back inside.

'Joe, the whole window is covered with prints and smudges and dust, except those two places. The one we were in before doesn't have any clean spots.'

The telephone rang, and it startled her. 'Hello?' she said, far too loud.

'Mike Lang here.'

'Yes, Mike,' said Elizabeth.

'I think it's going to be a long night. The poison turned out to be curare, of all things. It's in the glass where he soaked his dentures, in the dentures, and no place else. No container anywhere, either, and the Polident box is clean.'

'So it is murder,' said Elizabeth.

'I hate to pin it down that tight, but I'm damned if I see any other explanation. He couldn't have carried curare in without a container, and a man doesn't kill himself with his own false teeth. At least not if he's got any sense of dignity.'

'No. But curare? Are you sure? It's not exactly the American murderer's favorite form of poison, is it?'

'Of course I'm sure. And I don't have anything else to tell you that'll make it seem sensible. But at this point I'd be willing to listen to anything anybody else has.'

'I think there's a chance somebody came in from the balcony,' said Elizabeth. 'We're not sure yet, but it looks as though somebody had both hands on the glass, about chest high.'

'You mean they got prints on it?' asked Lang. 'Terrific!'

'No,' said Elizabeth. 'That's just it. Somebody wiped the glass off. Nobody who works for a hotel would wipe two spots on a six-by-eight-foot window. They'd wash it or forget it. And no guest would wipe the outside of a window for any reason.'

'Is Mistretta with you?'

'Yes, he's right here.'

'Then let me talk to him.'

Elizabeth handed the phone to Joe, who listened intently for a few seconds and then said, 'Yeah, it's possible she's right, but we're still looking it over.'

He listened again, then said, 'The police didn't think so. No. Too obvious, I guess. The window latch was the first thing they went for after the corpse was moved. They said no indication of forced entry.'

He was silent for a moment. 'Yeah, that too. Of course. We'll keep you posted.'

Mistretta hung up and chuckled. 'That's something, isn't it?' he said to Elizabeth. 'We earn our pay on this one all right. Which do you want to work on first? Proving a man came in through the locked fourth-floor window because there are no fingerprints, or figuring out how he arrived at the idea of using curare on the old guy's false teeth when he got here? I don't suppose the MO file will help much on this one, unless it was a South American pygmy we're looking for.' He shook his head and the false bravado began to fade.

Elizabeth wasn't looking at him, though. She was standing before the window with both hands in front of her. 'Pygmies don't live in South America,' she muttered absently, staring at her reflection.

'I suppose we'd better get the forensics people back up here,' he said, picking up the telephone again.

Elizabeth didn't turn, just said, 'Yes. I'd like to be here when they come.' She'd never noticed that before, she thought. When you press your palms against a flat surface, the tips of your fingers are just exactly shoulder height. If you allowed for shoe soles, five foot ten? Six feet? They'd measure it, though. You could always count on them to measure.

Hart came into the room, bringing with him his notepad, still scribbling on it. He said, 'I heard a phone ring. Was it the lab report?'

'That's right,' said Elizabeth. 'It was curare that was put into the glass where he soaked his dentures, believe it or not. Mixed with his Polident.'

'What's the report on the rest of his stuff? Any curare or containers for it?' He seemed to Elizabeth to be hiding his surprise at the poison and it annoyed her a little. How could he not be surprised?

'No,' she said tonelessly.

'Then I'd say we have only a few things we can check on,' he said. 'One is that somebody close enough to him to get into his luggage put poison on one of the Polident tablets and only one. Maybe his assistant or whoever packed his bags. Another is that somebody tampered with them between Washington and here.' He hesitated for a moment, but Elizabeth wasn't going to help him, since he hadn't had the decency to be surprised. Then he said, 'But I'd say the least unlikely thing is that somebody came in through the window.'

'The forensics people are on their way up now to check the window out,' said Mistretta. 'Elizabeth figured it out a little while ago.'

'Good thinking, Elizabeth,' he said, with apparent sincerity.

Elizabeth wasn't ready to accept the compliment. Patronizing bastards, all of them. She was past that part of it anyway, thinking about the killer. He had to be athletic, or at least fit, to be able to go from any other room to this one. No matter how it was done he

92

still had to get from one balcony to another in the cold and dark. That probably meant he wasn't over forty. He was between five foot nine and six feet tall. And he was sneaky. God, he was sneaky.

NINE

There was something clean about the sun in Las Vegas. Even in February there was a searing, blinding white light that made you feel as if you were being sterilized, even cauterized, so there wasn't a germ that could stick to you. Everything extraneous would be burned off your skin, desiccated and sucked dry, its empty husk blown clattering away in the hot wind out of the desert. Even the air itself felt like that – a breeze that carried with it tiny abrasive particles of ground-up quartz and topaz too small to see. You could feel them buffing and polishing away at you.

He rolled over on his stomach. Better be careful the first time out. Getting a sunburn on top of all those scrapes and bruises would be about the limit of what he could endure. He could already feel the sun gradually heating up his back and shoulders, breathing its energy into them so that moment by moment the temperature of his skin rose in infinitesimal gradients. In a few more minutes, he decided, he'd go back to his room and get cleaned up, then take a nice long nap before dinner. Your body heals faster while you sleep, he thought. There was no reason to think about anything at all until Friday night. Friday was payday.

The soft electronic female voices were alternating on

the public address system: 'Telephone for Mr. Harrison Rand. Harrison Rand, telephone. Telephone for Princess Karina. Princess Karina, telephone,' a steady murmur going out across the swimming pool from nowhere in particular, the volume just high enough to flicker across the corner of your consciousness. There was no more urgency to it than the constant whir and click of the slot machines in the casino. This, he thought, was the only place he knew of where clock time didn't matter. You measured time against the size of your bankroll – unless you were lying on a chaise longue next to the swimming pool, he remembered Then the sun would damned well remind you what time it was if you weren't careful. Enough for today.

He sat up and put on the dark brown terrycloth robe and zoris he'd picked up in one of the hotel stores this afternoon. Then he changed his mind again. The vast empty surface of the swimming pool sparkled at him. There was time enough for one more dip in the water, he thought. There was no reason not to do exactly as he pleased, and swimming was good for you – the best thing in the world for damaged muscles, and it would be time to stop when you didn't feel like it anymore.

The water was warm, almost hot, like a gigantic Roman bath. He swam lazily from one end to the other, testing the flex and fluidity of his muscles against the solidity and support of the water. It had always struck him as funny that they should have a heated pool that was twice the size of the ones they used in the Olympics, and that he should be alone in it every time. People who were serious about swimming didn't drive through the desert to do it. He stopped at the shallow end and let himself go limp in the warm water, feeling the deliciousness of it, held there as though by a broad, gentle hand. He floated on his back, surveying the people sprawled on lawn chairs, absorbing the sunlight. Most of them had probably been up all night, he thought. Gambling, drinking, fucking, and now they were recharging their batteries by the energy of the sun. No, they weren't swimmers, but it seemed to comfort them to be near all that water. Something to look at through your polarized sunglasses while you waited for night.

He swam back to the deep end, acutely aware of the workings of his muscles as he stroked. He was going to be all right. Everything felt exactly as he wanted it to. At least his body did. His head was going to take longer. It felt big and soft and sensitive today, a peeled pumpkin held in anxious balance on a neck too thin for it. Just so there weren't any scars on his face. The pain he could live with.

He pulled himself up out of the pool and flopped down on his chaise longue. In a few seconds he could feel the water on his body disappearing into the parched desert air, leaving his skin feeling tight. He let the sun settle its gentle pressure on his face for a few moments before he put on his sunglasses. Then he closed his eyes and let himself slip into a state that felt as good as sleep but wasn't quite a relinquishment of consciousness. 'Telephone for Mr. Arthur Walters. Arthur Walters, telephone. Telephone for Mrs. Natalie Beamish, Natalie Beamish, telephone,' crooned the soft unanxious voices in monotonous alternation.

'You do all that to yourself or did you have help?' said a voice above him. His eyes flicked open for an instant like camera shutters behind the sunglasses, and brought back with them into the darkness an imprint of the familiar, hulking shape. Little Norman.

'You know how it is, Little Norman,' he answered. 'You want something done right, you have to do it yourself.' He heard the scrape as Little Norman dragged a lawn chair across the pavement to his side. Little Norman. The first thing anybody said when he heard the name was that he never wanted to see Big Norman. Little Norman was six foot four without his hand-tooled Mexican cowboy boots, and must have weighed in at two-fifty without the two rolls of quarters he always had in his pockets. As if those fists needed the extra weight. And Little Norman was no longer young. He had to be at least fifty-five and semiretired, so that wasn't it either.

'What brings you to Caesar's Palace, Little Norman?' he said. 'I thought you hung around at the Sands.'

'Nice sunny day out,' said Little Norman. 'Good day to get a tan.' Little Norman was wearing his usual tailor-made suit and stiff-collared white shirt with pearl studs. Little Norman was also blacker than the bottom of a coal mine.

'You're right there. Been getting some myself, and doing a little swimming.'

'That's good, kid. That's what you need for those thumps you got on you. A little sunshine, a little exercise, a lot of rest.' He said it again, 'A lot of rest.'

He just nodded and let Little Norman go on.

'For excitement there's always the tables. You don't have to do anything spectacular to keep your blood circulating, you know what I mean, kid?'

'Sure I do, Norman.' He smiled. Then he said, 'I'm

not working. Nobody works in Las Vegas, you know that.'

Little Norman's long face broke into a broad grin. 'That's real sensible, kid. Coming in here with a face like that, people wonder. I'm not asking where you got it, you understand. But people do wonder where you got it and whether you're maybe a little mad about it.'

'If you see anybody like that, will you do me a favor?'

'Sure, kid, if I see anybody like that.'

'Tell them I'm not working.'

'I'll do that.'

'Thanks, Little Norman. I wouldn't want anybody worrying about my health.'

Little Norman stood up, straightened his tie, and said, 'If you've got some time on your hands you might stop by for a drink. You know where to find me, don't you?'

'Sure,' he said.

'I'll see you, then.'

He watched Little Norman's huge back moving along the edge of the pool toward the entrance near the casino. It hadn't taken long, he thought. He reached in the pocket of his robe and pulled out his watch. Four hours. He'd been in Las Vegas less than four hours before someone had noticed him and told Little Norman. But at least Little Norman seemed to be satisfied. For the next hour he'd be scurrying all over town telling rich, powerful old men that there was nothing to worry about this time. Their deaths hadn't been purchased yet. It really was a vacation. And the uneasy truce would hold until the next thing came up. He should have looked up Little Norman right away, he thought, and made sure the word got out before any of them got nervous. It was the polite thing to do.

TEN

In his room he closed the door, bolted and chained it, then took off his robe and walked into the shower. Little Norman worried him because it hadn't occurred to him that the way he looked would cause them alarm. It was never a good thing to come to the attention of any of the dozen nervous old men who lived in the fragile sanctuary of the open city. Each of them had survived to his present vicious senility through predatory cunning and the instinctive preference for striking first. And they wouldn't forget that. No matter if you were eighty-three years old and propped like a sack of rags in a wheelchair like Castiglione, you would remember that much.

As long as Little Norman did what the old men paid him for, it would be fine. And there was no reason to think he wouldn't. But now a slight trickle of fear had begun to mix itself into his bloodstream. It wasn't enough to spoil the pleasure of being safe and comfortable in Caesar's, but it was there. He decided that maybe it wouldn't be such a bad idea to go have that drink with Little Norman. He had told him he was on vacation, and now he'd damn well better act like it. Besides, he was on vacation. At least until Friday night.

*

When he woke up the room was dark and he could hear the voice of a man outside the door of his room saying, 'System, my ass. You see this place, Alice? It's made out of systems thought up by dumb women from Fullerton.' Then a door closed and he heard footsteps receding down the hallway. He couldn't hear what Alice said in reply, but the man's voice said, 'So you won once. That doesn't . . .' and then they were out of earshot.

He rolled over and looked at the luminous dial of his watch. Nine thirty. Perfect, he thought. Just the right time to start the evening. He lurched to his feet, turned on the lights, and went to the closet to lay out his clothes. The nap had done him more good than he'd dared to hope. He felt cheerful and clearheaded. If he hadn't caught sight of himself in the mirror he'd have said he was 100 percent.

It was Eddie who'd taught him about rest. Eddie had been the undefeated world champion of resting. He could still hear the quiet, patient voice: 'Never work when you're tired, kid. You have to be able to think straight, and you have to have the physical edge too. Each time it's a contest and if you don't come in first place every time you're dead.' Eddie Mastrewski had kept the physical edge all right. That frigid winter night in Philadelphia when the building contractor had spotted them on the street and tried to run away he'd seen it. All his mind had told him was that they couldn't shoot, and so he was paralyzed for a minute. But Eddie had just muttered 'Oh, shit,' reached over the seat to the back of the car, and taken off on foot after the contractor with the tire chain. He ran him down and garrotted him.

But Eddie'd had the build for it, he thought. A Pennsylvania Polack from the coal mining country – probably the toughest physical specimens on earth except for maybe central Asian goatherds who were supposed to live to be a hundred and forty. He could hear Eddie correcting him, 'I'm not a Pole, I'm a Lithuanian. There's a difference, kid. I just don't know what it is.' But Eddie had sure known how to sleep. He seemed to sleep whenever there wasn't some definite reason why he shouldn't. Even then Eddie seemed a little resentful and suspicious that the reason might not be good enough. He'd seen Eddie sleep on trains, buses, and airplanes; in stations and sitting up behind the wheel of a parked car. Over the years he'd learned that there was something to Eddie's theory. Sleep really did make a difference. Maybe Eddie hadn't had enough sleep the day he got it. Or maybe when you got to a certain age there just wasn't enough sleep to make up for all the years.

He put on the sport coat he'd bought in the hotel store this afternoon, took another look at the knot in his tie, closed his door, and began to walk down the hall toward the elevator. Then he hesitated. No, he thought, it's stupid not to. He returned to the room, bent over, and pulled a few tufts of lint from the bright azure carpet. He stuffed them between the door and the jamb about two inches above the surface of the red carpet of the hallway. It's always better to know than to wonder, he thought as he stepped into the elevator.

He made his way through the crowds and noise of the casino and out to the front entrance. The doors gave a wheezy sigh and opened automatically to pull him forward into the warm night air. The absurd magnificence of the oversized fountain along the drive seemed to be the focus of the unanimous eyeless contemplation of the genuine Carrara marble copies of classical statues that stood sentinel. Sammy Cohen had once called them The Stupefied Losers, but that wasn't what they looked like. It was as though they were staring in dumb amazement at waking up and finding themselves so far from the gentle, reasonable proportions of home.

He glanced at the line of taxis waiting in the loop, but dismissed them in favor of the stroll. There were hundreds of people walking up and down the sidewalks of the Strip in light summer clothing that changed colors as they passed under the garish incandescent auras of the gigantic marquees and glittering facades of the casinos. He stepped in among them, into a herd that was flowing along in the direction of the Sands. As they passed each doorway, came into the glowing circle of each new complex of lights and neon signs, a portion of the herd would be drawn off by the magnetism of it. Others would issue forth from the doors to replace them.

They were moving toward the center of the city, and as they did the white river of automobile traffic in the street seemed to slow down and constrict, the signs and lights to cluster together more tightly into a general undifferentiated blur and dazzle, until the doorways were just holes in the light.

Then there was a pause in the glitter, as though it were gathering itself up for some major effort, and then the monolithic marquee of the Sands burst forth to dominate the night. He peeled himself out of the moving crowd, walked up the steps, and crossed the

103

boundary into the air-conditioned cool of the casino. Inside the light, the air, the colors, the sounds were all different and belonged to the special exigencies of this place, where the world consisted of a low-frequency hum of unflagging agitation, like an itch or a hope.

He made one slow circuit of the casino, past the banks of winking, buzzing, clattering slot machines that spun gyroscopically on the periphery, then past the zone of roulette wheels and crap tables and along the rank of fan-shaped blackjack games ascending in order of wealth toward the roped-off sanctum of high-stakes baccarat, where the croupiers wore black tuxedos and the reverential faces of French financial consultants.

Little Norman wasn't in evidence in the casino, but he knew that someone would tell him. One of the unseen beings Norman kept on his personal payroll would probably be talking into a telephone right now. He made a leisurely path to the doorway of the Regency Room and slipped through the doors into the candlelit red-and-gold silence. He always had the sense that this place was insulated from the cacophony of the city by something more than walls, as though everything outside could explode into screaming atoms and you'd never know it by so much as the wavering of a candle flame. The maitre d' conducted him to a booth in the far corner of the room, where a waiter nodded his respect for the wisdom of beef Wellington and a middle-range Bordeaux with two glasses.

He had almost finished the beef Wellington when Little Norman came in and sat down at his table. 'Hello, kid,' said Little Norman. 'You come over here looking for me?'

'That's right, Norman. I thought I'd take you up on that drink. I suppose you've already had dinner?'

'Yeah, but since you got an extra glass I'll help you with the wine.' Norman poured it himself, sniffed the bouquet, and said, 'Not bad at all. Your idea or the waiter's?'

'Mine,' he said and kept eating.

'Then you've picked up a lot since you worked with old Eddie. I always heard that travel broadens you.' He chuckled.

'I've always heard that too.'

'Something on your mind, kid? You're not looking too cheerful. I mean besides the thumps on your face.'

'I'm fine. Nothing wrong that a few days of rest won't handle. How about you, Norman? You have a hard day? Run into anybody that was nervous about anything?'

'No,' said Little Norman, and smiled. 'I ran into one or two who used to be nervous, but I seem to have a natural talent for reassuring people. Should have been a psychiatrist, I guess. I'd probably have a lot more money.'

He eyed the heavy gold ring on the finger Norman had wrapped around the stem of the glass. The diamond, he calculated, was around five carats. It looked big even on Little Norman. 'I doubt it,' he said.

'I guess you're right,' said Little Norman. 'White folks don't want a big black psychiatrist, and black folks don't have the money for one. They just have to stay crazy, like I did, and learn to enjoy it.'

He pushed his plate away and noticed that Little Norman had emptied the bottle. 'Well, how about that drink, Norman? You want it here, or you want to go someplace else?'

Little Norman leaned back in his chair to let the waiter deposit the check where the plate had been. He paused to savor the last inch of wine in his glass, then said, 'You know, I think you've been working too hard. Seems to me like you're in a hurry all the time, like you forgot how to relax. I'm gonna have to take pity on you and remind you how it's done.' He waited while the waiter whisked the money away. Then he stood up and said, 'No sense in being crazy if you're not gonna enjoy it.'

'I know you wouldn't want me to learn it on the street, Norman,' he said, and got up to follow.

Elizabeth sat on the edge of the bed watching the forensic team going about its work. It took an extraordinary act of patience even to watch them. They crawled around on all fours, sighting along the edge of each smooth surface for latent prints, then wrote in pads, took photographs, stretched tape measures from one point to another, and made more notes.

It was already clear that they weren't going to find anything new in the room, she thought as she watched a sergeant crawl up to the coffee table and stare at the same spot for the third time. She said to Hart, 'Let's try something different.'

'Got anything in mind?'

'How about the other rooms on this floor? Do you have the list of who was in what room? Maybe we could start with the hotel register.'

'Mistretta's got it and he's checking them all out now. Not just this floor, either.'

'Well, it looks as if we've hit the point of diminishing returns in here.' The forensics people were packing their equipment in black metal boxes and preparing to leave.

'Whew!' said the sergeant. 'This has been a long day.'

Elizabeth said, 'Oh?' She was still a little resentful because they hadn't seen the importance of the absence of prints on the window.

'Yes, ma'am,' he said, 'two murders this morning besides this one, three breaking and enterings, all within a mile or two of here.'

The resentment came back without warning. Ma'am and sir were what policemen called outsiders. Whatever sympathy she had been prepared to feel for a tired cop who'd been crawling around straining his eyes for invisible marks went out of her. But she just said, 'Please have copies of those reports sent to us at the Bureau office, with the precinct log.'

'No possible connection, ma'am,' said the patient sergeant. 'The other two had their skulls crushed. Nothing subtle about it. Just a gang fight in an alley. The B and E's were all just the usual – an auto parts store, a housebreaking, and a stereo shop.'

She matched his patience. 'I want them anyway. It's important to learn everything that we can about what went on in this part of town last night.' At last she succumbed: 'If nothing else, it may tell us where the squad cars were when a murderer was swinging like Tarzan from balcony to balcony on the outside of this building.'

'Yes, ma'am,' said the sergeant. He picked up his fingerprint kit and stomped out the door.

Elizabeth became aware of Hart standing there watching her. She turned on him and said, 'I know it wasn't nice. But it happens to be true.'

Hart shrugged. 'The local police can be very helpful if they want to.'

'So I'll be extremely sweet to him when he gives me the logs and the investigation reports, and we'll be fast friends forever. But the local police might not be the kind of help we're going to need on this case. Has anybody—'

'Yes,' said Hart. 'The CIA was as surprised about it as we were, and they've spent the day trying to match it to their standing list of possibilities, apparently without success. Mike told me they've probably cabled their field offices and are waiting for something that sounds plausible to come back. He also told me it doesn't look as if anything will. McKinley Claremont was in the Senate for almost thirty years without doing anything very controversial in the area of foreign policy.'

'I suppose all we can do tonight is wait for the forensics people to work their way through the other rooms, then.'

'That and wait for our replacements to arrive,' said Hart. 'As of an hour ago we're no longer here just to establish a presence.'

'So they'll send in the first team?' said Elizabeth. 'We haven't done so badly, considering we've hardly had time to begin.'

'No, we haven't,' said Hart. 'But just the same, I'm not going to do much unpacking.'

'Speaking of that, has anybody told you where we're supposed to be staying?'

'They had our bags sent here a little while ago.' He reached into his pocket and fished out two room keys. 'That way we're easy to get hold of if they turn anything up.'

Elizabeth reached for the telephone and dialed a familiar number. An unfamiliar voice came on and said, 'Justice.'

'This is Elizabeth Waring. I want to leave a message for Roger Padgett,' said Elizabeth.

'I'll see that he gets it,' said the voice. 'What's the message?'

'I want his airline reports for last night and all day today wired to the Denver field office of the FBI. Everything within a five-hundred-mile radius of Denver. The information I requested previously I want telephoned to me at the Constellation Hotel.'

'That in Denver too?'

'Yes,' said Elizabeth, 'I'll give you a number.' She read the number on the telephone dial slowly. Then she held out her hand, and Hart placed one of the keys in it. 'Room 256.'

'Got it,' said the voice. 'Anything else?'

'No,' said Elizabeth. 'Thanks.'

Elizabeth sat on the bed feeling exhaustion beginning to flood into her mind, taking possession of whole sections of her brain at once like water rushing into a sinking ship. Too many things were going on at once, and she was beginning to lose the strength of will that kept them separate. Everything was beginning to get muddled together and hazy. She couldn't remember anymore whether she was collecting information that was supposed to lead in some particular direction, or just collecting information. Pervading all of it was an impression, a sense that an awful lot of people seemed to be dying. There was something unreal about it.

You knew they were dying because somebody told you so over the telephone, and by the time you got there, there wasn't even a body. At most there was a chalk outline like the one on the floor at her feet. The discreet efficient functionaries had already cleaned everything up, so there wasn't the palpable and substantial residue of an act of violence, just a question; the murder itself just an intellectual postulate and you were supposed to deduce its causes and corollaries starting with an infinite range of things that could have preceded it in time. All you had to work with was your ability to see the relationships, to pick the single thread of logic that might lead to the one who'd done it, and then follow it slowly forward, trying hard to take each step faster to bring yourself closer and closer to the present moment, where the murderer would be waiting for you. And all the time, the act itself was moving backward, further and further into the past. Everything you chose to look at put the act farther from your reach – trace the poison? check the airline records for suspicious travelers? check the police reports? the other rooms in the hotel? the Senator's personal life? the CIA's foreign agents? the world?

She was aware that Hart was saying something to her that had just battered against the tired receptors in her brain without their being fast enough to decipher it. 'Huh?' she said.

'I said I think we ought to go to bed.'

110

'So do I,' she said, and sensed in herself a tiny warm tremor of joy. Then she realized that part of her mind had heard him differently, and had rushed upward to meet him without being held back or delayed by the restraints. She caught it in time to keep it from blurting out, 'Oh, you mean each of us, not both of us.' She smiled to herself as she stood up and walked out the door. All the barriers seemed to be going at once; things were tearing through them without warning, things she hadn't suspected were there. This one would take some thought. Not that it meant anything, but it was interesting, like a dream.

They went out to the parking lot and got into Little Norman's white Mark IV, then drove to the Marina Hotel.

At the bar, which was set back and above the casino, Little Norman said, 'Grab a table where I can see the action; I'll be back in a second.'

He said, 'Where are you going?'

'Just a quick phone call, kid. I'm looking after your interests.'

He waited as Norman plowed through the knots of gamblers to a bank of telephones near a men's room. When Norman got there, he dialed and then turned back to face him, smiling as he talked.

The waitress leaned across him with Little Norman's drink, actually placing a breast on his shoulder for an instant. Everything here was different, he thought. It was calculated to put things that secretly delighted just out of reach, always as though it had been a fortuitous chance. They probably had a class that taught them to do that, as the last girl in the line of the dinner show at

111

the Lido had her G-string snap, always in the last few bars of the performance.

Little Norman said, 'To your health, kid,' and took a drink.

He responded, 'And yours,' and drank too, but only enough to wet his mouth and let the ice click against his teeth. There wasn't much point in overdoing it, and he would overdo it if he had to drink one for one with Little Norman. Besides, he had been on the road for over a month, and he never drank on the road. You had to keep your head clear on the road.

On the other side of the casino that crowd around one of the crap tables was two deep and growing. The man who was rolling was wearing a sport coat, but had stuffed his tie in a pocket and opened his shirt at the neck. He rolled again and a little cry went up from the table that was just loud enough to reach the bar. More people strolled over attempting looks of detachment, but joined the crowd and riveted their eyes to the table. From where he sat in the bar it was hard to tell whether they were betting or watching. The quick, mechanical movements of the croupier didn't reveal anything to him. From this distance they all just looked hungry.

'You a gambler?'

'I may try my luck a little later,' he said. 'Why?'

'Some people in that line of work are, some aren't. Henckel once lost twenty thousand in one night. Personally I didn't like it much until after I quit. Couldn't see the point in it. When you're old you need some kind of excitement that doesn't involve your body.'

Another cry reached them from the crap table across

the casino, not a cheer, exactly, but a wordless, spontaneous howl from all the throats gathered around the table, as though it were the collective sound of their blood pressures going up in unison.

'You're no more retired than I am, Norman,' he said. 'Just got a steady job now.'

'It ain't so, kid,' said Little Norman, his eyes suddenly open wide and his smile gone. 'I'm sixty-one years old. But once I was good. One of the best. Quiet and reliable. Maybe the best button man in the Midwest.' Then his eyes narrowed and the opaque smile returned. 'Not as good as you, though. I was real surprised to see your face like that. I never expected to see you looking like that. Not ever.'

'It happens,' he replied.

'I didn't say it couldn't happen,' said Little Norman. 'What I said was I didn't think I'd see it. That's a loser's face.'

Across the casino the man rolled again; this time he rolled into a silence, a deep-drawn inbreathing like a wall of anticipation. From the bar it was hard to tell whether he made his point, but the silence seemed to draw spectators even faster, like particles rushing to fill a void. When the stickman leaned across the table, bestowing and gathering in single economical movements, the man was still visible, standing with his back to the bar. But then the crowd shifted a little and he disappeared behind it.

'Maybe so,' he said. 'Hard to tell about winning until you count the money.'

'That's a fact,' said Little Norman. He gulped down the last finger of Scotch in his glass and stood up. 'Be seeing you, kid. It's always a pleasure.'

'Thanks for the drink, Norman.'

'Any time,' he said as he stepped down to the casino floor. For a long time it was possible to watch his head and shoulders moving along above the crowd, but then he was gone.

ELEVEN

He finished his drink and left the hotel. There wasn't any particular reason to leave. He wasn't hiding from anyone and didn't have anywhere else as a destination. It was just the normal thing to do, as automatic as the urge to blink his eyes, as automatic as going outside and then waiting beside the door to see if the next one out paused for a second to see which way he'd gone. He was on vacation for two more days. That was no time to let himself slide into a position where he'd feel uncomfortable.

He walked across the parking lot to the street, and joined the anonymous hundreds moving along the Strip from casino to casino. Just before they got to the MGM Grand Hotel he parted from his companions and took a shortcut through a closed gas station, then stopped in the shadows behind it. Nobody came after him, so he went on. If there was a watcher, he at least had sense enough to keep his distance and not be annoying.

He went in the front entrance of the Grand Hotel and moved quickly to the other end of the gigantic casino, where the blackjack games were proceeding in an atmosphere of spurious calm. At one table a man piled his remaining chips on the square in front of him and waited, one foot already on the floor to push his chair away from the table. The dealer's deft fingers peeled cards out of the shoe and made them rematerialize in front of the players, and the man found himself sitting behind a ten and a four. He didn't seem surprised or disappointed by it, just watched while the second ten appeared and the dealer's hand snatched away the chips. Then his foot pushed off and he relinquished his chair.

The dealer's face didn't seem to notice that the man was gone, or that he'd ever been there. Only his marvelous hands took note of the fact that there were no chips on one of the betting spaces, and passed by without leaving any cards. The face didn't acknowledge it when another man sat down in the seat to wait for the next deal. One of the hands snatched the five crisp twenties and tamped them into the cash slot, while the other left a stack of chips where the money had been. If the dealer's eyes had passed across the new face with its terrible bruise and the cut just above the hairline, they didn't linger there. The eyes were only there to direct the hands, and there was plenty for the hands to do.

When he sat down at the table he checked his watch. it was eleven thirty. It didn't make much difference to him where he spent the next few hours, but it was important not to lose track of things. He set out a single five-dollar chip and watched the hands of the dealer deposit his cards on the table. They were a queen and a ten, so he stood pat and waited while the dealer's king and five drew another king and busted. The hands fluttered over the green felt surface of the table, rearranging chips and cards, rewarding and punishing with the same even, imperturbable move-ments, but in any case obliterating the decisions that had just been made along with the combinations of numbers and symbols that had prompted them. Each time there was a new set of decisions, and then the hands performed their mechanical reckoning and dealt again. He kept a rough tally of how well he was doing, and it was no worse than he'd expected. The dealer had started on a losing streak, and busted about half of the first twenty hands. After that the normal order of probabilities had reasserted itself and the house's regular five-percent advantage had resumed. When he glanced at his watch again it was one thirty. Two hours was enough. He gathered his red chips and headed for the cashier's cage. When he went out the front door he had six twenties and a ten in his shirt pocket. It was mildly pleasing to him. He was no gambler and the minimum bets he had stuck to had just kept him there passing the time. But he figured it was better than losing.

Outside, the last big crowds of the evening were spilling out into the parking lots from the late shows. Caesar's Palace was practically across the street, so he joined a group walking in that direction and began looking for the watcher, who would have been alerted when he left the blackjack table. Hadn't he seen that older man in the gray suit who joined the crowd at the corner? Earlier, at the Sands. Only before there had been a woman in a white dress with him. People always went in pairs to the shows. He looked for her, but the man was alone, looking a lot like a middle-aged businessman from someplace else who'd left the tired little woman in the hotel room and gone out for some action on his own. If he wasn't, she'd turn up again in time.

He kept the man's location in mind without looking at him again. Then a portion of the crowd streamed into Caesar's and another portion split off into the parking lot to search for their cars. Once inside the casino he moved off along the edge of the forest of slot machines. There she was, a nice silver-haired lady from Missouri with that hypnotized look they all got, intently pumping dimes from a paper cup into a slot machine as though the wheels and gears couldn't spin fast enough to digest the coins. Only this time she was wearing a blue dress. The man in the gray suit walked past her and over to the elevators without either of them making a sign.

That was just fine. As watchers went they were tolerable. They didn't hang around close enough to be annoying, and now that he'd spotted them he could relax. He went to the second row of elevators and pushed the button for his floor.

The hallway was empty, so he made his way to his room and checked the space between the door and the jamb. The little ball of blue fuzz was still stuck there, an inch or two above the bright red carpet. Good. No surprises. They must be satisfied for the moment.

He swung the door open and for an instant struggled to remember if he'd left the bathroom light on. As the door swung wider he caught a glimpse of the television screen, which was casting a bright variegated display of moving colors into the dimness. He stepped aside and waited. Then a woman's voice said, 'Come in, baby. You've got the right place.'

He stepped across the doorway and caught sight of

118

the whole room at once. She was kneeling in the middle of the bed and she seemed to be wearing nothing. He poked the door all the way open and moved warily inside. There didn't seem to be anyone else. He ignored her for the moment and searched the room for hiding places. There was nobody in the bathroom or under the bed. He checked behind the curtains, then out on the balcony, but there was nobody. He retreated to the doorway and looked at her. 'What are you doing here?' he said.

'I'm a present, honey. Compliments of Little Norman.' She crawled toward him across the big bed and he took a closer look at her. She was small and dark, with long black hair and skin like cinnamon and big black eyes. Mexican or Puerto Rican, he thought. She couldn't be much over twenty.

'How did he get you in here?' he asked.

'Little Norman knows somebody,' she smiled. Then she stopped, poised for a second in a parody of thought, kneeling with her knees apart and her body erect to let him get a chance to look at her. 'No,' she said, 'Little Norman knows everybody.'

He locked and bolted the door, then leaned back against the wall and looked for something to block the window latch. Now she was off the bed and standing in front of him. 'Relax, honey,' she said. 'I thought you were supposed to be here to enjoy yourself.' Her voice was cool and soothing. Her hands were fiddling with his belt. 'So loosen up a little.' And then she was down on the floor, murmuring something in a soft, kittenish voice, but he couldn't understand it because she was also taking his penis into her mouth.

He stood with his back poised against the wall,

careful not to let his mind go completely out of his control, keeping back the tiny part he needed to look and listen, while she took possession of the rest of him. So now there were two of him – one that gave in to whatever she did and seemed all mindless yearning, a rush forward from some dim distant place, and the other part that looked over her shoulder for a flicker of shadow behind the curtain, and shut out the soft cooing sounds of her voice to hear a footfall in the hallway or a click of metal.

After a few minutes the one who kept watch was no longer tense and fearful. It didn't go to sleep, but it let the other part relinquish the safe wall, shed its clothes, and take the girl to the broad, ornate bed. It didn't stop listening and watching, partly because it couldn't, and partly because there was still the marker left in the door that somebody besides the girl had seen and replaced.

He lay sprawled on the bed pretending to be asleep. He had been pretending to be asleep for a long time now but she still hadn't moved. Maybe she wasn't the adventurous type. But how could she not be? Taking in every penis that pointed in her direction, just so long as it had an endowment of a hundred bucks or so to go with it – a few chips the dealers had missed. So now if she thought he was sleeping she'd leave, try to turn one or two more tricks before daylight.

Then he realized she had moved. One minute he had been touching her and the next he wasn't. He tried to sense her movement; he couldn't open his eyes, because he knew she'd be watching his face all the way out the door. She'd done this before, he thought. She

knew enough not to crawl on the bed with her hands
and knees; just seemed to slide across the sheets. It was
probably a talent that was worth a lot to her: when
she'd managed to temporarily exhaust a particularly
difficult client, or at times like this when she'd been
paid for the whole night in advance. He heard a very
quiet swishing sound as she pulled on her underpants,
but not even a snap of elastic. A few seconds later he
heard the click of a clasp or a button, but that was all.
Then he could sense her presence near the door, and
more whispers of cloth. It seemed to take a long time.
What the hell was she waiting for? Oh yes – the wallet
in his pants. She was the adventurous type.

Then the door opened and closed so smoothly that
he didn't hear the click of the latch, just felt it. He
opened his eyes and looked around the room. It was as
though she'd never been there at all. Perfect. He went
to the wall by the door and looked at the pile of
clothes he'd left there, picked up his pants and felt for
his wallet. Good. At least she hadn't taken the whole
thing. He looked inside and counted his money – still
better. She had been smart. She'd only taken about
four or five of the sheaf of twenties and left everything
else intact. Most of the time when she met the trick at
two a.m. and smelled liquor on his breath, she could
assume he wouldn't even know she'd taken anything.
At least he wouldn't be sure. He threw the wallet on
the bed and smiled while he chose fresh clothes from
the closet. He didn't begrudge her the money. He'd
have given her almost that much as a tip if she'd stayed
all night anyway. Then his smile turned into a chuckle.
If he'd been able to trust her, he'd have given her three
times that much to leave now and not tell Little

Norman. And as it was, he knew she'd never let Little Norman know she hadn't stayed with him in the room. Not if Little Norman had paid her. Not ever. Not on her life.

TWELVE

He was dressed and ready in a few seconds. It was time
to make some quick arrangements. If someone spotted
the girl before daylight they'd check to be sure he was
still in the room. He slipped out the door and down
the hall to the back stairway. Then he was outside
again in the mild, sluggish night air, making his way
down the street. He did his best to look inconspicuous,
but he knew that walking slowly with the few late
gamblers wasn't enough. If he was seen at all they'd
recognize him and after that their curiosity would be
insatiable.

The crowds thinned out and straggled as they moved
out on the Strip toward the Hacienda, and he felt his
protection slipping away from him. Then the last of his
companions turned off into one of the small motels
and he was alone again. It was no use trying to do it on
foot – he'd have to take a chance on a taxi. He strolled
up the walk to the parking lot of the Hacienda. At this
hour there were no cabs waiting in the loop, but he
knew there would be one in a minute. He kept to the
shadows near the street, strolling toward the front
entrance as slowly as he could without attracting
attention. Then a cab swung into the drive, bobbed to
a stop at the top of the loop, and unloaded a young
couple. He broke into a trot and reached the cab just

as the driver was getting back in. 'Can you take me to the airport?' he said, leaning down to speak so he would be practically shielded from the hotel.

The driver shot him an appraising look and said, 'Sure. Get in.' There was only a mile or so of empty highway between the Hacienda and the airport, and the driver accomplished it with a grim confidence. They still seemed to be accelerating when the cab swung into the drive.

The Avis Rent A Car agency was near the front entrance, the part of the airport dominated by candy counters and telephone booths. There would be two sets of watchers at the airport, he knew. The other set would be the one the police stationed there to see if any familiar faces were arriving under false names. But they would all be grouped around the ticket counters, baggage checks, and entrance gates; two sets of watchers, staring most of the time at each other. Now and then a face would appear that was a surprise to one side or the other, and then there would be a flurry of activity, one side attempting to surround the new face with disguises and distractions and whisk it away into obscurity while the other attempted to follow it unobserved.

But all of that was going on in the other part of the building, and the car-rental counters were as remote from that activity as any other part of this town could be. There was no trouble with the car. The Indiana driver's license and Mastercard in the name Frederick G. Ackermann weren't forged, after all. The bills were mailed to a post office box in Gary and forwarded. The fact that a nonexistent man paid his bills was sufficient identity.

He drove with a feeling of elation. There was no chance that they had noticed him at the airport, he could sense that. Now he did a few quick turns and then pulled over to the curb on a side street to be sure. After ten minutes he had seen no other vehicle, so that was that.

He drove the car back to the Strip and scanned the buildings and signs. It had to be now, so the stores were out of the question. The pawnshops were too dangerous because you could never tell what silent partners there might be – and what pawnshop would be open at four a.m., even in Las Vegas? No, the only chance was a gas station, the right kind of gas station, and the only way to tell if it was right was by location. He described it in his mind and using that description as a map, he drove out of town and straight through the moonlit desert to it and pulled up beside the air pump. If it were the right place there would be some opportunity. He got out and walked around the car staring at the tires with a look of puzzlement. Inside the lighted cubicle of the station a man in greasy work clothes sat reading a magazine with his feet up on the desk. Faint sounds of a radio floated above the occasional drone of a solitary vehicle rushing past on the distant freeway.

He checked the tires and added a pound of pressure to one of them, now and then glancing at the gas man in his cubicle. The gas man never moved, never looked up throughout the whole operation. He got back into the car and moved it to the gas pumps. He was glad that the car-rental companies had stopped filling the tanks before they rented them. He topped off the tank and entered the station where the still-motionless gas man sat reading. Now that he could see the magazine he noticed that it was a *Newsweek* dated June 15. That didn't seem to matter to the gas man, any more than it mattered that he hadn't turned the page. He must have found one that he liked.

'I owe you four fifty,' he said, waving one of his twenty-dollar bills.

To stand up the gas man only lurched forward, still bent slightly at the hips, as though something about the desert had baked the fluidity out of him while he was sitting there waiting for something to happen important enough to propel him out of that chair. He scuttled to the cash register and stood with his face close to the drawer and his shoulders hunched around it in an unconscious attitude that resembled an embrace.

In a second or two the gas man would be scuttling back to the chair, so there was no choice but to ask him. 'Is this place a store, too?'

'Store? Hell no. All the stores're in town,' said the gas man. 'Buy nearly anything there, lots of things you'd be better off not having.' He turned around and laid the bills in the stranger's hand without counting them, as if to say a grown man can damn well count his own change, and if he doesn't do it he's a fool. The stranger didn't move, so the gas man's eyes flitted longingly at his chair, but he didn't follow them: he stayed where he was between the customer and the cash register.

'Oh,' he said. 'Looked like a store, with all the stuff you've got sitting here.'

'That?' said the gas man. 'That's something, all right. It's not merchandise. It's security.'

'Security?'

'That's right. Folks leave Vegas sometimes without enough gas to get home to LA. They drive a few miles and then figure they're out far enough to find somebody dumb enough to give them a tank of gas on credit. I'm it.'

He only nodded and gave a knowing smile, so the gas man went on, well launched on his favorite proof of the utter folly of mankind.

'I've seen 'em all. Brand-new Cadillacs pull in here and no money at all to buy gas. So they'll leave things. Watches, diamond rings. Damn near anything. They'll swear up and down they'll be back in a day to give me the money and pick up what they left. Once in a while they do, but mostly not. Even had one once wanted to leave her two kids here for security.'

'So all this stuff was traded for gas?'

'No,' said the gas man, shaking his head and looking down at the floor. 'Security.' He pointed at a man's wristwatch hanging on a utility hook next to a crescent wrench. 'That watch was left over two years ago for a tank of premium. Fifteen gallons, it was. About ten bucks. Watch is worth two hundred easy, and I still got it.'

'Amazing,' he agreed. 'You ought to sell off some of this stuff. Probably make a hell of a profit.'

'You're right,' said the gas man. 'I ought to, but I don't get much chance. On the way into Vegas they don't stop out here, and on the way out they don't have any money. Just this stuff. Radios, suits, jewelry, guns, suitcases, whatever they brought with 'em and haven't figured out how to trade for chips. You see anything you want, make me an offer.'

127

'Maybe I will,' he said. 'What have you got?'

'Lots of things. All in the next room here, waiting for 'em to come and buy it back. Take a look.'

In the back room, which was also the gas man's tool-room, an entire wall was covered with the miscellaneous belongings of the travelers. It looked like the lair of a burglar. There were piles of suitcases, a rack of expensive clothing, and a pegboard covering the back wall that was hung with cameras, radios, binoculars, jewelry, guns, and even a painting of breakers crashing onto the beach at an imaginary Malibu that had been supplied by the artist with a few indomitable gray rocks. He casually surveyed the hoard, looking more closely at a pair of binoculars and a camera before he let himself turn to the guns.

'I'll give you a hundred for this one,' he said, tapping his finger on the graceful walnut stock of a thirty-ought-six with a scope.

'A hundred?' said the gas man. 'That won't do it. The scope's worth eighty. Man who owned it got a bighorn sheep with that rifle just a week or so before I got it.'

'He tell you that, did he?' he smirked.

'Well, it's a good rifle. I'll take two hundred for it.'

He studied the rest of the guns hanging on the pegboard for a second, then said, 'If you'll throw in this pistol I'll give you two-twenty.'

The gas man looked more closely at the rifle, then plucked the pistol off the wall and tested the action. It was a thin .32-caliber Beretta. He thought for a second and then said, 'Cash?'

He nodded and the gas man handed him the pistol. He put it in his coat pocket and counted eleven twenties from his wallet. The gas man counted the twenties a second time before he folded them and put them into the pocket of his overalls. Then he started to turn away, but stopped and added, 'Sell you some ammunition for those? I got no use for it.'

'People leave you cartridges too?'

The gas man chuckled. 'No, just one. Fellow had a whole case full of it. All kinds. Guess he was a collector or something. I'll give it to you for half the marked price.'

'I'm not really interested,' he said. 'I wasn't out here on a hunting trip, you know, but I'll take a box of each if it's not too old.'

'About a year, no more.' He was already bent over a crate in the corner, reading the small cardboard boxes he pulled out, one by one, until he'd found what he wanted. 'Let's see. That'll be eleven dollars.'

When he paid the gas man and took the two cartridge boxes he noticed the date on them was almost three years ago, but he'd only looked out of curiosity. It made no difference. At the car he set the rifle and the cartridge boxes in the trunk, taking only the Beretta and a dozen rounds into the front with him. He glanced at his watch as he pulled out onto the highway. Only twenty-five minutes – less time than it would have taken to fill out the papers in Los Angeles.

There was only one problem left, and that was where to put the car. It had to be available, close to Caesar's, and in a place where it would attract no notice. If you put it that way, there was no choice. He glided up the drive in front of Caesar's Palace, pulled to a stop in the middle of the only part of the parking lot that was still crowded at this hour, and got out. He

129

opened the trunk as far as he could without letting the light go on, loaded the rifle by the light of the moon, jammed it into the wheel well beside the spare tire so it pointed to the rear, and closed the trunk.

He was in the hotel's back hallway a moment later, skirting the casino and shops, and taking the back stairway to his room. There was no sign that anything had been moved. His clothes were still in a heap on the floor by the door, and the television was still glittering noiselessly into the darkness, throwing colored shadows across the crumpled white sheets of the bed. There was little chance anyone knew he had been out, and whatever searching they were going to do had been done early in the evening. He had managed to build himself an edge – not much of an edge, just a car and some guns that they wouldn't know about. But then he probably wouldn't need an edge. He was on vacation.

He loaded the pistol, went to his bag, and took out six large Band-Aids. He used them to tape the pistol tightly to the wall inside the closet above the doorway, the one spot where nobody ever looked. Then he took his pocket knife and cut a thin slit in the lining of his left coat sleeve just above the cuff and pushed the two car keys into it. It wasn't much of an edge, he thought, but at least it was enough to let him go to sleep. It was almost five in the morning, and it had been a long day for a man who wasn't working.

THIRTEEN

Senator Claremont's papers had been stuffed into a battered brown leather briefcase and flown to Denver in the baggage compartment of the airliner. They sat apart from the rest of his belongings on a little table in the corner of the laboratory, the latch of the case burnished to a dull gold sheen by daily handling.

Elizabeth sat sipping her morning coffee and staring at the soft, wrinkled leather. 'Has anybody gone into the papers yet?' she asked, her voice catching a little in her throat so that it came out almost a whisper. It reminded her it was the first full sentence she'd said this morning. Hart had left a note under her door telling her to take a taxi to the FBI building. She had yet to see him, and wondered vaguely where he was. Elizabeth cleared her throat and prepared to try again, but Mistretta had heard.

'Not yet. We're checking with the White House first. Protocol. The theory is you never know what might be in there. There's always a chance it might be something they don't want turning up as physical evidence at somebody's murder trial.'

'Are they sending somebody?'

Mistretta shrugged and went on with his work, which consisted of studying a long typewritten list and making a shorter list on a pad beside it. Elizabeth

131

decided against asking him what the list was. It looked too much like the sort of drudgery he might want to share.

She left him and went down the hall to the main office. As she came in the receptionist said, 'Miss Waring, this is just in for you over the line from Washington.' It was a computer printout. Elizabeth accepted it without bothering to look. She had seen Padgett's airline summaries too many times. 'Is there a place I can spread these out?' she asked.

The receptionist glanced at the sheaf, appearing to calculate its length and apply it to all available spaces. 'The best place is the conference room,' she said, indicating the room where Elizabeth had been the night before.

Elizabeth stepped into the room and considered closing the door, but didn't. It wasn't that the airline reports didn't require concentration, but that the concentration probably wouldn't produce any useful results anyway. She unfurled the long, continuous scroll on the conference table and then walked back to the head of the table where it began.

FLT 205 UNITED. DENVER CHICAGO: DEP: 0503. ARR: 0647. Underneath were the names and addresses of the passengers. She wasn't sure what to do with them. Padgett used the reports to spot the particular two or three hundred names he referred to as his 'friends.' All that took was programming the computer to remember the names, addresses, credit card numbers, and usual aliases. It was done in a second a day. But this was different, and would have to be done by elimination.

The murderer worked alone – one set of marks on

the window, a single person sneaking around in the darkness trying not to wake up a sleeping victim – it had to be one person. But would the person travel alone? It would be less suspicious to travel with someone else: a family, children and all. No, that couldn't be. If he traveled with someone else his companion would know. The camouflage wasn't worth the risk. So it had to be a single reservation. And it was probably a man, most likely between twenty and forty. The marks on the window were too high for any but the tallest women, and the climbing around on the balconies in the cold would require the kind of flexibility and stamina that began to disappear early even in athletes.

She went through the passenger list of Flight 205, crossing out all the obviously female names and the men who traveled with them, all the half-fare children's seats, all the men who were traveling in pairs on one reservation. That part worried her, so she thought it through again: who would the second man be? A partner? But if it were a partner, he would have to be responsible for doing something that was worth a share of the money, if there were money involved. But if the murder was political, there wouldn't be any distrust, and no money: he might be a contact, a controller, a spymaster. No, that was unlikely too. There was no reason for any organization to risk a second agent where he had no particular function. Then she remembered that there was still the Senator's briefcase. If something were missing from the briefcase the second man would be the one to take the handoff. If that were it, though, they wouldn't be on the same plane. They'd be on two different planes going in different directions, or no plane at all. The handoff would take place before anybody left town, and probably very soon after the murder. So he had to be alone. A young man alone. Elizabeth moved down the long conference table, crossing off the names on each flight. She lost track of the time it took, and when she reached the foot of the table and straightened up, her back was stiff. She noted it and forgot it as she walked back to the top of the list.

The next thing had to be times. The Senator hadn't gone to bed until after 11:30 Monday night. That meant nobody could have come in until midnight at the earliest. If everything went supernaturally well he could have been out by 12:30 and caught a 1:00 a.m. flight out of Denver. She sat down on the nearest chair and worked out the rest of it: a 2:00 a.m. flight from Cheyenne, a 3:00 a.m. from Pueblo, a 3:30 from Laramie, a 2:30 from Boulder, and nothing earlier than 6:00 from Salt Lake City. There was something else about times, but she couldn't quite identify it yet. It was too vague, just a feeling that she was missing something important. She opened her mind but it wouldn't come, so she stood up and walked down the list again, this time crossing out the flights that were too early.

Elizabeth studied the list and thought for a minute – of course, the addresses. If somebody had killed a senator and gotten on an airplane afterward, it meant he didn't live in Denver. That let out about half the remaining names, which she spent the next half hour crossing off. The list was getting short now, and she was able to tear out whole sheets and set them aside. She sat there and thought it out again from the beginning. There were still around five hundred names, too many to do anything with. But there was something else – it was all too neat, too logical, and she was getting farther and farther along, each step depending on the others, and if one step was wrong he could slip through the mesh. It all depended on his being logical too, setting everything up just as Elizabeth would herself. All he had to do to escape her logic was to do something foolish – have a companion he trusted enough to travel with – something of that sort. But there was still something else and she was near it now. She could feel it. He wasn't foolish. He'd done too much too carefully already, taken too many steps to get to the Senator and get out without faltering or wasting time. He made all the right choices, and some of them were crazy. They were crazy, but they were logical.

Elizabeth looked at the list and it was suddenly clear. She was looking at the wrong list. What she needed was the reservations list. She knew now that she understood him. He was a man who made choices. He hadn't climbed into the hotel room of a US senator knowing he was going to poison his dentures. That was what had bothered her from the beginning. It was too absurd. It was just that he carried with him a range of options in case he needed them. He wouldn't take a chance on not getting out, missing a flight or having it cancelled, and he couldn't be sure he'd succeed on the first try. If it was the first try. He'd be double-booked. He might have reservations on a flight every hour for several days. And there would probably be a car, and a bus ticket too. It didn't matter which one he finally used, whether he'd gotten on a plane or driven out or disappeared into thin air or stayed put. The point was, he'd have given himself all the options. Whatever he'd finally done didn't matter at all, and there was no sure way to resurrect it now anyway. The only thing she was sure of was that he'd be on more than one list. Elizabeth snatched up her printouts and walked out of the conference room.

'Where's your computer terminal?' she asked the receptionist.

'Room twenty-one seventeen,' said the receptionist.

Lang, the FBI man she'd met last night, was in the terminal talking to one of the programmers when Elizabeth arrived. He listened carefully as she tried to explain what she wanted. The programmer saw her theory immediately. He said, 'What's the flag?'

'What do you mean?' asked Elizabeth.

'What do we ask the computer to look for to establish a match?'

'Names, addresses, credit card numbers if there are any. Anything that comes up more than once. The idea is, he'd want to use several airlines, probably several nearby points of departure, and certainly several times, beginning with Monday night and ending when the Senator was scheduled to leave Denver. When was that, Mike?'

'This Friday night,' Lang said.

'Okay,' said the programmer. 'I'll begin with the airlines. You want car rentals, buses, Amtrak. Anything else?'

'No,' said Elizabeth. 'If that doesn't produce at least a double, then I'm wrong in the first place.'

'Right,' agreed the programmer, and began to type in codes with rapid, jittery fingers as though Elizabeth

136

and Lang had ceased to exist or had somehow been switched to another circuit that had nothing to do with him.

An electric voice that Elizabeth recognized as the ghost of the receptionist said, 'White phone, Agent Lang,' through the intercom. He went to the wall and picked up the telephone. Then he listened for a moment, said 'Understood,' and hung up.

He headed for the door before turning to Elizabeth. 'We can get started on the papers now, if you'd like to be in on that.'

'I suppose I would,' said Elizabeth. 'The reservations lists will probably take most of the day.'

In the laboratory Elizabeth expected to see the others already peering into the briefcases, but when she and Lang arrived the room was empty. 'Where is everybody?' she asked.

Lang said, 'Hart's on the poison with the forensics people. They're taking the samples to the Air Force's toxicology lab today and then hanging in for a theory on where it came from. Mistretta's investigating the people who stayed in the Constellation Hotel. The theory now is that whoever it was must have checked in, but not necessarily while the Senator was there. Anybody who would want to kill the Senator would have known enough about him to know that's where he'd stay when he came to town. Hobson's sweating through the police reports for all the precincts in Denver beginning last Friday. Davis is doing the same for state police. MacDonald – I don't think you've met him – is coordinating all the inquiries to other agencies, trying to get them to squeeze their informants – Alcohol, Firearms, and Tobacco; Narcotics, CIA, and so on. I've got other people collecting hotel and motel registrations all over the city, watching airports and train stations for old faces, and others transmitting everything to Washington for interpretation. So we're stretched damn near the limit around here. Within a couple of days we're going to have about all the raw data we're going to get. If we don't get a break or an inspiration pretty soon, somebody's going to have an uncomfortable time in the Senate.'

'What do you mean?'

'There's bound to be a special committee of inquiry set up to find out what happened. Somebody from the Bureau – probably the director himself – is going to have to go in there with whatever we can give him. If he doesn't have a culprit, he's going to have to prove there's such a thing as a perfect crime.'

'You don't really have much hope for it, do you?' she asked.

Lang turned to study her for a moment. A look of tired amusement seemed to flicker across his face, but he stifled it, took off his glasses, and peered closely at the lenses before taking out his handkerchief to clean them. 'No, I don't. I didn't at the start. Somebody who pulls off something like this and manages to get himself out of sight afterward without leaving a print or a witness is practically home free. He doesn't look any different from anybody else.' He put on his glasses again, as though illustrating his point, and added, 'What it amounts to is a burglar who didn't take anything.'

Elizabeth thought about it and sighed. It really was a lot like that. She was beginning to feel tired again, and it wasn't even noon yet. 'So we're just covering now, trying to look thorough, is that it?'

'Oh, no,' said Lang, suddenly flustered. 'We're not dogging it and neither is Washington. They're doing a real number on that end; looking for a motive, sending out their own people to follow every lead. I just meant we've got two things to worry about – doing our job and preparing to prove we've done it. So let's get going on that briefcase.' He went to the corner of the lab and picked up the briefcase. He stopped at a desk and pulled a printed form out of the top drawer and brought that back with him to the table.

'Here's how it goes,' he said. 'We take down an itemized list of what's in here, and then each of us signs it. Just a standard procedure when the owner isn't around to sign the slip, but let's be sure we don't make any mistakes on this one. A year from now I don't want a man from the National Security Agency to show up with this in his hand asking me how some document the Senator once initialed turned up for sale in Berlin or Hong Kong or Zurich.'

Lang took out the first thick sheaf of printed matter. He said, 'I'd say this is a copy of the *Congressional Record*, pages 1098 through 2013, twelve January through one February. With – let's see – penciled corrections and notes. Agreed?'

Elizabeth glanced at it, and nodded as she wrote down the description.

Next there were an address book, a set of airline schedules, an issue of *Time* magazine, a draft of a speech on income taxes. It felt uncomfortable and strange, not because she was going through a dead man's belongings, but because they didn't feel as if they belonged to a dead man at all. Everything was half finished, cut short: the magazine fresh and still smelling of printer's ink, the speech still lacking a conclusion as though someone had just stopped talking to answer the telephone in the middle of a sentence. But then she remembered that was all murder was, once you got beyond the blood and the pain and the momentary unpleasantness.

She wrote rapidly as Lang formulated the descriptions. They seemed overly precise, silly almost if you allowed yourself to think about them that way: 'Spiral-bound notebook. Quantity, one. Blue. Gem Corporation. Eight and a half by eleven, numbered pages to two hundred. Pages eight, nineteen, seventy-three, and one hundred and six missing. One, no, two packs of cigarettes, Sobranie, unfiltered. Wrappers unopened. Memorandum, dated February third, addressed to All Senatorial Offices from Mr. Deering of the General Services Adminstration, Re: Unnecessary Use of Electricity.'

As she scribbled the word 'electricity' she was saying, ' Got it,'

'That's it,' said Lang. 'Oh yeah . . . briefcase, brown leather with brass fittings. Initials MRC.'

They both signed the list and Lang held onto it. 'I'll go call this in to Washington now,' he said. 'They can reassure the White House that we're not sitting here looking for fingerprints on the plans for a new ICBM.'

'Can I get started on these papers?' asked Elizabeth.

'Sure thing,' he said. 'The only things that look promising are the address book and the notebook, but you might as well get started.' He went out and closed the door behind him.

The first few pages of the notebook were enough. She leafed through the hundred and seven other pages with writing on them, and they didn't get any better. The notebook was a sedimentary deposit of all the things the old man had wanted to remember. Appointments with other senators and appointments with his doctor crowded lists of groceries and fragmentary cryptic memoranda. *Bannerman Act – call N. G. Remind Carlson to invite d'Orsini et al. Sunday.* She wondered if she had a clue when she saw the double exclamation on *Clayburn!!* until she saw the triple exclamation on *Pretzels!!!* There were phrases from what appeared to be political orations: *The trouble is, they're trying to run the country like a poker game –* but there were no notations as to who had said it, where, why, or when.

Elizabeth sat and thought. There would have to be some kind of systematic grid that could be constructed to unravel it. It was rather simple, actually. Since the reminders and appointments would have to be written in before they happened, the exact dates could be pinned down by checking with the other people involved. The notations on each page would have to be transcribed in thematic divisions – to start with, the categories could be *appointments and reminders*, *political references*, *personal references*, and *miscellaneous*. There had to be a *miscellaneous*. It might be possible to retrieve almost all of it – whom he saw or spoke to, what he was doing each day of the past two months, what he was thinking about. It would take some time, though, and might not be of any use. After all, if there had been anything there, wouldn't the Senator have noticed it in time to save himself?

But there were shortcuts available. He'd had a staff, and they would be able to translate most of the notations, maybe all of them. There was the legislative assistant. What was his name? She leafed through the notebook again, and it was everywhere: *Papers on Calloway Bill – Carlson. Have Carlson call N. G. Re: Oil Depl. Allow.*

Elizabeth walked to the wall and snatched the white telephone. It rang immediately and then she noticed it had no dial. The voice that said 'Yes' was that of the receptionist. My God, she thought, doesn't anybody else work here? But she said, 'This is Elizabeth Waring in the Forensic Lab. Can you get me an appointment with Mr. Carlson, the Senator's aide, as soon as possible?'

'I'm sorry, Miss Waring,' said the receptionist. 'Mr. Carlson is on his way back to Washington. I'm sure we can put through a call to him this evening.'

'Damn!' said Elizabeth. 'Who told him he could go and why in the world would he want to?' She regretted it instantly, but already the receptionist's even, measured tones were answering, 'Mr. Lang spoke with him on the telephone only a short time ago before he left the hotel.'

'So he may not be gone yet?' said Elizabeth.

'His plane leaves this afternoon at twelve thirty and arrives in Washington at seven fifteen Eastern time.'

Elizabeth glanced at her watch. It was just noon. 'I'm sorry, but there's no dial on this phone. Can you call the airline and ask them to get him to a phone? It

142

could be important.' She was glad she'd said 'could be.' Her control was coming back.

'Yes. If we locate him I'll ring you in the lab.'

The telephone rang again in a few minutes and Elizabeth said, 'Waring.'

'I have Mr. Carlson on the line,' said the receptionist.

'Mr. Carlson?'

'Yes, Miss Waring,' he said. Behind his voice there was a huge hollow where random noises echoed. He spoke tonelessly and loudly as though he had his free hand pressed to his ear.

'I have a number of questions that you seem to be the only one who can answer, and I—'

'Miss Waring, I'm sorry, but I have a flight to Washington that's already boarding, and I'm about to miss it as it is. Can I call you back when I get home this evening?'

'I'm afraid that won't do. You see, I have something you'd have to look at to be able to explain. If you could take a later flight, I'd—'

'I've already been interviewed and grilled and investigated for over twenty-four hours, and – oh. Just a second.' Elizabeth could hear that another male voice was droning just outside the range of understanding. Then Carlson said something too. It went on for a few seconds, and then she heard him sigh into the receiver. He said, 'I've just missed my flight. I have to wait four hours for the next one.' He sounded sad.

'Where can I meet you?' asked Elizabeth.

'How about here, if it's just a few questions? I'll be at the American Airlines desk in about twenty minutes. I'll be in a light gray suit, looking impatient. And you?'

'I'll be the lady carrying the Senator's notebook.'

When she saw him he was standing at the ticket counter staring at his watch, then craning his neck out of the stiff shirt collar with his mouth slightly open as though to demonstrate to anyone in his vicinity that he was a man who was being unjustly delayed by petty matters. When he spotted her striding toward him with the notebook, he leaned back against the counter and pursed his lips in a look of sardonic displeasure.

Elizabeth tried to remind herself that he probably *was* being delayed by petty matters – by a piece of evidence that wasn't likely to be evidence of anything in particular – but she knew that the people in the ticket line were thinking that she was an incompetent secretary who had misplaced an important document and made her employer, the efficient-looking, carefully tailored and barbered man in the gray suit whose glasses were even now glittering little semaphores of disdain at her, late. She couldn't forgive him that. So when she was still seven feet away she said, 'Relax, Mister Carlson, you're not under arrest. We just want to have a talk.' She spoke in a voice that sounded as though it was meant to reassure a man who was essentially a coward.

His reaction brought to birth a smile she had to stifle: it was as though he had been prodded from behind. He was off and walking and she almost had to run to catch up. He didn't stop until he was no longer visible to the people at the counter. He was definitely annoyed. 'Miss Waring, I thought you people were much more discreet.'

Elizabeth just gave him a puzzled look, then

144

appeared to dismiss his odd behavior by placing it in some category well known to professional investigators who were accustomed to seeing people at their worst. She said, 'Well, shall we get started? I'd hate to have you miss the next flight.' It was said with what could almost have been taken as sympathy if they hadn't understood each other so well.

'All right,' he said, 'Where?'

'I've made arrangements to borrow a conference room.'

They were expected at the airport courtesy desk. The room was off the main lobby and contained ten chairs, three of which looked comfortable, and a long wooden table. There were no windows, but a painting of an undifferentiated landscape was hung along the far wall. They both chose utilitarian chairs at the table. Elizabeth opened the Senator's notebook and took out her own.

'Mr. Carlson, why were you going back to Washington today?'

'Because Senator Claremont is dead. There didn't seem to be anything I could do about it and Agent Lang said I might as well go. You people were through with me. Am I under suspicion?'

'No, of course not,' said Elizabeth, as though the idea had never crossed her mind.

'That's good, because if I am, we'll stop this right now while I get my lawyer.'

'I'd thought of that,' said Elizabeth, 'but that would be time consuming, and we didn't want to delay you any longer than necessary. If you'll just give me the best cooperation you can, I'm sure we can get through this quickly.

'Tell me what you know about this notebook.'

'It's not really a notebook. It's a scratch pad. The Senator liked to keep it by him so he could jot down things that occurred to him when he didn't have time to do anything about them,' said Carlson. 'He had a rotten memory and had the sense to know it, so he wrote things down.'

'Did it work?'

'Most of the time he'd remember to keep the rest of us informed. The appointments would get transferred to his calendar and so on. Sometimes he'd forget. Sometimes he'd even forget where he'd put the notebook – leave it in some hearing room or a press conference or someplace. But it always turned up.'

'I'd like to go through a few portions of it and see if you can help me understand it,' said Elizabeth.

'Sure,' said Carlson. He glanced at his digital wristwatch as though he were going to charge for his time beginning now. Then he opened the notebook and began to read it aloud. 'Dinner the seventh–S.A. That's the dinner the Saudi Arabian ambassador gave on the seventh of January. He never could remember the ambassador's name, which is Ruidh, so he gave up trying. Call R.T.T., that's got to be Ronald T. Taber, the congressman from Iowa. They were in on a farm bill a few years back, and now and then one or the other would call to compare notes on how it was working.'

Elizabeth wrote quickly, trying to catch as much as she could, and hoping that the order of it would help her put it back together later. Carlson went on, looking and talking as though it were a family album full of vaguely familiar faces. He was good, she had to admit. He seemed to know what everything was and how it came to be that way.

Finally he came to the list and stopped. 'I don't know what all this is,' he said. 'It must relate to the tax hearings that he was planning for the fall.'

'Relate in what way?'

'Well,' said Carlson, 'there was a special staff for the committee, which handled details for the hearings. They're more likely to be able to tell you for sure than I am. This isn't anything I handled.'

'But what does it look like?'

'It's a list of corporations – all sizes and shapes. See? Bulova, General Motors, Eastman Kodak. Then you get ones nobody ever heard of – Gulf Coast Auto Leasing, Standard Hardware, North Country Realty. A few that are utilities: PG&E, Comsat, FGE, Con Ed.'

'What do you think he was going to do with them?'

'Maybe use them in a speech, maybe subpoena their books, maybe call somebody to testify. I don't know. They have a staff for that.'

'Who would know?'

'Justin Garfield would. Staff counsel. This list is over a month old and if it has anything to do with the committee, he'd probably have been in on it by now. You can't call in General Motors and tell them to be there next week with a shoebox full of receipts and tax forms. It takes time to get it together in a form that one person can look at.'

Elizabeth turned the notebook toward her and glanced down the list. 'What does PG&E stand for?'

'Pacific Gas and Electric. Oh, yes, I forgot. You're from the East.'

'And FGE?'

'Probably Florida Gas and Electric.'

'Where do I get in touch with Justin Garfield?'

Carlson pulled a leather address book out of his inside pocket and read, '(202) 692–1254, extension 2. Should we go on?'

'Please.'

Carlson returned to his translation, moving from page to page with renewed confidence. It was clear that senators didn't get much time for solitude or much privacy either. Carlson knew whom the Senator had seen, whom he'd called, and what they'd talked about. Twice he had to turn to his own address book and match a telephone number with an initial, but that was only to verify. At last they reached the end of it and Carlson said, 'Is that all you wanted from me?'

'Yes, Mr. Carlson. Thank you for your cooperation. Where can I reach you if we need to ask anything else?'

'For now, in the Senator's ofice. If my situation changes, I'll let the FBI know.' He glanced at his watch again and said, 'Good-bye.' They didn't shake hands before he went out, closing the door behind him.

At the Constellation Hotel the only sign that there was anything that hadn't been planned and provided by a solicitous and efficient management was that the elevator wouldn't stop at the fourth floor.

It wasn't until she closed the door to her room that Elizabeth realized she had forgotten to stop at the Bureau to return the Senator's notebook to the lab. She cradled the telephone in her lap while she rummaged through her purse for Lang's number. When the

148

telephone rang she felt it and heard it at the same time. Her startled jump knocked the phone to the floor.

'Hello?' she shouted into it.

'Hi, clumsy,' said the voice.

'Hello, Padgett,' she said. 'What have you got for me?'

'A sore finger. I've been calling all day.'

'I was at the FBI working.'

'You don't have to tell me. I don't handle travel expenses. Making any headway?'

'We've got a little to go on, but it's mostly hunches and shaky physical evidence. Enough to keep us busy. Have you got anything new on the Veasy thing?'

'Just what you asked for. The company pension fund has been mishandled, from the look of it.'

'Ah—'

'Just mishandled. Stupidity, not crookedness. They've dumped most of it into pie-in-the-sky stuff, hoping for a killing. A lot of it's gone to the outfit you asked about – Fieldston Growth Enterprises. It looks legitimate, but they're speculators, pure and simple. Buying up a lot of undeveloped land in resort areas, things like that. Been at it about eight years, picked up a lot of paper profit but not a dime you or the union or the IRS for that matter could put your hands on.'

'Where's their office?'

'Las Vegas.'

'Why did I ask? Who owns it?'

'Biggest stockholder is Edgar Fieldston himself, at forty-two percent. There's not much information on him. No arrests, pays his taxes and all that. He's chairman of the board and draws a salary of seventy-five thousand. Second is the Machinists, who own fifteen percent. The rest are individuals, a couple of banks, all small percentages.'

'Where'd you get all this?'

'It's all public information – their annual report, "FGE for the Future." Then I checked with a few people in the SEC and the FTC to corroborate—'

'FGE.'

'Sure. Fieldston Growth Enterprises.'

'Is Brayer nearby? I've got to talk to him.'

FOURTEEN

He woke up to his own face; as though it were a separate entity that had moved into the room during the night and now filled a corner like a piece of furniture that would somehow have to be moved aside before anything else could happen. It was dry and angry and hot to the touch. He made his way to the mirror and confronted it.

It wasn't as bad as it felt, he thought – not infected, anyway. But it was going to take some time and even then it would leave a scar. The bruises and bumps would go away in a couple of weeks, but not the cut. The knee was stiff, but he could feel the blood beginning to course through it and loosen it a little.

He looked at his watch. Eleven o'clock already. He carefully shaved, ran the shower over his wounds, put on clean clothes, and went out into the corridor. It was time to pick up the watchers and get something to eat. They'd probably be waiting near the two most likely exits. He strolled along, testing the knee for hitches, but the elasticity of it seemed to have returned. He crossed the casino and made one circuit of the lobby before he turned to join the line at the ballroom. There middle-aged women in PTA dresses were ranged along a cash register to admit candidates for brunch, which they did with a stony and repellent efficiency, spotting

151

hand signals from the waitresses with the impassive eyes of casino pit bosses.

The watchers weren't easy to spot this time. He didn't see any familiar faces, and he didn't see anyone who made a habit of staring past him into the distance. He had known the old couple would be gone, but it hadn't occurred to him that they might not be replaced by someone as obvious. He flashed a glance down the line for someone. If the watcher weren't very good, he would pick that moment to turn away or adjust his glasses or at least touch his face; nobody did.

Inside the ballroom he found a banquet laid for the purpose of proving to the eye that any paroxysm of human greed or voracity could run its course and still be buried in inexhaustible plenty. Pyramids of champagne glasses filled beyond the brim towered over mounds of scrambled eggs and sausages; bleeding slabs of beef were being expertly shaved into pink pages by shining blades. Piles of chicken breasts seemed in danger of spilling over their silver bins to crush the ornately decorated layered pastries. People of all descriptions assaulted the tables in celebration of their acceptance into this place where there could be no such thing as lack or unfulfilled desire.

Mothers piled extra squares of pastry, oozing globs of hollandaise, and slabs of paté on the plates of their children; elderly people balanced second plates on their skinny forearms as they picked their way back to their tables.

They drank and ate and then rushed to the serving trays to accumulate more while their first plates still were heaped with untasted food. All around the ballroom the obsequious starch-coated functionaries circulated like gentle spirits, filling glasses, deftly clearing spilled food and broken crockery from the aisles, and always, unceasingly and untiringly, replenishing the splendor of the serving tables – all of it calculated to foster in each guest the illusion that he had somehow managed to encompass the whole banquet with the amplitude of his desires and to engulf all of it in his insatiability; the pitiful rodent-inroads he had accomplished on the feast were made to stand in his mind for the fulfillment of Gargantuan yearnings in the soul of a restless and heroic being. As it always did, the management had succeeded in concocting a substantial form to stuff into the yawning emptiness of the clients' dimly perceived insufficiencies.

He had to wait a little longer because he was alone, and the management always balked a bit before devoting a table to one person. But he knew there would be a waitress who remembered that a man alone tips more generously than he does when his wife is watching. It took a few moments before one of them noticed him, cut him out of the gaggle of detainees, and conducted him to her region of the ballroom. It was a tiny table for two along the far wall, where he could survey the entire room without seeming to.

It wasn't until he saw Orloff that he knew where to look for the watcher. Orloff's short, corpulent body bobbed up into the line of people waiting for a table, and a man in a light blue cowboy shirt nodded to him and left. It was typical of Orloff, he thought – always in a hurry, always running three minutes late for an appointment somewhere else. He'd waste a face so he didn't have to stand fidgeting in a line, his pudgy fingers wandering over the immaculate surface of his gray suit coat as though something important were in one of the pockets.

He watched as Orloff's fat white hands fluttered impatiently at a passing waitress, then pointed at his table next to the wall. The waitress nodded and Orloff waddled rapidly down the aisle toward him. When Orloff reached the table there was a dewy mist of sweat on his face, as though he had just passed through a cloud. He was a little out of breath, but it sounded more like agitation than exertion. He was taking gasps of breath through his thin red lips and blowing them out his nose in nervous little snorts.

He pushed the chair opposite him away from the table with his foot and Orloff settled into it, his elbows already on the table.

'Have you lost your mind?' said Orloff.

'Why, have you found one?' he answered.

'It's Wednesday, the fifteenth of February,' Orloff hissed, then paused to snort twice for emphasis. 'Our agreement was that you would pass through here on Friday the seventeenth in the evening.'

'I finished early.'

Orloff's face seemed to bloat suddenly with suppressed anger. At that moment a waitress appeared with a jug of coffee, which she poured with cool precision in a stream from the height of about a foot. When she disappeared Orloff pronounced with malicious triumph, 'You've made a serious mistake.' Then he shook his head, making his jowls wobble. 'It was not discreet. Not discreet at all.'

'Don't worry,' he answered. 'They don't give a shit about you. They just wondered if I was here working, and I've taken care of that.' He took a sip of his coffee, which he decided was rather good. It was a shame Orloff was here to distract him. He was getting hungry.

'Oh, I'm sure you have,' Orloff sighed. 'You show up three days early looking like that and then give me your assurances that everything's fine. You'll pardon me if I don't bubble over with confidence in your judgment.'

'Sure. I'm not your psychiatrist.'

Orloff almost smiled. 'The condition of your face would indicate you've miscalculated before.'

'If you're worried about it pay me now and I'll go away.'

'It's not that simple,' said Orloff, his hands beginning to flutter about in his suit coat again before he located his handkerchief and mopped his brow. 'It's a sizable sum and it isn't here yet. Which, if you had lived up to our agreement, would have been here at the moment you arrived.'

'Don't start talking breach of contract,' he said. 'You may be a terrific lawyer, but save it for a court. Nobody refuses to pay me.'

'You've made it much more difficult. How do you imagine it'll look to them when a large sum is passed from us to you? It's much more difficult.' He shifted his eyes to his coffee cup, staring at it as though he were surprised to see it. 'Much more difficult, more difficult and more expensive.'

'You'll get it. Nobody refuses to pay me,' he smiled.

Orloff cocked his head and stared at him. 'No,' he said. 'I suppose they don't.' He pushed his coffee away as though afraid he would spill it, then ascended to his feet like a freed balloon. 'Friday,' he said. He rushed back up the aisle, glancing at his watch.

He watched the fat man out the door, then went to the serving area to select some food. It was too stupid even to think about, he told himself. Orloff was afraid because he knew they would see the connection as soon as the money came out. But the first thing Orloff had done was walk right up and sit down with him in a public place where they were sure to be seen. What was that for? Maybe to prove to someone he wasn't afraid. Afraid of what?

None of the old men should care about it one way or another. It was a straightforward set of contracts between outsiders on outsiders. He carefully picked out fresh vegetables from the platter with a pair of silver tongs. Maybe it had something to do with the money: he'd said there was trouble getting it together. But they always said that, the lightweights and small timers – as if they were afraid he'd want more if they didn't pretend that was the last dime. Still, it didn't make any sense. Orloff was genuinely worried about something.

He moved along the serving line, picking small portions of food that looked as though they'd be good for him. By the time he had returned to his table he had worked enough of it out. There was a third party involved in it somewhere, a third party Orloff was afraid of. And if Orloff was more afraid of the third party than he was of him, he guessed maybe he'd better start worrying a little bit too.

Elizabeth tried to console herself as she struggled to get the airplane seat to lean back at the proper angle.

There wasn't much material to work with, but she tried. She'd been away long enough already, for one thing. It would be nice to sleep in her own bed and not have to worry that she was running out of ways to recombine the few outfits she'd had time to throw into the suitcase. She looked at the profile of Hart in the seat beside her: of course, his time was up too. The FBI had jerked him back to Washington as they'd said they would. Wednesday was the limit. It didn't matter that the two of them had spent most of the time shuttling from disaster to disaster like a pair of reporters, always just a few hours too late to do anything but visit the spot where something was supposed to have happened. And there would be lots of work waiting for her when she got back to the office; Brayer had made that clear. It might not be work that made any difference, but somebody had to do it no matter what, and she was drawing the salary so it would be she. Elizabeth watched the stewardess making still another circuit of the cabin with her tray of drinks, offering each passenger one more chance whether he or she showed any interest or not, awake or asleep, alive or dead for all Elizabeth knew. Every station had to be treated with exactly the same leisurely solicitude, even if the stewardess knew the next five didn't want to be bothered and the sixth was waving a twenty with one hand and an empty glass with the other. Standard procedures had to be followed and there was always a logical reason for them that had to do with statistics. Organizations did things with the long run in mind. It was only individuals that jumped at momentary advantages, took short-cuts, made mistakes. Then Hart was talking to her.

'It's not as bad as all that,' he was saying. 'You look pretty depressed for somebody who's going home.'

'It is as bad as all that,' said Elizabeth. 'I could tell we were getting closer to it. I could feel it. And now we'll go back and the whole thing will be buried in the files.'

'Sure,' he said.

'What do you mean?' said Elizabeth. 'Is it as simple as that? No results because they didn't feel like letting us do a real investigation? That's great.'

'I mean that we did what we were supposed to do – we looked around and got some information on two different matters, and it'll go into the files and maybe contribute to the handling of those matters. That's what it's all about.'

'Matters?' said Elizabeth. 'Jesus.'

'You can't think in terms of solving these problems yourself. What you do is contribute to a systematic information-gathering effort, and you'd better realize that or you'll find yourself being unhappy and frustrated most of the time. Maybe a decent dinner would cheer you up. We'll be in Washington at five thirty and I could pick you up at eight. I might have enough clout to get us a late reservation at Le Provençal or Sans Souci on a Wednesday. I've always made a point of grossly overtipping just in case of an emergency like this.'

She smiled as kindly as she could. 'No thanks,' she said. 'I'm tired and I want to see what I can do tonight about the way I look before I stagger back to work in the morning.'

He didn't seem daunted. There was something to be said for men who didn't seem daunted, she decided, but it wasn't enough to change anything. She listened as he tried to make his way back to neutral ground as gracefully as he could: 'It's a solitary hamburger for each of us then,' he grinned. 'Some other time.'

'Some other time,' she agreed. But would there be another time, she wondered. There was a mystery to these things too. Sometimes something happened and sometimes nothing happened. Whatever controlled it was too subtle and indistinct to make rules about. She settled back in the seat and watched the approaching stewardess. There was no reason not to have a drink, she thought. She wasn't going anywhere.

FIFTEEN

Thursday morning. He stared into the mirror and worked his fingertips over the skin of his cheeks. It wasn't too bad. He was still young enough to heal quickly, he thought. In another day or two the suntan and the soft life would take care of the worst of it, and he was beginning to think there might not be a scar. He lingered in the shower for fifteen minutes, trying to decide how to manage the next stage of it. There was too much he didn't know. He dressed carefully and inspected the results. Not bad – a real estate man from Phoenix having a little side trip on the way home from a business meeting or a winter vacation, if it weren't for the bruises. But the sunglasses helped.

At the end of the hallway he waited for a moment to see if another door opened, but there was no sign of anyone. It would be the maid, probably, who would be under orders to ring someone she thought must be an assistant manager as soon as Room 413 was unoccupied. He took the stairs to the casino and moved through the crowds in the direction of the front entrance. The telephones here were too closely flanked by slot machines. There was no way of telling who today's watchers were, or even if there were some electronic eavesdropping system. It didn't matter because if they could video-tape every hand at every blackjack table they could probably pick up a number dialed on the house phones too, and there was no way for him to know what happened to the tapes afterward.

On the street he stopped to buy a newspaper at a vending machine, then walked into Uncle John's Pancake House. He waited at the door to see if the watchers were following closely enough to be seen, then went to the telephone booth and placed the call.

He counted six rings before the voice on the other end said, 'Dapper Dry Cleaners.'

'Mr. De la Cruz, please,' he said.

A voice shouted 'De la Cruz' over the hum of machinery.

'Cruiser, I don't want to talk long, so listen. I have a little work I need to subcontract – maybe two days' worth and nothing noisy, so it can be any rummy as long as he doesn't stand out. Can you sell it for me?'

'Well, hello to you too, amigo. I heard somebody seen you but I didn't believe it. Bring me some shirts.' The line went dead. He said good-bye to the dial tone and went back to the line of patrons waiting to be served for breakfast.

He sat down at the counter and ate quickly, scanning the paper. It wouldn't do to keep the Cruiser waiting too long: his other interests might take him away from the laundry. As soon as he could get out without seeming hurried, he was back on the street.

It didn't look as though the maid had been to his room yet; at least she hadn't cleaned it. He built a pile of his dirty shirts and fitted the hotel's plastic bag around it. Once outside he walked the two long blocks to the Flamingo to lead whatever watchers there might be far enough from their cars before he got into a taxi. To his disappointment he didn't see anyone rushing for a car as he drove off. That had been one of Eddie's favorites: 'Always look as though you're doing one thing and do another; but do it smooth. Don't look as though you changed your mind. A stupid watcher will commit himself too early and walk right up your ass. If they're set up to cover you with a switch they'll usually look at each other, just like one was handing you off. They can't help it.' But that was only if they weren't good. If they were, you might see them and you might not.

When he came through the entrance to the laundry he could see the Cruiser waiting for him in the center of the dry-cleaning section. Clothes on hangers suspended from the conveyer track on the ceiling whisked past the Cruiser's dark, slouching form like frantic ghosts. Abruptly the moving track stopped and the dresses and coats swung forward once, then backward, then stopped too, and hung opaque like a curtain. The Cruiser stepped from among them.

'Hello, amigo,' he said, snatching the bag and shaking the shirts out onto the counter. 'What's happening?'

'Just some watching until tomorrow night. Nothing special.'

'How much?'

'Four hundred do it?'

'What's the bonus?'

'Another four for the best. One if I'm just sure he was awake and nobody saw him.'

The Cruiser smiled and thumped the counter once

with his fist and said, 'Sold' and then returned to sorting shirts. 'What's the name?'

'Harry Orloff. He's in the phone book. Want something up front now?'

The Cruiser nodded his head. 'All but the bonus.'

He looked up as he took the four hundred. 'You know I can't do anything without something to at least flash at them, amigo. And if you're not around Friday when I deliver these shirts – I'm not saying you wouldn't want to pay, but things happen – I'd be out that much. I gotta live here, man, and—'

'It's all right. Just get on it as soon as you can. I'd like the shirts at seven on Friday. That okay?'

'Sure, amigo. See you then. Earlier if there's something to talk about. You at Caesar's?'

'Yes. Four thirteen.'

'Okay,' he said, and disappeared behind the hanging curtain of clothes.

When he was back on the street he glanced at his watch. It was 11:30 already. The best time to return to the Strip would be after twelve when the first of the DC 10's and 747's from the East arrived and dumped their hundreds of passengers at McCarron Airport. Every day the taxis streamed onto the Strip to deposit them, disoriented and burdened with luggage too heavy for them to carry, under the gigantic roofed porticos of the big hotels. And then each taxi would roar out the driveway again to try for one more piece of this flight or the first passengers off the next one – the man who was first to the taxi stand because he was in a hurry and didn't mind tipping big to get to the casinos.

He decided to walk. Sunshine and exercise were the

best medicines in the world. He was feeling stronger already, even though his leg still didn't feel right. And maybe by evening he'd know what was bothering Orloff. It was probably just that somebody had seen him with Little Norman and gotten scared, but it could be anything. And for that matter, Little Norman hadn't behaved right either. As soon as he showed up with a bruise or two everybody had changed – as if he were an eyesore that was going to lower the going rates on hotel rooms or spoil the customers' appetites.

He reached the Strip at Sahara Avenue and crossed to the other side of the street. He passed Circus Circus, the Stardust, the Silver Slipper, and settled on the Frontier. It was a little quieter this time of day, and it was mostly blue inside. He established himself in the dark bar off the main casino and ordered a Bloody Mary. He didn't much like them, but if you were going to drink in the daytime you had to have what other people drank in the daytime.

As he sipped the Bloody Mary he could see that the midday flights must have begun arriving at the airport. Already on the other side of the casino the lobby was beginning to fill up with people wearing too many clothes for this weather, who apologetically stepped aside to avoid carts of baggage propelled with relentless efficiency toward the elevators by bellmen who seemed unaware of obstacles. In another half hour the first planes would be fueled and ready to take off again, and the scene would be complicated by the husbands in line at the hotel cashiers while the wives pumped the slot machine handles a few more times. If there were still watchers they would have to fight the crowds.

It was just about right, he thought. He wouldn't stay out of sight long enough to worry anyone; just long enough so the watchers would have time to pick him up again and pretend they hadn't lost him in the first place. Then he noticed that the bar was slowly beginning to fill up around him. In a few minutes more waitresses would appear, and when that happened the lights would begin to brighten imperceptibly so they could push the drinks without bumping into each other or losing track of anybody.

He edged farther into the shadows and watched the people coming into the bar. There were the usual couples – some middle-aged, husbands in sport coats and looking secretly pleased at the unfamiliar feeling of not wearing ties on a weekday. The wives in spotless unwrinklable pants outfits that were designed and manufactured to say money – some young, the pair not quite used to each other yet, the man still looking younger and greener than the woman in spite of what he thought of himself. Then there were a few solitaries, both men and women, all fortyish, who would sit down where they could get a good view of the casino. Usually they smoked heavily but didn't drink much – drank at all only because it was the price of the seats they occupied while they collected themselves from the long flight and scanned the casino to see which tables seemed to be paying off. After the first drink most of them would have to get change because they didn't have anything smaller than a hundred.

Then he noticed three men who didn't look right. Two were wearing business suits like junior bankers or insurance men, and the third was dressed like a cowboy in a magazine ad – boots and jeans and a blue shirt with snaps on the pockets. They all came in together, but sat alone in different corners of the bar. He couldn't decide whether they were inspectors from the Nevada Gaming Commission or the trouble-shooters the casino planted to keep the whores from hanging around and distracting the gamblers.

And then he spotted the old man crossing the lobby toward the elevators, his accountant in front of him to shield him from the possibility that anyone could come within eight feet of him, his lawyer beside him, eyes sweeping the surrounding area for any sign that something was out of place, and then, five paces behind him the porter pushing the luggage cart. It didn't matter who paid the men in the bar for watching the old man. Just the fact that Carlo Balacontano was here was enough reason to be somewhere else. The old man was an industry. There would be bodyguards, courtesy envoys from the semiretired Dons in the area, influence peddlers, favor seekers, business partners, all trooping in to get an audience with Carl Bala. And probably there would be cops, here to be sure he wasn't in town because he had a secret interest in a casino; and just as much, to be nearby if any of the people who hated him finally managed to have him killed – not to stop it, but to clean up afterward so the public order wasn't derailed too brutally or for too long. It wasn't a good place to be.

The old man had passed through and disappeared in a moment. He waited while the three men finished their drinks and left, then finished his own more slowly. He headed out through the aisles of jangling, buzzing, winking slot machines toward the side entrance to the parking lot.

Elizabeth was not fully awake and it was ten o'clock already in Washington. It was her third time zone this week; the fact that this was the one she was supposed to be accustomed to didn't help any. And being pulled away from her activity reports before she'd had fifteen minutes to burrow into the three-day backlog destroyed any illusion that she was settling back into the routine. As soon as he'd noticed her, Brayer had said, 'Drop that. Padgett needs your help.'

So now, as drudgery specialist for the entire office, damn them, she was doing Padgett's field reports while the computers in the room behind the glass wall ticked out more to be piled onto her own desk. Sometimes she imagined she could hear it, though she knew that was impossible. It wasn't just the work. It was that she was always at the mercy of contingencies, at any moment available to be pulled away from her own work to become what amounted to a clerical assistant to Padgett or Richardson or somebody. They were all supposed to be on a par: senior analysts. But when Elizabeth was in trouble you didn't see Brayer pulling them off anything to help her. And they didn't see it and wouldn't see it if they outlived the Washington Monument. It was just the way things were. Every time one of Padgett's 'friends' felt his hemorrhoids acting up and decided to see a doctor in Des Moines, Elizabeth had to drop everything and monitor field reports or do background checks or something. And when the 'crisis' was over and even the file report was already done because Elizabeth had done it for him, did anybody worry about Elizabeth's work? No, dammit, they didn't. They stood around in the lounge or took a much-needed day or two off.

This time it was going to be worse. There were four of Padgett's old mafiosi out of their neighborhoods at once, all in the Southwest, and now two had turned up in Las Vegas. These were old men, rich men. What else would they do in the winter but go to a warm spot? And of course they'd stop in Las Vegas. What on earth did John think? That they'd sit alone in the middle of the desert reading Gibbon's *Decline and Fall of the Roman Empire*, no doubt. And when Elizabeth had worked two or three weeks as Padgett's lackey, they'd all four have had enough of the big hotels and gambling and golf and hookers and go back home to rest up and so would Padgett.

But not Elizabeth. She'd go back to her own desk and work three more weeks of twelve- and fourteen-hour days to catch up. But she wouldn't say anything to them, because there wasn't anything to say that was sufficient to overcome the massive stupidity of it. If she tried they'd wink at each other behind her back and tell each other it was probably just that she was having her period. Well fuck them, she thought. And you can't even get the satisfaction of saying that because if you do they'll decide you're a slut and have that to hold over you too.

Suddenly she realized she hadn't been doing any work for some time – just staring at the field report and feeling sorry for herself. It wouldn't help. It just meant there was that much more to do besides her own work. She forced herself to read it: 'There are none of the standard indicators of friction or animosity at this time. Balacontano has been placed in a celebrity suite at the Frontier Hotel, which, although it has security design of B class, does not appear to indicate undue fear of violence. The suite also has superior facilities. The normal price of the suite is six hundred dollars per diem, and it is often used to house entertainers appearing in the hotel shows. As of this time there is no indication of the length of Balacontano's stay. The Learjet (leased from Airlift Transport, Inc.; Nutley, New Jersey, Registration Number N-589632) was refueled immediately after landing. No flight plan for another destination has been filed with the FAA, however. There has been no communication with persons outside the suite since arrival at eleven forty-five a.m. Thursday.'

Big deal, thought Elizabeth. Flew in and checked into a hotel room, in a thousand words or less. But they were edgy, she could tell. They always did that until something happened and then they snapped to. Every word would count then, but now it was just chattering to make the time pass, to keep the sense that there was somebody back here listening.

She looked up and saw Padgett rush by with a worried look on his face, carrying a voice transcript in his hand. So important – Man with a Big Job to Do – he was really in his glory now, she thought. Probably one of them ordered a martini from room service and the agent in place called for help. Padgett rapped urgently on Brayer's door, then passed in.

Elizabeth returned to her reports: 'Toscanzio is at the MGM Grand Hotel, where it appears he has been for at least twenty-four hours.' So that's part of it, she thought. Somebody lost track of one of them, and now the whole organization is supposed to compensate for the lost day by watching them all twice as hard, as though they could bring back that day.

'Elizabeth,' said Brayer from his doorway. 'Come on in. I think we've got something.'

Sure thing, Mr. Brayer, thought Elizabeth as she set aside the sheaf of reports and stepped to the inner office. It had to be an isolated farmhouse, she thought. The agents were getting edgy and it was about time for a farmhouse. Field agents seemed to live with the vision of an isolated house in the backs of their minds because they were weaned on the Apalachin conference and Boiardo's private graveyard. It was like the Holy Grail to them, and you knew they were getting eager when it started turning up.

'What is it?' she asked.

'All hell seems to be breaking loose,' said Padgett. So it wasn't the farmhouse. Maybe they were already up to the Man With A Rifle, always amended in final reports to man with a long, thin parcel (or golf club or broom or cane or pool cue).

'What, exactly?'

'Three murders in Las Vegas in the last two hours – at least two of them odd-job types. The other one seems to be some kind of businessman who just got in the way while they were taking out the first of the others. We're checking, of course.'

'What makes you think it's significant?'

'Because Balacontano made his first appearance in public while it was going on. Went down to the hundred-dollar tables and started betting the farm at the crap tables, not even looking to see if he'd won or lost, flashing a lot of money and attracting attention.'

Elizabeth noted that the farm had made its appearance in a new avatar, but didn't let it distract her. 'What about other people? Toscanzio? Castiglione?'

'All in an uproar for the first few minutes, then quiet. Shut up in their houses and hotels. But no soldiers in evidence anywhere, almost as though somebody got word to them and convinced them there was nothing to worry about. Like they were ignoring it for now. Or maybe they knew in advance. It's hard to tell at this distance, and the reports are all of the "we're standing by" variety.'

Brayer was still silent, staring at the transcript on his desk. Elizabeth waited for him to say something, but he didn't. She asked Padgett, 'Any idea yet on how it was done?'

'No,' said Padgett. 'Give me ten minutes. There's a call out for the report of the LVPD as soon as the homicide team gets back in.'

She glanced at her watch: twelve o'clock. That meant nine o'clock there. Friday. Too early for much of the reaction. Some of them probably weren't awake yet. The hourlies later in the day would be more reliable.

'What do you think, Elizabeth?' Brayer finally spoke up.

'I think we should check on the other two and see where they go. If there's a conference in Las Vegas and this is really Balacontano, I would guess they'd head for home. If they show up in Las Vegas this was nothing. If they don't, it doesn't prove they'd ever planned to, but it's still worth checking.'

'Agreed,' said Brayer. 'And Padgett, be as thorough as you can when you're checking on those victims.

171

Don't give up easy. If you can establish a connection with somebody in particular it'll tell us what's going on. We might as well know who's mad at whom.' Then he added, 'Even though it probably won't do us any good or them any harm.'

Padgett wheeled about and headed for the door and Elizabeth followed. Brayer sat immobile, staring at the transcript. Elizabeth almost asked for it, but thought better of it. There would be another copy at the monitor's desk. Brayer was either planning his next three moves or contemplating the vanity of his last three. If it helped to stare at a paragraph he'd long since memorized, so much the better.

SIXTEEN

'Amigo,' he said. 'I got some shirts for you.'

'I'll go pick them up.'

'Not a good idea, amigo. I'm on the road already. Ten minutes, no more.'

'Right.' The line went dead.

Shit, he thought. Any news had to be trouble, and it was – what? ten hours? before the shirts were supposed to be back. He looked at his watch. Nine o'clock. The Cruiser never did business at nine. Most of his customers wouldn't be up for hours. Even the cleaning business didn't open until ten thirty.

He scarcely had time to dress before he heard the knock. When he swung the door open the Cruiser slipped inward with it as though attached to it, then tossed the box of folded shirts on the bed.

'Amigo,' said the Cruiser. 'You really fucked me up.' The Cruiser was smiling, the first time he could remember having seen that exact expression: he was showing his bad teeth and his breath seemed to come in short gasps.

'What happened?' he asked.

'You said it was no big thing but it was. All you had to do was tell me it was. You know better, amigo. You should never have done it to me.'

'It's no big thing. Orloff owes me money.'

'Not now. He's dead.'

'How?'

'I sent a man to his office to watch. He was in a parked van all night and then I was going to send somebody else this morning. He was my cousin. Not smart, but I thought I'd let him have this easy one to make some money. But he wasn't smart, so I sent my boy Jesus at seven to see if he was awake. He was. God. Something to do was such a big deal he hadn't even lain down all night. Sat there in a chair staring at an empty office through a peephole he drilled. He sent Jesus to get him something to eat. Jesus got back to the block in time to see it. Orloff drove up to the office and started to get out of his car. Then three of them just appeared from no place. Jesus said he thought the one with the shotgun came out of the building, one came from someplace on the other side of the street where the van was parked. The other might have been in the bushes, but he couldn't tell. They just were there. Orloff just stood there next to his car shaking, and the one with the shotgun blew his head off. Jesus said my cousin panicked and jumped into the driver's seat and tried to start the van. He must not have seen the one near him. Jesus said the guy didn't look surprised or anything, just stepped to the side of the van and put a pistol to the window. He fired five or six times. After that Jesus didn't see anything else. He was already running.'

'I'm sorry it happened. Where is Jesus now?'

'Outside in the car waiting for me. I've got to get us all out of town.'

'Will a thousand do it?'

'I think so. You know I'll have to tell if they corner me, though. With Jesus and Ascención—'

'Sure. But try to give me time. Leave now and keep going. I wish I could tell you something that would help you spot them, but I don't know anything. He just owed me money and looked nervous. Did the kid tell you what they looked like?'

'No. Just three Anglos. One dressed like a cowboy and the other two in suits. They didn't even look like they came together.'

'Thanks for the shirts,' he said.

'Yeah,' said the Cruiser. 'See you sometime.' He slipped out the door and was gone.

He locked the door and sat down on the bed. It wasn't good. There was no way to tell if it even had anything to do with him. Anybody who had any dealings with Orloff would probably consider doing it sometime. Orloff was cunning and greedy, and he sometimes got nervous. But the three who did it had to be ones he'd seen in the Frontier, and that meant it had something to with Carl Bala – but what? They'd either been watching for Bala or just watching him. And there was the money too – a lot of trouble for nothing. His leg started to ache a little at the thought of it.

And now he couldn't leave. If he did, they'd think he'd done it – broken the rule and violated the truce the families had agreed to among themselves and imposed on everyone else for almost thirty years. Especially the way his face looked, and the fact that Orloff had been seen with him – the fat, stupid pig. Now he'd have to stay put and hope that would convince the dozen old men locked in their houses and hotels that he represented no threat or inconvenience

175

to them. At least with Orloff he could be sure whoever had wanted Claremont dead didn't know about him. Orloff had never been stupid enough to make his services as middleman unnecessary. He'd known his life depended on it. So he could forget about the three men unless somebody saw the connection between the pile of dead meat in the van and the Cruiser and had the resources and the persistence to find him. And Cruiser would probably be in Mexico by late afternoon.

The ringing of the telephone startled him. He snatched the receiver off the hook and snapped, 'Yes?'

'Hi, kid. It's Norman.' The deep, velvety voice was quiet and imperturbable.

He collected himself. 'Hello, Norman.' So it was starting already, the test. 'What can I do for you?' He added, 'It's pretty early yet for either of us, isn't it? What time is it?'

'Almost ten, kid,' said Little Norman. 'I figured you'd be up for hours by now. Maybe playing tennis. You like to keep in shape, don't you?'

'Sure, Norman.'

'Well come downstairs and I'll buy you breakfast. I'm in the coffee shop.'

'I'll be there.'

He quickly got undressed again, showered, shaved, and put on a coat and tie. At the closet he lingered for an instant, thinking about the gun taped to the wall, then felt ashamed. Whatever happened he wouldn't need a gun between the room and the coffee shop. This wasn't the time to indulge his nerves.

In the coffee shop Little Norman seemed to take up one side of the booth, his arms spread out along the

176

top of the seat in a gorilla's embrace so that the camelhair sport coat looked like upholstery. When he sat down, Norman didn't smile. 'You're having ham and eggs, kid,' said Little Norman. 'I ordered them while I was waiting.'

'Thanks, Norman. That'll be just fine.' He added, 'Sorry to keep you waiting, but you pulled me out of the sack.'

'I came to tell you something,' said Little Norman.

'What's that?'

'I just heard Harry Orloff died.' His dark eyes didn't flicker; they seemed to sharpen and hold him for impaling.

'So?' he said. 'Sorry to hear it. He should have lost some weight.'

'Don't play that on me, kid,' hissed Little Norman, leaning forward on his elbows so his big face loomed only a foot away over the table. 'I was the best before you were born. You were with him two days ago.'

'Sorry, Norman,' he said. 'What now?'

Little Norman leaned back again to give the waitress room to set the plates on the table between them. Finally he smiled. 'That's better.'

'I didn't do it, you know,' he said. 'I don't work in Vegas.'

'I know you didn't,' said Little Norman. 'I heard he owed you money.'

He picked up his knife and fork and started to saw at the slice of ham. 'Easy come, easy go,' he said.

'Not this time, kid,' said Little Norman. He leaned forward again and his voice dropped. 'You're gonna get paid, and then you're gonna leave. Tonight at nine you play blackjack at the Silver Slipper.' He didn't wait for an answer. He was already standing by that time, and then he was moving off toward the door, the broad tan back of his perfectly tailored coat swaying slightly as he leaned to the left to avoid a scurrying keno girl whose stacked wig barely reached his shoulder.

'What the hell does that mean?' said Padgett. The computer clicked and the lines of green print swept into view across the screen. 'A car stopped at a red light, was blocked in by two others, and three men walked up and shot a whole family inside it.'

'That supposed to mean something?' asked Brayer.

'That's the fourth, fifth, and sixth,' said Padgett. 'It has to mean something. How can it not?'

Elizabeth pressed the hard-copy button and waited for the machine to roll out the warm, damp sheet. She scanned the report of the Las Vegas police, and it suggested nothing at all. A husband, a wife, and a boy of ten. Stopped at a corner waiting for the light to change. 'If we had a little more it might tell us something,' she said.

'What do you want?' asked Brayer.

'Anything. What he did for a living, where they lived. What they had with them, I guess. And maybe which direction they were going.' She looked out the window into the second heavy snowstorm of the month, and tried to picture it: a bright, sunny morning in Las Vegas and the car stopped in traffic. Maybe the man and woman in the front seat, and the little boy in the back. And then screeching tires, cars lurching to a stop at odd angles, and the sound of guns blasting in the windows, the impact of the slugs at first punching

circular spiderweb shapes into the glass, then spattering the glass into tiny crystals like diamonds spread all
over the bodies. 'I guess that would be first,' she said.
'Which way was the car going?'

He was afraid. It was as if fear were a thick, oily liquid
that had somehow seeped into his entrails and stuck
there, holding him in a kind of paralysis. Somehow his
body had stopped digesting; his food had turned into a
greasy, immovable mass. He could feel it – his body
wanted to do something, fight, run, turn light and fly –
but the thing was in there, holding him down.

No. He'd seen it too many times. They'd sit there
staring at him, maybe their fingers fluttering involuntarily like birds while their eyes went stupid. After it
was too late they'd do something – the hands would
reach for whatever was nearest, or the leg muscles
would tense for a spring, but by then they'd be dead. It
wasn't going to be that way with him. He sat on the
bed and thought about it. Little Norman had said they
were going to pay him. That was something to think
about.

He felt a little better. They were going to pay him.
That meant that they acknowledged the debt and that
Orloff had done something else. No, that didn't work
unless they thought Orloff had told him where the
money was going to come from. And that he had some
way to make it worth paying him. He looked at his
watch – almost noon. Nine hours left, so he might as
well reassure them now.

He reached for the telephone and asked for the
United Airlines number. Even as he made his reservation he wondered who would take an eight o'clock

flight from Las Vegas on a Saturday morning. Probably the other passengers would all be people passing through – or maybe it was just that so many people arrived here on Saturday mornings that the only other choice was to fly the planes out empty. He'd probably never know, he thought.

It was going to be tough to give himself an edge in nine hours, most of it daylight. They'd be watching him too closely. He knew he'd have to get started if he was going to make it.

He looked about the room to see what there was to work with – the bed, the shower, the telephone, the air conditioner – all standard. It would have to be the Magic Fingers machine on the bed. He studied it carefully. The metal box had an electric alarm clock besides the mechanical massager. The coin box was impregnable, but the wiring was easy enough to get to. Once he had the back open it was fairly simple. The wires that went to the alarm buzzer fit through the crack in the back once they were stripped of insulation. He set the alarm for noon and tested the wires. The spark wasn't much, but it would do. He put the Magic Fingers machine back together and trailed the wires beside his pillow. Then he went to the dresser and brought back his bottle of after-shave lotion and read the label: 98 percent alcohol. He set the alarm, poured the lotion into a paper cup, set it on the bed, and arranged the wires. It wasn't much, but it might help. If he wasn't back by two a.m. there would be a fire in Room 413.

That was one of the things Eddie had been able to give him. 'Know everything. If there's nothing you can know that the mark doesn't know you better make something happen.' The main thing would be getting out. He had the car, and there was the off chance that he might use his plane reservation. Then there were trains and buses. He'd have to get those set up during the afternoon. But that late at night there wouldn't be many of them, and he might not be able to get where he had to be to get on one.

It was probably just nerves, he thought. They weren't going to kill him in the Silver Slipper, and they weren't likely to pay him two hundred thousand and then kill him. But nothing else about this seemed right either. There was no question that something big had gone very wrong, and now they were trying to clean it up. Whatever it was made it worth what they'd done to Orloff, and they'd never have done that in Las Vegas unless it was necessary.

Whatever it was, he'd have to stay out of sight until it was time for the payoff. If they were going to kill him it would probably be before rather than after. He checked the lock on the door, chained it, then moved the dresser in front of it. Then he went to the closet and pulled the pistol off the wall and checked the clip. Then he turned on the television.

SEVENTEEN

The air was cold now that the sun had been down for a couple of hours. The hot, steady current of the desert breeze had changed into something harsher and more petulant that whirled down the Strip in icy eddies, then pawed at him and buffeted him from above as he waited to cross the street. He hunched his shoulders and moved closer to the center of the crowd of people. It was as though the frigid emptiness of the mountains was rushing in to correct some imbalance that had been precariously asserted by all this light and noise and motion and color – as though some fragile barrier had been swept away. He pulled his coat tighter around him and felt the pull of the tape on his belly. The hard, sharp edge of the safety catch on the pistol irritated his skin a little, but there wasn't anything to be done about it now. There would be watchers around him already. It was the only place for it anyway. It had to be near his center of gravity, where he could forget about it. There was no way to carry an extra pound of steel attached to your side or your leg without involuntarily carrying yourself differently. One of the first things he'd learned was to watch for the man who held one arm an inch farther out than the other, or the man who stepped a little stiff-legged.

Before the light changed the first two lurched

forward into the street, and the rest of the people scurried after them. He stayed among them, measuring his steps to keep himself surrounded by their bodies. He looked at his watch again. He was still on time. It was just the cold that had made the walk seem endless. Above him in the dark night sky the gargantuan lady's high-heeled shoe beaded with white light bulbs spun absurdly.

In a moment the pneumatic doors huffed closed behind him like an air lock, and he stepped forward into the warm brightness of the casino. He kept moving deeper into the place. There was no question they had picked him up by now. Somewhere out of sight a telephone would have lit up and a voice would be saying 'He's here,' and that would be all.

He strolled along the line of blackjack tables, his eyes sweeping the green felt surfaces for a sign, then straying upward to the private, emotionless eyes of the white-shirted dealers. He spotted it without difficulty. A new brigade of dealers filed down the aisle from wherever their break room was, but this time one of them stationed himself behind an empty table, fanned the deck of cards across the felt, and stood with his arms folded on his chest in the customary pantomime of ostentatious idleness that announced the opening of another table. The placard at the dealer's elbow said ten-dollar minimum bet. So it was not to be private – it would be duly witnessed and recorded. The minimum was low enough to ensure that the table would fill up quickly. He waited to take a seat until two other players had rushed in front of him. The dealer swept his hand across the felt and the fan of cards closed into a thick deck. While the hands expertly performed the ritual of shuffling, the rest of the seats at the table were claimed.

The dealer's empty eyes seemed to stare out over the heads of the gamblers at some distant focal point as his fingertips tapped the fat deck into the shoe. The dealer looked young, his carefully sculpted hair blond from the sun, but already he had the ageless look of detached competence they all seemed to have worn into them. He clapped his hands once, held the perfect fingers up, turned them to show his palms, and said, 'Good luck, ladies and gentlemen.'

The cards seemed to fly from the shoe and appear in perfect order before the gamblers. The gamblers paid little attention to each other as each played his hand in turn, assessing the threat implicit in the dealer's up-card. He watched the dealer's hands float above the felt, collecting cards and moving chips with relentless unhesitating efficiency. He looked at the cards in front of him, a queen and a ten. The dealer's nineteen won the chips on four of the betting circles, and paid off one other bettor. The cards appeared on the felt again and the dealer busted; the hands moved in an arc along the semicircle, duplicating five of the stacks of chips. The cards appeared again and the dealer's seventeen had to pay four of the gamblers. As the game went on, the trend became clear. He was winning three hands out of four at minimum bets. Three of the others were getting random pairs of cards, sometimes good, sometimes bad. The dealer was using the other two.

One was a fat man in a blue plaid sport coat who was dealt an ace and a ten-point card every few hands. The other was a small, pinched-looking woman about forty-five years old who was playing a mysterious intuited system that seemed to be paying off. He wondered which one the dealer was going to bust first. He collected his steady income, letting the dealer deftly pay his winnings in larger denomination chips to keep the stack in front of him from looking too big, and watched the other two winners to see if he could sense it coming.

When the fat man began to double his bets, he knew. Slowly the trend changed. When the man lost, he doubled again. In a few minutes the chubby pink fingers extracted another pair of hundred dollar bills from the plaid sport coat and bought more chips. The cards kept coming, each pair the fat man got costing him more. Then he got up and left. When he pushed his chair back another man left too. By now the little woman was winning so steadily that the others took an interest. Nobody noticed that the nondescript man beside her was winning almost as steadily, or that he was now betting twenty-five-dollar chips. Two of them shrugged in sympathy when her luck ran out. One of them said, 'Good move,' when she climbed down from the stool while she was still ahead. One by one the rest of the players dropped out and were replaced by new faces, until he was the only one of the original players who remained. The new people won or lost and moved on, none of them allowed to remain long enough to notice that the quiet man in the gray tweed was on a big winning streak. And then the dealer paid him off for a hand just as a new dealer arrived to relieve him. The dealer clapped his hands once, held his fingers up and said, 'Good luck, ladies and gentleman,' and walked away.

Instead of watching while the new dealer began to

shuffle, he looked at the last stack of chips. The third one down was slightly smaller. He pretended to restack them and palmed the chip so he could look at it. In the center, where the others had the legend *Silver Slipper*, this one said *Flamingo*. He put it in his pocket, collected the rest of the chips, and moved away from the table. At the cashier's window the teller gave him almost ten thousand dollars.

It seemed even colder outside now. The Flamingo was several long blocks out on the Strip, but he didn't take a taxi. As soon as he had made his way to the blackjack tables he spotted the invitation. This time it was a middle-aged woman who looked a little mannish in the dealer's white shirt. The evening was approaching its peak now, and seats were scarce at the tables. The twenty-five-dollar minimum bet at her table didn't discourage anyone when she laid out the fan of cards. The game proceeded as it had in the Silver Slipper. Time after time he got nineteen or twenty. The dealer's seventeen or eighteen took most of the chips on the table; about a quarter of the time she went over twenty-one. He won steadily while the faces around him changed. After about an hour the dealer paid him with a chip from the Dunes. This time when he cashed in the teller gave him forty thousand dollars. As he walked to the Dunes he was beginning to wonder where he would carry the rest of it. But by the time he left the Dunes it was almost midnight, and the Friday evening gamblers were too busy to notice that the teller had counted out sixty thousand-dollar bills to the man in the gray tweed. At the Aladdin it was the same. By the time the dealer at the Tropicana gave him the chip

186

from Caesar's Palace he calculated that he must have the whole two hundred thousand. His pockets were full of money and they were sending him home. He had to admit it was sort of funny; they'd actually found a way to ring in their own dealers without the solid-citizen management types of all those big hotels even suspecting it. Anything happens, the hotels get the heat.

At the front entrance of the Tropicana the wind was now blowing in an unvarying, merciless rush up the street into the city. He checked his watch and saw that it was after one thirty. The fire he'd set up in his room would start at two if he didn't stop it, and the pedestrian traffic had died down at the outer end of the Strip. He took the doorman's offer of a taxi. 'Caesar's,' he said and the car roared down the driveway to the street, then stopped. The driver said, 'Excuse me, sir,' and got out. He bent down as though to check the left front tire.

It was a second before he realized what was happening, but when the two cars pulled up on either side of the cab he recognized the face of the man in the cowboy shirt. The man was out of his own car and reaching for the door handle of the cab already. The one on the other side was a pace or two slower. He chose that one.

He didn't feel the pain when he tore the pistol off his belly, just a sensation of cold where the tape had covered him and his shirt was open. The gun blast jerked the man backward a few feet, but he was out the door and had the pistol in the cab driver's face before the body toppled on its back. The cab driver's face had an expression of surprise when he squeezed the trigger. He knew the cowboy was on the ground somewhere behind the car, but there was no time. He jumped into the front seat past the steering wheel, threw the cab into gear and hit the gas pedal hard with his left foot. The cab jerked forward as he struggled to control it without showing his head above the seat. He heard shots as he wheeled out onto the Strip, but the sound of the cab's engine accelerating drowned out whatever he could have heard of the bullets smacking into the side of the car. He took the first right turn off the Strip and waited to see if the other cars had followed. After a few seconds he knew they had stopped to pick up the bodies, so he drove the cab into a parking space behind a closed gas station and got out. 'Jesus,' he said aloud. 'So it was the taxis.' They had offered him one outside each casino. And that was why they'd picked the casinos so far apart.

Damn them!

There was nothing he could do now except get out quickly. He'd have to make his way to the car in Caesar's parking lot and get out. But damn them! They hadn't needed to do it in the first place. He wouldn't have been a threat to Carl Bala, sitting up there in the Frontier surrounded by a dozen concentric circles of hotel security men and policemen and the syndicate faithful, all watching each other watching him. And he didn't even know if Bala was the one who'd ordered it. He loped along behind the buildings, moving parallel with the sidewalk out on the Strip, looking out at each alley to see if there was anyone to walk with, but each time seeing only empty sidewalk and the flash of passing cars. God! The stupidity of it! They could have sat there and done nothing, and he wouldn't even have known who owed him the money. He sure as hell wouldn't have shown up with his hand out at Carl Bala's door. If he had, he would have deserved this, for being a fool. They had wasted his life for nothing at all, as if he were some poor sucker who'd happened to be standing too close when a numbers runner came in for a handoff. It was a joke.

He was now behind the MGM Grand. Caesar's parking lot would be just a block up and a block over, but there didn't seem to be any way to get there. It was just too much empty pavement to cross alone and on foot if they were cruising the Strip in cars.

Behind the MGM Grand he had a thousand cars to choose from. He selected one he would feel comfortable with if he got stuck with it for the night, a dark blue Chevrolet. He hotwired it. He was out of the lot in a few seconds. At Caesar's nothing looked peculiar. There were still gamblers wandering from aisle to aisle looking for their cars, and even a few late arrivals pulling into the lot. He knew that for the moment they would be searching for him on the freeway only. They would think he was still in the cab until they found it behind the gas station. In a little while if it didn't turn up they might have the cab company report it stolen.

He glided up the driveway and found a parking space near his rented car, sat there and waited. Something about the place made him hesitate to disentangle the ignition wires of his stolen Chevrolet. The rented car was only thirty feet from where he sat, but that thirty feet would be enough for them if they'd thought to wait for him. And if they'd managed to find out about the rented car sometime during the week, it was all over anyway. They'd be sitting somewhere out of sight waiting for him to turn the key and blow himself into a hundred thousand spoonfuls of hamburger. So he sat there with his lights off and his motor idling, staring into the darkness around him for any of the signs – a parked car with the silhouette of a head in the driver's window, a man alone and on foot who didn't find his car right away, a car that circled instead of swinging out into the driveway at the end of an aisle.

He glanced at his watch. It was two ten already. By now the fire should have started in his room. The smoke sensor should have gone off. The fire engines should arrive in a few minutes. At this hour they'd roar down the Strip at fifty or sixty, their flashing lights visible for a mile or more, not downshifting once until they were abreast of the giant sign that said Diana Ross. He tried to spot the window of his room, scanning the fourth strip of glass up from the parking lot for a flicker of light. Damn them! They weren't thorough, they weren't smart, but there was no way to make yourself a break with them because there were so damned many of them, lumbering around like so many baboons. It didn't matter what you did, the weight of their stupid single-minded brutish persistence would advance behind you – either slowly like a glacier or fast like an avalanche and obliterate all your tricks and contrivances and you with them. It was too late to be cautious, too late even to be afraid. Somebody powerful, maybe Carlo Balacontano sitting in his suite in the Frontier, had become annoyed with Orloff, so Orloff and everybody in his vicinity must cease to exist. It was a miracle they hadn't torn Orloff's building apart the same day to eradicate every sign that such a person had ever walked the earth.

It was time to move. If he didn't do something soon there wouldn't be time to get out. He felt in the lining of his sleeve for the keys to the rented car, and clutched them in his left hand. He killed the engine, reached under the dashboard until he felt the line of fuses, and plucked them out of their clips one by one. There was no time to figure out which circuit controlled the dome lamps. When he opened the door he didn't want to be bathed in light.

He was out the door and moving quickly now. He heard no engine start, no sign of life as he accomplished the thirty feet to the car. If they were about, they hadn't moved. He bent down as though to tie his shoe or check a tire or pick something up, and scanned the surface of the asphalt around him for feet. While he was down he unlocked the door and waited.

Suddenly he could hear the thin, whining sound of the sirens somewhere down the Strip, screaming into the vast night sky that practically swallowed their shriek into its emptiness. But there was no question what it was. 'The cavalry,' he chuckled to himself. 'The fucking cavalry.' From here on it would be timing.

The sound of the sirens swelled as the trucks approached. He crouched, straining to prepare. At the moment when the first of the trucks flashed into view he slipped into the car, the interior flickering with light for only a second. If there were watchers they would be staring at the trucks, if only for that second; there was no way they could stop themselves. The first truck, a long hook-and-ladder rig, bounced up the driveway doing at least thirty, its siren wailing to a stop as though out of breath as the truck pulled up in front of the covered portico. Another like it burst into the parking lot by the side entrance and pulled around the building out of sight. Smaller trucks were materializing now, but he didn't watch them. Instead he scanned the parking lot.

He saw them at once. Three cars lit up to reveal the shapes of men swinging out to their feet. He ducked down and listened for the sound of running, but the noise of the big diesel engines was now flooding the air to replace the sirens. He saw one of the men dash past his window, but the man's eyes were fixed on the doorway of the casino. Now the fire trucks were all in place according to some prearranged contingency plan the fire department worked by. The watchers would be at the hotel entrances waiting for him to try to slip out with the frightened guests.

He had a moment of residual terror when he turned the ignition key, but he already knew there was no bomb. They would never have sat in the parking lot to watch it go off. He backed out of the parking space and drove onto the Strip. If any of them noticed him it was too late for them to be sure what they were looking at, because already there were four or five others driving away from the hotel as he'd known they would. The hotel guests would stay to clog the sidewalks and the parking lots and crowd the firemen, but the visiting gamblers would be heading for their cars to go someplace where there damn well wasn't a fire to close down the tables just when their luck was about to return to them.

He was out now, in a clean untraceable car with a full tank, carrying about two hundred thousand dollars stuffed into his coat. But as far as they were concerned he was dead already. He had been from the moment some old man's mind had settled on him and declared him a possible irritant. All that had remained was the mechanical, automatic translation of the thought to accomplishment, and the old man had probably lost interest in specifics of that sort years ago. Having given his frown or his nod or said, 'Take him out too,' his mind would have moved to other matters.

So he was dead. Well fuck them. He wasn't going to take that. They were damned well going to know he wasn't dead.

EIGHTEEN

She stood in front of John Brayer's desk with the computer copy in her hand. 'Fieldston Growth Enterprises,' Elizabeth said. When Brayer didn't react, she set the sheet in front of him and touched her finger to the line. He could hear her pointed nail tapping the glass top of the desk. 'Fieldston Growth Enterprises is the name of the building where this lawyer Orloff was murdered. It's also the name of the company that turned up in the investigation of the Veasy murder in California.'

'Oh, yeah. You didn't get anything much on that one, did you? Too bad we had to pull you out so fast. You're keeping up with what the locals are doing, aren't you?'

'John,' said Elizabeth, letting just a hint of the exasperation she felt seep into her voice, 'this company has turned up at least twice now in murders that might be professional within a week. It's a match as it is, and I think there's a third.' She waited until she knew he had to speak.

'All right,' said Brayer. 'It's slim, but I'm willing to pursue it, to a point. The third, if I remember, was that the initials turned up in something of Senator Claremont's, right?'

'You know it is,' she said.

'What's the name of the staff counsel on Clare-mont's tax committee again?' He matched her impa-tience with a fair imitation of sluggish complacence, but she saw that he already had the telephone receiver in his hand.

'Justin Garfield,' she said in a sweet alert voice he would probably have believed in another conversation.

'You might as well go wait for me at your desk,' said Brayer. 'If this guy says FGE is Fieldston Growth Enterprises, I'll want a report I can use to get a subpoena for their records before you get on the plane.' He started to dial the telephone.

'What plane?'

'To wherever this company is – oh, yeah,' he said, staring at the computer copy she'd laid on his desk. 'Las Vegas.'

He knew what he had to do without stopping to think about it. When he drove past the Frontier he spotted two watchers without even turning his head. One was in a Mark VI parked in perfect position to block the front exit of the parking lot if he slipped the hand brake and let it roll forward five yards. The other was just inside the lighted front lobby, waiting for a taxi within a few feet of a half dozen of them. He drove eastward toward the other end of the city.

There was no simple way to do it without making a lot of noise. He wouldn't have the kind of time it took to be clever, and there were sure to be a lot of people around who were ready to avert just this kind of thing. Castiglione was old, but he was old the way a retired president was old, living behind a high fence in a house that was built like a fort and cost somebody plenty. If you had a reason to see him it was hard enough to get in, but if you didn't have a reason it was worth your life to try. Still, it had to be Castiglione. He was the only one. He was the elder statesman, the one who had always had the juice to keep Balacontano and Toscanzio and some of the others in check. If he was out of the picture there would be confusion. None of the capos would ever believe that one of them hadn't done it, and the only reason to do it was to make a bid for ascendancy.

Eventually one of the others would come out on top, but it would take time for them to devour the losers. If he couldn't be sure of getting the one he wanted, this was the next best thing. He drove up Grayson Street slowly, a good citizen of Las Vegas trying not to wake up the neighbors after he got off the eight-to-two shift at the Thunderbird or somewhere. Grayson Street was a ruler-straight parkway with a hairpin turn at the end of it dominated by the imposing adobe facade of Castiglione's house. As he swung past the house he studied it carefully. There was nobody outside patrolling the grounds. It had probably seemed unnecessary to have somebody freezing in the cold desert wind to protect a man whose personal enemies had been dead for decades. The adobe wall around the yard didn't obscure the view of the house, which sat on a little rise in the center of a vast lawn. No shrubs had been allowed to grow within a hundred feet of the house, so anyone who approached it would be in the open all the way back to the street. And there would be lights, although at a glance he couldn't see them, big floodlights that would change night into day in the first seconds of danger. The windows of the place were negligible squares cut into the adobe of the house's Spanish-style facade, more because a blank wall that size without some variation would offend the eye than because old Castiglione would want to look outside at the shimmering heat waves of the desert floor.

It wasn't promising, he thought. Castiglione had been in too much danger for too many years before he'd come West. Besides the front entrance, there was a side door that opened on a stone walkway to the swimming pool. He parked the car in the driveway of a neighbor, facing the street. He took the rifle and began to walk the circuit of Castiglione's wall. Now that he could see the place clearly, it was even more forbidding. There were only the two doors he'd seen from the street, and at the back of the house even the small windows had been eliminated. He began to wish he had some dynamite. He couldn't see any lights burning in the house, but he knew that the old man who lived here would have someone awake, if only to be sure the telephone didn't disturb his sleep.

He felt frustrated and disappointed. It was going to be a pain in the ass. He carefully climbed the fence and approached the house, watching where he placed his feet. It wouldn't be out of the question for the old bastard to have the lawn booby-trapped. He cautiously walked around the house looking for points of vulnerability until he found what he needed. There was a barbecue pit big enough to roast a side of beef, and near the swimming pool were two cabinet doors built into the wall. When he saw them his heart began to beat faster. It could be done. He took his pocket knife and quietly jimmied the first of the doors. Inside was the hot-water heater for the house. Behind the second

197

door was a collection of miscellaneous objects: garden tools, charcoal and a can of fire-starter for the barbecue pit, bottles of chlorine for the swimming pool, a long hose already attached to a faucet. He leaned his rifle against the house.

In the darkness it was difficult to work silently, but he moved with care and deliberation. First he took the charcoal and the can of fire-starter and moved around to the front door of the house. He banked the charcoal against the gigantic wooden door and soaked it with the odorous liquid, getting as much as he could on the door itself. Then he left it to sink in and moved back to the patio. He took all of the garden tools and spread them on the pavement in front of the door. The hose he propped between two gallon jugs of chlorine so that it aimed from the side into the doorway. He checked the loads of his rifle and pistol and set the rifle on the deck next to the swimming pool. He looked around to see that everything was ready. The hot-water heater was the key to all of it, so it would have to be first. He turned off the gas valve and then disconnected the heater from the gas pipe. He went around to the front door and started the charcoal fire.

He trotted back to the patio, turned on the gas and lit the jet, then turned it up so the flame was high enough to lick the top of the cabinet. Then he turned on the faucet and adjusted the pressure so that a steady, hard stream of water rushed across the doorway. Finally he retreated to the swimming pool. He lowered himself into the water at the shallow end of the pool and gasped. It was colder than he'd imagined. He ducked down to wait, holding the rifle above the surface and shielding himself from the growing glare by clinging to the gutter of the pool nearest the house.

It seemed to be taking a long time. He peered over the edge of the pool at the house. There were still no lights on, but he could see the glow of the fire in the front of the house, and the gas jet was flaming steadily. The eaves had caught, and part of the roof. Already the facade of adobe was crumbling, and the plywood siding beneath it crackled into flames almost instantly. He began to shiver, whether from the cold of the water or the cruelty of the night wind he couldn't tell. It suddenly occurred to him that Castiglione might not be home. What if he wasn't even home?

But then the lights went on, one after another, each window now glowing. The fire from the hot-water heater must have eaten its way into the back of the house. He ducked down again. When they were ready to leave, the outside lights would blaze on. He listened to the muffled shouts inside the house, trying to gauge how many voices there were. There were doors slamming and the sound of running feet. He knew when someone reached the front door, because he heard a yelp that escaped into the night air, then footsteps back toward the rear of the house. The pool, he judged, was about seventy feet from the side door. He steadied the rifle on the cement deck and lined up his sights.

At last the side door burst open and a man ran out onto the patio. When he was sprayed by the hose he turned and shot at it, then swore when he stepped on a rake. He ran toward the hose, since it seemed to his dim, confused, frightened brain to be somehow the source of the trouble. He was easy to hit because when

199

he got near enough to see that there was no one holding the hose he stopped short, silhouetted in the growing light of the fire behind him. Another man made it far enough to kneel over his fallen comrade, then looked around him for someone to kill, before the rifle's sights leveled on him too.

Inside the house they couldn't tell what was happening. There had been shooting outside, and water coming from somewhere, but there was no way to put it together into a coherent idea that would tell them what to do. Somebody must be trying to put the fire out with the hose: he could tell that was what made sense to the two who rushed to the door next, because they weren't armed. He let one of them get almost to the gas jet before he cut him down. The other stood inside the doorway, unaware that his companion was dead.

From his spot in the dark swimming pool, he decided to take a chance. He shouted, 'Get the old man out!' then ducked down into the shadows and waited. There was the sound of movement inside the house and then he saw what he had been waiting for. A man in pajamas carefully eased a wheelchair into the doorway, and moved it out onto the patio. He aimed the rifle at the center of the chair's back and prepared to squeeze a round into it. Then he sensed something was wrong. When the attendant got the chair to the patio he moved away from it toward the front of the house, his gun drawn. It wasn't right. They wouldn't leave the old man alone, no matter what happened. He studied the chair through his telescopic sights. There was something in it, but now he was sure it wasn't the old man. Some hero? No, there were shoes on the footboard, but the leather back of the chair didn't bulge in the right places. He thought quickly. It couldn't be the front door. He could see that the front of the house was blazing now. There must be another way out. But where was it?

It had to be the garage. They'd want to get him away. The garage was behind him, too far to walk an invalid in an emergency. Suddenly it made sense. The place was built like a fortress, and yet the garage was a hundred yards away from the house. There had to be a tunnel under the yard. Then he realized that as soon as the ones who were left had made it to the garage, the old man would be driven away and then the floodlights would come on. He had to get out of the pool before they reached the safety of the garage.

He calmed himself and aimed at the only man he could see, the one in the doorway. He watched him fall backward. He dropped the rifle into the water and heaved himself out of the pool and began to sprint for the garage. He made it just as the electric door began to whir. He heard the car's ignition, and then the dark shape of the car, its lights out, slid forward beside him, inching ahead behind the rising door. He froze and waited until the driver was abreast of him, then fired the pistol into his face. The car kept sliding slowly forward of its own volition, no living foot on its brake to halt it. When the back seat slid into view beside him he saw the old man's face, held for an instant in a mask of surprise and terror like a photograph. When he squeezed the trigger the head jerked sideways as though it had been kicked. He walked along beside the drifting car and shot the old man twice more before he relinquished his place beside it.

He knew there would be only seconds now before someone turned on the lights. He sprinted for the nearest place the driveway ran along the wall and clambered over it. He didn't look back, just kept running, turning the seconds of remaining darkness into whatever distance he could purchase. As he came to the end of the wall he saw a crouching shape waiting for him, both hands extended in front of it as though to steady a pistol. He heard the man shout something just before he fired into the crouching shape. The man's gun went off in a last spasm of the fingers and he ran over the body before he realized that the man had said, 'Hold it.' Hold it? Why would he say that? He kept running, but glanced back for an instant and realized the body was wearing a white shirt and tie under its coat. Strange, he thought. At three o'clock in the morning? But he didn't have time to think about that. He was running hard along the house fronts. Behind him the floodlights went on and he heard the driverless car crash into something. When he reached the driveway where his car was parked, he jumped in, started it, and gave it as much gas as he dared without turning on the lights. In the rearview mirror he could see half the sky was lit up, a chaos of white floodlights and orange fire, and he could hear the first barking of guns back and forth across the deserted lawns and into the empty night. As he turned the corner and urged the car to fifty-five, he smiled to himself. He didn't feel so angry now.

NINETEEN

There was the climate-controlled humming tube of the airplane's interior; and then the two stewardesses standing at their station next to the Formica kitchenette like a pair of dancers from the chorus line brought out for a last bow in front of the curtain; and then the white, searing sunshine of the Las Vegas Saturday morning. Elizabeth squinted as she stepped down the portable stairway, staring down at her feet to avoid a glaring sun that seemed to explode at her from every direction at once.

There were no knots of happy relatives waiting at the terminal entrance for the passengers to arrive – everyone was a stranger here – only sober-faced preoccupied porters. As she looked about her for some sign that would tell her where to find her suitcase, a man's voice came over a loudspeaker.

'Elizabeth Waring, please come to the United Airlines Courtesy Desk, Elizabeth Waring. Elizabeth Waring, please come to the United Airlines Courtesy Desk, Elizabeth Waring.'

Brayer. No question about it, she thought. No doubt he'd forgotten to tell her something, and it wouldn't occur to him to wait until she got to the hotel. She approached the desk, and said, 'Elizabeth Waring.'

The man handed her a note, which said, 'Please

telephone John Brayer as soon as possible.' The please had to have been the airline's amendment. She went to the bank of pay telephones on the wall across the lobby and dialed. He answered on the first ring.

'Something's going on there, Elizabeth,' said Brayer. 'I'm not sure yet what it is, but we've got an agent down.'

'Oh God,' said Elizabeth. 'Are you sure? Who is it?'

'The Las Vegas police phoned a half hour ago. They found DiGiorgio this morning when they were going over a burned-out house. He's alive, but there were five dead men in the yard, and they're not sure if there were others inside.'

'What do you want me to do?'

'Sit tight for a few minutes. There'll be a police officer at the United desk to take you to the hospital. If they'll let you talk to DiGiorgio find out what you can. If they won't, get everything the police have and get back to me. When you've done that I should have a better idea. For the moment work through me. Don't try to get in touch with any of the field agents. I don't know what the hell is going on and I don't want anybody spotted until I do.'

'John,' said Elizabeth, 'I see the policeman at the desk now. I'd better get going.'

'Fine. Get back to me when you can. We've got people all over Las Vegas and if they're in danger we've got to know it.'

Elizabeth hung up and moved toward the desk just as the policeman turned to approach her. 'I'm Waring,' she said. The policeman nodded and touched the polished brim of his hat as they set off toward the

204

door. He was tall and his first two strides left her a yard behind.

'My luggage,' she said apologetically. 'I haven't picked it up.'

'Where are you staying?' he asked.

'The Sands.'

He looked a little surprised, but said, 'If you'll give me your stub I'll have it sent on.' He returned to the desk and gave the stub to the United man. He joined her at the curb outside, where his patrol car sat idling, its front door open and the radio squawking and sizzling.

She got in beside him and he swung out into the drive. 'How's DiGiorgio?' she asked.

'Critical,' said the policeman, his face stony. She decided that he didn't like women, but that it didn't matter whether he did or not, so she forgot about it. 'He lost a lot of blood before they found him. Upper chest. One shot from close up, small caliber.'

Elizabeth thought about it for a moment, but it didn't mean much. 'Does anybody know what happened?'

The policeman's eyes shifted to her face for an instant, then flickered back to the road. 'We'd hoped you might help us there, ma'am.' There it was again, she thought. The exaggerated politeness reserved for outsiders. Outsiders and women. 'He's your man.' It sounded like a reproof.

'He was assigned to surveillance,' she said. 'But it was supposed to be remote. He wouldn't have initiated any contact.'

The policeman nodded. 'That's what we thought.' Then he added, 'Of course, we didn't know he was

205

here. We were pretty surprised when we found his identification.' So that was it, she thought. A federal agent turns up and the local police didn't know he was there – the implicit assumption that somebody is probably on the pad. She let the thought lie there between them, because there wasn't anything she could do with it. It was just the way things were done and they both knew it and neither one was responsible for it, though it carried with it an insult to what he was and what he did.

He seemed to have thought through it before she arrived, and so he recovered first and determined to do his job. He went into his recitation. 'The house belonged to Salvatore Castiglione, so we're assuming that was who Agent DiGiorgio was observing.'

'Belonged?' she said. 'Is the house destroyed?'

'No,' he said. 'Castiglione is dead. So are five other men who were apparently staying there. Four of them were shot with a high-powered rifle. We found the rifle in the swimming pool. Agent DiGiorgio and Castiglione and one other man were shot with something smaller. Maybe by each other. We won't know until they finish with the ballistics reports and the autopsies.'

Elizabeth thought for a moment. Castiglione dead. She tried to put it together. DiGiorgio is spotted, Castiglione orders him killed, and DiGiorgio puts up a fight, killing – six men? And besides, there was the rifle in the swimming pool. And Castiglione had been watched for years. It was a fact of his life. He wouldn't panic now. No. Try again. DiGiorgio is watching Castiglione's house, and for some reason a fight breaks out between the men in the house. Shooting starts, one of them has a rifle; DiGiorgio goes to stop it and gets hit. But what about the fire? Try again. DiGiorgio is watching the house. Men come and try to burn the house, to kill Castiglione. Castiglione's men fight back. DiGiorgio is there, tries to stop it or at least to apprehend somebody, and is wounded. She kept trying the combinations, trying desperately to ignore the one that kept coming back into her mind: DiGiorgio is standing outside the darkened house with a high-powered rifle in his hands, waiting for the old man to come through the door to escape the fire. DiGiorgio has spent too many years sitting in cold cars outside fancy restaurants, checking license numbers on parked limousines, translating taped conversations into English. DiGiorgio is an avid hunter.

The policeman had the microphone in his hand and said, 'Go ahead.'

The radio clicked and farted, then the voice said, 'You may proceed to the hotel directly.'

The policeman said, 'Copy,' and slipped the microphone into its slot.

'What's that about?' said Elizabeth.

'I guess your man didn't make it.'

'That was quick,' said Brayer. 'What have you got?'

'Not much,' said Elizabeth. She was standing at the glass door to the balcony. It overlooked the swimming pool, where people were lying immobile in long deck chairs, their bodies glistening with oil as though they were being rendered for their fat. But what she was thinking about was that the layout was just like the room where Senator Claremont had been killed. She edged along the wall to catch the light so she could

207

study the finger smudges on the glass. 'DiGiorgio died before I could get to the hospital. I just got off the line with the local homicide people and they said he'd been in a coma since shortly after they brought him in.' She waited, but he didn't say anything. She added, 'I'm sorry.'

'So he didn't tell them anything either.' Brayer's voice was gruff.

'Nothing anybody can use,' she said. 'In the ambulance he was just raving. I think what he said was "a fucking war." '

'What?' said Brayer.

'A fucking war. Over and over again. It could have been that it reminded him of something in Viet Nam. I didn't know him well, but he was an ex-marine, wasn't he? Although from what I've been told, that wouldn't be too far off. You wouldn't have to be delirious to make the connection. There were six besides DiGiorgio, and the house was a ruin.'

'Including Castiglione,' said Brayer. He paused for a moment. Then he said, 'Look, Elizabeth. There's the possibility that he was just describing what it looked like. Agreed. But there's also a chance he was describing what he thought was happening. What if this Orloff character was involved in something? Say he was working for Castiglione, and somebody, maybe Toscanzio or Carl Bala, decided to take over and killed him? Then there was that family killed in their car. A reprisal? And there was another shootout in front of the Tropicana last night. Nobody knows what happened because when it was over the ones who were left standing put the ones that were hit into cars and drove off. But there was blood all over the pavement. So far

208

nobody has been reported missing and no doctor within a hundred miles of Las Vegas has treated anybody for gunshot wounds. We're monitoring for it. What's it sound like to you?' He didn't wait, just kept talking. 'I'll tell you what it sounds like. "A fucking war." '

'You think so?' asked Elizabeth. 'But who? And what do we do about it?'

'Well, obviously Castiglione was on one end of it. And I'll bet whoever comes up top dog is on the other end. God knows what we're supposed to do about it. I'll tell you what I'd like to do. I'd like to pull all our people, you included, about a thousand miles eastward and let those bastards kill each other off. If it weren't for the chance that it has something to do with Senator Claremont I think I'd damned well do it.'

She said, 'That and your curiosity.' She heard him give a humorless little chuckle.

'You're probably right,' he said. 'And DiGiorgio.'

'Yes,' said Elizabeth, 'I'm sorry about that, John. I didn't know him well, but I guess you must have.'

'Oh. Yes,' he said, without inflection. Then his voice became animated again. 'Jesus,' he said, 'I think what bothers me most about it is that he had no business there in the first place. He was supposed to sit tight and watch, no matter what happened. He probably died trying to save that old piece of scum from something he had coming to him for years.'

Elizabeth said nothing. She didn't see any reason to remind him that DiGiorgio was the only one found at the scene who hadn't lived there, that he'd been found in the yard, not in his car, where every regulation, every procedure of the department insisted he should

209

be. She knew Brayer had been thinking about that since he'd received the telephone call in the early morning.

'Now we've got to find out as much as we can without wasting time,' said Brayer. 'But don't do anything stupid.' He said it as though he had something specific in mind. 'You find out what you can about the company and that's all. The minute you see or hear anything that might be illegitimate you report it. And if it looks like it might be more than that you get on a plane and talk to me about it in person. You got that?'

'Got it,' said Elizabeth. 'Don't worry, John. I'm no hero.'

'I'll be satisfied if you're not a fool.' He hung up.

TWENTY

The building didn't look like a place where there had been a murder. It looked still less like a corporation that would appear in the notebook of a United States senator. It consisted of a single one-story cinderblock structure with a small sign that read *Fieldston Growth Enterprises*, and a tiny lawn protected by a frail cordon of thirsty geraniums.

When Elizabeth walked in the front entrance the receptionist stopped typing and smiled with some sincerity, and Elizabeth believed the smile. This had the look of a place where a receptionist could get lonely. There were only the wood-paneled walls, the typewriter, and the telephone.

'Hello,' she said. 'I'm Elizabeth Waring of the US Department of Justice.' She held out her identification, but the woman didn't look at it so she dropped it into her purse.

The receptionist was in her mid-forties but her hair was already tinted with a blue rinse, probably, Elizabeth decided, to draw attention to her vacant blue eyes. The eyes didn't flinch or flicker. Any visitor was obviously a treat.

'May I help you?' asked the receptionist, her smile broadening. Elizabeth revised her estimate when she saw the tiny crinkles at the corners of the mouth – mid-fifties, she thought, but takes care of herself.

'I'd like to speak with Mr. Fieldston, please.'

'Oh, I'm sorry, Miss Waring,' said the receptionist. She seemed moved by the disappointment she was about to inflict. 'Mr. Fieldston isn't in today.'

'I wonder if you could tell me where I can reach him? I'd like very much to speak with him.'

'Mr. Fieldston is out of town this week,' said the receptionist, as though he had vanished into a realm that was out of reach to any form of human communication.

'Do you have a number for him? I'm on a tight schedule.'

'I'm sorry,' said the receptionist. 'Mr. Fieldston is meeting with a client, and I'm never permitted to tell anyone where he is when he travels. I'm sure you understand.'

Elizabeth didn't, but she was interested now. 'Why is that?'

'The investment business is a difficult one. If Mr. Fieldston's competitors knew in advance what he was buying, the negotiations might be complicated by other bids. If people knew he was acquiring a particular holding, the price of all surrounding holdings might be artificially inflated.' The way she added, 'And so on,' signaled that the receptionist had either run out of imaginary excuses or reached the limit of her understanding of the business, but Elizabeth couldn't decide which it was.

'Let me leave my number then,' she said. 'I'm staying at the Sands.' She fished in her purse and found a calling card, and wrote on the back of it *Sands Hotel*,

Room 219. 'If Mr. Fieldston calls, please ask him to get in touch with me.' She turned to go.

'What can I tell Mr. Fieldston?' asked the receptionist, already prepared with a message pad. 'Is it about Mr. Orloff?'

Elizabeth hesitated, but she supposed that it was about Orloff, partly. 'Yes it is,' she said.

'A shame,' said the receptionist. Elizabeth could see her write *Re: Mr. Orloff* on the note, then watched, fascinated, as the receptionist stapled her card to the note and placed it in her *Out* box. It was the only piece of paper in the box.

Someone had brought her suitcase into the room during the day. Taped to it was a note on the front desk's stationery: *Please call Mr. Bechtman, Room 403.* The time on it was only four thirty. Two hours ago.

Elizabeth dialed 403 and the voice said, 'Elizabeth, stay where you are. I'll be there in a minute.' She sat down on the bed with the dead telephone to her ear. Brayer!

Brayer's seersucker sport coat and sunglasses weren't a disguise so much as a radical change in his personality. After more than a year of getting used to the dark, conservative suits that got shiny and wrinkled in the back from the long days he spent sitting at a desk, Elizabeth was fascinated.

'Great outfit, John,' she smiled. 'You look like a Cuban spy.' But she was thinking something else; he was perfect. He looked like another version of what he was – a middle-aged man from somewhere in the East. A man who had spent most of his years working too

213

hard and not getting enough out of it to soften the signs of wear – but who wasn't at the office today and meant to make the most of it. Maybe he was here for a convention; maybe he'd come with the little woman and managed to slip away from her for a few hours to look for some action at the tables.

But the voice was Brayer of Justice. 'What have you got so far?' he said.

'Still very little to go on,' she answered. 'Edgar Fieldston is out of town checking out some kind of investment. The secretary pretends she can't tell anyone where he is but she's probably lying and doesn't know herself. After that I went to the police station to see what they had. It wasn't much either.'

'You didn't ask them about FGE, did you?' Brayer snapped.

'No,' said Elizabeth. 'But it was just because there didn't seem to be any reason to. I figured you'd want to know about DiGiorgio—'

'Right,' said Brayer. 'What's new on that?'

'The place was clean. If Castiglione was doing anything special it was miles from his house. Except for Castiglione the men killed had no criminal records and were legally entitled to carry the guns found there. They were officially employees of a private security company – there's no question what they were but you couldn't have proven it in court. The rifle that killed them was manufactured over twenty years ago, and the last time it was recorded as sold was at a gun shop in San Diego in 1967. It'll take time to track down the man who bought it, if he's still alive. DiGiorgio, Castiglione, and the driver were killed with a .32-caliber pistol. What they think now is that it was done by three men – one near the pool with the rifle, one near the garage with the pistol, and one somewhere near the front of the house who started the fires and then probably stayed with the getaway car to control the front door, driveway, and street.'

Brayer listened intently, then nodded. 'Okay. So it's probably the three who got the Mexican family. And DiGiorgio saw what was happening but didn't see one of them or got distracted at the wrong moment.' Elizabeth could see he was imagining it, re-creating what must have happened, as a man re-creates the scene where he lost something valuable.

He sat down on the bed and took off his sunglasses. His eyes looked tired. 'Okay,' he said again. 'That's probably all we'll get on that. The rifle will turn out to have been lost or stolen years ago. The pistol was already at the bottom of Lake Mead or sawed into fifty pieces hours before the police got around to investigating. No surprises anywhere.'

She said, 'Sorry, John. I guess your trip was a waste of time.'

He looked surprised, his gaze suddenly widening, but turning sharp and predatory. 'No, we're just beginning,' he said. 'The reason I came is Fieldston Growth Enterprises. All your chickens have come home to roost.'

'What do you mean?' asked Elizabeth.

'I mean that there's something wrong with it. When I got through to Justin Garfield, I didn't see much in it. The list was only a statistical fluke. They programmed a computer at IRS to spit out the names of companies that had earned unusually high incomes last year but had reinvested most of them to avoid showing a big profit on the balance sheet at the end of the year – plowed the money back under. Senator Claremont was looking for instances where they might have disguised investments as operating expenses. He wanted to amend his tax bill to close the loophole. Fieldston Growth Enterprises had a high ratio of gross income to net profit and so it went on the list. It was no big deal. Garfield said it was possible the Senator might have decided to call in somebody from FGE to testify in next session's hearings, but it was just as possible he'd have deleted it. It might not be big enough to use as an example. The Senator had a preference for the dramatic.' He pulled a notebook out of his coat and stared at it.

'So what makes it look interesting?' asked Elizabeth.

'Garfield's people started poking around, doing groundwork for the committee. They came up with some odd facts. Edgar Fieldston started the company in 1971, so they began with him. He looked good. An old California family. They owned ranch land that got bought up in the thirties. They took a loss, but it didn't matter much because the money involved was still enough to make them as rich as anybody needs to be, and in those days nobody would have believed what the land would be worth in fifty years, or cared much either. Fieldston looked fine, except for one thing, and it wasn't much. In 1969 and 1970 his income taxes were in arrears. He was building up penalties.'

'So he started a business in 1971,' said Elizabeth, 'and came out okay.' She shrugged.

'Right,' said Brayer. His mouth turned up into something like a smile, but colder and harder. 'He couldn't pay his taxes for two years. In the third year he had enough money to pay the taxes, penalties and all, and start a business with an initial investment of, let's see—' he glanced at the notebook. 'Four hundred and sixty thousand dollars.'

'A silent partner?' said Elizabeth.

'Has to be.' Brayer closed the notebook and slipped it back into his breast pocket. 'And nobody got suspicious. He was the scion of an old family with money. Maybe he sold some land they had left somewhere, maybe a rich aunt died, maybe a friend loaned him the money. The rich have rich friends. Nobody asked any questions.'

'Until the name of the company started turning up around murders,' said Elizabeth. 'Until they got careless.' She was warming to the hunt now, her mind racing ahead for the next stage of it, but Brayer stopped her.

'No,' he said. 'Just the opposite. Until Garfield's computer spit it out by accident. I think Fieldston's silent partners got wind of it somehow and reacted to protect the company. Garfield's people were light-footed. They did credit checks, talked to bank officers, and so on.'

'But they wouldn't do that,' said Elizabeth. 'No. It doesn't make sense. We're off the track.' She was up now, pacing the hotel room. 'First, there's Veasy. A machinist in Ventura, California. He might have been a threat because he was critical of the union's investment in FGE, but not much of a threat unless he got in touch with the Senator's committee, and there's no way he would have known about it. And if by some chance he did, the last thing they'd do is kill him because that would bring the police and maybe the

FBI.' She walked back and forth, as though each step brought her closer to what she was looking for. 'And killing the Senator wouldn't do it either because there was still the committee, and Orloff was their man, their lawyer. No, John, it has to be something else. Something is missing.' She stopped and stared at him, but he was smiling that strange, cold smile, still sure.

He said, 'You're right about part of it, but wrong about the rest. Veasy was the first in time, but not in logic. That's what you're missing. The Senator was the main thing. If they got rid of him, the committee wouldn't go after FGE, because he was the only one interested in it. Garfield told me today the information on Claremont's inquiries has already been packed away. At the end of the next term it would have been shredded because it wasn't part of an official, permanent record and it wasn't part of an ongoing project. And nothing had happened yet. There was no reason for anybody to wonder if the Senator's death was linked to FGE, certainly not the police, because the only ones who knew he'd ever heard of FGE were the committee staff, and they'd never hear about Veasy or Orloff or the rest of it. All they'd ever know was that it was one of a hundred or so that they were supposed to check out for a hearing months from now.'

Elizabeth was still shaking her head. She said, 'There has to be more. A lot more. They knew they wouldn't get caught, agreed. But that was because no reasonable stretch of the imagination would connect them with the Senator – but that's still true. Because nobody would kill a US senator just because he might subpoena their books or call clean, upright Edgar Fieldston to testify.'

'I'll go the rest of the way for you,' said Brayer. 'And they wouldn't kill a machinist in Ventura because he was criticizing his union's investment in a company he'd never even seen the outside of.' But the smile was still there, still sure and maybe even a little smug.

'And there's still Orloff,' said Elizabeth. 'That has to be something different.'

'It's all the same,' said Brayer. 'It doesn't matter how it was done or in what order. The time doesn't matter at all for now. They were plugging leaks, getting rid of every liability they could think of at once. Maybe it was all done to protect something that was very important to them and might come out as soon as any government agency started to look closely at the company. Something close to the surface.'

'What?' asked Elizabeth. 'It can't be the silent partner. And yet it has to be.'

'There's a vulnerable point somewhere, and they knew it. And right now they're trying to cover it up. They'll succeed if we don't get to it soon. The one thing we've found that fits the pattern is that they've got a number of complicated investments – subsidiaries, really. One is an oil consulting firm. We're concentrating on that one for the moment. It'll take time to track everything down.'

'Why that one?' asked Elizabeth.

'Because it involves moving people and small amounts of sophisticated equipment from one place to another. A lot of it to other countries. There are a hundred possibilities: smuggling, a money-laundering operation, drugs, or maybe just an excuse to have somebody in particular on the payroll with a legitimate reason to travel.'

219

'A hit man!' said Elizabeth.

'Don't jump to conclusions,' said Brayer. 'That's the least likely of a hundred possibilities. For one thing, it would be the hardest to spot, and whatever they're worried about is more obvious. Maybe it's just an excuse to have bank accounts or investments in foreign countries.'

Elizabeth sat down again. 'So that's why you're here,' she said. 'It's a full-court press, isn't it? You're going to put the pressure on and watch to see who squirms. Who else is in on it? The FBI?'

Brayer's smile broadened a bit as he nodded, but then it disappeared. 'I'm afraid it's a little bit different this time,' he said. 'It's a full-court press all right. I didn't know you liked basketball, by the way, but it fits. The only thing is, we can't let them see all of it at once.'

She could tell that something was bothering him. It was a moment before she realized what it was. She said, 'And they've already seen me.'

He nodded. 'They've already seen you.'

She sat there for a moment, thinking about it. Then she stood up, straightened her skirt, and said, 'All right. What do I do first?'

'We've already requested a subpoena for their ledgers. It should be ready by morning. It lists you as officer of the court.'

TWENTY-ONE

The trees lifted naked branches toward a sky that seemed to be made of stone. Now and then an icy gust of wind would tear down the street bringing with it a scurrying herd of wrappers and dead newspapers. He had been on this street before. Three, maybe four years ago. That time he hadn't stopped, just checked to be sure he had the right address and then driven on. He'd been alone that day too, and he'd had some time and had promised Eddie he'd look. Eddie had been careful enough to last for a long time. It would have been stupid not to do what Eddie said. 'This is an address you might need sometime, kid. Don't ever write it down. Go there when you're in Buffalo and remember where it is. Chances are if you ever need to see him you're gonna be in a hurry.'

Most of the snow had been pushed off the sidewalks into the gutters, so he had no trouble walking if he avoided the thin patches of ice near the curb. There were only a few bundled figures leaning into the cruel wind as they walked. They scuttled close to the storefronts for shelter, veering outward only to avoid each other, their faces turned down out of the wind. Sliding steel cages accordioned across the doors and windows of the buildings. No business was open on Sunday morning on this stretch of Grant Street. He moved more quickly. The coat he'd bought last night was warm, but his ears were already numb. The collar wasn't high enough to do anything for them.

One more block. He wished for a moment that he still had the car. But that would have been foolish. He wouldn't be here until tomorrow night or the next day at the earliest – and in a car with Nevada plates. You couldn't drive through places like St. Louis and Cleveland in a car with Nevada plates and not attract attention.

There were houses now and he knew he was getting close to it. The houses were set farther back from the street and he missed the shelter of the storefronts. There it was. 304. He remembered what Eddie had said. 'Knock and ask for directions to someplace. It don't matter where. Don't ask for him or you won't get in the door.'

He made his way up the icy walk and then up the steps to the porch. He knocked and listened, but the wind was the only sound. 'His name is Harkness,' Eddie had said, 'and he's a nigger. Don't hang around out front for too long because your white face will attract attention.' There was still no sound, but the door swung open.

An old black man in a white shirt that was buttoned to the collar stared out at him, saying nothing.

'I wonder if you could tell me how to get to the Albright-Knox Art Museum,' he asked.

'It's cold out there,' said the man and stepped back. He followed him inside into the dark, warm hallway. The floor was carpeted but underneath he heard the creaking of hardwood floorboards where he stepped. Along the wall to his right there was a row of rubber boots; above them a row of pegs where thick, damp coats hung like effigies. It was quiet here, so quiet that he sensed there must be others in the house, waiting.

'Who told you to ask me?' said Harkness.

'Eddie Mastrewski told me to ask here if I got lost,' he said.

The old man stared at him, then spoke quietly. 'How is Eddie?'

'Dead,' he said.

The old man only nodded, then walked on into a large, dark living room and lowered himself into an overstuffed chair. The old man looked like a shrunken child in the dark embrace of the chair. After a moment Harkness said, deliberately, 'I know you.'

He waited, and the quiet voice came again from the half-invisible man in the chair. 'I know who you are.'

He shrugged. 'I can pay.'

The quiet voice said, 'I know you can. What do you propose?' Suddenly he knew why it had all seemed so familiar – this house, this old man, the furniture – it was the formal, quiet way his grandfather had moved and talked when he was a child. It was the way the men of that time discussed serious business.

He said, 'I'm in a lot of trouble—'

Harkness interrupted, not harshly, just talking into his sentence. 'You don't need to tell me that. Nobody comes here except he has his troubles. What you want from me?'

'I have to disappear, but I have to do some traveling first. It may take time.'

The old man sat motionless and silent, staring at him. 'I see,' he said. Then he said, 'It'll cost twenty

223

thousand dollars. More if it's longer than a month. That's if I can do it at all.'

He waited and the old man went on. 'Only two thousand is for me. The rest is to keep you alive while you go.'

'Why so much?'

'I said I know you. I don't want to know why you have to disappear, but I know it's not the law. If anybody found out how you traveled, the ones who helped you wouldn't go to some nice warm cell.'

'What do I get for it?'

'A bodyguard. Enough cover, if they're not too eager to find you.'

He frowned. 'A bodyguard? Hell, I can't travel with a bodyguard. They'd spot us.'

'You can with this one. She's the best I know of.'

All it amounted to was going in with the FBI's auditors and taking possession. You just handed the subpoena to whoever was there and let the auditors do the hard part. They'd know where to look and what to look for. That was what Brayer had said. 'Just stay out of the way. Don't worry. Those guys know exactly what they're doing. Pick up the search warrant and meet the auditors at the FGE office.'

She wondered what one wore to a raid. That's what it added up to. She got out of bed and tested the shower. The stream of water was hot and strong – where did the water come from in the middle of a desert? Oh, yes. Lake Mead. She slipped out of her nightgown.

The telephone rang and she turned off the shower – seven a.m. – it had to be Brayer.

224

Brayer's voice said, 'Elizabeth, are you awake?'

'Yes, barely,' she answered. 'What's new?'

'I just wanted to check. I don't want anything to interfere with the schedule. It looks good so far. They haven't got the slightest idea what's going on. The place has been watched since yesterday morning, and nothing has been moved out or destroyed.'

'Are you sure?'

'Of course. We've been through their garbage and their outgoing mail. There are only about four employees who work weekends, and they left empty-handed.'

'You've thought of everything.'

'Yes, I have,' he said. There was no irony in his voice. 'Just take care of your part of it and we'll be fine. Even if there isn't anything in the company records the raid's got to trigger some action from the silent partner. He'll have to wonder if there is.'

Elizabeth returned to the shower. She'd had just enough time to get wet and enjoy the sensation of waking up when the telephone rang again. She wrapped a towel around herself and scampered out into the bedroom. Brayer had changed his mind about something, no doubt.

'Agent Waring,' said an unfamiliar male voice. 'This is John Tollar, FBI Las Vegas.' It sounded like an address. God, they were a humorless bunch.

'Yes?' she said.

'We've been informed of a change. Can you meet me at the front desk as soon as possible, please?'

'I'll be there.' It didn't sound as though Brayer had just gotten impatient, she thought. Something was up. They must have panicked and made a move. Elizabeth dressed as quickly as she could and made her way to the desk. There wasn't any problem locating the FBI agents. There were two burly men in business suits at the elevator when she emerged. Their broad, tanned faces reminded her of a football player from the Pittsburgh Steelers she'd seen advertising cologne on television. They made her miss Agent Hart a little, but only for an instant: they were perfect for this job. Brayer had probably handpicked them because they looked like what they were; their beefy, unlined, and untroubled faces had a quality of merciless and efficient innocence that would terrify whoever saw them show up with a search warrant.

'Miss Waring?' said one. 'I'm John Tollar and this is Bill Hoskins. We have our car waiting.'

Elizabeth let her hand be engulfed twice by their hard, clean palms, then followed them down the corridor away from the casino and the lobby. John and Bill, she noted. Easy enough to remember the names, but hard to remember which was which. John had the dark gray suit and Bill the dark blue suit. She let one of them open the car door for her while the other assumed the driver's seat.

As the car moved out to the street, Elizabeth said, 'Why so early? Did something happen?'

Tollar said, 'I don't actually know if anything happened. We just got a call from the Bureau to move now.'

Something must have happened. It was typical that the Bureau office wouldn't have told them, and that they would refuse to speculate in front of her. But it wasn't like Brayer to pass up another chance to interrupt her shower with a telephone call. But this

226

was their show, really. They were the auditors and she was only – what? The decoy.

At the courthouse they pulled up to the front entrance and Bill got out to open the door for Elizabeth. For the first time she noticed he was carrying a gun in a shoulder holster. She felt a wave of affection for John Brayer. He was always cautious, always protecting his people. DiGiorgio's death must have torn him apart, but he wouldn't let anybody know how it felt; he'd just make damned sure it wouldn't happen again.

She quickly found the chambers of Judge Stillwell. The judge's clerk was already waiting with the warrant, and as soon as she'd flashed her identification he simply handed it to her. More of Brayer's work, she thought. All preparations made with quiet efficiency. Elizabeth scurried down the empty corridor and out to the car.

She glanced at her watch. Almost eight o'clock. They'd arrive just as the office was opening for business. John maneuvered through the morning traffic expertly and without visible effort. There was obviously nothing special about this job for them. It was just another warrant to be served, another set of ledgers to examine. They were probably a little jealous that other agents always made the arrests and felt the excitement. In a little while they'd be sitting in an office in their shirtsleeves tapping away at calculators. They took a shortcut to the Fieldston Growth Enterprises office, a long straight street that passed warehouses and lumberyards. They bumped over three sets of railroad tracks, past a junkyard piled high with the wrecked and stripped carcasses of automobiles. This was another side of the city, she thought, a place so foreign to the hotels and casinos that it didn't seem that the same name could be used to refer to both. She wondered if this was what truck drivers and railroad men thought of when they said Las Vegas – a gigantic depot in the middle of the desert where you delivered tons of liquor and bed linen, food and cigarettes, and then pushed on to Kingman, Arizona, or Albuquerque, New Mexico, before the sun got too high and began to overheat your engine.

But then they turned a corner and she recognized the squat building with the Fieldston Growth Enterprises sign. John parked the car in the rear of the building and the three walked in on the receptionist just as she was uncovering her typewriter. Her purse was still in her hand. She said 'Good morning' and looked pleased.

Elizabeth handed her the warrant and waited for her to read it. 'What is this?' she asked.

'It's a search warrant,' said Elizabeth, trying to manage a soft, kindly tone. 'We'd like to see your accounting department, please.'

The receptionist stared at Elizabeth blankly. Then it occurred to her that something she'd heard meant something to her. 'Last office,' she said, waving the warrant at the corridor behind her.

The auditors were two steps ahead of Elizabeth before she had time to move. They walked down the corridor and into the accounting office and flashed their identification wallets at the three clerks in the room, then immediately began opening file cabinets and taking out files. She left them to it and turned to the astonished clerks. She said, 'We're here for an audit. It won't take very long to get what we need and then we won't disrupt your office any further.' She tried to be reassuring, but she felt like the one in a bank robbery who says, 'Don't move and you won't get hurt.'

The two FBI men were working quickly, piling files on the nearest desk and then rummaging for more. Elizabeth felt too uncomfortable to stay. She wandered back up the hallway toward the front of the building. The receptionist was staring at the warrant, her purse still in her other hand.

Then Tollar emerged from the office carrying a stack of files, followed by Hoskins. 'Can I help you?' she asked.

'No, thanks,' said Tollar. 'Only one more load.' They went to the car. They returned to the accounting office and then appeared with another set of files. 'That's it,' said Hoskins.

Driving back to the hotel Elizabeth could think of nothing to say. They had the files and all she could do now was wait. The people in the office hadn't been criminals, she was sure of it. Whatever the files revealed to the FBI's experts wouldn't be anything that those startled clerks knew anything about. It was a little depressing.

In front of the Sands she got out. 'Let us know as soon as you have anything.'

Tollar said, 'We'll call,' and they drove off.

Elizabeth felt like having breakfast, but even more like going back up to her room to finish her night's sleep. She decided in favor of breakfast; it would be impossible to sleep, wondering what they were finding in the files. She looked at her watch again. It was only ten thirty now, and the raid was already over.

She was relieved to see that the Sands had a coffee shop. It was more in keeping with her mood than a full-scale restaurant would have been. And it was quicker. She sat down at the counter and ordered a prune Danish and a cup of coffee. It was the coffee she wanted, but it seemed somehow more respectable to eat something. When she finished she moved through the casino to the elevators and headed for her room. Brayer would want to hear from her.

When she opened the door to her room she nearly screamed. Brayer was sitting opposite the door. 'God, you startled me,' she said.

'Good,' snapped Brayer.

'Well, I'm back, anyway. It all came off as ordered.'

Brayer looked angry. 'What came off? And where the hell have you been? The auditors have been waiting for you for damned near half an hour. I said ten thirty, dammit.'

Elizabeth's heart stopped. What if – no, it wasn't possible. Just a communication snarl at FBI. She said, 'John, I served the warrant at eight and the auditors dropped me off here at ten thirty. If that's not what was supposed to happen we – I – may be in big trouble.'

Brayer looked both angry and confused, but said, 'No. Who told you to do that?'

'The auditors. Hoskins and Tollar from the FBI.'

Brayer sprang from the chair and picked up the telephone, his face now set in a look of maniacal concentration. He dialed a number and almost shouted into the receiver, 'Ray, do you have two agents named Hoskins and Tollar?'

Elizbeth searched her memory. She'd seen their identification cards, hadn't she? No, she had seen them flash something in the FGE office at some frightened civilians. She hadn't seen the cards herself. She started to feel light-headed.

But Brayer was saying, 'Then we need an all-points bulletin on two men as soon as you can get it on the wire. Here, I'll put someone on who can give you a description.' He handed Elizabeth the phone. She wasn't sure, but she thought she could get through this, through these moments, and even through the next hour. But sometime, she knew, she was going to be by herself, and then she was probably going to cry.

TWENTY-TWO

The faces in the room were not accusing. They were empty and cold and attentive like the faces of the men around the green felt tables downstairs. They weren't judging her for what had happened, she kept telling herself. But each time she tried to believe that, she remembered that she had already been judged by each of them in the first seconds and forgotten. They weren't thinking about what had happened except as it revealed to them what they must do next. It was just a fact, something that had to be taken into account – an agent had been lost because he hadn't followed standard procedures. A second agent had been stupid enough to hand over essential evidence to two men she'd never seen before because they looked like FBI agents.

Everyone was waiting for Martin Connors to speak. It was his prerogative as the head of the Department of Justice's Organized Crime Division, senior to everyone else in the room by virtue of his rank and his white hair but also because he had been the last to arrive, taking a special flight from Washington because one of his units was onto something big and blowing it.

Connors sat back in his chair and puffed hard on his pipe. 'All right, I think I understand the situation. The element that seems to connect the murder of the

Senator and this man Veasy is Fieldston Growth Enterprises. Then this lawyer, Orloff, is killed in front of Fieldston. An examination of the tax records seems like an interesting enough idea to warrant study, but two imposters steal the company's files: I guess that's clear enough. The question, then, isn't whether FGE was the place to look for the evidence that would connect the murders of Veasy, Senator Claremont, and Orloff, but whether it still is.'

'That's right, Martin,' said Brayer.

'That's not too good,' said Connors. 'Bad showing by both sides, I'd say.' He sucked his pipe again, and said, 'There's not much reason to doubt that whatever was on the premises that would help us is gone – they selected the files themselves.' Elizabeth could feel herself blushing.

The FBI Las Vegas field headquarters chief interjected, 'Of course we might find the two men, and we'll probably be able to put some of it together in other ways.'

'True,' Connors nodded. 'But it wasn't that kind of move. They were buying time, and they've got it, as far as I can tell. What are the chances you'll get them? I mean ever, not just while the files are still in their possession?'

The FBI man shrugged. 'Not much, and every minute means it's less likely. They could have parked the car in one of the hotel lots with the files in the trunk and it'd take a week to find it. And every third man in Nevada looks like a football player.' He looked a little like a quarterback himself, thought Elizabeth.

Connors said, 'Right. So for now we've got to forget what we've missed out on, and concentrate on what they've given us. What they've done is conceded that FGE is the connection. Somebody very important is, or was, vulnerable in at least two ways. First, the lawyer Orloff knew something – maybe just who the silent partner is. That's a dead end because they got to him. Second, the company records held some information they thought we could use. The point is, they got it in a very special way. They took a hell of a chance, for one thing. They should have been spotted going into the building. Why weren't they, by the way?'

Brayer answered, 'Just a screw-up, Martin. Our surveillance team saw Waring and figured the men with her had to be FBI, and the FBI thought they were ours.' He looked embarrassed. His superior stared at him but didn't say anything to reassure him.

Instead Connors turned to Elizabeth. 'All right, Waring. You've been in on most of this. What do you think is their next move?' Elizabeth stared at the carpet. She had to admire Connors' perception. Always ask the lowest-ranking person first, because the others won't be afraid to contradict. Once you ask a person's boss, you won't hear a peep out of him.

'I'm not sure, Mr. Connors,' she said. 'I agree that they're trying to break a connection. If that's true there are several people we ought to look for. The first is Edgar Fieldston. The others are the ones who have been doing the killing. And I think the murder of Castiglione ought to be included in this.'

'Why?' asked Connors. 'Of course we're interested. We've got a lot of people on it, but he wasn't the silent partner.'

'Because it's an enormous event for the people we're interested in. Why did it happen just now, and in this

234

town? It doesn't make any sense unless it has some connection with these other murders.'

Connors shrugged and puffed on his pipe. 'Give me a hypothesis.'

'All right, here's one. Castiglione was using FGE as a front for various operations, including a cover for professional killers. He had dealings with other powerful people – maybe heads of the other families. When the Senator's committee made inquiries Castiglione had him killed. The others whose dealings with him could have come out got nervous and decided to get rid of him and the company's lawyer and the company's records.'

'Plausible,' said Connors.

'Of course it's plausible,' said Brayer. 'Everything is plausible if you haven't got the answer. You have to go on what we know. What we know is this: somebody killed Claremont and Veasy and Orloff, and FGE is the common denominator. Somebody also killed Castiglione. Maybe it's connected, and maybe not. In any case the hits were all done by professionals, and the chances are we won't get professionals unless we get very lucky. So what's left?'

'You tell me,' said Connors. 'And make it good, because when we're through here I'm going to have to either ask the Attorney General's office to authorize the expenditures you'll need to pursue it or tell him I've scrapped the operation.'

'But it's not that simple, Martin,' said Brayer, his hands now clenched on the arms of his chair.

'I know. But this is an expensive operation, and what have we got to show for it? You've lost a man and spent a lot of time and money.'

Elizabeth could stay silent no longer. 'That's not how to figure it, Mr. Connors,' she said. 'What we've got is nothing but FGE. What we might have in a week is the man who killed a United States senator. Something big is going on, and this is just the start. They can cover their trail on FGE for a time, but we'll know more eventually. What we ought to be doing in the meantime is watching all of the candidates to see if we can catch one while he's trying to cut off the links with FGE.'

'Martin, look,' said Brayer. 'They're shooting each other down on the street over this. If we watch closely enough we've got a hell of a chance, and it won't be tax evasion or stock fraud.'

Connors sat immobile, still puffing little clouds of smoke into the room. Finally he spoke. 'I suppose there's no alternative. I'll speak with the Attorney General himself if I have to.' He stood up and nodded to the others in the room. 'John, my plane leaves in an hour, and I'd appreciate a ride to the airport. I'll arrive in Washington at nine thirty, and I'll expect a call with a list of what you'll need. You might as well include what it would take to find Edgar Fieldston and if necessary extradite him from wherever he is. I expect he's probably dead, but the extra funds will give you some leeway.'

His eyes opened and he was alert and present, as though he'd stepped through a doorway from sleeping to waking. It had been years since he'd allowed himself the luxury of even momentary uncertainty about where he'd been when he'd closed his eyes. Had he heard something? No, it was just his instinct telling

236

him it was time. The shadows in the room had deepened and melted together into darkness. He sat up and strained to see the dial of his watch. It was six thirty; the old man had been gone for over five hours.

He stood up and listened to the breathing of the empty house: the faint hum of the furnace in the cellar, the soft substantial sound of the clapboards standing up to the bitter wind. It brought back the feel of the house in Pennsylvania when he was a child, not so far from here, but too many years ago. It was as though he'd walked out, and when he looked back that world had been gone for so long that there wasn't anyone else left who even remembered it. The house was probably still standing, like this one was, but now someone else lived there.

'It's a safe house,' Eddie had said. 'Nobody talks about it because they might have to use it someday. But I know. People have gone through that door and nobody's ever seen them come out the other side. For all I know he turns them into niggers.'

He heard a sound outside the house. He drew out the Beretta and floated slowly and carefully into the kitchen, his ears tuned to the pitch of the first noise. It was the sound of footsteps making their way to the back door. He crouched at the kitchen door and leveled the pistol on the back hallway. He heard two pairs of feet, one scraping the pavement – probably the old man – and another harder and faster, clicking on the walk. That had to be the woman, taking shorter steps. But he didn't move. What was to keep the old man from selling him? In five hours he could have found out who the buyer was.

The key turned in the lock and the old man called into the darkness, 'It's me,' then opened the door.

'Come on in,' he said, and stepped back behind the doorway away from the sound of his voice. The light came on in the kitchen and he could see them. While the old man was struggling out of his overcoat, he studied the woman. She looked right. She was about five feet eight, not tall enough to be noticeable and not too small. She was pretty, he decided, but she was smart enough to be the kind of pretty that didn't strike the eye at first glance – she had done something to herself. It was the hair and probably makeup. The dark, shining hair was cut short and then waved so the angles of the face were softened into a kind of unremarkable pleasantness. He couldn't tell much about her figure, but she seemed slim even in the thick coat she was wearing. As long as the coat wasn't hiding gigantic breasts or a seventeen-inch waist she'd do – an attractive schoolteacher or maybe a secretary traveling, but not the kind that traveled with the boss – a secretary on vacation with her husband.

'This is Maureen,' said the old man.

He nodded to her, and she acknowledged it but said nothing. He said, 'She looks okay. When do we leave?'

The old man said, 'That's not up to me. I'm going in the other room to watch a little television while you work that out. After that I'm going to bed. Just leave my two thousand on the counter and lock the door when you go. If it's there when I get up tomorrow morning I never heard of you.' He walked through the kitchen door and closed it behind him.

'We can go any time now,' said Maureen. 'Everything I need is in the car.'

'I'll get my suitcase,' he said, and went back into the living room. The old man was gone, but he could hear the television in the bedroom. His suitcase was in the front hallway where he'd left it. When he returned to the kitchen he set the two thousand dollars on the counter and placed a coffee cup on top of it.

He let her out first, and followed her into the cold night wind. She took a different way, up the driveway and past a tiny garage. On the far side of the garage was another garage and a driveway leading to the street behind. He followed her to a three-year-old Chevrolet parked at the curb.

She handed him the keys and waited while he stowed the suitcase in the trunk. He let her in and took the wheel. The car's engine sounded well-tuned and healthy, and he could feel the heater warming the interior. As he pulled away from the curb and down the street, he could tell that it had gotten colder by the way the tires wobbled and crunched over the ice chunks.

'Do you know where you're going?' she asked.

'Yes,' he said.

'Good. Then we can talk while you're driving. You don't have to tell me anything. That isn't part of our deal. But if there's anything that will help I'd like to hear it.'

He thought for a moment, then made his decision. She was in all the way already. Even if she had an inclination to betray him she would know they probably wouldn't be able to get him without taking her out too. He decided to clinch it. 'I had a deal with a man who was working for somebody else. After I delivered, they killed him but made me think I was going to get my money anyway. I got out. That was two days ago. It could have been anybody, but Carlo Balacontano was there when I was.'

'Carl Bala,' she said. 'Shit.' She was lost in thought for a moment. Then she said, 'I just have to know one more thing, and I won't ask any more. How bad do they want you? Is it just the money or do they have some reason to be afraid of you? The old man said you were a pro.'

He looked over at her, but her face was obscured by the shadows. He drove on through the night. After a few minutes he found the entrance to the expressway and swung the car up the ramp into the rushing stream of southbound vehicles. It was over an hour before either of them spoke again. She asked if it was all right if she smoked, and he said it was.

TWENTY-THREE

Elizabeth studied the report. It could hardly be called a report, because it told her nothing she hadn't known for a week; in fact, there were two paragraphs that she had handed in as field notes for the Ventura police. Veasy, A. E. Death by detonation of explosives carried in vehicle. Probable murder. No suspects, no motive, no identification of the source of the explosives, no witnesses to the wiring of the truck, no similarities to other cases. Projected course of investigation: none. They were cutting it loose. No case with a report that said *Murder by Persons Unknown* could ever be closed, but the report had the neat and polished appearance of a document done for the archives. They knew this was a sheaf of paper they were going to have to live with. Damn.

She turned to the Senator's file. It was already five or six hundred pages of field reports, chemical analyses, interviews, and transcripts from consulting agencies. It wasn't really different from Veasy's file. It would just take longer before they could give up. But already the additions were beginning to take on that peculiar archival quality. Here and there she could see notations that said *substance not traceable* or *checked without result* instead of *investigation in progress*. It was just time, that was all. A week for a machinist, and how long for a senator? A month? A year? It didn't matter, because in another week or two the real investigation would have ended – maybe it had already. If there was evidence about the murders it had to be at Fieldston Growth Enterprises. And that meant it was gone. Because of Elizabeth Waring.

When Elizabeth looked up, Brayer was back. She returned to her work without speaking to him. Since Connors had left, the sight of John Brayer had been an irritant. She had placed him in a vulnerable position by her mistake, and he had accepted it and supported her. Now he was an irresistible temptation, the only possible source of approval that could assuage the guilt and humiliation of the last twenty-four hours, and she couldn't ask for it or even take it if it were offered. It wouldn't be offered because then he wouldn't be John Brayer, who approved what was efficient and productive, and disapproved of everything else.

The file had been kept up. After she'd left Denver the FBI had even followed up on Elizabeth's theory that the killer would have multiple sets of reservations. If he had, he'd been clever. He'd used more than one name, and possibly even used other blinds nobody had thought of. He was home free, she thought. He could run for senator himself, now that there was a vacancy.

'Elizabeth,' said Brayer. His voice sounded normal – happy, almost. She closed the file.

It couldn't be, she thought. They hadn't caught Tollar and Hoskins.

'We've got some action. I just got a call from the Flamingo. They've asked for a bellhop in Toscanzio's suite. It looks like he's headed for home.'

*

He woke up and looked at Maureen. She was still moving the car down the highway, her eyes peering through a pair of saucer-shaped sunglasses at the traffic. She'll do, he thought. Even if all she knows is driving a car and staying awake when I can't. I'm a respectable businessman on a trip with his wife.

The first stop would be the one that would tell him how to handle the rest. He'd worked in Detroit. There were people who knew him by sight. It had to be first, it had to be the test. He looked out at the bleak, rolling hills, a few trees between patches of old gray snow. Even like this it was familiar – especially like this. It reminded him of the man standing alone on the hillside, a man so alone he could have been lost on the surface of Jupiter or drifting in the darkness and silence at the bottom of the ocean. And as soon as the man had seen his face he'd known. The man had been a numbers runner, or was it a bookie? But the man had come up short. He'd been given chances, but he hadn't used them. But as soon as they'd gotten close enough for their eyes to meet, the man had known that this wasn't a warning. That was when the rest of the world had dissolved and he'd become the man alone on a hillside, a dark, motionless vertical object standing on the gray, empty snow. He hadn't bothered to say, 'Wait, I can pay.' He hadn't bothered to say anything, because when he saw who they'd sent to meet him he'd known that restitution and repentance and even money were things that pertained to people on a world a million miles away from him, a world that he was no longer a part of. He had stood there and then the bullet had smacked into him and toppled him over. The man lay there against the empty hillside, already dead with his blood leaking out into the snow, and he'd stood over the body and pumped the trigger until the clip of the big .45 automatic was empty. Later he'd dropped the gun in the river, a heavy military-model .45, inaccurate beyond a few feet, all square edges and with a kick that jerked his forearm when he fired it.

In Detroit he had let them use his face. He'd been young in those days and hadn't known any better. It hadn't occurred to him that this day might come and there might still be people around who had thought about that face during the long winter nights, wondering if it would be the last thing they ever saw.

They were nearing the city. He said, 'I'll drive now. Find a place to pull over.'

Maureen nodded and turned off at the next exit. It was a rest stop that consisted of a parking lot and gas station and a Howard Johnson's with a tiny souvenir shop attached to it. They got out and separated to the rest rooms, then bought gasoline before he swung back onto the highway.

He drove for another half hour, the traffic heavier now, as more and more cars poured onto the highway from the roads that converged on the city. At the Woodward Avenue exit he slipped from the current and guided the car down the ramp to the stoplight.

'What do you want me to do here?' said Maureen.

'Nothing,' he said. 'We make one stop and move on. In and out as fast as possible. I'm going inside and you stay with the car so we don't get a ticket.'

He inched the car down the familiar street from stoplight to stoplight, past large department stores and office buildings and banks. It hadn't changed much. He searched for a place to leave the car. Anyplace would do now. He passed the Midwestern Bank and turned right.

Maureen said, 'What about there? You just passed a parking lot. There's another one coming up.'

'No,' he said. 'Some of the parking lots downtown are owned by people I don't want to see. I can't take a chance.'

Just past the next corner a delivery truck was waiting to pull out. He stopped and waved the driver on, then pulled into the empty space. 'Stay here,' he said, and got out. He walked back up the sidewalk to Woodward Avenue and looked for a likely store. It took only a block before he found the side entrance to Hudson's Department Store. He had no trouble finding the right kind of briefcase. It was the kind that the men in this district carried – hard sides and a combination lock.

In ten minutes he was crossing the street in front of the Midwestern Bank. 'There is a magic elixir to make you disappear,' Eddie had said. 'It's money. If you have enough of it you can go anywhere and do anything and nobody will ask you where you got it. But that's only if you've got enough of it so you don't ever have to do anything to get more.'

At the teller's cage he said, 'I'd like to get into my safe deposit box, please.' He made sure she saw the briefcase. A man with a briefcase might be bringing something to put in the box, or might be making an exchange. You never knew. But he was probably taking a minute off from work, and might be pressed for time.

The teller said, 'Your name, please.'

'David R. Fortner.'

She made a move with her left hand and a man appeared beside her. He said, 'Please come with me.' The man conducted him to a tiny cubicle with one chair and a table in it, then took his key and reappeared with the box. He asked the man to wait outside; he'd only be a second.

When he was alone again he opened the box. Inside were the bills, exactly as he'd last seen them five years ago. There was no point in counting them; it took time to count a hundred thousand in hundreds. They fit neatly into the briefcase. He watched the man lock the box into its place in a wall of identical boxes, then took the key.

As he walked back to the car he looked at his watch. One thirty-five. It had been less than a half hour, and now he could move on, leaving Detroit behind.

Maureen sat in silence as he drove back toward the freeway. Every third block she glanced behind them at the traffic, but after they were on the highway she settled back and lit a cigarette.

He had planned to drive for an hour and then stop, but when the hour was up he kept driving, putting the monotonous miles between him and Detroit. It had gone beautifully, he knew. It had been in and out with little chance anyone could have seen him. But he still didn't feel what he wanted to feel, so he drove on, checking the mirror every few seconds to see if there could be a car that had been behind them for too many miles. It was just his nervous energy, he knew, and not the sure and reliable sense of caution he'd acquired over the years. But he drove on into the afternoon sun, building up the count of miles between him and the days he'd spent accumulating the stack of money in that box.

He drove past South Bend and Gary and was on the broad eight-lane expressway that poured the west-bound cars into Chicago when Maureen said, 'I think we'd better find a place to stop for the night.'

He said, 'Not for a while yet. We can move faster at night.'

Maureen said, 'I'm tired and I'm hungry, and I think we should. A vacationing real-estate man from Syracuse doesn't drive all night, and his wife doesn't have to look as though she slept in her clothes. Why don't we stop at a motel in the right price range and eat supper in the right kind of restaurant? We mustn't look as though we're running from something. Use your head.'

Of course she was right. Besides, he thought, they probably wouldn't want to try for us where it'd cause an uproar. They'd rather have us on a dark highway. If they spotted me. And they couldn't have. It might be a week before the word reached places like Detroit that a sight of him was worth money. And nobody had ever known about the safe deposit box.

He saw a Holiday Inn sign drifting toward them beside the highway. It was as good as anyplace: the right location for a couple who had been on the road all day and didn't want to get enmeshed in the city traffic, the right price. And there would be food nearby. He suddenly realized that he'd been hungry for a long time.

In the parking lot Maureen put her hand on his forearm and held him back. 'Here's where I start to earn my keep,' she said. 'Do what I say, and you'll be all right. I've been doing this for a long time, most of it with people who weren't much more than dead weight.'

'What do you want me to do?' he said.

'The cover is my responsibility. It's part of what you're paying for and I know it's good. We're Mr. and Mrs. William Prentiss of Syracuse until we're alone again. From now until we're on the road tomorrow the curtain is always up and you're always on stage.'

He smiled. 'That's a little extreme, isn't it?'

She shrugged. 'You're paying for it, you can decide. If the troubles you've got involve Carl Bala, it probably isn't. But you know more than I do about that, too. All I can say is I haven't lost a patient yet.'

He sat still for a moment and thought. Then he said, 'How thick is the cover?'

She said, 'It's about as thick as anything I've ever used. The car is registered to William Prentiss, the license is good, the address exists. If we use the credit cards the bills will get paid on time.'

'All right,' he said. He took out his wallet and examined the driver's license, the car registration, and the credit cards again. They were either very good forgeries or genuine. He got out and started walking toward the motel office.

'Wait for me,' she said, and caught up with him. 'From here on we stay together.'

In the office, he went to the registration desk while Maureen wandered to the other side of the room and pretended to look at a rack of postcards. When the desk clerk asked what kind of room they wanted, he hesitated for an instant, and Maureen said, 'A double bed will be fine.'

Once inside the motel room, Maureen walked all around, looking under the bed and behind the mirrors and in the bathroom until she appeared to have satisfied herself of something. Then she turned on the television, came close, and whispered in a voice he could barely hear, 'You haven't worked with a woman before, have you?'

He shook his head.

'You've got to think differently now. Look at me. If you were my husband, a young real-estate man from Syracuse, would you want twin beds? You might take them, sure. But you wouldn't ask for them. That's just the kind of thing that creep would snicker about, and maybe mention to a friend or two.'

Then she brightened and said, 'Give me a minute to make myself look human and we can go eat. Check the phone book and see if you can find a restaurant.' She leaned forward and brushed his cheek with her lips, and then disappeared into the bathroom.

The kiss startled him, but he did as he was told. He found a restaurant that appeared to be just the thing; the address was on the same street as the motel. The ad in the Yellow Pages was only mildly pretentious. There was no mention of entertainment, and that was the main thing they'd have to avoid. In some clubs in the Midwest, it was hard for singers and comedians to work unless they were sponsored by the Italians. There was always a quiet man in the audience studying the act, judging the applause, watching for the moment when the performer was ready to be booked into the big clubs in Los Angeles or Las Vegas or New York.

In a moment she was back. 'What did you find? I warn you, no more hamburgers.' He was starting to feel a little foolish. They hadn't eaten anything since they'd left Buffalo.

'This place,' he said. 'The King's Coach. It's just down the road, and it looks okay.'

Then she took on a look of concern that amazed him. 'Can we afford it?'

'I don't know,' he said. 'It doesn't look too fancy. But hell, we're on vacation now, you know.' He felt even more foolish, like a man who had been enticed out of the audience to blurt out a single line on stage.

'I won't argue,' she assured him, already making for the door. 'Come on. I'm starving. We can bring the bags in later.'

He locked the door and joined her in the car. 'What the hell was that all about?' he said. 'Weren't we alone?'

'I don't know,' she said. 'Get us moving.' He started the car and pulled onto the road. She said, 'I checked as well as I could, and didn't find anything. But we can't afford to stumble into one of those places that they wire to blackmail businessmen getting a little on the side. The best way to listen in is through the telephone or the TV, especially if the TV is on a cable instead of an antenna; but they're practically impossible to check unless you take them apart. A video camera is harder to hide. I don't think they have one in there, but they might.'

'If you thought they could be listening, why did you talk in there?' he asked.

'I had to make sure you knew enough to act the part. The TV will cover a whisper, but if you'd blurted something out in there we'd have been taking a chance to go back. If the place is a trap they didn't see or hear anything unusual yet. They'll pay attention to some-body else.' Then she laughed. 'Maybe a suspicious-looking couple who really are a real-estate agent and his wife.'

He said, 'You know a lot about it..'

Her brightness faded again. 'I didn't ask you where your money comes from, did I?'

'Okay,' he said. 'Then tell me about Prentiss. How much money do I make selling real estate? What can I afford to order in a restaurant?'

She thought for a moment, staring judiciously at him, and said, 'Well, you're pretty good at it, but no world-beater. I'd say you make between twenty and thirty thousand. You can afford to eat just about anything on the menu if it's the kind of place I think it is. But don't be too imaginative. You don't want escargot, for instance, because you don't eat things like that. As long as you stay on the steak-and-potatoes side of things you're safe. Wine is okay, but not anything extraordinary if your natural inclinations are in that direction. And take it if it's good or not. And don't overdo it on the other side either. Don't try to mispronounce the name of it while you're ordering. You're an ordinary guy, not a dunce. Just use your head. And straighten your tie.'

When he pulled into the parking lot at the King's Coach, Maureen said, 'Perfect. Pretty ordinary and there are plenty of cars in the lot. Maybe the food will even be good.'

He nodded. It looked safe enough.

'One more thing,' she added. 'If we have to wait for a table we'll go into the bar. I'll have a martini and you'll have a bourbon and water, or Scotch, if you like

251

that better. Do you feel up to talking about our kids, or do we have to invent something? I don't imagine you're up to much real estate, are you?'

'I think I can handle a little of each if I have to. What are the kids' names?'

'Tom is four and Jo Anne is two, so no talk about Tom being the captain of the football team or anything. Now let's eat. I really am starving.'

The meal proceeded uneventfully. They talked for a time, staying with their two subjects. By the time the waiter brought the check, he was reasonably comfortable as William Prentiss. That was the major part of a cover, Eddie had always said. 'You have to be who you say you are.' But he wasn't used to working with a woman, and it worried him a little. There were too many ways to get caught in the open.

At the car he said, 'All right, you're in charge. Back to the motel?'

She thought for a second, then said, 'Yes, I guess so. But be careful. When we go in I'm going to check the place out to see if anyone's been there. If they have, it'll probably be bugged. If I brush my hair with my right hand, it's probably all right. If I use my left, watch out. The next thing I do will be to walk over to the place where I think the problem is. Watch me and do anything I say to do. In any case, don't say or do anything out of character.'

'How will you know?'

'The usual things. You sat on the bed when we came in. There were wrinkles on the bedspread. I balanced a hair on the bathroom doorknob, inside. When I closed the curtains I left them a thumb-width apart. The first thing a small-time blackmailer will do is close them the rest of the way. He may remember to open them a little bit before he leaves, but he won't measure it. When I turned on the TV I put a smudge on the screen with my other hand. If they've put something in there they may change it, or even wipe it off.'

'Anything else I'll need to know?'

'Only the commonsense things. I'll have a gun in my purse. Use it if you need it.' She smiled. 'I know. I'm putting you through a lot when the chances are a million to one against trouble. But you know it's not wasted effort.'

'I know,' he said. The practice was never wasted. He had to learn to work with her, and it would have to be her way, if she was to provide the cover.

At the door to the motel room, Maureen prepared to enter first, her hand shuffling busily in her purse as her eyes darted about. He carried the bags, but set them down at the door to search for the key. He watched Maureen as she settled her eyes on the slightly opened curtains behind the window. She nodded and he opened the door, and then she pushed in ahead, her hand still in the purse. He breathed a sigh that he fancied could be the sigh of a husband setting down heavy luggage. He locked the door, regretting that there was no chain, then watched as Maureen made her inspection. She brought a hairbrush out of the purse, walked over and knelt in front of the television, and turned it on. Then she began the talk again, stood up, and walked into the bathroom, still carrying her purse.

He listened to her, waiting for some signal that all was well. 'And that waiter,' she was saying. 'I was waiting for him to pour your coffee all over the table and wipe it up with your tie. How can they always get the orders switched when there are only two people at the table?' The bathroom door closed.

He forced a chuckle, and stared at the screen, where a detective was grandly wrapping up his case, as he did weekly, by accusing his client of the crime. The client, as always, produced a pistol from nowhere, and jeered as he admitted everything in detail. In a moment the client would be running away from the detective, stopping occasionally to fire a shot or two in the general direction of his pursuer, then turning to run again, always up a stairway or fire escape, higher and higher until he was trapped. At the top he would run out of ammunition, hurl his pistol at the head of the detective, and lose the ensuing fistfight. In any case he would be on the pavement below in time for the commercials. He glanced idly at the bed as he took off his coat and loosened his tie. There were wrinkles on the bedspread. Were they the same?

In a moment the bathroom door swung open and Maureen came out, her head cocked to the side. She said, 'I'd like to have the recipe for the stuff they put on the asparagus though.' He didn't bother to answer. As he watched, she gave her head a toss, and began brushing her hair with her left hand. He had to force himself not to whirl his head around to look for it. What was it? A microphone? A camera? What? Watch her. He grunted and waited for her to move.

She stood firm in the doorway brushing her hair, but she seemed to be pondering. She said, 'I'm going to try to make it myself. But you'll have to help test it, because I want to get it right on the first try.' Then she smiled a too-broad smile, almost a wince, and added,

'God, the way the prices have gone up, we can't afford to miss the first time.' She still hadn't moved from the bathroom doorway. Then that was it. It had to be in there. He could see that light perspiration stains were beginning to appear under her arms. But still she held the grin and went on talking and brushing.

He said, 'I'm no cook. You said so yourself.'

She answered, 'Yes, but everybody should learn. It'll keep you alive if the real-estate business falls apart and you can't eat out anymore.'

Did she mean the cover was no good? She must. But that they wouldn't be able to run. He said, 'Okay, now let me in the bathroom.' He picked up his toothbrush and toothpaste and headed for the door. She stepped aside and said, 'All right, but save the shower for morning, okay?'

He froze in the doorway, not believing at first what he knew he felt. She had stopped brushing her hair. He looked at her eyes, which now held an approximation of a coquettish half-lidded sidelong glance, but there was behind it a kind of terror. The hand that held the hairbrush was trembling. He didn't bother to look down at the hand that was fondling his genitals.

He smiled and said, huskily, 'Jesus, I think I'll get that recipe myself. Give some to the girls at the office.'

Maureen turned and slipped away, and tossed the hairbrush on the table. As he brushed his teeth, he looked around him with an air of casual curiosity. The only thing that looked like a possibility was that there was no medicine cabinet. The mirror was attached directly to the wall. She had made a point of the shower. Was there something in it? Better not look. But it didn't make any sense. If there were a camera

255

and microphones, they would be trained on the bed. And they would both have to be there in a minute.

When he returned to the bedroom he was still confused, not knowing where to look. He was afraid that his eyes would rest on the spot, and they would know he was looking for something. Then he wondered if they would notice he was moving his eyes around too much. Only Maureen was safe to look at. She was sitting on the bed with her legs tucked under her, still brushing her hair with her left hand and smiling faintly to herself. He picked up his coat and started to hang it on the chair next to the bed. It had to be near, or he would never reach the Beretta in time. Maureen was busily turning back the covers, when she seemed to notice him again. She said, 'Mind if I check our finances?'

'Not at all,' he answered, and she sat back on the bed and whisked the coat to her. She fumbled for a moment in the pockets, then found the wallet. She dropped it on the floor. As she leaned down to pick it up, keeping the other hand on the bed for balance, he thought he saw a swift movement under the coat. Then both hands reappeared and she was peering into the wallet, moving her lips as though counting.

'Not bad,' she said. 'We should be okay at least until we get to Miami. Then we can use the traveler's checks.'

'That's what I figure,' he said. Miami. What else was there to say? He engaged himself in unbuttoning his shirt.

She tossed his coat back to him. When he caught it he was sure. The gun was gone. 'How about my wallet?' he said, and she tossed it to him. He set it on the nightstand and continued to undress. Somehow his mind resisted. For some reason his alarm had eddied and swirled around inside him and had finally solidified as a reluctance to be trapped naked. Yet he knew that the surest way to convince whoever Maureen thought was watching that he was something out of the ordinary was to remain fully dressed. He knew Maureen must have slipped the gun into the bed somewhere, but now she was on the other side of the room, rummaging in her purse.

For a moment he was terrified. She couldn't reach the gun, and he would need precious seconds to find it. If she had seen something, what – but then he remembered the gun in her purse. She hadn't forgotten. She was standing guard over him until he could get into the bed and find the pistol. He quickly finished undressing and slipped in between the cool, fresh sheets. He pretended to stretch, and in one motion grasped the Beretta in his left hand and pulled it down next to his thigh. Then he lay on his back with his arms folded behind his head, looking at Maureen.

She moved to her suitcase, then took out a filmy white negligee. He had forgotten about that – that it was her turn now, and it must be harder for her. If someone was watching, it was a man. He resolved to make it easier for her if he could. He turned out the lamp beside him, leaving only the one on her side. If she wanted that out, she could turn it off easily and naturally. He said, 'What do you think we ought to do first in Florida? I mean besides shopping.'

'I thought you were so excited about going deep-sea fishing,' she said, looking at him as she began to unbutton her blouse.

'Yeah,' he said. 'But what about you? What will you do while I'm out there hauling in the big ones?' He wanted to keep her talking, busy playing the part until the hardest moments were over and she could slip into bed and pretend to sleep. He tried not to stare as the blouse came off and she stepped out of the skirt.

She looked into his eyes from across the room, her lips turned up in a little smile as though she knew what he was thinking and thanked him for his two contradictory wishes. 'Oh, I'm going with you,' she said as she reached behind her and unhooked her bra. 'I'm the bait.' As she spoke she shrugged it down off her shoulders, and he couldn't help watching her firm round breasts jiggle slightly, the pink nipples standing out like tight little buds. When she slipped the silk underpants down her thighs he tried unsuccessfully to keep his eyes off the dark triangle of hair.

He said, 'And what if the fish don't like girl meat?'

She stopped in the middle of reaching for the wisp of nightgown, smiled again, and said, 'Then there's always the fisherman.' He could feel himself blush hotly as he realized that she was looking at the place where the thin covers rose over his erect penis.

She stepped to the bed in time to stop him as he reached across to turn out the other light. 'Leave it on tonight,' she said. As he started to turn she was already pressing against him, sprawled atop the covers, kissing his neck and giggling. She began to claw back the blanket, and he understood. She actually intended to go through with it. He snatched her wrist and said, trying to make it sound like a joke, 'Wait a minute, Miss. I'm a married man.'

She held his face in both her hands, still smiling her

false smile, but her eyes opened wide in a kind of pleading. She said, 'I know it. And if you don't start acting like one you won't live until morning.'

He pressed himself to her, fondling her breast and kissing her deeply. She gently drew him on top of her, one hand clenching and unclenching on his back and the other moving about under the covers. When she had found the gun he knew it. The hand stopped and she opened her legs. And then he was inside her, feeling at once the warm moistness of her, and the cold, hard impression of the gun on his leg. She began to give low, whispered cries, and kicked back the covers, keeping only one side veiled.

Whenever he opened his eyes, he could see her open eyes rolling about, as though in a kind of rapture. Her cries were coming more quickly now, and she moved almost with violence, her head rocking from side to side. He could see nothing but her head on the pillow beneath his, her hair spread like a flaming halo about it. At last the lids came down and she shuddered. A real orgasm, he thought. For a moment he was lost in the surprise of it, but he forgot it as her hips began to move again. He looked down at her face. There were tiny beads of perspiration now on her upper lip. Again she was moving her head from side to side. Finally her eyes narrowed for an instant before closing and they were both lost, falling weightless as the throbbing pressure exploded out of him.

For a moment they lay still, and her hand flattened on his back, while the other moved down it, then stopped. The hand raised slightly, and he heard the deafening bark of the pistol and felt a flash of heat. In an instant he had rolled clear, and found himself crouching like a wrestler beside the bed. At the foot of it he saw a figure of a man standing with an expression of pained surprise on his face, his eyes bulging and his mouth hanging open. As the figure tottered, two more shots slammed into his chest and he topped backward like a felled tree.

'Shit,' he muttered, and looked at Maureen, who was still pointing the pistol under the covers, where there was now a singed and smoking black hole. She said, 'See if he's dead.'

He bent over the body, but there was no uncertainty. There was no pulse, no heartbeat, no breathing. It was as though the thing on the rug had been part of the furniture of the unfamiliar room, or a bit of luggage left there by a slovenly porter. He looked at the face, frozen in its instant of outraged amazement. Then he said, 'We've got to get out of here.'

'Uh-huh,' she said. He looked up to see that she was already at her suitcase, taking out a fresh set of clothes. She turned to him and said, 'But we'd better make him disappear.'

He began to dress. 'Not much point in that,' he said. 'It'll slow us down, and it won't help.'

'What do you mean?' she said. 'We can't just leave a—'

But he interrupted her. 'I knew him.'

TWENTY-FOUR

'Twelve five p.m., Tuesday, February 20, Las Vegas: Subject Vincent Toscanzio. At 11:50 subject boarded TWA flight 921 for Chicago. He was accompanied by three persons: One registered as William Capell, positive ID Guillermo Montani. Others listed as Daniel Chesire and Richard Greene not identified. Photography will be forwarded to Justice.

'2:30 p.m., Tuesday, February 20, Las Vegas: Subject Carlo Balacontano. At 1.30 subject boarded private aircraft at McCarron Airport. Aircraft took off at 1:45. Flight plan filed for Nutley, New Jersey. No ETA.

'9:15 a.m., Monday, February 19, Palm Springs: Subject Antonio Damonata, AKA Tony Damon. Subject checked out of Royal Palms Hotel at 7:00 a.m. Wife, Marie Damonata, took Sun Aire connecting flight to Los Angeles, 8:30 a.m. and Pan American flight 592 at 9:50 a.m. Destination Miami, Florida. Subject and two other men in Cadillac El Dorado, Blue, California license 048 KPJ, left vicinity at 8:35, probable destination Los Angeles.

'5:40 p.m., Monday, February 19, Miami: Subject Marie Damonata arrived Miami airport flight 592. Flight was met at 5:20 by four men. One positive ID

Martin Damonata, son of Marie and Antonio Damonata. One probable ID Stephen LaTona.'

That was enough, thought Elizabeth. Brayer was right, and the last one clinched it. What the others were doing might have been open to question, but Tony Damon was scared to death. The murder of Castiglione had stirred them all up, and now they were on the move, scurrying back to their strongholds and getting the women out of sight.

It was coherent, she thought. Everywhere it was the same. The news had traveled quickly. 'Five eighteen p.m., Tuesday, February 20, Seattle: Subject Joseph Vortici. Vortici has not left his home since Sunday, February 18. Vortici's children have not been in school.'

They were all waiting for the next thing to happen, and it was clear they all expected it to be ugly. She put down the sheaf of reports and walked to the window. Las Vegas was a strange place. Even this building, FBI headquarters, felt like some sort of temporary structure thrown up in the middle of the desert. One-story, cinder blocks painted government green, an air conditioner every few yards. The only buildings that looked as if they were built by people who intended to stay were the giant hotels and casinos clustered around Las Vegas Boulevard like dinosaurs crowding up to drink at a stream. It was ludicrous, really. It was everything that everyone had always told her. What had Brayer called it? 'A monument to the Mafia's ability to cater to the lowest forms of lust in the souls of the American people; to give the suckers what they want. It's the biggest joke that's ever been played on the United States. Take a good look at it,' he'd said. 'You'll learn something. It'll show you why the best we can ever hope to do is yap at their heels.' It was true. It wasn't a regular city. All around were the most bizarre and outlandish temptations to do things you couldn't do at home – eat too much, drink too much, stare at naked bodies in feathers and sequins, but mostly, gamble. But you had to admit there was something about it. It wasn't exactly beautiful. It was – dazzling. For all intents and purposes, a place that grew up overnight, the night Bugsy Siegel arrived in 1946. Vanity Fair. If John Bunyan could have seen it he would have recognized it.

'Miss Waring.' She turned and saw it was the local FBI division chief. It was the first time she'd seen him since the meeting in the hotel. Where had he been?

'Yes?' she said.

'These gentlemen are agents Grove and Daly from Justice.' He left the office and closed the door.

She waited for them to say something, but they were busy pulling out chairs for themselves and shuffling papers in their briefcases. They looked vaguely familiar. She had probably seen them some time in a Justice hallway. She smiled and said, 'What can I do for you?'

Grove said, 'Miss Waring, we're from Internal Security. We'd like to ask you a few questions.'

She struggled to hold the smile, but she knew it must be fading. 'Sure. What about?'

Daly, a chubby man with thick glasses and a crew cut, spoke first. 'It's about the incident concerning Fieldston Growth Enterprises. Please sit down.' He sounded kind, soothing, almost the way some men did who had always been chubby and worn thick glasses.

Grove cleared his throat, and she suddenly realized

that this was going to be something she wouldn't like. The men were distinctly uncomfortable. 'To the best of your knowledge, who knew you had been ordered to serve a warrant on Fieldston Growth Enterprises?'

'John Brayer, of course,' she said. 'The FBI. There were two Bureau auditors, but I didn't get to meet them. I suppose the local FBI division head, the man who was just here. And there were two or three agents on surveillance at FGE.' Grove scribbled on a yellow legal-size notepad.

He said, 'Who else?' He seemed to know the answer.

She remembered. 'The presiding judge and I suppose his staff.'

He repeated, 'Anyone else?'

This time she was sure. 'Nobody I know of.'

Daly spoke up. His eyes looked apologetic behind the round magnifying lenses – big, sad, puppy eyes. 'Please try harder to remember, Miss Waring.' It seemed to be very important to him. 'Did you mention it to anyone? Family? A boyfriend, maybe?'

'No, of course not,' she said. 'I spoke to no one.'

He smiled. 'All of us who work in this field deal with a hundred details every day, a lot of them sensitive. We'd never intentionally reveal anything, but sometimes we make—' he paused, then chose 'errors. Maybe we have plans that have to be cancelled due to our responsibilities at Justice.' What in the hell was he getting at?

He smiled again. 'You know. You get a call from the boss – your Mr. Brayer, and then you have to break a date. My wife has gotten used to it, but believe me,' he chuckled, 'it took many years.'

She saw it coming, but had to wait. He said, 'You

call your boyfriend and say, "Sorry, can't go. I've got to serve a warrant." '

Elizabeth said, coldly, 'I just told you I spoke to no one. I have an excellent memory. Now tell me what's going on.'

This time Grove answered. He was a large man about fifty years old, with small, sharp eyes and a broad, expressionless face. 'We're here to find out why the people you're investigating seem to know in advance what the next move is. Your superiors consider you bright and perceptive, Miss Waring. Surely that must have crossed your mind.'

'Yes,' she admitted. In fact it had kept her awake until after two last night, but she wasn't going to tell him.

His expression didn't change. He said, 'Well, it occurred to Mr. Connors too. He's asked us to find the problem.'

She wondered whether she would be able to keep herself under control. Her head was beginning to throb. 'And so you're asking me.'

He nodded. 'And so we're asking you.'

She said quietly, 'But I don't know. I was just told to do it, and when I got a call from the two agents – but they weren't agents, were they? – I served the subpoena. I spoke to no one.'

Daly said, 'Do you have any suggestions for us, Miss Waring?' So there it was: the chance to serve as the anonymous accuser. 'We're not making much progress.' The methods of interrogators were always the same.

'No,' she said. 'I only know I'm not the one. I don't have any idea how they know what to do or when to do it. It might be they just figured it out. I was the agent in the open. I'd been to FGE the day before and gotten nowhere. The next logical move was to audit their records. Maybe they just put the pieces together.'

The two were already standing up and putting their notepads away.

Elizabeth felt a sudden desperation. She knew it was part of their craft, that they were trained to make her tell them things because she wanted to know what they knew, but she couldn't help herself. 'Wait,' she said. 'Whom else are you talking to?'

Daly's chubby face turned to her in a look of bright hope. 'All of the agents, I suppose. The judge and his staff. Are we missing someone?'

She said, 'No, I don't think so.' Watching them leave, she regretted having said anything.

Elizabeth shut the door and dialed Brayer's room at the Sands. When he answered she said, 'John, I've just been grilled by two men from—'

He interrupted. 'I know, I know. Internal Security. Don't let it bother you. They're looking for a leak.'

'I know they're looking for a leak,' she said in frustration. 'But I'm not it.'

'No,' said Brayer, 'and neither am I. But I had to put up with it too, and so does everyone else.'

'Then it's not because I was the one who—'

'No, dammit,' he said. 'It isn't. So forget it. I've got things going on here and I can't take the next hour to hold your hand. So get back to work.'

'What's going on?' she asked.

'More killings.' He hung up.

*

Elizabeth sat with the dead telephone in her hand. The field reports were still in a pile on the table, set aside to make room for the Internal Security men. But killings. Brayer had said killings. That made the field reports obsolete, she thought. Half of them were more than twelve hours old. The petty chieftains had been running for cover for two days. By now some of them could be anywhere – given twelve hours Damon could be in Hong Kong. Or dead. But Elizabeth had been assigned to the field reports, and the only way back into Brayer's good graces was to do what you were told. And she had been told to analyze the field reports. But how did Brayer know there had been killings? She picked up the pile of reports and leafed through them quickly. They were almost uniform. There were no reports of murders among them, just the opposite: what she held in her hand were thirty or forty individual ways of saying that nothing was happening. If there were killings, Brayer hadn't gotten the information from the field, because as soon as a call came in, the typescript was run off and distributed to everyone on the case. Her heart stopped. Oh, God, she thought. Was it the mistake or the suspicion that she was the security leak?

Elizabeth sat motionless for a moment, then remembered she was still holding the telephone, and set it back on the cradle. She thought it through again. No, it wasn't like Brayer to take someone off a case and say nothing. He wouldn't leave her in a quiet office with a pile of out-of-date reports to keep her out of the way while the others handled everything sensitive, would he? But then why hadn't he explained what was going on? Then it hit her. There was another possibility.

That was if the killings were local. The field agents would be reporting directly to the local controller. And the controller right now happened also to be the unit head. John Brayer.

There was one way to find out, she thought. If the agents were in the field the controller would call in the report to the FBI office, even if the controller was John Brayer himself. And if Brayer had called in and the report had been withheld from her, she decided, she was damned well going to know why.

TWENTY-FIVE

The car's headlights threw a bright wedge of light into the dark Illinois fields and the car rushed forward to occupy it, never quite fast enough to catch up. He drove in the silence of intense concentration. He knew he had to figure it out, but no matter how he arranged the facts, there was something he didn't know how to account for. It was the thing that was most dangerous.

Maureen spoke. 'I didn't sell you.'

'Huh?' he said.

'I said I didn't tell them where you were.' Her voice, coming from the darkness, sounded frightened. Of course.

'Oh, don't worry,' he said. 'No, do worry, but not about that. I know you didn't. You might be stupid enough to sell me to them and then panic when you realized they would take you out too. They're not stupid enough to send a face I knew. Not unless they didn't know where I'd be. You did fine. Your fee just doubled.'

He sensed in the darkness that her body relaxed from a rigidity that must have gripped it for some time. Stupid, he thought, both of us – her for being afraid and me for letting her sit there like that and not noticing. And the gun she must have near her hand will disappear now. She won't let me see it, and she'd deny it if I said it, but I know it's there. Probably under her skirt, between her legs.

'What now?' she said.

'Now we've got trouble,' he said. 'Did the old man know the cover?'

'Yes,' she said. 'But he didn't blow it. He wouldn't and anyway he couldn't be sure they'd get us both.'

'I suppose,' he said. 'But the cover is blown. We'll get rid of the car in a bit.'

She was silent, so he went back to his concentration. Something was going on. He thought about the comical surprise on Crawley's face when the slugs had ripped into him in the motel room. But that was just a distraction. Crawley was Bala's creature. What was he doing in Chicago? Chicago belonged to Toscanzio. It was Toscanzio's responsibility to get the man who'd killed Castiglione if he was in Illinois. It shouldn't have been Crawley; they'd never hire an outsider for the one who'd gotten Castiglione. It should have been Toscanzio's soldiers, maybe half a dozen. And they wouldn't have sneaked in to do it quietly. They'd have smashed in and demolished him, torn the whole motel down if they had to. It didn't make sense unless killing Castiglione had worked. He smiled to himself. There was no question about it. The bastards were at each other's throats.

'He looked just like that when we found him, Miss Waring. We haven't moved him yet because of the – the way it was done.'

'I see,' said Elizabeth. She walked back toward the front of the gift shop where the other one had been, the girl. She stepped behind the counter and stood at

270

the cash register, then scanned the room. You couldn't see the dressing cubicles from the counter. The tall racks of china objects in the center of the room were too thickly crammed for that – coffee cups that had *Las Vegas* and a pair of dice on them, ash trays that looked like roulette wheels. The killers had probably stood behind the rack of coats in the back. The front of the gift shop was where all the likely objects were placed: the jewelry, small carved figurines, and even the junk that wasn't worth stealing. In the back were the bigger things, the clothes and the imported coffee tables. They were too big for a shoplifter. There was a round convex mirror on the wall, but the girl at the cash register couldn't have seen behind the rack of coats. God, what a place. A rack of coats – sable and mink and silver fox, none of them to be had for less than seven thousand, and next to it a rack of T-shirts. Something for everybody.

The girl's body was gone, but the usual chalked outline was on the rug where she fell. Not that anybody needed it. It was amazing how much blood you had in you.

'Miss Waring, we're getting ready to move him now.'

Okay. One last chance. It wouldn't accomplish anything, probably, except to give her one more image for a nightmare. But you had to look. You always had to look, because they might have made a mistake, gotten too confident, let their flair for the dramatic get them into trouble. She left the counter and made her way back around the racks of souvenirs to the dressing rooms.

The police lieutenant was waiting for her. He pulled

open the curtain and stood back. A gentleman, she thought. Absurd. She stared in at the body. It was sitting on the bench, leaning in the corner of the little cubicle, the head lolling sideways as though he were trying to look over his own right shoulder. She could see the face in the mirror, the open eyes bulging, and a T-shirt stuffed in the mouth. It was hard to tell what he would have looked like when he was alive. He was big: fifty-three years old, they'd said, but he was broad shouldered and with a barrel chest. She looked down at his waist. Not much of a paunch – he had stayed in shape. A hard man to take into a busy gift shop and do this to. He'd been strangled and they'd broken his neck. She looked down to examine the shoes, but she couldn't get past the abdomen without stopping. For some reason that was the most horrible part of it. The joke.

The china figurine of a baby rabbit had been stuffed into the fly of his pants, so only the head and shoulders stuck out, the little face smiling shyly at nothing. She looked down at the shoes. They were beautifully polished, with no scuff marks. What was the leather? Lizard. At least two or three hundred dollars, she thought. A good match for the suit. She'd lost track of what men's clothes cost, but this one was expensive.

'Do you know what he did?' she asked.

'Did?' said the police lieutenant.

'Yes,' she said. 'What he did for a living. You know.'

The lieutenant shrugged and let the curtain swing across the body. 'Not really. Ferraro was from New York, and the response from NYPD didn't tell us much. The first round just said he was a probable. When they sent the rap sheet to us the last they had was 1958, assault, three counts. Nothing recent, but he's obviously come up in the world.' He nodded, and the ambulance men shouldered their way into the cubicle to begin maneuvering the body to their cart.

'What do you think happened to the girl?' said Elizabeth.

'Hard to tell,' he said. 'At the moment I think she probably saw something or heard something, and started toward the dressing room. But it's possible they wanted her too. She was shot four times. There must have been a silencer because nobody heard anything, and this is a big, busy hotel.'

It didn't matter, Elizabeth knew, because Brayer had been right all along. They had probably killed the girl because she'd seen their faces. There must have been two of them. It was Ferraro they wanted. But why in a gift shop in a bottom-level corridor of the MGM Grand Hotel? She looked out through the glass display window at the crowds moving past. It was easy to see how they'd done it, slipped in and done their work, maybe one of them at the door to pull the curtain and put up the *CLOSED* sign. Then in a few minutes they'd just come out and dissolved into the flowing current of people. And it might have been an hour before anyone had checked the door or wondered aloud why a hotel gift shop was closed at ten thirty on a Wednesday. But why? The only possibility was that Brayer was right. It was a struggle for primacy, and the opening gambit would have to be like this, terror tactics, each side telling the other that it would be best to submit. They were saying we can get you whenever and wherever we want to.

*

273

He returned to the car and carefully wrapped the money in the newspaper so that it made a neat, tight bundle. He wrapped the masking tape around it and slipped it into the padded book mailer, then sealed the mailer. Maureen watched, but said nothing, just stared out across the broad expanse of the parking lot while he worked. He left the car and returned to the post office, then printed boldly across the package, *PO Box 937, Tonawanda, New York 14150*, and dropped it into the mail slot.

When he was back in the car Maureen said, 'Is that what this is all about?'

He started the car and drove out of the lot. 'What do you mean?' he asked.

'You're collecting your nest eggs, aren't you?'

He nodded. 'That's part of it.'

'And you're mailing them somewhere.'

'It would be hard to deny that, wouldn't it?' he said. 'So what? I've got to travel light.'

'Nothing,' she said. 'I just hope you're not one of those guys who has a wife or a girlfriend somewhere waiting to pick it up.'

He chuckled then said, 'Maureen, are you jealous? I mean, you're a lovely lady and an outstanding fuck, but come on.'

'That isn't what I mean and you know it,' she snapped. 'I mean if wherever you mailed that isn't secure I want to know about it, and I want my money now, because I'm getting out of this. If there's somebody at that address they'll have the money and they'll have the place it was mailed from.'

He looked at her. She was staring at him and her jaw was tight. He said, 'Relax. It's a post office box.

I've had it for some time. I've got several of them, all over the place. Some I've used for people to get in touch with me when they had a job to offer. Some I use as addresses for the covers I need: a place to send bills for credit cards, license renewals, and so on. There's somebody behind all those boxes – me. This address is a money drop for me. I've only used it three times since I've had it, which is about that many years. I've never given the address to anyone, and nobody knows I've been there. Is that secure enough?'

Maureen didn't answer at first, just stared ahead at the road. Then she brightened and said, 'You're not such a terrible fuck either. Nothing special, but adequate, I suppose.'

He said, 'Then it's settled.'

She looked puzzled. 'What's settled?'

'That we get rid of this car, scrap Mr. and Mrs. William Prentiss, and disappear into the sunset. We're going to make a jump and then go under for a bit.'

They made Peoria at almost two o'clock. This time Maureen drove the car around the block and waited while he went into the bank. The money didn't fit in the briefcase, so he put the rest of it in his pockets. This, he decided, would be enough. There were savings accounts in seven banks in different parts of the country, but they could wait. None of them was large enough to be vulnerable, and the money would keep until it was safe to transfer it in small payments to the account of his next identity. In the meantime it would even draw interest. If he left it for a few years it would double.

The proportion was about right. He had at least eight hundred thousand dollars in those accounts, three hundred thousand in the post office box, and two hundred thousand with him when he returned to the street. He could wait. He could wait until Toscanzio and Balacontano and the others died or went off to retire in Italy, until Little Norman and everyone else who'd ever known him had died and been forgotten. Because he didn't have to work again. He was a rich man. He could take it day by day, living comfortably but not comfortably enough to draw anyone's attention. And each day he bought himself would make it less likely that the Italians would ever find him. Each day he would seem less dangerous to them, and each day would bring them something new that they'd rather think about because there was a profit in it. Someday they'd have forgotten all about him. In five years he'd be one of those problems that had solved itself. In ten, it would be hard to find anyone who could remember whether or not he'd been found and killed. Crawley had played a hunch and waited for him in Detroit and followed him. He'd have done the same himself. A sucker who had to disappear would try to get on a plane for someplace far away that he'd never been to, but you had to figure a pro would go to ground in a familiar place. But Crawley was dead. The only thing that still worried him a little was that Crawley had seen the car, and managed to find it again in the motel parking lot outside Chicago. Crawley had never been that lucky. Had he managed to do that alone?

He stood in front of the bank looking for the car. Maureen would keep circling the block until she saw him. The traffic downtown was heavy, he thought. It might take a few more seconds before she came around again, so he watched the people on the street. It wasn't a bad way to do things, he thought. There were other people standing in front of buildings across the street waiting for buses or the arrival of friends. He knew he didn't look appreciably different from the others, if you took them as a group. He was wearing a sport coat and carrying a briefcase. The only difference was that his was full of money.

He even counted two who looked a hell of a lot more suspicious than he did. One of them was a short, dark man with curly hair who was just standing on the corner across from him. He was wearing a gray three-piece suit and carrying a briefcase. He wasn't waiting for a bus, because he was right at the corner. Whenever the light changed, a herd of people would scurry across the street, but he'd still be there. Whatever he was waiting for, he didn't look impatient about it: he never looked at his watch and he never looked up and down the street to see if it was on the way. Maybe he was early. The other man was about a hundred feet from the corner, in front of the display window of a travel agency. He was waiting for someone too, but he was getting impatient. You could tell because he had been staring into the window for a long time, the way people did when they had been standing in one place long enough to wonder if they were attracting attention. It made them feel as though they had to be absorbed in doing something, or people would notice them. People would think, look at that schmuck standing there. He's been there for twenty minutes. She stood him up, and he's too stupid to know it, the poor bastard.

Where the hell was Maureen? His sense of time must

be off, because it seemed he'd been here long enough for her to go around the block at least twice. There couldn't be trouble, not real trouble. He hadn't been in Peoria in a year, at least. There was no way anybody could anticipate that he'd be coming to pick up an old contingency fund. The one thing they would believe was that he wasn't worried about money. They'd given him two hundred thousand less than a week ago. But what was keeping Maureen? Unless she'd decided to sell him after all, now that they were separated and he could be had alone. No, that didn't fit. She would wait for the forty thousand he'd promised her, because she could never suspect that he was worth more than that to them, not on what he'd told her. So where was she?

He began to feel a prickling sensation at the back of his scalp. He was vulnerable. He had to stand here in the open as long as it took. There was no plan to cover the possibility that one of them would get into trouble. He'd only been in the bank for ten minutes – what trouble would there be? But there must be a problem. And here he was. He didn't even have a gun. You didn't walk into a bank with a gun on you because it wasn't worth the risk.

Suddenly he saw the car swing around the corner. He felt the muscles in his neck and shoulders relax. He could see Maureen behind the wheel now, coming toward him. It was all right. Then he thought, if she stopped somewhere and went into a store to buy a new pair of panties or something I'll make her wish she hadn't. As the car approached he took a step forward toward the curb to meet it.

The car didn't stop. Maureen didn't even look in his direction, just drove on past him and kept going. His practiced reflexes took over and he completed his stride and made another step forward. He looked down the street into the distance as though he hadn't recognized Maureen. His mind worked at the problem. She had seen something and come here to warn him.

She was being followed. It had to be that, because nothing else would make leaving him here less dangerous than picking him up. Somebody was following her, and she thought they wouldn't make their move until the two of them were together in the car. So it had to be the car. Crawley hadn't been alone after all, and someone had spotted the car a second time. And now she would have to keep driving, leading them somewhere else until either she shook them off or they realized she'd seen them. That meant they'd backtrack until they found him, or they'd take her and ask her questions. He didn't bother to think about that. She'd tell. His forty thousand wasn't worth what they'd do to her. Nothing was.

So he had – what? Five minutes? Fifteen if she bought it for him. He looked at his watch, and then started walking down the sidewalk. The important thing would be to get off these streets as quickly as possible. He wished Peoria had subways. A taxi might do it, he thought, but he didn't see any. A bus? No, a city bus was too dangerous. If anybody saw you get on, he'd see the route number and he had your schedule for the next hour. He walked briskly, varying his pace to the hurried strides of the people around him. He was getting cold. He hoped it didn't show. A businessman wouldn't hang around on the street long enough to get as cold as he felt.

Across the street and ahead of him was a Sears store.

That looked like the most promising place. He stopped at the corner to wait for the light to change. Then he saw the man. It was the short man in the gray suit. He had moved down the block across the street, and now he was standing at the corner. He looked to see if there were a second man. Maybe the one who'd been staring in the travel agent's window? He couldn't see anyone who looked familiar. But the man in the gray suit was looking at him.

He started walking again. The man in the gray suit walked too, moving parallel with him across the street. So that was the way it would be. The man in the gray suit had intended to let himself be seen. He was herding him somewhere; it must be to a place where a second man waited in ambush.

He considered the situation. Something up ahead was a trap. The man in gray was herding him forward. He didn't look over his shoulder, but he knew that there would be somebody following at a distance to keep him from turning around if he recognized the tactic. If he went into a store, so much the better for them. They'd have time to prepare for him while he waited for an advantage that would never come. He knew the strategy, but it had a flaw. It depended upon the victim's natural inclination to wait while his chances slipped away. The ones who were following him, guiding him toward the pocket, would converge on him until it was too late for him to move, because any one of them was close enough to kill him. So he had to move now.

He watched the cars gliding past in the street. A taxi would be perfect, but his luck didn't seem to be running today. Still, it had to be that way, a jump that would put him outside the triangle that was closing on him. Then he'd have a chance. He stopped at the next light and waited. The light changed and all the other people crossed the street, but still he waited. The man in the gray suit was stopped across the street from him, and he knew whoever was behind him would be coming up fast.

The light changed again and the first car across was a Volkswagen. He waited for the station wagon behind it, then made his move. He ran forward and flopped onto the long, flat roof just as the car began to move. The driver seemed to know that something had happened, because he started to brake, but then horns sounded behind him, so he speeded up again. The horns were louder now, because the other drivers were alarmed. Then it must have occurred to the driver of the station wagon that he'd hit something. He pulled over to the curb, opened his door, and got out, but what he saw made no sense. A man was running away, carrying something – a briefcase, maybe. But he wasn't concerned about that so much as he was about whatever he'd hit. He started the long walk back up the street to the light. Jesus Christ, he thought when he saw the two men running down the street toward him. It must have been bad. He just hoped to God it wasn't a kid or a doctor. If you ran over a kid or a doctor they made you pay for the rest of your life. When the two men sprinted past him at full speed he felt a giddy relief. Then he thought, Oh, God, don't let it be a pregnant woman. Even a doctor would be better than that.

TWENTY-SIX

The afternoon had been exhausting. For once it wasn't that they didn't know anything. They had too much information from too many sources. It was too complicated to be coherent. It was just as Brayer had said. 'We're not looking at some gang fight. We're looking at a disruption in one of America's biggest industries. We don't even know what the hell to look at. Ferraro gets killed in a gift shop. Castiglione at his house. A guy named Crawley gets it in a Holiday Inn near Chicago – Christ, we don't even know what he was or who he worked for. But there was a booby trap in the shower of the room where he was killed – wired to electrocute whoever used it. The killing is what we're seeing. But how do we know that what we ought to be looking at isn't that one day the ice cream doesn't get delivered to a baseball game in Cleveland, or a chain of shoe stores in Massachusetts goes bankrupt because the banks won't give the company a loan?'

Brayer was right. It was ridiculous. The Organized Crime Division of the Justice Department was – what? three hundred people? And there was no way even to sort out the information that was coming in now from every agency whose jurisdiction included some avatar of the Mafia. Because that was everybody.

Elizabeth walked across the casino toward the corridor with its waiting elevators. When she opened the door to her room, she managed to stifle the scream before it got out, but not the jolt of adrenaline that seemed to pump into her veins. She could feel her temples throbbing as she said, 'What are you doing here?'

Grove was the one who spoke. He said quietly, 'Please come in and close the door.'

Elizabeth came in but didn't put down her purse. She remained standing. 'What are you doing in my room? Searching my luggage?'

'Oh, no, Miss Waring. You're in the clear. Completely. We're here for another reason.' It was Daly who spoke.

Then Grove again, 'We're here because there's a tap on your telephone. We've had a team in here half the day looking for bugs, but all they had was a remote on your line.'

Elizabeth sat down in the chair beside the desk. 'So you've found the problem.' It wasn't a question, it was a statement. She was relieved. They were here to tell her she wasn't under suspicion anymore. For a moment she almost felt grateful, but then it didn't seem appropriate. 'You've taken care of it?'

'Yes,' said Daly, 'we've detected the tap. But it isn't feasible to remove it. We don't know where it is, and we can't take it off without compromising other . . .' he paused, searching for the right word, 'sensitive parts of the investigation.'

'So what do I do?' asked Elizabeth.

'Nothing you wouldn't do otherwise,' said Grove.

He looked at his watch, then said to Daly, 'It's almost six fifteen.'

Daly said, 'Miss Waring, in a minute your telephone will ring. Just answer it and say the things you would normally say. But don't ask for more information than you're given, and don't volunteer anything.'

Elizabeth said, 'All right. Who is it, though?'

'It'll be Mr. Connors,' said Grove. The telephone rang and Elizabeth jumped. It was too quick.

'Answer it,' said Grove.

Elizabeth obeyed. 'Hello?'

'Agent Waring?' came a female voice.

'Yes.'

'Please hold for Mr. Connors.'

Connors came on immediately, and the secretary was gone. Elizabeth had the sensation that there were numberless people listening to him as he spoke. Her mind ticked off the ones she knew of. The secretary, Daly, Grove, a team of technicians trying to follow some electronic signal that could tell them where in the circuitry an extra milliohm of resistance occurred. And the wiretappers themselves. She couldn't picture them, of all the invisible listeners. There was no face, no idea what it would look like – there was just the sense that there was a person, an intelligence waiting between her and Connors, not breathing or moving, not necessarily even capable of breath or movement. Maybe it was just a tape recorder. Connors said, 'Miss Waring?'

'Yes, sir.'

'We've found the leak in the operation.'

What was he saying? Was he telling the wiretappers that Internal Security had found the tap? Why?

'Really?' was all she could say. And why was he telling her?

'That's right. And I'm positive he'll tell us everything he knows. We've finally got the break we needed.'

He? A person? She said, 'That's great, Mr. Connors.' She wasn't sure how enthusiastic to be, so she tried to modulate her tone to imitate his.

'We've got it set up so he'll have to talk. Immunity from prosecution, money, resettlement. If he doesn't talk we've got enough to charge him. So the problem turned out to be a bonus.'

'That's wonderful,' said Elizabeth. She almost asked him what he wanted her to do next, but she remembered that Daly had told her not to ask questions. She said, 'Thank you for letting me know.'

Connors said, 'Quite all right, Miss Waring. You can go on with the investigation from your end, and we'll handle the rest from here. Good-bye.' He hung up.

Elizabeth put down the receiver. 'Do you think that was long enough?' she asked Daly.

Daly was standing up and beginning to move toward the door. 'That was fine, Miss Waring,' he said. He seemed to be speaking to the carpet.

'But I always heard it took a long time to find a tap – ten or twenty minutes,' she said.

Grove and Daly were moving toward the door, but she stepped in front of them. 'Wait,' she said. It couldn't be the way it looked, but what else could it be? And if it wasn't, what was all that nonsense about finding a leak? She said, 'Tell me what just went on here. They weren't looking for the tap at all, were they? It was something else.'

Grove's face remained impassive. 'That's right. We're leaving the tap in place.'

Elizabeth's heart was pounding, and she could feel her temples beginning to throb again. She understood, but she was going to make them say it. 'So that's it,' she said.

Daly's eyes fluttered to her face and then back to the carpet. 'It was necessary,' he said. 'There is a leak, we're sure of it.'

'So you decided to set him up?'

'That's right,' said Grove. 'You did a good job. Now we've got to leave here and get on with our work. Thank you for your cooperation.'

'But you know what you did. They'll kill whoever it is.'

Grove nodded. 'Maybe they will. Judging from the rest of the case, they'll probably try, anyway. Good night.'

She said, 'But that's—'

Grove interrupted, his voice suddenly harsh. 'Who do you think that was on the other end of the line, lady? It was Connors. He authorized it, he made the call himself. So forget it. You've done your part. Thanks to you the leak has been neutralized.'

'You – we – just made sure somebody in Justice would be murdered,' she said. 'Maybe somebody in my office. And he won't even have any warning because there wasn't any real investigation. Nobody was even accused of anything.'

Grove's face didn't change. He said, 'What do you think this is, anyway? Do you think it's a game? Whoever it is was doing the same thing to you. Ever think of that? And if we got lucky and caught the bastard he was dead already. In jail or out of it his friends would have gotten him.' He stopped, and seemed to remember something. 'And by the way, don't stop using that telephone. Just remember not to say anything you don't want them to hear.'

Elizabeth sat down on the bed and watched them leave. She tried to decide what she felt. Then she identified it. She knew that a shower wouldn't wash it off, but she also knew that the shower was waiting for her in the next room and absolution was not.

'We've finally got something on Edgar Fieldston,' said Brayer. 'The SEC called a few minutes ago, and they think they've gotten a glimpse of his coattails.' He was smiling, but it wasn't his enthusiastic smile. Elizabeth waited for the rest of it.

'Yesterday a loan was approved at the United Free Bank of the Bahamas to an Edgar Fieldston – four million dollars' worth.'

'What was the collateral?'

'A portfolio of stocks. A lot of blue-chip stuff to sweeten the deal: IBM, Commsat, Xerox, ITT, but the main part was FGE stock. Almost five million dollars' worth, if you take it on today's market.'

'How did the SEC get wind of it? The Bahamas aren't subject to our reporting regulations, are they?'

'No, but the United Free Bank wasn't up to the transaction. They had to get in touch with First National in Miami. You see, the deal was for cash.'

'Oh, God,' said Elizabeth.

But Brayer continued. 'Even that wouldn't have done it, because bank-to-bank transactions aren't subject to reporting regulations. But First National couldn't spare that much cash, so they got in touch with the Federal Reserve Board. Federal Reserve likes to keep an eye on deals involving banks in the Bahamas, because some of them exist mainly for the purpose of moving dirty money. When they learned about the collateral they got in touch with the SEC to see if somebody happened to notice that he'd misplaced some stock certificates. The SEC didn't pick it up until it was too late. The stock wasn't stolen, and Fieldston owned it, so—'

'So he's wandering around in the Caribbean,' said Elizabeth, 'with four million dollars in cash. At least he's alive.'

'Maybe,' said Brayer. 'If he is, I'd say he doesn't intend to come back. If the FGE stock collapses, as I expect it will when we're through investigating their operations, he's just picked up four million dollars for about two hundred thousand in legitimate stocks and a whole lot of worthless paper.'

'But there's another possibility?' asked Elizabeth.

'Yes, I'll admit he could be on his way to someplace like Paraguay or Costa Rica or Haiti, where he can't be extradited and can live like a king on his "loan." But it's more likely he was getting the Mafia's investment out of the company.'

'If that's true, what then?'

'Then it may not even be the real Edgar Fieldston the bank gave the loan to. In any case, he's not likely to run off until he's paid whoever's behind him. They're not interested in niceties like extradition. All we know for sure is that somebody is liquidating the assets of FGE.'

'So what's being done?' Elizabeth asked.

'Oh, the obvious things. There's a list of the serial numbers the Federal Reserve board turned over to First National. It may turn up in interesting places, but probably it's already been laundered. The American consulates are alerted for Fieldston's passport. But I don't know what we can expect from any of it. With four million dollars he can go pretty deep, if he's alive and on his own. If he's not, the possibilities are endless. We'll never hear of him or the money again.'

'So what you're saying is that we're up against another dead end,' said Elizabeth.

Brayer shrugged. 'Maybe, but maybe we'll get lucky. The main thing is to keep on it. I'd say that as of yesterday Fieldston Growth Enterprises ceased to be a functioning entity. But that might be a break for us, if we can figure out who's carving up the carcass.'

He left the office and Elizabeth tried to return to the reports. The piles of information were getting bigger now. In another week they would be the size of a set of encyclopedias, and there would be nothing to show for it except paper. How many murders so far? A dozen? She began to leaf through the summaries, counting. Thirteen positive, and two more probable if you counted the two blood types found on the pavement in front of the Tropicana. And they still seemed no closer to an indictment than they'd been when Veasy the machinist blew up. And that too, she thought – the union. Veasy was dead, and the union's pension fund was somewhere in South America by now, maybe working its way northward through a dozen metamorphoses to become a certificate of deposit in some Caporegima's Swiss bank account. Even if the Justice

Department knew about it, the laundering would be so complete they'd never be able to prove it. At least then they'd know whom to watch – but so what? By that time what they were watching for would already have happened. It was worse than hopeless. All they could do was keep score and try to figure out what was next, always hoping an agent might be on the scene when the hit men arrived. Only this time she knew where it would be, and there would be an agent on the scene. Because she had helped put him in front of the guns. If thine eye offend thee pluck it out.

TWENTY-SEVEN

Just before the five-o'clock rush reached its peak, a businessman carrying a briefcase walked out of the big Romanesque central post office in Peoria, Illinois. There wasn't anything about him to distinguish him from the surrounding crowds of people, except that he seemed to walk a bit more slowly than some of them. Only the most perceptive of observers would have said he had a slight limp. But they would not have had the time to feel sorry about the limp, because as he reached the bottom of the broad granite steps, a young woman pulled up at the loading zone in a small blue Datsun and opened the passenger door for him. He got in, set his briefcase on his lap, and smiled at her as they drove away. He didn't kiss her, but that wouldn't have seemed unusual, because there wasn't time. She was already off to make room for others at the loading zone, and a moment later the Datsun had disappeared in the traffic.

'Maureen,' he said, 'that was very good.'

'I knew if you wanted to meet me it would have to be at the post office,' said Maureen.

'Is the car safe?' he asked.

'Sure. It's rented. I wanted to spend my last few hours on this job in relative ease.' She glanced over at him, as though she expected him to say something unpleasant.

He said, 'Again, very good. We just aren't going to make it together.' He took a package out of his coat and placed it in her purse on the seat. 'You don't have to waste time counting it,' he said. 'It's all there – fifty thousand dollars.'

'Fifty?'

'Yes,' he said. 'We'll get you on a plane tonight, but first there are few things I want you to get me. I'd better make a list.'

He watched the lights of the plane as it lifted into the dark sky and diminished to a pair of tiny blinking spots. The problem with airplanes was that they only looked that way – they were built in the shape of the prototypical image of untrammeled movement and freedom. But an airplane was only part of a complex of tubular corridors that moved you from one broad and brightly lighted lobby to another. There were no cutouts, no places to hide, no ways of modifying the predicability of their movement. A telephone call from one end meant that when you walked down the last tube at the other end there would be something waiting for you: maybe a quiet man who was carrying a box that looked like a present for grandma. But Maureen would be all right. They would have no idea who she was or where she'd come from, and they'd have to spot him again before they knew she was gone. He envied her. She was out of it.

He started the car and drove out of the airport parking lot. It was going to be a long trip, he decided, but the solitude and the darkness would give him time to think about what he was going to do. There was no question about his destination. The one thing he'd been sure of was that he could never go to Las Vegas again, but that had been before he'd realized how things were. They weren't going to forget about him. They had already devoted too much time and effort to finding him to let him sink out of sight into a comfortable retirement.

He had taken a couple of jobs for Orloff, and done them, and come to collect. It all seemed to have started with those two in the alley in Denver. As soon as he'd shown up with a few bumps and bruises, everything had changed. They all turned on him like sharks when one of them is bleeding. But that couldn't be it. It was too ridiculous. And they wouldn't have killed Orloff just because the specialist he'd hired had a black eye. But they'd ignored the moratorium that had held in Las Vegas for years, and killed everyone they could find. Now they were after him and they weren't going to give up. That meant that whoever had killed Orloff still felt vulnerable – but to what? He didn't even know for certain who was paying Orloff. It might be Balacontano, or Toscanzio, Lupo, even Damon.

Whoever it was had sent soldiers all over the country looking for a single man, even with Castiglione dead. Even the death of the old consigliere hadn't distracted him, although the families would now be spending most of their time watching each other to see who moved first.

So he had to find out. The one who paid Orloff had too much juice to ignore; he'd used Little Norman as his errand boy, and had watchers waiting everywhere. But whoever it was was worried about something, and the soft spot had to be in Las Vegas. The link was Orloff.

The more he thought about it, the more angry it made him. It was stupid. Uneconomical. He had taken the contracts on the usual terms. He'd dealt only with Orloff and never inquired about who was paying the bill or why he wanted Veasy and the Senator. He hadn't been curious about it. He'd done his work and that should have been the end of it. He hadn't even been that curious about the killing of Orloff, although it had seemed bad luck that it had happened before he'd been paid. He'd behaved like a professional. But they'd gone too far. They'd panicked and shot down everything that moved. And that was stupid. Because they should have left him alone.

When Elizabeth awoke it was dark, but she had the disconcerting feeling that she was already late for something. It was a feeling of urgency; something had begun and she was still in bed. She heard the knock on the door, and remembered the sound of it. Somebody had been knocking for several minutes. As she got out of bed she called, 'I hear you,' and the knocking stopped. She turned on the light and squinted at her watch on the nightstand – four thirty. It had to be Brayer, afraid to use the phone. Her bathrobe was draped across a chair, but even with that she felt naked. 'Just a minute,' she called. It was foolish, she thought, but was it more foolish than opening the door to a knock in the night? The gun fit into the pocket of her robe. She kept her hand on it when she unchained the door and opened it.

The man at the door was a stranger. He wasn't even

as tall as Elizabeth, but he gave the impression that he was big because his broad shoulders and belly seemed to belong to someone taller. His hair was dark, but beginning to turn gray.

'What?' said Elizabeth, not sure whether she was angry or not, but positive she was uncomfortable.

'You're Elizabeth Waring,' said the man. Elizabeth realized that it had somehow been intended as the answer to her question.

'I know that,' she said. 'It's four thirty.'

The man said, 'Please, can I come in?' He looked past her into the room as though he longed to be there. The look on his face startled her. Brayer hadn't sent him.

'What do you want?' she asked. Her grip on the pistol tightened.

'Please,' he said, 'I have to talk to you.' She hesitated, so he whispered, 'FGE.'

She let him in and closed the door. He said, 'Do me a favor, and take the gun out of your pocket. You can point it at me if you want, but in your pocket it might go off by accident and hit us both.' He sounded sad, as though he had resigned himself to putting up with a great deal of incompetence.

Elizabeth obliged him. She aimed the gun slightly to his side, but it was in sight. 'What do you want?' she repeated.

'I want to be a material witness. Turn myself in and tell you stories.'

Elizabeth said, 'Stories?' But she was thinking, it's happening; he really is one of them trying to come in from the cold. But he's coming to me, and I don't know what to do with him. I can't even call for help because the telephone is tapped.

'Yes,' he said, 'I want to make a bargain with you. I want immunity, a new name, protection. In return I'll give you information about some people I know, testify in trials, the works.'

'That all takes time,' said Elizabeth. 'And we hardly ever do it. How do we know your information and testimony are worth it?'

The man sighed. 'If what I know wasn't enough to do them some damage, why would I want protection bad enough to come here?'

It hadn't occurred to her before, but it sounded true. If a man was willing to get involved at all . . . but she decided not to pursue it now, while she was still disoriented from sleep. 'What's your name? Who are you?'

'I'm Dominic Palermo.' He shrugged. 'I don't imagine you know who I am. I was Ferraro's partner.' He corrected himself. 'Friend and partner.'

Elizabeth understood. 'So you're afraid they'll get you too. The way they got him in the gift shop. And that's why you came here, now. You didn't want them to know.'

He nodded and smiled, then seemed to hesitate. 'I came to you to turn myself in.'

'All right,' she said, 'the problem is, I don't know when they'll be able to get the Attorney General to agree to your terms. When do you plan to actually come in for good?'

'For Christ's sake,' he said, 'I'm standing in front of you. I'm here. Now.'

'But I thought you had conditions,' said Elizabeth. 'A bargain.' She didn't understand.

'That's only for what I tell you,' he said. 'Not for going in as a material witness.'

'You don't seem to understand, Mr. Palermo,' said Elizabeth. 'They won't consider you a witness unless you tell them something. You can't sit in a cell and bargain.'

'I'll chance it,' he said. 'Meantime I'll be alive.'

She thought about it. 'All right. What we've got to do is get you over to the Bureau. You know you would have been smarter to go straight into the FBI office, don't you? What if somebody saw you come in here?'

'No,' he said. 'I'm not turning myself in to them. It's to you. The Justice Department, not the FBI. Remember that, it's part of the bargain.'

'But it's exactly the same thing. The FBI is part of the Justice Department. We have to go there.'

'I won't,' said Palermo. 'Look, honey. You don't seem to know how to do this, so I'll help you out. We'll help each other out. Whoever brings in somebody like me is going to look terrific – you'll get promotions, bonuses, whatever you people give each other. And your organization has control of the information. Like your boss can say to somebody – the police commissioner in New York, maybe – "I know who's running heroin in at Kennedy Airport. What have you got for me?" So believe me, it's to your advantage to hold onto me. Knowledge is the most valuable thing in the world.'

She ignored the argument and decided to ground herself in facts. 'But the Justice Department doesn't have field offices like the FBI. Most of them are just offices where lawyers work on federal cases, and it's usually civil cases at that. There's no place to put a material witness, and nobody trained for that sort of work.'

'Look,' he said, 'I'm willing to talk, but you've got to go a little way on this too. I picked the Justice Department because they give the best terms, for one thing. For another, it's the highest.'

'Highest?'

'Yeah. If I have a deal with Justice, then five years from now the sheriff of Herkimer County can't decide he wants me for double parking.'

She had to admit to herself he was smart. His idea of the way jurisdictions worked was bizarre, but he was right about the way they'd work for him. 'All right,' she said, 'I can't give you any guarantees about what you're asking for. I can't even tell you if Justice will take you as a material witness. But I have to talk to my superior on this.'

'Don't use that phone,' he said. 'It may be tapped.'

She picked up the telephone and dialed Brayer. When he answered she said, 'John, come to my room right away,' and hung up.

'I'm not happy about that,' said Palermo. 'I'll go along with it because I'm stuck with it, at four thirty in the morning and all that, but I want you to know I'm not a happy man.'

'What's wrong now?' said Elizabeth. She sat on the bed, keeping the gun trained on an imaginary spot a foot to the left of Palermo's chest. She could see he was telling the truth – he wasn't a happy man – but she wasn't sure if she wanted him to be. She wasn't sure what was supposed to happen now, but if he was unhappy she must be in control.

Palermo began to pace back and forth in front of the door. 'Don't you people ever do anything on your own?' he asked. 'There's always got to be a Mr. Brayer or Mr. Farquhar or some damn thing. No wonder none of you can find your own ass with both hands. You're taking a lot of chances with my safety.'

Elizabeth said nothing, just let him walk back and forth, muttering to himself. Maybe Brayer could convince him to go in to the FBI office downtown – or better still, maybe Brayer and a pair of armed field agents would take him there.

She heard the knock on the door and stood up. Palermo was visibly uncomfortable now. She could see a thin film of sweat was beginning to appear on his fat cheeks. He said, 'Let me fling it open and stand behind. If it's anybody but your Brayer, blow his ass away.'

Elizabeth ignored him. 'Who is it?' she said.

'John, Elizabeth. Open up.'

When she opened the door he slipped in and locked it behind him. 'So. Who's this?' he said.

'John, this is Mr. Palermo. Dominic Palermo. He wants to turn himself in as a material witness on the FGE thing.'

'And a hell of a lot more,' Palermo volunteered. 'But I want protection. Immunity, resettlement, the works.'

'Why did you come to Miss Waring?' asked Brayer.

'I heard she was working on some things I know about,' said Palermo.

'Heard?' said Brayer. 'From whom?'

'I just heard, that's all. So what's the deal? Can you get me what I want?'

Brayer looked at him, then at Elizabeth, then back at him. He said, 'That depends. If what you know is worthwhile and you're cooperative, and you tell us the truth, I might – just might – be able to arrange something like that. But a lot of people I don't have the authority to speak for would have to agree to it.'

Palermo shook his head and stared at the carpet. 'Christ,' he said. 'Another one. So you've got to call somebody too. And then he's got to call somebody.'

'That's about the size of it,' said Brayer, staring hard at the fat little man. 'So take it or leave it.'

Palermo looked at him in desperation. 'What can you guarantee? Not what you might do if the President feels like it and the Attorney General's new shoes don't pinch his toes and there's enough humidity. Look, I'm no rummy. I got things you'd like to hear.'

Brayer shrugged. 'You came here because you think you've got something to sell. I can probably keep you alive, for one thing, and you wouldn't be here if you had the same offer from anyone else. So I'd say that's high bid.'

Palermo sat down on the bed with his shoulders hunched and said nothing. Brayer turned to Elizabeth and drew her to the other side of the room. At first she hesitated, but Brayer said, 'You don't have to watch him. What's he going to do to us?'

When they were out of earshot he whispered, 'What's he told you so far?'

Elizabeth said, 'He's a partner of Ferraro, the man they killed in the hotel gift shop, and he's afraid somebody's going to get him too. He's very particular about who protects him. He's set on the Justice Department. Not the police or even the FBI.'

300

'Anything else? What about FGE?'

'Just that. The initials. But he must know something, or he wouldn't be here.' She tried to remember the logic of it. 'He wouldn't need protection unless—'

Brayer nodded and said, 'Probably not. But if a war is on, it's hard to tell. He might be nothing. We can't take the chance, of course. The question is, how do we make the best use of him?' Brayer looked over at Palermo, who was sitting on the edge of the bed with his arms folded, staring at the floor.

'Why don't we get some guards and take him to the Bureau office?' said Elizabeth. 'We could even call them to come get him. Then we could start making arrangements with Washington for the bargain.'

Brayer's eyes narrowed. 'You know, he may be right about the FBI. For one thing, we've got him and nobody knows it. If we take him to the Bureau headquarters openly, we lose the best part of him. If we don't all his pals will know is that he dropped out of sight. See what I mean?'

Elizabeth nodded. 'Sure, but how do we do it? We can't keep him here.'

Brayer said, 'What I'd like to do is get him to Washington, but I don't think we could do that very easily without either being spotted in an airport or driving, and that'd be worse. It would take a week before we got a word out of him. No, we've got to get him somewhere safe and quiet by morning.'

'But where?' said Elizabeth. 'We don't even have a field office in Las Vegas, and anyway—'

'No,' said Brayer. 'But how about the capital? Carson City. We've got one there, and it's within driving distance. Besides, it would convince him we're going to meet him halfway on his bargain. Go get dressed.'

Elizabeth had a sick feeling. 'We're not going to do it ourselves, are we, John?'

'What else can we do?' he asked. 'If we start collecting agents here at quarter to five in the morning we might as well put an ad in the paper. In fact, if he's as valuable as he claims, he might even get killed.'

Elizabeth went to the closet and began collecting her clothes. Palermo looked up and said, 'So. You must have made a decision. What is it?'

Brayer answered, 'We're going to do what you want, at least as long as you're cooperative. We're going to take you to the Justice Department's office in Carson City for now. If we can get you that far without anybody noticing, we can fly you to Washington later.'

'Oh,' said Palermo, 'I get it. If I tell you enough in Carson City you're a hero and I get to go to Washington so you can show me off. If I don't, you don't have anything to show your boss, so you chuck me out.'

Brayer said, 'Could be. That's the chance you have to take. But don't worry. As you said, you've got things we want to hear. You're no rummy.'

'That's right,' said Palermo, his big, dark eyes glaring up at Brayer out of his broad face. 'I've got nothing to worry about.'

Elizabeth dressed quickly in the bathroom. Of course John was right. If they could get Palermo out of sight where he could be interrogated before anyone knew he was missing, it might be just the break they'd been waiting for. Whatever he knew would stay fresh as long as his bosses didn't know he was talking. As soon as they knew, things would begin to change, evidence would evaporate; they'd be raiding empty buildings and trying to arrest people who had already left the country.

She caught sight of herself in the mirror and shuddered. She must have been sleeping on her face; her eyes were puffy and her skin a sickly pale color she couldn't remember seeing on anyone who wasn't ill. A little makeup helped, but not enough, she thought. And if Brayer saw she'd taken the extra seconds to apply it – but that was something he'd have to let her decide. If he wanted her to be inconspicuous he'd have to wait.

When she came back to the bedroom, Brayer handed her a set of keys. 'Take the rented car,' he said. 'It's parked almost at the side door by the casino.'

'Aren't you going?' said Elizabeth.

'No. I've got to make the arrangements from here. And it's less likely to attract attention, just the two of you.'

She was about to argue, but she stopped herself. She couldn't say she didn't want to go alone because Palermo gave her the creeps. He wasn't dangerous; she was his best hope of living the year out. And she couldn't ignore the fact that Brayer was doing her a favor, giving her a chance for a major coup.

At the car Palermo said, 'I'll drive.' When she hesitated he said, 'Look, I know the way to Carson City. You don't even know the way out of town.' It wasn't until he had established himself in the driver's seat that he added, 'Besides, my nerves are shot already.'

She resented it silently. In a way it was comforting.

It seemed right that he should be thoroughly unpleasant.

He drove down a network of back streets. When he emerged on the highway she was surprised, but refused to be impressed. After all, he lived here. And this was the last driving he'd do for some time, she reminded herself.

Suddenly he said, 'You don't care much for me, do you?' The formality of it seemed incongruous.

She was caught off-balance and only managed, 'I don't know you.'

He said, 'I know. I'm a stool pigeon. Nobody likes a stool pigeon, even if it's a stool pigeon who gets them a promotion. I don't blame you. But I want you to know, I wouldn't have done it if they hadn't left me out here on a limb.'

'No, I suppose not,' said Elizabeth. She wondered how far away Carson City was. The world was supernaturally dark. She imagined desert on all sides, but could see nothing but the road.

'Damn right,' said Palermo. 'When Old Granddad was killed—'

'Old Granddad?'

'Castiglione. When he was killed they said they'd protect me. Told Ferraro that too. They protected the shit out of him, didn't they? Then I find out they've pulled out all the soldiers they had for some important project Carl Bala had on his mind. Nicky Palermo can go fuck himself. Well, we'll see.'

'So you feel betrayed,' said Elizabeth.

'Betrayed?' said Palermo. He drove in silence, staring off into the darkness. 'Yeah, I guess that's the word for it. For years it was Nicky, you're terrific,

Nicky you're a real friend, Nicky, I owe you. All of a sudden the roof collapses and what do I hear? Who's Nicky Palermo?'

'What do you mean, the roof collapses?'

'Lady,' said Palermo, 'I don't know what you people do all day, but it must not be much. You must know about Castiglione, right? It was in all the papers, for Christ's sake.'

Elizabeth said, 'Of course.'

'Well, he was the old consigliere. He kept the young bulls in line – Carl Bala, Toscanzio, Damon, Lupo, DeLeone, all of them.'

'But I thought he was retired.'

'He was, in a way. He had everything he wanted, so he wasn't interested in getting more. What he was interested in, I guess, was keeping the world quiet so he could hold on to it.'

'But if he was retired, how could he do that? He didn't have any soldiers, did he?'

Palermo chuckled. 'Neither does the Pope, honey. Or the head of the United Nations. When he made a decision it stuck. If it needed to be enforced, he'd get word to all the families and they'd do it. The smaller, weaker ones would be afraid the bigger ones would eat them up. The big guys like Toscanzio and Bala and Damon weren't interested in having twenty families come together against them. Besides, they couldn't trust each other. Castiglione they could trust. He didn't want anything but peace and quiet.'

'So who wanted him dead?' asked Elizabeth.

Palermo drove on, shaking his head. 'Figure it out for yourself, like I did. Who stood to gain anything? The little guys like Bellino or Lupo? Hell, they only existed because Castiglione kept the big fish off them. They're all scared shitless. It had to be somebody who was big enough to think he could step in and take over, gobble the small operations up.'

'Then you think it was Toscanzio or Bala who did it. Or maybe Damon.'

'No, I know who did it,' he said. 'There was supposed to be a meeting this week. Castiglione had called it. The only reason I knew was because it affected me in a way, or would have. I'd dealt with FGE a few times, and Castiglione wanted to talk about FGE.'

'Why?'

'He didn't like it. It was practically in his backyard, and it had been used for some things he hadn't agreed to. Things that might bring a lot of weight down on him.'

Elizabeth detected the slight shift in his tone. They were nearing some point he wasn't going to talk about: something he was planning to sell. She knew she had to steer him away from it or he'd stop talking entirely. She said, 'So they killed him rather than give it up, and killed Ferraro and Orloff and would have killed you.' He didn't react, so she took a stab in the dark. She had to get him back on the subject he was most interested in, himself. 'Because you killed Senator Claremont and that man in California.'

'The hell I did,' said Palermo. 'For Christ's sake, look at me. I weigh two thirty and I'm five eight. I'm over fifty years old. For the last twenty years I've cleared over two hundred thousand a year. Do I look like somebody who takes on wet jobs? Hell, they hired somebody to do that. A specialist.'

'Who hired him?'

Palermo laughed. 'I'm not going to tell you that,' he said. 'At least not now. Maybe later when I see what arrangements your boss made in Carson City.'

'But these are the people who are trying to kill you,' said Elizabeth. 'And if you don't get them, they'll get you.' She had stumbled into the spot he was protecting; all she could do now was pursue it until he refused to go on.

'No,' said Palermo, 'what they did was kill Castiglione and leave me alone in the open when the war started. They didn't warn me, they didn't protect me. Nothing. It was the other families who killed Ferraro and would have killed me.'

'Aren't you afraid?' said Elizabeth. 'When they know you've come to us, won't they send this specialist after you?'

'They might, if you let them know,' said Palermo.

'But we don't know what to do about a professional like that,' said Elizabeth. 'Look at all the assassinations. We can't protect you from that kind of killer unless we know who he is, or at least what to look for.'

Palermo shook his head, solemnly. He said, 'Jesus, you must think I'm stupid, pulling that on me. The specialist? Shit, him I'd give you for free if I could. Problem is, I can't. I never saw him, and I don't even know his name. When they talked about him they just called him "the butcher's boy." '

'Nice name,' said Elizabeth.

'Yeah,' said Palermo. 'Isn't it?'

307

TWENTY-EIGHT

What he was most worried about was time. Las Vegas was probably the most difficult place in the world to hide in. It was full of people who were in the business of noticing every new face and searching it for the means of extracting a profit: greed, lust, gluttony, stupidity. Plenty of them had seen him before, and whoever noticed him first would feel fortunate – they didn't have to cajole or deceive him or cater to his sexual appetite. All they had to do was mention that he was there. The only things in his favor were the huge number of newcomers that arrived each day – tens of thousands of them – and the fact that he wouldn't be expected.

Even taken together, the two didn't represent much of an edge, he thought. He'd have to find a way to reduce the chance of his being spotted to practically nil. He'd have to stay away from the big hotels. No, any hotel, he decided. There was no way to predict who really owned what, and who was a friend of whom. The airport and the bus station and the restaurants were out too. It would have to be done by a quick visit to town in a single night, and then more forays later if they seemed productive. He had to keep the time he was visible to a minimum.

He wished there were some other way. If only he'd

been more careless he'd know more, he thought. That was the irony of it. He'd always avoided personal connections with his clients. He never saw them more than once if he could help it, and never let them know where he lived. His post office box was all they'd known about him, and often he'd known even less about them. His lack of curiosity had been a form of protection. He let the middlemen, the brokers like Orloff, accept the danger of knowing. But now he wished he'd been curious, just this once.

Maureen had been helpful, he thought. Why wouldn't she be? She'd made fifty thousand dollars in less than a week. She couldn't have carried all that hardware on an airplane anyway. But it all helped, everything would help now that was done right. Weapons that couldn't be traced and hadn't turned up in a ballistics report would contribute something to his peace of mind, if nothing else. He knew the car was more important. There was no chance anyone would make a connection between him and a used car bought for cash by a single woman who'd just moved to Illinois to take a job in the local school system. The fact that in the fifteen-minute drive between the dealer's lot and the Illinois Department of Motor Vehicles the name A. Blake on the ownership papers had been changed to Mr. A. Blake would mean nothing to anyone.

He liked driving at night. He was a little disappointed when the sky began to acquire the blue luminescence that meant dawn would break soon. It was as though the sun were in a race with him, and now it was just behind him. In an hour it would catch up, and an hour after that it would be daylight in Las Vegas. He'd still be a day away.

It was getting light now, and Elizabeth could see the pink, craggy mountains jutting abruptly around the flat, empty basin that seemed to contain nothing but the road and billboards. She hadn't noticed when the change had come. She'd gotten used to the advertisements for Las Vegas, and then she'd looked again and they were all for Reno and Lake Tahoe. The pictures were the same – a gigantic girl decorated with a few feathers and rhinestones, her impossibly long legs and ripe breasts taking more space than the suggestion of an opulent building behind her – but the location was different. They had left the gravitational field surrounding Las Vegas, and entered the one that pulled cars into the complex in the north. They had passed some invisible boundary in the darkness.

She knew she should be feeling elated. Whatever value the man beside her turned out to be in court, he was a real asset already. At this moment she knew more than anyone about what was happening, and he hadn't even been interrogated yet. And what was more gratifying was that he'd confirmed most of the theories she and Brayer had developed. There was a war on between the families, and the key to it was Fieldston Growth Enterprises. One of the capos had even killed Castiglione over it. And Palermo knew who it was and might even be able to convince a jury. But almost as important for Elizabeth was that he knew what was going on at FGE. It didn't matter anymore that she'd let the company records slip away. She was bringing in something better, a man who could tell them anything the papers would have revealed, and more. Maybe she'd feel better after she'd eaten and slept.

Right now she felt a headache preparing to strike as soon as the sun rose high enough to pierce through the side window into her eyes. It had been over ten days since she'd begun shuttling around the country, and she'd gotten used to being exhausted. But the strain on her nerves had culminated in the arrival of Palermo in the middle of the night. And there was Palermo himself. She knew that was part of it. He was the break they'd been needing but hadn't dared hope would ever appear. He'd be more thoroughly protected than a visiting head of state, then resettled and watched and pampered for the rest of his life. In a way he was an admission of the hopelessness of it all. The Justice Department was just a better patron this week than whoever he'd been working for last week. And none of it seemed to change anything, really, she thought: if they weren't more afraid of each other than they were of the Justice Department, we wouldn't even have this man. And he's getting a free ride. The deal of a lifetime.

She felt the headache beginning to assert itself, and decided to think about something else. She was doing her job, and that was all anyone could do. There was another billboard. This time the girl was naked except for two pasties shaped like stars and a pair of net panty hose with a star on the crotch. It was the star on the crotch that made it ludicrous, she decided. Why couldn't the girl just be naked?

Palermo put on a pair of sunglasses. He was obviously prepared for the trip. There was probably a toothbrush in his coat pocket too. She turned away to

311

watch for the next billboard. The drive was beginning to seem impossibly long. All of the proportions in the west were wrong. You could drive for hours and see nothing but empty, harsh, hot land populated only by smiling giantesses in their feathers and sequins.

'Oh, shit,' said Palermo. 'Oh, shit,' he repeated.

'What's wrong?' said Elizabeth.

'Shit, shit, shit,' he said in rising cadence. He had begun to accelerate rapidly, looking anxiously from the road to the rearview mirror and back. 'Somebody's following us.'

'Are you sure?'

He was still accelerating, his head bobbing frequently to look in the mirror. Elizabeth turned to see the car herself. In the distance behind them was a car, still tiny, but definitely gaining on them.

'They know,' he said pitifully. 'Who cares how?' She could see he was terrified. He had the gas pedal to the floor now, the car straddling the broken white line in the pavement. Elizabeth looked behind again. The car was still gaining. It looked from the front like a Cadillac or maybe a Lincoln or a big Chrysler. She couldn't tell the difference. But it must be going at least ninety, steadily gulping up the distance that separated them from it. The white line in the road was just a blurred ribbon that snapped and quivered in front of her. She didn't dare look at the speedometer but she knew they must be going about as fast as their car could go. Behind them, the other car was still approaching. She took the gun out of her purse and checked the load.

'Shoot the bastards,' said Palermo. 'Now, before they get close.'

312

'But we don't know who it is,' said Elizabeth.

'Jesus Christ, who do you think it is?' shouted Palermo. 'They're going over a hundred. Shoot the bastards!'

The car was close now. Elizabeth could see it was a Cadillac. The dark green hood had an immaculate gleam that threw the sunlight back into the sky. It was drawing up behind now. There were two men in the front seat. She knew that at this speed all she'd have to do was hit the car. A punctured radiator or a blown-out windshield would stop them – maybe kill them. But what if it wasn't what Palermo said? What if it was just two morons opening up a big new car on a deserted highway? She said, 'No. Wait a minute.'

Palermo just repeated, 'Shoot them! Shoot them!' as Elizabeth watched the big car pull up behind. The car honked twice, and then the driver leaned on the horn.

Palermo had subsided into a muttered litany: 'Shit, shit, shit. Shit, shit, shit.'

Elizabeth watched the two men. If one of them pulled out a gun, or even looked as though he were about to she knew she'd have to shoot. The car pulled abreast. Palermo yelled, 'Hold on!' and stepped on the brake. Elizabeth saw the Cadillac flash past as her right shoulder hit the dashboard.

Palermo was gasping, slowing the car as the Cadillac diminished into the distance. Elizabeth managed to regain her balance, but only with difficulty. Palermo pulled to the side of the road and stopped.

The world sounded strangely quiet. Elizabeth watched as Palermo opened the door and walked out around to the back of the car. Her heart was pounding and her lungs didn't seem to be able to take in enough

313

air. Then she heard it. She didn't have to look. Behind the car Palermo was throwing up.

When he came back to the car she didn't say anything to him. He sat quietly while she drove. When she saw the little outpost a few miles down the road she still didn't say anything to him, just pulled off the highway and stopped at the gas pump. Palermo climbed out of the car and disappeared into the men's room.

The station attendant was young, probably just out of high school. His long blond hair was still wet from his morning shower, and his blue work shirt was crisp and clean. He yawned as he topped off the tank. The station must have opened at seven, she thought. Probably there wasn't much business out here at seven. You'd have to leave home at five to get here from anywhere.

She paid the boy and looked for Palermo. She almost felt sorry for him. No doubt he was in the men's room, white and shaking, his stomach turning itself inside out. She wasn't feeling too great herself. She parked the car away from the pump and went to the ladies' room. It was too late to prevent the headache, but aspirin might make it bearable until Carson City.

When Elizabeth returned she expected to see Palermo sitting in the car, most likely in the driver's seat. He wasn't. She got into the car to wait, a little angry. The longer he took, the longer it would be before she turned him over to the section chief in Carson City and went somewhere to sleep.

She wasn't particularly surprised when the green Cadillac pulled around the building and onto the highway. It was perfect that they should go that fast, only to stop in that godforsaken coffee shop. They'd probably make up the time by covering the next hundred miles in less than an hour. She watched them accelerate rapidly, diminishing into the distance at a speed she didn't feel able to estimate. Idiots.

Palermo. What was keeping him? This is what men are supposed to be built for, she thought. Big feats of strength and speed in a momentary emergency. Quick action, the massive infusion of adrenaline, and then a long period of repose. Not like women, built to last, the damned extra layer of fat for heat and cold and hunger, the nervous system tougher to stand pain. Babies.

Elizabeth looked at her watch. It was almost seven thirty. She remembered what he'd looked like when he left the car – pale skin, gasping for breath, his heart probably racing – oh God, his heart. That would be just about right. A heart attack in this place, fifty miles from the nearest doctor, probably. And nothing to do about it. Coffee and doughnuts. Air in your tires, sir? Better let me check your oil.

She got out of the car. The sun was warming the still air already. She walked to the gas station, past the boy, who was in the garage staring upward in consternation at the underside of a car on the hydraulic lift. She knocked lightly on the men's room door, listening as much for the approach of another man as for Palermo's answer. She heard nothing, so she tried again, this time louder. There was something absurd about it – no, everything about it was absurd. If she'd been a man she could have gone right in, or even gone with him in the first place. Maybe she should have anyway.

At this hour, in this place what difference did it make? But he wasn't really a prisoner. After the third knock she tried the doorknob. It was locked.

At the garage she said to the boy, 'I wonder if you could do me a favor? The man with me went into the men's room. I'm afraid he may be sick. Will you go in and check on him?'

The boy looked at her with sullen disapproval, then stared back up at the undercarriage of the car. It must be his, she decided. Then he said, 'How long has he been in there?'

She said, 'A half hour.'

The boy shrugged. 'Okay.' She followed him to the restrooms, and waited while he unlocked the door and sidestepped in, as though it were a tenet of his faith to protect the privacy of all men from the intruding gaze of the insistent woman.

From inside she heard the sound of his voice, 'Agh!' In a second he was back out, gaping at her in horror. He said to her, 'We've got to call a doctor,' and ran around the building toward the office.

Elizabeth rushed into the men's room. She could see Palermo's feet under the door of the stall, placed as though he were sitting on the toilet. But on the floor around them was a pool of blood. She slowly pushed the door open and looked at him. He was sitting there fully dressed, with his head hanging down on his chest as though he were engaged in some profound meditation. She didn't touch him, and didn't look more closely. She let go of the door and walked outside into the air. Then she remembered the boy. She knew she should go tell him to change the call. Anybody could see from Palermo's shirt what they'd done to his throat. The shirt had once been white. But there wasn't any hurry, really. She couldn't foresee any reason to hurry again. And out here the doctor probably doubled as the coroner anyway. The police would know. 47507Y. A blue license plate. Nevada.

TWENTY-NINE

It was just midnight when the sky above the black horizon began to glow pink, as though somewhere beyond this dark emptiness a city were burning. He was still twenty miles out when beneath the glow the impossible lights surfaced in a shimmering smear of white and blue and yellow and red.

His instincts resisted as the jumping, wavering apparition rose over the lip of the earth and began to resolve itself into the straight lines of bright streets and monolithic buildings bathed in color. He felt a strong urge to stay out here in the dark, empty desert, but he had to penetrate that eye of light. He had to have the name. Without it he could never be safe, because that man wanted him dead. The man wasn't to be distracted or fooled or misled by feints and sudden shifts because he wasn't even paying attention. He had signified the wish, and he was someone the others knew had the power to reward and punish at will, so it would remain a standing priority in a thousand minds until it was accomplished. That meant the name had to belong to one of fifteen or twenty men. That wasn't many, but each of them was like a celebrity or a petty monarch surrounded by retainers and sycophants and guards. There was no way to reach all of them, and each wrong guess would strengthen the one who wanted him dead. He had to have the name.

He avoided the exit ramp that led onto the Strip and its nearest neighbor. He took the third exit and moved up Flamingo Road across the Strip toward the complex of lesser streets beyond the lights. He had few choices. Little Norman knew, but there was no way to make him reveal the name. He had existed far too long by working for everyone and appearing to know nothing about anyone. If he caught Little Norman alone the best he could hope for was to kill him. Little Norman was a professional. Orloff had known the name. Orloff was dead, but there was still Orloff's office, the place where they'd killed him. Fieldston Growth Enterprises.

He drove around the neighborhood, carefully covering the streets for three blocks on each side. If there were a competent team of watchers in the vicinity, they would have cars at the most likely points of access to the major highways, out of sight of the building itself. There might even be a building nearby with a dim light in an upper window that faced away from FGE.

When he had satisfied himself that there were no watchers he drove up the street toward FGE. The street was quiet. All of the buildings in the area were closed, their darkened windows reflecting only the lights of his car as he passed. He parked on the street behind, and set off on foot toward FGE. He carried Maureen's pistol with the silencer in his coat pocket. He hoped that a small building like FGE that consisted only of offices would just have a burglar alarm. If the place contained the kind of information he needed, there would be no night watchman – they wouldn't want to seem excessively worried about security.

He approached the building from the rear, prepared to look for the most likely window. But there were lights on inside. Damn, he thought. A watchman. He'd have to find the watchman first. And it would be nothing like he wanted, a quiet visit that nobody knew had ever taken place. Whatever Orloff had that would give him the name would be hidden in a place where only Orloff could find it. Nobody would have missed it. But now there would be a dead watchman.

He started to make a circuit of the building, looking for the window that would give him the best view of the watchman. At the parking lot he stopped. There were two cars there, parked side by side. He approached the cars, and looked inside the first one. It had to belong to the security guard service, he thought. It had a radio under the dashboard, just like the ones the police used. He moved to the other car. Small letters of a decal on the trunk said, 'This car carries only bookkeeping material.' He thought for a moment. The first car had to be the watchman. What was the other? He moved to the building and looked in the window.

Inside, there were three men in shirtsleeves, working at desks. One seemed to be scanning files and putting folders in a cardboard box and the others were going through the drawers of the desks. All three were wearing guns in shoulder holsters. He moved away from the lighted window and returned to the cars. This time he looked at the license plates. They were both white and said *U.S. Government*. He kept walking.

He kept himself in the shadows as he moved toward

his car. He needed time to think. They had to be the FBI. Of course. Whenever there was a pretext, some possibility that one of these killings involved the crossing of state lines, the FBI moved in. But whatever they'd been doing in that office, it wasn't investigating Orloff's shooting. And the decal on the car had said something about bookkeeping. They were going through the files. What did they know?

He felt a sudden wave of panic, a surge of adrenaline. But the fear cleared his mind and subsided. No, it was all right. What Orloff had known about him was a post office box number. There would be a reference to him somewhere, but it would do him no harm. But the rest of it was disturbing. They knew that FGE was a blind. He hadn't counted on that. So now they were as likely to find the name as he was. But they were still looking, working through the night. And they were reading business files. Bookkeeping material, the car had said.

He smiled. There was hope. They were looking for the name, but they didn't know Orloff. They might figure out that Orloff was moving money, and they might find out where some of it went. Unless they found Orloff's private ledger they wouldn't find out where it came from. Not the name. They were looking at whatever Orloff had prepared to throw off the auditors and the tax men, not what he'd prepared to keep track of the real transactions. Because there had to be a ledger: Orloff wouldn't have taken the chance that he'd make a mistake. They were looking in desk drawers and filing cabinets, not tapping floors and walls for hollow places. They'd walk out with their files and maybe they'd figure it out eventually. But by then he might have the name, and they'd be wasting their time.

He was concentrating now. FBI men in Orloff's office. They didn't know what they were looking for. Maybe they didn't even know yet what Orloff was. If they didn't, would they have searched his house? He'd never been to Orloff's house although he assumed there must be one. It had never occurred to him to wonder where Orloff lived until he'd hired the Cruiser to watch him. He had little interest in the brokers and middlemen. He knew and accepted the fact that he wasn't the sort of man they'd want to spend time with, even if it hadn't been dangerous. And if Orloff had invited him there he would have been insulted. He did the work and took the money, but he would have resented any presumption that he cared who gave it to him, or took any interest in the problems and personalities that provided him with a market for his services. Orloff had been a pig. He had noted it, as he noted whatever came within the range of his consciousness, because it might present a problem or a solution, but it evoked no emotional response. But now Orloff was important to him because Orloff had known the name.

He contemplated Orloff as he searched for the address in the telephone book. Orloff had been greedy. So the house would be large and opulent. He memorized the address and returned to the car. But Orloff had been nervous and frightened most of the time, his greed conflicting with his natural cowardice to keep his fat body sweating beneath the custom-made silk shirts in fits of excitement and terror. So the house would be difficult to break into, no doubt protected electronically from whatever phantoms Orloff's brain conjured up when it contemplated the possibilities of the night outside the windows. That part presented no problem, because Orloff was dead, and unless he had a family still living there, there would be no one to turn on the equipment.

When he neared Orloff's house, he followed the same procedure he'd used at FGE. He circled the block searching for signs that the house might be under surveillance. He saw nothing that was questionable, so he drove past the house. There were no cars at all in the driveway. Orloff's car had probably been impounded by the police in the investigation, he thought. Maybe because it caught some of the slugs from the shotgun, although there must have been more than enough in Orloff's body for any practical purpose.

He saw no lights in the windows. It was the sort of house he'd imagined. The low, T-shaped structure gave an impression of careless, sprawling expanse, the two wings sheltering gardens of close-cropped yew and juniper, and yucca. Another eye would not have noticed that anyone approaching either of the two doors in the wings could be observed from behind through opposite windows in what must be the same room.

He parked the car around the corner and walked to the house. The windows were all tightly latched and bolted, so he contented himself for the moment with examining them to see if he could discern the contact wires or the glow of an electric eye that would show him how to disengage the burglar alarms. He peered through each of the windows, seeing only the dark shapes of the furniture. It took some searching, but at the rear of the house behind a fan-shaped shrub he found the electric meter. He read the meter and sat down and waited patiently for fifteen minutes, then read it again. It was as he'd hoped. The police had either notified the electric company to turn off the power or simply gone through the house in their methodical, unthinking way and turned everything off. In any case, nothing was drawing electricity. Whatever alarm systems Orloff had installed were so much dead metal.

He thought about the house. Probably one of the doors would be easiest, and it would be less likely to show signs of his entry than the windows. He took another look at the electric meter and froze. The meter wheel was moving. Something had been turned on. His mind raced – at two thirty in the morning what could it be? The alarm system would take steady continuous power. A light? No. At this hour the person would have to have been sleeping in the house and awakened. He'd been here over twenty minutes and they'd have to have sat in the dark at least that long. Then he remembered. Of course, the refrigerator. It was the only thing that turned itself on and off. He was safe.

He went to the side door and used a credit card to depress the door latch and let himself in. The door had deadbolts and chains, he noticed, but you had to be inside the house to use them. Orloff would have hated that, he thought, but the alarms would have consoled him. Now that he was inside he could see the two black boxes of the electric eyes, their sensors turned off.

He listened for the refrigerator. He tried to remember where the kitchen window was. He had a mental image of the house plan, and followed it to the kitchen. The refrigerator was unusually quiet – he couldn't hear it at all. He felt for the handle, turning his head away in preparation for the glare of the light. He didn't want to destroy his night vision. There was no light, and in the darkness he smelled the unmistakable odor of rotten food. He closed the door silently and thought. Someone was in this house.

He crouched low and remained motionless. Superiority in the darkness was largely a matter of concentration and patience. 'Get yourself a cat, like this one, and watch it,' Eddie had said. 'A cat will sit for an hour staring at whatever it's after and listening to it. As soon as the thing forgets what a cat is, the cat is on him, so fast you can hardly believe it. Forget all that jungle warfare shit they taught you in the service. You already know how to look like a fucking palm tree. A cat'll teach you how to look like a shadow, part of the house, a pile of garbage.'

He waited until his watch told him it had been five minutes. If he'd been heard by whoever was in the house, they'd either discounted the sound or forgotten it. It was a matter of shaping time to dimensions that didn't fit the normal sense of pace. If they heard a sound they'd listen for a few seconds to hear another. If they didn't, they'd stop listening.

He moved out into the living room, keeping low and close to the wall. When he reached the first chair he settled down again to wait, crouching beside it in the darkness, listening. Whoever was in the house had been confident enough to turn on a light. That meant he had the only advantage he would need. Now that his night vision was at its best he could see that the living room was large – fifty by twenty-five feet, he estimated. It wasn't a room that Orloff would spend much time in. It was designed for receiving guests in a fashion that would appeal to Orloff's vanity – small tables and lots of chairs, but mostly arranged around the walls, without a focal point. And the shapes of the furniture weren't the sort of thing Orloff would feel comfortable in – too little padding. The furniture would be different in the room he was searching for: thick and leathery, and with seats that wouldn't cramp Orloff's fat ass. But there would be time for that after he'd found the man in the house. He had as much time as he needed.

He decided to move again. Past the living room was a hallway leading to what must be bedrooms and bathrooms. That was where he'd find the room he wanted. Patiently he began to move himself by inches toward his goal, keeping himself low and close to the wall. His mind was cleared now of all thought except thoughts of sight and sound.

Years ago he'd done all of his thinking about what his body was now doing. Eddie had been wrong about cats – he'd learned that from Eddie's cat in the butcher shop. It wasn't that they shaped their bodies to imitate something else. All they did was make sure they didn't look like a cat. It was the eye of the prey that formulated the disguise. The instant that it would take the man he was stalking to decide that the shape in the hallway wasn't a chair, wasn't a shadow, was maybe a man, would be all the time he needed. That instant was the predator's moment, the cat's time.

At the first turning of the hallway he heard the man moving about in the darkness. He turned his head slowly from side to side to locate the exact point the sound was coming from. It was off to the left. It was then that the thin sheet of light shot out from under the closed door.

He stationed himself beside the door and listened. There was a sound of rustling papers, then a drawer opening, then a clicking noise. He listened, straining to sense the direction of movement, while someone walked from one end of the room to the other. There was another rustling, and then his ears detected the sound he was waiting for. The footsteps began to move away from the door. He snatched the door open and stepped into the room, his gun pointed at the sound.

A man whirled to face him, his expression the terrible mixture of animal and human that the instant of terror brought on him. A gurgling sound escaped from the taut muscles of his throat, and he dropped a briefcase on the floor. The instant passed, and the man said, 'What?' Then the man said, as though correcting himself, 'What are you?' His face betrayed the fact that he sensed that the question wasn't right. He tried 'What do you want?'

He studied the man. He was about fifty years old, wearing a charcoal gray suit. Not a burglar. Police? He said, 'Throw me your wallet and turn around.'

The man seemed to be relieved. He reached into his coat and pulled out a long, thin black wallet, and tossed it toward him, then turned his face to the window.

He didn't bother to catch it. That would only give the man a chance to do something he'd seen on television. He had only asked for it to see if the man had a shoulder holster on or handcuffs, and there were none. He kicked open the wallet. There was no badge.

Keeping his eyes on the man, he said, 'What's your name?'

The man said, 'Please, take the wallet. There's over a thousand dollars in it.'

He repeated, 'What's your name?'

The man said, 'Edgar Fieldston.'

Fieldston. Of course. There would be a Fieldston. An Edgar or a Ronald or a Howard or a Marshall. He knelt down and opened the wallet. It was true. Edgar R. Fieldston. A driver's license, credit cards, a Blue Cross–Blue Shield membership.

He said, 'Fieldston Growth Enterprises.'

The man said, 'Yes.'

'What are you doing in Orloff's house?'

Fieldston's voice changed. He assumed an air of authority. He said, 'Mr. Orloff worked for me. I needed some papers, and I have every right to be here. Now take the wallet and leave me alone.'

He sensed the wrong note in the voice. It wasn't the bravado of a man trying to scare the sort of perennial loser that held people up for their wallets. And he hadn't said take the money and leave the wallet. He'd said take the wallet. And to a man like this, the inconvenience of losing the license, credit cards, and identification could be more important than the thousand or so dollars. He said, 'No thanks, I've got a wallet.'

Fieldston's hands were in the air. Whatever resource he had been using to keep them from shaking now left him. When he spoke, it was with a slight tremor. 'What do you want?'

He said, 'You.'

Fieldston turned toward him, as though unable to control himself. 'No, wait a minute. You've got it wrong. I wasn't leaving the country. I'm here now, aren't I?'

He had to keep him frightened. He said, 'Bullshit.'

Fieldston pointed at the briefcase on the floor and said, 'Look for yourself. I was going to give it to him. Four million dollars. Hell, that's fifty percent a year on his investment.'

He had to get him to say the name. He just smiled and shook his head.

Fieldston was frantic now. His voice was shrill and strident. 'Yes!' he said. 'It's true. Here it is, and now we're even. I'll disappear where the police will never find me.'

He said, 'What were you doing in here?'

Fieldston said, 'I knew Orloff. He would have kept something here to use against us if there was an investigation. I knew him. Before I left I wanted to find it.'

He smiled again. Of course. He said, 'No. You wanted it for yourself. To use against us. To save your ass.'

Fieldston shook his head. 'No. Honestly. I know better than that.' He reached into his pocket and pulled out a checkbook. 'See?' he said. 'Here it is. It's a ledger of the transactions over the past five years. It's in his checkbook. I found it. We'll destroy it right now and you can tell them everything is okay.'

He said, 'You should have told them yourself.'

Fieldston said, 'But I was told never to use the telephone to talk to Mr. Balacontano.'

The name. He wasn't surprised, just glad it was over. He decided to make it simple. He aimed carefully and placed the single shot in the center of Fieldston's forehead. The pistol spat once, Fieldston's head jerked slightly, and the body crumpled to the floor. He looked at his watch. Not even three o'clock, he thought. Plenty of time.

THIRTY

When Elizabeth awoke there was a moment before she remembered. It was like the moment the mind realizes that the foot onto which the body's weight is about to shift should already have touched solid ground, but didn't. Then there was the rapid succession of feelings – remembering, alarm, and the mind's recognition of an emergency that is somehow already determined and familiar – not less unpleasant for the recognition, but a mishap of a particular kind and consequence, and therefore accepted with frustration instead of terror. Palermo was dead.

She sat up in bed and looked at the alarm clock. It was almost three o'clock in the morning. She had slept for over eight hours already. The sheriff had driven her to Carson City, and she'd taken a plane back to Las Vegas after waiting until two o'clock for the first flight. It was nearly four by the time she'd made it to the FBI office.

Why hadn't Brayer called her? He hadn't been at the office or at the hotel. If he'd taken a plane to Washington he should have arrived hours ago. And Connors or Padgett would be there to give him the message: Elizabeth had done it again. Palermo was dead. Go back and try to pick up the pieces of the investigation. It had to be her telephone.

She turned on the light. There was no point in trying to go back to sleep. She had used up the eight hours of unconsciousness she'd purchased with the exhaustion, the disorientation, and the shame of the morning. Now she had to face whatever was left of the night. It was six a.m. in Washington.

Elizabeth dressed. If she was doomed to spend the next few hours thinking about it, then thank God it was Las Vegas. Downstairs there would be something to eat, and crowds of people still gambling and drinking and living some life that didn't have to include an awareness of what sharpened metal did to flesh and arteries.

She took the elevator to the ground floor and walked through the casino. There were only a few tables open now, and people were playing blackjack and craps with a slow and leisurely alcoholic intensity in pools of light that swirled with blue-gray wisps of cigarette smoke. Elizabeth couldn't decide whether these were the serious gamblers who stayed on like permanent features of the landscape while the ephemeral hordes of tourists came and went around them, or just a straggle of losers who stayed on because there was nothing better to do than play away their last few chips, no place that offered more. It didn't matter. They were all here together at three o'clock in the morning – Elizabeth too.

She walked past the restaurants. They had closed hours ago. Nobody who was up at this hour wanted beef Wellington or sole bonne femme. The coffee shop was still ablaze with lights, but far off in the corner behind a stockade of upturned chairs a black man was following a vacuum cleaner in its jerky foragings beneath the tables. She picked a table away from the vacuum cleaner. She was only two tables away from a pair of beefy middle-aged men in gray suits, but at this hour it seemed best. It was inhabited ground, at least, and it made her feel less alone.

The waitress, she decided, had been pretty once. Maybe she was pretty still, but she looked tired and worn. The hairnet didn't help much either. She looked like a man wearing a beret. The waitress walked by on her way to the kitchen and slapped a menu on Elizabeth's table. In a few minutes she was back, standing over Elizabeth's table with her pad in her hand.

Elizabeth said, 'I haven't decided yet. What's in a Donna Summer sandwich?'

'Pastrami. Chopped liver. Cole slaw.'

It sounded about right, Elizabeth thought. She hadn't eaten in – how long? A whole day, at least. 'I'll take that. And coffee.'

The waitress nodded as she wrote. Her face retained its stony efficiency. In a very low voice she said, 'By the way, do yourself a favor.'

Elizabeth looked up, and saw that the waitress's eyes were sliding in the direction of the two men at the next table. Elizabeth said, 'Favor?' in the same low voice.

The waitress said, 'Don't try to sell it in here, honey.' She tipped her head so slightly in the direction of the two men that even Elizabeth wasn't sure at first that it meant anything. Then she said, 'Vice squad.'

Elizabeth's mind sprinted to catch up. Of course. The only women she'd seen in the casino had been a group of four motherly ladies in pantsuits at a blackjack table together, all giggling and silly like the teenagers they'd probably been the last time they'd been out late in a pack like this. She said to the waitress, 'Thanks,' and the waitress disappeared.

Elizabeth looked at her watch. Almost three thirty. On some other night it might have struck her differently. But now it felt as though she'd been slapped. Was it her clothes? She wanted to tell someone something that would prove they were all wrong. Had they all been thinking that? But the words that rose to the surface of her mind were, 'No, you're wrong. I got good grades, and worked hard!'

It was so peculiar it distracted her from the embarrassment. What had she stumbled on? Grades. Hard work and doing what they told you to do. Good girl. Ever so good. College. Scholarships. Business school. A government job. No mistakes, no flagging of attention, no momentary lapses, and you stayed at the top, the surface. Because just below the top it was dark and there was no way to see what lurked there. Something terrible. Everything terrible. And each step of the way was cumulative, like climbing up a ladder to avoid a flood. It got you farther and farther away from whatever was down there. Humiliation.

The waitress returned with the sandwich and Elizabeth started to eat. It was so thick it strained her jaw to get her mouth around it, but she decided she didn't care. And she didn't care about the calories either. Bad girl. She smiled. So what? Today I'm a failure. A fat failure. Who looks like a prostitute.

She began to feel better almost immediately. In another hour or two Brayer would turn up, and it would be a new day. And Palermo had told her quite a bit, after all. When she finished eating she'd go upstairs and write it all down, so it was ready when Brayer returned. And there was still Edgar Fieldston. He couldn't stay out of sight forever.

She was aware of a voice beside her. She turned to see that it was one of the men at the next table, leaning his pink face toward her and smiling, the angle of his head making his tight collar cut into his shaven jowl. He said, 'Would you like to join us for dessert?'

Elizabeth kept chewing and shook her head.

The man's smile only widened, his tiny white teeth like a string of pearls. 'Oh, come on. I'll buy.'

Elizabeth swallowed, then said, 'Shut up and go away. I'm thinking.'

He knelt over Fieldston's body and placed the towels underneath the head. It wasn't bleeding much, considering. In a little while it would stop, when the body cooled. Meanwhile, there was plenty to do.

The briefcase was exactly as Fieldston had said. He'd never seen so much money, he thought. Hardly anybody had. What had he said? Four million. Must be all thousand dollar bills. So maybe he hadn't been running. He could hardly have expected to spend those bills without being noticed, and without Balacontano's organization to launder them. So what the hell was he doing? All right, take him at his word. He was planning to pay Balacontano and then disappear, with Orloff's checkbook as the threat that would convince Bala to leave him alone. Which meant the bookkeeping at FGE was perfect unless there was a key. But that was practically impossible. How could it be that good? The fool. Balacontano would have helped him disappear all right.

He made a quick search of the house. Fieldston apparently hadn't touched anything in the other rooms. He must have known Orloff well. Certainly Fieldston wasn't smart enough to have found the room without knowing, not if he'd been stupid enough to think he could blackmail Carl Bala.

He went back to the body and searched the pockets. There were no keys. He thought about it. Fieldston must have taken a cab from somewhere or walked. Probably the airport. And he hadn't planned to go home, ever again, because he no longer even had a key to his own house. And he hadn't checked into a hotel, he had no hotel key. Fieldston had been frightened enough to make sure nobody at all knew he was in Las Vegas.

There was a lot of work to do, so he had to move quickly. No mistakes, nothing he'd forgotten about that he had to come back later to correct. It all had to happen between now and dawn. He looked at his watch. Three thirty. Two good, safe hours and then another one before the people who worked the day shift started to get up. He went outside and drove his car into Orloff's driveway with the lights off.

He went back into the house and looked around for something to help. Orloff's desk chair was about right and it had wheels. He got down on his knees, put his hands under Fieldston's shoulders, and hoisted him into the chair. Then he went to the bathroom and took two more large bath towels from the linen cupboard. Whatever else they'd done, he was sure they wouldn't have counted towels. He wrapped one of the towels around the upper part of the body and threw the other in Fieldston's lap. Then he pulled the office chair through the house to the door. He took the right arm and the body slumped forward onto his shoulders. He staggered with it to the car and shrugged it into the trunk. He arranged the towels as well as he could to keep the blood from escaping.

Then he returned to the house. He moved the desk chair back to Orloff's office, shuffling his feet on the carpet to remove the imprint of the wheels. He took a final look to see that everything appeared undisturbed, then put the wallet in the briefcase and went out. At the car he remembered. How had Fieldston gotten in? Fieldston hadn't had a key. He returned to the house and looked at each of the windows. It was the window to the guest bedroom, but Fieldston had been careful. There were no scuff marks on the sill, and the lock wasn't damaged, just scratched minutely. He took a last look around before he left the house. He pressed down on the trunk of his car just enough so the latch caught and drove off down the street. He took a labyrinthine route to reach the freeway without going down the Strip. As he felt the car accelerate onto the freeway, he had an impulse to laugh. By the time the sun came up he'd be in Kingman, Arizona, and maybe Flagstaff by the time the stores opened up. No telling how far a man might go after he'd been shot in the head.

The books he selected were paperbacks. In the supermarket he bought three, all of which said bestseller on their covers. In the bookstore he picked classics – books he remembered being forced to read in school. In the drugstore he found two that claimed to be something called novelizations of movies. When he

337

had enough, he sat in the parking lot to do the packing: one bill per page. It struck him as funny that the first of the paperbacks was worth over two hundred thousand dollars. It took more than an hour, but he couldn't afford to rush it. He was good at making packages, at tying and taping and arranging, and this was one package he wanted to make perfect.

By the time the post office opened he was there to watch the man unlock the doors. He sent the package fourth class, special book rate. It was a strange sensation to see the postman at the counter toss the package into the bin with a dozen others, all practically indistinguishable from one another. At that moment he knew there was no reason to think about it anymore. It was gone from his possession forever, and there was no way he could ever get it back. It was more money than he ever hoped to have, more than some towns were worth, probably. And now it was gone. He didn't linger at the counter to think about it. It had all been decided hours ago, while he drove through the cold air of the dark desert. It was the only way.

The sun was rising in the sky and he had to make every hour into miles. If he waited too long the bags of ice he'd bought would start to melt, and the seals on at least some of the bags would be defective. He couldn't afford to have water dripping from the trunk as he drove. If he kept at it he might make five hundred miles before he needed to change the ice, because the air rushing by would cool the surface of the car just as it cooled the engine. It was going to be a long time before he slept again, he thought. But there'd be plenty of time to sleep later on – twenty hours a day for the rest of his life, if he felt like it. All he had to do now was deliver Edgar. He said aloud, 'Keep cool, Edgar. It won't be long now.'

It was shortly after noon when he began to hear the sloshing sounds. Whenever he slowed down or accelerated there was a faint noise of water moving about in the trunk. By one o'clock he began to see drips of water hitting the pavement in his rearview mirror whenever the car gained speed too abruptly. When he stopped in Flagstaff to fill the gas tank he put his hand on the trunk and knew that his theory of air cooling had been wrong. The surface of the trunk was as hot as the metal fixtures on the gas pump. As he drove off he said, 'Edgar, we've got problems. You're getting parboiled in there. Afraid we've got to make another arrangement.'

It was in the Sears store that he bought the hacksaw and the shovel and the ice chest. He had to search another fifteen minutes before he found the ranchers' supply store. When he found it he shopped carefully for the lime, reading the labels on the big fifty-pound bags: calcium oxide – 95 percent; magnesia – 2 percent; total silica, alumina, iron – 2 percent. Water content no more than 1 percent guaranteed.

He moved the bags to the car in a cart, and was back on the road again. The bags of Blue Ice he bought at a liquor store in Winslow, because it was the first place he passed through that looked as though they might sell it already frozen.

It was mid-afternoon now and so hot that the endless, straight highway danced and quivered. Off in the distance dust devils swirled crazily and dissolved, the only signs of movement. He took Route 77 through Snowflake and Show Low, and then swung east again through Springerville and into New Mexico on Route 60. It was already night before he found the place he was looking for between Quemado and Magdalena, about fifty miles past the Continental Divide. It was a back road not shown on the map, but he could see it went somewhere. It had been over an hour since he'd seen another car, and the local ranchers would be shutting themselves in for the night. He turned off on a dirt road that wound through rocky hillocks and barrows, and kept going until he found a spot that suited him. He parked the car on the side of the road and got out.

Looking around and studying the place, he saw nothing but the gigantic, bright expanse of the sky, the stars incredibly clear and close above his head. He took the shovel and set off up the side of the hill. It was pretty country, he decided, even at night – bigger and emptier and cleaner than the land the main routes passed through. And if he worked steadily he could probably still make Amarillo by the time the sun came up.

THIRTY-ONE

The first half of the day Elizabeth had spent dreading the return of John Brayer. It was the fact that he must have been in Washington when he found out about Palermo that bothered her. In the first place, he would probably already have set up the appointment with the Attorney General's office before he found out. That meant he'd have to explain to them why he no longer needed to see them. But more than that she hated the idea that he would be there when the anger and disgust settled on him. He'd be right there in the office where they handled personnel cases, where Elizabeth's file was kept.

Sometime during the afternoon her feelings began to change. The FBI agents were coldly polite, but she could feel the weight of their resentment and contempt. And they were right. If only Brayer had let her take Palermo here, he'd still be alive. He might not be happy at first, but it really would have made no difference in the long run. The trip to Carson City had served no legitimate purpose. Something could have been arranged to keep Palermo under wraps here in Las Vegas. But now Brayer was comfortably out of sight in Washington or somewhere, and Elizabeth was still here in the Bureau office, taking the force of their resentment alone. And of course they all knew about it. Her report had included the rationale for making a dash to Carson City. The ones who hadn't read it had been told. She could see it in their faces. At four o'clock Elizabeth decided she had been a fool. If Brayer filed a request for dismissal, or even so much as a negative performance evaluation, she'd demand a hearing and fight it. He'd been the one who ordered her to handle Palermo that way, after all – a lone woman with an analyst's rating transporting a self-confessed criminal through an unpopulated area in the dark. She could have been killed too. If he filed any kind of reprimand, she thought, she'd make him regret it. By the time the hearing was over she'd have a special commendation.

At dinner Elizabeth began to wonder if she hadn't been too defensive. Nothing had come through from Washington all day that referred to Palermo's murder. Maybe Brayer was taking the blame himself, leaving her out of it for the moment. She'd seen him do that before, file a report in which somebody was just named as 'the agent in place' or 'the field agent.' That would explain why he'd been out of touch.

When she went to bed she was already feeling worried about him. He was in Washington taking the blame for the disaster, and the fact that he hadn't returned meant Washington wasn't taking it well. And Brayer couldn't be more than five years from retirement.

The next morning Elizabeth was certain of it. Brayer was taking the blame, and it was going hard. The best thing for her to do was to make as much progress as possible while he was in Washington. If she could only come up with something big enough, Washington would forget about Palermo and they'd both be all right. What she needed was another Palermo, somebody who knew the name of the silent partner in FGE and could prove the silent partner was killing people to protect himself. What she needed was Edgar Fieldston.

At the Bureau office Elizabeth pored over the field reports. Palermo had hinted that it was somebody big, and the biggest were Toscanzio and Balacontano.

'10:08 p.m., Wednesday, February 21. Saratoga Springs, New York: Subject Carlo Balacontano AKA Carl Bala. Subject has been secluded in his country residence since Monday, February 19. On Tuesday, February 20, he was joined by his wife, Therese Balacontano, his son Richard, and his daughter-in-law, Victoria, and their four children. Subject has received visits from a number of his associates. Key to: Lamborese, Antonio; Giambini, Robert; Montano, John; Guariano, August; DeFabiani, Daniel.

'9:15 a.m., Thursday, February 22, Evanston, Illinois: Subject Vincent Toscanzio. Subject has been in his home for four days. Subject's family, including subject's mother, Mrs. Maria Toscanzio, have arrived during that time and have remained on the premises. Members of subject's family were observed in the backyard making a snowman on Tuesday, February 20, but have remained indoors since then, possibly due to inclement weather. Frequent visitors, all employees of Diet Clubs of America, in which subject owns a controlling interest, except for the arrival on Wednesday of Antonio Damonata AKA Tony Damon, and two unidentified companions.'

There was no question about what was going on, but that didn't help. They were circling the wagons around the women and children and giving orders to their lieutenants. But that didn't solve Elizabeth's problem. The one she wanted was the one who'd started it, the one who had killed Veasy and the Senator and Orloff and Castiglione. Because she wasn't foolish enough to believe she'd get the other one. If he fell it would be a freak accident. But the one Elizabeth wanted was vulnerable. He'd been using FGE for something. Whatever it was had to be bad enough to take risks to keep it a secret, to kill off everyone who came near it. And whoever it was had missed the key man. As long as Edgar Fieldston was alive Elizabeth had hope.

The secretary didn't bother to knock when she came into the office with the reports. Why should she? thought Elizabeth. It's their office. I'm the interloper, the outsider they have to treat with grudging tolerance. The one they have to cooperate with who didn't cooperate with them when she had something to share.

It was the initial report on FGE's remaining papers. She scanned the inventory of records until she came to the summary. The papers weren't complete enough to prove anything yet. It would be like a problem in archaeology to figure out where the money came from and which accounts were padded. She supposed the FBI's accountants knew what to look for. Then she noticed the statement: *Recommended for intensive audit: Travel.* She leafed through the summary until she found the travel expenses. It was easy to see what had caught their attention. Calendar-year travel expenses were listed as $56,382.

She searched through the report for the breakdown. Most of it meant nothing to her. Orloff had gone to

New York, Los Angeles, and Chicago. Fieldston had spent a week in Buenos Aires, then gone on for another week to Rio de Janeiro. Did they have investments in those places, she wondered? But they'd check it, of course. For one thing, they were looking for Fieldston, and it would help to know where he had contacts.

She moved down the list. The other travelers were unfamiliar to her. Probably they were salesmen or something. The FBI would be working on that too. She moved down to the final entry and stopped. *Edgar Fieldston, round-trip ticket to Nassau, Bahamas, February 16.* She gasped. Round trip. Why hadn't anybody noticed? But then she rememberd. Of course he'd buy a round-trip ticket. If you had a return ticket the customs people didn't worry about you. They knew you wouldn't be stuck there when you'd spent your money. Damn! she thought. I'm seeing what I'm looking for, not what I'm looking at. Where the hell is Brayer?

The Parthenon Motel in Cleveland had four Corinthian columns across the concrete slab in front of the office. They didn't support anything, but they looked as though they might have supported the motel's sign before it had been redone in neon and the wiring had gotten too complicated. It was after ten but he had no trouble renting one of the rooms with a kitchenette. People didn't travel through Cleveland much in February, and those who did had no use for a stove and refrigerator, certainly not those for rent at the Parthenon.

He had been driving almost continuously for over forty-eight hours, and now he knew he had to sleep.

He parked the car outside his room and carried his suitcase inside. Then he went back to the car for his cooler. He brought it into the kitchenette and opened it. The Blue Ice he'd bought in St. Louis was still surprisingly cold, but he took it out and put it in the freezer to prepare for tomorrow. Then he said aloud, 'You too, Edgar. Got to keep fresh.' When he had finished loading the freezer he rinsed out the inside of the cooler, checked the locks on the door a second time, and lay down on the bed. He fell immediately into a nervous, troubled sleep. Late in the night he found himself partially awake, reaching for the pistol in his coat pocket. He took off the coat and laid it beside him on the bed. After that he slept soundly, dreamlessly, until the maid's morning knock startled him at eleven.

When he passed Buffalo in the middle of the afternoon he thought of Maureen. He supposed she must be somewhere nearby, taking a rest and counting her money while she waited for the old man to offer her the next job. She'd been expensive, probably not worth that kind of money, but he didn't regret what he'd paid her. She'd caught him at a time when he was in the mood to be extravagant, so she was entitled to it. That was part of the business.

He knew exactly where he was going. He'd seen the place once, when he and Eddie had been trying to fill the contract on Danny Lazaro. He'd owned a two-year-old filly named The Commodore's Pride, and Eddie had figured he'd come to Saratoga to watch her run. Eddie had been wrong, and they'd ended up watching the races and then driving around the area looking at the farms. It was a country composed of low, rolling green hills and small stands of ancient oaks and maples cordoned by the same white rail fences that lined the road.

'It's so the horses won't kill the trees,' Eddie had said. 'The fuckers are worse than beavers.' He'd made a note to ask somebody about that who knew something about horses, but he'd forgotten about it until now. Eddie had probably made it up. Eddie had lived in big cities all his life. If he knew anything about horses it was probably from carving them up to look like prime rib.

They drove past a large farm with a low stone fence, partitioned into paddocks and pastures where tall chestnut-coloured horses strolled in elegant leisure, and Eddie had said, 'Know who owns that place?' He'd shrugged, and Eddie had said triumphantly, 'Carlo fucking Balacontano, Esquire. That's who.'

That night somebody else had collected on Danny Lazaro. They'd found him in New York in a little French restaurant on the West Side, and when Eddie read it in the papers he'd said, 'No big thing. He missed a good race.' Rochester and Syracuse and Utica floated by as green signs on the New York State Thruway. It was almost ten o'clock by the time he swung north on Route 87 at Albany.

At eleven he saw the sign that said Saratoga Springs 15. He thought, I'll make the call by one o'clock, from Plattsburgh. I could be in Montreal by three, or New York City by four or five. It won't matter where I am, because in another day there won't be anybody looking for me. By tomorrow night they'll all know it's no longer worth the risk. Because they'll all believe the

347

man they hoped to please is beyond doing anything for them. Whatever he offered them will be just words. And they'll be thinking about something else. Some of them will lie low and wait to see who comes to the top in the five families and inherits New York, and some won't be able to wait for that: they'll run to Toscanzio or Tony Damon to anticipate the stampede.

He turned off at Saratoga Springs and drove to the farm. Even in the dark he recognized the white rail fences and the distant buildings. At the first boundary there was a small sign that said Montpelier Farms. And then in smaller letters, Arabians and Standardbreds. He wished he'd looked at the place in the daylight. Did horses get locked up at night? Did they even run loose in February? He drove along the fence studying what he could see of the acres beyond. There were three pastures, all empty snowdrifts and patches of frozen grass, and a smaller area near the stable that was trampled into mud. He decided that must be where they rode horses or trained them. Beyond that was a track, just like a racetrack only without a grandstand. On a knoll above the track stood the house. That was what power meant, he thought – so much empty land around Bala's house that he had to build a road to get to it, probably had to drive to see his own horses eating his own grass. He probably didn't come here more than a few times a year. And probably not at all in February. It was too cold out there for horses, he thought, too cold even to watch them.

It was going to be more difficult than he'd thought. There were at least two or three hundred yards of empty land between the highway and the house, and most of it was covered with snow. He couldn't drive it and he couldn't afford to leave footprints. And it was cold out there: the ground would be frozen solid. But there had to be a way. He'd come too far to give up.

He drove past the farm and thought about the problem. There was only one way to do it, and he knew he had to accept that. But it wasn't going to be pleasant. He turned the car around and drove back into Saratoga Springs. It took him a half hour to find a store that was open. It was a supermarket that seemed at this hour to deal mainly in beer, but he found what he needed – a pair of gloves, a knitted watch cap, a package of heavy plastic trash bags, and a roll of thick adhesive tape.

He parked the car a mile down the road from the farm in a closed gas station and made his preparations. He sawed the handle of the shovel off to the length of a foot and a half, then went around to the trunk. He shook out four of his plastic trash bags and placed them one inside of the other for extra strength, then opened the cooler. 'Come on, Edgar,' he said, 'last stop.' The walk was cold, but he knew it had to be done this way. Whoever Bala had to take care of his horses would be alarmed by a strange car parked close to the farm, and a car would be of no use to him now anyway.

When he reached the farm he walked along the white fence until he came to a point where another rail fence intersected it, dividing the two pastures. He was glad he'd bought the hat and gloves. He had to take off the gloves to fish out the adhesive tape. He put the shovel and gun inside one platic bag, and taped the two bags together to form a sling, which he threw over his shoulder.

He climbed up on the fence, his feet on the bottom rail and his hands clinging to the top rail. He began to sidestep along the fence between the two pastures, moving in the direction of the farm buildings. He inched along, slowly at first, but before long he found he could make good progress by keeping as much weight as possible on his feet. The pastures were empty, but now he could see horse tracks in the snow. They must let them out sometimes during the day, he thought. He wondered how the horses felt about it.

It took him over ten minutes to reach the place where the fence intersected with the section that ran along Balacontano's private road. He stopped to rest and read his watch in the moonlight. It was already after midnight, and there was no telling how long this was going to take. If only it weren't so cold. As he approached the house, he realized something was wrong. From the pasture side it looked as though every light were on. Cautiously, he sidestepped closer along the rail. Balacontano's caretaker wouldn't have all those lights on, and grooms and stableboys wouldn't be inside the main house. In spite of the cold he began to sweat. He leaned over the fence and stared at the snow on the driveway. It was crossed with what looked like a dozen treadmark patterns. There were the thick jagged impressions of truck tires, at least two different patterns of studded snow tires, and a few ruts made by the smoother treads of road tires. Shit, he thought, he's here right now, and he's got some of his people with him. Of course he'd be here. Nobody can get within three hundred yards of the house without being seen. He looked at the house again and thought, there might be twenty or thirty of them sitting around

350

in there to protect him. In New York City he'd have to make do with two or three.

He bent his knees and hung down behind the fence to keep from showing a silhouette. The area around the house was impossible. It had to be another way. He inched along the fence, with his body away from the house. It would have to be the stables. It was another ten minutes before he made it to the fence beside the long, low stable building. He studied the ground inside the exercise yard. There were only a few patches of snow, and the rest looked like mud. He cautiously tested the earth with one foot and smiled. It was mud all right but it was frozen solid into an uneven mold of hoofprints and footprints, ruts where wheelbarrows had passed, and tire tracks from what must have been a tractor. He set both feet on the ground and stood erect.

He walked along the fence across the yard to the stable. He could smell the strong acidic scent of the animals; he could feel their presence. He walked around the building and the scent grew stronger, almost overpowering in the cold, still, night air. He heard a horse's hoof clop on a wooden surface somewhere inside, and then a low neigh. They can smell me too, he thought. It's because I don't smell like horseshit.

He stood still for a moment to let the animals quiet down. As he waited he looked around. A few feet away was a mound of earth about ten feet high. No, he realized suddenly. That's not dirt. It's horseshit. That's why the smell is so strong on this side of the stable. It's a compost heap.

He moved away from the building to the other side

of the mound. As he came near he sensed a very slight steam coming from the mound. He took off his glove and held his hand six inches above the mound. It was actually warm. Keeping low, he took out the shovel and began to dig. The manure wasn't frozen, nor was the ground under it. He dug down about two feet before he hit the frost. He thought, sorry, Edgar. This is it. He put the pistol inside the other plastic bag, tossed in Orloff's checkbook, and buried the bundle. He took the shovel and headed back the way he'd come.

When he reached the corner of the stable, he heard a horse neigh again, and then something else. He stood perfectly still. It was footsteps. A man. Suddenly, above his head, a light came on. The whole yard was bathed in brightness. He moved back into the shadow of the stable and waited. If only he'd brought a second pistol, he thought. I'm here, half a mile from the road, with a shovel, and the bastards are awake.

Suddenly he heard other footsteps behind him, coming along the back of the stable. He opened a door, stepped into the stable, and found himself standing next to a horse. The animal seemed gigantic. The horse turned its long, wise face to stare at him, its eyes rolling to fix him in its gaze. Outside, footsteps scraped on the frozen ground. They passed and he could hear voices. One of them said, 'I don't give a shit what he thinks. If Toscanzio sends somebody it won't be through the stable. If he's so worried he should come out here and slide around on the horseshit himself.'

'Relax,' said the other one. 'We'll just make the rounds and go back inside.'

Guards, he thought. Balacontano has them doing regular patrols. The horse seemed to be getting nervous. It blew out a sputtering sigh and edged away from him in the stall. Just a few more minutes and I won't trouble you, he thought. Just a few more minutes and I'll be out of here, you big dumb son of a bitch. He thought, you're supposed to talk to them to calm them down. I can't risk it. He decided that patting the horse would help. It seemed so huge, looming beside him in the dark. He reached out and patted the horse's flank gently. He felt the skin quiver beneath his hand, then settle, but it was too late. The horse in the next stall seemed to sense his fear or the nervousness of the horse beside him. It whinnied and kicked the wall behind it. The noise was like a shot in the still night air.

He heard one of the voices say, 'What the hell was that?'

The other said, 'We'd better look in the stalls. Something's bothering them.'

He had no time to think. He opened the stable door and watched the horse turn and make its decision to go outside. As it passed him he leaped astride it and it trotted out into the yard. He was high in the air now, bouncing on the animal's back. Behind him he heard one of the men shout, 'Look.' He didn't know what to do, but he had to do something. He leaned forward. With his left hand he grabbed the horse's mane, and with his right he smacked the horse's flank with the flat of the shovel. 'Go,' he hissed. Before he was prepared for the response, he felt the animal's massive muscles tense as it leaped forward, almost unseating him. He clung to its mane with a grip that wrenched the muscles in his hand, and his legs hugged the horse's sides.

The men had left the gate open and the horse headed for it. He hung on with all his strength as it galloped through the opening and out across the pasture. Behind him he heard a shot, and the horse, terrified at the sound, dashed forward still faster, out into the darkness. He didn't dare look back for fear he'd fall off. At the far side of the pasture he saw the fence looming before him, a white barrier getting closer and closer. He said to the horse, 'Calm down, you bastard. Stop.' But the horse seemed to pick up speed as it neared the fence.

He thought, if I jump off I'll be hurt and they'll find me. He thought of hitting the horse over the head with the shovel, but there was no way to know what the horse would do, so he just hung on. And then suddenly he was airborne, and the fence floated past beneath him. He braced for the shock, but the horse landed easily and kept going, out across the second pasture at full speed.

When he saw the second fence he thought, I'm in for it again. But this time the horse ran up to the fence, slowed down, and trotted along it toward the far corner of the pasture. It doesn't like the road, he thought. It just wants to be away from the lights and noise. When it reached the corner the horse stopped. He jumped off and climbed the fence. His legs were sore, and for some reason his rib cage hurt almost as much, but he managed to bring himself to a run.

The important thing was to cover as much ground as possible. He sprinted in the direction he'd come from, but as far from the road as he could go. He was already to the next farm before he saw the first headlights on the highway. They were moving fast, at least sixty miles an hour, racing for the entrance to Route 87. The second set of headlights moved along the road at a slower rate. That would be the one searching for a parked car, he thought. He was careful to stay in the wooded areas now. A few minutes later more cars followed, but none of them stopped. There would be others moving off in the opposite direction too, he knew. None of them would try to follow on foot.

THIRTY-TWO

When it came it wasn't the way Elizabeth had imagined it. She was sitting in the Bureau office going over the morning field reports when the secretary came through and left the first of the afternoon communications in a stack on the table beside the door.

Elizabeth stood up and walked to the table. She was getting tired of being the one who had to come in here every day and suffer the silent enmity of a building full of people. All morning nobody had found it necessary to speak to her. And now the secretary had taken to leaving the reports in a stack by the door, as though Elizabeth were a prisoner in solitary confinement, or a pet that had to be fed but didn't require attention.

It was the sheet on top of the pile. It said, 'The following personnel will report to the office of the Organized Crime Division, Department of Justice, Washington, D.C., by 0800, February 28: Dornquist, William; Kellogg, Bertram; Smith, Thomas H.; Feiler, Eleanor; Goltz, Ann K.; Waring, Elizabeth. Travel authorized: air only.'

She read it through a second time. February 28. That was tomorrow morning. And now it was already two thirty. She looked at the timer readout on the transcript – it had only come in at 2:15, which meant 5:15 Washington time. That would be fifteen minutes after most of the people in the Washington office had gone home for the night. At least it wasn't just Elizabeth. It looked as though they were pulling out everybody still on detached service in Las Vegas. So they weren't necessarily calling her home to fire her. They were giving up on the operation.

She picked up the telephone and made a reservation on the next flight, then packed up her reports and her notebooks. For a moment she thought of leaving without saying anything to anyone, but it seemed too crude somehow. She walked down the hall to the Bureau chief's office.

He said, 'I heard you were leaving.'

Elizabeth said, 'Yes, it just came in over the wire.'

He tapped a pencil on his desk and cleared his throat. 'I suppose congratulations are in order.'

Elizabeth shifted in her chair and crossed her legs so the heavy reports wouldn't slide off her lap. 'Not that I know of,' she said.

He stared down at his desk and said nothing at first, but she could see he was angry.

'Have it your way. But just let me say one thing off the record. If you people would be a little less secretive things would be a lot easier for everybody.'

'I know,' said Elizabeth. 'I've been wanting to tell you too, off the record, that I was against taking Palermo to Carson City. It was orders and I tried to follow them and I lost Palermo. If it's any consolation, I think when I get back to Washington the first thing they'll do is—'

'Damn it,' he said quietly. 'I'm not talking about Palermo. That was two or three days ago. I'm talking about now. Do you think we're idiots?'

357

Elizabeth said, 'Of course not. What are you talking about?'

'Your whole team gets jerked back to Washington on a priority call, and then twenty minutes later, as an afterthought, they send us this message.' He tossed it on the desk and Elizabeth leaned forward to pick it up.

She read it aloud. 'Re: Edgar R. Fieldston. Disposition: Take no further action.' She said, 'So what? They know he's not here.'

Now he was almost shouting. 'So the case is closed and you're all on your way home. And nobody has the decency to tell us what in the hell's going on. Either we're in on it or we're not.'

'How can it be closed?' Elizabeth said. 'We don't know any more than we did a week ago, or at least I don't. And you saw every report I filed since I got here.'

He sat in silence for a moment, then stared at her. Very slowly, his expression changed. He said, 'All right. Maybe I was wrong.' He looked as though he wished he hadn't spoken to her. He added, 'If I was wrong I apologize.'

Elizabeth stood up, cradling the reports in her arms. 'I'm sorry about Palermo. But honestly, that's the only thing we didn't cooperate about.'

He looked a little sad, and more than a little embarrassed. He said, 'I guess there's something else I should show you. Or maybe I shouldn't, I don't know. But a few minutes ago, when I asked our own headquarters what was going on, this came back.' He handed her another transcript.

Re: Edgar R. Fieldston, F.G.E., and related matters: Effective immediately, second copy all reports to:

*Department of Justice, United States v. Carlo Balacon-
tano Trial Team, Attention Padgett.*

Elizabeth felt as though she'd been slapped. She
looked at him, and saw he was now staring down at
the desk. She said, 'They arrested Balacontano? I
didn't know.'

He said, 'I believe you didn't. I'm sorry.'

She said again, 'They didn't tell me.'

The Department of Justice office building seemed quiet
and cavernous at seven in the morning. The floors
gleamed and sounds echoed and died among the out-
of-date light fixtures along the high ceilings of the
corridor. Post offices and museums had seemed this
way to Elizabeth when she was a child. Even the smell
seemed the same, a mixture of floorwax and dust and
disinfectant and old paper; a substantial, official,
governmental smell.

She walked into the empty office and over to her
desk. It looked the way she'd known it would. When
the accumulation of daily activity reports had grown
too bulky for her desk they'd begun making a neat
stack of them on the floor beside it. In a day or two
somebody was going to have a lot of work to do.

She had only been there for fifteen minutes when she
heard the first footsteps in the hallway, the purposeful
clopping of male leather-soled shoes resonating in the
emptiness of the building. In a moment she realized it
was two men. And then one of them spoke and she
recognized the voice. Padgett. 'Just let me get a cup of
coffee and—' He came through the door and stopped.
He said, 'Elizabeth! Terrific. Glad to have you back.'
He started to pour himself some coffee. It was then

359

that the second man appeared. It was Martin Connors. He said, 'Good morning, Miss Waring.' Then he frowned slightly. 'I'd like to talk to you for a moment, if you don't mind.'

'No,' said Elizabeth and stood up. He was already walking down the corridor toward his office. Elizabeth had to trot to catch up.

Behind her she heard Padgett say, 'I'll bring you a cup, Martin.' Then he added, 'You too, Elizabeth?'

She didn't bother to answer. They walked in silence. He unlocked the door to his office and ceremoniously stepped aside to let her pass, then pulled a chair away from the wall for her. There was something about his manner that made her uncomfortable. It wasn't that he had the gestures of his own generation, but those of the generation before.

He sat down behind his desk, pursed his lips, and folded his hands. 'I'm glad you're here early, because I want you to be ready to help with this thing.'

Elizabeth thought, I'm not fired.

He leaned forward and said, 'You're the one who is most familiar with the case, and that makes it doubly important that you be here when it gets to the trial stage.'

Elizabeth thought again, I'm not fired. Then she thought, most familiar? She said, 'What about John?'

He said, 'John?'

'Yes, John.'

'You don't know?' Then he shook his head, and stared at his desk for a moment. 'John Brayer is dead.' He looked up at her again and said, 'I'm sorry, I thought you knew. Stupid of me.'

Elizabeth felt tears clouding her vision. She said, 'When? How?'

Connors shook his head again. 'Don't waste your tears on Mr. Brayer,' he said. It was an order. 'He was our informer and his friends decided he was too great a risk. It was in Las Vegas, shortly after the ... the Palermo incident. He was found in the desert somewhere outside Las Vegas. It took quite some time to identify him.'

'But nobody told me,' she said. 'Why didn't anybody tell me?' She was weeping now. Brayer was dead, and she'd been there, thinking – what? It was too wrong, there were so many things to remember. But she realized Connors had said something else too. Brayer the leak? She said, 'John wasn't the leak. What are you talking about?'

Connors became the formal superior again. He spoke very slowly, as though he expected to say it once and never have to say it again. 'When you and I spoke on your telephone we set certain wheels in motion. We both knew that. The result was that you and I both got an unpleasant suprise. The man who was killed was our John Brayer. So that's that. After he was killed we found he had a large amount of money in his home. Almost two hundred thousand dollars to be exact. And after that we received other evidence, which proves that John Brayer was the informer.' He formed his hands into fists. 'When I think of the things he must have told them—'

Elizabeth said, 'No. You're wrong. I knew him and—'

Connors shook his head. 'No, Miss Waring. The evidence I'm speaking of is conclusive. If you'll permit me to give you the most recent information, I'm sure you'll agree. I must caution you, however, that this information is sensitive. It must be released gradually and cautiously, at the right time. Some of it is very difficult to accept, but you must bear with me.' He looked almost fatherly now, his white hair no longer in its customary order. In her detachment Elizabeth thought with surprise, this isn't any easier for him than it is for me.

She said, 'All right.' She would be quiet. It was all she could do. But she knew Brayer hadn't had that kind of money. It must have been planted.

He almost smiled. He said, 'Good. Then let me fill you in. Early yesterday the police in Saratoga Springs, New York, received an anonymous telephone call telling them that they would find the remains of Edgar Fieldston buried on the estate of Carlo Balacontano. Actually, it's a place where they raise horses.'

'A stud farm,' said Elizabeth.

'Yes,' he said. 'On the strength of the call, the police got a warrant and raided the farm. What they found was, I'm afraid, not a pretty sight. It was the head and hands of Edgar Fieldston, and the pistol that killed him.' Connors looked down again. 'He was shot in the head.'

Elizabeth waited.

'They also found the missing bookkeeping from Fieldston Growth Enterprises. It was a checkbook and we've been able to match the balances to the accounts of Harry Orloff and others.'

Elizabeth said, 'Wait, Mr. Connors.'

He said, 'Honestly, Miss Waring. There is no question at all. When you see the evidence for yourself

362

you'll be amazed. Positively amazed. We have conclusive evidence that Carlo Balacontano was the silent partner in Fieldston Growth Enterprises and that he was involved in the killing of Edgar Fieldston and had him buried on his farm along with the secret bookkeeping of the company. You know, he used FGE to invest illegal profits amounting to over two million dollars. And another thing. Yesterday he received the money Edgar Fieldston got for the FGE stock in the Bahamas. Four million dollars. The serial numbers all match the list the Federal Reserve people made when the money was sent to Miami. It was mailed to Balacontano inside a package of paperback books.'

Elizabeth said, 'Wait. It must be a frame.'

'What are you talking about?'

'It's a frame-up. He wouldn't bury Fieldston's head and hands on his own property. He'd do the same thing with them he did with the rest of the body. Did you find the rest?'

Connors was flustered. 'No, but—'

'And the gun and his checkbook. It's ridiculous. Mr. Connors, a man like Balacontano must have people killed all the time. Why would he be so stupid? He could hire experts. People so skilled we'd never find anything. And who made the call to the police?'

Connors said, 'Miss Waring, I'm afraid you're asking questions that don't concern us. We have already compared the checkbook with what remains of FGE's records. What is there is genuine. The coroner has determined that Fieldston did die from a shot from the gun found with the, uh, remains. All on Balacontano's property. We have motive, body, weapon. Mr.

363

Balacontano is going to prison. I don't care who made the telephone call or why.'

'You know it's a frame,' said Elizabeth. 'I'm not saying he didn't own FGE, or even that he didn't have Fieldston killed. But somebody planted what was left of Fieldston, the gun, and the checkbook. That was who made the call. And come to think of it, that had to be the one who actually killed Fieldston.'

'I know no such thing,' said Connors. 'And you're stepping very far out of line. I'll ignore it because of your distress over recent events. When you've looked at the evidence you'll see how clearly it implicates Carlo Balacontano.'

Elizabeth just stood there knowing that anything she said would be wrong. Connors didn't want to hear the truth.

'I'll tell you what,' said Connors. 'You've had a hard time of it over the last couple of weeks. And you've built up a backlog of compensatory time off. I want you to take a few weeks. Go somewhere. Have you ever been to Hawaii? How about London?'

'I've been away a lot. It's good to be home,' she said.

Connors repeated, 'I'd like to see you take a vacation.'

THIRTY-THREE

Elizabeth closed her eyes while the plane hurtled down the runway and lifted itself into the air. That was the only part of it she minded, the moment when it was going too fast to stop, but still seemed to weigh tons of metal. Whatever it was that converted it from a freight train to a bird was still essentially mysterious to her. The explanation given by people who understand such things sounded perfectly reasonable to the part of her mind that made decisions; to the part of her mind that controlled her pulse and her eyelids, it sounded like nonsense. But again the airplane defied common sense and rose into the sky.

In the airport she'd bought some magazines to read, but now they seemed to belong to a world that was foreign to her. Sometime she'd care about new ways to turn a strict diet into an adventure, but not now. Soon enough, when she returned from this mandatory vacation. When she'd done her time.

Elizabeth had picked London because she remembered it as cool and wet and densely inhabited. It was a place that looked as though people had always lived there, layers and layers of them, one over the other through time. From there, if she still felt restless, she could go on to the Continent. She wondered if it would be in the London newspapers when she got there. Probably it would. American scandals seemed to have a peculiar appeal to the English. When the Senator's staff turned up FGE, Balacontano had acted to protect himself. That had been the week poor Veasy had picked to write his letter to the Department of Justice Organized Crime Division. His careful, semi-literate, handwritten letter explaining why he thought his union's pension fund was being looted had found its way through the bureaucratic labyrinth to the desk of the one man who had any knowledge of Veasy's problem. John Brayer. The papers would love that part of it.

The letter had been in Brayer's desk when Connors had ordered the search. That was the part that still kept Elizabeth awake at night. Brayer.

She heard herself sigh. She would try to stay abroad during the trial, at least the first part of it with its sensational revelations. She already knew the strategy the department would follow. They'd arrange to have the trial in Saratoga Springs, where the evidence had been found. Just the head and hands – the parts used to identify a body – and the gun and the checkbook, all buried together a foot or two beneath the surface. But she knew the evidence wouldn't matter to the jury, any more than it did to Connors. If Balacontano wasn't the one who had killed Fieldston, everyone knew he had ordered the other murders. Fieldston was just the one they could prove. So they'd use what they had, and the jury would go along with it. If the prosecutors played according to Connors' plan the jury would even come to believe that the lack of a whole corpse was especially damaging. You had to be a monster to cut a man up like that. A monster, she thought, or a man who wanted to move evidence from one place to another. But Balacontano would be convicted. And maybe the prosecutors would generate enough heat to convict the men found with him at the stud farm at the time of the raid. It might be a week or more before someone else moved in to fill the vacuum he left in the Northeast.

Elizabeth was out of it now. She looked around her at the other passengers in the cabin. There were the usual tourists, an elderly couple seeing the world outside Iowa before it was too late, a pair of college girls in bluejeans, and three businessmen staring at papers resting on their trays. The only passenger within the limited range of Elizabeth's vision who wasn't immediately identifiable was the man across the aisle from her. She pretended to read one of her magazines while she studied him. He was wearing a comfortable sort of sport coat that she decided was too informal for a businessman trying to impress people in London. He was traveling alone and she couldn't see any carry-on luggage. He was just a quiet, solitary man with nothing special about him. He was probably a professor. He was a professor of English or history making one of those professorial pilgrimages to England, hoping perhaps that if he could stand where William the Conqueror stood or walk where Chaucer walked he would have insights unavailable to mere reason.

As Elizabeth watched the man leaned his head back on the seat and closed his eyes. She felt proud of herself for her perception. He was a professor. And right now he's thinking about the fun he's going to have prowling around in castles and cathedrals and libraries where musty old books have sat on the shelves for centuries. The man shifted slightly in his seat. Elizabeth thought she caught just the slightest suspicion of a smile on the corners of his mouth. She felt an involuntary instant of affection for him.

The man's smile faded and the skin at the corners of his eyes tightened in concentration. He was trying to remember. It was ridiculous, he knew, but once the problem had occurred to him, it had bothered him for days. What was the name of Eddie Mastrewski's cat?

NIGHTLIFE

ONE

Tanya stood in front of the full length mirror on the bedroom wall and brushed her hair. She watched the other girl, in another room, wearing the same new blue skirt and tank top, using her left hand instead of her right to brush the long blond hair to a shine. Tanya had always secretly relished the existence of the other pretty girl who lived in the other room beyond the glass, like a fish in an aquarium. She loved the whole idea of a second girl who lived a second life.

In Wheatfield when she was little she had sometimes turned her mother's dresser so the mirror would be directly across from the full-length one on the closet door. She could make a whole long line of other girls, then kick her legs and look like the Rockettes, the nearest ones as big as she was, and the others smaller and smaller as their line stretched off into infinity.

She had dressed up in her mother's clothes sometimes, so she could change the girl in the mirror. She would be someone who had a good life, someone who was loved and cared for, someone who was beautiful and had everything she wanted.

She could invent things that the girl in the mirror could say, and practice them, whispering so the girl in the mirror would not be overheard. She would assume faces that were distant and just a little disapproving, and know that seeing them would make people frantic, trying to find ways to please her. She tried expressions designed to reward too, opening her eyes and mouth wide in a grateful smile that admitted no possibility of darker thoughts, nothing held back or hidden. Sometimes when she did that she would add a laugh at the end – not a small, forced sound, but a delighted laugh that made her eyes glisten and her white teeth show to their best advantage.

The alarm system's cool male electronic voice announced, 'Kitchen . . . door': Dennis was finally home. This was it. Tanya stopped brushing her hair, slipped the brush into her purse, felt for the other handle and gripped it once, then released it.

She could hear Dennis's hard leather soles on the slate floor of the kitchen. There was no sound of his dropping his briefcase on the kitchen floor, so he had set it down gently: he had brought his laptop home again. He was planning to spend the evening working. 'Tanya?' He was in the living room now.

She put her purse on the floor beside the dresser. 'Up here.'

She spent the next fifteen seconds considering him – turning him around and around in her mind and evaluating him. Women always said men had a hard outer shell but were soft and sweet and vulnerable inside, but she had found the opposite. They had a layer outside that was yielding and squeezable, but when you squeezed you began to feel the hardness beneath, like bone. She had squeezed him a lot in a short time, and she was already beginning to reach the hardness. He was getting ready to say no to her, to deny her things. Maybe he would even criticize her when the bills came and he could see everything added up. It was time.

Dennis's heavy shoes thumped on the carpeted stairway, coming closer. She already saw each step of the stairway in her mind, even though she had only been with Dennis Poole for a month, and all but a week of that had been spent in hotels. As he climbed step by step, she began to enumerate his unpleasant qualities. She didn't like his laugh. It was a quick staccato that made his voice go one octave higher, like a jackass's bray. A few times she had gotten up from her chaise next to him and gone into the hotel pool to cool her sun-warmed skin, come up from underwater, and seen him looking at other women in their bathing suits. He tipped waiters exactly fifteen percent and never a penny more, and was proud of it because it showed he could do the arithmetic in his head. He was not a sincerely appreciative lover. He pretended to care and be solicitous of her, but there was a practical quality about it. His concern was to please her, but it wasn't the right kind of concern. He wasn't a man unable to stop himself because he was enthralled. He was merely thinking about whether he was pleasing her enough to keep her.

Dennis had reached the top of the stairs. As she turned to look at him, her detachment was complete. He was a forty-two-year-old man with a soft belly and thinning hair who spent his days selling computer equipment to other men like himself. He was nothing. She smiled beautifully, stepped into his embrace, and kissed him slowly, languorously. 'Hello, cowboy,' she whispered.

He laughed as she had expected. 'I could get used to coming home like this and finding you waiting for me.' He looked more serious. 'You know, I'm glad you were here for another reason. I think we need to talk about some things.'

'Sure. We can talk, but first, don't you want to get comfortable? I should think you'd be tired after sitting in that office all day.' She knew that tone of voice. Anyone could tell he was getting ready to be cheap with her, to start complaining about money. She pulled back and said, 'I'll bet you're sick of wearing that suit. Why don't you get out of it, relax, and soak in the tub?' She looked down at his tie as she loosened it, not into his eyes. 'Maybe I'll join you.'

'Good idea.' He took his suit coat off and his tie, while Tanya went into the bathroom and turned on the water. The oversized Jacuzzi tub had jets that bubbled, so she turned them on too.

Dennis Poole was naked now, and he put his arms around her. She tolerated his embrace for a few seconds, then wriggled away and whispered seductively, 'Wait.'

She went back out to the bedroom and walked to the dresser, where she had left her purse. She waited until she heard him turn off the water faucet, so the only sound was the steady burble of the jets. She quietly walked into the bathroom.

He was lying in the tub with his head cushioned by a folded towel, looking self-absorbed and distant as the bubbles massaged his skin. Tanya reached into her purse, took out the pistol, held it about a foot from his head, and squeezed. The report was a bright, sharp bang that echoed against the tile walls and made her ears ring. She turned away from the sight of his corpse, the red blood draining into the bath, and stopped being Tanya Starling.

TWO

Hugo Poole's rubber-soled shoes made almost no sound as he walked along the sidewalk outside the CBS Studio Center's iron railings, past the soundstages on his way up Radford Street from Ventura Boulevard. He never would have set up a night meeting in the Valley, so far from the old downtown movie theater he used for an office, but he had often found that it was worth making small concessions just to learn what the other side wanted to do. There was no single precaution that would always work, and the least effective was never taking a risk. As soon as caution turned predictable, it became the biggest risk of all.

Still, he wished he could stay right here. He liked being near a television studio, because these complexes were usually on the itineraries of the people who heard voices telling them that God wanted them to punish a few actors. That ensured that there would always be plenty of jumpy security guards. He would have preferred to meet Steve Rao right here outside the gate, under the tall security lights.

Hugo Poole walked on beside the railing, now moving into the dimly lighted eucalyptus-lined blocks beside the big parking structure, and then he stopped at Valleyheart Street. He crossed the street to the city's chain-link fence and looked through it to the place where the concrete bed of the Tujunga Wash met the concrete bed of the Los Angeles River. On this hot midsummer night, the only water was the runoff from automatic lawn sprinklers, a steady trickle confined to a foot-deep groove a man could step across that ran down the center of each bed. In the rainy season this place became the confluence of two turbulent brown floods crashing together at thirty miles an hour and rushing south toward the Pacific.

Hugo Poole looked to his left, up the scenic walkway above the river toward the iron gate at Laurel Canyon that was designed to look like a big toad. At this hour nobody wanted to go for a walk above a concrete riverbed. He waited for the minute hand of his watch to reach the hour. Then he took out the key he had received in the mail. He unlocked the padlock on the gate above the wash, and slipped inside. Steve Rao's people had knocked off the city padlock and put on their own, then sent him the key to open it. Hugo Poole took a moment to close the gate. He reached into his pocket, took out his own lock, and placed it on the gate. He stuck Rao's key into Rao's lock, tossed them both down the hill into the bushes, and walked on.

He descended the sloping gravel driveway that the city had cut so its maintenance people could come down once a year to remove the tangle of dried brush and shopping carts from the concrete waterway before the rains. He reached the bottom, took a few steps onto the pavement of the river, and stopped to look around him. He could hear the distant whisper of cars flashing along the Ventura Freeway a few blocks away, and a constant dribble of water dripping out of a storm drain and running down the wall a few feet from him.

Hugo Poole's eyes adjusted to the darkness and picked out four silhouettes in the deeper shadow across the wash. They floated toward him, and Poole tried to pick out Steve Rao's short, strutting body, but couldn't.

The one who separated from the others was too tall to

6

be Steve Rao. 'What are you doing here?' the voice said. It was young, with a trace of Spanglish inflection.

It was the wrong question. Somebody Steve Rao had sent would know why Hugo was here.

Hugo Poole said, 'I'm not here to hurt you. That's all you need to know about me.'

The heads of the four shapes turned to one another in quiet consultation, and Hugo Poole prepared himself, waiting for them to spread out. There was a sudden, sharp blow to his skull that made a red flare explode in his vision and knocked his head to the side. He spun to see the two new shapes just as they threw their shoulders into him. His head snapped back and his spine was strained as they dug in and brought him down on the concrete.

They seemed to have expected him to give up, but he began to bring his knees into play as he grappled with them. They tried to hold him down on the pavement, but Hugo Poole fought silently and patiently, first separating them, then twisting his torso to jab a heavy elbow into a face. He heard a crack, a howl of pain, and felt his opponent fall away. He rolled to the other side to clutch the second assailant, and delivered a palm strike that bounced the back of the man's head off the pavement. The man lay still.

Hugo Poole was up on his feet again, sidestepping away from the two motionless bodies. The other four had made it only halfway across the riverbed toward him, and now they stopped with the shallow trench full of water separating them from Hugo Poole.

Poole put his head down and charged at the one who had spoken earlier. The young man hesitated, then looked at his companions, who showed no inclination to help him. They backed away, not from Hugo Poole but from their companion, as though if they could dissociate

7

themselves from his fate, they would not share it. As Hugo Poole leapt the trench, the young man spun on his heel and ran about a hundred feet before he turned to see if he was safe.

The other three interpreted his flight as permission to run too. They dashed to the far wall where the shadows were deepest, and then moved off into the darkness down the riverbed. Hugo Poole turned to see that the two who had been on the ground were rapidly recovering. One was helping the other to his feet, and then they hobbled off together up the inclined driveway toward the street.

Hugo Poole stood in the dim concrete riverbed and caught his breath. The right knee of his pants had a small tear in it; the elbow of his suit coat felt damp, so he looked at that too. It had a dark splash of blood on it from the first man's nose. He sighed: this was turning into an irritating evening, and it was still early.

Then Hugo Poole saw a new light. It began as a vague impression in his mind that there must be clouds moving away from the moon. Then the light brightened and the impression changed. The light was coming from somewhere down the channel. The wall opposite him began to glow, and then the light separated into two smaller, more focused circles.

A set of headlights appeared around an elbow bend in the channel and came toward him. He was aware that it might be a police patrol car, or the animal control people checking on the coyotes that used the concrete riverbeds to travel across the city at night. Either way, it would be best to stay still. It was especially important not to move if it was Steve Rao.

Hugo Poole stood and watched as the ghostly vehicle drew nearer, its headlights brightening until it pulled up beside him and stopped. Now that the headlights were shining past him, he saw that it was a black Hummer with tinted windows. Someone in the passenger seat used a powerful flashlight to sweep the walls of the channel and the bushes and hiding places up above at street level.

The flashlight went out, the passenger door opened, and a large man with wavy dark hair got out. He wore a lightweight black sport coat and pants of a color that looked gray in the near darkness. The driver got out, and Hugo Poole could see that he was wearing a sport coat too. Almost certainly the coats were intended to hide the bulges of firearms. The driver stood with his back against the door of the Hummer and kept guard while the other man approached Hugo Poole.

The man said, 'Sir, are you Mr Poole?'

'Yes.'

'Can you put your arms out from your sides for me, please?'

Hugo Poole complied, and stood with his feet apart so his legs could be checked next. He waited, staring into the distance as the man patted him down expertly, then stepped back. 'Thank you very much, sir.'

Hugo Poole said, 'You're an off-duty cop, aren't you?'

He didn't deny it. 'I'm a friend of Steve's.'

Hugo nodded and watched the driver open the back door of the Hummer. Steve Rao was perched on the edge of the high seat when the door opened. He was wearing black jeans and a black T-shirt with a dark windbreaker, as though he were out to commit a burglary. His shoes were half light and half dark, like bowling shoes. He slid to the end of the Hummer's back seat and then jumped down, smiling.

He looked proud of himself, his eyes and teeth reflecting the distant light from above. 'Hugo, my man. Thanks for coming. I hope it wasn't too inconvenient.'

'You saw?'

Steve Rao looked very serious. 'I didn't have anything to do with them, I swear to God.'

'I didn't think you did,' said Hugo Poole.

'It's terrible,' said Steve Rao. 'This isn't even gang territory. The city really has to do something.'

'I'll write a letter to the *Times*.'

Steve Rao's grin returned. 'You're still pretty mean, though, aren't you? You can handle yourself against these young kids even now.'

Hugo Poole did not smile.

Steve Rao gestured toward the two men beside his black Hummer. 'These two guys are my solution to that foolishness. You won't see me rolling around on dirty cement beating the shit out of no gang of kids. I learned that much.'

'I'll be honest with you, Steve. This night is beginning to wear on my patience. Why did you want to meet me in a place like this?'

'It's safe and secure.'

'It's safe and secure up there on the corner of Ventura and Laurel Canyon, and you can get a cup of coffee in Du Par's,' said Hugo. 'What is it you want?'

Steve Rao began to walk. Hugo followed for about two hundred feet, and stopped. Steve Rao noticed, so he stopped too, and spoke. 'I've been around for a while now. You know that?'

'I've noticed you for about five years,' said Hugo Poole.

'I haven't been lying around all that time.'

'I've noticed that too.'

'I've been busy. I've been talking to people, making deals, making friends.'

'No flies on you,' said Hugo Poole.

'It's worked out. I've gotten big.' It was a strange thing for a man Hugo Poole judged was about five feet five to say. 'It's time to make a deal with you too.' He glared at Hugo Poole. 'I've put it off for longer than I should have.'

'I'm listening.'

'I want ten thousand a month from you.'

'In exchange for what?'

'For being able to do whatever you want. For not having to worry. You can go on forever, just like you have been, and nobody will bother you.'

'Nobody bothers me now.'

Steve Rao stopped and pointed back at the Hummer, where the two off-duty cops were sitting. 'See those guys?'

Hugo Poole gave his second sigh of the evening. 'Steve, how old are you?'

'Twenty-four.'

'When you're a young guy, just starting out, you have to consider the possibility that the people who were here before you were born aren't all dumb.'

'What do you mean?'

'You should look around and say, "What are people already doing that works? What are people not doing, even though it's an obvious thing to do? And why aren't they?" '

Steve Rao glared at him again, then resumed walking. 'A lot of people are doing this. People have sold protection for a hundred years.'

'Street gangs. They shake down a few Korean grocery stores, a couple of small liquor stores. They ask for just enough so the payoff is cheaper than buying a new front window. The game lasts a few months, until all the gang boys are in jail for something else or dead. Grown-ups don't do this in L.A. And they don't use off-duty cops for bodyguards.'

'Why are you saying this shit?' Steve was quickly beginning to feel the heat around his neck cooking into anger. 'It's all shit! Half the rock stars in town have hired cops with them wherever they go.'

'I'm telling you this because I want to do you a big favor,' said Hugo Poole. 'That works great for musicians. Cops have to carry guns off-duty, so nobody has to make any guesses.'

'That's right,' said Steve Rao. 'So don't even think about trying to get out of this. I might as well be made out of steel. Anybody opens up anywhere near me, my cops will drill his ass for him. They got my back. Nobody can do anything to me.'

'That's probably true,' said Hugo Poole. 'But what can you do to anybody else?'

'Anything,' said Steve Rao, but he sounded uncertain.

Hugo Poole said, 'Off-duty cops will keep people from killing you if they can, just like they do for rock stars. But they won't let even the biggest rock stars grease somebody else.'

'We have an understanding.'

'They understand you better than you understand them.'

'They're mine. I bought them.'

'You're paying cops money to stay a few feet from you. They can see you make deals, they can hear what you say. When they've seen and heard enough, they're going to arrest you and all of the people who do business with you.'

'You're full of shit.'

'Steve, these guys know the system. They know that if they get in trouble, you won't be able to do them any good. The only people who can help them are other cops.' He paused. 'You aren't going to collect any money from anybody, Steve, because you can't hurt anybody in front of two cops. You just put yourself out of business.'

'Hugo, I always heard you were supposed to be the smartest man in L.A. But this is pitiful,' said Steve Rao.

He took a small semiautomatic pistol from his jacket. He didn't point it at Hugo, just shifted it to his belt. 'I want your ten grand tomorrow by five, and then once a month. Be on time.'

'Ask me how I knew they were cops.'

'All right. How did you know?'

'They're wearing microphones,' said Hugo Poole. 'See you, Steve.' Hugo Poole walked down the concrete riverbed, away from Steve Rao.

'You don't walk away from me,' said Steve Rao. 'You wait until I walk away from you.' His voice sounded strained and thin, as though his throat were dry.

Hugo Poole walked on, his pace the same smart stride he always used on the street that kept his head up and his eyes on the world in front of him and let him scan the sights beside him. He had decided that it would be best not to return to the street by the same path he had used to come down here, so he walked on for what he judged to be an extra two blocks before he came to the next ramp built for the flood maintenance people. At the top of the path he had to climb an eight-foot chain-link fence, something he hated to do, but since his suit was beyond repair, he supposed he could hardly ruin it twice.

He swung himself over, dropped to the ground, then walked back up to Radford. Just as he was coming out of the dimly lighted, quiet street toward Ventura Boulevard, he heard the distant pops of four shots in rapid succession, then seven more. They seemed to echo from the direction of the river. As he walked along, he considered the eleven shots. Eleven was a bad number for Steve Rao. The magazines for pistols like Steve Rao's held no more than ten in a single stack.

THREE

Hugo Poole parked in front of the Hundred Proof Bar and slipped a twenty-dollar bill to the bouncer outside the door in exchange for protecting his car from the tow trucks. The frightening late-night clientele of the Hundred Proof would keep the hot-wire artists away. As he walked along Sheldrake Avenue toward the Empire Theater he looked respectable but tired, like the bartender of an intermittently violent nightclub. He wanted to get this suit off. He would get a shower, put on a clean shirt and a new suit, and feel right again. Hugo Poole never wore a tie, because during his formative years he had watched a fight in which a man had been choked out with his Windsor knot.

He walked under the big, ornate marquee that announced EMPIRE THEATER CLOSED FOR RENOVATION. He stepped into the alcove across the terrazzo inlay of 1920s bathing beauties and stopped beside the ticket booth in front. He stared up and down Sheldrake Avenue. Hugo Poole did not simply glance: he took his time, his eyes narrowed to impart sharpness and definition to distant shapes. When he decided he had outlasted any possible duckers-behind-corners or walkers-the-other-way, he took a full turn and stopped with his back against the door to be absolutely sure he had not been followed. He had not. Hugo Poole unlocked the door to the movie theater, opened it, slipped inside, closed it, and tugged it once to be sure it had locked behind him.

He turned. The dim pink glow of the light inside the candy display case let him see the gilded plaster-cast sconces and the ancient painted murals of women who seemed half nymph and half movie star getting out of long antique limousines. Behind them, aimed upward in the sky, were beams from big spotlights. He heard a noise and turned to the carpeted stairway across the lobby that led up toward the balcony.

'Evening, Hugo.' Otto Collins and Mike Garcia came into the lobby from upstairs. They had been waking up the building, doing the evening walk-around, turning on lights and unlocking the inner doors.

'Hello, guys,' Hugo Poole said. He was not about to forget that the easiest way for somebody to kill him was to pay these two to do it here in the theater, but he had already studied them and acquitted them for tonight. Every night he looked at them for signs that they were going to betray him.

Hugo Poole was not watching for nervous twitches and smiling, sweaty upper lips. These were men. They worked for Hugo Poole, and they could be expected to behave with a certain amount of self-possession. What he was looking for was the opposite: excessive self-control. He had seen it come upon serious men when they were contemplating risky behavior. He knew that on the day when he was going to die Mike and Otto would grow cold and distant.

Hugo Poole knew that he was reputed to be a deep thinker, and it was a useful myth to cultivate. He was only premeditative, but to many people that made him seem clairvoyant. He made his way upstairs to the carpeted upper hallway, past the door marked PROJECTION ROOM, opened a wooden door that seemed to be a part of the paneled wall, and went inside.

Hugo walked to his desk and sat down, then glanced

at his watch. It had taken him forty-five minutes to get back here from the Valley, and he judged that to be enough time. He consulted the telephone book on the corner of his desk, picked up his telephone, and called the police precinct station in North Hollywood.

He said, 'This is G. David Hunter. I'm an attorney under retainer for Steven Rao, R-A-O. He hasn't shown up where he was expected this evening. Could you please check to see whether he has been taken into custody tonight?' He listened for a moment, then said, 'Shot dead? You did say "dead"? I'm shocked. When did this happen?' He listened for a few more seconds, then said, 'Thank you. No doubt you'll be hearing from me in the future. The body? I'm not sure. Let me talk to the family. I'll have to get back to you. Good night.'

He sat back, stared at the wall, and thought about this evening. He supposed he might have to anticipate some sort of retaliation from the two cops who'd had to shoot Steve Rao. They were certainly smart enough to know why Rao had turned on them. Hugo would have to postpone a few of the schemes he had been prospering on – removing small numbers of items from cargo containers at the harbor and replacing them with stones to keep the weights constant, having women pose as hookers so Otto and Mike could be the vice squad who burst in to confiscate wallets – and substitute a few that seemed a bit less flagrant.

He searched his memory for ideas that were safer. He had recently seen a television program in which a crowd of middle-class people stood in line carrying old possessions so that a team of antique dealers could appraise them. He had noticed that some not particularly prepossessing articles were assigned very high prices.

He had also noticed that in almost every case, the more scarred and damaged an item was, the more likely the experts were to revere it. He had become fascinated by the way the antique dealers talked. No matter what obsolete and arcane castoff the expert was appraising, he could always talk about 'the collectors' of that very item.

There was no doubt in Hugo Poole's mind that there were ways to make money from his discovery. How could he not make money off people who were willing to haul a five-hundred-pound sideboard to a television studio and then stand in line for hours to have some guy with a fake accent look at it?

There was a rap on the door. Hugo Poole automatically crouched low and moved to the left, where the steel filing cabinets full of books and papers would stop a bullet. He eyed the Colt Commander .45 that he kept duct-taped to the back of the cabinet against his day of doom. It was just possible that Steve Rao's untimely death was not being taken well by somebody. Hugo Poole waited a moment, but nobody kicked in the door.

'Who is it?' he called.

'Just me. Otto.'

'Come in.'

Otto said, 'There's a call for you on the house phone down there, Hugo. It's a woman who says she's your aunt.'

Hugo squinted at Otto for a second, then stood up and hurried past him to the stairwell. It was unusual for anyone to call in on the Empire Theater's telephone number, and during the daytime there was usually nobody here to answer it. When Hugo, Otto, and Mike were here, they were usually asleep.

He went to the small office off the lobby near the candy counter and picked up the telephone. 'Hugo Poole here.' He listened. 'Hi, Aunt Ellen. How are you? What? Dennis? Oh, my God.' He closed his eyes and listened for a few seconds. Then he rubbed his forehead. 'I'm so sorry, Aunt Ellen. I never imagined that anything like this could happen to Dennis.'

FOUR

Joe Pitt looked up at the chandelier. There were a few hundred tear-shaped crystal pieces like diamond earrings hanging above him, the light that came off them bright white with glints of rainbows. It was like heaven up there.

He looked down again at the green felt surface of the table, gathered his cards, and glanced at them. It was not heaven down here. Three of clubs, six of diamonds, four of spades, ten of diamonds, nine of hearts.

Joe Pitt watched his four opponents pick up their cards. Jerry Whang's tell was that he always blinked once when he picked up a really good hand. It was as though he were closing the shutters of his mind, because when he opened his eyes again, he revealed nothing more. There was the blink.

Stella Korb picked up her cards and looked sick. She'd had a Botox injection today to deaden the muscles under her facial skin, but it didn't change her eyes. The new guy that Pitt thought of as the Kid, who had the repulsive habit of wearing a baseball cap indoors, retained the same dumb look after seeing his cards.

Delores Harkness squeezed her cards open with her thumb, closed them again to look around, then thumbed them open once more to be sure she had seen what she had seen.

She opened with a single twenty-five-dollar chip, patiently trying to keep all of the others in as long as she could before she started murdering the last optimists. She succeeded, each of them tossing in a chip until it came to Joe Pitt. He set his cards down. 'Have a good evening, everyone. I'm out.'

Billy the dealer swept Pitt's cards away. 'See you, Joe.' Pitt stepped off, heading past the crowds of gamblers toward the front door of the card club. He walked outside, sniffed the night air, looked around himself, and listened. Just beyond the far side of the parking lot he could see headlights flashing past on the freeway and he could hear the constant swish of tires on the pavement. For once he had managed to lose all of the money he had allowed himself for the evening and not go to the cashier's window with a credit card. He supposed that was a kind of half victory, like getting into a crash and having the car still run well enough to get him home. Then why didn't he feel better?

He stared at the aisle of the big parking lot where he had left his car and sensed that something was not right. His right hand moved reflexively to pat his left side once, a gesture that was so habitual that most observers would have missed it. He was still permitted to carry his pistol in a shoulder rig under his sport coat: for the rest of his life there would be the chance that someone who had gotten to know him during his twenty years as an investigator for the DA's office would finally get around to killing him.

He opened his coat and stepped forward, away from the lighted front of the casino. Joe Pitt had a willingness to pay attention to vague sensations, and when he sensed that something was threatening he went toward it.

He had built his reputation by solving murders, and he had done it by moving toward whatever didn't feel right. Offices closed on weekends, but every day on the calendar the killer was a killer, and Joe Pitt was working his way toward him. Any suspect who had not understood it that way had found himself at a severe disadvantage. It wasn't some theoretical entity called the State of California that was after him; it was Joe Pitt.

He selected a row of cars three spaces to the left of his car, and began to walk up the aisle. It took a moment before he saw the heads in the car parked beside his. As he walked his angle changed, and he could see more: there was a male driver in front, and a second man sitting in the back seat. Maybe it was a rich guy with a chauffeur, and maybe it was an easy way of putting two shooters into position to fire at him.

Joe Pitt stopped beside a car, pretended to unlock it, then went low, as though he had gotten into the driver's seat. He stayed low and scurried along the spaces between parked cars until he was beside the car where the two men waited. He stood up slightly behind the passenger, with his gun in his hand close to the open window.

The passenger looked at him. 'Hello, Joe.'

Joe Pitt's hand tightened on the gun. 'Hello, Hugo.'

'You know my friend Otto?'

'Of course. How are you, Otto? Congratulations on your early release.'

'Thanks,' said Otto. 'It's nice to be out. And yourself?'

'I'm fine, thanks. What's up, Hugo?'

Hugo Poole looked up at him. 'I need to talk to you. If you feel safer doing it inside the casino, I'll send Otto in to arrange for a private space.'

'I'm not afraid of you. I'm just not interested.' He put his gun away.

'It's worth money to you.'

'I have money, thanks,' said Joe Pitt.

'You have a weakness for women and a gambling problem, and nobody's got enough money for those. Three different guys have come to me in the past year or so to sell me that information. I only paid the first one, but I remembered it. We don't have time to bullshit each other. Tonight when I found out I needed you I knew where you would be.'

'The gambling isn't a problem. It's the losing. What do you think you need me for?'

'Will you get in so we can talk? You're safe with us.' Hugo Poole pushed open the door and then slid to the other side. Joe Pitt hesitated, then got in beside him. Otto Collins drove the car up the aisle and out to the street.

Pitt said, 'I know that a few times when I needed information, you arranged for somebody to miraculously turn up to give it to me. I got the solution to something that was puzzling me, and you got – whatever it was that you got. That may have made me forget to add your name to a list of menaces to the public welfare. But life isn't the same now.'

'You're the same, I'm the same. What's different?'

'I'm retired from the district attorney's office. I'm out. I can't affect the outcome of some investigation. Whatever it is that you want, I'm not in the position to give it to you.'

'You're a private detective now. You're getting famous.'

'Everybody's got to do something. But I don't do anything for money that can send me to jail.'

'I assumed that. You wouldn't last long enough to get to the front of the chow line. If it were anything illegal, I wouldn't waste your time with it,' said Hugo Poole.

'So what do you want?'

'Yesterday my cousin Dennis got shot to death in Portland.'

'What for? Was he working for you?'

'No. He's never worked for me. I haven't even seen him in about four or five years.'

'So what was he into?'

Hugo Poole frowned. 'Nothing. Dennis wasn't into anything. He was a computer salesman.'

Pitt's face was expressionless.

'Dennis was a straight businessman. He had a store up in Portland and a warehouse, and he sold computer stuff wholesale and over the Internet. He was good at it. He made money. I want to know what gets a guy like that killed.'

'That's what you want? You want me to find out what happened?'

Hugo Poole held up his hands. 'I can't just leave this to a bunch of shitkicker cops in Oregon. I need somebody on this who knows what's what.'

'Portland isn't a small town, Hugo. They have homicide detectives who can handle an investigation,' said Pitt. 'And I don't think an outsider has much chance of finding anything they won't. It's their city.'

'It's not just their city I'm worried about. I need someone who will be able to make the connections between what went on there and what goes on here.'

Pitt's eyes settled on Hugo's face. 'You think your cousin's killing had something to do with you?'

'Dennis may have had some enemies of his own. He may even have been into something that I don't know about. But until somebody proves that, the only reason anybody had to shoot Dennis was that he was related to me.'

'What do you think I can do for you?'

'Fly up there. Cops all over the country know who you are, and the cases you solved when you were the DA's investigator. They'll hear your name and think you can help them find out who killed Dennis. So I want you to do it. I'll pay you a lot of money.'

Pitt stared at him, unblinking. 'Then what if it is

about you? I'm not interested in being paid to go up there and steer a police investigation away from you.'

'You wouldn't. I can keep myself out of trouble without any help from you. If the investigation starts pointing back in the direction of L.A., you'll be able to tell them where to look. Even if it's toward me.'

Pitt said, 'Then you'll need time to clean up your act, won't you? Or have you already started phasing down your operations?'

'Tonight I'm clearing up loose ends so you can go after this guy without tripping over my feet. I'm pulling my feet out of the way.'

'If I get into this, I'm not going to point the finger at some guy so you can kill him.'

'I want you to help the cops find the killer – the real one, not some poor bastard they decide to pin it on. If you do that much for me, then you did your job.'

'How much are you offering?'

'A hundred thousand plus expenses if you agree to make a serious effort. Another hundred when they get the guy.'

'You must really feel guilty.'

'If you won't take the job because it's my money, then say it.'

'No, I'm like a doctor,' said Joe Pitt. 'If you've got a heartbeat, I'll work on you until it stops or your bank account runs dry.'

FIVE

Joe Pitt followed Sergeant Catherine Hobbes up the driveway of what had been Dennis Poole's house. He couldn't help letting his eyes spend more time looking at her than was practical. He estimated that she was about thirty, but it was hard to be sure. She had a rounded athletic little body, but she had tried to blur the contours with a masculine gray pantsuit, and she had tried to harden her pretty face by pulling her strawberry-blond hair into a bun and wearing little makeup. Joe Pitt watched her step over the POLICE LINE – DO NOT CROSS tape, climb the steps to the door, where she ignored the big sticker that said CRIME SCENE – DO NOT ENTER, and unlock the door.

'Nice place,' he said.

'I hate this kind of house. It's pretentious – way too big for the lot it's on, and everything inside it was made to be looked at, not used.'

He said, 'I wasn't asking you to move in with me. I just meant it looks expensive.'

'It's that, all right.' She stared past him as she swung the door open, and stepped inside to hold it so he had to go in ahead of her.

Catherine Hobbes had been surprised to see how fine Pitt's features were, and how alert and intelligent his eyes looked. But for her there wasn't anything endearing about his attractiveness. He talked with the kind of easy familiarity that meant he was aware that he had an advantage with women.

She was irritated at Joe Pitt already, but she was determined to be polite to him. She had orders, and she was not about to get in trouble just because he was arrogant. If she could tolerate him long enough, she could learn something. He was a well-known investigator who had, in his prime, solved a number of murders. If she had to endure his banter to learn what he knew, then she would do it. 'There isn't any sign of forced entry here. The other doors are bolted from the inside.'

Pitt looked around. As a concession to the rainy Portland climate there was a small foyer with a black-and-white marble floor and a long wooden seat for changing boots, a coat rack above it, and an umbrella stand. Beyond that the thick carpet began, and everything in sight was beige or white.

'Where did he get shot?'

'Upstairs in the master suite. I'll show you.' She went to the long straight staircase, and they climbed to the landing.

Pitt walked into Dennis Poole's bedroom, which was big enough for four bedrooms. He surveyed the furnishings. On the wall there was a plasma television about six feet wide, and below it on a cabinet a set of videocassette recorders and DVD players. There was a big desk with more computer equipment on it than anybody needed. There were shelves with so many books and magazines on them that they reminded Pitt that he hadn't seen any evidence of a book downstairs. The bed looked like the oversized king in a good hotel suite. 'Was he in debt to pay for all of this?'

'We haven't found any debt yet. Considering his income, the house isn't at all extravagant,' she said. 'He bought it about a year after his divorce, when he was twenty-eight. That was fourteen years ago. He lived alone, and he cleared three to four hundred thousand a year. There's no sign of expensive hobbies or collections, no trace of drugs in his blood or the house, no history of gambling.'

'Anything missing?'

'He lived alone, so we haven't got anybody who really knows. There are no dust spots where things have been removed, or marks on the walls from missing paintings or anything. We took a couple of people from his office through the house, and neither of them could remember seeing anything here that's gone.' She held him in the corner of her eye. 'Maybe you can tell me.' Instantly she wished she had not said it.

He looked around him as though he had not heard. 'Where was the body?'

'In the bathtub.' She led him into the bathroom. It was big too, with an enormous black tub and a room-sized glass-walled shower with showerheads on three sides and a slate seat along one wall. Most of the surfaces were covered with fingerprint dust. 'One shot to the head.'

He looked down at the tub, then moved his face close to examine the blood-spatter pattern on the wall above it. 'And you're sure he didn't just pop himself ?'

'The gun wasn't found with him. Anyway, the angle was wrong.'

'How?'

'Sort of like this.' She pointed her index finger at her own head. 'See? The angle is too high. You can't get a gun up there and point slightly downward, and why would you?'

Joe Pitt nodded and walked farther into the bathroom, examining the shower and the sinks without touching anything. 'Was he taking a bath or did they just shove him in there to keep the job from getting messy?'

'He was naked. There was soap in the tub, and a towel under his head like a pillow.'

Pitt left the bathroom and stared at the bedroom again. 'I assume your people didn't find anything in the rest of the house.'

'It's all just like what you saw on the way up here. The rooms look like no one's ever used them. It's white couches that nobody ever sat in, and glass tabletops without so much as a fingerprint. The kitchen is beautiful, but there's hardly anything in the refrigerator but drinks. He ate out three meals a day.'

'He seems to have lived up here.'

'That's how I see it,' she said. 'The television gets something like two hundred and fifty channels, about fifty of them sports. He could sit up here forever watching one game after another, and never go downstairs except for more beer.'

'Who dusted the white couches and washed the windows?'

'He had a contract with Mighty Maids. They have a whole crew of women come in at once, clean the hell out of everything, and go away. That was how his body got found. His crew came twice a week during business hours, when he was usually at work. They had a key, but they also had an alibi – people who saw them cleaning houses at the time of death. They came in yesterday and there he was.'

Joe Pitt stood in the center of the room and slowly turned all the way around, studying every detail. 'Have you pieced together the sequence?'

She nodded. 'He left work earlier than usual, but didn't have to tell anybody why, because he was the boss. He was wearing a dark gray suit that day. He was home by four, set his briefcase down in the kitchen, and came up here. He took off the suit and tie and hung them up in here.' She walked to the huge walk-in closet and pushed the door open so Pitt could see the neat row of

28

coats and trousers hanging along the pole. At least four were shades of gray. 'They're in the lab, of course. Next he threw his shirt, socks, and underwear in the hamper, went into the bathroom, ran the water in the tub, and got in.'

'So he was still doing everything voluntarily – no chance of force?'

'There are no abrasions or contusions on him to show a struggle, and there was no water splashed around when the maids found him. At some point, the killer probably slipped in, approached him from behind, held the gun a foot from his head, and fired once. The entry wound is behind the right ear. The neighbors on both sides and across the street were still at work, and nobody else in the neighborhood remembers hearing a shot.'

'You figure it was intended to be a faked suicide at first?'

'I think so, but it was botched. Maybe Mr Poole heard the guy at the last instant and flinched. Maybe the killer just got too eager and fired early.'

'Was the gun Poole's? Did he have one that's missing?'

'He didn't have any firearms registered to him.'

Pitt looked down at his feet. 'This isn't going to be easy, is it?'

'No,' said Catherine Hobbes. 'He seems to have been secure and prosperous. He had no enemies anybody knows about. He just came back from vacation a couple of weeks ago, and the people at work said he seemed happy and relaxed.'

'What about women?'

'What about them?'

'Did he like them? Did he like one in particular?'

'That's one of the things that's been worrying me. The trace evidence people found some long, straight blond hairs. There were two on suits of his, a few on the carpet in here, one on a bathrobe. The women on the Mighty Maids crew are all black or Hispanic.'

'Any blonds at his company?'

'Two, but the hair isn't a match for either one. Nobody seems to remember seeing him with a blond woman lately. There are no female relatives who live in town, and his mother says none have long, straight blond hair.'

'This blond woman seems like the most promising thing I've heard,' said Pitt. 'She could have been married. That would give Poole a reason to try to keep the relationship quiet, and a good motive for the husband to kill him.'

'We've been concentrating on her, and we've found nothing yet. On the other hand, we do have one odd thing that turned up unexpectedly.'

'What?'

'You.'

'I don't feel like an odd thing.'

She shrugged. 'I got an order from my captain that I'd be cooperating with an expert from Los Angeles, a former DA's investigator who will help with the case. I looked you up on Google and found lots of articles about you, mostly in the *Los Angeles Times,* but in national magazines too. Pictures of you and everything.'

'Anything interesting?'

'You're retired from the DA's office – honorably, it said – and now you make a gazillion dollars a year doing private investigation. At that point, I was ready to invite you over for a home-cooked dinner and a shot at meeting my parents. Then I talked to my captain and found out you were working for the cousin.'

'You lost interest?'

'Let's say the nature of my interest changed.'

'It doesn't have to,' said Pitt. 'I'm not here to do anything wrong, and I really do make a gazillion dollars.'

'You're working for a bad guy,' said Hobbes. 'Lips that have touched Hugo Poole's ass will never touch mine.'

'Your ass?'

'My anything,' she said.

Joe Pitt nodded. 'So up here, when a known criminal asks you to investigate his relative's murder, you say no?'

'We don't actually consult him. When there's a murder we go after the killer, whether anybody wants us to or not.' She patted his arm and said with mock sympathy, 'It's not you, Joe. It's me. I just don't like people taking money from a crook to keep him out of a murder investigation.'

'I wasn't hired to do that,' he said. 'Hugo Poole agrees with you. He thinks the killing is a reprisal for something he did down in L.A. If you want to pursue that, he'll try to help you. But it's not what happened.'

'You don't know that.'

'If it's a reprisal, they wouldn't try to make it look like a suicide. They'd make it as big and ugly as they could, and make damned sure Hugo knew why.'

Joe Pitt stalked around the room, looking at things. 'This place has been cleaned up. I asked you before if something was missing, and you didn't know. I know now what it is. It's the mess.'

'But he wasn't messy,' she said. 'Downstairs each room looks like a department store window.'

'Because he didn't live down there. He lived up here, in this suite. But there's nothing random, nothing out of its place up here. I know it wouldn't look like a room in a fraternity house, but this isn't the way it looked when he died, either. It's been sanitized. The only person who would have done that is the killer.'

'You think the killer took the time to go through this whole suite wiping off prints and picking up fibers?'

'Yes, I do,' he said. 'But I think that what the shooter didn't want us to know about wasn't his prints. I think he was removing signs of the blond woman. The killer came in and shot Poole – one round, no struggle. At that point, he could have exited without much risk of leaving anything of himself. But instead he straightened the suite, put everything away, vacuumed the carpets. He missed a couple of blond hairs on the floor and stuck to Poole's clothes.'

'The blond hairs on the suit don't mean somebody cleaned the place. Maybe that's all there were.'

'You said the Mighty Maids were all black or Hispanic, and they cleaned the hell out of this place twice every week. That takes hours of hard work, a lot of it on their hands and knees. So where are the fibers from their uniforms? Where are the dark hairs?'

'Oh, God,' said Hobbes. He was right. Damn him. 'What if she was what it was about?'

'Could be. Maybe some other man came here to take her – or take her back.'

'I've got to find that girl.'

SIX

The girl felt some sadness, but she was satisfied. She had thoroughly experienced Dennis Poole, so she was not disappointed in herself. She was proud of herself for overcoming her shyness and fear in the hotel bar in Aspen, and being the first to speak. That alone was an accomplishment. She had found something about him appealing – his tall, slightly awkward body, the clothes he wore that seemed to be right out of the box, as though he had never worn anything all year but a business suit. She had sat in the bar at a small table near the window that looked out on the mountains, then feigned surprise to find him sitting nearby and said, 'What a wonderful sky. I love the color of the sky just after sundown.' How could he not reply?

After she had talked to him for a few minutes, she had found that she almost instantly knew what to say to him and how to say it. There had never been more than a few moments when she had needed to doubt herself. She had listened to him carefully, begun to accumulate a small trove of facts about who he was and what he liked, and then made herself the woman that he wanted. He owned a small, dull business and he was on vacation, so she became a perfect vacation companion. She was the lively girl who was always happy, always on the edge of laughter, ready to go to the next place just to see what was there.

She had experimented with liking him – pretended to find him more interesting than he was, better looking than he was – and found that after a couple of days she actually did like him. She looked back on it now and missed him. She remembered the cool, clear nights of early summer, when they walked out on the balcony of his suite and looked up at the stars and there seemed to be about three times as many as usual.

As she drove along the gently curving highway, she said aloud to the image of Dennis, 'At least we had a good time.' Her face felt so right when she said it that she held the expression, and flipped down the sun visor to look at her reflection in the makeup mirror.

Perfect. The full lips pouted, the sparkly blue eyes were wistful and wise. She revised the words slightly. 'At least we had fun.' The way the row of small white teeth touched the lower lip to say 'fun' was worth going for.

She flipped the visor back up and returned her eyes to the road. The darker hair she had given herself made her look a bit more serious than she had looked as Tanya, too sophisticated to bleach her hair platinum blond. She liked the subtle reddish highlights.

She felt good today. There was something hopeful about driving south, away from rain and toward warmth and sunshine and flowers. She had saved enough money from the month with Dennis Poole to be happy for a while. As soon as she had met him, she had begun pointing a finger at expensive, shiny things in stores and wishing aloud. She had loved it when he had bought them for her, and had rewarded him with affection.

Sometimes she would be about to leave him for the spa or the pool and ask him to give her some money for tips or drinks. A couple of times she had taken money from his wallet while he was asleep. After he had persuaded her to visit him at his house in Portland, she had come with only one suitcase, let him talk her into staying longer, and got his permission to pay for the extra

34

clothes she would need by borrowing one of his credit cards. Dennis had been a satisfying experience, but Dennis was over.

Who to be now? Being a brunette made her feel sedate, understated, aristocratic. Her new name should be something old-fashioned, even biblical, but Anglo-Saxon – no Catholic saints, and nothing faux French. Sarah would be good, or Rebecca. No, both were too common. Rachel. That was just about right.

She had always favored names that sounded like rich people's names, but nothing too heavy-handed. She didn't want to call herself a name that was also the name of a company: it would be hard to pass as a Ford or a Pillsbury. She thought about her new self for a few minutes, and decided that she should have roots in New England. Maybe a place-name. Stamford? No. Sturbridge. That felt right: Rachel Sturbridge – how do you do?

Rachel Sturbridge held the car to the south, and began to wonder where to stop. San Francisco was the next city she had heard about along the way, so she decided to aim for it and stop to see if it felt right. She drove half the night and reached the city at three a.m., then parked the car in a big structure near Union Square. She made her way downhill to the square, then walked around staring at the big buildings, the quiet, lighted entrances to hotels and the dark display windows of stores. She loved seeing a city late at night, after all of the superficial busyness and crowding and knotted traffic had been stripped away. She decided that she would stay. Then she returned to the parking structure and slept in the back seat of her car until people began starting the cars near hers and driving off.

In the morning Rachel used her Tanya Starling identification to rent a small furnished house, then added the name of Tanya's roommate, Rachel Sturbridge, to the lease. That afternoon she rented a post office box in both names, then placed a fictitious-business-name statement in the ad section of the *Chronicle*. It said that Rachel Sturbridge and T. Starling were doing business as Singular Aspects, and gave the post office box as the address. She went to City Hall and bought a business license for Singular Aspects, which she said on the form produced a 'mail-order newsletter for alternative lifestyles.' She was pleased with the fact that the description was utterly meaningless.

Before the banks closed at six she managed to start a Singular Aspects bank account with the two women as signatories and a deposit of four thousand dollars. At the end of each day for the next two days she made another cash deposit. When the balance reached twelve thousand dollars, she made out an application for a business credit card in the name of Singular Aspects. She flirted a little bit with the manager on duty, a young man named Bill, and he took the application without asking any embarrassing questions.

Dennis Poole had been dead three days. On the way home that night she bought the Portland newspapers at a newsstand and searched for stories about what the police were doing, but there was no mention of an investigation. There was only a short obituary that said his death had been declared a homicide. Since there was no mention of a woman, she supposed that meant her part in the episode was over, and decided that in the future she would remember only the good parts.

The next morning Rachel went to a copy center and selected a pack of ten sheets of heavy white paper with high rag content and a blank CD. She paid for them at the counter, rented a computer, and went to a Web site that she had found once before. It was a fan site devoted to every aspect of the life of the actress Renee Stipple Penrose. There were pictures of her parents' home in Barnstable, Connecticut, including some taken by a camera aimed through the windows, pictures of her elementary school and her high school, and – because there was a controversy about her real birth date – a clear and sharp image of her birth certificate.

Rachel copied the image to the computer and removed the original names and dates without altering the signatures or seals. She copied the blank birth certificate onto the CD for future use, and put the CD into her purse. Then she selected a matching type font and filled in the form to record the birth of Rachel Martha Sturbridge twenty-five years ago, and printed the new certificate onto one of her sheets of official-looking paper.

Rachel still had a driver's license she had obtained in Illinois as Tanya Starling. Now she found a matching type font, typed her new name a few times, and printed it out on a sheet of thin white paper.

When she was in her house that night she patiently scratched the old name off the license with a razor blade. She took the printout with the name Rachel Martha Sturbridge on it, cut it out in a narrow strip, placed it in the groove on the license she had created with the blade, and used a drop of clear glue to hold it there. In the morning, when it was dry, she placed a laminating sheet over the front of the license, and trimmed it carefully.

Two days later she went to the Department of Motor Vehicles office, flashed her Illinois license and her birth certificate, took a written test, and received a new California driver's license in the name Rachel Martha Sturbridge. She was so pleased that on the way home she joined the Auto Club and applied for a library card.

She let a week pass before she placed an ad in the *Chronicle* and sold Tanya Starling's car for fifteen thousand dollars. She deposited the check in the Singular Aspects account so Rachel Sturbridge would be able to write checks against it. Then she bought a six-year-old Nissan for five thousand in cash. The whole process of changing names was like watching a candle burn down and begin to gutter, and using its flame to light a new one before it went out.

She had made the change now, and it was time to think about the future. She needed to keep working at building her savings. Her goal was that someday she would be rich, and she knew that even though she was only at the beginning of the process, her progress was going to consist of hundreds of small decisions. For now, she had to keep her expenses under control and devote most of her time to finding the next man.

It had always seemed to her that the best kind of man wanted the sort of woman who went to plays and concerts and art exhibits, so she began to read the Datebook section of the paper and then buy tickets to events. While she was there she scanned the crowds for men who did not already have women attached to them. She liked being out, but even when she saw the right sort of man in the lobby before a play or a concert – or, more often, caught one looking at her – the event would be imminent, they both would have to find their way to widely separated seats, and the lights would go out. A few times, when she had seen a promising prospect, she had even stayed in the lobby afterward and given him a chance to find her. He never did.

Sometimes, late at night, she would go to the girl in the mirror and help her become Rachel Sturbridge. For her expeditions into high culture she had developed a rapt expression to indicate artistic appreciation. If she listened to a piece of classical music it might include a satisfied nod or a slightly troubled look around the eyes, as though she were comparing the performance with an invisible score. But her best new look was a serene, smooth-faced expression that was at once benevolent and superior, the habitual demeanor of a just queen.

She decided to try expensive restaurants in the Union Square district. One evening she sat in the bar at Postrio having a martini before dinner, her coat on the stool beside her. She liked the bar because it served as a long, narrow anteroom, where every customer had to pass by on the way to the staircase leading down into the restaurant. There was a grill at the far end of the bar, where three chefs dodged flames under a big copper hood, and there were a few booths along the wall, where patrons ate informal versions of the food served downstairs. The French doors across from the bar opened into the lobby of the Prescott Hotel, and new people entered every few minutes. She watched for unaccompanied men, dismissed several, and then saw one who looked right.

Rachel smiled to herself as she sipped her martini, feeling the icy glass on her lips and then the fire of the vodka warming her as it moved down her throat. She pretended not to see him. He stood for a moment talking with the maître d', then stepped into the bar.

She turned her head and looked up, her face assuming its new regal expression. The man was tall, wearing a navy blue sport jacket and a pair of gray pants. It was one of the uniforms all men wore when they weren't actually working, and it would have been difficult for most women to evaluate him, but Rachel Sturbridge had become a shrewd appraiser. The coat was a good cut, the fabric was finely woven wool, and the tie was tasteful and expensive. He had come in through the French doors, not the street entrance, so he was undoubtedly staying at the hotel. Shoes and watches were the best indicators, but she could not see either just yet in this light. He surveyed the bar, looking for a seat.

She caught his eye. 'Nobody is sitting here.' She indicated the bar stool next to hers. She took the coat onto her lap.

'Are you sure you don't mind?'

'No,' she said. 'It's all yours.'

He grinned, sat down, and said, 'Thank you. If you're waiting for someone to meet you or something, I'll be happy to give it up when he comes.'

'No need,' said Rachel Sturbridge. 'I'm alone.'

He ordered a Macallan single-malt scotch, which showed he had some standards, but he wanted the twelve-year-old instead of the eighteen, which meant he wasn't showing off. He turned to her. 'Can I get you another martini?'

'No, thank you,' she said. 'I just started this one.'

She decided he was probably the sort of man Rachel Sturbridge would like. He was tall and manly looking, and he was friendly in his manner but polite, and he hadn't leaned over her to talk, the way some men did when they met an attractive woman.

He sipped his drink and looked straight ahead. She sensed that if she wanted to talk to a gentleman like him, she would have to give him a signal she was willing. 'I like this place, don't you?'

He appeared mildly surprised, as though he wasn't quite sure that she had intended her question for him. When he turned and she met his eyes, he seemed pleased. 'So far, I like it very much. I haven't been here before, but I've heard good things.' He glanced at his watch, and the gesture gave Rachel Sturbridge two competing sensations. The indication that he might be bored made her stomach feel hollow, but her heart's tempo picked up when she recognized the watch, a Patek Philippe that sold for around six thousand dollars. She was relieved when he added, 'It's pretty crowded. I didn't have a reservation, but they said they'd try to fit me in. It's nine now. I have to hope somebody cancels.'

The young maître d' appeared beside Rachel and said, 'Miss Sturbridge, we can seat you now.'

Rachel smiled. She had favors to dispense. 'Come along. You can share my table.'

The man was delighted. 'Well, thank you.' The maître d' returned to his podium and the hostess arrived just as they were going about the awkward business of getting down from adjacent bar stools. Rachel noted that he quickly slipped off his, stood back, and held her hand to keep her from falling. They both left their barely touched drinks, but the hostess gave an invisible signal to a passing waiter, who snatched them up and followed.

The dining room at the bottom of the stairs was bright, lit by large bowl-shaped ceiling fixtures, and the light was reflected up from bright linen tablecloths. In the light, Rachel's companion looked a bit more attractive but a bit older, and she revised her estimate from forty to fifty. While they were getting settled at a table near the far side of the room, she held her compact in her palm to see what the lighting was doing to her, but quickly verified that her makeup had kept her from losing her color, and the new brown hair shone exactly as she had intended. She slipped the compact back into her purse.

He said, 'I'm David Larson, and I thank you for your gracious invitation. I was kicking myself for coming without a reservation, and I find that it worked out better this way. I may never call for a reservation again.'

She detected a faint accent, but couldn't quite place it – the South?

She liked it that he was confident enough to give an exaggerated compliment, and she liked the way his blue eyes transmitted sincerity without awkwardness. She decided to encourage him. 'My name is Rachel Sturbridge, and it's a pleasure to have your company.' She delivered her words with a condescending ease, like an actress stopping on the red carpet outside a movie premiere to speak to a camera.

Larson said, 'Usually I have my assistant make all my reservations from home, but this time I didn't have much notice. It was one of those times to throw some clothes in a bag and head for the airport.'

'Where is "home"?'

'Austin,' he said. 'How about you?'

'At the moment, I'm living in San Francisco,' she said. 'I've only been here a short time.' If he was from Austin, the safe place to be from was the Northeast. 'Originally I'm a Connecticut girl.'

They had to devote some attention to the menu, because the waiter had begun to hover nearby. Larson ordered salmon, and Rachel decided her first compliment to him would be to order the same entrée, the same salad.

He ordered a good bottle of wine without any consultation that would have forced her to acknowledge his extravagance, and she liked that. When the waiter had departed again, he said, 'What brought you to San Francisco?'

'Business,' she said.

'What sort of business are you in?'

She devoted a half second to the thought that she should have said it was a vacation. He was obviously a businessman, and now she was going to have to talk about a subject he knew. All she could do was try to sound sensible. 'I'm trying to start a magazine. This is a good place to do that. There are plenty of artistic people who will work cheap on the speculation that when the magazine takes off, so will they. There are almost too many good technical and business types who used to work for deceased Internet companies. There are lots of printers and good shipping facilities.'

'What about the rents?'

'They're expensive, but not like New York, and I can work out of my apartment and my post office box for a long time before I need to expand,' she said.

'I can tell you're a practical businesswoman,' said Larson. 'And I know a little about that. What's the title of your magazine?'

'I'm calling it *Singular Aspects*. It's going to be about alternative lifestyles.'

'What does that mean?'

'It means nothing and everything. Americans love to think they're special. Every last one of them, no matter how much of a conformist he is, wants to believe he's a maverick, an innovator. What people want to believe is what they'll buy, and lifestyle is everything. So I can do clothes, furniture, houses, music, books, movies, art, food, relationships, and say it's about them. It doesn't take much of a pitch to get them to buy an attractive version of themselves. They already like themselves.'

'And you think San Francisco is a good place to do this?'

'Not just a good place,' she said. 'The very best place. More huge fads have come out of San Francisco than anywhere, block for block. This was the place to be a beatnik in the fifties. Practically the whole hippie movement in the sixties came from the corner of Haight and Ashbury. The food-worship fad came from restaurants like Chez Panisse in Berkeley in the seventies. The computer revolution came from just down the road in the eighties. It's wave after wave. Not only will fad watchers pay for the latest from here, but advertisers will pay to be part of the next wave before it leaves here.'

He laughed. 'Well, that's just great. I like everything about it, and I think it's a good bet to succeed.' He stared at her for a few seconds. 'I think it's the best idea I've heard this trip.'

She saw her chance to move the conversation onto him. 'You've heard others?'

'Well, yes,' he said. 'I feel so comfortable talking to you that I keep forgetting that we don't actually know each other yet.' He took out his wallet – she caught a thick sheaf of green bills and a platinum card – and slid a business card out with his thumb, then handed it to her.

There was a logo with a pair of longhorns, and a business address in Austin for David Larson Ventures. She held it out for him to take back, but he said, 'No, please hold on to it.'

She slipped it into her purse. 'So what are David Larson's ventures?'

'Oh, I make investments.'

'In what?'

'Young companies, mostly start-ups. Anything where I can evaluate the product, the market, the competition, and the costs. I came to meet some people and hear some pitches.'

Rachel Sturbridge let the topic drop to see whether he was going to be a bore who didn't talk about anything but business. Instead he talked about other restaurants he knew in the Bay Area, an art exhibition he wanted to see while he was in the city, a book he had read on the airplane.

She silently cursed the waiter when he delivered the check. She had not had enough time. When she

44

reached for the check, Larson's big hand was on the little tray, covering it. He said, 'Please. I already know you're the kind of person who likes to pay her own way, but you would be doing me a kindness to let me have it. You did a great favor to let me join you, and it's all I can do in return.'

'Well, all right.' When the waiter took his card and went away, she said, 'Thank you.'

She pretended not to pay any attention to the check after that, but she had found that the way people treated servers could be an early indication of unpleasant qualities. She excused herself to go to the ladies' room at the right moment and looked down at it over his shoulder. He was a generous tipper. When she returned, she said, 'I would like to take you out for an after-dinner drink. There's a place near here that's quiet.'

He seemed taken aback. 'I would be absolutely delighted.' He stood up, then said, 'How near?'

'Two hundred feet.' They walked down the street to the bar of the Pan Pacific hotel, just off the huge white marble lobby. They sat at a table and ordered drinks. He said, 'I gave you my business card. Have you had any cards printed yet?'

'No,' she said. 'I haven't hired my designer yet, and I want to be sure everything has the right look.'

He produced another card of his and a pen and set them on the table in front of her. 'Then please write a number where I can reach you.'

She hesitated, then wrote the phone number at her house. They had their drink, but before either of them had finished it, she said, 'I've got to get up early and meet with a photographer to look at his portfolio.' He put her in a taxi in front of the hotel, and she went back to her house feeling pleased with herself for timing her exit to pique his interest.

The next day she got up early and walked to a news-stand on Market Street to buy the Portland *Oregonian*, then had a cup of coffee and a bagel while she searched it for new information about Dennis Poole. She found no mention of him, and she walked home feeling relieved. She turned the television to the local morning news for company while she read the *San Francisco Chronicle*, but didn't bother to turn it off when the news was replaced by reruns of a situation comedy. At eleven, her telephone rang for the first time. Nobody had her number except David Larson, so she hurriedly muted the television set before she answered it, smiled to herself, and said, 'Singular Aspects.'

The second dinner with David was at the Dining Room at the Ritz-Carlton on Nob Hill, and it went better than the first for Rachel Sturbridge. Just after their entrées were served, he said, 'You know, I've been thinking. I would like to buy a half interest in your magazine.'

She smiled and shook her head. 'There is no magazine yet. How can I sell it?'

'That's why I'm offering now. I'm betting you're going to be so successful that it will be too expensive to buy in later. I bring you capital and business knowledge, and you bring me the idea, the talent, and the effort. That's how start-ups work.'

'That's very flattering,' she said. 'But let's not be in a rush.'

'Why the delay?'

'I'm going to ask for fifty billion dollars, and I need to give you time to raise it.'

He laughed and touched her hand. 'That's it,' he said. 'That's why I'm willing to bet on you. I wanted to make you the offer before I left for Austin, but that doesn't mean I need the answer by then.'

'When are you going back?'

He looked unhappy, as though he had been dreading the subject. 'On Friday. I hate to do it, but I have a meeting that afternoon, and I've already postponed it once.'

'That's only two days.'

'One, really. I leave early Friday morning.'

'Is it that important?'

'Yes, I'm afraid so. People are coming from New York and London.'

She couldn't let him go this way. She knew that he had been enjoying his time with her, and that she was rapidly making an impression on him. But he was a rich man in his fifties. He had met a great many attractive women by now, and he probably met more every month. She had not yet had time to reach the point where she would not simply fade into his memory with all of the others. She had to do something quickly. 'Then you'll have to go. But can I take you out for a farewell dinner tomorrow night?'

He looked surprised. 'Thank you. I'd love that. But it shouldn't sound so final. You and I are going to be partners, just as soon as I raise that fifty billion.'

The third dinner was at the Fairmont. Once they were past the lobby, with its high, vaulted ceiling and marble columns, David seemed to relax. There was a quiet, comfortable quality to their conversation. He told her stories about his childhood in Texas, his business associates, his friends. When the waiter asked whether they would like anything else, Rachel said, 'No, thank you.' He asked, 'Would you like to charge it to your room?' She said, 'Yes.'

David met her eyes, and she shrugged. 'Another cat out of the bag.'

He said, 'You're staying here?'

'I reserved a suite when I made the reservation. The

47

view from the tower rooms is one of the best in the city. I thought it might be a nice way to be sure you didn't forget me as soon as you got back to Texas.'

'Not likely,' he said.

She had prepared herself in advance for a night of closing her eyes tight and enduring, but she was pleasantly surprised. He was a gentle, considerate lover with an easy, appreciative disposition that made her feel less self-conscious. When they were not making love he was a cheerful, affectionate companion.

Late that evening after he fell asleep, she lay awake considering the best way to make use of him. She had been wise to resist the temptation to sell him a half interest in her imaginary magazine. She had been very close to yielding. He seemed accustomed to risky investments, and he would probably forgive her when she faked an attempt at a magazine and didn't return any money. But she could afford to let her bet stay on the table. She was beginning to think that maybe the way to get her money was the way lots of other women had done it. Maybe she should marry it.

The next morning they said good-bye in the room. He called a cab to take him to the Prescott to check out and then to the airport. Rachel took a second cab back to her house. She put his business card on her refrigerator with a magnet and waited.

On the third day, a FedEx package arrived. Inside was a velvet box. She opened it, and found a white-gold pendant with a single large diamond. The velvet box said Van Cleef & Arpels, but that was only a box. She took off the shade of her reading lamp and held the diamond close to the bulb. She could tell it was a good stone, about three carats, and very bright. It must have cost him at least ten thousand dollars, and possibly much more.

Looking at the light sparkling in the facets of the diamond made her feel lucky. It had probably been dangerous to get involved with another man so soon after Dennis Poole, but there had seemed to be nobody looking for her, so she had begun to look for a new man.

Men were a difficult way to make a living. All any of them really wanted was sex. It made them easy to attract and easy to play for a little money, but not necessarily easy to control. They got jealous and watchful, and at times the sex could be troublesome, too. At least with David it wasn't unpleasant or especially demanding. She took his card off her refrigerator, went to the telephone, and dialed the private number he had written on the back. When he answered, she said, 'You certainly know how to keep a girl's attention, don't you?'

A week later David was in San Francisco again. He called her from the airport, then picked her up at her house and drove to a hotel in Carmel that consisted of a group of luxurious cabins on a wooded cliff above the ocean. They had dinner in the restaurant in the central building, watching the waves crash against the rocks below, then walked along the path through the pines to their cabin, and sat on the couch before the stone fireplace, listening to the crackling of the wood fire.

After a time, he said, 'I've been thinking a lot about you.'

'Good,' she said. She leaned close and kissed him softly.

'I've even been trying to find ways to help you get your magazine started.'

'You're sweet.' She kissed him again.

'While I was doing it I found out a couple of things that made me curious.'

'What kind of things?' She turned her body on the couch to face him. She could feel the hairs on her scalp rising. It wasn't exactly fear, but an intense anticipation.

49

'Well, you said you had never been married.'

'That's right.'

'I'm wondering if you changed your name at some point.'

She kept her eyes on his face. 'You've hired somebody to investigate me?'

He smiled. 'Now, please don't get mad at me. It's a normal thing to do if you're thinking of making an investment in a start-up. I have a standing account at the Averill Agency in Dallas. Whenever I'm about to make a seed-money investment, they routinely do a quick rundown on the principal players, just to be sure none of them has a tail and a pitchfork. It's no different from asking your mechanic to take a look at a car you're buying.'

Rachel leaned forward, her eyes searching his. 'And?'

'As you know, they didn't find any problems, because there are no problems. But they did have trouble finding out much else about you. They said that either you'd had a marriage at some point that you forgot to mention, or maybe had petitioned for a name change.'

She stared at him coldly, sensing the urge to make him suffer. 'Rachel Sturbridge isn't the name I was born with. My family was well-off and respected, but it looked good only from the outside. From the inside, it wasn't a group you would want to belong to. There wasn't a lot of love.' She paused, as though bravely controlling her emotions. 'What there was, was a lot of cruelty. After I grew up I spent years trying to get over it, and on the advice of my therapist, I severed the connection completely. Being really free of them meant using a different name, so I do. You're the only person I've ever had to explain this to.'

He was embarrassed at his mistake. 'Rachel, I'm sorry. I just cared so much about you that I couldn't know enough.'

She stood up.

He looked horrified. 'Please. I never imagined that talking to you about it would bring back bad memories. Stay with me.'

'I'm tired, and I'm going to sleep now. We can talk in the morning.' David had carried both of their suitcases into one of the bedrooms when he'd unloaded the car. Now she went into that room, took hers into the other bedroom, and quietly closed the door.

When she awoke in the morning she knew that two things were going to happen. One was that David Larson was going to buy her a big present. The other was that she was going back to San Francisco. She went into the bathroom, stood in front of the mirror, and began to pull herself together. 'I'm heartbroken,' she told the girl in the mirror. It was well said. She would use it.

During the time while he was in Austin she had allowed herself to grow overconfident. She had formed plans that carried them both years into the future. She had pictured them spending time in Europe together – maybe in the Greek islands, which looked beautiful and warm in the magazines, or Provence, which sounded in articles as though it existed solely to serve food and wine to people like her. She was sure David had accumulated enough money already. It seemed to her that the only reason he still traveled around chasing investments was that he'd had nothing better to do until he'd met Rachel Sturbridge. She could have made those years wonderful for him. But that was before he had betrayed her.

She watched herself in the mirror as she said, 'I'm heartbroken' again. She meant it. He had told his stupid private detectives to pry into her private life looking for incriminating information, and she was just lucky they had not found anything. It had been a cold, calculating thing to do. Men always wanted you to do impulsive, risky things because you let your passion for them get too strong to resist. They wanted you to trust them completely, holding nothing at all back to protect yourself. But then, after your body and soul had gotten to be things they had, rather than things they wanted, they announced that they had reserved the right to be suspicious and cautious about you.

When David knocked and asked if she would go to breakfast with him, she called through the closed door, 'No, you go ahead.'

Rachel spent the next hour working efficiently and methodically to make herself beautiful. She had started beautician's school the summer she had turned sixteen, and had learned some cosmetology and hairdressing before she had missed a tuition payment. But she had learned her most valuable tricks years before that, in the long succession of beauty pageants her mother had entered her in beginning at age four. She had been born with good skin and small, symmetrical features, and she had a quick, practiced hand with a brush, eyeliner, and mascara.

She was good at dressing herself because she had a hard, objective eye. That was something else the pageant circuit had done for her. She could look at herself the way a contest judge would, with no sentimentality and no mercy. She accentuated her figure's best points and hid the flaws. She tried all three dresses she had brought, chose the one that would give him the most haunting memory of her body, and put on spike heels.

Rachel packed her suitcase, stood it upright on its wheels, and extended the handle. Then she went to the living room, arranged herself on the small couch, turned on the television set, and waited. David returned about an hour after that.

When he opened the door and saw her, she could tell her effect was what she had intended. He stopped at the door and simply stared for a moment, then took a couple of deep breaths and walked toward her. 'Rachel,' he said. 'I need to talk to you. I'm really very sorry. I never imagined I was going to hurt your feelings or remind you of anything that caused you pain.'

She raised her face to him. Her eyes were cold, as though she were looking at him from a great distance.

He said, 'I brought you a little something.' He took a velvet jewelry box from his coat pocket and held it out to her. 'Will you please forgive me?'

Seeing another jewelry box nettled her, partly because it showed he thought she was childish enough to be mollified by it, and partly because she wanted whatever lay inside the box. Her expression didn't change. 'I waited here for you only because I felt that I should say something to you for the sake of clarity. If you'll remember, I never asked you to invest in my business.'

'I never meant to imply—'

'Please let me finish. I won't be long.' She glared at him, holding him in silence for a breath before she continued. 'It was a purely personal relationship, from my point of view. I never offered you anything or asked you for anything. When you asked questions about my business I answered them. When you offered to invest, I repeatedly refused your money. You called in detectives anyway and had me investigated. Well, that was a deal breaker. I'm leaving now. I want you to tear up my telephone number and forget my address.'

'But Rachel.' He tried to sit beside her, but she recoiled and stood up. He held out his hands. 'Can't we talk about this?'

'No. We can't. If you want to do something for me you can order your detectives to shred whatever files they have on me. Beyond that, I have no further interest in anything you do or say.' She turned, walked to the bedroom, grasped the handle on her suitcase, and pulled it to the door on its wheels.

David Larson stood up, looking pained. 'Please don't go, Rachel. It was a terrible mistake. I'm trying to make it up to you.' As he raised his arms in supplication, he noticed the velvet box in his hand, and held it out. 'This was for you. Won't you at least take a look at it?'

'No, I won't. Good-bye.' She pushed the door open, dragged her suitcase out, and let the door swing shut behind her. She went down the steps and up the paved drive to the main lodge, and had the concierge call her a cab.

On the long drive to San Francisco she contemplated what she had done, and decided that leaving David Larson had been her only possible choice. She couldn't continue the relationship after he'd had her investigated. If she stayed, he would have the detectives resume their poking and prying. It was quite possible that they would find out that she had once been Tanya Starling, and maybe even that she had known Dennis Poole. It was also a bit late to allow him to buy into her imaginary magazine, and then make the money disappear on imaginary expenses. Now that the detectives had been called in, she couldn't even continue to play him for gifts and support.

Her only possible move had been to sever any connection with him. The paradox was that his having her investigated had made her want to kill him, and the only thing that was preventing her from doing it was that he'd had her investigated. Before his body could cool, his detectives would be there to give the police a whole dossier on her.

The next afternoon at one, there was a knock on her door. She looked out the window to decide whether to answer, and saw it was the Federal Express man. She opened the door, signed for the thick envelope, and took it inside to open it.

The envelope contained three items. The first was the typed report that David Larson had received from the Averill Detective Agency in Dallas, Texas, saying that there wasn't much about Rachel Sturbridge to know. The second was a file folder, stamped AVERILL AGENCY: CONFIDENTIAL. It had *Sturbridge, Rachel* on the tab, and contained about twenty pages of handwritten notes describing things checked unsuccessfully, credit reports on Rachel Sturbridge that had yielded virtually no information, a copy of her business license, and some photographs. There were pictures of her coming and going from her house, as well as a few close-ups of her face made from blowups of more distant shots.

The third item in the package was a note from David Larson. It said, 'You asked that I destroy the background check. These are the only copies. Please accept my apologies. David.'

Rachel searched the kitchen drawers until she found some matches. She took the note, the file, and the report out to the tiny square of concrete below her back steps, then made a small bonfire. She looked at each piece as she added it to the flames.

The detective had been called off, and she was watching the collection of incriminating information burn up, page by page. She was confident that David was feeling contrite and apologetic, not suspicious of her. But this wasn't enough. She looked at the rented house, then down the hill at the city. She picked up a stick to stir the ashes and make sure there was nothing left of the paper. She would have to disappear.

SEVEN

The videotape was grainy and distorted, and the colors seemed faded. It had been taken through a plastic dome that covered the video camera in the hotel hallway. The shot angled down from the ceiling. A white-haired couple walked under it and up the hallway to the elevator alcove. A few seconds later, a man appeared, coming from the direction of the elevators. 'That's him. That's my cousin Dennis,' Hugo Poole said.

A thin blond woman caught up to Dennis while he stood at the door of his hotel room.

'Look at the hair,' said Sergeant Hobbes.

'It's just about the right length,' Joe Pitt said.

On the monitor, Dennis slid a key card out of his wallet. The woman stood facing Dennis, talking to him, waiting for him to push the card into the lock and turn the handle. Hugo Poole waited impatiently for the girl to show her face. Dennis Poole opened the door to let the girl in ahead of him. 'Turn around, for Christ's sake,' Hugo said. 'Turn around!'

The girl half-turned to go inside, and Detective Hobbes froze the tape. The blond woman was held in place, her image quivering slightly, a band of static moving upward from the bottom of the screen, disappearing, then reappearing at the bottom. Her face was attractive but not distinctive – just small, regular features. She seemed to be one of those women whose eyelashes and brows were light, so that her eyes disappeared into her face until she put on her makeup each morning.

Detective Hobbes turned to look down at Hugo Poole, her expression controlled. 'Well, Mr Poole? Have you seen her before?'

'Never.' He kept staring at the girl's image, scowling.

Joe Pitt asked, 'How did you get this tape?'

'Dennis Poole had been on vacation until two weeks before he died,' said Hobbes. 'His credit card slips gave us the hotel in Aspen where he had been staying. We asked the hotel for their security tapes, and I went down to watch them. The ones from early in his stay were all erased, but a few of the later ones survived. This is the clearest, I'm afraid.'

'Do you know who she is yet?' asked Pitt.

'Her name is Tanya Starling. She was registered at the hotel for two days before he arrived. After he had been there for about three days she canceled her room and moved in with him.'

'Did the hotel have a home address for her?'

'Yes,' she said. 'An apartment in Chicago. The phone number was out of service, so we asked the Chicago police to find out whether the number had been changed, but the whole account was closed. They checked with the company that manages the place and found she had moved out before she left for Colorado. She left no forwarding address.'

'Is the apartment still vacant?'

'No such luck. It's a fancy high-rise with a view of the lake, and there was a waiting list. They cleaned and repainted it right away and new people moved in a couple of days later. There's no chance of lifting prints now.'

Hugo Poole broke his silence. 'It's not right.'

Catherine Hobbes frowned. 'What's not right, Mr Poole?'

'I know you don't like me, but I'm trying to tell you something about my cousin.'

57

'And I assume you don't like me, but I'm listening.'

'The girl shouldn't be like that.'

'Like what?'

'She's wrong for Denny. He was a forty-two-year-old computer geek. He had a stupid laugh, he was tall in the wrong way – kind of big-footed and narrow-shouldered. He didn't talk about anything women could stand to listen to.'

Joe Pitt said, 'That sounds like a million guys, most of them married. If she moved in, she was interested.'

'Too good-looking,' said Hugo Poole. 'When I saw him with women, they were always on the same step of the food chain that he was on. She should be a nice fat girl with bad teeth.'

Catherine Hobbes studied Hugo Poole. 'What do you think was going on? Do you think she's a hooker?'

'I doubt it. She was with him for, like, three weeks,' said Hugo. 'He'd have died broke and still owed her money.'

'That's what I thought,' said Hobbes. 'Besides, the Chicago police would probably have picked up that kind of information. She could have been some single woman willing to give a guy like Dennis a little slack. His spending a lot of money on her would be flattering. She was on vacation, so the rules and standards sometimes slip a little. Somebody she wouldn't go out with at home might do for an evening in a strange place.'

'Okay,' said Hugo. 'Lightning strikes and guys like Dennis get lucky. But there's no way a woman like that would stay for more than one night unless something besides Dennis was the attraction.'

'All right, you two have convinced me,' said Pitt. 'There was a hidden reason why she was with him. So what was it? If she moved out of her fancy apartment in Chicago and took off for Colorado, maybe she was hiding. Maybe Dennis got killed by somebody who was after her.'

'You mean an old boyfriend or a jealous husband?' said Hugo. 'Dennis Poole killed by a jealous husband?'

'It might explain what she was doing moving in with him,' said Catherine Hobbes. 'Living with somebody who's paying for everything makes a woman hard to spot. She could also have been the one who killed him.'

Pitt said, 'Do you know whether any of his money is gone?'

'Nothing so far,' said Hobbes. 'He had some charges from jewelry stores, and some women's clothing stores. We've found about twenty thousand dollars' worth.'

'Are you sure he was the one who made all of the charges?' asked Pitt.

'He was alive on those dates,' Hobbes said. 'And he didn't report a lost credit card.'

'Then I'll go with the odds,' said Pitt.

'What are they?' asked Hugo.

Pitt said, 'That when you have a murder scene and a woman is missing, it's not because she was the perpetrator. Usually when you find her, she's the second victim.'

'Thanks for coming up to Portland and cooperating with us, Mr Poole,' said Catherine Hobbes as she turned off the tape and took the cassette out of the VCR. 'I'm sure that Mr Pitt will let you know the minute we find anything else.' She walked out of the interrogation room.

A half hour later, Catherine Hobbes sat alone in the interrogation room in front of the monitor, watching the videotape of herself, Hugo Poole, and Joe Pitt watching the hotel security tape. She studied the reactions of both men to everything that was seen or said. Then she got to the part she had been waiting for: the sight of herself walking out of the room.

She watched the tape of Hugo Poole as he stood up and looked at Pitt. 'What the hell did you do to *her*?'

Pitt went to the door ahead of him and reached for the knob to open it. 'I went to work for you.'

'I was expecting her not to warm up to me. This was about you. Whatever you're doing to her, you ought to either cut it out or do it better.'

On the monitor, Catherine Hobbes watched the two men walk out the door. If either of them had anything enlightening to say about the murder of Dennis Poole, he had not been foolish enough to say it inside the Portland Police Bureau.

EIGHT

Rachel Sturbridge emptied the vacuum cleaner bag into the garbage dumpster outside her rented house. She went inside, put on disposable rubber gloves, and walked one last time through her house with a bottle of Windex and a roll of paper towels. She stood at the window that faced north. Between two apartment buildings she could just see the taller office buildings along Market Street. She stepped to the side, sprayed the glass, and wiped it once more. It was important to be sure that she had not missed any surface as smooth as a windowpane.

She sprayed and wiped all of the handles, knobs, and latches, then took broad swipes over all of the flat surfaces where she might have rested her fingertips in the past few weeks. If David Larson had been lying about calling off his detectives, the least she could do was to deny them the gift of her fingerprints.

Rachel took a final look at the furniture that Mrs Halloran, the landlady, had supplied with the house, trying to find any hairs that she might have left on a cushion. She wrote 'Eve Halloran' on an envelope, slipped her house key into it, and left it on the mantel. Then she picked up her suitcase, went out the door, and pressed the lock button. Only after she was outside the house and in her car did she take off her thin rubber gloves.

She was out on Highway 101 by noon, driving south, away from the city. San Francisco had been a terrible disappointment to her, and she wanted to get away, but she had no destination in mind. Today it seemed to Rachel that the world was a cold and treacherous place, and the only act that was appealing was to keep moving.

For a few hours she drove and thought about her dissatisfaction with David Larson. He was a foolish man, one who had no idea what a wonderful future he had thrown away when he had betrayed Rachel Sturbridge's trust. He really deserved to die, and it bothered her that she had been forced to let him go. It didn't seem fair.

When she began to feel hungry, she looked at the clock on the dashboard and noticed that it was five o'clock. She stopped at a restaurant in Pismo Beach and stared out at the highway while she ate, wishing she could see the ocean.

She refilled the gas tank and drove all the way to the Los Angeles County line before she stopped again. She found a hotel off the Ventura Freeway in the west end of the San Fernando Valley and registered with her Rachel Sturbridge credit card. When she awoke in the morning, she showered, ate, and dressed, then settled her bill in cash. It was time to begin making herself safe from whatever problems David Larson might have caused.

She needed to be anonymous for a time while she rested and decided what she wanted to do next, and the nondescript neighborhood where she had stopped looked like a good place for that. All of Los Angeles seemed featureless to her, a vast sameness. A young, white middle-class woman could avoid notice for a very long time if she paid attention and didn't do anything stupid. She rented an apartment in Woodland Hills not far from the Topanga Canyon shopping mall by putting down money for the first month, last month, and security deposit in cash.

She went to a copying store, just as she had in San Francisco, rented a computer and printer, and took out the CD where she had stored the blank birth certificate.

During the long drive from San Francisco she had been thinking of using the name Veronica, but the girl who waited on her was pretty and energetic, and she was wearing a badge that said, 'Nancy Gonzales, Sales Associate.' The name Nancy seemed cheerful, so that was the one that she chose. She filled in the blank with the name Nancy Mills.

Next she bought a hair dye kit and lightened her hair again, then went to a salon to have it cut. She had worn it long and loose as Rachel Sturbridge, so now it had to be shorter. Long hair gave her an advantage with men, but she had decided it would be better if she didn't attract any more of them for a while. On the way home, she went to an optometrist's shop in a strip mall and bought some nonprescription contact lenses in different eye colors.

Two days later, when she went to the Department of Motor Vehicles to apply for a new driver's license, she wore the brown contacts, so in her license picture she had brown eyes and shoulder-length, light brown hair. She thought of the look as drab and ordinary, which was exactly what she wanted.

She sold Rachel Sturbridge's car through the *Pennysaver* to a woman she told she needed money to pay off a credit card debt. She could walk to restaurants, movie theaters, and even a grocery store from her apartment, so she decided that she could do without a car for the moment. Nancy Mills needed quiet and anonymity and solitude. She was disillusioned by her experience with David Larson, and had no desire to go anyplace where men might see her and talk to her, so she stayed away from health clubs, restaurants that had bars, and other spots where she had found men before.

After her first week in Los Angeles, Tanya Starling and Rachel Sturbridge had been erased. Nancy Mills was already nearly invisible. She would wait and watch and see if something troublesome had followed her from San Francisco.

NINE

Catherine Hobbes and Joe Pitt walked down the hall of the San Francisco police station, watching the numbers over the doors until they came to 219.

The door was open, so Catherine stepped inside. There were several desks in the room, where plainclothes officers gazed at computer screens or talked on telephones. She approached a group of three who were leaning over to look at a file opened on a desk, and said to them, 'I'm looking for Detective Crowley.'

'I'm Crowley. Welcome to San Francisco,' said a tall, thin cop with a bald head. He straightened and held out his hand. 'Are you Sergeant Hobbes?'

She flashed a smile and shook his hand. Crowley looked over her shoulder expectantly, and she remembered Joe Pitt. 'This is Mr Pitt, who is conducting an investigation for the victim's family. Do you mind talking to both of us?'

Detective Crowley shook his head, then reached past her, his arm almost touching her shoulder, and shook Pitt's hand enthusiastically. 'Not at all. I've known Mr Pitt for about a hundred years. How you been, Joe?'

Pitt said, 'Can't complain, Doug. I hear you've got Tanya Starling's car.'

'Well, we've found out where it is. We haven't impounded it. She sold it here about four days after you lost track of her in Portland. There was an ad in the *Chronicle*. The man who bought it is named' – he picked up a written report and scanned it – 'Harold Willis. He bought it for fifteen thousand.'

Pitt asked, 'Was that a good deal?'

'It was close to the high blue book price, so it wasn't a steal or anything. She wasn't just unloading it fast.'

'And did Harold Willis recognize the photographs of Tanya Starling I sent to you?' asked Catherine Hobbes.

'Yes. He said it was definitely her. She went on a test drive with him, took his check, made out a bill of sale, signed over the registration, and wished him luck. That took maybe two hours, so he had plenty of time to look.'

'Where did the sale take place?' asked Hobbes. 'Her place?'

'No. Her ad just had a phone number. She called Willis and brought the car to his house.' He anticipated the next question. 'She was alone with him all that time. She wasn't kidnapped or under duress. If she had been in trouble, she could have told him about it, or driven to any police station.'

Pitt said, 'How about the bank account where she deposited his check? Do you have anything on that yet?'

'It was a business account at Regal Bank.' Crowley handed Pitt a piece of paper. 'Here's the address of the branch where she deposited it, the account number, and her home address.'

'Great,' said Pitt. 'Thanks.'

Hobbes calmly reached over and took the piece of paper from Joe Pitt.

'Could be better,' Crowley said. 'We called on her and found that she's moved on again. She had signed a lease for a house with a roommate named Rachel Sturbridge. They paid three months' rent in advance, according to the owner, a Mrs Eve Halloran. She says they moved out about a week ago. The date is vague, because they left without telling her.'

'Did she have a job while she was here?' asked Hobbes.

'I'm not exactly sure,' Crowley said. 'The two of them had run a d/b/a announcement in the paper and took out a license for a business called Singular Aspects. It lists a newsletter, which I assume was a catalog. If it was a store, they didn't stay long enough to open.'

'That's what you think it was – a store?'

'I don't know. That's my guess, from the sound of it. I defer to you, though, Sergeant Hobbes. Doesn't it sound like a women's clothing store? Anyway, less than a month later, the bank account was closed and they had both moved on.'

'That's the part we need to know,' said Hobbes. 'Where did they move to?'

'We've got nothing on that yet,' said Crowley. 'Neither of them left a forwarding address at the post office or with their landlady. Before they left, they closed their account at Regal Bank, so there's nothing there, either. They might easily have found a good location somewhere nearby, like San Mateo or Richmond, and moved. By now they could also be in China.'

'Either way, Tanya Starling doesn't seem to be in any danger, and she certainly isn't dead,' said Hobbes. 'But she's still our only potential witness on why Dennis Poole is.'

Pitt said, 'Did Tanya buy another car before she left?'

'No. Rachel Sturbridge has one, and maybe they drove off in that.' He handed a piece of paper to Pitt. 'Here's the DMV printout on it. A six-year-old Nissan Maxima, black. License plate and VIN are supplied. It's registered to the address they rented here. So until she gets wherever she's going and reregisters it with a good address, we won't know where she is. If she's in-state, she probably won't get around to it until next year.'

'Keep us in mind, will you, Doug?'

'Sure,' said Crowley. 'When we get anything more, you'll have it.'

Catherine Hobbes said, 'Thank you very much, Detective Crowley. Here's my card. There are numbers for my direct line, the homicide office, my cell, and my home. It doesn't matter what time of day it comes in, I would appreciate it if you'll call.'

'Of course,' said Crowley.

She and Pitt walked out of the police station, and Pitt drove the rental car to the house where Tanya Starling and Rachel Sturbridge had lived. As soon as Pitt found a parking space at the foot of the long, inclining street, Catherine Hobbes got out and began to walk. Pitt locked the car and trotted to catch up. By the time he'd succeeded, he was winded.

'What's bothering you?' asked Pitt.

Catherine Hobbes walked along the street, her quick strides keeping her a half pace ahead of him so she wouldn't have to look at his fake concerned expression. 'Nothing.'

'Come on,' he said. 'You're going to give me a heart attack walking up this hill at this speed. Something's bothering you.'

She stopped and looked at him. 'We're not in some boy-and-girl relationship that requires your helping when something's bothering me. I'm a police officer working a homicide case. Your role is not to delve into my female sensitivities so you can talk me out of them. You're here with me only because my captain thought you might be able to contribute to the progress of the investigation. That was not an opinion I shared.'

'It's Crowley, isn't it?'

'Do *not* tell me I'm imagining things.'

'I won't. But—'

'I'm also not interested in being told it's not his fault because you knew each other twenty years ago, or because he's too old to get used to women in homicide, or because you two are from California and I'm not.'

'Okay,' he said. 'It's just that it's a waste of time to get mad at me.'

'I'm not.'

'Or even at him.'

'I'm not mad. I'm a woman cop. I'm used to being ignored, and to much, much worse. I'm looking for the house number.'

'Okay,' said Pitt. He followed her along the street for another half block, until they came to a narrow one-story house.

They walked up to the steps and Hobbes rang the bell, then listened for a moment to the door being unbolted and unlatched. It swung open to reveal a woman around sixty years old with dyed red hair wearing a pair of jeans with knee pads over them.

'Mrs Halloran?'

'I've been waiting for you,' the woman said. 'I was just finishing up on the trim. Come on in, but don't touch any woodwork. Everything else is dry.'

They went inside. The furniture in the small living room had been pushed together in the middle of the hardwood floor and covered with one large canvas tarpaulin. She pulled the canvas off on one side to uncover three chairs. 'You must be Sergeant Hobbes.'

'That's right,' said Hobbes. 'This is Mr Pitt. He's a private investigator cooperating with us on this case.'

It was not lost on Mrs Halloran that Joe Pitt was handsome, and closer to her age than to Hobbes's. She kept her eyes on Pitt as she said, 'Here, this is the only place we can sit right now.' Mrs Halloran sat on one of the chairs. 'You said "case." Tanya Starling is involved in a case?'

69

'We're looking for her so we can ask her a few questions. A man she knew in Portland was the victim of a crime.'

'What's his name?'

'His name was Dennis Poole.'

'Oh, my goodness,' said Mrs Halloran. 'No wonder she left in such a hurry. You mean you think she killed him, or that she's in danger?'

Catherine Hobbes allowed some of her frustration to show. 'We just want to talk to her. She knew him, and we would like to know anything she can tell us. She left Portland, so we haven't been able to talk to her.' Hobbes reached into her folder and pulled out a photograph. 'Can you identify the woman in this picture?'

Mrs Halloran held the picture a distance from her face, then close up, then farther away. 'Yes. That seems to be Tanya. But you should try to get a better picture. It's so fuzzy.'

'It's copied from a videotape. Did you talk to her much?'

'When I rented the house to her, we talked a bit. She said she was moving here from Chicago. Was that a lie?'

'No,' said Hobbes. 'Her last permanent address was in Chicago. We think she was only in Portland for a short visit.'

'That makes sense. She had nothing much with her. Her roommate hadn't even arrived yet.'

'What was the roommate's name?'

'Rachel Sturbridge.'

'What was she like?'

'I never met her. She was going to arrive separately in a few days. I let Tanya sign the lease and add Rachel's name to it, but Tanya paid the rent and security deposit in advance with her money, and initialed the lease to agree to all of the provisions, so for the time being, she was my tenant. I assumed that later on, as a matter of course, I would meet the other one. But as a rule, when you rent to young people, you don't want to hang around all the time. You risk becoming a second mommy to them. And what you don't know won't hurt you.'

'And you didn't see her when they moved, either?'

'No. They didn't tell me ahead of time, and if they had – I don't know – maybe I would have come to be sure they didn't leave the door unlocked or walk off with any of my furnishings, but they didn't anyway. They were perfectly nice. Later, when Tanya called and told me they had moved out, she said I could rent it to someone else right away. I asked if I could send her a refund at her new address, but she told me to keep the money for the trouble of renting it twice.'

'Very thoughtful,' said Catherine Hobbes. 'Do you remember the date of the call?'

'Let's see,' she said. 'It must have been about a week ago.'

'Did she say where she was calling from?'

'No, I don't think she did. She was in a hurry, and she said she was just taking the time to let me know about the vacancy, and had to go. I didn't want to keep her on the line.'

Catherine Hobbes said, 'Here's my card, Mrs Halloran. We're very interested in talking with her, so if you hear from her again, or remember anything that might help us, please get in touch. You can call me collect. In fact, I'm going to add my home phone number so you can reach me anytime.' She quickly wrote it on her card.

Mrs Halloran took the card, glanced at it, and stuck it into the pocket of her jeans. 'All right,' she said.

'Thank you.'

As soon as they had walked far enough from the house to avoid being overheard, Joe Pitt said, 'Are you getting the same feeling I am?'

'Oh, yes. She knows somebody is looking for her, and she doesn't want to be found.'

'This Rachel might be helping her lose the guy who killed Dennis Poole – if they use Rachel's car, and pay for things in Rachel's name, he'll have a hard time finding Tanya.'

'But we won't,' said Catherine Hobbes. 'Now that we know about her it gives us two chances for a hit. When we find one, we'll have the other.'

TEN

Nancy Mills found her walks through Topanga Plaza relaxing. There were gangs of old people who did power walks every morning before the stores opened, going the length of the mall, then clambering up the stalled escalator to the upper galleries and striding along beside the railings. Nancy was more subtle than they were, but she had begun to use the place for conditioning too, weaving through the crowds after the stores opened.

Nancy Mills didn't go on shopping binges the way Tanya Starling often had, and Rachel Sturbridge did once or twice. Nancy still owned all of their new clothes from Aspen, Portland, and San Francisco, and at the moment, her activities were too simple to require a big wardrobe. But she liked to look at clothes.

It was Thursday morning. The plaza was sometimes unpleasantly crowded on weekends, but Thursday was still perfect. She was in Bloomingdale's trying to decide which jar of bath salts had the right scent when she became aware that a man at the next counter was staring at her. He was in his early thirties, well groomed and nicely dressed. He wore a dark sport coat and shined Italian shoes. She assumed he must be a store floor manager or a salesman for one of the cosmetics lines, but she couldn't see from this angle whether he had a name tag without actually staring at him. Part of his job was to hang around being friendly to customers, so she dismissed him from her mind.

The saleswomen behind the counters were eager because Thursday mornings were slow, so one of them came right away to sell her the bath salts while another tried to raise the stakes by showing her the rest of that company's line of products. Nancy resisted the pitch and paid in cash, as she always did. As one of the women counted out her change and the other put her receipt in the bag, Nancy became aware that the man had not gone away.

She turned to look, their eyes met, and she had a horrible moment when she wondered if she knew him, then another when she had to endure his smile. It was at once shy and hopeful. There was even a trace of the conspiratorial, as though he and she shared a secret. He looked so familiar. Could she possibly know him?

She turned away, irritated. She wanted to say aloud, 'I wasn't looking because I was interested. I just sensed that someone was staring.' She took her bag, pivoted away from him, and walked back into the mall. She moved past the first couple of stores, then felt an uncomfortable sensation. She stopped and looked at the next store's window display, then quickly turned to walk to the other side of the mall.

She had been right. There he was again, a grown-up, smartly dressed man, following her around a mall like an awkward teenager. She supposed she should be flattered by the attention, but his behavior was very bad news: she had shortened her hair, dyed it a dull shade of brown, and worn clothes that weren't supposed to be eye-catching. All that seemed to have accomplished was to make her appealing to creepy, awkward men.

Nancy turned again, intending to leave him behind, but he was already at her shoulder, so when she turned she was nearly face-to-face with him. 'Excuse me,' she said, and stepped to the side.

'I'm sorry,' he said. 'I was almost sure I recognized you, and I wanted to check. I'm—'

'I don't think we know each other,' she said, and took a step.

'Regal Bank? San Francisco?'

She froze. Now she remembered who he was.

'I was the man who helped you open your commercial account at the bank. Bill Thayer. I'm the branch manager.'

'I do remember you,' said Nancy. 'What are you doing down here?'

'I have family here. I'm visiting. What about you? Are you expanding into the Los Angeles area? I still remember the name of your business — Singular Aspects. Right?'

He didn't seem to know that she had closed the account. She had to be extremely careful, because if he got curious, he could look things up when he got back to the office. 'No, actually, we decided that San Francisco wasn't right for us, and we're thinking about starting the business here instead. Well, nice to see you.' She stepped off.

'Miss Starling? Wait.'

She stopped walking. This was awful. She had forgotten that to open the account in San Francisco she had called herself Tanya Starling so she could cash Tanya Starling's check from the old account in Chicago. This Bill Thayer didn't know it yet, but he already possessed enough information to destroy her. He had seen her in this mall in Woodland Hills, just a few blocks from where she lived.

He said, 'I wondered if you would have dinner with me tonight.'

'Gee, Bill,' she said. 'I can't tonight.'

'I know it's kind of sudden, but I won't be here long, so I thought I'd better take a chance.'

She was afraid: she was afraid to be with him, and afraid to let him walk away. She knew that dinner was impossible. He would go to his parents' house and say he was going to miss dinner tonight because he had a date. Unless they were comatose, one of them would say, 'What's her name?' He would tell them who she was and where he had met her. She smiled. 'I do have some time now, though, if you'd like to have coffee.'

'That sounds good,' said Thayer.

'Do you have a car?'

'You can't go anywhere in L.A. without one. I rented it at the airport.'

'Then you can drive. There's a really great little place on Topanga just south of the freeway.'

They walked out of the plaza to the parking lot. His rental car was parked about a hundred yards off, almost by itself. When she saw it she was surprised. It was a Cadillac that looked enormous to her. 'Wow. Do you drive your mom and dad around when you visit?'

'Not much,' said Thayer. 'They think I've gotten rusty driving up north, so they don't trust me. The big car is for taking clients around. Whenever I come down I usually try to see a couple.'

They drove down Topanga past the freeway, and she said, 'Keep going. It's quite a bit farther, toward Malibu.'

'Is it on the left or right?'

'The right. Oh, look. There's a nice little park up there. Can we stop for a minute?'

'I guess so,' he said doubtfully. 'Sure.' Thayer drove off the road and stopped on the shoulder beside a grove of trees with picnic tables in it.

Nancy got out of the car with her purse over her shoulder. 'I've been looking for a good place to have a small party. I wonder if I could do it as a picnic, right here.'

Thayer didn't seem to know what to do. He got out of the car slowly, and scrutinized the ground before he took each step, as though he were afraid of getting his shoes dirty.

'Come on,' she said. 'Let's get a better look.' She took his hand playfully and began to walk among the trees.

Thayer looked a bit doubtful, but he began to stroll with her in the deserted grove, past picnic tables and trash cans. Nancy let go of his hand and moved off a few feet to disapprovingly rock a picnic table that was set on uneven ground. He strolled on, and got a few steps ahead of her.

She looked at her watch. It was nearly ten-thirty. It wasn't surprising that people weren't here in the morning, but someone could arrive before long to set up a picnic lunch. She looked back at the road. There were no cars going past, and she couldn't hear any coming. There was nobody nearby yet. It would have to be now. She let him get a few more steps ahead of her as she reached deep in her purse.

He suddenly stopped and turned to look back at her. He said, 'What are you looking for?'

She smiled brightly at him. 'My camera. I want to take a couple of pictures so I can compare it to some other places.'

He turned away and walked on.

Nancy Mills gripped the pistol and lifted it out, then held it tight against her thigh as she walked to catch up with him. She took one last look over her shoulder and listened for the sound of a car on the road. Then she raised the gun and fired through the back of Bill Thayer's skull.

His head bobbed forward in a sudden nod and his body followed it, toppling straight onto the ground. She squatted beside him to take his wallet out of his back pocket, then pushed him over on his back so she could reach his car keys in front.

She stood and walked calmly to the car, started it, and drove back the way she and Thayer had come, north on Topanga Canyon. She parked his car in the mall parking lot, wiped the steering wheel and door handles clean with one of the alcohol-soaked antibacterial wipes she carried in her purse, then picked up the bag containing her bath salts and walked away.

Nancy thought about the morning's events as she headed back toward her apartment. She had not wanted to harm Bill Thayer, but he had made it impossible not to. He'd had no right to keep pestering her. What could he possibly have been thinking?

Of course, she knew what he had been thinking. When he had seen the woman he thought of as Tanya Starling, it had probably made him feel excited. He already knew her slightly. She was a small business owner, and he was the manager of her bank. Not only could she be sure he was respectable, but he was powerful. He could raise her credit limit and get her loans approved. He could also get in her way, make things difficult for her. He was a shy, quiet man who had made so little impression on her the first time she'd met him that she had not recognized his face when it was three feet from hers this morning. But he had exercised his power over her, following her from the store, making her talk to him, keeping her from leaving, then making her agree to go somewhere with him. She'd had to get rid of him.

When Nancy reached home, she put on a pair of the rubber gloves she wore to do the dishes and sat at her kitchen table. She took Bill Thayer's wallet from her purse and examined it. The credit cards were too risky to keep, but he had also been carrying almost a thousand dollars in cash when she had killed him.

A lot of people carried extra cash when they were traveling, but this was better than she had expected. Nancy took the money, wrapped the wallet in a paper towel to disguise its shape, and put it in an opaque trash bag.

Somewhere in the back of her mind was a feeling, almost a physical sensation that had not yet developed into a coherent thought – something pleasant, even titillating.

Her need to end the fear had been like an ache. When she had at last been able to pull out the pistol and blow a round through Thayer's head, there had been a feeling of release. When she had left his rental car in the plaza parking lot and walked off with her Bloomingdale's bag, she had felt herself smiling.

Nancy had not allowed herself to acknowledge it yet, but she had been missing the excitement that she took from men. She had missed the anticipation of watching and waiting for the right one, and then the care and calculation of drawing him to her. She had missed the thrill of the next phase, the charged, anxious period of flirtation and speculation, and then the longer game of divulging and concealing, withholding and succumbing. She had especially missed the sweet, warm, lazy time after that, when she was secure in the man's love, soaking in the attention and the luxury.

Now she was beginning to notice the puzzling fact that she liked the bad parts too. When Dennis had begun to disappoint her, the resentment and anger had made her feel powerful and dangerous and clean – not like a victim, but like a judge and avenger. The building anger had made her feel energetic and purposeful. The single shot had been the best possible climax to the relationship.

She had liked the killing. The breakup with David Larson had shown her that perfectly. When David had betrayed her, she had enjoyed the process of getting angry and rejecting him and punishing him. Seeing his devastation had given her the chance to know how beautiful and desirable she could be. But it wasn't enough. What was missing was that she had not gotten to kill him.

She took the bag with the wallet out with her garbage late that night and stuck it in the bottom of the dumpster behind an apartment building three blocks from hers. Her gun stayed in her purse. It would be foolish to get rid of her gun just when she had started to enjoy it.

ELEVEN

'Hello? Mrs Halloran?'

Eve Halloran wasn't quite sure, but the young female voice made her think it just might be. 'Yes?'

'This is Tanya Starling calling. I'm very sorry to bother you, but I wondered whether anyone had tried to get in touch with me since I left, or asked about me. There might have been a man named David?'

'No, dear,' said Mrs Halloran. She spoke with barely suppressed excitement. 'I haven't heard from anyone like that. But a couple of days ago I did have a visit from a pair of police officers.' She stopped, waiting for a reaction.

'Police? Why? What did they want?'

Eve Halloran relished the suspense, loved holding back and tantalizing, but she could hardly withhold this information. It was too dramatic, too delicious. 'There were two of them, a man and a woman. They came all the way from Portland, Oregon. They said – I don't know how to break this to you – that a friend of yours has been the victim of a crime. It sounded as though he's been murdered.'

'Who?'

'I think they said Dennis Poole.'

'Oh, my God. Dennis Poole?'

'That's right.' Now Eve was feeling better. That last exclamation had carried the sort of emotion that she had been hoping for. What could that man Dennis Poole have been except Tanya's lover? 'I'm very, very sorry, honey. I hated to tell you this way, but there just wasn't any other way.'

'I can't believe it. How could he have been murdered? He was such a sweet man. He had no enemies. Was it some kind of robbery?' There were tears in her voice. Eve Halloran could hear the tension in the throat, the higher voice.

'They didn't say, but I don't think that was it,' said Eve Halloran. She allowed herself to give in to an ungenerous impulse. 'That was what they wanted to talk with you about.' She felt a tiny bit of guilt about holding back the next part of what they'd said, but she was still too curious. 'They seemed to think you might know something about what happened. They said you had left town just about the time when he was killed.'

'You mean they think I had something to do with Dennis's death?'

There. That was said just as Eve Halloran had imagined it. She didn't mind that she had to say the next part now. 'Oh, no, dear. They said you were not a suspect. They definitely said that. I didn't mean to imply anything of the kind. Stupid me. I should have said that right away, first thing.'

'I'm just overwhelmed. It never seems as though something like this can happen to anybody you know.'

Eve Halloran said eagerly, 'Were you very close?'

'I just can't believe it.'

That answer was unsatisfactory. In fact, it had been an evasion. 'Was he your boyfriend?'

'No.'

Mrs Halloran waited, but there was no more to the sentence. 'Well, it's very sad. I'm sorry.' Eve Halloran was growing tired of this conversation. She had built an expectation of a flood of intimate details, but she had been repeatedly disappointed.

Tanya said, 'Did the police say how I was supposed to get in touch with them? Did they leave a number or anything?'

'I'll see if I can find it.' Her voice was glum. This had been a disappointing conversation, and the fact that there was no further excuse to prolong it made her feel even more frustrated. She had taped the card to the wall right above the phone, but she stood leaning against the kitchen sink with her arms folded for thirty seconds. Let Tanya wait. She had become awfully demanding for a former tenant, calling up at night and expecting Eve to be her message board. After a time she sauntered back to the telephone. 'Tanya? Still there?'

'Yes.'

'Have a pencil?'

'Yes.'

'The name is Detective Sergeant Catherine Hobbes. She's on the homicide squad.' She added that part with a tinge of malice. She read off the various telephone numbers and the address of the police station, slowly and distinctly, to prolong the time of feeling important while Tanya silently copied down every word, probably with her hands shaking. When she had read everything on the card she said, 'Got all that?'

'Yes, thanks. I'll give her a call.'

Eve said, 'Have you thought about hiring a lawyer?'

'No. I just heard about this.'

'Well, from what I hear, the time to think about lawyers isn't after you've talked to the police, it's before.' She was spiteful now.

'I'll think about it.'

'You do that.'

'Thanks, Mrs Halloran.'

'You're welcome.' She was about to add a little jab

about how she was going to tell the police that she had talked to her, but she realized that the line was dead.

Nancy Mills stood beside the row of telephones in Topanga Plaza, gazing at the food court. She looked down at the little spiral notebook she had bought at the stationery store to prepare for this call, and reread the phone numbers of the cop who was after her. The name disturbed her: she had never expected that it would be a woman.

TWELVE

Catherine Hobbes sat in the homicide office. She had finished a long list of telephone calls that had not made her happy. Tanya Starling was turning out to be difficult to find. There was nothing helpful in her past – no way to find her family or her history. The apartment she had occupied in Chicago seemed to be an insuperable barrier: nothing was visible on the far side of it. A man named Carl Nelson had rented the apartment in his own name nine years ago. Tanya Starling had not been mentioned in the lease. At some point during those years she had moved in, and at some point Nelson had moved out, leaving the place to her. His accountants had continued to pay the rent until April, when she had moved out.

But it was as though she had come into existence in that apartment. Running a criminal records check on her name yielded nothing at all. She'd had an Illinois driver's license, and it had given the apartment as her address. None of the Starlings that Catherine Hobbes had found listed in Illinois had ever heard of Tanya.

Hobbes looked up and saw Joe Pitt appear in the doorway. She stood up and said, 'Come on, Joe. I'll buy you a cup of coffee.'

'Really?' he said.

'Really.'

'I'm flattered.'

She brushed past him and walked to the break room,

then put a dollar in the machine and watched the paper cup rattle into place, and the stream of hot black liquid fill it. She handed it to him, then bought one for herself. She went across the hall to the conference room, looked inside, then held the door open. 'Let's talk.'

He went in after her. 'You have something new?'

She sat on the table, sipped her coffee. 'Yes. I wanted to tell you alone. It's been mostly a positive experience having you come up here to cooperate in the investigation. You've been very helpful, and I've tried to learn what I could from your experience.'

'But?'

'But. It's time to cut you loose.'

'It is?'

'Yes. You've helped me to clarify a whole part of this case in my mind, and saved me quite a bit of time. I'm now convinced that this didn't have anything to do with Hugo Poole. At the same time, having a person acting as Hugo Poole's representative in this investigation isn't going to help us when we have to go into court for a conviction. So you've got to go.'

'I understand.'

'You don't sound surprised.'

'I'm not. Does Mike know about this yet?'

'Mike Farber? My captain?'

'Yes.'

'I told him this morning that this was what I was going to do.'

'And he agreed?'

'He agreed that it was my case, and that I had the right to make the decision. I made it, not Mike Farber.'

'Then I guess I'll try to stop and say good-bye to him before I leave. I wish you the best of luck on the case, and after watching you work, I have confidence that you'll handle it.' He held out his hand and she shook it. He smiled. 'See you,' he said, and he walked out the door and closed it.

Catherine remained perched on the table for a full minute, sipping her coffee and thinking. She knew that this decision had been inevitable and right, and she was relieved that it had gone so smoothly. She was also just a bit regretful, and she wasn't sure why.

She had to admit that was not exactly true. During the investigation she had begun to forget the imposition that Joe Pitt represented, and become used to having someone she could talk to about the case – not just some other cop who had a dozen cases of his own to think about, or a superior who had administrative details clogging his mind. When she had talked to Pitt she could talk in shorthand, and he knew exactly what she meant. She could test her ideas on him, and expect him to have ideas of his own.

Catherine tried to analyze her feelings. When Mike Farber had first called her in to tell her he had assigned her to work on a murder with Joe Pitt, she had felt insulted. If her captain thought she was so incompetent and inexperienced that she needed help from some out-of-town retiree, then she should get out of homicide. A moment later, when she had heard what a hotshot Joe Pitt was, she had wondered how it could be anything but an insult to her sex. Would Mike Farber have expected one of the men to serve as tour guide to a visiting potentate? No, it had to be the woman, the pretty face to please the visitor, and because the visitor was so great, all the hostess really needed to be was pretty. Joe Pitt would solve the case.

She had tested Joe Pitt – maybe tormented him a bit – and found that he wasn't so bad. She had come to feel comfortable with him. Why was she putting it like that? She had liked him, felt attracted to him. Maybe that was the worst thing about him. She couldn't afford to have him around any longer.

She jumped down, took her coffee to the break room, and poured it down the sink, then walked back to her desk in the homicide office.

Catherine's telephone rang. Maybe this was it. Maybe this was Tanya Starling. 'Homicide. Hobbes.'

'Hey, Hobbes. This is Doug Crowley in San Francisco. Has Tanya Starling called in yet?'

'Not yet.' Hobbes had been near her desk almost the whole shift. 'Mrs Halloran said that Tanya promised she would call, but she doesn't seem to be in a hurry to do it.'

'Well, I have something else that might be useful. The DMV has a hit on the roommate, Rachel Sturbridge.'

'What is it?' asked Hobbes. She sat at the edge of her chair and pulled her yellow pad toward her.

'It's her car. She's sold her car.'

'Her too? They both sold their cars? When and where did she sell it?'

'Los Angeles, about two weeks ago. The new owner just got around to registering it with the DMV. It was already registered in California, so she didn't think there was any hurry – she wouldn't get pulled over or anything. Her name is Wanda Achison, and she lives in a suburb called Westlake Village.'

'Has anyone talked with her yet?'

'As soon as we got this information I gave her a call. She sounded a little upset, because she was afraid it was stolen and we were going to take it away from her. She calmed down after a minute, though.'

'Did she buy it from Rachel personally? No intermediaries or dealers involved?'

'Yes. Rachel advertised it in a local swap sheet, Miss Achison called the number, and Rachel drove it to her house to let her check it out. Miss Achison said Rachel was in her late twenties, long dark hair, five-five, one fifteen to one twenty. Rachel told her she was selling the car to pay off a credit card debt.'

'That wouldn't be too unusual among people trying to start a business. Did she still have her address and phone?'

'No, but the paper did. It was a motel, and they don't have a record of Rachel Sturbridge staying there. I figured Tanya might have been the one who had signed the register, but they didn't have her down either. There must be a third person.'

'Maybe,' said Catherine. 'Can you give me Wanda Achison's address and phone number, please?'

He read the information, and she copied it. 'Thanks, Detective Crowley.'

'No problem.' He sighed. 'Are you and Joe going down there to do an interview?'

'Joe isn't involved in the investigation anymore.'

'He isn't? May I ask why?'

'Yes. He's been very cooperative, provided some information that eliminated some dead ends for us. Obviously he doesn't need a testimonial from me. But I don't think a civilian belongs in a homicide investigation.'

'I've always liked Joe, and I was glad to see him,' he said. 'But I don't either.'

'Thanks for all of your help,' she said.

'Don't mention it. And let me know if you need anything else from us in San Francisco.'

'I will.'

She hung up the telephone, then picked up the photograph of Tanya Starling that had been made from the surveillance tape. There she was, caught from the side, entering Dennis Poole's hotel room. Catherine Hobbes stared at the face. Tanya was just a small-boned woman who appeared to be in her late twenties, her expression untroubled. The blond hair that had obscured the features for most of the tape happened to have swung to the other side of the face for this instant, so all of the features were visible. The outlines were just vague enough to frustrate the viewer's eye as it tried to focus perfectly on an image that could never be any clearer. The bright, shiny hair drew the mind's attention more than the face did.

Catherine opened the file and scanned the lists of other agencies that had been cooperating in this case. She found the telephone number she wanted, then called the Illinois Department of Motor Vehicles to make her formal request for the driver's license photograph of Tanya Starling. She had waited long enough for Tanya to turn up or respond to her inquiries. It was time to go after her.

Catherine thought for a moment. Crowley had said that Rachel Sturbridge's car had been registered in California, so that meant the driver almost certainly was too. She dialed the number of the California DMV and requested the license photograph of Rachel Sturbridge.

THIRTEEN

Nancy Mills sat in her small apartment, staring out the window. It was eight-thirty, the time of each evening that made her want to open the door and go. She could see the sky through the west window. It was taking on that beautiful shading, the lower edge of it red, then above that a blue that began as only a little bit darker than the daylight sky, but as the eye looked higher, the sky darkened into an indigo canopy, with a few stars beginning to show.

She could almost hear her mother's voice calling. This was the time of evening when she always had to come in from play, and she used to come home dirty, the dust sometimes held to her little bare legs by dried sweat. She hated having to come home when the air was full of promise and expectation. Big, important things were about to happen. She knew that they were good things, marvels and pleasures that the grown-ups kept all to themselves.

She would usually let the sky get too dark before she made it home, so she would have to come up the street running. She remembered the sound and feel as, breathing hard, she made her sneaker pound on the bottom step of the front porch, and she pushed through the screen door into the living room.

Her mother and the latest boyfriend would already be in the bedroom getting ready. Her mother's skin would be pink and moist from the shower, the tight straps of her bra making depressions in the fat on her back. She would dance to tug the panty hose up over her hips. If the girl came in right at dark, her mother would be in a cheerful mood, the morning's hangover and remorse erased by the afternoon's nap, and her mind set on the adult evening that was coming.

The bathroom would be steamy. She remembered the boyfriend picking up the hand towel from the sink to wipe off the mirror so he could see to slide the razor along his bristly jowl, leaving a swath in the white shaving cream, pink and irritated but hairless, his mouth pursed and squeezed to one side to present a smooth, tight stretch of skin to the safety razor. She thought of it as a joke name for something that left small bright cuts on his chin so he had to stick bits of white toilet paper there, and let the red blood hold it in place.

It was a summer memory tonight because of the summer sky outside. The man in the memory changed, because there were so many of them. They were both a series and a progression, the nicer, younger ones all part of earlier memories, and the older ones coming later, when her mother's body began to thicken and her skin to loosen and wrinkle. Each man was the same in every way that mattered – the drinking and the yelling – but they differed in small ways, like how much hair they had or what color it was, or their names.

The boyfriend would get ready, and be standing around getting irritable before her mother would really begin. She would go to the other bedroom she had converted to her closet in her panty hose and bra, and then begin to try on each of her dresses in front of a big mirror with a frame that was supposed to hang on a wall, but was propped against a chair at an angle.

Each night the dressing would proceed all the way to its end several times. She would choose a dress, put it on, then go into the bathroom to apply her makeup and brush her hair, and suddenly discover some invisible flaw in the way the outfit made her look or feel, and take it off again. The earrings, necklace, and shoes were specific to the outfit, so they had to go too. Then she would put on another dress and the same thing would happen. Eventually, she would announce she was ready and would emerge, suddenly impatient to go, as though someone else had delayed her.

The little girl would look at her mother in amazement. Already it was clear that they were not going to look alike. Her mother was short, with big blue eyes and skin like cream. The girl was tall and bony, with pale skin and stringy hair. Her mother would look at her on her way out the door as a kind of afterthought.

'Lock the door after us,' she would say. 'Don't open it for anybody.'

Her mother and the boyfriend would go out and stand on the porch until the mother heard the click, and then they would get into the car. Usually they would be gone until just before dawn. The girl would sit alone in the house, feeling the loss as the sky darkened and deepened.

Often she heard voices outside her house in the calm night air as people passed by. Sometimes they sounded as though they were young, even her age. She was forced to stay in, lying on her bed in the dark, listening, while they were out there doing things and knowing things that she could not.

She would sometimes get up and go into her mother's room to look at the pageant trophies she had won. Her mother kept them in her own room, where the girl wouldn't break them or touch them and make them corrode. She called them 'my trophies,' just as an owner of a show dog would.

Nancy Mills had been inside this apartment every night for weeks. She'd had one problem turn up from San Francisco, but it had just been one of those rare coin-

93

cidences that Bill Thayer had been here visiting his parents and seen her. The fact that it had happened once would seem to prove that it couldn't happen a second time. It was just too unlikely. Besides, this was night. There were fewer people out, and the darkness would help protect her from being recognized. As she was pacing back and forth thinking about it, Nancy Mills had picked up her purse. She noticed it, gave herself permission, and walked to the door. She went out and closed the door behind her.

She didn't know where she was going, and it didn't matter. She had been staying out of sight since she had arrived, never going out after dark, going nowhere even in daylight but to the plaza, and she had not left this apartment for several days. She felt as though a rope had been tightened around her chest so she could barely breathe. As soon as she was on the street again, the rope seemed to loosen. The warm night air filled her lungs.

She walked to the plaza, used a pay phone to call a taxi, and waited for it outside Macy's. She said she wanted a ride to La Cienega Boulevard in Hollywood. When the dispatcher asked for the actual building number, she didn't know. When the dispatcher asked for the name of the nearest cross street, she didn't know that either, so she said Sunset. He said a yellow cab would arrive in about fifteen minutes. Nancy looked around her and began to feel bored and awkward standing alone in front of the store, so she reached into her purse and found the notebook where she had written the policewoman's phone numbers.

She carefully dialed the home number and waited, her eyes closed to help her concentrate.

'Hello?'

'Uh, hello,' she said. 'I'm looking for Catherine Hobbes?'

94

'This is Catherine Hobbes.' The voice was high and feminine. It sounded like a teacher. Nancy wasn't sure what she had expected, but this wasn't it.

'Hi. My name is Tanya Starling. Mrs Halloran told me that you had come by the apartment in San Francisco to speak to me, but Rachel and I had already moved away.'

'Yes,' said Hobbes. Her voice was tentative, almost preoccupied. Tanya knew that she was probably reaching to turn on a tape recorder or even pressing some button to tell somebody to trace the call. Nancy would have to do this quickly. Hobbes said, 'I have been trying to reach you. We need to ask you some questions. Mrs Halloran didn't have a forwarding address for you. Where are you living now?'

'I'm still on the road. I stopped for the night, checked into a motel, and started to clean out my purse. I found the piece of paper where I'd written your number, and realized I should call you.'

'Then I need to have the exact location where you are right now.'

'I'm in Southern California, off the freeway in a small motel. I don't know the exact address. I'm leaving for New York tomorrow, but I don't know where I'll be staying yet.'

'Please listen carefully. I want you to go to the nearest police station. Give the officer in charge my number. I'll fly there to talk with you.'

'You know, that's not possible tonight. Why don't you just ask me your questions right now? I mean, my memory isn't going to get any better staying up all night waiting for you.'

'I'm trying to help you, Tanya. But you have to cooperate, and you have to tell me the truth.'

'I called you, remember?'

95

'I know that you're afraid. It's not a bad thing to be right now. You had a relationship with Dennis Poole, and then he was murdered.'

'Are you implying that I had something to do with that?'

'I don't know any such thing. Someone killed him, and they could be after you too. I want to hear your side of the story. I want to know anything you can tell me about Dennis Poole. I want to know why you decided to leave Portland right after it happened.'

'This is stupid. I'm just trying to be polite, return your call, straighten this out, and get past it. Rachel and I had planned for a year to go to San Francisco and start a business together. I wasn't running. I didn't know anything had even happened to Dennis until I talked to Mrs Halloran. She was the one who told me.'

'I need to get through to you, Tanya. You and Rachel are both wanted for questioning in a murder investigation. You don't seem to be grasping the seriousness of that.'

'Well, sure I am,' said Tanya. 'That's why I called, so you could cross my name off your list and go on to somebody who knows something.'

'I don't think you're understanding me. Even if you are telling the truth and you're not withholding any information about the death of Dennis Poole, you could still be charged with fleeing to avoid prosecution, obstruction of justice, and about fifteen other things. They're all serious, and they all involve jail time. I can make sure that those things don't happen, if you will just do as I ask.'

'I will, if you'll ask for something I can do. I'm a thousand miles away from you, heading in the other direction, with very little money. I can't just leave everything I own in my car and park it in a lot someplace while I sit in a police station.'

'Listen carefully. Wherever you are, you're on a telephone. Just ask the operator to connect you with the local police. Tell the police you've spoken with me about going in for questioning in the Dennis Poole case. They can find where you are, bring you in, and keep your car and belongings safe. Give them the piece of paper with my number on it, and they'll call me. I'll handle everything from there. All right?'

'This isn't a reasonable thing to ask. You're trying to get me put in jail.'

'I'm trying to get you into a police station to talk to you. If you're running because somebody else killed Dennis Poole and you're afraid, the police will protect you. I'll make sure they do. If you're running because you're afraid the police will hurt you, then you can stop worrying about that too. It's a lot less scary when you go in voluntarily. I'll ask them not to put you in a cell.'

'I told you. I'm not running. I'm just moving, trying to get on with my life.'

'This is a detour you're going to have to take sooner or later.'

Nancy paused, unable to think of what to say. Finally, she said, 'I . . . I really don't think I should do that without a lawyer.'

'That's fine. If you'd like, you can have one before you answer any questions at all. They'll get you one. But you've got to do this, Tanya.'

'Let me think about it.'

'How long?'

'I don't know.'

'Tanya, the police are looking for you, not just here but all over. Right now nobody knows why you're not making yourself available, so they have to assume that you're dangerous. If you come in on your own, no harm will come to you. If you don't, then it's hard to predict what might happen. Go find a lawyer, and ask him to come with you when you turn yourself in. Tanya?'

Tanya didn't answer.

'Tanya? Please.'

Tanya thought about how much better it was to be Nancy Mills, out on a summer night in Southern California. She was too restless to stay on the line. She lifted the telephone to its cradle and pressed it down. The soft, warm breeze blew across the ear where she had held the telephone, soothing it. She was free, and she wasn't going to risk that. She saw the cab prowling along toward the front of the building, so she waved her hand and trotted to it.

She got in, rolled her window halfway down, and looked greedily out at the buildings and the people on the streets all the way to Sunset.

When the driver let her off on Sunset and La Cienega she began to walk. She passed the big faux-ramshackle structure of the House of Blues, then several restaurants. She wasn't in the mood to go into a formal restaurant and sit in the middle of a lot of tables with men and women on dates. What she needed was a hotel bar. She knew there were a couple of hotels along the Strip that had famous nightclubs, so she decided to find them.

She walked along the sidewalk beneath huge lighted billboards of the beautiful people in movies. Paintings of giant women covered the brick sides of tall office buildings.

The dry air was electrically charged, as though it would soon reach some peak voltage and emit sparks. The cars were nose-to-tail on Sunset, moving ahead in small surges. She could feel the eyes on her, not one man that she could see but many at once that she knew were there behind the glare of headlights or beyond dark tinted windows. She knew that when one of them looked, he was evaluating, trying to see if she was Someone, or even the one they had been searching for. The once-over lasted only for the time it took for her image to move from the windshield to the rearview mirror, but then the man in the next car was already looking at her.

Nancy's anticipation grew until she reached the Standard Hotel. It was low – only three stories. She stepped in the front entrance, trying to see everything but also trying to look as though she knew where she was going. She saw two security men – this was Sunset Boulevard, and what stepped in off the street could be literally anything – and smiled at them as she moved past the front desk. There was a girl with a pretty white face and gleaming straight black hair standing there to check people in, and behind her head was a greenish glass panel like a huge aquarium, where another girl who was naked napped on a clear inflated mattress, so that she appeared to be floating there.

This was the kind of place she had imagined. It was a sign of her magic that she had made it here. While she was still in her stuffy little apartment off Topanga Canyon she had only conceived a sense of how she wanted to feel, and what sort of place would make her feel that way, then moved toward it. She kept going until she found herself in the rooftop bar.

On the way to the ladies' room, Nancy studied the other women she could see standing near the long curved bar and sitting at the tables. They all seemed young, thin, and attractive. A few of them wore skirts or pantsuits, but most of them wore tight jeans and tank tops. Nancy felt reassured. At the moment when the urge had taken her she had been wearing a good pair of pants she had bought in Aspen and a Juicy Couture velour jacket over a little T-shirt she had picked up in San Francisco, so she was all right.

She studied her reflection in the mirror, brushed her hair, and wiped off her makeup. She had been wearing daytime shades, so she put on thicker eyeshadow, eyeliner, and mascara, darkened her lips as she listened to the chatter in the ladies' room. She could tell that these were not women staying at the hotel but local women who came here for the social scene. That was fine – so had she.

Nancy needed to set herself apart somehow, and be in a place where she didn't have to compete for attention with all of these women. She went to the bar and waited for a couple of orders to be filled so she could survey the room to evaluate the men and let them see her, then ordered her martini. When she had it, she took it outside, onto the big open stretch of blue Astroturf surrounding the pool.

She sat on one of the white lounge chairs and gazed down the slope at the city, the billions of tiny distinct lights shining upward from the streets and buildings to make the air above the city glow.

The first man to follow her out had long, skinny limbs covered in an off-white suit and a black T-shirt. He had glasses with thick black frames, and hair that had receded into a widow's peak. She glanced up at him and sipped her drink.

'Aren't you the girl from behind the front desk?'

'No,' said Nancy. 'She's still there. Go check.'

'I mean the one who pretends to be asleep. The naked one.'

'I know you do,' said Nancy.

'The girl from last night looked just like you. She's beautiful, and so are you.' He paused for a moment, studied her, and then said, 'You and I aren't going to be friends, are we?'

'Nope. Thanks for the compliment, though.'

'You're welcome. Good night,' he said. He turned and walked back into the bar.

After ten more minutes, another man came out. He walked to the pool, bent over and touched his hand to the water to test the temperature, then straightened, turned, and seemed to notice her. He was dark-skinned, with wavy black hair, and she imagined him to be Brazilian. When he spoke, the impression was destroyed. 'Oh,' he said. 'I didn't see you there.' He had an accent from New York, maybe New Jersey. 'Have you been in the pool yet?'

'No,' she said. She made a quick decision. 'I just came out here to be alone.'

'Me too. Would you like to be alone together?'

'No, I like to do it the usual way.'

'Oh,' he said. 'Well, see you.'

He walked back into the bar. This wasn't very promising, she decided, so she went back into the bar too. She moved to the wall, scanned the men in the room, and decided to choose one. He was standing a few feet to her right, looking over at her, when their eyes met. He was about thirty, with hair that must have been blond when he was a child but had turned brown later as hers had, and now lightened only when he had spent time in the sun. 'Hello,' she said. 'Do I have spinach stuck on my teeth?'

He came closer. 'Sorry if I was staring. What's the attraction out there?'

'It's really clear tonight. It's L.A., and you expect some smog.'

'Yeah,' he said. 'Otherwise you feel like you're not getting your money's worth.'

'They might have flown you to Bakersfield, and just told you it was L.A.'

'There's smog there too. And when it clears, you're still in Bakersfield.'

'I'll have to take your word for it. Or somebody's.'

He took a step closer and leaned against the wall beside her. 'Are you here on business?'

'Me?' she said. 'No. I'm here for a cold martini.'

'I can see you got one,' he said. He lifted his drink toward her, a faint gesture to simulate clinking glasses. 'Here's to it.' He took a sip. 'What I was trying to say was, you're a gorgeous person, and are you busy for the next few days doing work-related tasks all the time, or are you interested in meeting someone like me, getting married, and bearing my children?'

She made a show of appraising him, looking from his toes to his face and down again. Then she shrugged. 'It depends. Where would I have to live?'

'We could live anywhere you want. Right now, I'm based in Miami. But it's negotiable.'

'Based? What are you? A navy?'

'No. I just sell sound-imaging machines to doctors and hospitals, and that's where the office is. I'm Brian Corey.'

'Pleased to meet you. I'm Marsha.'

'No last name?'

'Corey. I'm going to be Marsha Corey, right?'

'True,' said Brian. 'Will you join me at a table, or do we have to keep our distance until after the wedding?'

'Now that we're engaged, you're welcome to sit with me, if you'd like.'

They stepped to a small empty table nearby. He moved a chair so he could sit beside her and look out over the city. 'I hate to descend to this kind of question, but where are you from?'

'I live here now.'

'At this hotel?'

'No, this is just where my martinis live. I recently moved to Los Angeles. I used to live in Chicago.'

'Why did you move here?'

'Because I was cold. There are a lot of songs about Chicago. But is there one that says you'll freeze your ass off? No.'

'Oh, I thought you might have come here to be an actress.'

'You mean you think I might be stupid.'

'I can only hope. But you are beautiful, and you did move to Los Angeles, so it was a possibility.'

'Are you disappointed that I'm not an actress?'

'No. I don't think that kind of career would leave enough time for me and the children.'

'Very smart of you to think ahead.'

'Ah, yes. Thinking ahead. Have you got plans for dinner yet?'

'Gee, we're barely engaged, and already you want me to cook.'

'No, I was going to take you to dinner, if you're willing.'

'After the kids and moving to Miami, dinner seems pretty easy. I'm willing.'

'We can drive out to La Parapluie, which is in Beverly Hills, where I happen to have a reservation for dinner in about a half hour. Or we can have another drink first, and take our chances that by the time we get there it will be so late that we won't need a reservation.'

'A quandary. My drink is dead, but since you mentioned dinner, I'm beginning to get hungry.'

'Let's try to have it all. We'll go down to La Parapluie, and order drinks at dinner.'

'Whatever you say, dear.'

Brian Corey had rented a car to make his sales calls, and the valet parking attendant brought it. He was an experienced driver who knew enough to get off Sunset right away, and they were in La Parapluie within ten minutes. It was a large, noisy room with lots of white walls and linen and some bright mediocre minimalist paintings, but the waiter brought Nancy a martini with a tiny iced carafe of vodka on the side, so she forgave the restaurant its decor.

While they were sipping their drinks, Brian said, 'I've been thinking about this since I met you, so I've got to say it: you really are beautiful.'

'Thank you. I was rather pleased when I got you into the light, myself. I guess it's a marriage made in heaven. What do you like on this menu?'

'I've only been here one time, but I had the swordfish, and it was good.'

'I'll try it, then.'

'Anything you'd like. For tonight, you're the queen of my expense account.'

'I'll have to tell you up front I'm not going to buy an ultrasound machine.'

'Then I hope you're willing to pretend to choke on a fish bone, so all the doctors in the place will rush to help, and I can deliver my pitch.'

'Of course. If we want the children to go to Harvard, I'll have to do that every time we go out.'

They ate dinner, and talked happy nonsense all through it. Nancy Mills was filled with manic energy. She felt that she should never have talked herself into believing that she had to stay out of sight.

After dinner they tried to move into the bar, but it was nearly midnight now, and the crowds of people in the restaurant had swelled. The knot of drinkers ordering at the bar was just the beginning of a line that stretched outward and made it an evening's labor to get another drink. Brian leaned close to her and said, 'I've got a mini-bar in my room, and a better view than this. It's on the eighth floor of the Beverly Hilton.'

She looked at him closely. 'All right. Let's go check out your bar.'

They drove to the Beverly Hilton and took the elevator up to his room. It was not the huge suite she had been hoping for, but it was a pleasant single room, and it had a balcony that was directly above the patio and a little to the left of the pool. He made her another martini while she leaned over the railing for a different view of the city.

She took her martini and sipped it. 'Thanks, Brian. Considering the primitive conditions, that is not a bad drink.'

'Thanks,' he said. 'I've found that I'm about as good a maker of third martinis as anybody.'

'I guess you're right,' she said. 'It probably tastes like lighter fluid, and I don't know the difference. I guess I shouldn't drink so much.' She walked past him into the room and set her drink on the desk.

The whole evening's adventure had been leading to this, hadn't it? She had sleepwalked her way here. She was with the right kind of man: she had chosen him. She stepped into him, snaking her arms around his body. He held her and kissed her gently. She remembered how much she liked this feeling.

His arms were thick and strong, and she could detect the definition of the muscles, but she could also feel his hands making soft, slow swirls on her back that made her feel small and sleek, like a cat. The nerves of her spine and shoulder blades shivered, waiting their turn to be touched, and she found herself moving to make him touch her there.

The kisses and caresses grew in intensity, building quickly with her impatience. She was excited by the rightness of whatever she thought to do tonight. Her impulses all seemed to be gratified instantly. Later she lay on the bed with the blankets tumbled in a heap at the foot, feeling the fresh night air blowing in over her body, cooling and soothing her. She stared at the ceiling, feeling her breathing slowing down and becoming even again.

Brian was out on the balcony, leaning on the rail and craning his neck to look down at something. He still had no shirt, but he had put on his pants in order to go out there. She studied him, gauged the attitude of his body. He was leaning on his elbows, a picture of relaxation and ease. Minutes passed. It was time now for him to come back in and lie down beside her and say nice things to her, or at least put his arm around her again, but he didn't. He didn't even turn and look at her, to see how beautiful she looked lying on the white sheets, her hair spread around her head in a halo. She began to be a little disappointed in him.

She gave him a reprieve. Was it possible that while she was lying here sending him a signal, she was missing the signals that he had been sending her? Maybe he wanted her to get up and come out on the balcony with him.

Nancy slipped into the bathroom and snatched the thick white hotel bathrobe from its hook behind the door. She tied the belt at her waist and came out behind him. He didn't seem to hear her coming. She put her arms around him and pressed herself against his back, rocking slightly from side to side. 'That was really nice,' she whispered.

He took a deep breath and let it out in a sigh. 'Yes.'

She felt her muscles tighten. 'That's all? You don't want to say something sweet to me?'

He turned, and that disengaged her arms from him. He placed his hands on her shoulders and held her there while he looked into her eyes, then kissed her forehead. 'I loved this evening. I think you're a really special person, and I feel lucky to have met you.'

'But?'

'I should have told you before. I have a girlfriend back in Miami. She and I have been together for over two years.'

Nancy shrugged, knowing it made her look good and that the top of the bathrobe would open a bit wider. 'I'm really not that naive, Brian. I knew when I saw you that I wasn't the first girl you'd ever met, and it's not like I thought that other girls wouldn't be interested in you.'

'I really haven't been honest with you, or with her. I loved tonight, but I didn't really have the right to be with you. I was standing here thinking how unfair I've been.'

She embraced him tightly. 'I understand. This was just a one-time thing. It was only for tonight, and when it's over, that's it. But why ruin it? What if this turned out to be the last night of your life?'

'That's a funny way to look at it.'

She smiled up at him, and she knew she was alluring. 'It's the only way to look at it. If it was the end of your life, how would you want to have spent it – alone or with me, the way you are?'

'With you.'

'Are you sure?'

'Yes. Absolutely.'

'Then smile.'

He gave her the smile she had asked for, and took her in his arms. They moved off the balcony and into the room. It was a moment before the bathrobe dropped to the floor and they were together on the bed again. This time there was something better than the eagerness and haste of the first. She imagined them to be a pair of lovers who had become old friends, and somehow had learned to enjoy each other without all the pain and hurt feelings and failed attempts to connect that people had when they were actively in love. She moved into a cycle of pure selfish wanting and receiving and appreciating and wanting. Then she lay motionless on the bed again.

Nancy waited until Brian got up and went out to the balcony again. Then she crawled to the side of the bed and swung her legs to put her feet on the floor near her pile of clothes. She dressed silently and efficiently.

She moved closer to the balcony, and she could see past him to the city below. It was the darkest, quietest time. The lightbulbs that were ever going to be switched off were off now. The fog had slid in from the Pacific, and dimmed even the streetlamps and traffic signals.

She took her first step on the concrete surface of the balcony, then the second, each quicker. If he heard her, he expected her to come up from behind and put her arms around him, just as she had done before. He did not move. He was still leaning forward, his arms crossed and his elbows on the railing.

Nancy went low, clamped her arms tightly around his knees, her legs already straightening to lift him up over the railing. Brian's head and upper torso had already been past the railing and leaning before she'd arrived, and he began toppling over the edge before he had any notion of what was happening. His arms started flailing now that there was nothing but air for him to grasp, and he half-twisted to try to face her, but his sudden movement only helped to propel him over. In an instant he was free of restraint, falling. As he went he said something that sounded like 'Unh?' Nancy stopped herself against the railing and watched him accelerating toward the earth.

It took a long time for him to fall eight floors. She watched until he hit the concrete walkway beside the building, bounced upward a foot or two, and then lay still. She could already see that there was a splash of blood where he lay, but she had no more time to look. She snatched his wallet, then wiped a towel over the glass she had used and the doorknobs and faucet handles, and quietly closed the door behind her.

Nancy knew without having to think about it that it would be best not to be in an elevator, so she stepped into the nearest stairwell. She took the stairs all the way down to the bottom, moving as quickly as she could. The door was locked where it met the parking garage, so she had to go up one flight, come out on the lobby level, and go outside. She avoided the parking attendant, hurried around the building to the entrance to the lot, went down and found Brian's rental car with the key under the visor. She got in, started it, and drove up the ramp onto the street.

She turned to the east and then north, and drove as far as a public parking lot on Hollywood Way near the Burbank airport. She parked the car, then walked to the airport. She waited two hours until the first flights of the morning arrived at seven, stepped out of the terminal in the middle of a group of arriving passengers, and waited her turn for a taxi.

FOURTEEN

Catherine Hobbes placed the two photographs together on her desk, and looked from one to the other. Then she picked up the telephone and dialed the captain's office. 'Mike, this is Hobbes. I've got something I think you should see.'

She released the telephone and walked down the hall to the last office. She opened the door, then walked to the big desk where Captain Mike Farber, chief of homicide, waited for her. She reached across the desk and set the driver's license photograph of the young blond woman in front of him. 'This is the Illinois DMV's latest license picture of Tanya Starling. It was taken less than a year ago.' She set the second photograph directly below it. 'This is the picture the California DMV sent us from the driver's license issued to Rachel Sturbridge. It was taken a month ago.'

Mike Farber was a big, broad man about fifty-five years old, with bristly gray hair. He leaned down for a moment to study the photographs, then looked up at Catherine Hobbes. 'Looks like you're not looking for an innocent witness anymore. What do you want to do about her?'

'I think it's time to get a new notice made up and sent out to other agencies,' she said.

'We'll want to get the DA's office in on this right away. I'll handle that. We can get a warrant on the false ID at least, and possibly intent to flee. That way we can get her held wherever she turns up.'

'She has turned up, in a way,' said Catherine. 'She wouldn't tell me where she was calling from, just Southern California. The phone company says it was a pay telephone somewhere in the 818 area code. That's the northwest part of Los Angeles. It's where Rachel Sturbridge's car was sold. I'd like to go down there to see if I can pick up her trail.'

He studied her for a moment, then nodded. 'Hand off the cases you have and go get her, Cath.'

It took Catherine Hobbes two hours to clear her desk of the cases she had been working on by giving them to the other detectives, and to prepare to make another trip out of Portland. The first plane to Los Angeles she could get left early that evening.

On the plane she kept working her way through the telephone conversation she'd had with Tanya Starling. She had sounded very young, and maybe a little bit slow. Catherine had spent much of the time trying to persuade her that being wanted for questioning in a murder case was a serious matter, not something that she could ignore. She had worried about Tanya, because it might take a certain amount of common sense for a person like her – a potential suspect who appeared to have fled – even to get arrested safely.

But as soon as Catherine had looked at the two photographs on the two driver's licenses, she had begun to get a different feeling about Tanya. Innocent bystanders and slow learners with nothing to hide didn't turn up with two driver's licenses in different names.

As the plane came closer to Los Angeles, Catherine couldn't help remembering that Los Angeles was where Hugo Poole and Joe Pitt lived. She kept catching herself constructing scenes in which she would call Joe Pitt to let him know what was happening. He would offer to help her get around the unfamiliar city, and maybe to help her get the best cooperation from the local police. Every time she caught herself thinking about calling him, she shook her head and cut the vision short. She knew that she had only been imagining these things because she had somehow allowed herself to think about him in a romantic way. She could recognize the idea of calling him for what it was – not a rational plan of action but the foundation for a fantasy.

Joe Pitt had everything wrong with him. He was too old for her, and he was a gambler. He was in his forties but had never been married, and he talked to every woman as though he had already been to bed with her. He was also a drinker. He was a jovial companion, the sort of guy everybody loved to have a couple of drinks with after work. When he had offered, she had always said no.

It made her feel a hot wave of humiliation to think of it now. She had managed to convince him that she was too prissy and rigid to have a drink with him. What Joe Pitt knew was the warm, easy face of alcohol, the evening gatherings with friendly people when he ordered a round and everybody went home feeling relaxed and happy. But Catherine Hobbes had a special knowledge about drinking.

When Catherine had been in college in California, she had known the pleasant side of drinking too. She'd always worked hard all week on her studies, and on weekends she had gone out with her friends to parties where for a pretty girl the price of a drink was holding out her hand to accept it. She had been funnier and more fluent when she talked, sexier and more uninhibited when she danced. She had felt that way, at least. But near the end of her junior year, she had noticed things that had scared her. She had awakened some mornings and spent an hour lying in bed waiting for the sick headache to fade and trying to remember what she had done the night before. She could retrace the stages of her night, but more and more often there were periods that were simply blank.

The problem had gone away. She had not been cured, only distracted. One night, just after she'd accepted her first drink at a party, Kevin Dalton appeared and began to talk to her. She did not have another drink that evening, and beginning the day after that, she and Kevin became inseparable. During her senior year she didn't have any free weekends to go to bars or parties with her girlfriends because she was with Kevin. They were married the summer after graduation and bought a condominium in Palo Alto. She did not make a decision about drinking. She simply forgot to drink.

Five years later, after the marriage had detonated and blown apart, she remembered to drink. The hard side of drinking came on her gradually. She began to go out after work with some of the other young brokers each evening. They all worked long days that began at five a.m., when the New York markets opened. They all lived in the same atmosphere of controlled panic, each of them paid on commission and all of them doomed to be fired the first time their sales figures fell enough to get the managers' attention. They drank and joked together for a few hours, then went home feeling a little better.

On most evenings, she was one of three women in a group that was overwhelmingly male. She somehow found herself more comfortable talking with the men than the women, and soon she was drinking with them glass for glass, listening to their jokes and their complaints, and making a few of her own. Early in the evening the other two women would go home, and then the party would be only Catherine and the men. Often, after she was home alone in the empty silence of the condominium where she and Kevin had once lived together, she would pour herself one last drink of whiskey to put herself to sleep.

One night she stayed late until the group dwindled down to Catherine and a friend named Nick. She let him take her home, and then she slept with him. Catherine fended off feeling ashamed by telling herself that the whole event had been good-natured – something that had happened between close friends – but they both felt awkward seeing each other at work after that, and the friendship diminished to a tacit agreement not to mention the incident again.

A couple of weeks later, it happened with another one of the men in the group. This one was Derek, a tall, thin British broker with a sallow complexion and an overbite. This time she had not even thought about being with Derek. He had simply paid the last tab, conducted her out of the bar, and kissed her. Derek drove her to his apartment, and they slept together.

In the morning she called her supervisor, said she was sick, and spent some time wondering why she had slept with Derek. All she could do was shrug and tell herself that she'd just had too much to drink – it wasn't her fault. But it wasn't the first time, and it was her fault. She brought back every moment of the night and analyzed it. She had not especially wanted to be with Derek, who wasn't a close friend like Nick, and wasn't even attractive. The alcohol had made her feel a lazy acquiescence: she had lost control of her will in exactly the way she had lost control of her arms and legs. It had just seemed like too much effort to exert them.

Later that day she quit her job, poured her supply of liquor out in the sink, and packed her belongings into her car for the drive home to Oregon. Driving back to Oregon was a desperate retreat. During every mile of the drive, she was afraid. She had failed to keep her husband, and she had run away from her career as a broker. She had developed such a taste for the forgetfulness and indifference that alcohol gave her that she had kept drinking even after she had done things that made her ashamed. She had slept with the two men who had asked, but it could just as easily have been five, or ten, or none. Things had just stopped mattering. The landscape behind her – the past, the people, the places where she had lived – was as dead and comfortless as a pile of bones.

She had no business considering a relationship with a man like Joe Pitt. She couldn't take the risks, and he shouldn't have to tolerate the rules she had made for herself. He didn't have any incentive to be constricted by her vulnerabilities and her past. She couldn't bear even to tell him about them. By the time the plane landed in Los Angeles, she was ashamed of herself for even considering speaking to him.

A few minutes later she was in Los Angeles International Airport, pulling her rolling suitcase along the concourse toward the escalator down to the car rental counters. She walked past the gift shops, looking in as she went. On the back wall were always racks of paperback books and magazines. There was the jumble of stuffed animals, hats, and T-shirts, all purporting to be from Hollywood or Beverly Hills. And in front of the store were racks with newspapers.

The New York Times and *Los Angeles Times* were in stacks, but the *Daily News* had one paper propped up where she could see the big color picture above the fold. The picture was a blurred security-camera shot, and that might have been what made her notice the resemblance immediately. The young woman seemed too much like Tanya to be anyone else. This time she had somewhat shorter, brownish hair, and she was wearing pants and a little sweater with a hood.

Catherine Hobbes read the caption above the picture: WOMAN SOUGHT IN SUSPICIOUS DEATH AT HOTEL. Beneath the picture was 'If you recognize this woman, please call the Tip Number . . .'

Hobbes started toward the cash register, then, on second thought, came back for another copy. She bought them, took them to a seat in a waiting area off the concourse and looked at the picture once again, then scanned the article.

The woman had been seen at a hotel with a young man named Brian Corey, who had later jumped, fallen, or been pushed from the balcony of his eighth-floor room. The detective who had spoken with the reporter was listed as James Spengler of the Hollywood Division.

Hobbes held the paper on her lap, got her cell phone out of her purse, and realized that her hand was shaking. She took a deep breath, then asked the information operator for the number of the Hollywood Division. When she reached the station she was transferred twice.

Finally, she heard a male voice say, 'Homicide. Spengler.'

She took another deep breath and tried to speak calmly and distinctly. 'This is Detective Sergeant Catherine Hobbes of the Portland, Oregon, Police Bureau. I just arrived in Los Angeles a minute ago and saw the front-page picture in the *Daily News*.'

'That was fast,' he said. 'What you've seen is tomorrow morning's edition. You don't, by any chance, know the woman in the picture?'

'Yes, I do.'
'Do you have a name and address for her?'
'I've got several.'

FIFTEEN

Nancy Mills had been awakened by the sun, which had somehow found a way through the blinds and made her pillow glow with painful brightness. She had dressed quickly and gone out, eager to be moving again. The killing of Brian stayed on her mind, even though he had been dead over a day now. She walked for a time, ate breakfast at the Red Robin in the plaza, then walked to the Promenade Mall and back. She spent most of the day wandering, finding anything she could to keep from staying in one place.

She tried to think clearly about killing. She remembered that she had felt a kind of emotional satisfaction after she had killed Dennis Poole: the act of shooting him had served to purge a great tangle of complicated feelings that she'd had about him. Then she had felt frustrated, interrupted, when she had not been permitted to end the relationship with David Larson the right way. The chance meeting with Bill Thayer had been pure adventure – a strong dose of fear, some quick thinking, and then it was over. But it had left her with a peculiar tingling, a pleasant excitement. The night with Brian Corey was different from all of the others. It had been wilder, riskier, and more exciting.

She loved being with men and feeling the strength of her ability to attract them. She liked the way they looked at her. She liked having sex with some of them. But afterward, she always detected in herself a surprising resentment for what they had taken from her. Even though she had gone out hoping that she would have the chance to make this happen, and had then struggled to get their attention, she didn't exactly wish them well – she just needed them to want her. With some of them, she suspected that they felt superior because they had cajoled and flattered her into bed. Even when she was with the best of them, the physical act made her feel that they were controlling her, making her feel one sensation, then another, always at their discretion. After she had put all the effort into seducing them, she felt as though she had been coerced.

She had felt that with Brian from the beginning. There had been a joy in attracting him, and in spending the beautiful warm night with him, but there had been another kind of pleasure in knowing that all along she was fooling him, manipulating him, spending the whole time patiently moving him toward that balcony.

It was getting to be dinnertime again when she walked back to the apartment. She still felt the energy that wouldn't let her rest, but she knew that she must be as close to invisible as she could manage. She went up the steps and opened the door, walked through the little lobby, past the mailboxes, and had entered her hallway when the door across the hall opened. 'Nancy?'

It was Nancy's nearest neighbor. A woman of about sixty, she always looked worn, haggard, and upset, as though she were engaged in some great task in her apartment when the door was closed. What was her name? The label on her door of the big mailbox in the lobby said M. Tilson. They had met down there several times. What was it – May, Mandy, Marcie, Marilyn? No. Just Mary. 'Hi, Mary.'

Mary Tilson pulled her door open wide and touched her short brown hair nervously. 'Do you have a second?'

Nancy stepped inside. Mary seemed anxious, a bit more upset than usual. Nancy had never been inside her apartment before. She could see that the layout was exactly the same as hers, only on the other side of the building, reversed like a mirror image. There was a lingering smell of chlorine, as though Mary had recently scrubbed her sinks with cleanser. Nancy imagined her as one of those women who were always scrubbing and cleaning things, and a glance around the apartment confirmed it. The light beige carpet looked new, and the shelves filled beyond capacity with horrible china dogs were free of dust.

Mary hurried to the well-waxed dining room table, snatched up a newspaper, and hurried back. Nancy could see it was the *Daily News,* the smaller Los Angeles morning paper. 'Honey,' said Mary. 'I'm glad I heard you come in.' It seemed an odd way for a woman who didn't know her very well to talk. 'I just came in myself. I was out at the grocery store, and I picked up both papers, because I like to see the early edition.'

'Oh?' said Nancy. 'What a smart idea.' It didn't seem to her to be a smart idea. It seemed sad. She sensed that Mary was going to be a neighbor who bothered her with bulletins about tiny aspects of her daily life. Soon it would be recipes and coupons for the supermarket. She made a resolution to avoid being cornered like this again.

'Yes,' said Mary. 'I started doing it with the Sunday papers, because they came out on Saturday afternoon, and there was so much extra stuff in them.' She seemed to struggle to get past these topics that made her comfortable, and into something that was making her uncomfortable. 'I don't know how to tell you this, but I think I have to.' She handed the newspaper to Nancy. 'Is this picture you?'

Nancy held the newspaper in both hands and stared at the picture on the front page. She realized that she was in a state of amazement that was making it hard for her to think past the brute fact of the photograph. How had anyone taken a picture of her in the hotel? How could they have it in the newspaper? The picture was a random blow to her, like a runaway car suddenly veering off the street to run her down. She knew she had to force herself to react, to talk. 'That's something, isn't it?' she said.

'Is it you?'

'Of course not,' said Nancy. 'I guess there are a lot of girls who look like me, or sort of like me. What's the story about?' As she chattered, she was trying to scan the two columns of print below the picture, but she was too agitated to keep her eyes on the print and too impatient to decipher it. She knew what it had to be about. She had instantly recognized the lobby of the Beverly Hilton hotel, recognized Brian, recognized herself, recognized the clothes she had been wearing.

'It's . . . it says that the man this woman was with the other night fell out of a hotel window.' She seemed alarmed by the way she had said it, then gave a nervous laugh. 'I'm glad it wasn't you. That would have been really awful. The man who fell, or jumped, would have been somebody you knew.'

Nancy handed the newspaper back to her. 'Well, thanks for checking. If it had been me, I guess I'd want to know.'

'No trouble at all. When I saw it in the store, I just couldn't believe it. I said to myself, "It can't be." And I was right. It wasn't. What a relief.'

Nancy started toward the door. She had been so edgy and full of restless energy when Mary had stopped her that she had barely been able to force herself to enter, and now the smells and the impression of clutter from the unnecessary furniture and the china dogs and clusters of framed pictures made her want to run.

'Wait.'

Nancy's mind was racing. She stopped because she knew she had to. But she needed to get out and think, and her mind kept jumping from one thought to another, never settling on one. She fixed an inquisitive, friendly expression on her face, and turned to look at Mary. 'What's wrong?'

'I was thinking. That picture looks so much like you. I wonder if you ought to call the police and tell them it's not you.'

'What?'

'It looks just exactly like you. There will be other people who see it. What if everybody in the building calls them, and the people at the supermarket and everywhere else you go call them and say that the picture is you?'

'I could hardly blame them,' said Nancy.

'Well, then would it be better to call the police and say, "I know you're going to get calls saying that's me," so they know they can eliminate you ahead of time? That way, they're not going to come looking for you. It could save you a whole lot of trouble and unpleasantness.'

'What kind of trouble?'

'The paper said they want to talk to you about that man's death, which they said is suspicious. You know what that means. If they come, they might arrest you.'

'I doubt it. I'm a pretty harmless person.'

'I saw this show on TV not too long ago about this young black guy who got arrested because he looked like this other young black guy who had robbed a liquor store and shot people. He was really a teacher, and he was just driving home from coaching the debating team, and they ended up convicting him of murder. When the real killer confessed, he didn't even look all that much like the innocent guy. Not nearly as much as you look like that picture.'

Nancy shrugged. 'If I have time tomorrow, I'll give them a call. I might end up saving them a trip. Thanks.'

'Would you mind if I called them for you in the meantime?'

'Why would you do that?'

'Because tomorrow morning, when this picture is on doorsteps all over the city, it's going to be too late. We could have a SWAT team here kicking down the door.'

The restless energy that Nancy had felt since the moment when she had pushed Brian off the balcony was beginning to overwhelm her again. She could feel her neck and shoulders tensing, and she clenched her hands like claws to keep them still. 'I wish you wouldn't do anything like that.'

'I'm giving you the chance to do it yourself.'

In the next instant, Nancy's distraction and nervousness died away. She saw the events of the past two days and the next two days at once. She knew now that she should never have gone out and found Brian Corey. It had been a horrible lapse of judgment.

She knew that Mary was right about the picture in the paper. At seven tomorrow morning there would be copies on thousands of doorsteps. People would remember seeing her at stores and restaurants in the plaza, in the apartment building, on the nearby streets. Tomorrow morning might be optimistic. It was a sensational story, the kind that might turn up tonight on the local television news. She had to get out of Los Angeles as quickly as she could. It would take only a few minutes to pack her clothes and her money. But that wasn't good enough. There was no time to get a car, and no time to build a new identity.

She looked at Mary. 'You're right.' She knew that

what she was considering was a form of perfection. It would fend off all of the people who wanted to do her harm, and it would give her a way to supply all of her immediate needs. It was so right that it began to happen without her choosing to do it. She didn't plan. She simply started.

'You're absolutely right. I wasn't really thinking clearly. In fact, I'd be doing them a favor too. Eliminating the need to investigate calls from fifty people is probably as good as a tip.'

'At least it helps. And if they've already been called about you, it might be important.'

Nancy gave an apologetic smile, and a shiver. 'I'm actually a little nervous. I don't know why.'

'Then let's do it together. Here. Let's have some iced tea. That'll help us cool off and calm down. Then we can make the call.'

Mary walked to the small kitchen and Nancy followed closely. Nancy's eyes and ears had been so sensitized by the excitement and agitation that they almost hurt. She saw Mary reach for the refrigerator's door, and she saw the black grips of the kitchen knives sticking out of the slits in the butcher-block holder on the counter. She snatched a big one out and had it in motion before Mary's hand could close on the door handle.

She stabbed it into Mary's back in the spot below the left shoulder blade that she judged must be the heart, but it hit a rib and she had to push it upward and over before it would go in.

Mary's arms flew out from her sides, she tried to turn, and she cried loudly, 'Oh! Oh! Oh!'

Nancy had to silence her. She tugged out the knife, clutched Mary's hair, wrapping it around her fingers, and jerked the head back. She drew the knife blade across Mary's throat under the jaw. She had heard someone use the term 'ear to ear,' so she did it that way, trying to make the slice as deep as she could.

Mary's hands came up to her throat. There was a hissing, gurgling noise, and spurts of blood spattered the white metal surface of the refrigerator door like carnations, then streaked down to the floor.

It was horrible. Why wasn't she dead? Nancy held her there, her hand still caught in Mary's hair. She hooked her right arm around Mary from behind and plunged the knife into Mary's torso just below the center of the rib cage. She knew she had missed the heart again, so she pushed down on the handle to lever the blade upward, then grabbed the handle with both hands and drew it toward herself.

Mary's knees buckled and she collapsed to the floor. Nancy released her hair and stepped backward, leaving the knife in her. Nancy looked down and saw that her arms were covered with blood from the elbows to the fingertips, dripping into the pools that were merging into each other beside Mary.

Nancy turned and stepped to the sink. She ran the water to wash the blood off her arms, twisting every few seconds to see whether Mary had moved. Was she finally dead? Maybe she was, but it seemed that as long as the pool of blood kept growing, the heart must still be pumping it out onto the floor.

Nancy knew that her jeans and her top probably had droplets of blood on them somewhere, but she couldn't see them and she was clean enough to accomplish the next tasks. She took the rubber gloves that Mary had left on the sink beside the cleanser and put them on.

Mary's purse was easy to find. She had left it in plain sight on the counter near the telephone. Nancy opened it and examined the contents. There were Mary's keys. The apartment key was exactly like Nancy's. The car key had a black plastic sleeve stamped with an *H* for Honda. There was a small wallet with Mary's credit cards and identification, but no cash. Nancy unzipped each of the handbag's inner pockets until she found one with a zippered change purse. Inside was folded currency, and on top were some fifty-dollar bills.

Nancy stood in the kitchen and looked through the doorway at the rest of the apartment. Here was the grotesquely crowded living room, one bedroom, and a bath, all laid out facing hers across the hall. She knew she should spend very little time searching the place, but she knew she wouldn't need much. If something of value wasn't in the bedroom, it had to be hidden in the kitchen – in the freezer, or inside the pots and pans, or high on a shelf in a sugar bowl.

Being near Mary made her feel uneasy. She wasn't really sure that Mary was dead yet, and she had the feeling that Mary was lying there awake, looking at her and listening to her as she went about her business. She had a curiosity about how Mary's bedroom would look, so she chose to begin her search there.

Nancy hurried to the hall and stopped in the bedroom doorway. It was just as she had expected. The furniture was pseudo-Victorian, heavy and dark, with scrollwork all over it. The bed had six ruffled pillows propped on a flowered duvet. There were corner shelves with china and glass objects, and thick brocade curtains in an ugly green smothered the windows.

Nancy switched on the light. She knelt and looked under the bed, but found it was where Mary stored out-of-season coats and boots in see-through plastic boxes. She searched the closet, then moved to the dresser. She was disappointed to find that there were only clothes in the drawers, and the jewelry box on top contained nothing that was worth stealing.

When she moved to the nightstand beside the bed and opened the top drawer, she felt herself flush with excitement. In the drawer, where it would be ready and within reach while she was sleeping, was a small, short-barreled revolver. Nancy picked it up cautiously and examined it. The gun was silver-toned, with white plastic handgrips. She aimed it at an imaginary target and saw the brass bullet casings at the back of the cylinder. Mary had stored it loaded.

It occurred to Nancy that she was lucky she had chosen to kill Mary right away and in the kitchen. If Mary had been in here, or even in the hallway or the closer parts of the living room, Nancy might have been the one who was lying on the floor bleeding. The thought of it made her heart beat harder again. She had never imagined that someone like Mary would own a gun. She had been ambushed and lured into this apartment by a woman who had a gun hidden ten feet from the door. Nancy had narrowly saved herself.

Why would Mary even own a gun? But then Nancy remembered that in one of their first encounters at the mailbox, Mary had warned her that rapists sometimes waited in the dark parking lots behind big apartment buildings. It had sounded as though rapists were a regular part of the landscape, swarming around like hornets. In other conversations she had seemed obsessed with some horrible crime she'd seen reenacted on television that had happened to some unwary single woman. It was probably inevitable that she would have a gun.

Nancy looked deeper in the drawer. There was a box of ammunition, so she took it. There was also a key that looked as though it belonged to a safe-deposit box, but she couldn't think of a way to use it. She found a canvas tote bag in the closet that had an ugly picture of a rose on it. She put the gun and the box of bullets inside, then moved to the kitchen and took the wallet, keys, and change purse.

She found a plastic bag in a drawer, took off the rubber gloves, put them in the bag, and dropped them into her tote. She moved close to Mary, careful to keep from stepping in the blood, and touched her bare leg. It felt cold. She had to be dead. Looking down at her now, Nancy realized that she must have been hysterical to have imagined that Mary was not dead before.

Nancy took one moment more to take two paper towels from the roll on the counter. With one she wiped off the handle of the knife that was stuck in Mary's chest. As she passed the table she picked up the copy of the newspaper with her picture in it. She used her other paper towel to keep her hands from leaving prints when she turned the doorknob. She locked the door and went to her own apartment.

Nancy's nervous energy was not an infirmity now. It was the power that might save her. She quickly packed her clothes and personal effects in her two suitcases, closed them, and took them to the door. She went to the sink and ran water over a dish towel. She began in the kitchen and wiped every surface with the towel, using the wetness to tell which surfaces she had wiped and which she had missed. She even cleaned the undersides of appliances, then put the few cups, dishes, pans, and silverware she'd bought in the dishwasher and ran it on the pots and pans setting.

She moved into the rest of the little apartment and wiped every window, every handle, all of the smooth surfaces of every piece of furniture. It was a quicker, more efficient process now than before, because now she was used to doing it. She never hesitated, never needed to stop or decide. Her manic restlessness kept her working. When she had finished, she made one last stop. She went to the mailboxes in the lobby, opened hers, wiped it off inside and outside, then relocked it.

She returned to her apartment, slipped her suitcases into a plastic trash bag so anyone who saw her would think she was taking out the garbage, locked the door, and hurried down the back stairs to the parking garage below the building. She had to search for a minute to find the Honda. Mary's car was hidden by two elephantine sport-utility vehicles that couldn't fit into their own spaces and overlapped Mary's.

Nancy put her bag in the trunk of the car, started it, and listened to the engine for a minute while she located the various controls and adjusted the seat and mirrors to fit her taller body. The engine sounded good, and the gas tank was full.

Nancy backed up to get out of the space, and drove up the ramp onto the street. She turned right onto Topanga Canyon and headed for the freeway. She took the southbound entrance because heading into the city would bring her to the tangle of interchanges onto other freeways. She brought her new Honda's speed up to merge into the moving river of cars, then glanced down at the tote bag beside her that held her new wallet, her change purse full of money, and her new gun.

SIXTEEN

Catherine Hobbes sat in the unmarked blue police car beside Detective James Spengler, watching the streets of the San Fernando Valley slide past her window. It was early morning but it was already hot, and the traffic coming eastward toward them was virtually stopped. The sun reflected off the windshields, so that she kept seeing flashes and then a lingering green glow on her retina. When she thought of the West Coast, she thought of her part of it – Portland, Washington, California as far south as San Francisco. Los Angeles was hard to get used to.

'You seem pretty calm about this,' said Spengler.

'It's an act I developed to keep male cops from thinking I'm emotional.'

'Right.'

'I promise I'll get excited when this woman is in custody and I know for sure she's Tanya Starling,' she said. 'You'll think you've won a football game. I'll be running around high-fiving you guys and slapping you on the butt.'

'You spotted the picture as soon as you got off the plane. She sure looks like the same one.'

'Your picture of a girl looks like my pictures of a girl. But we don't know if the apartment where we're going belongs to her. And whenever you put out a picture to the public, it strikes a lot of people as the spitting image of somebody who doesn't look that way at all.'

'Three calls tipping you on the same person don't usually turn out to be nothing.'

'That's why I'm nervous,' she said. 'I've been gritting my teeth for an hour hoping this is Tanya. But I've learned not to be too quick to assume anything about her. When we began this investigation, we all thought she was probably a kidnap victim. I'm still not sure whether some guy killed Dennis Poole because he was jealous over her and she's still running from him, or she's running because she killed him herself.'

'You want a prediction?'

'Sure.'

'Your first version is right.'

'Which one is that? I forgot.'

'The killing will turn out to be about her, but she didn't kill the guy. After you get her, you'll find out she was a drug mule who took off with somebody's shipment. Or she's a hooker who had a particularly possessive pimp, who wasn't about to let her go off with a client.'

'One of those was *my* first version?'

'I'm just going with the odds. You said before that they met at a hotel in Aspen and she came to visit, but nobody at home ever saw them together. That sounds like there was something about her that kept him from showing her off. And women don't usually do a gunshot murder on a guy unless they're married to him.'

'If you want to kill somebody bigger than you are, and you've got a gun, you use it – no matter who you are.'

'Maybe. But then there's the death of Brian Corey in the Hilton. They met in a bar, had dinner in Beverly Hills, and went up to his room and had sex. Afterward, she leaves alone, and so do his wallet and his rental car. What does that sound like?'

'It sounds like a hooker.'

'Right. And there was no gun, so she couldn't have

done the murder. The girl I saw in the picture didn't throw a full-grown man off a balcony. It had to be a man, or maybe two men – somebody like the pimp. In fact, it would have to be a really uneven match, somebody who could completely overpower and silence him. There were no signs of a struggle in the room, and nobody on the floor heard a fight.'

'You can push an elephant off a balcony if he's off balance and you give him a shove at the right time.'

'Joe Pitt agrees with me.'

It took an effort to hide her surprise. 'Joe Pitt? When did you talk to him?'

'He gave me a call when he saw the picture in the paper. He told me he had been working on this with you, and the girl looked like the one on your tapes. He also asked us to give you our best cooperation.'

'He did?'

'Yeah. He's very complimentary about you. But when we were talking about the Brian Corey thing, he figured there was no way she could have done it herself.'

'Let's concentrate on getting her into custody,' she said. 'Then we'll find out.' Catherine looked away. She had been thinking hard about Tanya Starling, but the mention of Joe Pitt was distracting her now. She wasn't sure what to think. She'd had a pleasant sensation when she had heard that he had complimented her, but then there was a suspicion that maybe the compliment had not been about her police work. He and Spengler were men, and they talked like men. And after all, he had told Spengler he disagreed with her theory. She was irritated at Pitt for calling Spengler and talking about her at all. What business did he have interfering with her investigation? No, that wasn't fair either: he had recognized Tanya's picture in the newspaper, and it was his duty to call the cops. But why hadn't he called her?

'Here's the street. The apartment is coming right up.' They glided up the street and a moment later the other two unmarked cars turned off Topanga Canyon after them. Spengler pulled the car into a parking space near the front steps, the next car drove around the back of the building, and the third pulled in beside Spengler.

'Well, let's see if we can scoop her up quick,' he said. 'Then, while she's telling us who killed those two men, you'll have plenty of time to congratulate me on being right.'

'Just don't assume she's not dangerous until she's handcuffed,' said Hobbes.

Spengler got out and conferred for a moment with the two officers in the car beside them, then joined Hobbes on the front steps.

The two officers stationed themselves at the building exits while Spengler and Hobbes stepped into the lobby. Hobbes stopped to check the names on the mailboxes. 'Mills' with no first name was on box 5. They went up two steps into the hallway on the right, and knocked on the door to apartment 5. They waited a few seconds, listening. Then Spengler knocked again, harder. After a minute, he knocked a third time. There was no answering call, no sound of movement in the apartment.

'Let's try across the hall,' said Hobbes. She knocked on the door across the hall, waited, then knocked again. 'Nobody's home in number four, either.'

Spengler said, 'Let's hunt down the manager.'

'Apartment one. I checked the mailboxes.'

They walked back to the lobby and into the opposite hallway, and knocked on the door. There was a small sign taped to it that said R. NORRIS, MANAGER. R. Norris was an unshaven man about forty years old who seemed to have been awakened by the knock.

Catherine Hobbes stood back and waited while

Spengler said, 'Mr Norris, I'm Detective Spengler, Los Angeles Police.' He held his identification up so that Norris could compare the photograph with his face. 'I'm very sorry we have to bother you this morning, but I have a warrant for one of your tenants. It's Miss Nancy Mills, in apartment five. She doesn't seem to be answering her door, so I'd like you to open it up for us.'

'She goes out most days. She walks a lot.'

Hobbes took a step closer. 'You mean for fitness?'

'In the morning she goes out and jogs. Then around ten or so, she goes out again. She doesn't have a car.'

Hobbes looked at Spengler. He reached into the inner pocket of his sport coat and produced some papers. 'Sir, here's a copy of the warrant. I'd appreciate it if you could open the apartment for us. It will save us all some trouble if we don't have to break the door down.'

Norris stared at the warrant, uncomprehending. After a moment he either found the part that permitted a search of Nancy Mills's domicile or he simply gave up. 'Hold on a minute. Let me get the key.'

A moment later, he returned with a set of master keys. He led the way down the hall to the apartment, unlocked it, and stepped back.

Spengler said, 'Thank you, Mr Norris.' When he swung the door open, he looked in and said, 'She's certainly neat, isn't she?'

'That's not it. She's gone,' said Hobbes. 'She's moved out.' She slipped past him into the kitchen and examined the cleaning supplies on the counter.

'Are you sure?'

'It's a furnished apartment. There's nothing here that's personal.' She stepped carefully along the edge of the living room to the hallway, her eyes on the floor to keep from disturbing any evidence. She continued into the bedroom and looked into the open closet.

She turned and saw Spengler standing behind her, his eyes on the empty hangers on the pole in the closet. He took the radio off his belt. 'Don't hold your breath, guys. She's out of here. She must have seen her picture in the paper.'

Hobbes heard a couple of tinny voices on the radio. 'Roger.' 'Got it.'

Hobbes said, 'Can you please call for a forensic team? I'd like to be sure it's the same girl I've been looking for.'

'Dave, call this in to the station,' he said into the radio. 'Let them know we'll need a forensic team. Everybody else come on in and help us canvass the rest of the tenants, and see if anybody knows where she went.'

Catherine Hobbes had tried to stay two steps behind Jim Spengler. Even though she carried a badge and a gun, she was only a guest in Los Angeles, and this was officially the investigation of the death of Brian Corey at a Los Angeles hotel. But it became evident almost immediately that she was a less intimidating interviewer than Spengler, so she began to take the lead.

The man in apartment 8 was not able to recall ever having seen the woman in the picture, nor could the couple in apartment 9. The others seemed to know very little about her. The person who lived across the hall from Nancy Mills was the one Catherine wanted most to talk to. She went back to knock on the door again, but the neighbor still wasn't at home.

After about twenty minutes, the forensic team arrived and set to work in Nancy Mills's apartment.

Catherine Hobbes had conducted enough interviews to persuade her that the woman who had called herself Nancy Mills had kept to herself and revealed very little. Catherine left the other detectives and returned to apartment 5, where two men and a woman were crawling on the living room carpet with rubber gloves, plastic bags, magnifiers, and tweezers, searching for physical evidence. The woman technician looked up from the carpet, and Catherine said, 'Catherine Hobbes, Portland Police.'

'Hi,' said the woman. 'I'm Toni.'

'Have you noticed the streaks yet?' asked Catherine.

'Streaks?'

'Yes,' said Catherine. 'Look at this coffee table, and you can see what I mean. You can see it best if you look at it from the side.' Catherine knelt beside the coffee table, and Toni joined her. They sighted along the top, then along the side. It was marked with a striated pattern. 'See the streaks?'

'They're from washing it,' said Toni. 'It's been washed with a rag that was soaking wet. If you use furniture polish or wax, it forms a coating. This was just wet.'

'Any fingerprints on it?'

'Not yet. And we're finding this everyplace. It's on all the furniture, the windows, the counters, even the walls. Every surface has streaks on it, because it's been washed down with a rag or cloth. You can see white cotton fibers in some spots. There were a couple of places that were still wet, so this wasn't done long ago. Maybe last night.'

'No prints at all?'

'Not yet,' she said. 'It's pretty hard to keep prints off everything, so we undoubtedly will find some. But she sure didn't want us to. Right now we're collecting hairs. So far all of them are ten to twelve inches, light brown.' Toni leaned over and picked up some hairs with a pair of tweezers. 'Oh-oh.'

'What?'

'More hairs. But these didn't fall out. They were pulled out.'

'You mean violently?'

'Yes. See, even without magnifying them, you can spot little bits of tissue. That's the root. Judging from the length, it's probably a woman's hair, but it's a different woman. This is thicker and wavier, like a perm, and it has a gray root, so the brown is almost certainly a dye job.'

Catherine Hobbes said, 'Excuse me, Toni.' She went to the doorway and looked down the hall. She could see Jim Spengler talking to the manager in the lobby. She walked up to them.

She said, 'Mr Norris, can you tell me about the tenant who lives across the hall in apartment four?'

'Her name is Mary Tilson. She's almost always there this time of day. I'm surprised she isn't now. She usually doesn't go out until the afternoon.'

'How old is she?'

'Maybe sixty or so.'

'Can you describe her hair?'

'Her hair?'

'Yes. Is it long and straight, short, blond or brunette?'

'It's brown. It's not straight. Kind of wavy, maybe almost to her chin.'

'Thanks. Can you excuse us for a second?' She took Spengler's arm and pulled him a few feet off. 'The forensic tech just found some hairs that had been pulled out of a woman's head, like in a fight. They're six to eight inches long, brown and wavy, with a gray root.'

'You mean you think they belong to the woman who lives across the hall?'

'It wouldn't hurt to take a quick look in her apartment. If she's not there and everything looks normal, fine. But somebody got some of her hair pulled out, and Toni says they don't belong to Nancy Mills.'

Spengler said, 'Mr Norris, can you come with us, please?'

They reached the door of apartment 4, and the manager unlocked it. Spengler pushed the door open a few inches, and his eyes focused on something. He said, 'Thank you, Mr Norris. We'll take it from here.'

He turned to Catherine as Norris was moving off. 'It's not good.' He stepped into the apartment, and Catherine followed. She could see the woman lying on the kitchen floor in a pool of blood. Spengler was already hurrying to the woman, but Catherine had noticed that the outer edges of the big pool of blood were dark and dry, which meant she had been there a long time. Spengler touched her carotid artery. 'She's been dead a while. Her throat was cut. And a knife – looks like a regular butcher knife – is still in her.'

'I'll call the forensic people over from the other apartment.'

'Yeah, thanks. We'll get them going on this.'

Catherine stepped across the hall and said, 'Toni, we've got a deceased victim in apartment four.'

'Oh, man.' Toni began to put her equipment back into the tackle box on the floor. 'I had a feeling about this,' she said. 'Too many hairs. Come on, guys. Let's see if we can get anything fresh over there.'

Jim Spengler was gathering the other detectives in the hall to tell them what had been discovered in apartment 4. Catherine approached.

She said, 'The manager says Nancy Mills didn't have a car.'

Spengler said, 'That's right. Ron, get a description of Mary Tilson's car, check the parking spaces downstairs and see if her car is gone. If it is, run her name and get the license and description on the air. Dave, get on the radio and let them know what we've got here.'

He saw the forensic team move to the doorway and peer inside before stepping in. 'Toni, you want us to call for reinforcements?'

'Thanks, Jim, but I'll call them myself as soon as I've taken a look.'

'Fine.' He turned back to the other police officers. 'Al, see if anything is missing in the apartment, especially credit cards or ATM cards. If they are, get started on finding out if they've been used yet.'

The detectives moved off, and Catherine went down the hall to Mr Norris. She said, 'I'd like to take a look at Nancy Mills's rental agreement.'

They entered Mr Norris's apartment, and he produced a file from a desk drawer. Inside were five-page lease agreements for all of the tenants. Catherine leafed through them carefully until she found the one that said Nancy Mills. Norris said, 'You can take that one if you want. I've got a Xerox copy in the file, and the rental company has a duplicate original.'

'Thank you,' she said. 'Do you have a spare file folder or an envelope?'

'Sure.' He handed her a manila envelope.

'Thanks very much,' she said. She slipped the agreement inside, and walked out of the room. She went down the hall and found Toni in the kitchen of apartment 4.

She said, 'Toni, this is the rental agreement for Nancy Mills. I'd appreciate it if you could take it to the lab and examine it for latent prints.'

Toni took it. 'Sure thing. I'll try dipping it in ninhydrin to bring up the amino acids, and give you a call.' She put it into a cardboard carton with her growing collection of plastic evidence bags.

Catherine turned to Spengler, who was staring down at the body of Mary Tilson. He said, 'I guess this just about finishes the idea that the girl is the one doing this stuff. I can't see her cutting a woman like that and leaving her to bleed out on the floor.'

Catherine walked out of the room, down the hall, and outside, where she leaned against the car and took a few breaths of air. Her mind had been fully occupied since the moment she had arrived, but now it was still racing, and there was little for her to do until either the crime-scene technicians or the officers searching for the girl gave her something new to interpret.

Her mind kept returning to Joe Pitt. She was tempted to call him and tell him what she thought of him for interfering with the relations between her and the Los Angeles police. But this was his town, where he had been the DA's investigator. She had no right to tell him what to say to the L.A. police, and any homicide detective here would know him personally. He had seen the photograph in the paper and recognized Tanya, and he'd had to report it. But why had he called the L.A. homicide people, and not her? She could think of two answers, without even asking him: the newspaper had said to call Spengler, so he had. And she had essentially told him not to bother her again, and so he hadn't.

SEVENTEEN

As the girl drove along Interstate 15, the brightly lighted hotels appeared against the sky in the distance, and minutes later the town rose up around her. She was afraid to stop, but she was too tired not to. She had been up since sunrise, spent the day on her feet, and then been forced to defend herself from Mary's ugly demands and clean up afterward. The hours of driving since then had drained the last of her nervous energy.

She saw the exit for the Mandalay Bay hotel, and then she was on it, and then in the thick traffic on the strip. The first place where she was able to make a right turn was the entrance to the MGM Grand, so she gave her car to the parking attendant there and watched him drive it into the parking structure.

She wanted to check into a hotel and sleep, but she didn't dare. If the police were searching for her, one of the things they would do right away was get in touch with the Las Vegas hotels. She was hungry, so she went inside to the long promenade where the restaurants were and looked into a few. The customers had all moved into the drinking phase of the evening, so she kept going.

She found a coffee shop farther on the promenade, bought a piece of lemon cake she saw in the glass case, and ate it. She rested her eyes and cradled her head in her arms for a moment. When she awoke, there was a tall man in a dark blue suit standing over her. As he leaned closer, she could hear low-volume radio chatter coming from his coat pocket. He said, 'Miss? Are you all right?'

'Huh? Oh my gosh,' she said. 'I must have dozed off.'

His sympathetic concern vanished. This was not a medical emergency. 'You can't sleep here.' It was as though he had already heard and penetrated the lie she had not told yet.

She stood, took her purse, and strode off. She had the feeling that he was behind her, talking into the radio about her. She never decreased her speed until she was out of the building.

For the next few hours she was one of the thousands of people walking from casino to casino. She had stopped in Las Vegas to rest, but there seemed to be no way for her to do it. When she was too tired to keep walking she would sit at a table in a bar and order a soft drink. She caught another catnap at six a.m. on the couch in a ladies' room in Caesars, but the attendant politely woke her as soon as she had entered deep sleep. Later in the morning she ate brunch at the Aladdin. When big groups of people began to check out of the hotels at ten-thirty, she joined the line at the entrance to the MGM and had the valet retrieve her car.

She drove out the Boulder Highway toward Henderson, and stopped at a shopping mall. She left her car inside the parking structure, where it would be less visible, and walked to the mall's cinema complex. She bought a ticket to the first movie that was showing. It was an awful film about two evil children, and there were few other people in the theater to watch it, so she found a seat in the middle of a row and fell asleep. She spent the whole afternoon and evening in the complex, going from one small theater to the next, each time sleeping for an hour or two and waking when the lights came up and people shuffled out.

When she felt that she was able to drive again, she ate dinner in a Denny's in Henderson. It was eleven-thirty when she drove into the desert to the east. She had wasted a whole day in Las Vegas, and she was nearly as tired as she had been when she had arrived.

Her troubles were building up. She had done a rash, unconsidered thing, but it had not really been her fault. She had not set out to kill Mary Tilson. She just had not been able to think of a way to avoid it. Mary Tilson wouldn't shut up, and she wouldn't leave her alone, and she couldn't be dissuaded from calling the police.

She was just a regular person who had always wanted what everybody else wanted – to be happy. She had been smart in school and had been accepted to the University of Illinois. She remembered that the letter had arrived in April, and she had taped it to the wall of her bedroom so she could look at it every morning when she woke up, and every night when she went to bed. The habit had lasted until June. It was a Sunday when everything had changed.

She remembered waking up and seeing the letter that morning: 'Dear Charlene Buckner: It is my pleasure to inform you . . .' She had used a single small piece of tape on the top so she could take it down in September and bring it with her in case she needed to prove that she had been accepted.

As she always did, she lay in her bed, looked at the tone of the light, and touched the wall beside her bed to see if it was warm or cool, because that side was the outer wall of the house. She could feel that it was warm. In those few seconds she sensed that something was wrong. The house was more than quiet. It was a vacuum, because something big had moved on, and nothing had yet filled the space. She knew what it was.

She got up and stepped to the door of her mother's

bedroom. The drawers of the dresser were still open, a little askew and out of their tracks because her mother had been in a hurry to empty them.

Charlene walked through the little house, moving from room to room and looking. She was not exactly searching for her mother, just looking at her world to see what it looked like without her. There was a note on the kitchen table, a glass placed on it to hold it down, as though a wind might blow through and take it. Charlene picked up the glass and smelled the strong, turpentine scent of whiskey, so she set it in the sink with the other dirty dishes.

She picked up the note. 'Dear Char, I had an unexpected opportunity, and I had to take it. If you need to reach me, write to me care of my sister Rose. I'll check with her later. Don't forget to ask the college for scholarship money. Bye for now. Mommy.' The o had a smiling face drawn in it. Charlene put the note in the garbage bag and began to clean up.

She rinsed the dishes and put them in the sink with very hot water and detergent to soak a bit while she went outside to pick up the Sunday newspaper from the sidewalk. She had always done that to keep the neighbors from noticing that her mother stayed out late and slept for the first half of the day. It was a warm, sunny morning, and there were flowers blooming in the neighbors' yards. She went back inside, closed the door, and locked it.

She was halfway through the dishes before she really felt what had happened to her. She was as alone as a person in a raft in the middle of the ocean. She spent a few minutes thinking about how it must have happened.

Her mother had been in one of her depressions lately, because of her most recent boyfriend, Ray. About two months ago, Ray had hit her and then left. The next day she had pretended that she had gotten tired of Ray and made him leave, then bumped into a kitchen cupboard in the dark because she'd been trying to get a glass of water in the middle of the night without waking Charlene. But Charlene had awakened and heard her sobbing, pleading with Ray not to leave: 'Ray, I wasn't even interested in him that way. It just happened. It didn't mean anything. Please don't leave. I'll never do it again.' Her mother's voice had been the shrill kind that carried, but Ray was a mutterer, with a deep voice, so Charlene couldn't make out anything he was saying. She hadn't needed to.

Charlene's mother had hated being alone. It wasn't clear to Charlene from the contradictory stories she told when she had ever been alone, but the experience must have been terrible, because she was willing to do anything to keep from being alone again. Some of the time when a boyfriend moved out, she had heard her mother saying, 'I'll do anything,' and known that she meant it. Charlene was sure she knew what the opportunity in the note had been. Somebody had offered her a chance not to be alone.

It struck Charlene at first that since her mother was so scared of being alone, it was odd that she would abandon Charlene. But she always had been that way. If the weather was hot, then she was hotter than other people. If there was only one piece of meat left, then she was hungrier than anyone else. Charlene should have seen this coming, from the moment when she had received her letter from the college. Her mother had read the letter on the wall too, and to her it had meant that Charlene was going away.

Charlene didn't like her mother very much, but she missed her in some deep, awful way. After another day, however, she realized she still had to get herself through the rest of June and graduate, then find a way to survive July and August on her own and get to college. The remark about a scholarship in her mother's letter had been her only mention of money. That had been her way of saying that she had not left Charlene any.

That morning, as soon as Charlene was showered and dressed, she went to the only place she could think of in Wheatfield to find work. It was the Dairy Princess on Highway 19. It looked almost exactly like a Dairy Queen place, but it actually wasn't. It was a transparent counterfeit, relying on the notion that people would see what it was imitating and then pull over, exactly as though it were a Dairy Queen. They would realize that it wasn't, but they would forgive the small imposture.

The summer manager was a boy named Tim she remembered from high school; he was two years older than she was, and was already off for the summer. There was a line at the order window, so she waited until it was her turn. She said she wanted to see Tim.

When he came to the window, he said, 'Hi, Charlene. What can I get you?'

'I need a job, thanks. Do you have one that's open?'

Tim looked at her for a long time. She could see him trying to calculate, and he actually looked worried, as though he couldn't figure out the answer. 'If you're willing to work hard, there's one left.'

'Okay,' she said.

She started right away. At first she worked only on weekends, because that was when most people wanted ice cream and hamburgers. When graduation came and summer began, she worked six days a week, from twelve until nine. She got minimum wage, which wasn't much, but she ate something during her break each night that served as dinner, and once in a while some man would give her a tip.

She took her mother's advice and wrote a letter to the admissions office at the university, informing them that she was going to need a scholarship. She told them that the reason she had not applied before was that her mother had never managed to fill out the Parents' Confidential Statement about her finances, but that her mother's finances no longer mattered because her mother had moved on. Two weeks into the summer she received a gently worded letter that said it was too late for this year, and included some application forms for federal loans.

Charlene remembered sitting in her empty house at the kitchen table reading the forms and feeling absolutely bereft. The next two nights she came home tired and worked on the forms. The third night, she finished at midnight and walked to the letter box outside the post office to mail them.

Charlene made a friend at the Dairy Princess named Alice. She was a woman of about twenty-nine who had a little boy but lived with her parents not far from where Charlene lived. At seven each night they went outside, away from the heat and the smells, and while Alice smoked, they talked. She had seen Charlene staring at Tim when he wasn't looking.

Charlene had not let her thoughts about Tim get beyond the speculation stage, where she felt a small tingle when he was near her in the narrow, hot kitchen and they accidentally brushed against each other as she was carrying food to the pickup window. She didn't have any room in her life for another person. But Alice had caught her looking at him, and from that day she spoke to Charlene about her crush on Tim.

One night when Charlene left at her usual time, Alice offered to close the store so Tim could go too. Charlene noticed him walking along the street twenty feet behind her, so she slowed and gradually they began to walk together.

He said, 'Alice told me you're having a hard time saving the money you need to start at college.'

She was alarmed, humiliated. She had not formed close relationships with other girls in high school, because they always seemed to turn any confidence into gossip. Alice was so much older that Charlene had assumed she wouldn't behave that way or betray her. She fought the panic and answered, 'I guess it's true. I've got to pay my own living expenses, because my mother is away right now.'

'I heard that too. It must be hard.'

'I don't miss the company. I'm out most of the time anyway. It's just that I got used to having her pay for things.'

They walked along the dark streets toward her house. They talked about the day's customers who had looked strange, or acted superior, and about the pressure Tim felt to keep the receipts at the Princess high so the owner, Mr Kallen, wouldn't give him a bad recommendation when he left in the fall. He knew he wouldn't be fired in the middle of the summer, and his parents had enough money to pay his tuition at Purdue whether he worked or not, but he was convinced that a bad recommendation in his first supervisory job would ruin his future.

Charlene walked along beside him, most comfortable while he was talking but feeling something like stage fright whenever a topic had been exhausted and another hadn't replaced it. She became ashamed of the fact that the items that occupied her mind weren't theories or ideas, only the personal obsessions and problems that consumed her – the fact that she wasn't paying the rent on the house or the utility bills, just trying to ignore the increasingly ominous late notices and not answering the telephone in the hope that she wouldn't be evicted before September, the fear that people would know she was alone in the house and too young to have any rights – and she didn't want him to know any of them.

When they reached her house they stood for a moment in silence on the porch in the dark, and he kissed her. It was a shock for her, a soft, sweet moment in a life that had turned into an emergency. She had come to expect days full of sweat and the smell of burning grease and overflowing, fly-swarmed garbage cans. As he held her, she seemed to be floating, her eyes closed. When he released her, she stood motionless for a few seconds.

He said, 'I've been thinking about you a lot. I watch you in the Princess.'

'You do?'

'Yeah. You're the best-looking girl in Wheatfield.'

'Of course, Wheatfield is so huge. There must be twelve girls. And I'm not, anyway.'

'I'm serious. Everybody knows it. I remember when you came into high school. I was a junior. Everybody was blown away.'

She looked down, afraid that she might be blushing and that he could see it, even though they were under the porch roof, so the moonlight didn't reach them. She couldn't think of anything to say, so she said, 'Thank you.'

They kissed again, and she began to feel her nervousness being replaced by a relaxed, lazy sensation that she sensed might be a sign of danger. If she didn't stop, she was going to let him go too far. She broke off the kiss. 'I'd better go in now. Thanks for walking me home.' Then she grinned. 'And everything.'

She found her key chain in her purse and turned to unlock the door. He said, 'Can I come in?'

She said, 'I'm sorry. I can't tonight. See you tomorrow.' She slipped inside and locked the door.

The next day Alice watched her and watched Tim during the day. At three, when they were outside for their break, she said, 'Tell me exactly what happened.' After some hesitation, Charlene did tell Alice.

Alice said, 'That's it? That was all?' She seemed disappointed.

Charlene was slightly offended, but she realized that a woman twelve years older than she was, with a child, was probably used to more than that. She was tempted to embellish the story, but she didn't know what to say that would be satisfactory, so she decided to wait and see whether anything else happened.

That Saturday, Charlene stayed late to help Tim lock up, so that he would walk her home again.

This time when they reached the porch, she said, 'Would you like to come in for a minute?' He came in. She felt the heat of shame as he looked around him. She had always been aware that the house was smaller and less fancy than other people's houses, and her mother's boyfriends had been a problem, because she didn't want to introduce them and then have to explain who they were and what they were doing here. Now they were gone, and she had spent hours over the past few days cleaning the house, washing curtains, arranging furniture, and putting fresh flowers from the front yard in jars.

She reminded herself that it was different now. She was only seventeen and this was her own place, where she could do anything she wanted. Tim still lived with his parents, and he was two years older. She had bought a six-pack of cola, so she offered him a drink, and brought it in one of the glasses her mother had only used for adults. Then she sat on the couch with him.

He kissed her, but it wasn't the same as it had been the first night. He seemed more eager, but not more affectionate. He was insistent, implacable, barely letting her take a breath. She still liked him, but tonight she was a little bit afraid. She let him unbutton her uniform shirt, but then he took it all the way off, and her bra too. Once he had done that, it didn't matter when she put her hands on his and tried to keep him from taking her other things off too. He just did it. She whispered, 'At least turn the lights off,' but he said, 'No. I like to see you this way.'

Pretty soon he picked her up, carried her into her bedroom, and set her on her bed. She said, 'Tim, I don't think we should do this. I don't want to. I'm still a virgin,' and 'Stop. Don't.' Finally he hesitated, and she thought he had realized it wasn't a good idea, but he had only paused to slip on a condom. And then he took her.

When it was over, she wrapped herself in the covers and lay there, quietly crying. He put on his clothes right away and tried stroking her hair and her bare shoulder, saying softly, 'Please don't cry. I'm sorry. I really like you, and I couldn't help it. I thought you liked me too.'

Charlene hated him, and she loved him, and she hurt. She wanted him to go away, and to die, and to stay forever, being nice to her now that he'd had what he wanted. Then, without expecting to, she stopped crying. It was like a fever that abruptly broke. 'Go home now,' she said. She heard his heavy steps on the floor as he walked out of the room, then heard her front door open and close.

The next day she didn't go to work. The day after that, she went in at the usual time, started working, and wouldn't look at Tim or answer him when he spoke. She didn't go and sit outside with Alice during the three o'clock break, because she couldn't bear to answer her questions.

At quitting time she left without a word. He left too, and walked beside her. As soon as they were on a dark street and alone, he said quietly, 'I really care about you, Charlene. I want you to know I couldn't sleep for the last two nights. I didn't mean to make you hate me or anything.' They walked on for a dozen steps. 'Charlene?'

'What?'

'Aren't you going to say anything?'

'Okay.' She walked in silence for another few seconds. 'You raped me.'

'No, I didn't. It was just—'

'You did. I said no, and you did it anyway.'

'I thought you were just saying that, like "no, no, no-oh," and then you stopped saying it. I thought that meant you really wanted to.'

'I was crying, Tim. You didn't even notice.'

'I'm sorry. I'm really, really sorry,' he said. 'I didn't think I was doing anything you didn't want me to. If I'd thought I was, I would have stopped.'

They were at her house now. She climbed the porch steps and turned to face him, but he stayed down in the shadows by the railing. She took her keys out of her purse and unlocked the door. 'Come in.'

'That's okay,' he said.

'No. It's not okay. You're coming inside. Now.'

She held it open, and the light from the lamp she had left on so she wouldn't have to come in alone in the dark was shining on his face. He looked down, but he came up the steps and followed her into the house.

Charlene shut the door and locked it. She didn't turn on any more lights or offer him a drink. She said, 'You were horrible. I liked you so much, but you hurt me and treated me like you didn't care what I felt. You were like an animal or something, and you made me feel like one too. You were a pig.'

'I feel terrible. I don't know how to make it up to you.'

'You've done it. You can't undo it. But you're not going to leave me feeling like this.'

'I can't go back to two days ago. What am I supposed to do now?'

'You're going to do it one more time. People say the first time is awful for everybody, but once you're past that, it's nice. You have to be sweet to me. Do it the right way this time, not mean.'

All these years later, she remembered the look on Tim's face – shock, then something like relief. He treated her gently, as though she were made of porcelain, like the dolls in the window of the antique store. He was very slow and cautious, very patient. This time it was the way she had always imagined it would be, and she almost liked him. He stayed until three-thirty, then hurried home so he would be asleep before his parents woke.

For the rest of the summer, she allowed him to think of her as his girlfriend. At the Dairy Princess he did all of the heavy lifting that was involved in her job, then did the cleanup and walked her to the local hangout, where his friends were already drinking and talking with older girls.

Alice began to resent Charlene. She made a remark about how nice it must be having somebody to do her share of the work. Once when Charlene yawned, Alice told her she should sleep alone sometimes, then turned and went to the order window, leaving her alone. Charlene felt as though she had been slapped. She thought about it for a while, and then decided that Alice didn't matter. Charlene just had to endure a few weeks, and summer would be over.

By mid-August, Charlene's unpaid bills had all been turned over to collection agencies, and their attempts to get the money from her became more aggressive. She had to unplug the telephone to keep from being called all the time, but then when she plugged it in to make a call, it wouldn't work.

The customers of the Dairy Princess had moved into the strange frenzy that seemed to hit people just before each summer ended, and made them frantic and selfish. She knew they were trying to get the last few days of pleasure before things turned dark and cold and wet again, so they lined up at the Princess in surly, sweating queues, crowding the lot in front of the store on the way home from some activity that had left them discontented. The sweet residue of ice cream and sugary drinks they spilled made the wasps drunk and vicious.

Charlene waited one night until she and Tim were alone and cleaning up before she said, 'Tim, I'm pregnant.'

His mouth was open and he seemed to reel, as though he didn't have enough air. She waited a few seconds, then said more loudly, 'I'm pregnant.'

'I heard you,' he said, the slightest tinge of irritation slipping into his voice. She waited for him to say it, and he said it, exactly as she had imagined he would: 'What are you going to do?'

'I don't know, exactly,' she said. 'What are you going to do?'

'What do you mean?'

'You're the only one I was with,' she said. 'Ever. It's yours too.'

'I know that.' This time the irritation had shaded off into sadness. 'Of course I'll do what I can. What do you want me to do?'

His suffering resignation inspired her to torment him.

'I guess we could get married. I'll be eighteen in a few months.'

She could see that behind his widened eyes a film was running at great speed. It was about the things he wanted desperately – education, good jobs, prosperity, a beautiful young wife who would come into his life in about ten years – moving beyond his reach forever. He looked faint. 'I don't know. I want to marry you,' he lied. 'But that's – I don't know. You're not even eighteen, and I'm only twenty. We don't even have a job after the first of the month.'

'Wouldn't your parents help us? They must have some money.'

'I don't know. My father will be pissed. My mother – God, I can't tell her this.'

'It's their grandchild. I'm pregnant, and I can't even afford vitamins.' She was very proud of that one.

'Oh, God,' he said. 'We always used protection. How did this happen?'

She looked at him with distaste. 'Obviously, once it didn't work. It leaked or something.'

He said, 'We've got to think this through. How pregnant are you?'

'My period was supposed to start eight days ago, and I'm never more than a day or two late. I bought a test, and I took it yesterday. I bought another today, and used it. I wanted to be sure, and now I'm sure. I called the doctor because he doesn't charge to talk on the phone, and he said the accuracy of the test is almost a hundred per cent.' She gave a sad little smile that she had practiced for this moment. 'He told me congratulations.' Then she made herself cry.

Tim held her and rocked her back and forth, but she didn't stop, so he released her and finished closing the store. They walked to her house, but when she asked him to come in, he said he needed to be alone to think.

For two days, they exchanged looks of worry in the kitchen, where Alice and the customers couldn't see them. Three days after that, when she arrived at the Dairy Princess he was waiting for her outside the back door, and they walked to the park. He was so nervous that she could see the sweat on his forehead. They sat on a park bench and he said, 'I've thought about this. I have something for you.' It was a plain white business envelope. Inside were some green bills. He said, 'It's twelve hundred. Most of what I saved this summer.'

'You're trying to buy me off?' Tears came to her eyes. 'For twelve hundred dollars?'

'No,' he said. 'It's not to buy you off.'

'Keep it.' She tossed the envelope on his lap. 'I can't live on it if I have the baby, and I'm not getting an abortion.' She stood up. 'I thought by now you would have talked to your father. You can't keep him from knowing this.'

Tim was horrified. His eyes were swimming, but he wasn't crying. It looked the way a person's eyes watered when he was hit in the nose. 'You're not going to go to him. He'll kill me. He'll disown me. Really.'

'We'll see.' She got up and started to walk.

'Wait. You're right.' When she heard him running to catch up with her, she kept going. 'Please,' he said. 'Give me one more day.'

The next morning when she was almost dressed for work there was a loud knock on the door. She could see from the shadows on the curtain that it was two men. She was afraid it might be the sheriff's deputy with an eviction order, but when she pushed the curtain aside a quarter inch, she saw it was Tim and an older man wearing a business suit, who didn't look happy. She smiled into the mirror, fixed her hair, then went to the door.

When she opened it, Tim surged forward. 'Can we come in?'

The older man held Tim's arm in his hand and pulled him back, then stepped in ahead of him. 'I'm Tim's father. I know who you are.'

'I'm Charlene.'

'Tim tells me he knocked you up.'

'That's right.'

'You've both been very foolish. Neither of you had the right to do that. I'm here to try to settle this right now, while we still can.'

'How?'

'Tim tells me he offered you some money, and you told him it wasn't enough.' He reached into the inner pocket of his suit coat, took out an envelope, and held it out. Charlene could see it had come from the same box of envelopes as Tim's had.

'How much is in it?'

'Enough to see you through the pregnancy, or to get you an abortion. Three thousand dollars. In return, you sign this paper, saying he's not responsible.'

Charlene said, 'I appreciate your coming here to help me. But I haven't decided what to do yet.'

'What do you mean?'

'The first time it happened, Tim forced me.'

Tim's father's head spun to face the boy, his eyes protruding. He looked like a bull. Tim's eyes stayed straight ahead, staring at her as though he had been punched. 'Charlene . . .'

Charlene said, 'He was my boss at the Dairy Princess. I was afraid to tell, and afraid to say he couldn't do it again. It was the only job I could get in town. I needed to work to pay for college, and I'm only seventeen, so I couldn't work in a regular restaurant where there's a bar. I'm thinking about talking to somebody about it – maybe a lawyer.'

Tim's father's eyes blinked as though he had a pain in his stomach. She could tell he had a suspicion about her, but he did not dare voice it without knowing the truth. He had to assume that this meeting was his only chance to settle her complaint quietly. She knew he was considering letting Tim take his chances, but the risk was enormous – greater than Tim knew. If she really was seventeen and pregnant, and told that story in court, Tim could end up in prison.

He said carefully, 'Charlene, I'm sorry. I didn't really understand the situation until now. I want to pay for your medical care and your first year at the university – tuition, room, and board. I make that about—' He looked up at the ceiling. 'Three thousand medical. Fifteen thousand for the university is eighteen thousand.'

'Is that how much it costs?'

'Yes. I'll be honest with you, that doesn't include a lot of frills. But it should cover things.'

'All right, then.'

He said, 'Here's the paper.' He handed it to her, then held out a pen.

She took the paper but ignored the pen. 'By the time you get back here with the money, I'll have had a chance to read it.'

Late that afternoon, she packed and stripped the house of the few items she cared about that fit in her two suitcases, and counted the money Tim's father had given her. The next morning she was on the early bus to Chicago.

Tonight, as she drove along the dark highway in Mary Tilson's car, she remembered how much she had enjoyed the day when she had left Wheatfield on the bus. Lying about the pregnancy had given her some satisfaction – planning it all summer, then springing it on Tim's father like that, right in front of Tim, when she hadn't left him a way to even deny any of it – but what she had enjoyed most was the money. She remembered sitting on the bus staring out the window at the long line of telephone poles going by, and thinking about the beautiful things all that money would buy.

EIGHTEEN

Catherine Hobbes sat at a stainless steel table in the crime lab and watched Toni Baldesar pouring epoxy into a small dish. Toni carefully placed the kitchen knife in the vapor chamber, then lifted the dish of epoxy onto the hot plate, closed the door, and began to heat it. She turned to Catherine. 'All we can do is wait and see if the epoxy vapor makes some latent prints show up. If they match the ones I got from the rental agreement, we'll have her.'

'I don't think there will be any,' said Catherine. 'She's not careless. She's got an obsession with cleaning things and wiping off surfaces to be sure she doesn't leave anything. I don't see her leaving prints on a murder weapon.'

'I know, but you'd be surprised at how often I get lucky with things like that. They get emotional, and then everything is such a mess, and they have so many things to think about at once. Sometimes I think that a person's brain just skips over the things that it doesn't want to think about – especially things that involve getting blood on them or going back to touch the body.'

'Maybe,' said Catherine. She had a blown-up copy of the driver's license photograph of Tanya Starling on the table in front of her, and while she waited she was using a pencil to fill in the background to make the hair shorter. 'And it's just possible that my theory about her is wrong. Some man may have come looking for her and killed Mary Tilson because she saw his face.'

'I'd rule that out,' said Toni.

'Based on what evidence?'

'Based on no evidence – no evidence that a man has been in that apartment since the day the plumbing was installed,' said Toni. 'No prints, no hairs, no shoe marks, nothing.'

'That's what I've been telling people,' said Catherine. 'So far I've got two of us convinced.'

Toni was staring through the small window in the front of the vapor box at the butcher knife. The epoxy vapor had filled the small chamber. She flipped a switch and an exhaust fan cleared the vapor. She opened the door and examined the knife with a flashlight, then turned it over. 'Score one for the pessimists. She wiped the handle clean.'

'What have we got left?' asked Catherine.

Toni looked up at the clock on the wall. 'It's nearly eleven. What I've got is a load of laundry and a sink full of dishes waiting at home.'

'I'm sorry,' said Catherine. 'I know I kept you here half the night.'

'No,' said Toni. 'You didn't. When we've got one that fresh, I always try to squeeze all the information I can out of the trace evidence the first day. Sometimes you find something that helps catch the killer that day, and not just convict him two years later.'

'I know. That's why I've been hanging around.'

Toni carefully poured the warm epoxy back into its jar. 'How long have you been a cop?'

'Seven years. Four in homicide.'

'You went through the ranks fast.' She began to sponge off the counters where she had been working.

Catherine shrugged. 'It's a small department and I'm good at taking tests.'

Toni looked at her for a moment. 'I'll bet you are.'

'How long for you?'

'Fifteen years this June. For me, it's a little different. I see some horrible things, but I don't have to chase anybody down and drag him off to jail. There's less stress.' She took off her lab coat and hung it on a hook. 'And no fear.'

'Well, thanks for staying late tonight,' said Catherine.

'I'm sorry we didn't get everything we wanted, but we'll keep working on it.'

'Thanks to you, we know for certain Nancy Mills is Tanya Starling, and we can place her in the victim's apartment. That's plenty for one day.' Catherine folded her picture of Tanya Starling as they walked toward the door.

'Do you need a ride to your hotel?'

'No, thanks,' said Catherine. 'I have a rental car.' She stepped out in the hallway and Toni locked the door of the lab. 'Good night.'

She went to her car in the police lot and drove through the dark streets toward her hotel. Talking with Toni had made her think back on her first days as a police officer. She had not grown up planning to join the police bureau. She had decided to apply to the academy during the long drive home, away from the wreckage of her life in California. It had been an act of desperation, just grasping for something in her life that made sense and didn't need an excuse or an explanation. The months in the academy that followed, the grueling physical training and the Spartan discipline that bothered other recruits so much, had been her salvation. At times she thought it had saved her life.

She remembered the first day after she had graduated from the police academy. She reported for work at the police bureau more than an hour early, all dressed in her uniform with her shoes shined and her heavy gear creaking against her leather belt. She had been assigned to the precinct station on the northeast side of the city.

When she walked in the front entrance and approached the desk, a big man with a military haircut and a neck that seemed to overflow from his starched collar stepped in from the side and said, 'Hobbes?'

'Yes.'

'I'm Lieutenant Morton. Come with me.'

She followed, watching his broad back swaying from side to side with his rolling gait. He went into his office and closed the door, then glared at her with bloodshot eyes. His face seemed to have some kind of pink, irritated rash on it that she later came to believe was a reaction to contained anger. He said, 'Catherine Hobbes.'

'Yes, sir' was all she could think of to say.

'Your father is Lieutenant Frank Hobbes, and your grandfather was the first Frank Hobbes. Is that right?'

She smiled. 'Yes.' She felt a moment of pride, and maybe some relief.

'I hate dynasties.' He paused, then narrowed his eyes. 'A police force is a government operation, which means that nobody in this town owns any more of it than anybody else. It doesn't matter whose daughter or granddaughter you are. You are the greenest of green rookies, and you will be treated like all of the others in every respect. You got that?'

'Yes, sir,' she said. 'I never wanted any special privileges.' Her stomach began to sink, and she knew her face was beginning to turn red.

'You are also a woman,' he continued. 'I'm very suspicious of that.'

'Of what – that I'm a woman?'

'Being a woman and wanting to be a cop. In this precinct we deal with a lot of street crime. Every day a cop has to go out and drag somebody back here in handcuffs or push somebody around. You coming here and exercising your constitutional right to wear that uniform has grave implications for the rest of the people I put out there. You coming here means to me that you must be assuming that some male cop is going to be willing and able to do his share of the physical stuff and yours too.'

She knew that her face was bright red, but there was nothing she could do about it, and she was not going to retreat. 'I'm not—'

'Being Frank Hobbes's daughter, you cannot pretend that you didn't know what a cop does. You can't possibly imagine you're going to take down some crystal meth monster who's six feet six and two eighty.'

'No, sir,' she said. 'Most of the men in my academy class aren't up to that either. But any one of us will do our best to help subdue a person like that if the occasion comes up, and to use our brains to be sure it doesn't come up often.'

He glared at her for two seconds, then smiled, and said. 'You are Frank's girl. Welcome to my shop. Now get to roll call and go to work.'

NINETEEN

Nancy Mills drove deeper into Arizona in the night. She had hoped to be better off than this by now. When she had seen Carl for the last time in Chicago, she had said she would have more money than he had within one year. It had been most of a year already, and what did she have so far? Forty thousand? No, less. She probably had thirty thousand left, and she was driving a dead woman's car along a highway that had signs telling her to watch out for elk. Carl would have laughed at that if he could have known.

Carl had hated nature. He had told her that golf courses were about the wildest places he ever wanted to be. He said that people who went on hikes in the wilderness or liked animals were stupid. Now that she could look back, she knew he had thought that most of the people he knew were stupid. Compared to Carl, they probably were.

She had met Carl in a restaurant in Chicago. She had just finished her final exams for the fall semester, and she had taken herself out to dinner to celebrate.

The celebration felt due, because the semester had been a difficult time for her. Charlene had come to Chicago on the bus four days early. She had slept in the bus station the first night, then rented the only lodging she could afford, a room in a dirty motel not far from the campus. She had walked past her dormitory each day to see if it was open yet, and then sneaked in on the fourth day at seven a.m., when the last of the janitorial crews were cleaning up after the painters who had given the hive of cubical cinder-block rooms a fresh coat of bile green.

She had dreaded the way the first day at the dormitory would be. She had seen simulations of that day in movies and television shows – the happy, eager students, the resigned, tearful mothers, the proud, worried fathers all haunting the dormitories – and had known there was no place for her in that event. For her it could only be an unmasking. Everyone would see that nobody cared about her, and that she was nothing.

She put her clothes into one of the two dressers in her room, left a note to claim one of the beds, and went out until evening, after the other girls were settled and their families gone. She told the girls on her floor that her parents were living in Europe, and couldn't come with her.

College began badly and became an ordeal. She had hoped college would change her life, but the girls snubbed her, the city was gray and filthy, and the work was demanding and monotonous. The world was pretty much the same everywhere, and her status in it was fixed at the lowest slot. Nothing Charlene Buckner ever did was going to make more than a minor change that would probably be temporary and might not even be an improvement.

Near the end of the semester, Charlene began to make her first visits to another life, one that existed because she chose it. She bought two good outfits at Marshall Field's. One was a black cocktail dress that was on deep discount because there was a tiny tear in the hem that she could fix in a minute. The other was a sleek black skirt and three different tops to go with it.

She found a good pair of black shoes on sale because they had heels too high for most women to bear. Her mother had trained her from the age of four to dance in high heels for the beauty pageants, so she loved them. There was also a pair of black flats that she could wear in less formal places, and a small, elegant black purse. The coat she bought was intended as a raincoat, too light for a Chicago January, but she knew it looked right, so she tolerated the cold. She began to dress and go out alone at night.

Charlene would call for her reservations in various names that she made up while she was standing at the dormitory pay phone, like Nicole Davis or Kimberly De Jong. She would go into the bar after dinner, and when men asked her name, she would give them the latest one. During the long weeks of classes she was Charlene, but once or twice a week, there would be a night when she became Nicole or Kimberly or Tiffany.

She discovered that she could attract men. Occasionally she would go out on a Friday night, meet a man, and then not return to the dormitory until Saturday, or even Sunday. If anyone asked where she had been, she would say she had gone to visit an old school friend in Boston, or met her parents for dinner in New York. But the other girls had so little interest in her that they seldom asked.

She loved the nights when she was someone else. The only disappointment was the men. They excited her at first because they were a few years older than she was, but they were all so involved with their careers as stockbrokers or sales representatives or junior executives that they were unable to convey anything to her about their lives that she understood, except that they worked very long hours.

On one of those Friday evenings, at a restaurant called Luther's, she met Carl. She'd walked in from the dining room and stepped toward the bar when she became aware that someone was close behind her. There was a tap on the shoulder, and she turned to see Carl. He smiled and said, 'Please join me at my table.'

Carl was older than the men she had been meeting: he looked about forty-five. He wasn't exactly handsome, but he was trim and had good posture, and his dark suit was beautiful. For a second when she had first turned around she'd thought he might be a hotel employee who was going to check the forged identification she'd bought outside the student union. But she looked at his expression and saw his eyebrows raised in an offer rather than knitted in anger, so she assumed a look of self-assurance she had been practicing, and went with him.

He introduced himself as Carl Nelson, and said he had noticed her at dinner and had not been able to let her leave without meeting her. He spoke without any embarrassment or uncertainty, a feat that she could not imagine any of the younger men performing. Everything he said seemed effortless. He told her she was a young woman who deserved to be congratulated on her beauty and told her that seeing her gave him pleasure.

She was so pleased that she invented a name for the occasion. She said she was Tanya Starling. It came to her because Tanya had always seemed to her to be foreign, and therefore frankly sensual. Starling was the corrective, a word that made her sound tiny and vulnerable, a way of protecting herself from the Tanya part.

Carl liked her name, and he liked her. When the waiter arrived, Carl didn't ask her what she wanted. He simply ordered two vodka martinis, up, with an olive. When they arrived, cold and clear, she recognized them. As a child she had always imagined her mother in an elegant place like this with a man like Carl, drinking something from a stemmed glass that moved back and forth to throw off reflected light when she lifted it.

Carl was a lawyer. Unlike the younger men, he didn't say much about his work, but it was clear he had made money. Tanya didn't exactly lie about what she was doing, but she made getting a bachelor's degree into 'studying the arts at the university,' so it would sound like a whim of an older woman.

When she went back to the dormitory she had to tell her roommates that she would take any calls for her friend Tanya. Two days later, Carl called her and took her to another good restaurant. After that he took her out every couple of days, and called her whenever he happened to be thinking of her. He sent her flowers because they reminded him of her. He began to see other things – a set of sapphire earrings that would set off her blue eyes, a dress that would make her proud of her tiny waist.

He called one day at the end of February, when the ground was covered with dirty snow that had partially thawed and then frozen into ice, and the wind was punishing. He said, 'Honey, I'm going to Florida for a few days on business. I thought you might like a little break, and I'd like some company.'

'Florida?' was all she could say.

'I've got to meet with a client in Palm Beach. That part won't take long, but I'm staying until Friday. Can you spare the time for me?'

She packed her two suitcases with the few good clothes she owned, said good-bye to her roommates early in the morning, and told them she'd be back in a week for midterms.

That day she learned what life with Carl Nelson would be. When they arrived in Florida a limousine waited to take them to the hotel and then to the country club for lunch with the client. The client was about sixty years old with impossibly white capped teeth, a pair of red-tinted glasses, and a suntan of a depth that had not been stylish during Charlene's lifetime.

Carl introduced them by saying, 'Tanya, this is Richard Fellowes. Richard, this is the most beautiful girl in the state of Illinois, and her name is Tanya.'

After only a moment she realized that Carl had brought her there to be decorative, so she imitated the haughty, bored look of the fashion models of her childhood and kept all of her movements graceful, while showing no awareness that the men were having a conversation. She answered direct questions and smiled politely at Richard Fellowes when it seemed necessary, but smiled much more warmly at Carl.

The lunch told her a bit about Carl. Fellowes had owned a chain of dry-cleaning plants in the Midwest. Carl had helped him sell his controlling interest in the business at a large profit and move to Palm Beach a few years ago. Fellowes had remained on the board of directors, but now that the new owners were considering selling it, they wanted to buy his remaining shares.

Carl went over the papers with Fellowes while Tanya Starling gazed out over the shady veranda at the deep green lawns and the first hole of the golf course, a tree-bordered straight stretch of grass that looked to her about the length of an airport runway, with, at the end of it, a tiny flag. The only sight beyond the flag was the blue of the ocean she had never seen before.

Carl's voice was deep and calm and reassuring. She could tell he was smart, that he had instantly seen what he had needed to in the contract and knew exactly how much of it to explain to his client. At the end, he handed Fellowes an onyx fountain pen and had him sign. When Fellowes said, 'What's this?' he answered, 'You're just initialing there to show that you know I'm also getting a fee from the company' Tanya let her face reveal nothing. Carl was being paid by both sides.

On the way back to the hotel, Tanya wanted to say something to Carl about the opulence of the country club, but she didn't. She wanted him to believe that she was sophisticated from birth, a creature of natural taste who belonged in luxury because she was unimpressed by it.

When the week in Florida was over, they flew back to Chicago at night. There was no discussion about Tanya going back to the dormitory. Carl simply had the driver go directly to his apartment in a high-rise building overlooking the lake. The driver carried their bags to the lobby, and the doorman put them into the elevator and transported them to the apartment on the top floor. Carl put her two suitcases in the guest bedroom and said, 'You can have the closets and bathroom in here to yourself. When you're undressed, come into our bedroom.'

After two weeks Tanya thought to make a telephone call to the office of the dean of students and let them know she wanted a leave of absence. The next day she went to the university in a taxi, found the boy outside the student union who had sold her the fake driver's license she'd used to get served in bars, and ordered identification in the name Tanya Starling.

She wanted to be the perfect mistress, but it took her some time to realize what Carl expected her to be and to do. She went about it with the discipline she had been taught in the beauty pageant competitions when she was a child, and the determination that had gotten her to college. She used the pocket money Carl gave her to buy custom-mixed makeup, and had the store's experts teach her the latest looks and application techniques. As soon as Carl left each morning, she entered the home gym he had installed in the apartment, and exercised. She studied the articles in women's magazines about how she should look and what she should wear, and what men liked in female behavior but didn't necessarily know they liked, and how to improve her skin, hair, nails, body, and small talk.

In the evenings when she went to parties and dinners with Carl, she closely observed the other women. Some were attorneys or clients, but most of them were wives or girlfriends of very successful men. They were all a few years older than Tanya, and very elegant and poised. She studied manners and personality traits that she envied, and took them for herself.

From the beginning, some of the men Carl knew would find ways to be alone with her for a moment and try to interest her in meeting them somewhere without Carl. She was extremely careful to be unremittingly loyal to Carl, but never derisive or threatening to the suitors. She understood instinctively that making enemies of Carl's friends and colleagues could only lead to trouble for her. As she got better at her new vocation, she gained knowledge of what men were really thinking and feeling. She saw that they might have complex minds full of information she was not capable of understanding, but in their dealings with women, they were no more able to think beyond the mere prospect of sex than Tim had been.

Carl dressed her expensively, took her to wonderful places, and treated her as his protégée. His conversation taught her things – which paintings in a gallery were the best, which wines were the right ones to serve, which writers were the ones to read, which orchestras were the ones to hear.

Carl was a recreational talker, a man whose own voice enchanted him so much that for him speech was like singing. As soon as he was home each evening, drinking the martini she had mixed for him, he told her anecdotes about what he had done all day and what he had thought, and shrewdly analyzed the people he had seen. They were all minor players in his personal story, which was essentially comic, because he always triumphed.

He taught her how much to tip various people who provided services, and to remember that it was wise to tip the most when the service was still in doubt, not afterward, in gratitude for something she already had. Once, when Carl needed to leave her alone for a few days, he opened a drawer in the bedroom and showed her where the gun was.

He picked it up, then said, 'It's loaded, see?' He moved the cylinder to the side to show her the bullets in the holes, then flipped it back. 'It's smart to consider all of them loaded, but this one always is. If somebody knows I'm gone and thinks that makes it a good time to break in, you hold it like this, arms extended in front of you, and pull the trigger. Fire three or four times. It's a .357 magnum, so I guarantee it will stop him. It's got a bit of a kick, so hold on.'

'You mean it's legal to kill someone because he's trying to break in?'

'It's not murder if he breaks into your apartment and tries to harm you. If he's still outside in the hall when you shoot him, drag the body inside before you call the cops.' Then he added, 'And if he's not dead, shoot him again, in the head. If they live, they sue.'

For nearly nine years, she lived with Carl Nelson and learned from him. In return, she was even-tempered and companionable. She was aware that his attraction to her was sexual, so she cultivated the attraction. His manner in bed was much like his conversation. He was affable and he wanted to charm her and be the one directing the proceedings, teaching her things he thought she would like. All she really had to do to please him was to be available and submissive, willing to be impressed.

Just before Tanya's twenty-eighth birthday, Carl Nelson came home from his office early. He didn't sit where he usually did, on the couch where she had been waiting for him. He sat instead in the chair across from her. He said, 'I'm finished with the Zoellner case. I'm going to Europe for a while.'

She said, 'Wonderful. Should I call to make arrangements with the travel agent?'

'No, thank you. They've already handled that at the office.'

She understood then, from the way he said it. He was going. She was not. She controlled herself as well as she could. 'You deserve a break. When will you be back?'

'In about a year. I'm taking a sabbatical. I'll be doing some work while I'm over there, handling some things for regular clients.'

'You're taking a secretary, aren't you?'

He nodded. 'Mia is going with me.'

She had seen Mia at his office. Mia was nineteen years old and already a failed model. She was taller than Tanya – taller even than Carl – and she had striking green eyes. She was Tanya Starling's replacement.

Tanya stood up and said, 'Excuse me, Carl. This is hard for me.' She went into their bedroom, crawled onto the bed, and cried. She stayed there for a long time. Then she heard noises. It was Carl in the big walk-in closet. There were sounds of hangers scraping sideways along the pole, and drawers opening and closing.

Tanya went into the bathroom, spent a few minutes fixing her hair and makeup, then stepped into Carl's closet. She said, 'Packing? You're leaving that soon?'

'My flight is at ten tomorrow.'

She could feel herself beginning to lose control. Tears

were coming, and her knees felt weak. She said, 'I'll have my stuff out of the apartment as soon as I can. I think the doorman will let me leave a few things with him while I find a place.'

'There's no reason to do anything like that, Tanya. In fact, I've been counting on you to stay here while I'm gone.'

'For the whole year?' Maybe he was going to have the secretary for a while and then come back to her. Men loved variety. That was okay. Her mind was already accommodating itself to the idea. Maybe he would even send for her.

'Sure. It will give you the time to figure out what you would like to do with your life, and get a start on it. You're smart, beautiful, and you should be doing something. Maybe real estate, or decorating. Take some time and think it over. And your staying here gives me somebody I know I can trust to care for the place and keep an eye on it. I'll have the office pay the bills and send you an allowance.'

'Sure.' The word *allowance* was a deliberate reminder of her dependency, but he would have had to maintain the lease anyway, and pay someone to occupy the apartment and care for his tropical fish, his paintings and antiques.

She considered taking Carl's pistol out of its drawer and shooting him. She considered simply slipping the loaded gun into his suitcase, so he would be arrested at Heathrow or De Gaulle or wherever he was flying to. But then she detected a contradictory impulse. She stopped being angry because she wanted him to stay. She began to be impatient for him to leave.

She spent some minutes exploring feelings she had not acknowledged before. She was humiliated, hurt, shocked, but now she realized that her situation was not so simple. She had been exploited, certainly, for her sexual attractiveness and her docility. In return, she had been educated, entertained, and pampered for nine years. The part that she was astounded and ashamed about was that she had not anticipated this moment or prepared herself for it.

Carl's ability to appreciate women was limited to girls of about eighteen. He found them interesting only during this phase of their lives. His was an entirely sexual addiction, but it wasn't because they were at their best. The exercised, massaged, and rested Tanya Starling looked much better, even younger, than the lonely, sad, frightened Charlene Buckner had, and she was more adventurous. And Tanya had seen Mia, who was going to take her place. Mia was pretty, but not prettier than Tanya. The attraction was that she was the right age: Tanya no longer was.

Tanya couldn't be taught which clothes to wear or which wines to serve, how to behave at a cocktail party or how to please a man in bed, because by now she knew. She couldn't be taken to a great hotel and stare in awe at the paintings on the domed ceiling, because she had already seen others as good. She had heard Carl's stories, and he could never tell them to her for the first time again. She was no longer a protégée, just a sycophant massaging his ego, more desperate each day to keep him fooled, so she would not lose her increasingly unpleasant job.

He had betrayed her, certainly, but he had also set her free. He had supported her so lavishly that she would never have been able to translate her vague feelings of dissatisfaction into the irrevocable act of walking out the door. Now he was sending her away. It didn't feel good, but it felt overdue, like a task she had been putting off.

Tanya went to bed in the spare bedroom, but when, a couple of hours later, Carl finished his preparations for his trip and climbed into the bed with her, she didn't object to having sex with him. He seemed to believe he had one more night due him, and she didn't feel like fighting. It gave her a chance to observe the extent to which she had only been going through the motions, and to try to think back to the time when sex with him had still been exciting. She realized that tonight, when she had no feeling except impatience for his departure, was not much different from the last fifty nights.

The next morning, Carl was up at five. He wrote her a big check and placed it on the antique table in the entry. 'Cash this,' his note said. 'It's just in case you need anything. Call the office any time you need more.' At the door, he turned and noticed that she had stepped into the room to watch him. He set down his suitcases and embraced her. 'I know you're a little scared, but you'll be fine. I know you're going to be a very success-ful woman someday.'

She remembered her answer: 'In a year, I'll have more money than you do.' She had looked through the win-dow to the street far below and watched the cab moving off, the tailpipe spewing steamy white exhaust into the cold morning air.

Tanya spent the next few months looking for work in the daytime and looking for a man in the evening. The evening hunting was better, but she didn't find the sort of man she needed. Rich men were nearly all married, and they were all aware that the most expensive catastrophe likely to befall them was a divorce. They were willing to spend lots of money on her, but they weren't willing to stay the night.

She went through a period in which she stopped look-ing for work and applied for readmission to the university, then spent her days trying to devise a course of study that would help prepare her for a career in law. Her observation of Carl had taught her that his clients paid him lots of money for very little work, as long as he kept them afraid.

She had begun to feel optimistic when she received a telephone call. She thought she recognized the voice on the other end as Arthur Hinman, one of the other partners in Carl Nelson's firm. He said, 'May I speak to Miss Starling, please?'

She wasn't absolutely positive it was Arthur, so she said, 'This is Miss Starling.'

'This is Arthur Hinman, one of Carl Nelson's partners at Colefein, Park and Kayslander. I'm calling to let you know that Mr Nelson has died.'

'Oh, my God. How? Where?'

'I believe he had a heart attack, but I'm not sure yet. He was in Spain.' He paused a full breath, which was his mourning period for Carl Nelson. Then he said, 'We're handling his estate, and the lease for his apartment is being terminated. We'll be closing it up to inventory his effects. That means your services won't be needed anymore.'

'Arthur,' she said. 'Don't act as though you don't know me. You've been here dozens of times. You know I'm not the maid or something.'

'I'm sorry. I know it's inconvenient. But please be out of there by noon tomorrow. You can leave the key with the doorman downstairs.'

She hung up the phone and went to work, taking everything from the apartment that she was sure Carl would have missed but the law firm would not. The art and antiques, the huge record collection, the old books were probably all insured. The cash Carl kept in the toe of a shoe on his upper closet shelf, and his cuff links, tie clasps, and tuxedo studs were all small enough to take.

His watches were probably insured too, but nobody would be able to prove he hadn't lost one in Europe, so she took his Rolex. Then, as an afterthought, while she was tossing things into her suitcase, she opened the drawer that contained Carl's gun, and slipped it into her purse.

TWENTY

Catherine Hobbes sat in the homicide office of the North Hollywood station. She had borrowed a table beneath the whiteboard where someone had drawn a crude diagram of Mary Tilson's apartment, with a body that looked like a gingerbread man. She shut the sounds of ringing telephones and the voices of the detectives out of her mind, opened the file, and looked at each of the crime scene photographs again, and then at the list of fingerprints from the two apartments that had been identified so far. There was the copy of the print that belonged to Nancy Mills. Staring at it gave Catherine a strange feeling: this was more than something that the woman had touched. It was more intimate, the touch itself.

Catherine had spent a career listening to the confident voices of experts who assured her that there were no mysteries, and that the physical evidence always told the story. This was a physical world, every cubic centimeter crammed with molecules. Any motion created a disturbance that left a trail, and anything the killer touched stuck to him. They were right about Tanya: she was leaving a growing collection of trace evidence behind her. But where the hell was she?

Jim Spengler came into the room. 'I brought you some coffee.' He set a white foam cup on the table, then sat in the folding chair beside her.

'Thanks. I'll bet when you do interrogations, you're always the good cop.'

'I would have brought it sooner, but I've been checking to see if there have been any other homicides since she got here that might have something to do with her.' He looked at the photographs in front of her. 'I heard you were in the lab half the night. Anything new?'

'No. I think Mary Tilson let her in, and they went together into the kitchen. I think Miss Tilson was turned to the left, maybe getting something out of the cupboard or refrigerator. When she turned away, I think Nancy Mills took the butcher knife out of the holder and stabbed her.'

'You don't think a man did that?'

'I'm looking at the list of prints Toni's people found. I don't see any male prints anywhere in the apartment, identified or not. I don't see a forced entry.'

'So she let him in.'

'A sixty-year old single woman like Mary Tilson is going to be nervous about letting a man into the apartment if she's alone.'

'So Nancy Mills was with him. She let them both in.'

'Even if the man is with Nancy Mills, he doesn't go into the kitchen with Mary Tilson and wait until she turns her back.'

'Why not?'

'Because she won't let him, and if he comes, she won't turn her back. If a single woman comes over to see another single woman, they both might go into the kitchen while they talk. The guest at least offers help while the hostess gets refreshments. If it's a stranger, a man, he doesn't go in the kitchen, he stays in the living room. If it's a man with Nancy Mills, the one who goes into the kitchen is still Nancy, not the man.'

'Why not both?'

'Because. It's just the way it is. I've been a single woman for long enough so I know all the moves.' She shrugged. 'And there's no evidence that there was a man.'

'You're also assuming that the stab in the back came first, not the throat.'

'That's right. If you cut the throat first, the victim is as good as dead. If you stab her first, maybe she's still up to making some noise, even fighting. That's when you have to cut her throat – to keep her from yelling. We know the stab in the lower chest was last, because that's where the knife ended up.' She glared at him. 'I know what you're going to say next: No woman would do that.'

'I was still back on the part about single-woman etiquette. You said you've been single for a long time, as though you weren't always. Have you ever been married?'

She frowned. She had been careless, because she hadn't been thinking about herself, or about him: she had been thinking about the sequence of events at the crime scene. 'Yeah,' she said. 'I was.' She avoided his eyes. Could he possibly not know that bringing up a woman's failed marriage would cause her pain?

'When were you married?'

'None of your business.' She still didn't look at him.

'Come on. What am I going to do, gossip? Nobody knows you down here, and all I asked was when. That's a public record. I could look it up.'

She turned to him, feigning boredom with the topic. 'A long time ago. We were young, just out of college. It was a classic starter marriage. After a couple of years we both started to realize that we'd made a mistake.'

'What was your reason?'

All right, she thought. Evasion would just prolong the badgering. 'He had a problem with the "forsaking all others" part.'

'So you got a divorce. And that's how you got to be an expert on women living alone.'

'Correct. Divorce is a costly way to find out how to choreograph murders of single women, but it works.'

'Okay,' he said. 'For the moment, we don't have any sign it was a man. But my gut is telling me there is one.' He looked over the lab reports.

From across the room Al Ramirez, one of the officers who had been at the apartment building, called out, 'Detective Hobbes? There's a call for you from your department. Captain Farber.'

She stood. 'That's my boss. Where can I take it?'

'That phone on the desk in the corner. I transferred it.'

'Thanks.' She stepped over and picked it up. 'Mike?'

She noticed that Jim Spengler had found something to do that kept him nearby, in earshot. The captain said, 'Hi, Cath. What's up?'

'Tanya Starling was here in Los Angeles, using the name Nancy Mills. She seems to have pushed a man off an eighth-floor balcony at the Hilton hotel in Beverly Hills the night before last.'

'How do you know it was her?'

'She got herself on another hotel security camera.'

'Pushing him?'

'No. Picking him up in a bar earlier that night. The LAPD released a picture of her with him. She seems to have seen it and panicked. She packed up, cleaned her apartment, killed the woman in the apartment across the hall from hers, and went off in the victim's car.'

'You really think she's doing all of this herself?'

'You sound just like Jim Spengler, the homicide detective in charge of the case.' She looked at Spengler, who shrugged. 'Who also sounds like Joe Pitt, and everybody else. I can place her in Dennis Poole's hotel room in Aspen with a picture and witnesses, and her hair places her in his house. I have pictures that can put her in a room in the Hilton hotel with the second victim, Brian

Corey, and a fingerprint that places her in the apartment where Mary Tilson was murdered. What I can't do is find a single bit of evidence that there was an unknown man with her, or after her.'

'I've seen a few pros who could come looking for her, kill witnesses, and take the evidence with them. I'm just saying, don't rule out the man just yet. I assume the LAPD has the car's description and plates out to every department.'

'Yes. I think we're about twelve hours behind her. I think she'll get as far as she can in a day or two, and then dump it.'

'So what do the L.A. cops need you for?'

'I suppose they don't. I'd like to stay at least another day in case the car is found and she's still in it.'

'All right. You've got a day. And I know how I want you to spend it. We still don't know for sure that Dennis Poole's murder wasn't some kind of reprisal against his cousin Hugo – whether the girl did it, or someone helped her, or someone came for Dennis and she became an inconvenient witness.'

'How can I eliminate a reprisal against Hugo Poole?'

'Find out if Hugo Poole is fighting back.'

Catherine Hobbes parked her rental car on Sheldrake Avenue and dialed the number of the homicide office on her cell phone.

'Spengler.'

'It's me. I'm on Sheldrake and I can see the theater.'

'I hear you.'

'All right. Here goes.' She put the cell phone into the compartment on the side of her purse without ending the call, got out of the car, and walked toward the old movie theater. Long experience made her dislike being on foot and alone in this kind of neighborhood: there was nobody else walking, and there seemed to be no place to take a defensive position, only big brick office buildings with bars across their doorways. She considered the possibility that Hugo Poole cast such a big shadow that it kept minor predators away from his door.

When she reached the front of the theater, a tall, muscular man about thirty-five years old was waiting on the other side of the glass with a set of keys. He unlocked the door and held it open for her, then scanned up and down the street before he closed and locked it again.

'I'm Sergeant Hobbes, Portland Police.'

'I know.'

'And you are—?'

'We're not in Portland.'

The man turned, and she followed him into a big, ornate old lobby with an empty glass candy counter and faded art deco murals on the walls. He climbed a carpeted staircase to the upper hallway. On both ends of the hallway were loges, but in the middle there was a wall of dark polished hardwood. It took her a moment to see that there were two doors cut into the wood. One had worn gold letters that said PROJECTION, and the other was unmarked. The man knocked on that one, and a muffled voice said, 'Come in.'

The man held the door open for Catherine Hobbes. 'Thanks, Otto,' said the voice inside, and Catherine entered.

Hugo Poole stood behind a big old desk that must have been part of the theater's original furnishings. He came around it, smiling. 'Hello, Catherine. Or is it Cathy?'

'It's Sergeant.'

'Oh. Should I be asking to see a warrant?'

'I'm just here to chat. When I called, I figured you would have Joe Pitt with you. Is he on his way?'

'No. I paid him off, and he went back to gambling full time.' Hugo Poole looked at her suspiciously, and for a moment she wondered if he had sensed that her question had a personal interest behind it. But he said, 'I don't know if you're wearing a wire or not. I often have Otto frisk visitors who might mean us harm. With you that policy seemed fraught with difficulties.'

'Yes,' she said. 'Fraught.'

'So I'll have to assume you are wired.'

'Suit yourself.'

'Are you here to tell me you've finally caught Tanya Starling?'

'No, I'm here because a disturbing suggestion keeps coming up as we search for her.'

'What's that?'

'She seems to be doing things that some of my colleagues believe she couldn't, or wouldn't, do – at least alone. They think that your cousin Dennis was killed by some man who was trying to hurt you, and she was either a witness or an accomplice.'

Hugo Poole stared at her unhappily, but said nothing.

She said, 'Two days ago, another man she had been with in a hotel fell off an eighth-floor balcony. There are pictures of her on the hotel security tapes, just as there were with your cousin Dennis. The day after that, the woman who lived across the hall from her was stabbed to death with a butcher knife. LAPD is saying that it seems as though a dangerous, angry man is looking for her, and killing anyone who tries to protect her.'

'I've heard that theory.'

'What do you think of it?'

'Not much.' He stared into her eyes. 'But I don't know much about these things.'

'No?'

'No. You're the cop. I'm just a small businessman. But

it seems to me that all of these theories are based on the idea that women don't kill people.'

'True.'

'It seems to me your colleagues aren't willing to see anything that isn't statistically likely, because they're afraid of looking stupid.'

'You could be right. But it's hard to prove that somebody isn't after her. And the only person anybody can think of who has a motive to hunt for her, and might have found it necessary to kill anyone near her, is you.'

'I haven't been out of town since I was in Portland with you.'

'The last two were in Los Angeles. The hotel was right up there on Wilshire.'

'I haven't been in any hotels lately. You said there are pictures of her on the security tapes. Did you see any pictures of me?'

'No. But I didn't see any pictures of anyone else, either.'

'Then she did it herself.'

Catherine hesitated. 'I'll be honest with you, Hugo, but I need you to be honest with me too. I think she's the only one. But if there's anything going on down here that would have made someone kill your cousin, I need to know about it. Now.'

Hugo Poole shook his head and held out his hands. 'I don't have any active enemies that I know about. I haven't heard a word from anybody taking credit for Dennis and threatening me. And I didn't kill any of these people or pay anybody to do it.'

'I noticed that you didn't say that you've never killed anyone.'

'And I noticed that the cops haven't been able to find one young girl in all this time, even though she's been leaving bodies all over the place.'

'She'll be found. Be sure of that.'

'Is there anything else I can do for you?'

She looked at him closely. 'No. I just had to check and see if you knew anything I didn't.'

He walked to the door and held it open for her. 'Then you'd better be going. The traffic gets bad in this part of town right about this time of the afternoon.'

'Well, thanks for your time, Hugo. Take care.'

She walked past him into the carpeted upper level of the theater and let Otto conduct her to the front door. When Hobbes was outside and walking toward her car, she took her cell phone out of her purse and pretended to dial it. Then she said in a voice too low to be audible beyond a few feet, 'Did you get all that?'

Jim Spengler's voice said, 'Sure. I haven't heard the recording, of course, but it should be fine.'

'Thanks for doing it,' she said. 'Not that it got us anything.'

'Do you think he was lying?'

'No,' she said. 'I didn't see any sign that he was lying, and I'm good at spotting it. I think he was actually glad to see me at first, because he thought I'd come to tell him we had Tanya Starling.' She reached her car. 'Well, I'm at my car. I'll be there in a half hour or so.'

'Wait,' said Spengler. 'I've got news.'

'What is it?'

'Remember that I was checking other homicides that happened since she came to town? Well, after you left, the detective who was working on another case came to talk to me. He was investigating the murder of a young man a couple of weeks ago. The victim was a bank branch manager from San Francisco named William Thayer. He was here to visit his family. He was found shot in the head in a picnic area in the hills above Malibu. His car was found in the parking lot of the Topanga Plaza, about a mile from the apartment building where Nancy Mills lived. It seems the dead guy was the manager of the bank branch where Tanya Starling and Rachel Sturbridge had a joint account.'

'Shit.'

'What?'

'Nothing. I'll be there soon.'

Inside the lobby of the Empire Theater, Otto locked the front door again. He watched Detective Hobbes get into her car and drive away, then turned to see Hugo Poole standing behind him, watching too. Hugo asked, 'Did she say anything to you on her way out?'

'No. Anything I need to know?'

Hugo Poole nodded. 'Yeah. All this time has gone by, and they're no closer to finding the woman who killed my cousin than they were two months ago.'

'They're not?'

'No. She was back here to see if I did it. She's starting over.'

'Is there something you want done to speed this up?'

'See if you can reach Calvin Dunn. Tell him I want him.'

TWENTY-ONE

It was three-thirty a.m. and Nancy Mills seemed to be getting used up. She had been driving for hours and she was on the outskirts of Flagstaff, Arizona. At night like this, the city looked like an outpost on another planet. She found a street on the southwest side of the city where there were a few run-down apartments, parked Mary Tilson's car by the curb in front of an empty lot, and opened the trunk. She needed to cut down on what she was carrying.

She put her money and the drabbest, plainest clothes she had into one suitcase. She put the Colt Python pistol that had been Carl's into the zippered pocket on the outside of her suitcase, checked to be sure the smaller pistol she had taken from Mary Tilson's bedroom was loaded, and slipped it into her purse. She closed the trunk, then drove until she came to a shopping center, and cruised along the back of a row of stores until she found a dumpster. She placed the unwanted second suitcase into it, and drove off again.

She was lost in a way that felt hopeless, because there wasn't any place she was looking for, or any reason to believe that anywhere she stopped was going to be safe. She knew that she had to find a way to get some sleep. When she turned onto the next street, she saw that there were cars parked all along the curb, below some apartment buildings. She let the car coast to a stop and looked around her. Maybe if her car was parked with so many others, she could sleep in the back seat and nobody would notice her until morning.

But she couldn't let herself be here in the morning. The sun would come up, the new day would already be under way, and she would be caught in the light in the open.

She had to think hard, but she was so tired that getting her brain to do more than keep the car on the road was too much effort. She drove on for another mile of flat pavement, each side lined by one-story bungalows on plots of land that had ornamental stones or desert brush instead of grass.

She realized that it was the car that was making her vulnerable. The police would be searching for it, and without it she would look just like anyone else – just an anonymous girl. That gave her an idea, and she drove on, following the signs toward the airport. She parked the car in the long-term lot, wiped off the steering wheel, door handles, and trunk lid, took her suitcase, and caught the shuttle bus to the terminal.

She went inside the baggage area to the row of courtesy telephones for local hotels, picked the ones near the airport, and began trying to find a vacancy. When she found a room at one called the Sky Inn, the man at the desk asked for her name. She hesitated. The police were looking for Rachel Sturbridge and Tanya Starling, and probably Nancy Mills by now, so she said, 'Nicole Davis.' It was one of the names she had used in college when she had gone out alone. She stepped outside and into the first taxi at the curb.

When she arrived at the Sky Inn, she saw that the clerk who had talked to her was in his twenties but had taken on the mannerisms of middle age. He never smiled, and the only thing that seemed to give him pleasure was his own efficiency. He spoke in a monotone, as though he were reading, held the registration card so that it faced her, and used his pen to point to the room rate, the check-out time, and the place for her signature. As she signed, he said, 'And I'll need a major credit card.'

She stared at him, and her mind was blank for a second. She had become so exhausted she hadn't thought this through. She reached into her purse and pulled out a stack of bills. The rate was a hundred and sixty-five dollars a night, so she placed two hundred-dollar bills on the counter. 'I'll pay in cash. I don't use credit cards.'

He looked at her closely for the first time, but she sensed that it was only because she was a curiosity – a person who had gotten herself into trouble because she didn't know when to stop charging things. He took her money, went to the back room, and returned with her change. He handed her a small envelope with her key in it. 'Up the elevator behind you to the second floor, then turn right.' As Nicole Davis left, the young man busied himself clicking the keys of his computer terminal.

She entered her room, locked both of the locks and set the chain, put her purse where she could reach the gun, took a hot shower, and collapsed on the bed.

Several hours later she awoke and sat up, then reminded herself of what this room was, and that she was Nicole Davis. She stood and opened the curtain on the window just an inch, and the light blasted in to illuminate the whole room. She squinted out at the parking lot. The sun splashed off the roofs and windshields of the cars and into her eyes. She retreated.

The idea of stopping here to sleep had seemed brilliant last night. She had been on the edge of collapse, driving a car that belonged to a dead woman. She had felt she needed to be rid of Mary Tilson's car, and she was at least four hundred miles from Los Angeles. But now she was stranded.

She was in a hotel in a place where she had never been before, and she had no easy way out of here. How long had she slept? She looked at the clock by the bed, then picked up the watch she had left on the nightstand. It was nearly noon, check-out time. She remembered that geek downstairs saying it in his monotone voice. She stepped to the bed and picked up the telephone, then pressed the button for the front desk. 'This is Miss Davis in – what is it – room 256. I'd like to stay another day. Is that all right?'

'Let me see.' This time it was a girl's voice. A child's voice. 'Um . . . you paid cash in advance for one night. What credit card did you give us?'

'I didn't. I don't carry credit cards, but I can come down there in a few minutes and pay for another day in cash.'

'Well, there's a problem. I'm afraid your room, the one you're in right now, is rented for tonight. We might be able to move you to a new one, but check-in time isn't until four.'

'All right. I'll just wait. Give me a call when the new room is ready.'

'I'm so sorry. The thing is, we need the room you're in, and it's check-out time now. The staff has to clean it and change the sheets and so on before the new people arrive. They can't wait until four to do that. See?'

'So I have to check out now, and then check back in at four?'

'I'm afraid that's the only way we can accommodate you.'

Nicole Davis had to be very, very careful. She closed her eyes to keep the frustration from turning into a red, blinding rage. 'I can do that. I'll be right down.'

She dressed quickly, then went through her suitcase. She removed all of the cash she had been carrying there, and the jewelry that David Larson had given Rachel Sturbridge, and put it into her purse. She closed her suitcase, and then opened it again. She couldn't leave the two-pound .357 magnum Colt Python with its four-inch barrel in the outer pocket the way it was. Somebody might brush against it or read its shape in the bulge it made. She slipped it inside the suitcase among her clothes and locked the suitcase.

She took the elevator to the lobby. At the front desk she found the female clerk she had spoken to, and she was glad she had kept her temper. The clerk was a small blond girl who seemed to be about seventeen. She smiled and tried to be helpful, but she didn't have enough authority to accomplish much.

Nicole Davis made a formal reservation for the first room that became available, and managed to force the girl to take the money for it in advance. Then she said, 'Can I leave my suitcase with you and go out for a while?'

That was something the girl knew how to do, so she came around the desk with a label, wrote 'N. Davis' on it and attached it to the suitcase, then wheeled it around the desk into a back office.

Nicole Davis found that it wasn't as hot outside as she had feared. The sun was bright and the sky cloudless, but the altitude in Flagstaff was much higher than she was used to along the coast.

Nicole was uneasy. The police were looking for her, and Flagstaff wasn't big enough to hide her for long. She needed to get out of town, but how she did it made a difference. She couldn't get on an airplane or rent a car without identification, and the police were waiting for her to use ID that said Tanya Starling or Rachel Sturbridge. When she thought about the police hunting her, she always pictured the woman cop from Portland.

That Catherine Hobbes had followed her to San Francisco, and she was still thinking about her every day, waiting for her to make some tiny mistake.

Nicole needed a car. She couldn't buy one at a car lot, because they would ask to see a driver's license. She needed to find a car on the street that had a For Sale sign on it. She would give the owner a few grand in cash and drive away with it. She began to examine every car parked along her way for a sign, but she couldn't find one. Then she turned a corner and saw something better – a bus station.

Nobody who was looking for Tanya Starling would imagine her getting on a bus. Everything they knew about her habits would lead them to look in the most expensive hotels or expect her to turn up at the luxury car lots. They knew Tanya Starling. But what they knew was a person she had invented. They didn't know that she had ever been anything but rich and spoiled. They didn't know that she knew how to be poor and alone.

She walked into the bus station, stepped to the counter, and picked up a copy of the printed bus schedule. She could see that business was slow today. There were a couple of men who looked like drunks slouching in and out of sleep in the waiting area, a couple of old people she decided were Indians, and a middle-aged woman with two children who looked the right ages to belong to her daughter. The bored man behind the window seemed to have nothing to look at but her, so she left with her schedule.

Thirty feet away, Tyler Gilman let his small blue Mazda coast to a stop at the traffic light on South Milton near the bus station. He looked at the clock on his dashboard. It was twelve forty-nine, and he still had to park and carry the five lunch orders to the women in the insurance agency on the next block by one.

He let his eyes drift to the sidewalk and saw the girl step out into the bright sunshine, looking down at a bus schedule she held open in her hands. Tyler's lazy glance settled on her and he didn't want to look away. She had straight brown hair that she had tied up in a neat bun like a dancer's, because it was so hot on the street. The sunlight caught the wisps of hair at the back of her delicate white neck. As though she sensed someone was staring, she abruptly looked up, then, not seeing Tyler behind his tinted side window, looked down at the schedule again.

He had seen her wrong at first. She was older than he was – not a girl of sixteen or seventeen but a young woman, at least twenty-five. Tyler felt a sadness that he knew was irrational. He knew he would have had little chance of attracting a female like her at any age, but her extra years moved her entirely out of his reach. Looking at her, he regretted it profoundly. He studied her rounded hips and breasts, feeling cheated. Wanting her wasn't his fault: she was a creature who had been deliberately designed to arouse his sexual longing. In his peripheral vision he caught the red light going out and the green coming on. He stepped on the gas.

Tyler drove to the next block, stopped in front of the insurance office, and turned off the engine. As he got out of the car, he looked back along South Milton, but he couldn't see the woman anymore. He leaned into the back seat to pick up the box of bagged orders from El Taco Rancho and thought about his reaction to her. He knew it was another odd thing about him he could thank his parents for. When he had started to be curious about sex at the age of nine, they had insisted on sitting down together to explain it to him. They were both religious people, so everything that existed was God's plan to accomplish something else. God wanted people to be fruitful and multiply, so he made women in a shape that you could barely keep your hands from touching, and that you kept thinking about and couldn't get out of your mind, even while you were asleep and dreaming.

Tyler kicked the car door shut, hurried across the sidewalk, and leaned his back against the door of the insurance agency to ease his way in with his box.

'Tyler! Where have you been?' It was Mrs Campbell. She was a big, broad-faced blond woman who sat at the desk closest to the door. She went to the same church his family went to, and she seemed to think it gave her a special right to criticize.

He said, 'I had to put your orders together, then drive over here from the restaurant.'

'At Domino's, if your order doesn't arrive in twenty minutes, it's free.'

'At El Taco Rancho they don't have that,' said Tyler. 'I'd have to pay for it myself.'

'Maybe if you had to, you'd be faster.' She was up from her chair, blocking his way and opening each of the five bags, looking inside them at the food.

Tyler began to sidestep. 'Where can I put this down?'

Mrs Campbell glared at him, but she pointed at a long table nearby, where there were a couple of coffee cups. He set the box down and stepped back while she continued to paw through the bags.

The four other women had heard her voice. They came out of the back offices and pulled chairs to the table where Tyler had set the food. Two of them were old, nearly retirement age, but the other two were young, and one was pregnant. The other young one gave him a smile as she passed close to him, and he watched her as she went to the table to identify her lunch. Tyler had written on the bags with a marker what was inside, so she took only a second.

The pregnant one said, 'Whose turn is it to pay for lunch?'

'Julie's,' said one of the older women. Nobody disputed her.

Julie was Mrs Campbell. 'How much is it?' she asked.

'Thirty-four eleven,' said Tyler. He held out the cash register slip. He was sure that she had been the one he had told on the phone when he had taken the order. None of the others sounded anything like her.

'I'll get a credit card,' she said. She took her purse from her desk and reached in.

'We don't take them,' he said. 'I mean, we do at the restaurant, but I can't do that here. I asked on the phone if it was cash or charge.'

Mrs Campbell took out her wallet. 'All I have is a hundred-dollar bill.' She held it out, sensing a victory.

'I don't have that much change.'

Mrs Campbell looked triumphant. 'Then you'll have to come back for the money tomorrow.'

'But I'll have to pay when I go back. The managers count the receipts against the orders every night, and everything has to add up.'

Mrs Campbell took a breath, but the pregnant woman said, 'Don't worry. I'll get it this time, and Julie can take my turn tomorrow.' She walked over to a desk, opened a drawer, and took out a purse. Tyler waited, avoiding Mrs Campbell's eyes while the pregnant woman counted out the money, hesitated, then added three dollar bills. 'And that's for you.'

'Thanks.' The amount of money didn't matter now. She had saved him.

Mrs Campbell snapped, 'I wouldn't tip him. He didn't

bring extra salsa or extra hot sauce, or even enough extra napkins.'

Tyler clenched his jaw and turned toward the door. He could feel his cheeks burning in anger and humiliation. He wanted to kill her. He wanted to go to the trunk of his Mazda, take out the tire iron, come back in, and swing it through her skull. But he couldn't. He couldn't even say anything back to her. She was in his parents' church.

As he reached the door, she called, 'I'll be talking to your parents about the way you do your job, and the way you treat your elders.'

As he opened the door and stepped out, he heard a voice say, 'Oh, Julie.' He closed the door behind him, walked quickly to his car, got inside, and started it. In the car it was quiet, and a stream of cool, breathable air surrounded him. The car was a place of sanctuary. He put the transmission into drive and moved ahead a few feet, but he saw Mrs Campbell come out the door and step toward him. He quickly pulled out into traffic and moved up the street away from her.

Tyler drove around the first corner, then came along the back of the bus station, turned right again and looked at the front entrance. The pretty young woman he had seen was gone. He wasn't sure why he had felt he needed to look at her again, and then he knew. At that moment he had felt reckless enough to offer her a ride. It was probably a good thing that he had missed her, instead of suffering the embarrassment of having her look at him with contempt.

Tyler charged that loss against Mrs Campbell too. She had held him up until the pretty woman had disappeared, as though Mrs Campbell was acting on behalf of the church. He knew the young woman was nearby, probably waiting inside the station out of the sun, but he had no more time. Already he was going to have to apologize to the other people who worked at El Taco Rancho for taking such a long time. The worst part was that what he really hated was not Mrs Campbell. It was the way his parents had put him in the power of all of the people like Mrs Campbell.

He knew that she really would corner his parents after church next Sunday and tell them that he was lazy and slow and disrespectful, and hint at causes for it that were worse. She would tell other people too, and he would see them looking at him with suspicion. His father and mother wouldn't defend him. They never did, and never had. They would believe Mrs Campbell. Even if all four other women in that office said he was a good person and a responsible worker, it would make no difference, because Mrs Campbell was saved, and the others weren't. They were members of false churches.

Tyler was sixteen years old and working full-time by himself while his parents went on vacation. He always got good grades at school and had competed all winter on the wrestling team and started all spring at second base, but they would believe that rotten old bitch instead of him. They would punish him, take something away from him. It would probably be his car, because they knew he loved his car. It had been his mother's for several years, but now it was his on the condition that he worked all summer for it.

Maybe they would even have a conference with Pastor Edmonds. Then he would have a chance to add on new punishments for Tyler too. They had done it when he had gone with Diane O'Hara to that party, because she was a Catholic. And then they had searched his room and found that magazine. Tyler's parents were gullible and weak and more worried about what a lot of people in the church thought than they were about their son.

They had never protected him from anything – unfair teachers, the older guys who beat him up after school, people who said things about him.

He wished he could kill Mrs Campbell and get away with it, but he knew he was being foolish to think about it. He was only concentrating on her because he didn't quite want to face the fact that the ones who most deserved to die were his parents. They had done what Joseph's brothers had done to him in the Bible – delivered him into the hands of his enemies – only they had done it over and over again all his life. He wished he could kill all of them, all of the tormentors and the betrayers who told him what to do and never left him alone.

Tyler made it back to El Taco Rancho, swung into his space near the dumpster, and trotted inside. It was already one-thirty, and the lunch rush was over. Nobody seemed to care that he was late. Danny and Stewart were busy scraping the griddle clean, and the girls were all refilling salt shakers and napkin dispensers in the space beneath the television set on the wall. Maria stepped up on a chair to change the channel to a station where a woman dressed up as a judge shouted at people who wanted a divorce.

Tyler started wiping down the tables and chairs with a dirty rag. A few customers straggled in while he worked, but most of them only wanted cold drinks, so one of the girls would leave the television set to draw the drinks and take the money. After a while, when Tyler was mopping, the sound of the television changed. Instead of voices there was urgent music. He looked up and saw the words 'Breaking News' in red on an orange background. He stopped and watched.

There were two pictures of the pretty woman he had seen at the bus station. One had long blond hair, and the other much darker brown than she had now, but it was definitely the same woman. The news man was calling her a fugitive, armed and dangerous. Tyler's chest expanded with excitement. He had seen her. He knew where she was. He looked at the clock on the wall. It was two fifty-three, almost time for the three o'clock break, when half the staff took off for a half hour. The others would go at three-thirty and be back at four to prepare for the dinner rush.

Tyler thought about the woman, and he felt that she was his, in a way. If he wanted to be a good citizen, he simply had to take out his cell phone and call the police. If he wanted to be a hero, he could drive there and make a citizen's arrest. He had seen her, and he knew that she wasn't really dangerous. Knowing about her was power, and having power was a new feeling for Tyler. He had to guard it. He pretended that he had not noticed the television. He moved off, mopping the floor near the front window, where he could not see the television screen, and thought about the pretty young woman and what he should do with her.

At three o'clock, Tyler took the mop and bucket he was using into the back of the kitchen, leaned the mop handle against the wall, and continued out the back door. He got into his car and drove it toward the bus station.

Nicole Davis had stopped for a quiet lunch in a small Mexican restaurant a block away from the bus station, and looked at her bus schedule. There was a bus leaving for Santa Fe, New Mexico, tomorrow at ten in the morning, so she had returned to the station and bought a ticket. She would get another night's sleep, then take the bus to Santa Fe.

She knew she was probably too early to get into her new room, but she seemed to have accomplished what she could for the moment, so she began to make her way back. She headed in the right direction, but after a time she did not see any buildings she remembered. She had somehow gone past the street where she should have turned. At each intersection she stared up the street and down, until she recognized the sign above a store on the corner two blocks to her left.

She considered correcting her course, but the street she was on had a long row of two-story buildings that threw shade across the sidewalk, and the shops had window displays of jewelry with turquoise and coral set in silver, weavings that might be Indian, and pretty clothes.

As she walked she could see that she was going to approach the hotel from the back, and that seemed fine to her. But as she came closer, she saw something else. There were four cars parked near the loading dock, all of them big American-made sedans that had short antennas sticking up on their trunks, identical but in assorted colors: navy blue, white, black. There were two men inside one of them. One seemed to be talking on a radio, and the other had his head bent down as though he was writing something.

Nicole stopped and retreated a few steps, until she was out of sight of the cars. She wanted to run, but she had to control herself, and fight the panic. She told herself there was no good reason to assume they were here for her. She walked back the way she had come for two blocks, then turned, making a wide circle around the building, trying to see more of it without being seen.

From the front, the hotel looked exactly the same. There were no police cars, no big men standing around. When she came to the parking lot side, she picked out the window of the room where she had spent last night. It was on the second floor, three windows from the elevator shaft. The curtain was open, and she saw a man walk past the window and disappear.

She walked quickly back toward the bus station. As she walked, she took out her bus schedule and scanned it. There was a bus leaving for Phoenix in thirty minutes. When she arrived, she bought a ticket for that bus, then sat in the dismal waiting room to stay out of the sun. But after a few minutes she began to be aware that somebody was staring at her.

A teenaged boy must have come in the side entrance while she was buying her ticket, and now he stood near the wall watching her. He was tall and thin with sandy blond hair, and when she looked at him, his blue eyes would turn away, toward other people in the station, then look out the windows at the street, and then return to her again, staying on her unblinking until the next time she caught him at it.

She went outside and waited near the pay phone until she saw her bus arrive and discharge the passengers from its last leg. When their luggage had been unloaded and the driver was standing by the door taking tickets from the line of new passengers, Nicole stepped to the telephone and dialed the front desk of the hotel. She heard the young girl answer, 'Sky Inn. May I help you?'

Nicole Davis said, 'This is police dispatch. Are any of the officers who are waiting for the female suspect close to you now?'

The girl said, 'Yes. Would you like to speak with one of them?'

Nicole Davis said, 'Cancel that. We've just reached the one we wanted by radio. Thank you.' She hung up and walked toward the line of passengers waiting to board the bus.

Suddenly the teenaged boy who had been staring at her came out of the side door of the bus station, stopped a few fect ahead of her, and said, 'Come with me. Hurry.' His expression was anxious and scared, and even though he was as tall as a man it made him look young, like a boy.

She said, 'What?'

'I know you,' he said with quiet urgency. 'I saw you on TV. I can get you out of here. I've got a car.'

She looked at him for a moment, then at the bus. She put her ticket into her purse and walked toward him. She followed him from the station at a distance of about ten feet all the way down the block. He went to a small, dark blue Mazda with dark tinted windows that was parked beside the curb. He opened the door for her and she got in.

When he sat down behind the wheel, she was staring at him. 'How old are you?'

His blue eyes clouded, and his soft, unlined face seemed to flatten with disappointment. 'I'm sixteen. Now you don't want my help, right?'

'Yes. I want your help. Please.'

He glanced into his mirrors, then cautiously pulled away from the curb. The sound of sirens reached their ears. He looked at her furtively as he drove down the street away from the bus station. 'The cops are coming from the other direction, where their station is.'

'And where are we going?'

'My place.'

TWENTY-TWO

It was Catherine Hobbes's last night in Los Angeles. Mary Tilson's car had not turned up, and Catherine had a reservation for a morning flight to Portland. She sat at the desk in her hotel room making an inventory of the duplicate case files from the murders of Brian Corey, William Thayer, and Mary Tilson before packing them. As she leafed through the collections of photographs, lab reports, interview notes, and drawings, she began to feel a sensation of dread. All of this had happened in a period of just a few weeks since Tanya had arrived in Los Angeles.

Catherine had seen videotapes of Tanya and spoken to her on the telephone. Tanya had seemed very young and harmless, maybe even a little empty-headed, someone Catherine had needed to explain things to. But what had been behind Tanya's pretty face and her soft, feminine voice had been this – the capacity and intention to cause the horrors in these files.

A knock on the door of her hotel room startled her. She left the files on the desk, flopped on the bed to reach into her purse, came up with her service pistol, then stepped to the door and looked through the small fish-eye lens into the hallway.

She held the gun behind her right thigh and opened the door. Joe Pitt stood in the doorway wearing a sport coat and a shirt that seemed better than the ones she had seen him in before. 'You?' she said. 'I thought I'd already given you the brush-off.'

'You did,' he said. 'I've never been so thoroughly dismissed in my life.'

'I just wanted to get that straight. So what are you doing here?'

'I'm not making any money on this visit, but it's business related. I'd have to say it's not going to make you happy.'

'As long as it doesn't involve my making you happy, you can come in.' She stepped away from the door, and he could see she had been holding her gun in her right hand. She slipped it back into her purse.

He advanced past her into the area near the window, where there was an armchair. 'Kill any bellhops?'

'Not when they were on duty.' She closed her files and piled them on the desk, then sat down on the bed. 'Go ahead. Make me miserable.'

'I heard something tonight that you need to know.'

'Hugo Poole sent you to tell me he didn't kill anybody. I already knew that.'

'I don't work for Hugo anymore. He paid my fee and we parted company.'

'That was a great job. You didn't even have to show up.'

'During the twenty years I was the DA's investigator, I never had an easy one,' he said. 'Not once. Now that there's money involved, it seems to happen a lot. Funny, isn't it?'

'Not to me. What did you want to tell me?'

'That Hugo Poole has hired Calvin Dunn.'

'Who's Calvin Dunn?'

'He's sort of a well-known figure in this part of the world. If you don't know anything about him, you should have Jim Spengler run his record for you. Dunn does investigations. I don't know if he's still got a license or not, but it doesn't matter.'

She shrugged. 'So Hugo replaced you. I wouldn't work with you, and I won't work with him, either.'

He shook his head. 'Calvin Dunn doesn't want to work with you.'

'What do you mean?'

'He works for people who would never go to the police for any reason. If a criminal has a relative kidnapped or a shipment hijacked, he wants to find out who did it. Calvin Dunn will find out. He's not one of us. He's one of them. He goes down the rabbit hole, and when he comes back he's got blood on his teeth, and there's no rabbit problem anymore.'

'When did Hugo hire him?'

'Today, I think. It could have been yesterday.'

She stared at the wall for a moment. 'Why did you decide to tell me this?'

'Because Calvin Dunn is dangerous. He isn't going to be out collecting evidence or something. He's not interested in seeing the girl go to trial. Even if you see him go through two sets of metal detectors, you should assume that he's armed and doesn't mind if you're the one he needs to hurt to get to her.'

'Thanks. I appreciate the warning. I probably won't be the one to run into him, though.'

'Why not?'

'I've got to leave for Portland in the morning. My captain let me stay this long only because we thought the California police might stop her on the road. But there are other cases in Portland, so he wants me back.'

Joe Pitt shrugged. 'I suppose he's right. She could turn up anywhere at this point, and L.A. probably isn't the most likely place now that she's been here.' He brightened. 'You know, since you're just going to spend tomorrow in airports, you could come downstairs and have a drink with me.'

'I don't drink.'

'Then come and have a soda with me.'

She gazed at him for a moment, wavering. She detected in herself a kind of affection toward him, maybe just because she had worked with him and then expected not to see him again. She had been feeling very alone, and maybe even depressed tonight. 'All right. Just for a little while. Then I have to get to sleep.' She took her purse, went to the door, and opened it for him.

As she walked beside him to the elevator, she sensed an odd feeling of familiarity, and then realized it was walking beside a man in a hotel corridor. It reminded her of being with Kevin.

She dismissed it, irritated at her own stupidity. Joe Pitt was very different from Kevin. The two had absolutely no shared qualities except that they were both about the same height and weight. That had been all that was necessary, she supposed. The voice came from about the same distance above her ear, the sound of his shoes on the hotel carpet was the same, and so it had set off the feeling of loss again.

It was ridiculous, because it wasn't Kevin that she missed. She missed having another presence, the other person who was seeing things at the same time and reacting, so that her thoughts were not just voices inside her own skull.

She had been surrounded by male colleagues most of the time since the academy, but she had never allowed her relationships with them to become close, let alone romantic. She had exerted her will to ignore any inconvenient feelings. It was like forcing herself to tune out a particular sound so she wouldn't hear it, and listen instead to the other sounds that competed with it. Any approaches from other cops that she could not ignore she had brushed aside with humor.

But now and then she would be surprised by a feeling, a memory, a sound.

She analyzed her vulnerability. Joe Pitt was very male and he was smart, and the fact that he seemed to like her had surprised her, so that forbidden part of her mind had been switched on when she had not been guarding it. All she had to do now was switch it off again.

'I'm only going to stay for ten or fifteen minutes. I've still got packing to do, and when I get home I'll have to try to catch up with what's been piling up on my desk.'

He pressed the elevator button and the elevator took them downstairs to the lobby. She was surprised when he stopped at the bar, ordered two colas, and carried them to a small table for two. She took hers and said, 'I thought you were a drinker.'

He shook his head. 'Been known to, but tonight I'm driving.'

So maybe he wasn't a problem drinker. She found that she was losing one of the barriers that had kept her distant from him. She had to build others, distract herself, keep everything impersonal. 'What do you think of the fact that she's killed a woman this time? They were always men before.'

'Don't you ever think about anything besides the case you're on?'

'I'm still learning. You've seen more killing sprees than I have. I've seen solitary men, or pairs of men doing strings of killings. I've seen one where there was a man taking his girlfriend along for the ride. Have you ever worked a case where a woman traveled around alone killing people?'

'Is learning the only interest you have in men, or is it just me?'

'I don't think I know what you mean.'

'You're interviewing me. I feel as though there's a tape recorder in your purse. Why not let yourself relax? Your subconscious will still be working on the case, I promise.'

'I'm just making conversation,' she said. 'The case is what you and I have in common.'

'We have lots of things in common. We just don't know each other well enough to know what they are. We need to tell our life stories.'

'No, we don't.'

'I'll start. I was raised in Grand Island, Nebraska. I dropped out of college, spent four years in the air force, and then became a state trooper. Then I was a police officer in Los Angeles, and finally became a district attorney's investigator. I retired from that a couple of years ago, and now I'm a private investigator.'

'Okay,' she said. 'I was raised in Portland a few blocks from where I live now. I graduated from college, got married instead of going to law school, dropped out of the marriage, and then went to the police academy. I'm still in the first law enforcement job I ever had.'

'See? Our lives are exactly alike.'

She laughed. 'Uncanny resemblance.'

'If I fly up to Portland tomorrow, will you have dinner with me?'

'No.'

'Why not?'

'I don't date people from work.'

'Wait a minute. You've made it very clear that you and I are not working together, and that we aren't going to be working together. We don't live in the same city, or even the same state. There's no way I can be considered to be "from work."'

'I guess that's probably true,' she said. 'But people up there know who you are. They know we were on the same case, traveling and sharing information. If you turn up when I do and take me out, it will put me in an uncomfortable position.'

'Why?'

'People will think that we're sleeping together.'

'Do you always behave like this – all these rules?'

'Yes.'

'Then they won't think that.'

She laughed again and shook her head. 'I'll go out with you. I *am* out with you. It's nine o'clock, and I haven't had dinner. How about you? Are you hungry?'

'Starving.'

'Then let's go across the lobby to the coffee shop and see if we can get a booth.'

'No,' he said. 'I want to take you to a place I like. My car's outside.'

'That's too hard. I'd have to change, and then it would be too late.'

'You look beautiful, and I'm past fixing. The place is not far, and the food is better than the coffee shop. Come on.' He was already standing, and he took her arm so that in a moment they were out of the bar and on their way.

He drove her to the Biltmore Hotel, let the valet parking attendant take his car, and led her into the ornate lobby, to Bernard's. 'This is really formal,' she said. 'You implied that this was going to be some kind of interesting dive.'

'I don't think I implied it was a dive,' he said. 'I distracted you by reminding you that you were beautiful.'

The restaurant was large and dimly lighted. She could see that in her business suit she was dressed as well as most of the women, so she began to feel more comfortable.

When the waiter came, Pitt said to Catherine, 'Would you like a drink before dinner?'

'No thanks,' she said. 'You can have one if you like.'

But he looked at the waiter and shook his head. When the waiter was gone, he said, 'So tell me about your family, your pets and hobbies. All women have them.'

'I don't have any pets right now, and not much time for hobbies except reading and exercising, which are just two aspects of the same futile, late-onset urge to improve myself. I do have parents, though – one of each. My father is a retired cop. How about you?'

'My parents are still in Nebraska wondering where they went wrong.'

'Where did they?'

'Nowhere, actually. They're terrific people. Everything I've done to myself is my own fault.'

'What have you done to yourself ?'

'Oh, I don't know. I guess what I've done is spend too many years doing nothing but thinking about murder cases. When I came into your hotel room before and saw you with three case files open on the desk, it reminded me of myself. I used to lay them out everywhere in hotel rooms – on the bed, usually. Then, one day, I noticed that about twenty years had passed. I had cleared a lot of cases. I'd made a succession of DAs who were elected because they had good hair look smart. But I hadn't gotten married or had kids. I didn't even own a house.'

'How sad.' She smiled. 'I'll bet you lived just like a monk.'

He laughed. 'I didn't say that. And since I retired, I've bought a house. It's pretty nice.'

In spite of her misgivings, she liked him. He was realistic about life, and yet he had a cheerful, optimistic temperament that seemed to have come through the sad and ugly things that he had seen in his career. She kept asking questions to listen to him talk.

Catherine ordered too much food and ate all of it because she didn't want the dinner to end. She knew that as soon as it did, she would have to get back to packing and preparing herself to return to her town, her house, her job.

Finally, he asked the waiter for the check. On the way back to her hotel she was quiet, thinking hard about the way she had been conducting her life. She had been reasonably contented for the past few years, because thinking about nothing but her job had been better than being in a marriage with a man who had seemed more and more often to hate her. The life she had constructed for herself was good, but this evening with Joe Pitt was better. She wondered how much of her pleasure was just a sense of release after years of discipline and solitude.

He pulled the car up at her hotel and started to get out to let the valet take it. She said, 'Uh-uh. Don't get out. I really do have to get packed and go to sleep now.'

He got out and opened the door for her, but waved the parking attendant off. 'Then have a good flight home.'

'Thanks for dinner, Joe.' She stood beside the car for a second, uncertain. The evening had been something that could only have happened unexpectedly, something she had tried to avoid and thought about at the same time. What was she hiding from? At this moment, what she wanted most was to make him want to see her again. She leaned into him, put her arms around his neck, and gave him a soft kiss on the lips, then stepped back. 'If you do come up to Portland sometime, I will go out with you.' Then she turned and strode into the hotel lobby and was gone.

TWENTY-THREE

Except when he was desperate to get somewhere quickly, Calvin Dunn liked to travel by car. Today he was driving a new one, a customized coal black Lincoln Town Car. It had steel plates fitted into the door panels and a front end that had been reinforced with steel bars. The rear seat sat on a false floor so that he could carry a few extra pieces of equipment without subjecting them to public scrutiny.

The extra space permitted him more ways of administering rewards and punishments. At the moment it contained fifty thousand dollars in cash, eight pairs of plastic restraints, a set of night-vision goggles, three pistols, a short-barreled shotgun, and a 7.62-millimeter rifle with a four-power scope.

His customary attire included a black sport coat with thirty hundred-dollar bills zipped into an inner pocket and a ten-millimeter Smith & Wesson pistol in his shoulder holster.

He was in a good humor today. He was in the business of doing things nobody else would do, so usually his ego didn't get much involved, but Hugo Poole had given him the sort of compliment that meant something to him: a great deal of money and the promise of more.

It was a pleasure for Calvin Dunn to work for a man like Hugo Poole. He didn't have to explain the things that every adult male ought to know. Dunn had not needed to say, 'You will pay what you owe me on time and in cash, or I'll have to come take it and leave your body in the desert for the coyotes.' Hugo Poole had not needed to say, 'If you rat me out, I'll find you in prison and drive a sharpened toothbrush through your temple.' They both knew how business was done.

Hugo had given him the names the girl had used so far, and this morning Calvin Dunn had driven to the police station in the Kern County town of Paston, where he lived, and obtained a photocopy of the police circular. The circular had good photographs taken from driver's licenses and her accurate height and weight. There was some confusion about eye color, but if he got close enough to see that, the job was as good as done.

Outside the police station he studied the printed information on the circular, then started his engine. He knew where to begin the hunt. He drove to Los Angeles County and found the address in the San Fernando Valley near Topanga where the girl had lived under the name Nancy Mills. He parked his car where he could easily see it from the windows at the front of the apartment building, then went inside and knocked on the door of the building manager's apartment.

The man who opened the door had a short beard that looked like a permanent three-day growth. Calvin Dunn held up a small leather case with an identification card in it that had his picture in an official-looking format and an embossed gold badge under it that had no insignia and didn't say he was anything in particular. But Calvin Dunn was tall and had muscular arms, so he looked like a cop.

'My name is Calvin Dunn, and you are—?'

'Rob Norris.'

'Pleased to meet you. I'd like to ask you a few questions about a tenant, the young lady who called herself Nancy Mills.'

Calvin Dunn's stare transfixed the manager. Dunn's pale gray eyes appeared to be focused on a point two inches deeper than the manager's forehead, inside the manager's skull. It was an uncomfortable feeling for him, and he felt an urge to close the door.

'Can I come in?'

The manager had no desire to let him in but no confidence in his power to stop him, so he said, 'Okay.' He stepped back just in time to prevent Calvin Dunn from colliding with him. When Calvin Dunn arrived, violence was not a remote possibility but something already present in the room with him. The manager sensed that his task was to keep it from becoming overt.

The manager watched Dunn standing in his small living room, his hands clasped behind him as though to emphasize the difference it might make if they weren't clasped, and rocking toe to heel on his shoes. 'I'm afraid I'll have to ask you some of the questions you already answered,' said Dunn.

'Okay.'

'Tell me about Nancy Mills. Why did she decide to live here? Did she know anybody here?'

'No. She just called up and said she liked living near the mall.'

'How did she pay for the rent? Did she have a credit card?'

'She gave me cash. It was a lot of money, when you add up first, last, and security deposit. Over three thousand bucks. I had to deliver it to the company that owns the place that day, because I didn't want to keep that much around.'

'Just like that? Didn't you do a background check to see if she was a problem tenant?'

'What do you mean?'

Dunn was patient. 'A deadbeat, who skipped on her

last landlord. Or a drug dealer, or a prostitute. That's the kind of person who has lots of cash.'

'I don't do that kind of checking. I think that the company does sometimes. On the application they ask for a lot of information. They want the last three addresses and phone numbers. They ask for references too, including an employer they can call.'

'Do you have her application here?'

'No,' said the manager. 'The company gets it as soon as the place is rented.'

'I'd like you to see if you remember anything at all about her that might help me find her. Does she like to wear particular colors or a special style of clothes, for instance?'

'She has a nice little body, so she tends to wear pants and tops that are sort of snug. Not tight, exactly. Fitted. I never saw what she wore when she went out at night, but the picture from the hotel camera looked like the kind of thing I always saw on her. It was pants and a yellow top, and a matching yellow jacket thing over it, with something written on it.'

'You mean like a brand?'

'You know, there's always some smart-ass thing written on it, like to tease you. Maybe the brand is mentioned, maybe not.'

'Oh. Any friends, anybody she talked to a lot?'

'I don't think so. I guess she must have talked to Mary Tilson, the woman across the hall from her.'

'Nobody else? No guys?'

'None that I ever saw. If you're an apartment manager, you have to kind of watch for that too. You get a sweet-faced little babe into an apartment, and then all of a sudden there's a boyfriend living there and his drinking buddies are in and out all the time, making noise and pissing off the other tenants.'

'What did she do all day? Did she work?'

'I don't know. She used to go out for a run in the morning, then come back. After that, I guess she would go for the day. Now and then she'd come home with bags from stores.'

'Interesting. I'd like it if you'd let me into her place now, so I can have a look around.'

'I'm not really supposed to do that. The police won't let me rent it out or anything yet.'

Dunn said quietly, 'If you help me, I'll pay for your cooperation. If you don't, I'll still get what I want, but you won't.'

The manager noticed again the strange way that Calvin Dunn looked at him, his eyes appearing to focus on a point inside the manager's forehead. 'All right.'

They went to the apartment, and Dunn waited while the manager unlocked the door, then ducked under the yellow police tape across the doorway and into the room. Dunn looked at everything closely, and sighted along the woodwork where the police had dusted for prints. There didn't seem to be any spots where they had put tape down and lifted a print. Then he examined the furnishings. 'Did she pick out this stuff, or did it come with the place?'

'It's furnished. The company buys it in lots, I think. It all looks the same. They have a lot of other buildings.'

Calvin Dunn spent a few more minutes looking for anything that Nancy Mills might have left, carefully opening and closing cabinets and drawers with the edge of his hand, but looking only experimentally, to be sure the police had already searched. Then he said, 'Let's go back to your place.'

When they were in the manager's apartment again, Calvin Dunn reached into his inner coat pocket and handed the manager three hundred-dollar bills. 'This is for your cooperation.'

'Thank you,' said the manager.

'You're welcome. Now get me the application.'

'I already told you—'

Calvin Dunn held up his hand to interrupt. 'I want you to think about it. You just saw that I'm a truthful man. No harm came to the apartment and you got a reward. Look at me. Do you want me to be your friend, or do you want me to be your enemy?'

The manager said, 'I can't give you that.'

Dunn lunged forward, his right arm across the manager's chest, and flipped him backward over his hip so that he landed facedown on the floor. Dunn held the manager's wrist with both hands and placed his foot against the manager's back. 'You keep a copy of the application. Where is it?'

Norris gasped. 'In the desk. Over there.'

'Thank you,' said Calvin Dunn. He released the manager, walked to the desk, pulled open the deep file drawer, and found the applications filed alphabetically. He took the photocopy of the one that Nancy Mills had filled out, and examined it closely. Then he set it on the desk. 'That will do it for me. Don't worry, your arm will be okay in a day or two.' He stepped to the door. 'You look too smart to say anything to anybody about my visit. Are you?'

The manager looked up from the floor. 'Yes.' And then Calvin Dunn was out the door and gone.

TWENTY-FOUR

The boy drove Nicole Davis to a long, one-story suburban ranch house with a low rail fence at the sidewalk and a small rustic wooden sign on the lawn that said THE GILMANS. The boy used an automatic garage-door opener, drove all the way in, and closed the door behind them before he got out of the car.

Nicole Davis looked around her at the garage in the dim light. It was big, made for three cars, and the little Mazda seemed lonely in the center of it. When the boy went to the wall and switched on the overhead light, she could see a workbench along the back wall with a vise, and a pegboard with outlines of hand tools traced on it, most of the tools in their places. She got out of the car. 'The Gilmans. Is that you? Are you a Gilman?'

'I'm a Gilman. I'm Ty. That's for Tyler.'

'Where are your parents?'

'Don't worry about them. They're at Lake Havasu right now. They won't be back for almost a week. On the way home they're going to swing by my grandmother's house in Scottsdale.'

He went to the side of the garage, unlocked it, and let her into the kitchen. She took in everything quickly. It was small and a bit worn. There were dishes in the sink and the floor was dirty. He wasn't coming in with her. She looked back to see him going to the car. He noticed her watching. 'I've got to get back to work now. I'll be home around eight. Make yourself comfortable, but don't let anybody see you. Okay?'

'Okay.' She closed the kitchen door, then listened while he opened the garage door, started the car engine, backed out, and closed the garage again. She went through the kitchen to the living room, knelt on a chair, and moved the curtain aside a quarter inch to watch him drive off.

She looked around her and had a feeling of unreality. Being here was strange and sudden. She had been rushing to get on the bus, and now she was here, alone in this quiet suburban house. He had said he'd seen her on television, so she went to search for a television set. The living room was the kind that she suspected the family seldom used. The furniture had awful patterns on it that looked defiantly fresh and clear, and there wasn't a book, magazine, or anything else on the coffee tables.

As she explored the house she wondered about the boy. She felt sympathy for his awkwardness. He looked to her as though his hands and feet had grown too fast and the rest of him had not caught up yet. His sandy blond hair had been cut short and tousled with his hands instead of combed, which unintentionally accentuated his baby face and thin neck. She could almost see his ribs through his shirt, and his pants seemed to be barely held up on his hips. He had earnest, open eyes, and his chin and cheeks were still smooth and looked soft, because his beard had not been shaved enough times to make it bristly and rough.

He had saved her life a few minutes ago. That horrible girl at the hotel had undoubtedly told the cops about her call, because it had taken them practically no time to head for the bus station. They had probably stopped the bus and dragged the people off it looking for her.

What had Ty seen on television that had induced him to get in the way of that? She kept looking for the television set. Had she missed a small one in the kitchen? No. There was a cookie jar that looked like a fat puppy on the counter. The clock in the wall was supposed to look like a sunflower, so the dark part in the center had hands on it. It said five o'clock. She went to a door past the pantry and found a kind of den, a room with only one window high on the wall, a couch, an easy chair, and a big television set.

Nicole located the remote control and turned it on, then worked her way through the channels until she found a local news show. The newswoman assumed a fake-sorry face and said something below hearing. As she was replaced by another young woman, this one dark-haired, standing in front of the Sky Inn, Nicole turned up the sound.

'. . . a murder suspect who police say was on the run from California. She apparently arrived in the Flagstaff area last evening and was scheduled to stay a second night at the hotel, but became suspicious at some point and fled, leaving her suitcase. Police have made photographs of her available.'

The scene was replaced by two pictures that Nicole recognized. One was the Illinois driver's license she had gotten years ago in the name Tanya Starling, when she had been given her first car. The other was the California license of Rachel Sturbridge. The excited voice of the young woman said, 'She is five feet five inches tall, approximately a hundred and twenty pounds. When last seen she had brown hair and blue eyes, but she has been known to wear colored contact lenses and dye her hair to alter her appearance. If you see her, call the police immediately. The number is at the bottom of your screen. Do not try to apprehend her yourself.'

Nicole switched the remote control to move from channel to channel. 'The manhunt continues for—' There was her picture again. '. . . is considered to be armed and—' This time it was a pudgy middle-aged man in a police uniform standing at a podium outside a building she didn't recognize. '. . . will be cooperating with law enforcement authorities in California, Oregon—'

She turned off the television set and realized she was hearing an unfamiliar sound, then recognized it as her own breathing, coming in shallow huffs, amplified by the intense silence in the house. She had to think. She had to make a plan, invent a way to get herself out of here.

She couldn't collect her thoughts, and she knew that the plan had to be based on knowing what the police were doing, so she turned the television set back on. The pudgy cop was saying, '. . . are now completing a building-to-building search of the blocks around the bus station where she was seen. We ask that people take alternate routes to avoid that area until we've given the all clear. We know that she purchased bus tickets to both Phoenix and Santa Fe, so authorities in both cities have been notified.'

He looked attentive while he listened to a question from a reporter, then said, 'She may have just been getting some sleep so she could go on to the next place.'

Nicole said, 'Then why are you chasing me, you fat asshole?'

She turned off the television again. All it was doing was making her so agitated that she couldn't think. Things were bad out there, but she wasn't out there anymore. She was in here, thanks to Ty.

She spent the next half hour examining the house to learn about him. What she saw confirmed her first impression. There was a mother. She had more sweat-pants than a track star, and about four or five outfits for going out, besides whatever she had taken with her. She was at least three inches taller than Nicole, but thin, like Tyler.

The father seemed to have a job that involved more physical labor than paperwork. He had three pairs of brown ankle-high boots with steel toes, and several pairs of dark blue pants that looked like the work pants that janitors and mechanics sometimes wear – almost a uniform, but not quite.

Ty's bedroom was at the far end of the house. It contained relics of his childhood – his baseball glove and bat, trophies for various sports, a row of three-inch robots on a shelf. But he was growing up. She saw a DVD player with headphones, a computer, huge posters of female rappers striking provocative poses as they danced and shouted openmouthed into wireless microphones. Ty had quite a few more expensive gadgets than Charlene had owned, but things had not changed too much.

She wandered the house to satisfy herself that everything conformed to what she had seen so far. When she reached the kitchen again, she drew the curtain on the window over the sink, just in case some neighbor had a view across the backyard. Then she washed the dirty dishes.

She could tell that they had accumulated over a couple of days, at least. There was sour-milk residue in the bottoms of half a dozen glasses, and egg yolk hardened on two plates. She decided she liked Ty's laziness and disorganization. He was still a kid and would wait until his parents were practically pulling into the driveway before he washed a dish. After a time she began to regret waiting so long to start the housework, because the sunlight was getting dimmer, and she did not dare turn on a light.

She found a bucket and mop in the laundry room off the kitchen and mopped the kitchen floor. She took a sponge and got down on her hands and knees to wash the most neglected and dirty areas near the sink and the cooktop. When she had finished the floor, she looked at the sunflower clock again and saw that she still had an hour before Ty would return.

She knew it was not a good idea to turn on the television again before his car was in the driveway, because the screen would throw light that the neighbors could see. It didn't matter. She had driven for a day without stopping, had had a partial night's sleep, had walked all over town, and had been afraid for so many hours that she was too tired to be afraid anymore. She lay on the couch in the television room, listening to the unrelieved silence in the empty house. Then she was asleep.

She awoke, startled. The light was in her eyes, and a big male shape was standing over her. She quickly rose to a crouch, and heard his voice. 'It's only me.'

'Oh,' she said. 'I guess I fell asleep.'

'Yeah, I guess you did.'

She rubbed her eyes and smoothed her hair with both hands to be sure it wasn't horrible. She made herself smile. 'How did everything go, Ty? Your job and everything.'

'No problem. When I went to find you I was on my three o'clock lunch break. I made it back and nobody paid much attention.'

'Where do you work?'

'At the Taco Rancho restaurant, up by the interstate. That was where I saw you on TV. They have the TV on all day. A lot of people think it makes the day go faster, but usually it's on some crappy thing like those fake courtrooms where people sue each other and a fake judge bitches at them.'

She smiled. 'I hate that too.'

'Well, they cut right into it today – one of those breaking-news alerts. At first everybody thought your picture was up because somebody had kidnapped you.' He shrugged. 'I could tell you were wanted, because they showed two pictures of you with different hair.'

She made her eyes wide and innocent, and kept them on his. 'I didn't do it.'

'Do what?'

'What they said I did. I want you to know I'm innocent.'

He looked down at his feet thoughtfully, then nodded. 'I brought some food. You hungry?'

'I guess I am,' she said. 'You didn't have to do that, though. I would have cooked us something.'

'It's okay. Every night I bring stuff home from the restaurant.'

'I hope you didn't buy too much more than you usually do. Somebody could notice things like that.'

'No,' he said. 'I fill my own order, pay for it, and get my own change. I got us two El Pollo Grandes and a bean burrito. We can split it.'

'Sounds great.' She reached for her purse. 'I'd like to pay you back.'

'Don't,' he said. 'We can talk about that stuff later. Come on.'

She followed him to the kitchen, where he looked around. 'Oh. You washed the dishes, huh?'

'Yes. The floor, too. It appeared as though you hadn't had time lately.'

He looked at her as though he had not liked the gentle chiding, then turned and opened the cupboard and pulled out two glasses, set them on the table, and got two plates. They sat at the kitchen table and he divided the items from his El Taco Rancho bag with scrupulous care.

'I watched TV after you left,' she said. 'They seem to be looking for me everywhere. Did you hear anything while you were at work? Do you think I'll be able to leave tonight?'

He finished chewing, then said, 'I saw a bunch of cops. They're eyeballing people in cars, and stopping some of them, mostly women driving alone.' He shrugged. 'They haven't given up.'

'Then would it be all right with you if I stay longer?'

'I think you have to. If they catch you, then I'm in trouble too.'

'Why did you help me?'

He stared at her for a few seconds, then looked away. 'I saw your picture. I thought you were nice looking. I wanted to do you a favor.'

'You could go to jail for it.'

'I know that.'

After dinner, they sat in the den on one of the couches and watched the television again, but there were no more special bulletins. At eleven, the local news shows repeated the whole story, with the same reporters standing in front of the hotel again, even though there was nothing to see. But one of them also showed a roadblock at an entrance to Interstate 40, where police officers shone flashlights on the faces of women in the cars, then waved them on.

Nicole felt her pulse rate increase again. She stood up and said, 'I'd like to take a shower. Is that okay?'

Ty said, 'I guess so.' Then he said, 'Can I watch you?'

She was paralyzed for a second. 'What?'

'Can I come and watch?'

'Why?'

He shrugged. 'I want to see you naked.'

She tried to laugh, but it came out hollow and false. 'Of course not. That isn't what you really want.'

'Yes. It is what I want,' he said. 'I've been thinking about it since I first saw you.'

'I'm so much older than you are. I'm twenty-eight, twelve years older. It would seem weird. I'd be embarrassed.'

'It's not much to ask. If I hadn't come, you'd be in jail now. Or maybe dead.'

'I'm grateful for what you're doing. I want us to be friends. That's just not the way.'

His face was darker and grimmer. He was feeling resentful, more and more unappreciated and ill-used, and she could see anger growing behind his eyes. She said, 'Haven't you ever seen a woman before?'

'No. Just movies. Pictures.'

She was desperate, miserable. She couldn't afford to make him angry and resentful. 'Look, Ty. You don't have to feel rejected, or that I'm just too selfish to give you what you want. I like you. I really do. And I know that what you're thinking about seems like something you really want, but this isn't the right time. I'm not the one.'

His eyes were fixed on the wall ahead of him. 'It's not that big a thing to you. You take off your clothes in front of doctors, people like that, people who haven't done anything for you.'

She said, 'Please, Ty.'

'Please yourself. Please.'

She sighed. 'All right then, I suppose.'

'Now?'

'If I have to.'

TWENTY-FIVE

As soon as Catherine Hobbes had learned that Tanya had been sighted in Flagstaff, she had taken a plane to Arizona. Now, as she sat in the passenger seat of the police car, staring out the window while Officer Gutierrez drove, she wondered if she had missed her again. At night Flagstaff didn't seem big enough to hide Tanya Starling. There didn't seem to be enough places for strangers to sleep, enough people on the streets to keep her from being seen. There didn't seem to be enough men.

Gutierrez was about forty years old and the sort of officer that Hobbes would have appointed to guide a visitor if she had been the one to pick. He was proper and experienced and pulled together like a military man, in a fresh uniform with razor creases and spit-shined shoes. All the steel on him shone in the dim light of the dashboard.

He drove past the hotel and around to the parking lot, then kept the car idling. 'See the window up here with the blinds drawn and the bright lights?'

'Second floor, third from the end?'

'Right. That was her room.'

Catherine Hobbes looked around to determine the lines of sight from the nearest street. 'Think she saw somebody waiting for her in her room?'

'I don't know,' he said. 'I know there were a few unmarked cars parked back here, so she might have seen them. Or maybe she's just getting into the habit of calling places to see if there are cops before she shows up. Whatever it was, she picked up the signs.' He pulled into a space. 'Ready to go in?'

'Can you show me the bus station first?'

'Sure. It's just up on South Malpais Lane.' He pulled across the lot and back out onto South Milton, drove a couple of blocks, then turned left. 'It's up ahead, there. It's been about eight hours since she's been here, though.'

'I'd like to take a look anyway,' she said. 'I'm trying to get to know her, and I'd like to see what she saw.'

Officer Gutierrez drove a few yards past the station entrance and stopped the car at the curb, then got out with Catherine Hobbes. Catherine could see the pay telephone attached to the stucco wall at the front of the building. It could have been the one Tanya had used to call the hotel, but there were probably others inside or around the back in the boarding area. It was too late to take prints from any of them now.

She pushed through the glass doors, into the station. It was late evening, but she could see that the station had the forlorn, always-two-a.m. look that bus stations had, the fluorescent lights just bright enough to make a person who was stuck here feel defeated. She walked over to the counter and picked up one of the small folded bus schedules.

While she was examining it, Gutierrez said, 'The first ticket she bought was to Santa Fe for ten o'clock tomorrow morning. She bought the one to Phoenix just before it was due to leave at five after three. That was the next bus out.'

Hobbes went to the front door, stepped out, and looked at the city. 'The hotel is about four long blocks in that direction, right?'

'Right,' said Gutierrez. 'Maybe a half mile.'

Catherine stepped back inside, then walked to the door on the opposite side of the waiting area, underneath the sign that said BOARDING – TO BUSES. She went outside again and stood under the overhanging roof. A bus came up South Malpais and made the wide turn, shouldering up the slight rise onto the blacktop, then emitting a hiss as it came to rest. The lights came on and the doors opened. The sign above the windshield that said FLAGSTAFF changed to HOLBROOK.

As Catherine watched, an assortment of people slowly made their way, one by one, down the bus's narrow steps to the pavement. They were the people Catherine had become accustomed to seeing on sweeps through the bus stations in Portland: old men and women who stared down at their feet as they walked, or very young, solitary men with faces that were pinched with watchfulness, or teenage girls in twos or threes, talking and laughing as though the rest of the world could not hear them.

The driver and a ticket agent opened the luggage compartment on the side of the bus, hauled suitcases out, and set them in a row, where passengers came to claim them. Then Catherine saw the people she had been waiting for, the first of the riders for the next leg of the bus's journey, forming a line. They were like the last group, people too young or too old to drive, people who had no money for a car. Catherine got into the line behind a lady carrying a large carpetbag, looked around her, then moved close to the bus.

She said to the ticket taker, 'Do city buses stop here? I don't see a bus stop.'

'They don't stop at the station. The nearest stop is on the corner at South Milton.'

'Thank you.'

Gutierrez stepped up to Catherine, curious. She said, 'I think somebody picked her up.'

'What do you mean – like she had someone waiting for her?'

'No. She came in here and bought the ticket to Phoenix just before the bus was going to leave. She walked to the front door, made the call to the hotel, then got into this line to board the bus.'

'Right. That's what the witnesses said.'

'But when the state police stopped the bus she wasn't on it.'

'I'm with you.'

'Well, something happened while she was standing here, right where I am, waiting to board. Something changed her mind, diverted her from the bus. But from this spot, you can't see any alternatives. There aren't any taxicabs, or rental cars, or anything else. If she had just turned and started walking, she would have been spotted. The police units arrived within a minute or two after she called the hotel, and they searched for blocks around the station, questioning everybody who might have noticed her. The only possibility is that she met somebody, and he or she gave her a ride out of the area in a private car.'

'You think she could do that? She works that fast?'

'You saw her picture. She looks young and sweet and vulnerable.' Catherine looked around her at the entrance to the station. 'The only thing I'm wondering about is who it could be. The reason people are in a bus station is that they don't have cars.'

'Whoever it is, he's going to get a big surprise.'

As Catherine stepped away from the line with Gutierrez and they walked along the street toward his police car, Calvin Dunn took a step backward behind the idling bus to keep the headlights of a passing car from shining on his face. When he had seen the two of them behind the bus station, the woman standing in line and then going with the cop, he had experienced a moment of interest. She was about the right age, size, and shape. But apparently she was just another damned cop.

TWENTY-SIX

Nicole Davis lay on the bed, her eyes open wide, staring into the darkness. She tried closing, then opening her eyes, but the darkness looked the same. She wanted not to be here, not to be who she was. She turned and listened to Tyler asleep beside her, snoring a little in his dream. She knew what he was dreaming about.

She had foreseen exactly what would happen as soon as he had gotten his wish. She had known what his next wish would be, and that there would be no way for him to resist, and no way for her to stop him. Of course she had known, because for the first time in her life she was the one who had lived enough to know what he would feel before he felt it. So now she had become the knowing seducer and the unwilling victim, both at the same time. Ty had been all eagerness and joy at what was happening, while Nicole tried to be patient and instill patience, to teach.

She felt that time had fractured and slipped, two sides meeting in the wrong place, like a break in a fault line. She should have been with him when she was sixteen too, and they would have been a match. They would have groped their way into the same experience at the same time. She would have been the way he was now – amazed. After that, she would have been so happy with a boyfriend just like Ty all those years ago, on the other side of the chasm. It would have made everything different, every moment of her life after that.

She felt a pair of wet tears spill from her eye sockets

and streak down both sides of her face to her ears. She had come a very long way from sixteen, and none of it had been the way she had imagined it.

Events seemed to be coming faster and faster now. She was being forced to make choices without warning, without having the time to consider the consequences. Whenever she made a move, the reaction to it seemed to come instantly. If she took a step, the police sirens were wailing before she could take the second step.

It was that woman cop she had talked to on the telephone: Detective Catherine Hobbes. She was probably still all the way back in Portland, but what was happening here in Flagstaff was her fault. In fact, everything that had happened since Dennis Poole had been because of Catherine Hobbes. She was the reason why there were all of these cops blocking the roads tonight.

Dennis Poole's death had been the end of a private dispute, a contest between equals. Dennis had been getting ready to accuse Tanya of taking his money. He could have gotten her sent to prison, and that would have been the end of her. She had shot him in self-defense. All that Catherine Hobbes had needed to do then was report it as a homicide, fill out her stupid police forms, hand them in, and go home. But instead she had decided to use poor Tanya Starling to transform herself into a hero. It was disgusting.

If it had not been for Catherine Hobbes, there would have been no reason for her to protect herself from people like Bill Thayer or Mary Tilson. There would have been no reason to give in to the sexual fantasies of a sixteen-year-old boy in Arizona. She lay in the dark and closed her eyes until she fell asleep.

At daybreak she awoke and looked at the sleeping face of Tyler Gilman on the pillow. It was untroubled, almost blank. He was in absolute repose, his mouth closed and his eyes unmoving.

She slid off the bed and walked to the bathroom where she had left her clothes. They were still hanging from the hook behind the door, where she had hung them as she took them off. She carried her clothes to the living room before she quietly put them on, because she wasn't ready to be with Tyler yet. As she sat alone, hugging her knees, her bare feet on the couch, she concluded that she had done the only thing she could possibly have done. If she had refused, he would not have done anything else for her. She needed for him to do much more, or she was going to be caught. It was that simple.

Now she needed to decide what she wanted him to do for her. She wanted to get out of Flagstaff. That required waiting several days, until the police had searched everywhere in town that they could search, and then having Ty drive her to another city. It should be outside Arizona.

Eventually she would need her own car, and she would need a suitcase full of clothes that didn't look much like the ones she had left in the hotel. She would have to think of a way for Ty to acquire those things without drawing attention to himself. As she considered her situation, she realized that it probably wasn't too bad. All she had to do was control Tyler Gilman.

She heard him stirring. There was a thump as he bounced off the bed to the floor. She heard him pad up the hallway toward the living room, then felt the vibration as he walked across the room to her.

He was standing in front of her, a blanket wrapped around him. 'I woke up, and I was afraid that you were gone – that you had left while I was sleeping.'

She slowly lifted her head to face him. 'I'm not gone. It's just that you made me do a serious, important thing last night, when I didn't want to. That's why your mind did that to you.'

'I'm sorry,' he said. 'I mean, I'm not sorry I did it. I'm just sorry for you, that you feel bad.'

'I understand. I told you last night that I understood why you wanted that. It's the way men are.' She stood and walked toward the kitchen. 'I'll make your breakfast. You like eggs, don't you?'

'Are you mad at me?'

She looked at him pensively. 'It's too late for that now. You did something big and risky for me, and then in return you wanted something big from me, that's all. So now it's another day. What kind of eggs do you like?'

'Will you ever let me again?'

She cocked her head. 'I don't know. After we've had breakfast and a shower and brushed our teeth, I might think about it. Now go sit down at the table.'

He walked toward the kitchen. As he passed close to her, she noticed that he lowered his eyes. He would be fine.

TWENTY-SEVEN

Calvin Dunn sat in a winged armchair in the farthest corner of the Sky Inn lobby, so that his back was against the wall in the corner next to the stone fireplace. There was no fire tonight, because the temperature had been in the nineties today, and the heat lingered in the brick walls of the building. Calvin Dunn read the newspaper.

It seemed to him that the story of the female serial killer had already begun to get overripe in Flagstaff. It was not on the front page anymore. There were enough car accidents and killings of local people by their friends and neighbors to keep the cops busy and provide the reporters with copy. Nobody seemed excited anymore by the girl's visit to town. She was like a cloud that had passed overhead without getting anybody wet.

He lifted his eyes over the newspaper and watched the young man at the front desk. It was after two a.m. and the last guest had come into the lobby an hour ago, but the clerk was always busy looking busy, trying to keep himself in line for a promotion to – what? Head night clerk? He was the only night clerk. This time of night he was running low on things to do, so he polished his counter with a can of Pledge and a hotel washcloth. He was aware of Calvin Dunn's presence, and looked up at him occasionally.

Calvin Dunn folded his newspaper under his arm, stood up, and walked to the desk.

The clerk said, 'Can I help you, sir?'

'Do you happen to be the one who checked in that girl I've been reading about in the newspapers?'

'Yes, sir. That was me.'

Calvin Dunn looked interested. 'That must have been something. What was she like?'

It was a momentous question, one the young man had probably been asked many times at first, but that people had stopped asking since the girl had disappeared. 'She was really nice looking. That was the first thing I noticed, the first thing anybody would notice. But then, when I asked her for a credit card, she said she didn't use them. She didn't look like the kind of person who doesn't use them. She didn't look poor, or political, or anything.'

'She's a criminal,' said Calvin Dunn. 'I would have expected a criminal would be eager to use a credit card – somebody else's, of course.'

'I wouldn't really know,' said the clerk. 'But she had a purse full of cash. I could see it when she paid for her room. I thought for a minute that maybe she was, like, a movie star who didn't want to be recognized.'

'Happen to see a gun?'

'No. I'm sure she probably had one, but she didn't let me see it.'

'You know, you might have been killed.'

'I know,' said the young man. He seemed pleased that at last somebody had realized it.

'The thing is, you were brave to turn her in.'

'Not really,' he said. 'I was at home, and I happened to see her picture on television. I called the police from my apartment.'

'That's what I mean. You were the only one who recognized her, and turned her in.' He paused. 'The only one.'

'I was?'

'Yeah,' said Calvin Dunn. 'She's probably given a lot of

thought to you during the past couple of days. Of course, there were other people later who said they remembered her going by one place or stopping in another. You and I know that it's mostly because people hate it when anything big happens right in front of their noses and they don't see it. So they convince themselves that they did see it. The point is, you were the only one who really did notice and got the police after her.'

The young man seemed uncomfortable. 'Are you a police officer?'

'No,' said Calvin Dunn. 'I work for the family of one of the victims.'

'I wondered why you were sitting by the fireplace reading the newspaper so late at night, so I thought you were the police, watching me.'

'You're not far off.'

The young man looked into his eyes and understood. 'You've been waiting for *her*, haven't you? You think she's going to come back here and try to kill me.'

Calvin Dunn said, 'The thought had crossed my mind.'

'Oh, man.'

'It's just a precaution. The police are watching the bus station and the car rental places and the airport and even the highway entrance ramps. They've got all the rational places covered. They know what she looks like, and if she shows up where they are, they'll probably get her.'

'You sound as though you don't think she will.'

'She's got another side besides the rational one, and that makes all the difference. She looks as though she wouldn't say boo to a goose, but once in a while, she pulls out a big old pistol and shoots a guy through the head. That shows that she doesn't necessarily do what other people would do.'

'But she wouldn't get anything from killing me.'

'It's hard to say what she got from killing those other

people either. Some killers get a thrill out of it, and some are just pissed off.' He shrugged. 'I'm a little surprised that the police haven't considered the same thing. They're acting as though they think she's already a thousand miles from here.'

'You don't think she is?'

'I don't know, and neither do they.'

'Are you planning to stay here until my shift ends?'

'If you don't mind.'

'Not at all,' said the young man. 'Make yourself comfortable.' He held out his hand. 'My name is Donald Holman.'

Calvin Dunn shook his hand. 'I know that. Calvin Dunn.'

'You know, the light up here in the lobby is better for reading. Hardly anybody sits by the fireplace in the summer.'

'I noticed that. But it's the only place where someone outside can't see me through the windows.'

'Oh. Yeah. Well, if you need anything while I'm on duty, just let me know.'

'You know, there is just one thing. Do you, by any chance, have a woman staying here named Catherine Hobbes?'

Donald looked troubled. 'I'm really not supposed to talk about any of the people staying here.'

'I didn't ask for her room number or anything. I could go over to the house phone over there and ask the operator to connect me with her room.'

'I know,' said Donald. 'It's a silly rule. She is staying here. She flew in from Portland to interview me a few hours after I reported Tanya. After that Detective Hobbes checked in, and one of the local cops told me she wanted to be in this hotel because she likes to see everything that Tanya Starling sees.'

'Maybe that works for her. What it does for me is put you both in one place, and that makes this the place to be.'

Donald frowned. 'You think she's in danger too?'

Calvin Dunn shrugged. 'She's a detective hunting for a serial killer, she's in a strange town where the serial killer is – or was – and the killer knows her name. The thing that keeps cops alive isn't that they're especially smart, which most of them aren't, or tough, which a few of them are. It's that they come in bunches, an inexhaustible supply, like ants. But she's here alone.'

'I guess you're right. She's probably as much of a target as I am.'

Calvin Dunn was leaning on his elbows at the counter with his arms folded. He straightened, and his right hand opened his coat to reach into his inner pocket. Donald saw the knurled handgrips of the big pistol in its shoulder holster, but the coat closed again and Calvin Dunn held a thin stack of hundred-dollar bills. 'Tonight I expect to be in sight of you until your shift ends, but maybe I won't be tomorrow. This is five hundred, and here's my card. I would like you to call my cell phone number any time Detective Hobbes goes out or has a visitor. If you happen to overhear anything, I can promise you a lot more.'

'Gee, I don't know . . .'

'Please take it. She's a dear friend of mine, and she's just too proud and stubborn to let me protect her.' Then he had Donald's wrist in a grip that wasn't hard, but it was so strong that Donald was afraid to let any of his muscles contract for fear the grip would tighten and break his wrist. Dunn put the money into his hand, then released him.

'I shouldn't be taking this money, or spying on a policewoman.'

'It's for her own good, and yours. This way I can keep an eye on both of you at once.'

'But I don't feel right about taking the money.'

'I'm going outside to look around the parking lot now,' said Calvin Dunn. 'And don't worry about my money. The only reason to have money is to help your friends.'

TWENTY-EIGHT

It was Thursday morning, and Nicole sat at Tyler Gilman's computer in his bedroom. The scanner he had beside his printer had given her an idea. She scanned the pattern from the back of an honor roll certificate that had been posted on Ty's wall onto a blank sheet of paper. She did it on four sheets, then turned over the paper and did it on the reverse side. 'Ty,' she called. 'Help me think of a new name.'

He lay on the bed, staring up at the ceiling. 'How about Tara?'

'Too unusual.'

'You are unusual.'

'No. I want something that sounds like everybody else's name. I want to fade, Ty. I want to be invisible for, like, two years, and have a life.'

'Victoria? Veronica? Melissa?'

'Too long. Maybe I'll be an Anne. Let me see. Foster, no, Forster. Anne Forster.'

'That's good,' said Ty. 'That's really good.'

She reached into her purse, took out the disk she carried, and put it into the computer. She opened the file containing the blank birth certificate. She selected the type font that fit the rest of the document and filled in the blanks to make Anne Forster a woman born twenty-two years ago, on the nineteenth of July. She put one of her sheets of paper with the filigree patterns on it into the printer and printed the certificate. Ty reached for it, but she said, 'Don't touch it. The ink will smudge.'

He stopped himself, and held his head at an angle to see the certificate in the tray. 'It's just like the real thing. What should my name be?'

'Your name?'

'Yeah,' he said. 'It should sound real too. How about Joshua? Josh Forster.'

'Uh . . . not quite right.' She managed to conceal her surprise, but her mind was not moving quickly enough. 'Who are you?'

'What do you mean?'

'Why do you and I have the same last name? What are you trying to be?'

'Your husband.'

She smiled indulgently, but she shook her head. 'That's so sweet. But Ty, you're twelve years younger than I am. That difference is three-quarters of your life. Nobody would believe we were married. More likely, they'd think I was one of those teachers who run off with one of their students. They'd call the police.'

She saw his eyes begin to cloud, and he lay back on the bed and stared at the ceiling. She had said too much, and she had to fix things instantly or she was in trouble. 'How about my brother? You could easily be my brother. That way, if we traveled together, people wouldn't think anything of it.'

'I don't want to be your brother.'

'Ty, please. Don't insist on taking extra risks. Our lives could depend on this. We can't be lazy-minded and draw attention to ourselves.'

'I don't even look like your brother.'

She thought about what she had seen of his parents' room. 'Does your mother dye her hair to get rid of the gray?'

'Yeah.'

She got up and went into the master bathroom off Ty's

parents' bedroom. When Ty caught up with her she was opening cabinets and drawers. She knelt at an open cabinet under the sink, and took out a hair dye box with a picture of a beautiful woman on the front. She stood and pulled Ty to the mirror, then held the box up beside his hair. 'Look. Her hair color is exactly the same as yours.'

'You're going to dye your hair the color of mine?'

'Yes.'

'Our eyes are different.'

'My eyes are a paler blue than yours,' she said, 'but I have blue contacts. And brown and green. But I'll wear the blue. We'll look amazing.'

He said nothing, just stared unhappily into the mirror at her. She looked at him from the corner of her eye. 'Brothers and sisters can stay in the same hotel room at night. They do it all the time to save money.'

He smiled.

'Come on. Help me.'

'Now?'

'Yes, now. Ty, we've only got about three days left before your parents show up. Anything we need to do to prepare has to be done well before then. And some little thing might be what saves us.' She tore open the top of the box.

'What if she notices it's missing?'

'I don't know,' she said. 'She probably won't notice, at least right away. She's got three boxes. I do know that if she can't find a box of hair dye, what she does about it isn't going to be calling the police. That's all I care about.' She started to take small bottles and plastic gloves out of the box and set them on the sink.

'This looks really messy.'

'It is.'

'Then let's do it in my bathroom.'

'But that's smaller and darker.'

'If they come back and we're gone, you don't want them to figure out what happened right away. If there's a stain on the counter or something, they'll know the exact color you dyed your hair.'

She stared at him. He kept surprising her. She followed him into his bathroom and set up her kit on his sink. She pulled her top off over her head, and heard the intake of breath from Ty. 'Don't,' she said. 'Not now. I just can't take a chance that I'll stain my clothes. I don't have any except these.'

He said, 'I . . . I'm sorry. I should have thought about that. I have, like, three hours before I have to go to work. I can go out and buy you some now. I'll bring them when I get back from work.'

'Where were you thinking of going?'

'I don't know. The mall?'

'Go someplace big, where nobody pays any attention to you and you put stuff in a shopping cart. Is there a Wal-Mart or a Target or something?'

'Yeah. Both.'

'Then I'll give you a list of what I need, with my sizes. Buy some stuff for yourself, too, and mix it all together, like it's for your family. Okay?'

'Sure.'

She stepped into his room, took a blank sheet of paper from the printer, and wrote out her list. She picked up her purse and took out some money. 'This is six hundred dollars. If you spend all of it in one place, they'll notice you.' She handed him the list, and watched him read it. 'Can you handle all of that?'

He shrugged uncomfortably. 'I can do it. I've bought things for my mom.'

'Just do your best, Ty. Be careful.' She leaned close and kissed him slowly, passionately, then held him at arm's length. 'The thing I care about most is that you keep yourself safe. If anything in or around the store doesn't seem right, then avoid the place. Don't go in.'

'Okay,' he said.

'Then go. Get the exact sizes I said. Try to stick with dark colors and earth tones. Don't worry about the lengths of the pants. I'll shorten them if they're too long. And try to find me a small, cheap suitcase with wheels, about the size to hold the clothes.'

She kissed him again, and he looked a bit dazed. He didn't want to go. His arms lingered around her, until she grasped his wrists and removed them. She spun him around and pushed him toward the door. 'Get going!' She snatched a pillow from the bed and hurled it in his direction. He sidestepped it easily and was out the door.

She listened to his footsteps going out, then the sound of the car. She went into the bathroom, took off the rest of her clothes, and opened the bottles. The strong, acrid odor of the chemicals filled the room. Some people hated that smell, but for her it brought back very early memories. The first time she had smelled that smell she had been five. Charlene and her mother had arrived in the downtown hotel the night before the Tiny Miss Milwaukee pageant, and she and her mother had gone down to the ballroom to watch the other contestants being brought in by their mothers for registration. As they watched the other little girls, her mother had looked increasingly worried. Finally she had locked Charlene in their room, gone to a drugstore down the street, and come back with two hair-dyeing kits. The next morning at the opening of the pageant, Charlene and Sharon Buckner had appeared with the same fresh golden hair and the same carefully applied makeup. They had looked almost alike, the pretty daughter like a miniature of the pretty mother.

As she worked, she reflected that it was a relief that

Ty was gone. The dyeing wasn't difficult to do, but it did require that she pay attention to the time, and he was always trying to distract her.

She finished, and she could tell even while it was still wet that she had done a very good job. She went to her purse, found the little plastic case with her colored contacts in it, selected the blue ones, and put them in. She stood in front of the mirror. 'I'm a Gilman.'

TWENTY-NINE

Catherine Hobbes waited until Officer Gutierrez had pulled into the long-term parking lot at the airport and come to a complete stop. 'This is probably about as close as we ought to get,' he said.

They both got out of the patrol car and Catherine walked toward Mary Tilson's small gray Honda. She could see uniformed officers outside the perimeter of yellow tape that had been set up around the car. They were stringing more tape to force cars coming into the lot to go up another aisle, one that led away from the technicians who were working around the Honda.

Catherine reached the tape, and a police officer in a pair of suit pants and a white shirt with a lieutenant's badge clipped on the pocket stepped up to meet her.

When he talked she could see him making decisions. Even though he must have seen her get out of Gutierrez's patrol car, he had to verify that she was Hobbes. 'Hello. Are you Sergeant Hobbes?'

'Yes,' she said.

Next he had to tell her that he was in charge. 'I'm Lieutenant Hartnell.'

She held out her hand so he could shake it. 'Pleased to meet you.'

She saw him decide that he wanted to have her think he was informal and spontaneous, not the sort of man who made decisions every time he spoke, so he said, 'Steve Hartnell' as he shook her hand.

'My name is Catherine.' She had her small notebook in her hand, and she compared the California license number on the plate of the Honda with the number in her notebook, then put the notebook away.

Hartnell said, 'We've got it roped off so we can screen the area around the car for footprints, dropped items, and so on. The flatbed will be here in a few minutes to bring it in so we can have the trace evidence people give it a closer look.'

'Do you know the time when it was left here?'

'The ticket is on the floor on the passenger side, as though she tossed it there after she took it and the automatic stile went up. It says three forty-eight a.m., two nights ago. In a way, it's a relief. It means she went to the terminal and took a taxi right to the Sky Inn. She didn't have time to stop off and kill a family of six.'

Catherine ignored the last sentence because she was thinking about Tanya. 'She must have been exhausted.'

Hartnell looked at her as though he wondered about her sanity.

Catherine saw his expression. 'She killed a woman in Los Angeles early in the evening, cleaned her whole apartment, packed up, and drove off in the victim's car. She must have stopped somewhere for a day and traveled after dark, but it took her until three a.m. on the second night to get here. I think she must have been worn out.'

'I'm not exactly moved to sympathy,' said Hartnell.

'I'm just ruling a few things out in my own mind,' Catherine said. 'I don't think she had somebody here that she was trying to reach – somebody who would take her in or help her get away. At four a.m. the person would almost certainly have been home, and she would have gone there. Instead, she ditched the car here and went to the Sky Inn. I think she probably stopped here because she was falling asleep at the wheel.'

'But somebody picked her up within a minute after she called the hotel from the bus station the next day,' said Hartnell. 'She could have made an arrangement for that during the daytime. Maybe the accomplice worked nights or wasn't home until then.'

'I don't think so,' said Catherine. 'She seems to be an expert at getting people to help her, to take an interest in her. Usually it's a man, but it doesn't have to be. I think that's what got Mary Tilson killed. She befriended the young woman who lived across the hall in her apartment building. She had invited her into her kitchen and started to get her something to eat or drink when she got stabbed.'

'Do you have any way to use that?' asked Hartnell.

'I think we've got to concentrate on the person who picked Tanya up. If he drove her someplace, we need to know where he let her off. If he's still with her, we need to persuade him to turn her in.'

Hartnell seemed to be making one of his decisions. He said carefully, 'I'll talk to the chief about having a press conference.'

'Great,' said Catherine. 'I also think we ought to check with your missing persons section to find out if there's anybody with a car who hasn't been seen in the past two days.'

'Good idea,' he said. 'See you later.' As he walked to his unmarked car, Catherine knew that she had gone too far, trying to tell a lieutenant in another state how he ought to organize his investigation. She had alienated him. She watched him start his car and drive out of the parking lot.

She turned to look at the car again, and thought about Tanya. She had been stuck in Los Angeles, on the verge of being discovered because of the photograph on the front page of the *Daily News*. She must have reacted desperately to get herself out – gone across the hall and stabbed her sixty-year-old neighbor to death just to steal her car. She had driven the car just about as long as she could without getting spotted: she had probably known that she had to get rid of it before daylight. When she had run out of time, she had ditched the car here. She had picked a place where she could leave it with a collection of other cars, and not have anyone wonder about it for a few days. She had been trying to buy time. She was pressed. She was running hard, and she was feeling vulnerable and scared.

Officer Gutierrez appeared at Catherine's shoulder. 'Looks as though she didn't leave any footprints or anything. The tow truck is here.'

'We may as well go,' Catherine said. 'Can you drop me at the station?'

'Sure.'

Gutierrez drove her to the station and let her out at the front entrance. 'What are you going to do now?' he asked.

'I'm going to try to persuade Lieutenant Hartnell to get me a chance to talk to Tanya.'

THIRTY

Driver's licenses were difficult, and they were the form of identification that counted. She judged that the Rachel Sturbridge driver's license from California was the best one to scan. It had been issued most recently, and it had the greatest number and variety of devices on it to deter counterfeiters. There was a large color picture of her on the left side, a smaller one on the right, and lots of overlapping silver hologram state seals with the letters DMV. But once she was out of California, the address and numbers had no meaning to anyone.

She scanned the Rachel Sturbridge license onto a CD, typed in the name Anne Margaret Forster, her new eye color, hair color, and birth date, printed and cropped it, then inserted it into the plastic sleeve in her wallet. With the slight clouding, the license looked perfect.

She scanned Ty's high school group picture, and began to play with the images. In a few minutes she had separated Ty's face from the others and superimposed it on the image of the California license. Then she typed in the name James Russell Forster. She put in a new eight-digit number in red and changed the birth date. Then she printed it and cut it to size.

She took off her clothes and washed them with Ty's. While the clothes were in the dryer she took a hot bath. Before it got dark she found Ty's mother's nail kit and did her nails. In the last of the natural light she did her makeup and brushed her hair.

When she heard Ty's car come up the driveway, she moved to the kitchen to wait for him. She heard the garage door open and the car glide in. Ty closed the garage door, then came to the kitchen door, opened it, and turned on the light. He was carrying a bag of food from El Taco Rancho.

'Welcome home, Ty.'

At first he was startled, but he recovered quickly. He stepped closer to her, looked at her hair, stared into her eyes. 'Unbelievable.'

'Do you like it?'

'It's awesome. You look like my aunt.'

'Now I'm your aunt?'

'I didn't mean that,' he said. 'You just look a little bit like her. Not like she looks now. It's my aunt Darlene, my mother's sister. You're a lot younger, but I bet that's what she looked like when she was young. She was supposed to be hot. My father says she was a piece of ass, but now she's just a pain in the ass.' He walked around her in a circle. 'I can't get over this. You look so different. Your eyes and everything.'

'So it looks all right?'

'Yeah, it does. It's a turn-on.'

'You're a sixteen-year-old boy. Everything is a turn-on to you.'

'Everything about you is.' He set the bag of food on the counter and put his arms around her, so she had to kiss him. When his hands began to move from her waist, she grasped them and held on.

'I've got some other things to show you. Come on.' She pulled him to his bedroom, where she had the new birth certificate and driver's license for James Russell Forster.

He picked them up and looked from one to the other. 'Man, I can hardly believe this. It's . . . like, perfect. Can you make me one that says I'm twenty-one?'

She laughed. 'You mean so you can get into bars?'

'Yeah.'

'I want you to use this one when we're traveling.' She grinned. 'But later I'll do my best.'

'That's all I ask.' He went to his closet, opened the door, and took off his uniform shirt. As he pulled out a clean shirt, she saw something.

'Is that a gun?'

He reached into the corner of the closet and grasped it by the walnut foregrip and pulled it out. 'Yeah. See? It was my father's old one, the first one he ever had, when he was my age. It's a thirty-ought-six.'

She touched the smooth wooden stock, the bolt, and the scope. 'Have you ever fired it?'

'Hell, yes. A million times. I'm a great shot.'

'What have you shot at?'

'Deer, elk.'

'You kill deer?'

'We didn't last year. My dad had to work weekends for practically the whole season, and I had football practice.'

'But you've used it?'

'Yeah. Now you're going to tell me you hate me because I iced Bambi's mom, aren't you?'

She realized she must have had a lapse of concentration and let him see her disenchantment with hunting. She touched his arm. 'There's nothing about you I don't like, Ty. You're a special person.'

He put the rifle back in the closet, turned back to her, and said, 'Shit. I forgot to bring in all the stuff I bought. It's still in the trunk.' He hurried out of the room, then came back a few minutes later with three large shopping bags.

He reached into his pocket. 'I had about sixty bucks left from buying that stuff.'

'Hold on to it. I need to give you more, so you can get some supplies tomorrow for the trip.'

He studied her. 'Is that when we're leaving?'

She shrugged. 'The longer we wait, the safer it is. But I'd like to be out of here at least two days before your parents show up.' She frowned. 'Why don't they ever call you?'

'They do. They called me about five times while they were in Lake Havasu. I think they were feeling guilty. Or maybe they just wanted to be sure I was going to work. Since then I called them twice on my cell phone.'

She grinned. 'You don't want me to hear what you're saying, huh? Do you call them "Mommy" and "Daddy"?'

'No,' he said. 'I just don't want any trouble. If they heard you talking or I sounded like somebody was with me, we'd be screwed.' He asked, 'Where are we going? We haven't talked about it at all.'

'I don't know.'

'Where were you going before?'

'I didn't know then, either. We need to get out of Flagstaff, out of this part of the country, where people expect to spot me. Beyond that, it doesn't matter. Every place has something nice about it.'

'But we have to be heading somewhere.'

'I have an idea. After dinner, why don't you go on the Internet and see if you can work out a route heading east, with maps and everything?'

'Okay,' he said. 'I'll map out a couple of ways, in case the first one is too dangerous.'

'Good idea.' Then she added, 'Jim.'

'Thanks, Anne.'

After dinner she cleared the table and went into the living room to examine the clothes he had bought. She looked into the first bag with trepidation, but in it she found two pairs of pants – one black, which was perfect, and one brown, which was ugly – a pair of blue jeans, and a pair of Nike running shoes. The tags told her he had bought the sizes she had given him. She was relieved.

In another bag were six pairs of socks, six pairs of panties, and three bras, supposedly obtained for the price of two. She thought of Ty going into that section of the store to buy those things and it made her smile. He had bought himself a jacket, as though to assuage his embarrassment.

The third bag had a couple of T-shirts, one of which had a picture of a cat and said 'Cat-fight Boxing'; the other said 'Hotel Juicy.' The sweatshirt with them mercifully said nothing. There were three other tops, one a hideous pink, one sky blue, and the other the sort of green that people wore on St. Patrick's Day. All of the tops were completely wrong for her, but with the exception of the green top, none of them stood out, and all seemed to be the right sizes. She had never been seen wearing anything like them before. The more she considered the clothes, the happier she was.

She noticed that Ty was standing in the doorway, looking at her anxiously, so she said, 'Ty, this is just fabulous. You did a wonderful job, much better than I ever expected.' She put her arms around his neck and hugged him.

'Did I get the right sizes?'

'I haven't tried them on yet, but the tags say you got what I asked for.'

'How about the suitcase?'

She took it out of the bag, unzipped it, and said, 'It's perfect. Thank you so much.' She busied herself removing all of the tags and pins, and throwing them in the trash with the plastic bags. Then she went into Ty's parents' bathroom to try on the clothes. She went through the process quickly, and found that everything would serve its purpose. Since she had been trying to hide, she had found little in the refrigerator, and nothing Ty had brought home from El Taco Rancho was more than marginally edible, so she had lost weight. She put on the black pants and the sky blue top, and went back to Ty's bedroom.

She opened his closet and studied herself in the full-length mirror that was attached to the closet door. Today she had made some good progress. She studied her eyes, her hair, her clothes. She looked like a new person again, and felt strong. She heard the sound of the ink-jet printer taking in a sheet of paper, and raised her eyes slightly to look into the mirror at the part of the room behind her.

Ty was printing his maps and directions, but he wasn't looking at the printer. He was staring at her now, looking at her longingly, hoping that the lightning was going to strike again.

She looked into the mirror at herself. 'They fit,' she said. She locked her eyes on his. She had to keep him happy, just a little bit longer. She began slowly, deliberately, to take off her new clothes.

Two hours later she lay on the couch in Tyler's bathrobe with her head on his lap. As he held the remote control and flicked from channel to channel, she said, 'Stop.' The policeman with the potbelly that hung out over his silver belt buckle was behind the podium again.

Behind the chief were four severe-looking men in suits and a woman in a navy blue pantsuit with the cuffs and collar of a white silk blouse showing. She liked the look of it, she decided. She would probably look good in navy, now that her hair was light again.

'Nicole?'

'Anne. Learn to call me Anne. Get used to it, Jimmy, because we leave in a day. We're Anne and James Forster.'

'Do you think—'

'Hush,' she said. 'I want to hear this.' She took the remote control out of his hand and turned up the volume.

The chief said, '. . . and now I would like to let Detective Sergeant Catherine Hobbes of the Portland, Oregon, Police Bureau have the microphone.'

'Oh, my God,' Anne whispered. 'It's her.'

'It's who?'

Someone off camera shouted, 'Sergeant!'

'I'll be around to take questions after the conference,' said Catherine Hobbes. 'I just wanted to speak for a moment to Tanya Starling. Tanya, we've spoken on the telephone, so you probably recognize my voice.'

'You bet I do, bitch.'

'If you're anyplace where you're able to hear me, I want to appeal to you to turn yourself in now. If you can't get to a police station, just dial nine-one-one, and officers will come to pick you up and take you there. At this moment police organizations in at least fifteen states are watching for you, and it's only a matter of time until you're found.'

In the pause, Anne said, 'Fuck you.'

'I know you're frightened,' said Catherine Hobbes. 'But everything I told you on the telephone still holds. I can guarantee your safety if you will come in voluntarily.'

'You see?' said Anne. 'She's threatening me, trying to scare me and get her face on television at the same time.'

Tyler Gilman gaped at her. He had never seen her when she wasn't in control of her emotions. She seemed to be irrationally angry.

'She's hounding me. She won't leave me alone until she runs me down and gets her cops to kill me.'

'She doesn't seem like that,' said Tyler.

Catherine Hobbes left the podium, and the chief took her place. He said, 'We believe that someone picked up Tanya Starling and gave her a ride away from the Flagstaff bus station in a private car. I urge and appeal to this person to call the police immediately. We need to know where you took her, what name she is using, and anything else that might hasten her apprehension. I caution you that her appearance is deceptive. We believe she is armed and extremely dangerous. If you are with her now, you are in peril. Get as far as possible from her right now and dial nine-one-one. You need not fear prosecution. We believe that you merely intended to help a stranger in need.'

'Liar!' said Anne Forster. 'He's lying.'

'Him too?'

'They all are. She's just the worst, because she's decided I'm going to be the one that makes her into a success.'

'It'll be okay.'

'No, it won't. People think the devil is a cartoon character, all red with horns, but that's not what it is. It's a person like that, all self-righteous and sure that anything they do to you is right because you have to be punished. She keeps trying to tempt me. She says, "Come in," like she was asking me to come to the doctor's for a checkup. But as soon as I let them know where I am, the cops will come and nobody will ever see me again. They'll take me out into the desert and shoot me.'

'You really think they'd do that?'

'Do you believe her instead of me? Did she come to your house because you said to, and have sex with you to prove that she was a sincere person?'

'Obviously not, but—'

'But what?'

'Don't worry about her,' Tyler said. 'She can't do anything.'

'You look at her, and I know you only see that she's pretty, and she's talking with a soft voice, so you think she must be telling the truth. She's not. Take a look. See her standing there? That's what death looks like.'

The press conference vanished from the screen, and the television stayed on, but neither of them was watching or listening to it, so after a half hour, they turned it off, went into Tyler's room, and collapsed on the bed.

She awoke early the next morning and started to make her preparations for departure. She packed her suitcase, then went to Ty's closet and dresser to pack a suitcase for him too. When they spoke they practiced calling each other Anne and Jim.

Later that morning she sent him out to run errands. The first was to fill the Mazda's tank with gas. 'Jimmy, when you're trying to get away from a place, you don't take a single risk that isn't necessary, and you prepare. Stopping for gas anywhere near here later with me in the car is foolish, so we won't do it. You do it alone ahead of time, when it's safe.'

'Sure,' he said.

'And go to the grocery store. I made a short list, and here's the money. Buy at least twelve bottles of water, some nuts – peanuts, cashews, almonds – a few candy bars, some apples, and pears.'

'What's all that stuff for?'

'The drive. We don't know how long we'll be on the road. In this heat we'll need water, and the nuts have fat and protein, so they prevent you from being hungry, and they keep. And by the way, Jimmy. Don't just buy gas. Check the oil, water, tire pressure, and whatever too. We get one chance at this.'

'I guess I'll get started,' he said. 'What time do you want to leave?'

'Tonight. Right after you finish work.'

'Why then?'

'Because your going to work gives us extra time before anybody notices that anything else is wrong. Just before you leave, tell your boss you want to take tomorrow night and the next night off. Your parents have car trouble in Lake Havasu and you have to go get them and leave the other car there to be fixed.'

'I don't think he's going to be okay with that.'

'You say, "Gee, I'm sorry, but I don't have any choice. If you have to fire me for it, then you do."'

He looked at her with admiration. 'That's really good.'

'Either way, it keeps anybody from noticing you're gone until your parents get home, which gives us two full days. Now get going.'

He went out, and she listened to his car going up the street. She selected the clothes she wanted to wear for the trip and laid them out on the bed: the black pants and the blue top, with the sweatshirt out where she could reach it if she got cold during the night drive. She took out some clothes of Tyler's too.

Now that she was used to Tyler's computer and scanner and could make birth certificates and driver's licenses, she made sets in the names Barbara Harvey, Robin Hayes, Michelle Taylor, Laura Kelly, and Judith Nathan. She spent hours diligently performing the kind of cleaning that she had done before in the other places where she had lived. She managed to finish wiping down the surfaces in the master bedroom and bathroom, the den, and the living room before Tyler returned with the supplies.

She cooked a steak and baked potato for Tyler's lunch, and served it on plates from the best set she could find in the cupboards, with crystal stemware for his milk. 'This is the way you deserve to be cared for, Jimmy. I want you to know what it's going to be like when we get settled somewhere.'

Before noon he left to go to work. She made such a big event of his departure that she was afraid for a moment that she had done too much and he would refuse to leave her for his final night of work. While he was gone she cleaned the rest of the house of all traces of her presence, did the rest of the packing, showered and washed her hair, then searched the shower stall for any hairs of hers that might have fallen. She knew that her hair was exactly the color of Tyler's mother's, but she did it anyway.

She dressed and then prepared herself, sitting alone in the house that had now fallen into darkness. When Tyler came in the kitchen door he had to walk through the house, looking for her. He found her in his bedroom, sitting on the bed, looking grave. Beside her on the bed lay his rifle and two boxes of .30-06 ammunition.

'What is it, Anne? What's wrong?'

'You know,' she said. 'You saw last night.'

'What do you mean?'

'All day I kept telling myself what I always do – that next time it will be better, next time things will be different. But it won't. There's really only one thing we can do.'

'What do you mean?'

'We've got to get rid of her.'

THIRTY-ONE

Catherine Hobbes had been in the Flagstaff police headquarters for eighteen hours, and she was tired. She had helped to work the leads that developed every time Tanya made a move – the abandoned car, the witnesses at the hotel and in the stores between the hotel and the bus station. As the time of the press conference had approached, she had been gripped by nervous energy that had lasted until she finished speaking in front of the cameras and then left her feeling drained and anxious. Finally she had spent hours sorting through the dozens of calls from tipsters, all the time waiting for a call from Tanya, hoping that something she had said would persuade her to pick up the phone.

There was no way of knowing whether Tanya was hiding in a place where there was no television, or had managed to escape beyond the range of the television broadcast, or had heard Catherine's plea and ignored her.

Everything Tanya Starling did made Catherine Hobbes uncomfortable. Serial killers usually had patterns and compulsions that made them perform a series of killings in the same way, often with elaborate planning and victims who were similar. Tanya didn't seem to do anything the same way twice in succession. Maybe she killed people out of fear.

It was confusing, because she didn't act as though she was afraid. She didn't hide from potential victims; she seemed to seek them out. She went to resorts and hotels and restaurants to find them. Tanya appeared to form relationships with strangers effortlessly. She cultivated them, made them trust her. She convinced them that she was smart and attractive and personable, and they didn't seem to notice that she was missing something. She was like a machine that didn't have some crucial part. The motor whirred and the wheels turned, but it didn't work right.

Hobbes had wanted to try to talk to her one more time. Tanya seemed to be susceptible to self-interest, and that implied that if she were approached in exactly the right way, she might be persuaded to come in quietly. Hobbes had now made two attempts, and both had failed.

Around eleven-thirty, after the press conference had been repeated on the eleven o'clock news, the telephone calls had increased for a while, then gradually stopped, and the police officers in the station had begun to look at her with curiosity, obviously wondering when she was going to give up.

She stood up, stretched, stepped out of the station, and got into her rental car. She drove along Route 66, then turned down South Milton Street toward the hotel. It was going to be another night when she arrived at the hotel long after the kitchen had closed, and it was too late for dinner.

She supposed that it wasn't so bad. There was something awkward and depressing about sitting in a restaurant alone late at night. People at that hour in restaurants were in groups or couples, and they always seemed to her to be looking at her strangely. Men were either considering offering her their company or forming theories as to why she was alone. Women seemed to think either that she was to be pitied or was up to something, possibly attracting the attention of their husbands.

She knew it was the aloneness that made her think about Joe Pitt again. He had begun to make more frequent appearances in her consciousness over the past few days. She was still not sure whether their relationship was going anywhere, but she missed him. He had called her in Portland the day after their impromptu dinner, and they had stayed on the phone for half an hour, talking like teenagers. But when she had received the news that Tanya had been sighted in Flagstaff, she had left Portland without letting him know. She wasn't used to calling men, but maybe she should.

Catherine gave a silent huff of air as she drove, a laugh at herself and her firm rules and requirements. She had a big foolish crush on him. As soon as she reached her hotel room, she would be forward and give him a call. He would undoubtedly be out at this hour, doing everything that she didn't like to imagine him doing. He might not be, though. If he answered, she would ask him for an opinion of what she had been thinking about Tanya's motives. Having something sensible to talk about would help preserve a little bit of her dignity. She saw the hotel's sign and turned into the entrance to the parking lot.

A blow like a hammer strike hit the car, the force of it making the frame shiver slightly; she could feel it in her back and feet. Catherine was so startled that her hands jerked the wheel sharply, and the car wobbled as she corrected it. Then she hit the gas pedal.

It had to have been a rock. Somebody had thrown a rock at her car, and all she had to do was get out of range and see who it was. She stared into her rearview mirror, but could not see either the rock or the thrower. He was undoubtedly some jerk who had decided to scare some defenseless young woman from out of town who was staying at the hotel.

She decided to do what she would have done if this had happened in Portland. She kept the car going about a hundred feet to get out of effective range, hit the brake, and spun around in the parking lot to swing her car's front end toward the rock thrower, then hit her high-beam lights.

Her car swayed a bit from the spin and settled, a smell of burned rubber from her tires pervading the air. She saw no human shape, and there was no hiding place, only neatly trimmed grass on either side of the driveway. She turned in her seat and craned her neck to see if she had missed him. Her eye passed across the metal strut just ahead of the rear window. There was a clean, round bullet hole just above it at the edge of the roof.

Catherine saw the side window behind her explode into the interior, bits of glass like little cubes of light spattering the back seat, stinging her right cheek and temple with a pain that seemed to intensify into a burn during the first second. The window on the opposite side of the car was gone, blown outward by the bullet, so she knew the approximate direction of fire.

She guessed that it was probably a hunting rifle, because the time between shots was too long for a semi-automatic assault rifle. It felt to her like the time it took to cycle a bolt, and it was due again . . . now.

Bam! The next shot punched through the door behind her. She swung the car to the right and accelerated again, slouching to bring her head and body down as low as she could and still see out the windshield to drive.

She knew that the shooter was lining up the next shot at the back window of her car as she drove away from him. That made her almost as easy to hit as she would have been standing still, so just as she felt it was time for another shot, she jerked the wheel abruptly to the left.

She heard the distant report of the rifle – a miss – and

swung the car to the right, up an aisle between two rows of parked cars. She turned at the end of the aisle and put two more rows of cars between her and the shooter, then pulled into an empty space.

She killed the engine, switched off the dome lights, opened her door, and slid out to the pavement. Catherine held her sidearm with her right hand and dialed her cell phone with her left. After a half ring, the operator answered, 'Emergency.'

'This is Detective Sergeant Catherine Hobbes of the Portland Police. I'm under fire from a person with a rifle in the parking lot of the Sky Inn on South Milton Street in Flagstaff. The sniper is on the west side of the hotel, firing from a distance.'

There was another loud bang as a shot punched into her car's trunk, and then the report of the rifle. She said, 'I would say from the sound that he's about two hundred yards west of the hotel. He's probably up high.'

'We're dispatching units to your location now. Have you been hit?'

'No. I'm staying low in the parking lot, and I'm about to move to a spot where I don't think he'll be able to see me. Remind the officers not to overlook the possibility that the shooter might be a woman.' She closed her cell phone and put it into her pocket, then dashed across the open aisle. There was the sound of a bullet burying itself in the asphalt behind her, and then the report as she reached a tall truck in the next row of vehicles. She ran around to the front of it, where the height of the cab would hide her from sight.

Calvin Dunn's black car accelerated out of the delivery entrance of the parking lot on the other side of the hotel, sped two blocks up South Milton, and pulled to the curb. In a heartbeat Calvin Dunn was out and running. He ducked between two buildings and trotted up the alley behind the row of stores. He wasn't sure exactly where the shooter was, because the shots had come from a distance and the reports had echoed among the buildings, but he had seen Catherine Hobbes's car, and he could make an educated guess. He just had to make it to the right spot without tripping over the sniper.

As he trotted, he kept his body in the deepest shadows close to the back walls of the buildings, where the light from cars and streetlamps could not reach him. When Calvin Dunn approached the end of a large store with a loading dock, he judged that he must be near the shooter. The buildings along here were the right height, and the ones on the next block didn't have a clear line of sight to the hotel. He slowed to a walk and began to hunt with his ears.

He kept moving steadily in the shadows toward the area where he knew the shooter would be, keeping his head up and his eyes scanning for human silhouettes or movements. He knew that this time he might be looking for the much smaller, slimmer shape of a girl. Beyond that, the size and sex didn't matter. A person with a gun was mostly gun.

There: he had seen a change in the borders of a shadow high on the fire escape of a four-story building directly ahead. What had looked like a part of the black iron railing moved, and the bigger shadow behind it shifted. There was the sharp bang of the rifle's report, and in the muzzle flash a man with a rifle appeared and disappeared again.

Calvin Dunn advanced another twelve feet closer while the man was staring through the scope to see if he had hit his target, and another ten while he was flipping the bolt up and pulling it back to eject the spent brass, pushing it forward to seat the next round, and down to lock it again.

By the time the hot brass casing flew from the rifle and went spinning down to the pavement thirty feet below, Calvin Dunn was close enough to have reached out and caught it. He stared upward to find the ladder suspended below the fire escape. It was on a weighted cable that made it rise above the reach of a burglar when nobody was on it, but Calvin Dunn could see how the shooter had gotten up.

Dunn took off his sport coat, wrapped his gun in it, and set the bundle in a doorway. Then he climbed to the top of a dumpster, took the bar that was meant to slide across the lid of the dumpster to lock it, stuck it between the bottom two rungs of the ladder, waited for the next shot, and pulled it down. He began to climb carefully and silently toward the man.

Calvin Dunn could see him on the third-floor landing of the fire escape, staring through his telescopic sight at the distant hotel parking lot. As Dunn climbed, the man fired again. Dunn knew from experience that the noise of the rifle would cause a ringing that would deafen the shooter for a second or two while he was fighting the barrel down after the kick, and then he would make noise working the bolt. Dunn used the time to climb closer.

The shooter prepared himself again, holding one of the vertical supports of the railing with his left hand to form a solid rest for the rifle's foregrip. Calvin Dunn was almost there. He climbed slowly and steadily, watched the man take careful aim. He heard him blow the air out of his lungs, then squeeze off a round. The shooter cycled the bolt and ejected the brass, but Dunn could tell from the sound that the gun must be out of ammunition. The shooter fiddled with the magazine release, removed it from the underside of the rifle, reached into his jacket for more ammunition, and heard Calvin Dunn's feet on the steel steps of the fire escape.

The shooter was seated with his legs in front of him and his knees bent, so getting up in time was impossible. He pushed a couple of rounds into the magazine and clicked it into place, then twisted his torso to bring the long gun around, but Calvin Dunn was already there. Dunn gave a quick tug on the barrel to stimulate the man's reflex to yank it back toward himself, and then pushed it up violently so the butt plate pounded into the man's face.

The voice that grunted 'Uh!' sounded young. It was a kid, and his left hand went to his injured face. Dunn snatched the rifle out of the boy's right hand, swung it around, and worked the bolt to bring the first round into the chamber.

Dunn stood with his back against the wall of the building as he stared down at the young face, now streaked with blood from the nose and mouth. 'Listen carefully. I'm going to give you one opportunity to tell me exactly where Tanya Starling is at this moment. Do not waste your one chance.'

The reply was surprising, even to Calvin Dunn. The boy opened his bloody mouth, revealing that a couple of front teeth were gone. He took a deep breath, and let out a bellow. 'Tanya!' The yell was a louder sound than he would have thought the boy could make, a howl like an animal. 'I'm caught! Get away!'

Dunn pulled the trigger, the rifle kicked, and the bullet tore through the boy's chest. Dunn leaned over the boy and noted the location of the hole. He was dead.

Dunn left the rifle on the fire escape beside the body and climbed down the fire escape stairs until he came to the ladder. He stopped there to wait for the police car he could see at the entrance of the alley to drive all the way to the end.

THIRTY-TWO

Catherine Hobbes sat on an uncomfortable wooden chair at the side of the interrogation room while Lieutenant Hartnell sat down at the table to question Calvin Dunn. As she looked at Calvin Dunn, she understood why Joe Pitt had warned her. The face below his graying hair was smooth and almost unlined, devoid of emotion. The pale eyes revealed no concern, or even much indication of an interior life. They were merely watchful.

As soon as she had heard the name of the man who had killed the sniper, she had asked to be in the room while he was interrogated. Lieutenant Hartnell had said, 'You're welcome to watch the video monitor, or even have a copy of the tape afterward.' But she had said, 'I want him to see me.' Then she had told Hartnell what Joe Pitt had told her about Calvin Dunn.

While Hartnell prepared to begin, Catherine watched Calvin Dunn. He took note of each of the people in the room and looked up at the video camera suspended from the ceiling, but nothing he saw surprised him. He turned his attention to Hartnell, and Catherine could see that it made Hartnell uncomfortable.

Hartnell said, 'Your name, please.'

'Calvin Dunn.'

'I'm Lieutenant Hartnell, Flagstaff Police Department. I would like to ask you a few questions about what happened tonight. I want you to know that you have the right to refuse to answer them. What you say could be used against you in court. You also have the right to have an attorney present while we talk to you. If you cannot afford an attorney, we will get you one before we proceed. Do you understand your rights?'

Calvin Dunn never took his eyes from Hartnell as he listened to the recitation. 'Yes,' said Calvin Dunn. 'I think that for the moment I won't need an attorney, thank you.'

Hartnell did not like the exaggerated politeness. 'I assume that you're saying that because you think that you won't be charged with anything?'

'I can't control what somebody might accuse me of. But I won't be convicted of anything. That's not a possibility.'

'What makes you so certain?'

'Because there was only one gun up on that fire escape, and the dead man brought it with him. I climbed up there carrying no weapons. While I was struggling to take his rifle away from him to prevent him from using it on me and others, it went off.'

'Mr Dunn, your identification says you live in Los Angeles. What are you doing in Flagstaff?'

'I'm a licensed private investigator. I'm searching for Tanya Starling.'

'Why were you at the Sky Inn tonight? Are you registered at the hotel?'

'No. I was watching for Tanya Starling.'

'Why? She hasn't been seen at the hotel for several days.'

'Hasn't been seen. Right,' Calvin Dunn said. 'That doesn't mean she hasn't been there, or wasn't nearby, just out of sight, doing the seeing.'

'All right. You know she hasn't been seen at the hotel, but you were waiting for her to show up anyway. Why would she do that?'

'Because of that lady right there.' His right forefinger pointed directly at Catherine's heart. It made her want to flinch, but she controlled the impulse. 'I went there at first because that was where Tanya Starling had been spotted last, but then I developed a hunch, and verified that Miss Hobbes was staying there. And that made it a good place for me to be.'

'Explain.'

Calvin Dunn looked directly at Catherine. His pale eyes made her uncomfortable, but she met his gaze. 'You can't just follow a killer around and hope you'll catch up with them. You have to think about what makes them want to do it.'

'Can you elaborate on that?'

'Sure. There are some people who kill once because they lose their temper or they're drunk and don't think it through. Others do it because they get a charge out of it, like sex. Tanya Starling isn't either kind. She solves problems that way.'

'Solves problems? What kind of problems?'

'Whatever comes her way. She goes along doing what she wants until somebody becomes a problem. She solves it by killing them.'

'And how in the world did that theory lead you to sit in the parking lot of the Sky Inn tonight?'

'The place you want to be isn't where the last victim was. It's where the next one is going to be.'

'You thought that Tanya Starling was going to the hotel to harm Detective Hobbes?'

'It seemed likely.'

'How long would you have stayed?'

Calvin Dunn turned to Catherine Hobbes. 'How long would we have stayed?'

The others sat in silence, and Catherine realized she had to answer. 'I can't say.'

Calvin Dunn turned to Hartnell. 'We can't say.'

'Why would she think killing Detective Hobbes would solve her problems?'

'Miss Hobbes was the one who investigated Tanya's first killing and has been after her ever since. If it wasn't for her, nobody would care about Tanya Starling. Cops don't get much appreciation from the general public. But you can bet there's one person who knows exactly who you are and exactly what you did in each case. I figured Tanya has to know who's after her.'

Hartnell sat still with his lips pursed. 'It must have been kind of a disappointment to you that the shooter turned out not to be Tanya after all.'

'It *was* her,' said Dunn. 'That kid up on the fire escape was doing it for her.'

'I'm sorry to cast doubt on your theories, but we have people killed around here that have nothing to do with Tanya Starling.'

'Did he fire at anybody besides Miss Hobbes? Are there any bullet holes in any of the hundred other cars in the hotel parking lot or the two hundred that went up the street past him while he was waiting for her?'

Hartnell's eyes shot to Catherine, and she could tell he wanted to throw her out of the room. But Hartnell's voice remained calm and deliberate. 'Mr Dunn, I think you need to remember that it's my job to ask the questions.'

'I'm just pointing out that the kid was doing it for Tanya.'

'I caught that,' said Hartnell. 'Let's concentrate on you. Had you ever seen the sniper before you saw him on the fire escape?'

'I think I probably did. It's probable he was one of the people who drove by the hotel parking lot a bit earlier tonight. I was mostly looking for women, but I did take a look at everybody I saw.'

'What do you suppose he was doing?'

'I don't know.'

'Come on, Mr Dunn. You have a theory on everything. Was he looking for Detective Hobbes?'

'More likely, her car.'

'How did he know what her car looked like? How could he possibly know?'

'I would guess he might have seen that press conference in front of the police station on television, then driven by the station parking lot and looked for a rental car. I don't imagine there were a lot of them out there.'

Hartnell knew Dunn was right, and that made him more frustrated. 'All right. You were in the parking lot of the Sky Inn at around eleven-thirty, when the first shots were fired. Is that right?'

'Almost. I think it was around eleven-forty.'

'Take us through the rest of this. What did you do then?'

'Well, I saw the car with Miss Hobbes in it come up the road and signal for the lot entrance, so I started looking at the cars behind it to see if Tanya was following her. The first shot looked like it drilled the rear strut, just in front of the rear window. Miss Hobbes jammed the gas pedal, hit the brakes, and spun around. Then a second shot hit the side window and went through the car, so she drove off across the lot as fast as she could. But because the bullet had hit both windows I could tell which direction the shot came from.'

'Did you try to help her?'

'Help her do what?'

'Get to safety.'

'She was already doing what I would have done, which was to drive like hell to get behind something to block the shooter's view. She was weaving around a bit to give him a harder shot.'

'Did you call the police?'

'No. I knew she would do that.'

'So what did you do?'

'I drove around the hotel building to get out on a side street, then drove toward the place where I thought the shooter was.'

'And you thought the shooter was Tanya Starling.'

'I didn't have any other candidates in mind at the time, but I didn't know who it was.'

'But your theory that told you to be there suggested that that was who it was. So you didn't call the police or try to help the potential victim to safety or warn the innocent bystanders who might drive into the lot. What did you do?'

'I went after the shooter.'

'And where did you find him?'

'Perched on the fire escape of one of the taller buildings, about two blocks west of the hotel.'

'What was he doing when you found him?'

'Shooting.'

'He wasn't trying to get away?'

'No. From up there he had a pretty good view. He probably figured he would see any police cars in plenty of time to get away.'

'What do you think? Was he right?'

'If he was wrong, he would still have been up on that balcony with a thirty-ought-six and a couple of boxes of ammo when the first cop cars came up that alley. Then you would have had a couple of those bagpipe funerals.'

Hartnell was clenching and unclenching his teeth. Catherine could see his jaw muscles tightening and relaxing. 'So when you got there, he was still shooting.'

'Yes. Otherwise, he probably would have noticed me, but he had his eye in the scope.'

'Why didn't you shoot him? We found your gun in your coat.'

'I've been deputized by the sheriff of Delacruz County, California, as an auxiliary officer, and if you found the gun you found the concealed-carry permit with it. Arizona and California have a reciprocal agreement.'

'Answer my question. Why didn't you shoot him?'

'Because I wanted to try to get him alive.'

'Why?'

'So he would tell me where she was.'

'So we're back to Tanya Starling again?'

'We've never been anywhere else.'

'Who hired you to find her?'

'A victim's family.'

'What's the client's name?'

'It's the Poole family.'

'Hugo Poole hired you to kill her, didn't he?'

'He hired me to find her.'

'You thought the boy on the fire escape was Tanya Starling, so you climbed up there intending to kill her. It must have been an incredible disappointment when you saw it wasn't even a woman. It was a boy.'

Dunn said, 'I can see the friendly part of our talk is over. Now you can get me a lawyer at your expense, and I'll be ready to continue.'

Hartnell turned to the uniformed officer beside Catherine and said, 'Put him in a holding cell for now.'

Calvin Dunn stood up and faced Catherine while the police officer handcuffed his wrists behind his back. 'Be careful for the next couple of days, darling. It looks like I won't be around to watch your back.'

THIRTY-THREE

Anne Forster heard the news on the radio at seven in the morning, when she had already driven halfway into New Mexico. She had the radio tuned to the strongest signal she could find, the Albuquerque morning drive-time program.

The woman who served as sidekick to the funny morning man read the story. 'There's a bizarre twist to the hunt for Tanya Starling, the woman wanted for questioning in multiple murders in several states. Last night in Flagstaff, Arizona, a sniper opened fire on a police detective from Portland, Oregon, who has been pursuing the case. Police say the sniper shot at Detective Sergeant Catherine Hobbes in the parking lot of her hotel. The sniper, in turn, was killed in an attempt to apprehend him, and remains unidentified. There is no word on the whereabouts of Tanya Starling.'

'I'm sorry, Ty,' she said quietly. The words sounded really good to her, with just a small break in her voice. She said it again, and it was even better. That bad-little-girl voice would have made Tyler's knees buckle. The thought made her miss him for a moment.

She was irritated that the woman on the radio was trying to make everything sound like her fault. Was she supposed to feel guilty now that this Catherine Hobbes had killed a sixteen-year-old? Anne's eyes passed across the items that Ty had left in the car when he had gone off with the rifle. He had left his baseball cap, some pocket change he'd been afraid would jingle, his jacket. She reached into the jacket with her right hand and found his cell phone.

She set it down and reached into her purse. She found the little notebook where she had written the phone numbers of Catherine Hobbes in Portland, Oregon. She dialed the home number and listened to the recorded invitation to leave a message.

'Hello, Catherine,' she said. 'It's me again. I'm thinking about you.' She was pleased with that. She had not practiced or even planned it, but it had sounded scary. 'I just heard on the radio that you killed the boy. He saw the press conference where you and the fat cop said nothing would happen to him. I told him to trust you. But you killed him. That was a disgusting thing to do. Good-bye, Catherine. I'll be thinking about you.'

She turned off the telephone and smiled: pretty good. If she had made the call any spookier, it would have seemed intentional. She left the telephone open and dropped it out the window, onto the pavement. This route – Interstate 40 – was one of the busiest east-west roads in the country. In a few seconds one of the big fourteen-wheelers she had been passing for hours would come along and crush Ty's phone to powder.

She put on Tyler's baseball cap so the brim would help shade her eyes as she drove east, toward the rising sun. She glanced in the mirror on the back of the sun visor. She looked cute. Maybe she should wear hats more often.

When she reached Albuquerque, she watched the signs and took the turn at one that said I-25 North. She wasn't sure where she was heading, but soon she began to see signs that listed cities, as though they were items on a menu: Santa Fe, Colorado Springs, Denver, Cheyenne. She would have to start avoiding little places, where people remembered everyone they had seen in their whole boring lives.

She called me again.' Catherine Hobbes stood in Lieutenant Hartnell's office, still holding her cell phone in her hand.

Hartnell lifted his eyes from the file on his desk. 'Tanya?'

'Yes. She called my house in Portland and left a message about a half hour ago.'

'Can I hear it?'

She lifted her cell phone, tapped the keys to replay her message, and handed it to him. He listened to it, then took a small tape recorder out of his desk drawer, turned it on, and hit the 1 key on Catherine's phone to replay the message beside the microphone. Then he pressed the 2 to save it, and handed it back to her. 'She seems to think that you ambushed him.'

'She seems to,' said Catherine. 'The phone company says the call came from a cell phone, and the origin was Albuquerque. Here's the number.' She handed it to him on a sheet from a desk message pad. 'They say it belongs to Tyler Gilman, of Darling, Arizona.'

'That's just down the road, outside of town,' he said. He stood up and went to the door, then beckoned to someone. When one of the detectives came in, he said, 'I need you to find out what you can about a Tyler Gilman. The address is in Darling. I think he's either another victim or he's our sniper.' Hartnell turned and came back to his desk.

'Well,' said Catherine, 'Thanks for letting me in on the investigation. I'd better be going now.'

'Going?'

'The call came from Albuquerque. I've got to see if I can get on a plane.'

'You know she definitely talked that boy into trying to kill you?'

'Think of it. She can talk somebody into that, and I can barely get my dates to open a door for me.'

He didn't laugh. 'If you know, then you ought to take some precautions.'

'I spend all my time with other cops.'

'Think about tomorrow or the next day,' said Hartnell. 'She could do it again. Some man you never saw before could walk up and put a bullet in your head, just to win points with her.'

'Absolutely true,' said Catherine Hobbes. 'It's always been a crummy job.' She stopped to his desk, leaned across it to hold out her right hand. 'Thanks for everything.'

THIRTY-FOUR

Anne Forster was exhausted from driving, but she was excited. Denver was big and busy and had lots of traffic. There were crowds of pedestrians on the downtown streets who walked past one another without really looking, just as they did in Chicago or Los Angeles. Their memories must be so overloaded with faces that ones they saw on the street left only an impression that blurred and faded within seconds.

As she came into the central part of the city on I-25, she saw a sign for something called City Park, so she took the exit. When she got to the park entrance, she pulled into a lot and turned off the engine. There were hundreds of people in the range of her vision, and they were all sorts – most looking relaxed and happy, walking or sitting, throwing Frisbees, chasing children. She got out of the car to hide her purse in the trunk, but on the way she glanced in at the back seat. She had brought along a blanket from Tyler's bedroom in case she wanted to nap while Tyler drove. She hid the small pistol she'd taken from Mary Tilson in the pocket of her jacket, locked the trunk, took the blanket with her to the shade of a big tree on the vast lawn, and arranged herself on it.

She rolled the jacket up and used it as a pillow. She knew that since she didn't look either poor or crazy, nobody would object to her dozing off under a tree in the park in the daytime. All she really had to worry about was the very slim chance that somebody who had seen her picture on television would come by and recognize her despite her dyed hair and new clothes, or that a patrol car would pick out Tyler's car among the hundred parked in the lot. She listened to the sounds of the people and gradually slipped into sleep.

She slept peacefully until seven, when a car drove along the edge of the parking lot with a booming bass beat on its stereo, and she sat up quickly with her hand on the jacket and looked around. The young mothers and their toddlers, the old men and women had all gone home now. They were being replaced by teenagers, mostly slow-strolling couples or gangs of boys patrolling the park for girls. She decided it was time to go.

She stood up, put on Tyler's jacket carefully so the gun would remain unseen in the pocket, and folded up the blanket. She stared up at the big trees and decided that she liked Denver. It was going to be the place where she would make herself safe again. She walked to the car, put her blanket in the trunk and got her purse, then went into the public restroom to wash her face and brush her hair.

She drove until she found the right kind of restaurant, a diner with vinyl booths. She ordered a big dinner, and while she ate she thought about the steps she needed to take, each in its place in the logical order of things.

The way to survive was to find someone to be. She had read somewhere that the best place to find the sort of information she was going to need was in people's trash, and she decided that the best kind of name would belong to a middle-class home owner. She drove through nice neighborhoods until she found streets where there were garbage containers rolled out to the curb to await the morning collection, but she did not stop. Instead, she kept driving until she knew the boundaries of the next day's pickup area.

She chose neighborhoods as though she were buying a house. She wanted houses that were recently painted, solid buildings with good landscaping and no signs of neglect or disrepair. She stayed away from the homes of the very rich, because she had a suspicion that the richest people must have security patrols watching their neighborhoods late at night.

At one a.m., after she had selected the right block, she parked and walked to a set of cans. She began to open the lids, lifting and touching the trash bags. The ones that felt heavy and solid or gooey she put back. The ones that felt as though they contained paper, she took with her. She went on for an hour, collecting bags of garbage and putting them in her car trunk. When she had collected all the car would hold, she drove to a shopping mall and parked away from the lights near a dumpster.

She used the flashlight from Ty's trunk and began to go through the garbage bags, working quickly. She set aside all of the pieces of paper that looked like bills or receipts. She dropped the bags in the dumpster and went out to get more. She kept working in the same way for four more trips. By dawn she had a big pile of other people's discarded papers in the back seat.

When daylight came she parked in the shade of a tall, windowless self-storage building and went through the bills and papers. After an hour she had gone through all of the papers but had not found any of the information she needed.

At seven she drove to a part of the city park where she had not been before, found a parking place, and lay on her blanket under a tree to sleep. At three o'clock, the sun had moved far enough so she was lying in the sun. She awoke with a terrible glare in her eyes, and reached up to feel her face. It was hot but not tender, so she had hope that she had avoided a sunburn. She had to be careful, because people who lived on the street all seemed to have faces damaged by the sun. She had to look middle-class as long as she could.

She went to the nearest public restroom and examined her appearance as she washed and brushed her teeth. She was still okay, still clean looking and undamaged. But the fear had been planted, so she went to a drugstore and bought sunblock, shampoo, conditioner, and moisturizer, then drove back into the park to a restroom near the zoo. She washed her hair, gave herself a sponge bath, and rubbed her skin with lotion, then put on fresh clothes.

She went to the telephone beside the restroom and used the phone directory to find the addresses of three hospitals. Tonight was going to be a hard one for her, but she judged that it had a better chance of bringing her success than last night had.

She drove to the first of the hospitals, a sprawling newly expanded place with several wings and several driveways. She picked one and drove the perimeter of the hospital. There were dumpsters all around the building, but all of them had their tops locked down. When she reached the driveway where she had entered, she left. She had not been thinking clearly. Probably the hospital had to lock the dumpsters, because otherwise addicts would be there looking for half-used bottles of painkillers and narcotics.

She widened her search to the surrounding neighborhood. There were always medical office buildings within a block or two of major hospitals. The hospital might have strict security procedures, but all of the clerks who worked in all of those doctors' offices couldn't possibly be that careful. People just didn't care that much.

She spent the evening finding and searching the dumpsters outside the office buildings surrounding the three big hospitals. At four a.m. she found something that looked right: a carbon copy of a physician's office-visit checklist. On it the doctor had checked off the exams he had performed and the tests he had ordered for a patient. The patient's name, birthdate, and social security number were on the sheet. It was not going to help her in the way she had hoped, because the patient's name was Charles Woodward, and his age was seventy-one. But she put the sheet in her pocket and kept working.

At seven she went back to the park to sleep. When she woke for dinner at four, she was already breathing hard – panting, almost. She had a panicky certainty that she had been letting time go by without doing the right things, or doing them assiduously enough. She decided she was already running out of time. She had left Flagstaff on Friday, and it had taken all night and most of the next day to drive here. That made it Saturday afternoon when she had arrived in Denver, so now it was Monday. She had to get moving.

She drove to a mailbox-rental store, paid in cash to rent a mailbox in the name Solara Estates, and took a couple of business cards so she would remember the address. After it was dark, she went to a big Kmart and bought an adjustable wrench, a screwdriver, and pliers.

She drove to a street where there were auto repair shops, muffler shops, tire stores. One of the cars that had been left outside a mechanic's shop caught her eye. It had a cover over it, and she looked beneath it to see that the hood had been removed and so had the engine. She stole the license plates, drove to a dark alley down the street, and used them to replace the Arizona license plates on Tyler's car.

She drove to the Aurora Mall, went to the ladies' room near the food court, washed, and did her hair and makeup. She went to Nordstrom's, bought a purse, a pair of black pants, shoes, and a top like the ones she had always worn by preference, and changed into them. As she studied herself in the mirror she judged that she had held up surprisingly well. Sleeping in the park during the day had not been something she would have chosen, but she had actually gotten more undisturbed sleep than she'd had since she'd left Chicago. The work of wandering the city and hauling trash bags around by night – or maybe the one meal a day that she had eaten – had kept her trim. She looked good, even healthy.

When she returned to her car she opened her suitcase and put on some medium-good diamond earrings that Dennis Poole had bought her and a matching tennis bracelet. She put her Anne Forster driver's license into the little ID wallet that came with her new black purse, then stuck a hundred dollars in with it. She locked everything else in the trunk, and kept the keys in her pocket.

She found a singles bar near Larimer Square early in the evening. There was a line outside, and it gave her a chance to see the kinds of people who thought the bouncers and doormen should admit them. It was too early in the evening to see the staff make any difficult decisions. They turned away only a couple of young men, who seemed to have done something the night before: 'Sorry, man. If the boss sees you two in there after last night, I'm going to be looking for a job.' They didn't turn any women away, which was a good sign.

When she reached the head of the line, she held her homemade license inside the wallet, but the bouncer barely glanced at it before he waved her in. Inside, the light was dim and the recorded music was loud. There was a DJ in a booth high above the dance floor choosing cuts and operating the colored lights that strafed the crowd. The line at the bar was already three deep, and the five bartenders were lip-reading and pouring drinks methodically.

She had to have a drink to hold in her hand, so she ordered a 7UP with a lime twist, which looked enough like a gin and tonic in the changing light. As soon as she was away from the bar, men started asking her to dance with them, so she did. She had an extremely clear vision of what she had to accomplish tonight, so she used the dancing, making turns to watch the way the crowds were forming and reconfiguring.

As she danced, she could see groups of single girls sitting at the tables in the corner of the room just off the dance floor and farthest from the front door. Men lingered near that spot or walked by, surveying the selection while pretending not to, and the women made their own evaluations and decisions while pretending not to.

When she had danced enough to be sure that the young women at the tables had become used to her, she bought another 7UP and went to the women's area to sit on the upholstered bench that ran the length of the wall beyond the tables. She began to make overtures to the women around her. 'This is a great place,' she said to one of them. The woman appeared not to be able to hear her over the noise of the music. She tried the one on her other side, a thin blonde who seemed to be there alone. 'Wow. I absolutely love those shoes. Would you mind telling me where you got them?'

'Zero Gravity.'

'Can you tell me where that is? I'm new here. I just moved here from Florida.' She laughed. 'I don't know anything.'

'It's on Colfax, not far from the capitol building. It's really a great place.'

'Thanks so much. Do you know a good place to get a jacket? The fall stuff is out already, and I thought I might pick up a jacket now. With the altitude here and everything, I'm freezing half the time.'

'Zero Gravity would be a good place to start for that too. Or, you know, there's a mall in Aurora that has just about everything.' The woman's eyes left hers and rose to focus on someone standing over them.

'Would you like to dance?' asked the man. He was looking at Anne.

She said to the blond woman, 'Would you mind watching my purse for a minute?'

The woman said unenthusiastically, 'Okay. Sure.'

She got up and danced with the man. He was tall, skinny, and young – so young that she wondered if he had used a false ID to get into the bar. She smiled at him, wondering if the blond woman she had chosen was right. If she had chosen wrong, the woman would be gone and so would her purse, fake driver's license, and hundred in cash.

When the song was over, the young man said, 'Want to dance again?'

'I shouldn't. I left my purse with that girl.'

She went back and found the blonde still there. She said to her, 'Thanks for watching my purse.'

She worked to shape the evening and make it conform to her vision. She talked with the woman and made observations, tried to make her laugh. They moved to a table when its occupants left. They became more and more comfortable with each other, and their smiles and laughter attracted another man. The blonde got up to dance with him, and she said, 'Your turn to watch my purse, okay?'

'Sure.'

She waited until the girl had disappeared into the surging crowd of dancers, took out her little notebook and pen, and reached into the purse. She kept the purse beneath the table, her head up and her eyes on the dancers, so even if the lights had suddenly come on it would have been difficult to say she had been searching the purse. She looked down only when her fingers had identified something.

The driver's license gave the blonde's name as Laura Murray, her address as 5619 LaRoche Avenue in Alameda, and her date of birth as August 19, 1983. She copied quickly, then found the health insurance card, which gave an identification number that started with XDX and ended in a social security number. She looked into the wallet to see the issuers of the credit cards. Then she closed the purse and put away the notebook and pen. The whole process had taken barely sixty seconds.

The young woman came back after ten minutes to find her slightly bored and tired. They talked for a few minutes longer, and both went to the ladies' room. As soon as they returned, the young man who had danced with the blonde before asked her to dance again. At that moment, Anne caught the blonde's eye, pointed at her watch, and waved. The blonde smiled and waved back.

She stepped outside into the cool night air and breezed past the doormen, feeling eager. It was going to work. She knew it was going to work. She walked back to her parked car, retrieved her real purse with the gun and money in it, and drove to a 7-Eleven store that had a pay telephone on the wall outside. She searched the directory for an all-night copy service that rented computers, then drove there.

When she reached the copy center, she was pleased. This seemed to be a business that served people from the university. The customers were all her age or younger, and there were at least two dozen of them, even though it was after midnight. There were a dozen using the self-service copying machines, paper cutters, and laminating machines. There were another dozen people using the computers. She claimed one and went to work.

She went to bank Web sites and found one that would

allow her to apply for a Visa card online. She brought up the application and checked her notes to be sure it wasn't one of the banks that had already given Laura Murray credit. She entered Laura's name, address, birth date, social security number, and driver's license number. She said Laura was an executive trainee, effective a month ago in case the credit check revealed some other job, and that she made approximately fifty-one thousand dollars a year. Then came the question 'Have you moved within the past two years?' She said yes, typed in 'Solara Estates,' the mailbox number, and the street address of the mailbox-rental store. She put the effective date as today, and clicked that address as the current one.

She had noticed that the application form she had filled out had asked, 'Would you like to apply for a second card for another person on this account?' It gave her an idea. She applied for two cards in the name of Charles Woodward, the elderly man whose medical record she had stolen. After filling in his name, social security number, and birthday, she said he was retired. His annual income was eighty-seven thousand dollars. Yes, he did want a second card on his account. It was for one of the names she had made up for herself, Judith Nathan. She said her full name was Judith Woodward Nathan, and that they both lived at Solara Estates.

She checked to see that the copy center was still safe, then used the scanned images of her Illinois, California, and Arizona driver's licenses to make the paper fronts of licenses for Judith Nathan and Laura Murray, and signed off. She used a copier to copy the backs of her licenses, used a laminating machine to join them to the front sides, and a precision paper cutter to trim them to size. They still were not good enough to fool a policeman in their home states, but if she put one of them into the plastic holder in her wallet, it looked real.

When morning came, she bought a *Denver Post* and searched for furnished apartments. The place she found was an old motel that had become less and less desirable to travelers and was living an afterlife offering rooms by the week at cut-rate prices. After a few days of sleeping during daylight in a park, she was not critical of the place's faults. She was delighted to have a shower and a door with a lock on it, and there was even a television set.

She drove to a hardware store and bought four sliding bolts. Late on the first night she installed two of her sliding bolts at the top and bottom of the door, and one bolt on each of the two windows. When she had done that, she slept with Mary Tilson's gun under the spare pillow beside her head.

She slept ten hours a day, exercised, took long showers, gave herself facials, treated her skin with moisturizer, and did her nails. She watched television, thought, and planned. She went out only to buy food and newspapers and check her Solara Estates mailbox.

On the tenth day, she found her first credit card, in the name Laura Murray, in her mailbox, and on the thirteenth, the one for Judith Nathan. By the twenty-first day, she was ready to drive again. Judith Nathan packed her suitcase and began the long drive toward Portland, Oregon.

THIRTY-FIVE

It was five-thirty in the morning. Catherine Hobbes stood at the big window of her dining room, sipped her coffee, and stared down at the city of Portland. Each morning since she had returned from Albuquerque, she had gone to work at five-thirty so she could spend an hour or two before her shift trying to follow cold leads to Tanya. It had been a month since Tanya had made the call to this house from Albuquerque and then disappeared again, and Catherine had begun to let a new possibility enter her mind.

Not all serial killers got caught. Catherine had thought Tanya would turn up in Albuquerque, but there was no guarantee she would ever be recognized again anywhere. At some point people would say, 'Maybe she died.' Or, 'Maybe she's in a prison somewhere for something else.' But she wouldn't be, and from time to time, when the urge came on her again, she would kill someone else.

Catherine put her coffee cup in the sink and went to find the lightweight hooded raincoat she kept for unpredicted rains. She slung it over her forearm, checked her watch, and appraised herself in the mirror near the stairs. The gray suit looked good, so she ran an inventory of the gear by touch: the belt with her gold badge clipped to the right of the buckle, the handcuffs at the hip, the pistol on her belt to the right side of her spine under the tailored coat.

She went downstairs and out to the garage, got into her teal blue Acura, and conceded that she was letting her mood weaken her. She had even failed to keep herself from thinking about what day this was. The divorce had happened long enough ago so the day shouldn't matter anymore. It was the twenty-first of August – Kevin's birthday. He would be – what? Thirty-five – today.

Each year had made her feel it less and less, and after eight years, Kevin was no longer real. He existed only as a part of her mind now, an altered point in her brain. What would the doctors call it? A lesion. Everything in medicine was a lesion, from a mild scratch to a fatal tumor.

The part that was hard to believe now was that Kevin had been the other half of the conversation for so long. She had been with him for years and talked without any dissembling, and eventually without filtering or even reserve. When, at any time during those years, she had said something funny or profound, he was the one who had heard it, and probably the only one. For years after the divorce there had been times when she would catch herself in a forgetful impulse to describe something, and then remember that he wasn't there anymore. There were other times when she would be talking to someone else – a friend, a colleague – and realize that the point she was making was something that she had heard Kevin say.

The birthday was not a good memory. It had been on his twenty-seventh birthday that the quiet explosion had occurred. She had taken a half day off from her job at the brokerage. At just before noon she had rushed out, bought a birthday cake, and gone to his office to surprise him. She remembered that when she had grasped the doorknob of the office on the fifth floor, she had sensed that something was different. She had felt odd, almost dizzy, and she had attributed it to the elevator ride, but it didn't feel that way. It had felt as though she were holding on while a subtle tottering of the universe occurred, a tremor.

She opened the outer door of the office and walked into silence. The sales center wasn't the sort of place where customers simply walked in, because the company worked on enormous construction projects. Usually somebody stayed to watch the office during lunch, but the desks were empty. It occurred to her that maybe the whole office had shut down and taken Kevin out to lunch to celebrate. It was a young, social group, and Kevin was a popular manager. She should have called ahead instead of surprising him, she thought, and then she could have gone too. He would have loved that.

The thought gave her an idea. Maybe there was a notation somewhere, a scrawl that would tell her where they had gone. Paula, the receptionist, would be the one likely to have made the reservation, so Catherine looked first at the notepad on her desk, then the Rolodex, to see if the card that was showing was a restaurant. It wasn't.

Catherine went past the empty desks in the outer office, through the bay past deserted cubicles, to the hall-way that led to the offices of the sales executives. She knocked on Kevin's door, then opened it.

He wasn't there. She went to his desk to see if there was anything on his calendar. There were a few scribbled lines – his morning appointments, a meeting at four. She put the cake on his desk, then sat in his chair and typed on his computer, 'Happy birthday, Kev. I just stopped by for a minute to tell you I love you. See you later, Catherine.' She highlighted it, made the type twenty-eight point and red, and left it on his screen.

She was pleased with that, because it implied that she had just breezed through in a rush, and not that she had blown half a day of work for nothing. He would feel happy instead of disappointed or guilty. She stood up, stepped out of the office, and heard something down the hall. It seemed to be a muffled female voice, as though one of the salespeople had stayed and was on the telephone. There was the voice again. It was definitely a woman's. Maybe she would know where Kevin was.

She followed the sound to a door down the hall. She put her ear to the door. She knew. There was no way to introduce doubt, no way for Catherine to save herself. Catherine had no right to open the door, but she did.

It was Diana Kessler's office, obviously. Diana was bent forward over her desk, her skirt up over her back, and Kevin was behind her. They didn't hear Catherine open the door. She stood there, paralyzed and speechless, for two or three seconds before she took a step back and closed the door again. Catherine remembered the cold, empty feeling in her chest, the tightness in her throat. She had simply stood there, listening to their alarmed voices, the rapid, hurried rustling, and the quick footsteps.

When Kevin flung the door open and saw her, his eyes widened with what looked like fright. He tried to cover, forcing a smile. 'Honey! Are you here to surprise me? I'm so glad to—'

'I saw,' she interrupted. 'I opened the door while you were with her.' She turned and began to walk back along the hall toward the outer office.

'Wait. Please. Let me talk to you.'

'I don't want to talk.'

His voice became jocular, but it was unconvincing. 'Come back. I don't know what you think you saw, but you misinterpreted it. You're wrong.'

She stopped walking and turned to glare at him. 'Kevin. You don't seem to have heard. I saw. I am not "wrong."'

His brows were knitted in worry and unhappiness. He put his hands on her arms, as he had a thousand times, and looked into her eyes. 'Diana can tell you. It's a mis-understanding. Let's talk. The three of us.'

He seemed to have lost his mind. 'I don't want to talk to Diana, and Diana doesn't want to talk to me. Now let me out of here.' She shook his hands off her arms, spun, and walked out of the office. That had been the explosion, and it had propelled her away from his presence, his life.

When she thought about it, she usually summarized the story as though she had caught him one day and never seen him again. It wasn't that simple. There had followed months of surreal scenes with him. There were meetings with him to sign off on the property settlement, two meetings that were supposedly by chance when he was clearing out, and others she couldn't quite bring to mind now. But she had been forced to hear his denials, then his excuses, then his anger.

During those months all of their mutual acquaintances seemed to discover the need to unburden themselves of their knowledge about some girl who had slept with him. Two had even admitted to having done it themselves. They felt that they, too, belonged to a larger category of women mistreated by Kevin. It had all ended eight years ago, and every one of those people had vanished from her life.

THIRTY-SIX

She drove through the city, toward the bureau. Portland was not huge, so if she was up early enough she never had much trouble getting across the river and into the homicide office in fifteen minutes.

She was there before six, and went to work immediately on the next phase of the search. Today she was sending copies of the photographs of Tanya Starling to Department of Motor Vehicles offices in major cities all over the country, warning them that Tanya Starling would probably soon be applying for a new driver's license somewhere.

Catherine was nearly finished with the flyers for the motor vehicles departments when she looked up and saw Captain Farber approaching her desk. 'Catherine, I need to assign you to help Tony Cerino this morning.' Cerino specialized in missing persons complaints. She could see him standing beyond Mike Farber's shoulder in the entrance to the homicide office, so she didn't protest. Instead she turned to Cerino. 'What can I do, Tony?'

He stepped closer. 'I've got a three-day missing person. It's pretty straightforward on the surface, but when Ronny Moore did the interviews, he thought there was something hinky about the whole thing. I want to bring a homicide officer with me to the second interview.'

She shrugged. 'It feels that wrong?'

'Well, the husband says she's only been gone for three

days. The parents say that she usually calls every day, but she hasn't in a week. They filed the report.'

She put her circulars into a file folder and stuck it into a desk drawer. 'Let's go.'

The house was a low bungalow painted green with a roofed porch in front. It seemed identical to most of the others on the street, but this one had a chain-link fence along the sidewalk. Catherine had been a police officer long enough to open the gate cautiously and wait to see what sort of dog responded, but Cerino said, 'The dog belonged to the previous owner.'

Cerino knocked on the front door, and a man came to open it. He was small but muscular, with sandy hair combed to the side over his balding head and the sort of expression that Catherine classified as habitually dissatisfied. He was wearing blue jeans and a short-sleeved pullover that seemed tight over his biceps. She manufactured a smile. 'Are you Mr Olson?'

'Yes,' he said. He was somber, but she noticed that he looked relaxed and well rested.

'My name is Sergeant Hobbes, and this is Sergeant Cerino. We wondered if we could come in and talk to you.'

He opened the door and let them in, then went to sit in a worn wing chair in the living room. The gesture made Catherine almost feel reassured about him, because it was so human: he was in a nightmare, and he instinctively went to the chair for comfort. But there was something about his movements that made her uneasy. His limbs seemed to be rigid, mechanically stiff. 'Have a seat,' he said.

Cerino sat on the couch to the left, and Catherine moved to the chair directly in front of Olson. She kept her back straight and both feet on the floor.

'You found her body, didn't you?' said Olson.

Catherine looked into his eyes and she knew. She had no evidence yet that this call concerned anything more than a woman who had taken three days off from a lousy marriage. The missing woman's parents had told Ronny Moore, the first officer on the case, that she had gotten into arguments with her husband and left him before, so this could easily be just another spat. But Catherine knew it wasn't.

She shifted almost imperceptibly in her chair to keep the back of her coat from impeding her reach for her gun. 'No,' she said. 'We're just conducting a preliminary inquiry. We're hoping that she hasn't come to any harm. Usually if somebody's missing for only two or three days, they come back on their own.' She paused. 'Do you know if there is any reason to believe she might not have left of her own free will?'

His face assumed an expression of frustration, as though he were trying to make himself understood by people who barely spoke the language. 'She left here on her own. She went grocery shopping. She should have been home two hours later at the most, but it's been three days. What I think happened is that there was a guy in the parking lot waiting for somebody like her. She went to put her bags in the trunk or something, not paying attention to what was going on around her, and there he was behind her with a gun.'

Catherine kept her face attentive and sympathetic, and recognized that she had just heard the story he was going to be pushing. She knew too that when his wife's body was found, it would have bullet holes. 'I certainly hope that's not what happened,' she said. 'Please excuse this, but we have to ask some personal questions. It's part of the procedure. Has she ever left you like this before?'

'No,' he said. 'She hasn't left me now. She's missing.'

'I mean, has she ever gone away without explaining where she was going, and possibly stayed away overnight?'

'I just answered that. She hasn't ever done that. Three days ago she said she was going to the supermarket, and never came home.'

'Which one?'

'The Safeway, on Fremont Street. At least that's where she usually goes.'

She turned to Cerino. He answered, 'We've checked the lot and all of the parking areas nearby.'

She turned back to Olson. 'Did you have any kind of disagreement during the day or two before she went shopping?'

'No. We didn't. We always got along just fine.'

'You never had arguments?'

'Once in a while. But never anything that mattered much, and nothing that day,' he said. 'Look, if I had any reason to believe that she had just gotten pissed and run off, I wouldn't call the police and embarrass myself, would I?'

'*Did* you call the police?'

'Well, no. I guess her parents called first, but I would have today.'

'But you had thought she would be back in an hour or two. After a day passed, weren't you scared? Afraid for her?'

'Yes. But I always heard the police don't consider anybody missing unless they've been gone for at least three days.'

'So you didn't call us. What *did* you do?'

'I called some other people. I drove around to the store to see if her car was there. Things like that.'

'Whom did you call?'

'Let's see. Some people she worked with. The neighbors across the street.'

'Did you call her parents?'

'Yes. No. I think they called me first.'

She handed him a pen and a piece of her notebook paper. 'Can you write down for me the names of all of the people you called?'

'Gee.'

'And if you can remember their phone numbers, that would help too.'

He frowned and began to write, then crossed something out, then wrote some more. 'This isn't as easy as it looks. I was in a real panic, and I'm probably forgetting some.' He glared at her. 'What's this for, anyway?'

She took the paper. There were only three names, one of them crossed out. 'If you think of anyone else, you can add the name later.'

He shrugged. 'Why aren't you out looking for her?'

'There are other people doing that,' she said. 'They'll be interviewing lots of people, asking questions and comparing notes.'

'Oh, I get it. I'm going to be the suspect, right? Whenever somebody gets killed, it's the husband.'

'I certainly hope not,' she said. 'Most of the time when we receive a missing person call, it has a happy ending. People get depressed. They get upset or overwhelmed by something in their lives. They go off by themselves for a while to think. Those are possibilities we always have to look into.'

'All right. I understand. I'm just worried about her, that's all.'

Cerino took his turn. 'Was your wife on any medication? Insulin, lithium, antidepressants, anything she had to have regularly?'

'No.'

'No recreational drug use? Alcohol wasn't a big factor?'

'No.'

'You said your marriage is in good shape,' Cerino said, looking down at his notebook as though he were checking off items on a list. 'Does that include all aspects? Neither of you had a sexual relationship outside the marriage that you know of?'

'Absolutely not.'

Catherine caught Cerino's eye. 'I'd like to look around a bit.'

Cerino turned to Olson. 'With your permission, we'd like to examine the house to see if there's anything that will point us in a new direction.'

Catherine watched Olson. His shirt was tight across his chest, and she saw his breathing stop for a moment, then start again. She nodded to Cerino.

Cerino said, 'Do we have your permission?'

'What do you want to search here for? I told you she left to go shopping, and she hasn't come back.'

Catherine said, 'It's just one of a few dozen steps we have to take in a case like this. It's part of the checklist.'

'I can't think of one reason for you to search my house.'

'I can think of a lot of reasons. A wife who has been secretly planning to leave her husband might very well leave signs of it somewhere – correspondence from another man, brochures about some destination. A suicidal person might leave a note or a secret journal.'

Olson's forehead was moist now, his jaw muscles working. He looked as though the room temperature had suddenly risen twenty degrees. 'My wife could be less than a mile from here right now, pleading for her life.'

Catherine knew she was hearing small hints of what had really happened, his mind simply throwing out the first thing it stumbled on. The wife really was less than a mile from here. Maybe she had begged him to spare her life. Catherine said, 'All you have to do is say yes, and we'll be able to get started. Your quick cooperation might make all the difference.'

'It's not logical,' he said. 'You're not trying to find her.'

Catherine looked at Cerino. She had found a weakness, so she increased the pressure. 'Sergeant, would you mind calling in our request for a forensic team on the radio? If you go to the captain, I'll bet we can have them here in fifteen minutes.'

Cerino wasn't sure he understood what she really wanted. He stared at her as he slowly got to his feet, reluctant to leave her alone with Olson.

Olson said, 'I just told you, I don't want you people in here tearing up my house.'

Catherine said, 'They won't tear up your house. They don't have to.'

'What are you talking about?'

'They can eliminate certain things quickly. They can spray luminol on a surface, and it will show if there's ever been any blood on it. The spot glows in black light. It doesn't matter how thoroughly it's been washed. It will still glow.'

The more she spoke, the more his face went limp and blank, like the face of a poker player. She knew she had hit another of the vulnerabilities. Whatever had happened, it had been here. There had been blood somewhere in the house. She said, 'Go ahead, Sergeant. I guess we'll need a warrant.'

Cerino walked out the front door.

Olson's anger was more apparent now that he was alone with Catherine. 'You don't seem to be hearing me. You can't do this.'

'Mr Olson,' said Catherine. 'I'm sorry you haven't decided to cooperate, but this isn't a violation of your rights. There's the suspicion of a crime, and my partner is requesting a search warrant. As soon as it's granted, we'll be—'

Olson's lunge came so quickly that she was barely able to react. She ducked sideways and down, and his fist caught her forehead instead of her nose and mouth. She dodged off the chair to the floor before his spring brought him into it. He went over her, hitting the chair back and taking it with him to the floor. He pushed himself away from it and stood, then turned and took a step to begin his run toward the back of the house.

Catherine swept out her leg, caught the tip of his right foot, and tripped him just as he was bringing it forward for the second step, and he went down. As he sprawled on the hardwood floor, Catherine heard Cerino fling open the front door.

Catherine flopped across Olson's legs and clung to them while he tried to kick free, and Cerino dashed to straddle Olson's back. The three struggled in silence for a few seconds. Catherine snatched her handcuffs off her belt and handed them to Cerino, who closed one on Olson's left wrist, then dragged the right behind his back to force it into the other cuff.

Catherine recited the Miranda warning, then said, 'Do you understand these rights?' She poked his leg hard with her knuckle. 'Do you?'

'Yes.'

Cerino twisted his body to look at Catherine. 'You okay? Looks like you got hit in the head.'

'I'll live. Give me your handcuffs.'

'Here,' said Cerino.

She took them and closed them on Olson's ankles. 'That ought to do it. Watch him for a minute, okay?' She got up and took a few steps away from them, and when Olson didn't move or try to struggle, she trotted out to the police car and made the call. 'This is One-Zebra-Fifteen. We need a unit to transport a prisoner and we need a forensic team. The address is 59422 Vancouver.'

She went back into the house and entered the kitchen. She didn't touch anything at first, simply looked. The kitchen was extremely clean and tidy. Everything seemed to be in its place, freshly washed and put away. She opened the refrigerator without touching the handle. The shelves were packed with closely arranged items – jars that still had the plastic around the tops because they had not been opened, fresh fruits and vegetables. She looked through the transparent side of the meat drawer at the packages on top. There were a steak and lamb chops dated September 19. That was two days ago.

Catherine kept going. She went up the stairs to the bedrooms. There was a guest room that was neat and empty, with a well-made bed, the sheets pulled tight and tucked with hospital corners beneath the bedspread. She moved to the master bedroom. The room had been cleaned. There were two dressers, but only the tall one without the mirror – the male one – had anything on its surface. She looked into the closet. There were clothes for Olson and his wife on hangers, with an empty space between them.

She moved to the bathroom. There were items that had to belong to the missing wife, but they had all been moved to a small space at the far end of the long tile counter.

She was sure that he had wanted to get rid of his wife's things, but doing so would have been evidence that he knew she wasn't coming back. As soon as her body was found, he would have been able to do it. But Catherine had another intuition about Olson. He had been calm and controlled until the final moment when he had been sure he had lost the argument and she was going to order a search of the house. Then he had panicked. The reason he had decided to run was that there was something here that he knew would convict him. It was something big and obvious that a search could not miss. She had an idea of what it might be.

Catherine went downstairs and then into the garage. There were two vehicles in it, and an empty space for the Toyota Camry Myra Olson had supposedly taken to the supermarket. Catherine looked at the floor, and she could see the faint images of stains on the concrete that had been cleaned. They didn't seem to be blood, but she could not be sure. She turned her attention to the two vehicles. One was a Lexus sedan, and the other a big Cadillac Escalade.

She walked toward the Escalade. Catherine had worked homicides for four years, and she knew exactly what she was looking for. In the back of the SUV near the tailgate, there would be a plastic tarp or a rug, and it would be rounded, probably tied. Maybe there would be a shovel. She opened the driver's door so that the light went on, flicked the switch to unlock the rest of the doors, and looked. The back was empty, except for a neatly folded blanket on the floor of the rear cargo area. She slammed the car door.

She heard something. It was a low whining sound. It seemed far away, but it couldn't be. She stood still and listened. Then there was a faint knocking sound.

Catherine followed it. She walked slowly, listening, her heart beating fast. The sound stopped, and she stopped too. She put her hand on the trunk of the Lexus. This time when there was a rap, she felt it from the heel of her hand and up her arm like an electric shock. 'I hear you,' she shouted. 'Hold on.' She patted the surface, then turned and ran into the house.

Cerino had lifted John Olson so he could sit on the couch, but his wrists and ankles were still cuffed so he couldn't attack Cerino. Catherine said to Cerino, 'Did you find any car keys on him?'

'No,' said Cerino. 'There weren't any keys. No wallet either.'

'Where are your car keys, Mr Olson?'

'I don't know.' His face looked angry, spiteful.

She marveled at it. He was caught, trussed up and about to be exposed, and yet he was taking some last bit of sadistic pleasure out of frustrating her. Catherine remembered the direction he had been running after he had hit her, and extended his trajectory.

She entered the kitchen, checking the counters and opening drawers. As she searched, she took out her cell phone and called the emergency number. 'This is Detective Sergeant Catherine Hobbes. I need an ambulance at 59422 Vancouver. We have an injured victim here. Thank you.' She kept going to the back door. There were some jackets hanging on pegs beside it. She patted the pockets of a jacket, then felt the hard shape of the wallet and heard the clinking. She reached in and pulled out the key ring.

She dashed out to the garage. First she tried the wrong key, and then found the right one. The springs of the lid made it pop up a few inches, and instantly the smell of fear – urine and sweat – came to Catherine in a wave. She raised the lid the rest of the way.

The woman rose to the light like a drowned body rising from the depths to break a calm surface. She had streaks of dark dried blood that had run from her nose and lips, and from a cut at her hairline. All of them had run in stripes on both sides of her face as she lay there in the dark. The bleeding seemed to have stopped a long time ago, so the blood was cracked like old paint. She was naked, and Catherine could see purple bruises on her arms, ribs, hips. Her wrists had been tied behind her. A separate strand of cord had been tied to keep her elbows back and make it harder for her to move. Catherine helped her sit up, and untied the cords. 'Are you Myra?'

The woman nodded and her chin began to tremble.

'I'm Sergeant Hobbes. It's over now, and you're going to be all right.'

'Did he kill my parents? He said he had already killed them. He had insurance on all of us.'

'No. They're fine. They're the ones who called us.'

'He said he had already killed them, and that he was going to kill me today.' She began to sob.

'Don't worry, Myra. They're just fine, and you'll see them later. Don't worry. He can't hurt anybody again. You don't have to worry about anything. Let's get you out of there.' She helped Myra ease one foot out of the trunk to the floor of the garage, then the other. She opened the Escalade, snatched the blanket, and wrapped it around her.

'You're safe,' she said. 'It's all over now.' She held her in a gentle embrace and rocked her back and forth. In the distance there was a siren.

THIRTY-SEVEN

When Catherine got home and picked up her telephone, there was a message tone. She dialed her code and listened. 'Catherine, this is Joe Pitt. You said you would go out with me if I came up to Portland. Well, I'm here. Meaning Portland. I'd like to see you tonight, and I'm making reservations for every half hour from eight until ten at different restaurants. Give me a call whenever you come in. I'm at the Westin hotel.' He recited the telephone number, but Catherine was not ready to write it down.

She replayed the message, wrote down the telephone number, and then dialed it. When Pitt answered, she said, 'Hi. You're pretty sure of yourself, aren't you?'

'No. As far as I can tell, there's nothing in our history together that would give me the least bit of confidence,' he said. 'I just haven't been able to pin you down on when I could come, so I figured I would come now and wait until you have time to go to dinner with me.'

'What a speech. I'd have to be a fool not to go. What should I wear and how much time have I got?'

'Dress up – really fancy. You have five minutes.'

'I might be able to make it to your hotel at eight, so keep the eight-thirty reservation.'

'See you then.'

When she arrived at the hotel, Joe Pitt was standing inside the entrance in a dark suit. Catherine was glad that she had taken him seriously and worn her only recently purchased fancy outfit, a black cocktail dress. She had also put on her white-gold necklace that had been her grandmother's. Pitt walked outside as soon as he saw her, and told the valet, 'Take her car, please, and bring mine.' He handed him a ticket.

She got out and watched her car disappear down the ramp to the garage, and said, 'What – you don't want to be seen in a working woman's unpretentious Acura?'

'No. I just like driving when I'm on a date, so I rented a car.'

The valet returned with a Cadillac, and she smirked at Joe Pitt. 'You can't impress me with that. I used to pull those things over all the time with a crummy Crown Victoria Interceptor.'

'Me too,' he said. 'But I always wished I had one.'

They drove to the restaurant, and the maître d' conducted them to a table. They ordered their dinners, and ate while they talked about Catherine's near miss in catching up to Tanya in Flagstaff, and then her failure to head her off in Albuquerque. Joe Pitt said, 'I'm sort of surprised you haven't told me about your day.'

She frowned. 'You know about that?'

'Yes,' he said. 'But I'd be delighted to listen to the story again if you'd like to tell it.'

'How?' she said. 'How do you know already?'

'I called your office at around noon, trying to reach you. I talked to Mike Farber, and he told me about it.'

She looked crestfallen. 'That's why you came? Because you heard about the Olson thing and felt sorry for me?'

'Sorry for you?' he said. 'I came because I thought you'd be in a good mood and let me celebrate with you. You're a hero,' said Joe Pitt. 'In the next couple of days the wire services will pick up the newspaper stories, and the networks will pick up the television news.' He sat back to let the waiter clear their plates.

'I hope they run my picture,' said Catherine. 'I'll be able to cash a check at my bank branch without having to show my ID anymore.'

'Probably not. But next time the promotions get handed out, there might be something in the goody bag. They need people like you, and they know it.'

'Why say "like you"? I'm me, other people are other people, and we're not alike.'

'"Like you" means cops who actually got to a murder victim before the guy killed her. When the brass see a young, beautiful homicide detective who saves an abused victim – probably by minutes – they want to throw a party. You're the proof that what they're doing makes sense. With that bandage on your forehead that you're bravely trying to hide under your hair, you're a photo op they couldn't buy for anything.'

'It's a Band-Aid, and I put it on myself.' She smiled. 'Want one?'

'No, thanks.'

'You certainly do bring a better brand of malarkey than you used to.'

'Malarkey? I don't think I've heard that word in about thirty years.'

'Ladies don't say "horseshit."'

'Oh?'

'At least not to somebody who flies a long way and takes them to a nice restaurant.'

'If compliments embarrass you, I'll stop talking about it.' He lifted his wineglass. 'I'll just drink to your courage and sagacity.'

She lifted her glass of water. 'And I to your discerning taste.'

They sipped, and put down their glasses. Pitt looked at her closely. 'You never drink. Did you ever?'

'Sure,' she said. 'When I was young. Not for a few years, though.'

'Are you an alcoholic?'

She was taken aback. 'What?'

'A lot of friends of mine who will never touch a drink are alcoholics. A lot of them are cops. I wondered if you were.'

She felt defensive and angry for a second, but as she looked at him, she detected nothing but honest sympathy. 'I don't know,' she said. 'Let's just say that alcohol does things to me that I don't particularly want done, so I stopped drinking.'

'Good for you,' he said. 'But bad for me. I'll just have to try to seduce you with my wit and charm alone.'

She smiled. 'I guess your strategy doesn't include surprise. I did like the flattery, though.'

'It was admiration,' he said. 'And I really meant it.'

'Now that I know your intentions, I'll have to be a bit skeptical.'

He looked at her with a serious, contemplative expression. 'My intentions have been on the surface since the beginning. I'm not here just to confer with an esteemed colleague. I asked you out on a date.'

'Asking for a date is kind of ambiguous,' she said.

'Maybe to you.'

'To everybody. To the world.'

'It isn't to me, and only I can say what I meant. When somebody asks you out on a date, you can accept or not, and your acceptance means whatever you want it to mean.'

'And what does your asking mean?'

'It means that I've already watched and listened to you and thought about you enough to have made my decision about you. I'm not window-shopping.'

She picked up her glass of water and took a deep swallow. Then she put it down and said, 'That's what it meant when I accepted.'

He looked into her eyes for a few seconds before the smile reappeared on his face. His eyes focused on the waiter and he nodded, and the waiter approached. 'Check, please?'

Hours later, Joe Pitt rolled onto his side, leaned on his elbow, and looked down at her on the pillow beside him. 'What made you change your mind about me?'

'I haven't changed my mind about you. You're exactly the way I always thought you were.'

'You always acted as though you didn't approve of me, but here you are.'

'Yep. Here I am. I'm lying naked in a hotel bed with a man on a first date. I guess that means I'm pathetic.'

'If you're fishing for compliments, I can give you a few thousand new ones now. I've been holding back.'

'Spare me.'

'You can't really feel bad about this.'

'No, I'm glad we're here. I was just afraid you'd want to talk about it.'

'You don't believe in talking about sex?'

'No, I don't. There's nothing anybody can say about it that isn't embarrassing and stupid. Yes, it was as good for me as it was for you. Yes, you're the best ever. As if you didn't know. If I didn't say that, you'd kill yourself, after all those years of practice.'

'I just want you to be happy – about tonight, about me, about you. No regrets.'

'There is one part I regret. It's that the minute I let you look at the Poole crime scene, all the old boys were thinking, "Hmmm. She's not bad. I wonder how long it'll take good old Joe to get her in the sack." And here I am. They were right, and I hate that.'

'What old boys?'

'Jim Spengler and the homicide guys in Los Angeles, your buddy Doug Crowley in San Francisco. My own friends up here.'

'Do you think it's possible to be too conscious about what other people might or might not be thinking?'

'No.'

'Oh. So I take it you don't do this kind of thing often.'

'Practically never.'

'I hope that will change.'

'If you want it to, it will.'

'Really?'

'Yes. I make big decisions carefully, and with both eyes open. I wouldn't have done this once if I didn't think I might be interested in something more lasting.'

'Would you consider having an exclusive relationship with me?'

'That's pretty quick,' she said.

'I make big decisions with both eyes open too. Will you?'

'Only if you're willing to do it sincerely,' said Catherine. 'If it isn't working out, we'll see it right away.'

'Then what?'

'Catch and release.'

'Sounds humane.'

'Practical too. Neither of us has to bury a corpse.'

'Deal,' he said. 'As of some hours ago – I don't have my watch on – you and I have been seeing each other exclusively, with serious intent.' He lay there for a time, staring at the ceiling. 'You've always insisted on being professional, so we don't really know anything about each other. We'll have to start talking about personal things from the start. How many children were you thinking of?'

She pushed him over quickly, rolled onto his chest, and kissed him. 'Oh, boy. I've got to take you to meet my parents before you come to your senses and get away.'

THIRTY-EIGHT

It was shocking. Judith Nathan could hardly believe what she saw in front of her on the television screen. She stood up and stepped closer to the cabinet where the hotel had secured the television set and squinted to be sure that it wasn't just someone who looked similar. No, it was Catherine Hobbes, absolutely. She was getting out of an unmarked police car with a tall male cop. Now she came around the front of the car and they both pulled another man out of the back seat. He was a shorter man wearing a short-sleeved pullover shirt that looked tight. He seemed to be a bodybuilder.

The picture cut to Hobbes and the other cop, standing outside a police station, and it must have been later. Hobbes was saying, 'During our visit Mr Olson became agitated and tried to run. We searched the house and found Mrs Olson bound and locked in the trunk of Mr Olson's car. The hospital says she's in stable condition and will recover from her injuries.' She listened to a reporter's virtually inaudible question, then touched a spot on her forehead where there seemed to be a bruise and a scratch. 'This? Yes.' She smiled. 'It was a lucky punch.' She turned away from the reporters and went inside.

'Bitch,' said Judith Nathan. 'You horrible bitch.' Catherine Hobbes was becoming a celebrity, practically. She was placing herself in front of the television cameras all the time now. Was anybody supposed to believe that it had been just little Catherine Hobbes fighting with that man? What had that big male cop been doing while that was going on? The man they had in handcuffs didn't even look like a bad person, just some ordinary man the cops had scooped up to use as a fall guy. He would be destroyed to give Catherine Hobbes one more moment of glory. Disgusting.

Everything had turned into a disaster. She had not been given time to start living. Every time she began to get settled, Catherine Hobbes would start in again, telling lies about her, circulating her picture everywhere she tried to live. Every time she went anywhere, Catherine Hobbes seemed to show up a day later. Maybe Judith should have taken Catherine Hobbes more seriously. She had thought that coming back to Portland was a clever idea, because it was the last place anyone would expect to see her. But the price was that she had to live in the same city as Catherine Hobbes.

That night she lay in bed, unable to sleep. Staying free could not be that hard. There seemed to be lots of people who had done things but never got found. It all seemed to depend on who was looking. The main one who was looking for her, the one who kept traveling around and convincing everyone that they had to drop everything and search for small, solitary Tanya Starling, was Catherine Hobbes.

The video clip of Catherine Hobbes on television kept repeating in her memory. It was like one of those dreams she sometimes had that reminded her there was something important that she had forgotten. There was something she was supposed to do that she had not done.

In the morning Judith Nathan left her hotel room, bought a newspaper in the lobby, and went out to begin searching for an apartment. She found one early, and gave Solara Estates in Denver as her last address. Because she had just arrived in town and had no local bank account yet, the landlady didn't mind taking her rent and deposit in cash.

Judith Nathan drove Tyler's Mazda to see a garage that was for rent about a mile from her new apartment building. The entrance was in an alley, and the rent was cheap, so Judith Nathan paid the owner in cash for six months' rent in advance. Judith stopped at a hardware store and bought a good combination padlock for the bolt on the garage door.

Over the next few days Judith Nathan drove to stores where she could buy the things she needed to furnish her apartment – unassembled furniture, a few lamps, and a television set. The apartment had a refrigerator and stove, so she bought groceries.

She was comfortable now, so she filled Tyler's Mazda with gas, drove it to her rented garage, parked it inside, and locked the garage door. As she walked home, she began to make her next set of plans. It was time to find out what Catherine was doing.

THIRTY-NINE

Hugo Poole sat in his office beside the projection room of the Empire Theater. He was thinking seriously about going out to a club tonight, just for the sake of being seen. Since Dennis had been killed he had virtually shut himself away, and that was not good for business. Just as he stood up, the telephone rang. He picked it up, and said, 'Yeah?'

'Hugo Poole?'

'You got me.'

'This is Calvin Dunn.'

'What's happening?'

'I called to find out what Joe Pitt is doing in Portland.'

'Joe Pitt? I don't know.'

'You don't?' said Calvin Dunn. 'It's a relief to me that you don't know. I would really hate it if you were trying to set up a competition.'

'A competition? Why? So I could take bets on who bags her?'

'Sometimes people who are smarter than anybody else think too much. They figure out ways to get themselves twisted around and meet themselves coming back.'

'Not me, Calvin. I paid him off and thanked him for his efforts before I ever called you. Where did you see him?'

'He's at the same hotel where I'm staying,' said Dunn. 'If you didn't send him, then he's just part of the mix. I'll change hotels. This girl has popped about four people now, so it's possible somebody else hired him to find her. I'll let you know when it's done.'

Hugo Poole put his telephone down and stared at the office wall. It was clear that he had just managed to duck while Calvin Dunn's resentment had whistled past him. Dunn was said to be very good at what he did, but he was too temperamental. Hugo didn't like having to be tolerant of jealousies and fits of egotism.

The call made him wonder what Pitt was doing. It could be the little policewoman, Catherine Hobbes. She was single and a very nice little handful. The whole thing could be completely harmless – Pitt going up to Portland to spend time with Catherine Hobbes. Hugo reached for his telephone, but held his hand. It was not a good idea to call back. Calvin Dunn had seen her in Flagstaff, and he was smart enough to figure the rest out. If Hugo was right, he gained nothing, and if he was wrong, he would weaken his position with Calvin Dunn.

Calvin Dunn was not somebody he had ever wanted on his payroll. Hugo had resisted the idea for a long time. He had tried waiting for the Portland police to handle things, and then tried hiring Joe Pitt – a reputable detective who had some appreciation of the complexities of Los Angeles life that might have caused a killing way up there in Portland. What more could anybody expect? Hugo had been as patient as he could be, but he'd had a limited period of time.

He had needed to be sure that unfriendlies in L.A. didn't get the idea that Hugo Poole would permit someone to kill a member of his family without paying for it. He had to be sure that the friendlies didn't get the same idea and conclude that they had to make common cause with the unfriendlies. He had to be sure that the people who worked for him weren't put in danger by the rumor that he couldn't protect or avenge them. He had been in this life for so long that he had seen all of the moves in advance. He had given the authorities all the time that he could. Then he had hired Calvin Dunn.

He had also owed it to his aunt Ellen to do something. She was his aunt because she had been briefly married to his father's brother. She had barely known Hugo's mother, who had never even lived with his father, let alone married him. Hugo had been conceived on a late-night pickup in a bar. After Hugo's mother died, Ellen had come to the funeral and then driven him back to the apartment to pack and come with her.

She had put him into a bedroom to share with her son, Dennis, and explained that they were cousins. Then she had treated them exactly the same. Everything she had bought for Dennis, she had bought two of and given one to Hugo. Anytime she'd gone out, she'd carried three pictures in her wallet – her ex-husband, Dennis, and Hugo.

When he was seventeen, Hugo had left Ohio and come to California. He had not talked to Aunt Ellen again for four years, then called her on the telephone and asked her how she was. She had cried so much that he had barely understood anything except that she had been worried about him. He had told her that he was sending her a present, and he had mailed her a check for fifty thousand dollars.

He had kept calling her and sending her checks. Half of every conversation had been about Dennis – some degree he had earned, some job he had gotten, some promotion he'd won. When Dennis had started his own computer business, Aunt Ellen had put up half the money. It had come from Hugo's checks.

A few days after Hugo had heard about the new business, Dennis had called him. 'Is this Hugo?'

'Yeah?'

'This is Dennis.'

'Hey, Dennis. I hear from your mother that you're doing great, starting your own business and everything. I'm proud of you.'

'Thanks, Hugo,' said Dennis. 'That's really why I called after all this time. I wanted to tell you about it. The place is a computer sales business. I'm good at the technical part of it, but I'm finding that I need help. I wondered if you want a job. You could be vice president, and help me handle the people.'

Hugo had been paralyzed for a moment: Aunt Ellen had not told Dennis where the money had come from. Dennis had simply decided that because he'd had some luck he would share it with his cousin Hugo. Hugo had needed to answer. 'Dennis. I want you to know that I'm honored. It makes me happy that you would do this. But I can't accept.'

'Why not?'

'Here are three reasons. I've got a good job here, and I'm happy in L.A., and I don't know a thing about computers. I really appreciate it, though, Dennis.'

He remembered hearing his own voice and being shocked. People always said that they regressed when they talked to their parents, became themselves as children. Hugo didn't have any parents. What he did that day when he talked to Dennis was go all the way back to the fork in the road – the day he had left Ohio – and take the other choice. He sounded like the Hugo who would have existed if he had stayed in Ohio.

Hugo might be a failure and an embarrassment to people like his aunt Ellen and his cousin Dennis, but he was considered an enormous success in this part of the world. It was a place where things were for sale. If a man had a name for his wish, or if he could only describe it, somebody could be paid to make it happen. At least Hugo could do this. He could get the one who had killed the poor, ignorant sucker Dennis.

FORTY

As soon as her telephone service was working, Judith bought a laptop computer and printer and signed up for Internet service. She entered the online telephone directory and typed in Catherine Hobbes's telephone number to find her address. When she had it, she began to get restless.

The night was coming again, and Judith was always restless in the early evening. It was the time when other women were putting on their most attractive clothes and makeup. She had always loved dressing to go out at night. Even when she was a little girl on the pageant circuit, she had pretended she was getting ready to go out dancing instead of just out past the flat pieces of scenery and the electrical circuit board and onto the stage. The beginning of an evening out was the best that a person ever looked, the best that she could be – the most beautiful, the most excited, and the most eager.

Judith Nathan could not dress that way tonight. She slipped on the black pants and sneakers, the blue sweater and the jacket Tyler had left her, then put on Tyler's baseball cap and went out to walk. Night in Portland was much cooler and wetter than she liked, but she knew that she could get used to it if Catherine had. She walked toward the Adair Hill neighborhood, overlooking the west side of the river south of the downtown section, because that was where Catherine lived. It was a long walk, but she amused herself by watching the few stragglers driving home from work, while others were coming out of their houses in nice clothes, getting into their cars to go to restaurants and bars.

People didn't really see her as she walked by, her hair under Tyler's baseball cap and her hands in the pockets of the jacket. In the dark she was just a shape that was merely human, and even when the headlights from a turning car swept over her and she became female, she was just another young woman who walked after business hours to keep in shape.

She found the right street at around ten. She stared up the block cautiously, getting a feel for it before she dared go farther. It seemed fitting that Catherine would live up a hill, where she could look down on the city but not be touched by it, or even seen.

Judith studied the neighborhood, but saw nothing that looked threatening. It seemed to be the kind of residential area where people walked, but there was nobody out now to see her. East of the Willamette River and to the northwest of it, Portland was laid out on a north-south, east-west grid. It was only here, below West Burnside Street, that streets angled off a bit, and Catherine's street wound and cut back to get up the hill.

Judith liked it, because the curves in the road kept headlights from settling on her for more than a second or two. Before a car came around a bend she would see the cones of the headlights shining on the trees, and then the pair of lights would appear like eyes opening for only a second, and they would go past.

Catherine probably walked along this street fairly regularly, Judith decided. Maybe she even ran. Judith had not been going for her morning runs since she had needed to leave Los Angeles, and she could feel this climb exercising her calves and thighs.

Because she was on foot, Judith could watch the house numbers closely, and she became aware of each house that she passed. The core of the neighborhood was old houses built in the 1920s and '30s, and the details and proportions were different from the few brand-new houses. The old ones had narrow, arched doorways and steep, pointed gables that held small windows divided into many panes. The trees and shrubbery had been given whole lifetimes to grow and thicken around the walls, so some of the houses looked as though they were from the illustrations of children's books.

As the road climbed, the trees thinned and the yards were less heavily planted and impenetrable. At the top, the land leveled to become a rounded bluff, and there was a whole row of small, nearly uniform houses that seemed to have burrowed into the cliff. Each had two stories, with a garage on the lower level. There was a set of steps on the left side of each house leading up the hill to a back door.

There it was, number 4767. It was white with a bright yellow door. The lights were off except for a couple of automatic outdoor floods that had sensors to switch them on at dusk. Judith stood across the street where the lights did not reach her, studied the house for a long time, and then moved on.

Three nights later, Judith began to wonder what was going on in Catherine Hobbes's life. There seemed to be something going on, because every evening when Judith walked by Catherine's house on Adair Hill the windows were dark. Judith kept taking her walks later and later, and still Catherine was out. Judith began to be afraid that Catherine Hobbes was out of town scouring some other city for signs of Tanya Starling. She didn't want her doing that. Catherine Hobbes had to be home. She had to be in her bed up on the upper floor, in a deep, peaceful sleep.

On the fourth evening, she arrived on Catherine Hobbes's block at one-thirty a.m., just as the garage door below Catherine's living room opened and a small car pulled into the garage. Judith Nathan sidestepped onto the grass strip in front of the nearest house and knelt behind a fragrant, flowering bush to watch. Judith could see the car was a new Acura, teal blue. She wasn't sure how she knew, but she knew Catherine had chosen the model and color so it wouldn't be anything like the unmarked cop cars that Catherine drove at work. She saw Catherine get out of the car in the lighted garage, then walk to the side of the garage and press a switch on the wall. As the door rolled down, Catherine's head, then shoulders, then torso, legs, and feet disappeared.

The lights on Catherine's main floor came on. Judith walked past, looking at the other houses in the row. Judith could see that all of the houses must have been built by one contractor from a single set of blueprints. All of them had balconies facing the river except Catherine's; she had a set of greenhouse windows in place of the balcony.

Judith could see identical bowl-shaped light fixtures in the center of the ceilings of two of the houses, and the rest seemed to have replacement fixtures in the same spot. The garage doors were wide enough for two cars. The straight, plain staircases to the upper floor were all on the left sides of the houses. As Judith walked home, her body seemed weightless, her step was light, and it seemed to her that a day was beginning instead of ending. Things were starting to seem clear to her. That was really all that Judith asked, that she be able to discern what she should do.

In the morning she got the *Tribune* and the *Oregonian* and began to look at the ads for Acuras. The dealers were really the only choice, because she wanted hers to be in exactly the right color, and no private owner who had one seemed to be trying to get rid of it. She needed to have exactly the right one. She decided to let the question simmer in her brain for a time while she concentrated on settling into the new city. Judith kept herself busy most of the time, and she found that it gave her a kind of contentment. She had missed the sense that everything she did contributed in some way to a practical goal, and now she had it again.

Judith decided two days later, as dusk came on, that it was time for her to go out for the evening. She had a special problem, because her photograph had been on television many times, and probably most often in Portland. The color and style of her hair were different now, but she would have to be careful.

In Portland there was seldom a reason not to be dressed for rain, so Judith Nathan could wear a black raincoat with a high collar that she could use to abbreviate the profile of her face, and carry a small umbrella. She tried on the outfit and the coat and studied her appearance in the mirror. Then she put on some flat black shoes and walked to the bar she had selected. It was called Underground, and it was decorated to look like a London tube station.

Judith Nathan walked comfortably in the dark. It was her time. She had Mary Tilson's revolver in her coat pocket and her right hand on the grips. It amused her as she walked to study the men who passed her on the street, imagining each one of them recognizing her from her picture. She would anticipate how each one would go about his offense – rushing toward her, or pointing at her and yelling – and then think through exactly how she would free the gun from her raincoat, aim, and fire. The pistol she was carrying wasn't like Carl's .357 magnum. She would have to fire five or six times to silence a full-grown male. She would place three in his torso to put

333

him down, and then be sure to fire one into his head. She was sure she could do that.

She found the bar, and looked at it warily as she walked up. It was impossible to determine anything subtle from outside, but she could tell that it was crowded, and that the lighting came indirectly from some tiny spotlights behind the bar and some jars with candles in them on the tables. She could see that men wore coats and women wore dresses and business suits.

Judith Nathan slipped in the front door and used the bodies of a group of tall men to shield her from view while she verified her impressions. It was the sort of place where people went after work. Most of them bought their drinks at the bar and stood around talking rather than sitting at tables and waiting for the waitress. The one difficult part was that she had to come in, make her choice, and establish a relationship almost instantly. She glanced at the three men in front of her, and then sidestepped into one of them.

He was about six feet two and had a sculpted body that he showed off by taking off his sport coat just inside the door. His only imperfection was that he had a terrible complexion. His face was rough and pitted by acne scars. She smiled up at him and said, 'I'm sorry. I was just trying to slip through to the bar. If I've hurt you, I'll buy you a drink.'

He seemed to overcome years of shyness to say, 'I've got a longer reach. I'll buy us both one.'

She said, 'Thanks so much. I'll have a vodka martini.' Then she looked around her and said, 'I'm right in the doorway. Can you find me if I go to a table?'

'Sure.'

That gave her a chance to pick a dark corner of the room and claim it while she waited. She sat down at a table and blew out the candle.

The arrangement she had made held its own dangers for her. She knew nothing about this man, but she had grown up in a world that included date-rape drugs like GHB and Rohypnol, so watching her drink was a reflex. She saw the bartender ice a martini glass, pour vodka and vermouth in the silver shaker, fill the glass. She kept her eye on both of her new man's hands as he held the two drinks level and made his way through the crowd to her.

When he sat down at the small table she had chosen, she gave him another expert smile before she accepted her drink and took a sip. She felt the bright, icy liquid travel down her throat, and then a sudden glow as it reached her stomach. She had always imagined that reaction as small magic, a sudden warmth that exploded under her heart and spread outward to her toes and fingertips.

She looked over the rim of the glass at the crowd around her. This was the first time she had dared come out to a nightspot since she had been in Portland. There was always a chance that somebody in a bar would have seen a picture of her on television and be able to spot her even with her new light hair and different makeup. But this was a very dark bar, she was in the darkest corner, and the rest of the people here were fully engaged in trying to pick each other up. 'Thank you very much,' she said.

'You're welcome. I'm Greg. And what's your name?'

'Judy,' she said. 'This is a really good martini.'

It was enough to trigger his prepared sequence of small talk. He said, 'I haven't seen you here. Have you been here before? Were you brought up in Portland? I was. What do you do? I design software. Where did you go to college? Are you dating anybody?' with such relentless rapidity that it was like a series of combination punches he had practiced so there would never be a moment of awkward silence.

Judith Nathan needed to help him avoid the silences, so she answered each question, some of them as though she were blocking or diverting his blows, but others more carefully. She said, 'I'm not working right now. I'm going to be an entrepreneur, but I haven't figured out the best business to be in right now. It's a tricky economy.'

'What have you done before?' he asked.

'I've tried a couple of things, but I haven't hit the right one yet. I tried starting a magazine, and I wanted to do a gift-buying service for men but couldn't get funding. If you've got any surefire ideas you'd like to share, I'd be delighted to hear them.'

She also answered the one about college. She said, 'I went to school in the East, at Boston University. I was only there for about three years, and then I left.'

'Why did you do that?'

'Fatal pragmatism.'

'What's fatal pragmatism?'

'I was out alone like this. And I met a man.'

'I'm sorry. I guess I was being nosy.'

'Don't be sorry. There's nothing mysterious. He was older. He had some money. I just compared what I was doing – being snubbed by snotty girls in the dorm and writing term papers – with what he was doing. His life was better, so I decided to do what he was doing.'

'What happened? Did you get married?'

'No. We broke up and I moved on.'

She had him within the first two minutes. Because he was shy, she was saying enough to make it clear that having a relationship with a man she met like this had a precedent. But in order to build on her progress she had to help him win himself over. He had to feel that when he was with her he could be smart and attractive.

She said, 'What is it like to be a software designer?'

'I like it a lot, but it's probably boring to other people.'

'That's perfect job security,' she said. 'If it looked like fun, everybody would be doing it.'

'I guess that's true,' he said. She could see he was beginning to trust her enough to forget his fear of seeming dull and foolish. He said, 'It's actually a lot more exciting than it looks. The code we write is moving to the edge, and changing a lot of things fast.'

'You mean things in people's lives?'

'Sometimes. Okay. You've got all these machines already, with incredible capacity. Every two years the next chip doubles the speed of the machine, and the minute you have a new machine you can make a hundred million of them. The competition, the hard part, is that somebody has to think up the killer application and then write code to make a computer do it. It's like—' He paused. 'I don't know, because the second I say it, somebody's already doing it. Say you want to control your house with your cell phone.'

'Control my house? Why?'

'Just say you do. Set the temperature, lock and unlock doors, turn lights and appliances on and off, take a look to see what the dog is doing, set the alarm. There's not a bit of new technology involved. It's all a lot of simple operations using pieces of equipment we already have. But somebody has to design a new chip for the cell phone and program it both to send intelligible signals to a phone receiver in the house with a chip that would serve as a switcher, and to receive messages to tell it the status of each of the appliances. You can't change the thermostat if you don't know what the temperature is.'

'That's what you do?'

'It's a dumb example, but that's the general idea. What we do is a lot more complicated than that. Most of it has to do with defense.'

'But that's really exciting. That kind of thinking

extends the range of things a person can do. It makes us stronger and smarter. Is that what you meant by being on the edge?'

'What I think of as the edge is the next step – moving into code that's computer generated.'

'That's the next step?'

'For me it is. That's what I work on. The idea is that the computer gets designed and programmed to recognize the points in the world around it where there could be an application. It will say, "You're doing this task this way. Why not do it a different way and save a step?" Or "Can you combine this task and that task?" See? It's computers suggesting their own applications.'

'What a great idea.' She had him. He was absolutely hers now, a possession like a pair of shoes or a car.

He said, 'Then once you have this machine analyzing your operations for things to do, you give it the capacity to write code. Computers do most operations faster than we can, and they have digital memories that are theoretically unlimited. We could have the computer see and analyze a task, go into its memory or online to find existing programming that can accomplish the task, customize it in a second or two, and do the task.'

'That would put you out of business, wouldn't it?' she said.

Greg was delighted, intoxicated with the unfamiliar pleasure of having an attractive woman listen to what he was saying. 'It will put us out of one part of the business – the dull part, where you're just writing derivative code, testing, finding bugs, and making patches – and into a hundred others.'

'Wow,' said Judith Nathan. 'I envy you so much. You're working on such exciting things. You must jump out of bed in the morning and run to work.'

He said, 'I do run to work.' He had finished his

scotch, but he didn't notice it until he picked the glass up, put it to his mouth, and had the ice clink against his teeth. 'I think we need another drink, don't you?'

She looked at her martini judiciously. 'I don't usually have more than one of these, but I don't usually have anybody interesting to talk to. Okay.'

She watched him bring two more drinks to the table. He drank his while they talked, but Judith Nathan simply brought hers up to wet her lips now and then.

She manufactured a special evening for Greg. What he said was brilliant, because she was impressed by it. When he tried to say something mildly witty, it was hilarious, because she laughed at it. He became physically attractive, because she focused her attention on the parts of himself he was proud of. When she laughed, she touched his biceps or leaned on his shoulder. When he spoke she stared directly into his eyes, never letting him remember that she must have noticed his rough, pitted skin.

She knew that he had, at some point in his teens, begun doing exercise to compensate for the attractions he lacked. He had studied to compensate for the fact that he wasn't clever or charming. He was a man who had learned one thing well – that patient, tireless effort would be his salvation – and he was slowly developing confidence.

When the bar began to lose some of its customers, she said, 'Well, Greg, it's getting late. I'm glad I met you. I was beginning to think that there weren't any men left who were smart enough to talk about something that hadn't been on TV.' She pushed her chair away from the table.

He said, 'It's been a pleasure talking to you. I – uh – wonder, would you give me your number?'

'Sure,' she said. 'I thought you'd never ask.' She took a pen out of her purse, wrote it on her cocktail napkin, and handed it to him. She stood up, and he stood up with her, but she didn't move. 'I'm waiting to be sure you can read it. Can you?'

He held it up and scrutinized it in the dim light. 'Yes. I can.'

'Good. Then if you don't call me I'll know that wasn't it.' She quickly turned and walked to the door. Just before she went out, she glanced back at him. He was leaning close to the table, transferring her number to his Palm Pilot. She kept moving, trying to keep from being face-to-face with any of the patrons lingering near the doorway.

The night air had turned cooler now, and after she had walked a few blocks it began to rain. She found that she was in the mood for walking, so she opened her umbrella and kept going. It took her forty-five minutes to get home, and it seemed to rain harder and harder as she went. When she arrived she was wet, so she slipped inside, locked the door, and undressed in the entry. She went into the bathroom and took a long, hot bath. She was winning again. It seemed to have been a long time since she had felt that way.

FORTY-ONE

It was still raining in the morning when Greg called Judy Nathan. He spoke as though he had read some article that said women liked to be approached in surprising ways at surprising times, but she tolerated the call anyway. She accepted his offer to take her out to dinner, then said, 'Wait a minute. You know, I have an idea. The weatherpeople say it's going to be raining all day and all night, and maybe we don't need to get all dressed up to tromp around in the rain. Why don't we just have dinner at my place? It'll be really simple, I promise. I have this tiny apartment and I don't have the equipment here to cook anything elaborate anyway. Come on. It'll be nice.'

He protested feebly, but she seemed not to have heard. She said, 'Good. I can't wait. Be here at seven, and don't get dressed up.'

'Be where?'

She told him the address and was ready to hang up when he said, 'There was one other thing I wanted to talk about.'

'What's that?'

'Do you want a job?'

'What?'

'A job. Our company, Prolix Software Design, has an opening. It's not a huge salary, but it's okay, and it would put you in a better position to start your business.'

'It would?'

'Well, you can save money, or at least stop living off

your capital, and you'll learn more about the city and the business climate and all that.'

'Let me think about it later,' she said. 'Right now I'm busy planning dinner.'

She heard a smile in his voice. 'Okay. Just keep it in mind.'

'Sure. See you at seven.'

The clock above Judy Nathan's stove said exactly seven when she heard the door intercom ring. She said, 'I assume it's you?' and heard Greg's voice say, 'I hope I'm not late.' She said, 'Think I'd eat without you?' and buzzed him in. She opened the door and waited in the hallway for him to appear.

He came up the stairs carrying a bouquet of flowers that had the distinctive paper wrap of Fleuriste, and a paper shopping bag from a gourmet shop that held two bottles of wine, one red and the other white. She stood on tiptoes to kiss his cheek. 'Somebody raised you right.'

'Thanks,' he said. 'I'll call my mom and tell her.' He was looking around him anxiously.

She took the flowers and the bottles. 'These aren't wet. Did the rain stop?'

'No. I kept them under my raincoat.'

He took off his raincoat and she saw that he had followed her orders to the extent of not wearing a coat and tie, but he had on tailored pants, a cashmere sweater, and a pair of shoes that were too good to wear out in the rain. 'What beautiful shoes.'

'Huh? Oh, thanks. I got them on sale about a year ago.'

'You did not,' she said. 'They're new. Somebody told you that women are impressed by nice shoes. Take them off, and your wet socks. I'll get you something to wear.'

He waited while she took his coat to her bedroom and hung it up, then snatched a pair of wool socks from a drawer. He held them in his hand and looked at them. They were just about his size. 'Why do you have these?'

'One time I didn't notice somebody had put some men's socks on the women's rack, and I bought a few pairs in a hurry.' She had bought the socks this morning while she was out preparing for the evening.

He put the dry socks on and followed her toward the kitchen area. The open kitchen was separated from the living room only by a high counter with two high stools. She had moved the dining table and chairs out of the kitchen, to the other side of the counter. She arranged the flowers in a vase she had bought this morning, and placed them on the dinner table.

'I have some scotch if you'd like that before dinner,' she said. 'I noticed that was your drink.'

'Thank you,' he said.

She poured him a scotch and water that was a good facsimile of the drink he'd ordered last night. Then she brought canapés and caviar to the coffee table, and sat on the couch with him.

He said, 'I thought this wasn't going to be fancy.'

'I said it was going to be simple. You don't cook caviar. You just open a jar. So how was your day?'

'It went kind of slow,' he said. 'I spent most of it looking forward to coming here.'

She grinned. 'Wow. Where are you getting this stuff? Is there some men's magazine that tells you exactly what to say? I thought all they had were pictures of naked girls.'

'If there is a magazine like that, I'd like a subscription,' he said. 'I'm always blurting out the wrong thing because I'm nervous. With you I just feel happy, so I don't get as messed up, I guess.'

'Another good thing to say. Maybe I'll start a men's magazine and let you write for it.'

'Have you thought about the job I told you about?'

'Not yet. I will, though. What is it?'

'It's support – a lot of filing and typing and answering phones. But in little companies you can make your own way quickly. You tear off as much work as you can do, and pretty soon that's your job, and they hire somebody else to answer your phone.'

'How many people in the company?'

'Only thirty. Our section is ten. There are ten in sales, ten in administration. They're all young, and get along okay.'

'Would I work for you?'

'No. You'd be in admin.'

'I don't know. I'll think about it some more.' She stood up. 'Time to get dinner going. Just vault over the counter if you want to see me be domestic.'

He followed her into the cramped little kitchen, and she said, 'I promised you cozy. This is cozy, isn't it?'

'I like it, and I like what you've done with it.'

She smiled. She had spent most of the day buying the prints that hung on the walls, the dishes and flatware on the table, the cookware and the food, the sheets on the bed and the bedspread.

The dinner seemed to materialize rather than be prepared. The lobster tails and the filets mignons were broiled and the asparagus seared, the wines poured. Judy had never been interested in cooking, so while she had lived in the apartment high above the lake in Chicago she had developed a few very basic meals that she could make by simply applying heat and butter. She poured the wine liberally, and drank sparingly. When they had eaten the main courses, she produced a plate of tarts and napoleons she had bought at a downtown bakery.

Greg had experienced so few occasions when any woman had even tried to impress him that he could barely

344

contain his delight at each part of the evening. After dinner she walked into the living room carrying cognac in small snifters, but Greg said, 'If I have this, I'm not going to be able to drive home.'

She said, 'Who said I wanted you to go home?' and sat on the couch to kiss him.

Later that night, she lay on her back in bed, listening to his breathing. Now and then a deep breath would end in a little snort, but she didn't mind. She knew that when she wanted to sleep, she would. She decided that she was satisfied with her progress. She had only picked Greg out twenty-four hours ago, and she knew that by now he would do anything she wanted.

The difficult part had never been getting a man interested in her. All men seemed to be doomed to hunt for sexual partners all the time, like restless, lonely ghosts. The problem was in choosing the right man, but she was almost certain she had chosen well in Greg. He appeared to be convinced that he was in the romance of his life, the one that made all of the conventional rules and precautions seem ridiculous.

The next morning, while they were eating the breakfast she had bought yesterday with the knowledge that he was going to be here to share it, he said, 'I hope you'll take that job.'

'I've decided against it.'

'When?'

'Last night. At the same time when I decided you weren't going home.'

'Why?'

'I hate complications.'

'What complications?'

'If you and I break up, I couldn't stand to work there. If you and I don't break up, other people couldn't stand to work there.'

He let it drop. She had to wait a whole week before he brought up the topic she was waiting for. He was taking her home after a dinner in a dark, romantic restaurant when he said, 'You never tell me about driving anywhere. Don't you have a car?'

'No.'

'Why not?'

'I'd like one,' she said. 'I know exactly the kind I want and everything. But I can't.'

'Why not – money?'

'No,' she said. 'Can you keep a secret?'

'Of course. Let me tell you all of the secrets I've kept.'

'Seriously. Do you promise?'

'All right.'

'Well, I have a lot of tickets from when I went to school in Boston. There was never any place that was legal to park, so I have parking tickets for all three years – about seven thousand dollars' worth. If you couldn't make it to class, you couldn't pass, so it seemed to be the only choice.'

'So you're an outlaw parker?'

'Yep. I left Boston, and figured that was the end of it. But I found out that some judge had issued a warrant for my arrest. I tried to register a car in Colorado once, and my name came up on the computer. They wouldn't let me register a car unless I paid the fines. I didn't have that kind of money at the time, and so I didn't do it.'

'I've never heard of anything like this,' said Greg. 'At least not for parking.'

'Neither had I until it happened to me. But here I am. I can buy a car. I just can't register it or get insurance for it.'

'Not to be too obvious, but have you thought about solving the problem by paying the fine?'

'Of course. At first I didn't take it seriously. It seemed

346

like everyone was doing it. Then I got kind of mad, because it's just a way for the city to make money off all these disenfranchised students from other places. Then I figured I'd better pay it. But by the time I was in Colorado it wasn't seven thousand dollars. Those penalties had been growing for seven or eight years. It was up to about fifteen, and now that there's a warrant, we're talking about lawyers, and going back to court in Boston. They could put me in jail to make an example of me. Anyway, now you know why I don't have a car.'

'It's a bad situation,' he said. 'Let me think about it.'

'I'm not asking you to solve it,' she said. 'It's my problem.'

Three days later, while they were on their way to a movie, he said, 'Did I get it wrong, or did you tell me you have the money for a car?'

She shrugged. 'Yes, I have the money. But big deal.'

'I've got an idea. You give me the money, and I'll buy the car. I'll add your car to my insurance, which will also make it cheaper. Second cars cost practically nothing to insure.'

'But then my car will be registered in your name. What happens if you get tired of having me around?'

'You'll be driving a car that's registered and insured in my name. What happens if you decide to drive it through the front wall of a nursery school?'

'I guess we have to trust each other.'

She forced tears to well in her eyes, put her hand on his knee so he turned to look at her, and then kissed him on the rough skin of his cheek. 'I think this is the best thing anybody ever did for me.'

'So be nice to me forever. What kind of car do you want?'

'An Acura. Teal blue.'

FORTY-TWO

Catherine Hobbes stood in the outer lobby of the airport, her hand on Joe Pitt's arm. 'I think this is as far as I go.'

He said, 'You're a cop. You could flash your badge at the security guys and they'd let you go to the gate with me.'

'How about if we put you in handcuffs, and I say I'm escorting you to trial in California?'

'I wish you would escort me to California.'

'Me too. But I can't leave here now. I've got three cases that are heating up and one that's getting cold, and that's scary. It's the one we're both interested in.'

'The only thing about that case I'm interested in is you. My client let me go, remember? Then he replaced me with a professional psychotic.'

'I haven't been replaced, and I'm going to do my job before I go anywhere with the likes of you. Stop stalling and go to your gate, or you'll miss your plane.'

He held her and she put her arms around his neck and gave him a lingering kiss. 'That's not going to make things easier,' he said.

'Who said it was supposed to be easy?' she said. 'Now move it.'

She watched him as he turned and hurried up the escalator, taking three steps at a time until he came up behind a lady who was stopped on a step above him, then turned and waved. A moment later, he was at the top and gone.

Catherine walked out of the terminal and headed across the street toward her car. She had delayed driving in to the police bureau on North Thompson Street by telling the captain she thought she ought to drive Joe Pitt to the airport. It had not aroused his suspicion, but it had not exactly been honest. She had not said that since their collaboration was over she had been dating him.

For the thousandth time she had the same thought, that the words for the dealings between people of the two sexes were always wrong. She wasn't dating him. She had thought about him for a long time and then started sleeping in his hotel room with him and then rushing home every morning to get ready for work, or just spending the evening with him and driving home at one or two a.m. for three or four hours of unconsciousness. They didn't have dates. When one of them was hungry the other would say, 'Let's go eat,' and she would drive them to a nice restaurant, because Portland was her city. On three rainy nights when the restaurants had been near her house, they had slept there instead of driving back to his hotel.

The words were always wrong. If they kept getting along, then there would be a time when he would be called her boyfriend, even though he was over forty and already much more intimate than any friend, and she would be his girlfriend, even though she was hardly a girl and had already been married and divorced. The only time the words were right was when people changed their behavior to fit the words. When people were married they tried to fill the space made by the word, behaved the way they had sworn they would – all of them except her ex-husband, Kevin, anyway.

Was she going to marry Joe Pitt? When she had met him she had experienced the standard reaction. She had wondered, 'Is he the one?' but she had gone to the

Internet to learn about him, asked the older male detectives if anybody knew him, listened to what they said, and decided that he almost certainly wasn't husband material. But maybe that was just another case of the words setting up an expectation that wasn't real. Right now he was the one. That was the only word she could think of that described the relationship: the one.

She got into her car and drove through the early-morning traffic to North Thompson Street to get to work. She still went in as early as she could every day to work at finding Tanya Starling while her mind was fresh and she had solitude and silence. Today she was starting late. She could spend only a half hour reviewing the information she had about Tanya Starling and searching bulletins and circulars for anything that might relate to the case before the other homicide detectives began to arrive. This morning her in-box was full, but there were no signs in it that Tanya Starling had been seen anywhere.

Catherine had a theory about what was going on. Tanya would be living in a very quiet way in an apartment in a distant city, working at developing a new identity. She would probably be dyeing her hair again, making herself fake identification, and constructing a reason for being where she was. She would try to wait long enough for all of the law enforcement agencies all over the country to be buried in circulars about other people.

Catherine knew her, and yet the feeling of knowing was like being gagged. The things she knew weren't things that she could prove to anyone or translate into action. Tanya had been born with a reasonably agile mind, and whatever had made her into a killer – or maybe the actual experience of killing – had made her an avid learner. Tanya was learning at a phenomenal rate. Every day that went by while she was free seemed to make her better at staying free. Every time she killed someone she did it differently. The other detectives had all interpreted the range of methods she'd used as proof that someone else had been in charge all along, and Tanya was just the companion. Catherine had known since Los Angeles that it wasn't true – no man had been in Mary Tilson's apartment, and no man had been on the security tapes going into Brian Corey's hotel room. Tanya had no companion. Tanya's methods were new each time because she was learning.

Tanya had learned some things between Portland and Flagstaff that made her much more dangerous. She had learned how to isolate victims, she had learned that there were lots of ways of denying blood to the heart and brain, and then she had learned that she could induce other people to do the killing for her. Now anything could happen.

At ten, a fresh homicide case arrived on Catherine's desk. The previous night there had been a burglary in the house in Arlington Heights where Marjorie and Jack Hammond lived. When Catherine arrived at the house, Marjorie Hammond had been so carefully made up, coifed, and dressed that to Catherine she looked as though she had been sitting for a portrait. The responding officer's report said Marjorie Hammond was forty-two years old, but like some beautiful women, she seemed to be without age.

She had been present when her husband had shot an intruder in the dark house in the night, and they had tried uselessly to stop the bleeding until the ambulance had arrived. The downstairs entrance and hallway were still blocked off with tape, so Mrs Hammond met Catherine at the kitchen door. Catherine sat in a spotless, cheerful sunroom at the back of the house while Mrs Hammond brought tea on a Chinese lacquerware tray.

Catherine said, 'I know it's hard to talk about what

happened here last night, but you understand that we do have to be able to explain all of it.'

'I understand.'

'Do you mind if I record our conversation? It helps when I make out my report.'

'No.'

Catherine took the recorder out of her pocket so Mrs Hammond could see it, turned it on, and said, 'This is Detective Sergeant Catherine Hobbes. I am recording my interview with Mrs Marjorie Hammond at . . . eleven-thirteen a.m. on October fifth.' She put the tape recorder back into her coat pocket. 'Let's see. You and your husband told the responding officers last night that you had never seen the intruder before. Is that right?'

'Yes.'

'By the way, where is your husband right now?'

'Jack?' She looked shocked. 'He's at work. I thought it would help him get through the experience if he went back to his routines right away. Men are creatures of routine, aren't they?'

'Are they?'

'Of course. Their work habits rely on it, and even the things they do for pleasure they do exactly the same each time. Once you've watched fifty football games, what can be new in the fifty-first, or the five thousandth? But it seems to give them some kind of reassurance.'

'What about you? Are you getting through the experience?'

'I'll be okay.'

Looking at her, Catherine sensed that it wasn't going to be that easy. She seemed too put together, too perfect. He should be here. 'I guess I can interview him separately,' said Catherine. Alarm signals were everywhere, but Catherine wasn't ready to decide exactly what they meant. 'Tell me what happened.'

'Well, Jack was working late last night. He had been in Seattle at a trade show. He sells power tools, mostly for the construction industry, and they were showing off a new line. I was upstairs in bed, asleep. Jack arrived home around midnight, came upstairs, and started to get ready for bed.'

'Did he wake you up?'

'Yes. I heard him trying to undress in the bathroom, so I turned on a light by the bed and called out to him. That was when we realized that there was someone else in the house.'

Catherine's eyes went to the doorway across the sun-room to the alarm keypad near the back door. 'Was the alarm system turned on?'

'He turned it on when he came in. I should have done it before I went upstairs, but I forgot because Jack usually does it, and so I didn't think of it.'

'Does he go away on business often?'

'Not really. There are conferences sometimes, or training sessions he has to go to so he can demonstrate new machines. Once in a while he goes somewhere to make a sale and stays over. It's only a few nights a year.'

'What time did you expect him to come home last night?'

'Actually, I didn't know he was coming home. I thought he'd be home tonight. But he got his meetings in early, and he caught a flight yesterday.'

'And when he goes away, do you usually forget the alarm?'

'I don't usually forget. I guess I was sleepy last night. That's all.'

'Okay. So you said you realized there was someone in the house. How?'

'Jack was the one who noticed. When I called to him that I was awake, he answered, then started down the stairs. He had left his suitcase in the entry because he didn't want to wake me up clunking around with it, but since I was awake, he decided to go down to get it. When he reached the top of the stairs he heard something. He ran back to his dresser, where he keeps the gun. He told me to get ready to call nine-one-one, and went down to search the house.'

Catherine was having the experience again of listening to someone lie, but not being quite sure of what the lie was. The secret that all police officers knew but that other people seemed not to was that truth and lies were not mutually exclusive. They were always mixed together in a kind of stew and had to be separated. Every person who told a police officer a story was lying. Sometimes they were only making themselves look braver or more sensible than they really had been in a crisis, and sometimes they were fabricating whole incidents to hide the fact that they had committed a crime. But while they spoke, Catherine always detected the same signs of lying in their faces and bodies. 'So he went downstairs alone?'

'Yes.'

'Where were you and what were you doing?'

'First I asked him not to do it, but he wouldn't listen. Then I took the phone off its cradle and brought it with me to the top of the stairs.'

'Did you turn on the lights?'

'No.'

'Why not?'

'We had heard someone making noises down here.'

'What kind?'

'Footsteps.'

'Walking or running?'

'Walking, at first, I guess. Then, when Jack came down, I think it was more like running. The man was trying to get into a good hiding place before Jack got there.'

'What then?'

'When Jack got there he started looking around. The man jumped out of the closet at him, and Jack fired.'

'How many times?'

'Once. No, twice. We called the police.'

'Who did?'

'I did.'

'And you told the responding officers that you didn't know Samuel Daily.'

'Oh. That was his name, wasn't it? I remember the police officer looked at his wallet and said it. No, we didn't know him.'

Catherine said very carefully, 'Before your husband arrived, did the intruder touch you?'

'No,' she said.

'Sometimes women don't say anything when something like that happens. I don't know if they're too traumatized to remember it clearly, or they block it out entirely, or if they have some misguided feeling that it must have been their fault. Maybe they're afraid their husbands will have the wrong idea. But nothing like that happened to you?'

'No. I already told you,' she said. 'I was upstairs asleep. He was downstairs.'

'Do you have any idea what he might have been after?'

'I don't know.'

Catherine was getting close to it, and she sensed that as Mrs Hammond got more agitated, she was beginning to forget the tape recorder. 'Sam Daily is the part of this that I can't quite get to fit,' Catherine said. 'He had no criminal record. He had a good job. He was a shift manager at a big supermarket. It's the Mighty Food

Mart down on Tillamook.' She paused. 'Have you ever shopped there?'

'No.'

'Are you sure? It might explain a lot.'

'What would it explain?' She was confused, wary.

'Well, he doesn't seem to have stolen anything in your house, or even tried to. And he came here on one of the few nights when your husband was away. If he had noticed you in the store, he might have been stalking you. If you pay with a check, they have your name and address. He might have begun to watch you, seen your husband leave with a suitcase or seen that his car was gone, and come for you.'

Mrs Hammond's mind seemed to be working hard to evaluate the suggestion. 'You know, I may have been there once or twice. It's not my regular store. But I'll bet you're right. I'm lucky my husband came home when he did.' She was grasping for the story, trying to make it her own.

'It's a theory, anyway,' said Catherine. 'It's possible he wanted to incapacitate your husband or kill him, so he could sexually assault you. Some of them even like to make the husband watch.'

'That's terrible,' said Mrs Hammond.

'You're right. We'll just have to wait for the rest of the information to come in and tell us which speculations are right.'

'What do you mean?'

Catherine watched her face. 'Don't worry. We'll try everything. We'll be looking at your financial records – credit cards, canceled checks, and so on – to pinpoint exactly when you were in that store, and then check the store's payroll to see if he was working those days. We'll be interviewing your neighbors to learn whether they've seen him hanging around. We'll ask his co-workers if he had any pictures of you, if he had any absences at odd times, like a few hours during the day when he might have been spying on you. We'll look at his phone records to see which numbers he might have called to find out your husband's travel schedule.'

Marjorie Hammond looked sick. 'What – what can possibly be the point? We know he was here, and he's dead. It's over.'

Catherine was sure now what the lie was. She had to keep pushing. 'Not for the police bureau. It's an open case. The forensics people were already here from twelve-thirty a.m. until around nine this morning, right? I haven't seen their report yet, of course. It will tell us a lot.'

Mrs Hammond said, 'I want my lawyer.'

'What?'

'Turn off the tape recorder. I won't speak to you anymore without my lawyer.'

'Do you have a lawyer?'

'I'll get one.'

'Okay. I'll read you your rights, and then I'll turn it off.' She recited the warning, then took out the tape recorder, turned it off, and put it back into her pocket. She said, 'And, of course, you'll have to come with me to the police bureau and wait for your lawyer so we can have the rest of our conversation.' She stood up and took out her handcuffs. 'Turn around, please.'

Marjorie Hammond was shocked. 'I didn't do anything.'

'I believe you didn't shoot anyone,' said Catherine. 'All you were doing was spending time with Sam Daily. Your husband came home early and caught you together.'

'No,' she said. 'It's not true. None of it is true. The whole thing is a lie.'

Catherine switched on the tape recorder in her pocket.

'You said you wanted your lawyer. You know that when I read you your rights it meant that you don't have to say anything to me at all, right? You'll have an opportunity to say whatever you want after your attorney is present.'

'Yes. I know that. But I'm telling you the story you made up isn't true. I didn't do anything. There was nothing going on between me and Sam Daily.'

Catherine knew Mrs Hammond was walking right along the edge, and in a moment she would topple over. 'Don't worry. If what you're saying is true, the physical evidence will prove you're right.'

'What physical evidence?'

'From the crime scene people. They search for blood, hair, fibers, fingerprints. If they haven't found any DNA from Sam Daily in your room, your clothing or bedding, and they didn't find any of yours on him – hairs, saliva, and so on – or any traces of your makeup, then probably the case will be closed just as you said.'

Catherine clicked the handcuffs shut on her wrists, and the voice came again, but it was changed. This time it was a whisper. 'Sergeant. Please.'

'What?'

'Please don't let them do that.'

'Why?'

'I told you the truth. It's the truth.'

'Do you mean it's what you want to have been true?'

'It's what happened. My husband didn't come in and catch us. He came home and started to get ready for bed. Sam really did hide in the downstairs coat closet, and when Jack opened the door, Sam did jump out at him. Jack's gun went off. It was an accident. Just a horrible accident.'

'Do you mean that Jack didn't intend to pull the trigger?'

'No. I mean yes, I suppose he did. But it was because he thought Sam was a burglar, trying to kill him. It was dark, and how could he know that Sam didn't have a knife or a gun too? He thought he had to shoot – that he was protecting his life, and mine too. Neither of them had ever seen each other before, and neither wanted to hurt anyone. It was just a terrible misunderstanding. An accident.'

'So your husband, Jack, really thought he was being attacked, and Sam thought he was about to be murdered and jumped out to defend himself?'

'Yes.' Mrs Hammond sat down on the couch, crying, her body bent over and shaking. 'Yes. It was my fault.'

Catherine looked down at her. The woman was so wretched that for an instant Catherine's strongest sensation was relief that she was not Marjorie Hammond. She was not this woman bent over and sobbing, crouching on the edge of the couch with her wrists cuffed behind her, unable even to wipe the tears that were streaking her face.

Catherine knew that she was about to do something foolish, and was violating department procedures. But she leaned down and used her key to unlock the handcuffs. She removed them, put them in her purse, and handed Mrs Hammond a tissue. 'Here.'

Mrs Hammond was rocking back and forth, crying steadily and silently. Almost inaudibly, she said, 'It's so stupid. It's just so stupid.'

'What is?'

'I always loved Jack. I love him so much. There was nothing wrong with us.'

'Then why?'

'I don't know. It just happened. I used to see Sam at the store every week, and we said hello. Sometimes we talked for a minute if he was approving a check, or I was asking him where something was. It was nothing. Then one time when I was out in the afternoon, I stopped for coffee at a Starbucks downtown, near Pioneer Square, and he was in there. He came up to me while I was waiting at the counter, and we sat together. We were there for about two hours, and we talked in a way we never did in the store – about our lives, what we thought and felt. He said he always came there on his days off, Tuesday and Thursday, at one, right after lunch, when he'd finished his errands. About a week later, I was near there again, and I went in.'

'Was it because he was there?'

'No, it wasn't. I didn't even remember it was Thursday. I happened to see the sign, and I remembered the place as pleasant. Then I got there and saw him, and I realized that the reason I thought it was pleasant was because of him. This time I went and sat with him.' She stopped and cried some more. 'He was just so nice. He was good, and smart, and he'd had such a sad life. He and I talked about everything, and then the afternoon was gone.'

'How long did this go on?'

'For a couple of months. I would think to myself that having coffee with a man wasn't a good idea, so I would miss Tuesday. Then Thursday came and I would ask what the harm was, and it didn't seem like there was any. So I went, and he would look up from his paper and he'd say how pleased he was that I had come. He would notice things about me, and be able to tell how I was feeling. He was interested in everything I had to say. Pretty soon I would think about it ahead of time, look forward to going to meet him.'

'Was he married too?'

'No. He had been engaged a few years ago, and then she'd changed her mind, and he hadn't been able to get over it for a long time.'

'But he knew you were married from the start, right?'

'Of course. Jack was the center of my life, and so a lot of the time what I talked about was Jack and me. Sometimes I would tell Sam about fights or hurt feelings I had. And then one day I realized that I'd fallen into the habit of telling him things that I had not even told Jack. If there were problems he didn't always have answers, and that was a kind of wisdom, too, to know that if the answers were that easy, I would have found them myself. Or even if there was an answer, he knew that I knew it too, but that I wasn't ready to admit it to myself yet. At those times he would just listen and let me work it out. I tried to do the same for him.'

'When did the relationship move out of Starbucks?'

'After a couple of months. That was my fault. I let that happen. I was feeling really good one day, and what was making me feel good was that Sam knew me so well and still liked me so much. When he saw how I was that day, I think the contrast may have been what struck him. He was kind of subdued and maybe depressed. I asked him what was wrong, and he told me. He said his life was empty and he needed more.'

'More?'

'A real relationship with a woman. He said he didn't want me to ruin my marriage and break up with Jack. He knew that it was the most important thing in my life. He just wanted to be with me.' She sobbed for a minute or more, while Catherine waited patiently. Then she looked up, almost pleading. 'You understand? Jack and I were happy, and that was what he wanted, and I wanted it for him too. I just sat there at the table looking at him, and the words "Why not?" came into my mind. I couldn't think of an answer that was real. The only answer was that I wasn't supposed to. He wanted to so much, and I did too. Sam knew that I would never leave Jack. So when I said, "Why not?" this time, it was out loud. We went right from there to a hotel across Pioneer Square.'

'That was the start. How long did it go on?'

'We still met on Tuesday and Thursday afternoons, at one. Sometimes we would go to his apartment. Sometimes we would drive somewhere, and he would have reserved a room. It's been about six months, from March until now. A couple of times, things just seemed wrong, and I would start to break it off. But then I couldn't.'

'When was that?'

'A few times. I remember once, standing by the car outside a hotel in Fairview, and we were saying good-bye for the last time, and it was raining. I was crying because I cared so much about him, and we were both getting wet, and then I could see his face was wet too. It wasn't just the rain. And I took it all back and we kissed and went back inside, even though we knew we could be late getting home and I would have to make up a lie for Jack's sake. I knew I was using up one of my lies, because I knew I wouldn't have many of them. You can't lie to someone about why you're late on Thursday afternoons more than about twice, or they'll know. It would have hurt Jack so much.' Saying it seemed to remind her of what was about to happen. She began to cry again.

'I'm sorry,' said Catherine.

'Everything is ruined, and there's nothing to make any of it better. Sam is dead. Jack's life is ruined. My life is ruined.'

Catherine needed her to get the rest of the story out before she stopped talking. 'Was last night the first time Sam stayed over at your house?'

'No. There were a few times before. I couldn't go to his place at night, because Jack might call our house from his hotel. But this time Jack didn't call. He just came home to be with me. When Sam and I heard the car pull into the driveway, I was terrified. I looked out the bedroom window and saw the headlights on the garage door, and then the door started to open. I made Sam grab his clothes and run downstairs to hide, so as soon as Jack came upstairs, Sam could slip out.'

'But Jack heard him?'

'Sam must have stumbled in the dark or dropped his shoe or something. I told Jack he was imagining things, but he wouldn't listen. I went to the top of the stairs and yelled at him not to prowl around – not just to persuade him, but to warn Sam too – but nothing worked. He opened the closet and Sam jumped out at him.' She stared up at Catherine, her eyes red and swollen, her face a mask of anguish. 'It's really the same as I said at first. I told you.'

Catherine said, 'I'm sorry. I'm really very sorry.' She gently took her to the car without taking out the hand-cuffs again, and drove her to the police bureau to get her statement on paper.

By the time Catherine was finished with the statement and her report and had signed the transcript of the tape recording, it was too late to answer any of the telephone messages that had piled up on her desk. She used her cell phone to call Joe Pitt while she drove toward Adair Hill.

He said, 'You're going home late. Solve another murder or something?'

'As a matter of fact, I did. Not a happy story, though.' She told him what had happened, then said, 'Oops. Joe, I need both hands to drive now. Sleep tight.'

'Good night. Love you.'

Catherine had started closing her cell phone before she heard it, and now she cursed herself for ending the call. Had he really said that? If he had, what could it possibly have meant? It had sounded automatic, like a formula. She thought about it as she drove up the curving road. She decided to ignore it. If he really had intended to tell her he loved her, then he would do it again.

She stopped in front of her parents' house and went inside. 'Mom?' she called.

Her mother appeared from the kitchen. 'Hi, honey. Just coming home from work?'

'Yeah,' she said. 'I hadn't seen you guys in a couple of days, so I thought I'd come and brighten your empty lives.'

'You mean you don't feel like making your own dinner?'

'That's right. Where's Dad?'

'He's upstairs. He'll probably be down in a minute. Want some leftover turkey?'

'Sure. Let me get my own.' She walked into the kitchen and got herself a plate, then took the Tupperware container with the neatly sliced turkey breast in it, added some broccoli, and put it into the microwave.

Her mother watched her. 'How is your new boyfriend working out?'

She turned her head in mock surprise. 'How's your crystal ball?'

'It's not that hard. I called your house the last five evenings and you've been out late. So how much are you going to tell me?'

'I'll spill my guts. His name is Joe Pitt, and he was just here for a few days. I have absolutely no business going out with him. He's too old and too rich and has a bad boy reputation that I think he probably earned. Naturally I'm getting more interested by the day. I'll let you know when I need to come over and cry about how it ended.'

'Well, that's nice,' said her mother. 'I'll set aside some time.'

There was the sound of her father's heavy footsteps on the stairway, and then her father appeared. 'Ah, the princess has returned.'

'Hi, Dad.'

He sat down in the chair beside hers, smiling. 'Working late, eh?'

'Yeah,' she said.

'Anything interesting?'

'Nothing you haven't seen a hundred times. Husband comes home early from a business trip. He trusts his wife, so he thinks the guy hiding in the closet is a burglar.'

'Bang bang,' said her father. 'It's a rotten job. I told you that from the time you were a child.'

'Practically from birth,' she agreed. 'This is good,' she said to her mother. 'It must have been nice to be one of the invited guests for its first appearance.'

'Then answer your damned phone,' said her father. 'We tried.'

'Sorry,' she said. 'I was busy trying to have a life.'

'Anybody we know?'

'No. He was a cop for a while, then an investigator for the Los Angeles DA. He's retired from that and working as a PI now.'

'Sounds too old for you.'

'He is.'

'Of course, you're getting older by the day.'

'Thanks for noticing. I guess the bloom is off the rose.'

'The second bloom is more luxuriant than the first,' he said. 'You seem kind of down. It was that case, wasn't it?'

'You know how it is. Half the people you see are dead. The other half you're seeing on the very worst day of their whole lives. It makes you tired.'

Her father stood up, kissed her on the forehead, and

went out into the living room. In a moment, she heard the television.

She finished her dinner and rinsed the plate and silverware, then put them in the dishwasher with the ones from her parents' dinner. She talked to her mother for a time about the things that had been going on in her parents' lives. Then she and her mother both drifted into the living room and watched the meaningless activity on the screen with her father.

Suddenly she caught herself falling asleep. She stood up, kissed them both, and drove the rest of the way up the hill to her house. As she pulled into the garage, she thought she saw something move, just beyond the reach of the lights on the eaves of her house. But she knew that sometimes that happened when a person had not had enough sleep for a few days – the mind supplied the monster that it feared.

FORTY-THREE

Judith Nathan filled the small backpack with the quart cans she had bought, and then lifted it. She had not expected it to be this heavy, or this hard and lumpy. She took everything out, wrapped the cans in a towel, put them in the backpack, and slipped another folded towel into the space between the cans and her back. She put the straps on her shoulders to repeat the test, and the pack felt more comfortable.

Judith dressed in her black pants and her running shoes, put on her black sweater and her raincoat. She inspected herself in the mirror, then looked at her watch. It was just after two a.m.

She opened the cylinder of Mary Tilson's revolver and made sure all the chambers were loaded. She put it into the deep right-hand pocket of the raincoat and examined herself in the mirror once more to be sure it didn't show. She took six extra bullets from the box and put them into her left pocket. Then she went outside and locked her door.

She had always been able to make herself feel better by going out into the night. When she was about six she had sometimes waited until her mother and the current boyfriend were back from their evening at the bars and had fallen asleep. Then she would slip on some clothes, quietly open the front door, and go out. The first time, she started by just stepping out on the front porch, looking and listening.

The night was not black, as it had always seemed from inside the lighted house. It was made of gray-blues, deep greens, and the white moonlight. She could see the familiar trees, sidewalks, and houses, but all of them were now silent, and everything was motionless. The people had not just gone. In the deep night they did not exist. The world was quiet.

At first she crouched on the porch with her back against the front of the house, far from the railing and near enough to the door so she had a fair chance of getting to safety ahead of whatever might leap out of the shadows to eat her. She stayed there for a long time that night and on several others before she was sure that no such thing would happen, and then stepped forward to the railing.

After that she moved to the porch steps, and it made an enormous difference. The porch roof had kept her in the shadows and hidden her, but it had also hidden the stars and the sky from her, and blocked her from the gentle current of slowly moving air. What she could hear once she was away from the house was a silence that had a range, that came to her from a great distance, from everywhere the dark could reach.

By the end of summer she had moved away from the house to the sidewalk, and on into the world. By the time she was eight she was in the habit of sneaking out every night and walking the streets. First she walked the streets of her neighborhood and looked at the houses she had always seen in daylight. Then she got into the habit of walking to school. The night walk became a tour of all of the places where she had been during the day. It was a chance to revisit scenes where things had happened. At night, the places were only hers.

She would look down at a spot on the concrete steps of the school and remember it was where Marlene

Mastich had stood and said Charlene's hair was dirty. She had stood right there to say it to the other girls, not an inch to either side. But now this spot, this step, this whole school, belonged to Charlene, and all other people were only memories, disturbances left in her brain from an ugly day. People weren't even real now, only the ground where they had stood. There was only Charlene in the night world. The trees were real, the dark stores with iron grates across their windows were real, and Charlene was real. That was all.

Charlene was Judith Nathan tonight, and it was time to move. She stepped around the building to the row of carports along the back. She wasn't worried that she would wake up any of the other tenants. Each carport had a cage at the rear of it where people stored things, and behind that was the laundry room. The first room where anybody slept was one floor up, and it was Judith Nathan's.

She drove her Acura far across town to the foot of Catherine Hobbes's street. Then she parked it a block away in a line of cars that seemed to belong to people asleep in a row of big old apartment buildings. She put on her backpack, walked to the foot of Catherine Hobbes's street, and began to climb.

The houses along the way were all dark and silent. After a minute of walking she began to feel again the peculiar sensation that had comforted her as a child, that the world was empty except for her. In the flat places downtown there were always people out and driving around, businesses with lights on. But up here on the winding, tree-shadowed street where people were all asleep, she was alone.

Judith had walked these same steps a number of times since she had arrived in Portland, but now the feeling was different. She was taking possession of the place.

The neighborhood had moved into the few hours of late night when all of the people had fallen into unconsciousness.

She walked along comfortably even though her small pack was heavy. She was used to exercising and jogging long distances. The weight of the pack made her breathing seem louder to her own ears, but she took the extra weight in her thighs and calves instead of her back, so it wasn't a strain.

Judith reached the row of houses along the crest of the hill and sat down on the curb across the street to study them. She yawned to be sure her ears were clear and she was hearing every sound. It was two forty-five a.m., and the silence was still unbroken. When she felt ready, she stood and noticed that up here along the ridge there was a slight breeze. Good. That would help.

Judith walked across the street slowly, careful not to disturb the perfect quiet. She climbed the steps beside Catherine's house and walked around to the back door. She looked in the window at the kitchen. It was pretty. The color of the walls seemed to be a pale yellow, but it was difficult to tell the exact shade in the darkness. She could see that here, as in most houses, there were no smoke detectors in the kitchen, where cooking would continually set them off. Judith took off her pack, pulled out a can, opened the spout, and poured charcoal starter on the door and the wooden footing below it.

Judith poured the rest of the can of charcoal starter on the clapboards of the house, letting extra pools of it soak into the sills of all the windows. She put the empty can back in the backpack, opened another, and kept going along the side of the house, searching for the things she had noticed in previous visits. When she reached the narrow door set into the wall outside the house, she slowly and cautiously opened it to verify that it covered a gas water heater. She took the adjustable wrench out of her backpack, unhooked the gas line from the heater, and closed the door. Then she poured some charcoal starter on the door and the walls beside and below it.

She tried to keep a steady stream of charcoal starter going as she walked beside the house, soaking the lowest few rows of clapboards. Whenever a can was empty she put it back into the pack and opened another. She took her time, trying to be thorough. There was a front entrance at street level that she knew opened into a narrow hallway with a side entrance to the garage. From there an interior staircase climbed to the living areas on the upper floor. She had glimpsed it the night when she had watched Catherine pull her car into the garage and open the door to go upstairs. Judith poured a whole can of charcoal starter on and around the front entrance and another on the garage door.

Judith still had a couple of cans left, so she used them on the wooden clapboards along the side of the house as she made her way again along the steps up the hill to the back door. Then Judith put on her pack. It felt incredibly light now. She took out her matches, and listened once more to the world. She could hear nothing, not even a distant swish of traffic from the city below.

Judith wanted to do this in a particular way. She wanted the fires in the back of the house to burn unnoticed for a time. She would light them first, beginning with the one that would block the back door and eat its way into the kitchen, where there were no smoke detectors. After a time the fire would spread to the petroleum-soaked wood on the sides and front of the house, blocking the other exits. They were the lowest parts of the house and they faced the river, where the wind was coming from tonight. Once the back of the house was engulfed, the fire in front would run right up the stairs to meet it.

She struck a match, listening to the scrape and then the hiss as the match head flared. She dropped it into the pool of charcoal lighter that had dripped to the foot of the back door. The wet fluid lit and the flames began to flicker up the surface of the wooden door. She moved a few paces and lit the next match, which she held against the lowest clapboard where it met the concrete footing below.

The saturated boards began to flare up, and the flames moved along the back of the house more quickly than she was walking: Judith had overdone it. The flames were running along ahead of her now. She stopped, turned, and hurried along the back of the house the way she had come. She had no time to go the long way, because the little house was already ablaze. The flames were blistering and peeling the layers of old paint to get to the dry wood beneath, then blackening it and beginning to devour it.

Judith trotted down the steps beside the house toward the street. She could feel the breeze making the short hairs along her hairline move, and she knew she had to escape. The fire was moving too quickly. Judith reached the bottom of the steps. She had to block the front exits, or it would all go wrong, so she struck another match and dropped it in front of the garage door. She watched flames unfurl from it, rolling up the surface of the garage door.

Judith whirled and started down the street. The flames were bright and yellow now, and her shadow stretched ahead of her on the empty asphalt of the street. She began to trot. She needed to get away from the neighborhood before the fire trucks and police cars came up that road. She had trotted only a few paces before she realized that the faster she went the better she felt, so she broke into a run, pumping her arms and pushing off with the balls of her feet.

The sidewalk was too treacherous, a series of tilted blocks and cracks to catch her feet, so she moved to the middle of the street. She sprinted, dashing for the first curve that would get her out of the light of the fire. She made it around the first corner and the light was dimmer. She ran hard for a few seconds, but then the light seemed to get brighter again.

Judith turned to look behind her. It was a set of headlights brightening the trunks of trees. She could hear the car coming fast. The car stopped a few feet from her and the driver was out, crouching behind his open door. He had a gun in his hand. 'Hold it.'

She said, 'What? What do you want?'

The man said, 'You. I've been waiting for you, honey. I've been watching, and waiting, and here you are.'

'Who are you?'

'My name is Calvin Dunn,' he said. 'Put the knapsack down and step away from it.'

Calvin Dunn. That was the name in the newspapers, the man who had killed Tyler. She knew that she had no choice except to do what he said. She set the backpack down on the street and took a few steps away from it, stepping to the side to get the light of the burning house behind her, trying to see Calvin Dunn's eyes.

They were focused on her. He said, 'All right. Stop there.' She could see the fire's reflection in his eyes, the glow flickering on the retina. Calvin Dunn took two steps from the car. His eyes moved to the backpack.

Judith's right hand slipped into the pocket of her raincoat and grasped the pistol. She sensed from a slight change in his posture that Calvin Dunn's brain had registered his mistake. She saw the eyes flick back to her and his body begin to tense, trying to raise his gun.

She fired through her pocket. The round hit his chest, but he didn't go down, so she leapt to the side. He fired at her, but she reached the barrier of a parked car. She heard Dunn running too, so she popped up and fired. This time when she hit him, he slowed as though the loss of blood was weakening him, so she fired twice more. He toppled to the pavement, and she stepped closer to fire into the back of his head.

The return of the silence seemed to waken her, and she began to run again. She took a half dozen steps down the center of the street, her gun still in her hand, before she remembered the backpack. She couldn't leave it lying on the pavement beside Dunn's body. She turned and ran back, snatched up her pack, and dashed down the street carrying it. She saw the end of the street bathed in light from the streetlamps, and she pushed the gun back into her pocket and ran toward the light. When she reached the bottom of the hill she tried to slow down, but her legs refused to obey her. She ran until she was around the corner and at her car. She fumbled with the keys for a second or two, but got it started and drove.

Catherine was in the midst of a dream she'd had many times. In it she had bought a huge, rambling house full of long turning hallways, attics, and secret rooms. She knew there was something in it that she had forgotten to take care of, something that was getting worse every second. She heard a shot, then another. Her brain worked to fit the sounds into the dream. Then there were three in a row, and she wasn't in that dream house anymore. She was in her bed. For a moment she felt the relief that awakening brought, the reassurance that the impressions had not been real. But something was still wrong.

She opened her eyes, and she could see there was light beyond the blinds in her room. She glanced at the clock, but it was only three-ten. Catherine sat up. The light in the cracks between the blinds was flickering and moving as though— She was up on her feet, and the air was thick and hot. She went down to the floor and began to crawl. As she did, the smoke detector overhead began to shriek at her, and she had to fight panic.

The lights were flickering beyond all of the windows. She had to get to the front of the house, where there were more exits. She crawled to the closet and pulled an armload of clothes off the hangers. There were a pair of pants – the silky black ones that were from her best suit – and a navy peacoat that she sometimes wore in cold weather. She put them on and crawled to the bedroom door. She reached up cautiously and touched the doorknob. It felt warm, as though it was beginning to heat up, but she could still grasp it. She turned it gingerly and opened the door.

She could see the sky through the greenhouse windows across the room at the front of the house, but there were flames moving along the walls on both sides of the room. The only windows still free of flames were the greenhouse windows, and they didn't open. Catherine rose to a crouch and rushed to the dining room table. She lifted one of the chairs and swung it hard into the greenhouse window. There was a crash and a spray of glass, and she pushed the chair the rest of the way out.

She wrapped the tablecloth around her right hand and forearm, used it to clear the glass shards from the bottom of the window, draped it over the sill to protect her while she put her feet out, then slid her body out after them and held herself there. She extended her arms, looked down, then dropped.

FORTY-FOUR

Judith Nathan's alarm clock gave an insistent buzz. She reached across the pillow to turn it off, and sat up in bed. She had been asleep for barely two hours, but she had wanted to be awake at six. She walked out into her living room, turned on the television set, sat in front of it, and waited.

The local morning news began with a lot of oppressively energetic music, quick cuts of cars on highways, shots of office buildings downtown, and idealized stills of the couple who read the news.

The man said, 'Good morning. Our top story this hour is an arson fire in the Adair Hill district that's linked to a murder.' Judith stood up, the excitement building. Had she caught Catherine Hobbes in the fire? 'Our Dave Turner was live on the scene with police lieutenant Joyce Billings this morning.'

The image changed to a shot of a woman in her fifties wearing an uncomfortable-looking blue police uniform who frowned at a hand that thrust a microphone into her face. She said, 'The fire at the house is now out. The firefighters say that the house will be a total loss, but they were able to contain the fire and limit it to the one building. Fire department investigators have already declared it an arson fire. There is conclusive evidence that accelerants were used.'

The voice of the man holding the microphone said, 'Is it true that this was a police officer's house?'

'Yes, it was. This happens to be an officer who has been involved in a number of high-profile cases during the past few months. We don't know whether this has to do with one of those cases or not.'

'What can you tell us about the shooting?'

'At approximately three a.m. there were calls to report both the fire and, about a block from here, gunshots. The fire trucks arrived first, to find the street blocked by what appeared at first to be a disabled car. Firefighters got down to push the car out of the street and found a Caucasian male about forty years old lying nearby. A gun was found beside him. We believe that he was killed during a shoot-out with an unknown assailant. We won't release his name until after his family has been notified.'

'Was he a suspect?'

'No,' said the lieutenant. 'He was not a suspect in the investigation.' She turned away, and the camera panned quickly from the microphone up the arm to the face of the young male reporter who had been asking the questions. Behind him Judith could see Calvin Dunn's car, which was now pushed to the curb. There were cops milling around measuring things with long tape measures and talking. Among them was a shorter, possibly female figure in black clothes.

'This is Dave Turner, live for KALP News . . .' Judith kept her eyes on the figure in black. It was definitely a woman, but maybe only a curious neighbor. '. . . coming to you from the scene of a very mysterious fire.' He gave his serious look, and the woman behind him turned to say something to someone. It was Catherine Hobbes.

'Shit!' said Judith Nathan. 'How did you get out of there, you bitch?' Catherine Hobbes disappeared and the scene changed to the studio, where the news couple sat behind their desk. It didn't matter. Judith knew how Catherine Hobbes had survived. She had been afraid of it since the moment it had happened. It had been the shots. It had been that stupid Calvin Dunn.

He must have been sitting in his car somewhere above Catherine's house, waiting. She had walked past the house on several evenings before, but he had not been there. He must have known that Judith would come for Catherine late at night, when she was in her deepest sleep. Of course Judith would do it then. Catherine Hobbes was an armed cop, and she spent all of her days surrounded by other armed cops.

He probably had not seen Judith arrive. She had not seen his car, so probably it had been parked beyond the curve, where Catherine wouldn't see it either. But he had seen the fire. He had driven down the hill and seen Judith come away from the house in a hurry, and he had seen her running. The only thing all night that he had not seen in time was where Judith had carried her gun. He had thought she had it in her backpack.

Judith switched channels, going to each of the local stations to hear their versions of the same story. Some of them showed the same police spokeswoman from slightly different angles, and some had video clips of the burning house and the firemen.

At least Judith had shown Catherine what it felt like to be hunted. She had wanted her to know what it was like to be alone and afraid, to have to run for her life. She supposed that she had accomplished that much. It was a good start.

FORTY-FIVE

Catherine Hobbes hurried into the department store with the envelope full of cash. All of her identification, her checkbook, and her credit cards had been incinerated with her purse when the house had burned. The money she had now was from the bureau's cash fund for emergencies. It had taken the captain's written approval to get the loan.

She was still wearing her black silk pants and peacoat. Abby Stern, one of the other female detectives, always kept a spare blouse in the office, and she had let Catherine borrow it.

Catherine could have gone to her parents, both for the money and the temporary clothes. But she had been busy with the firefighters and the police investigators, and had barely had time to call her parents at seven to tell them about the fire before they saw it on television. She supposed it had been more a question of efficiency than actual time. She knew that her mother would insist on having her stay with them, and she knew that she didn't want to. There would be an argument, and her father would eventually reassert his ancient authority to make her stop arguing with her mother. That was something that could happen only if she did exactly as her mother said. The only way to avoid it was to rent an apartment somewhere before she allowed the discussion to begin.

She held a patrolman's radio in her hand as she shopped, because her cell phone had burned with everything else, and she needed to stay in touch with the bureau while the hunt for Tanya was on.

Catherine picked out some underwear and three outfits that she could wear to work. The requirements were that there be a coat that was slightly oversized so it would hide the gun she sometimes wore under it, and that the pants would allow her to run or fight if she had to. Beyond that, the outfit had to be fashionable enough so that she would not stand out in a crowd. The last purchase was the two pairs of shoes. They took longer than the suits, but she was finished quickly.

As she hurried toward the door of the department store, she decided the shopping trip hadn't been bad. When she had bought her first uniform in the academy, it had come as a shock to her that the uniforms were still all cut for men, and that the regulation shoes came only in men's sizes. When she had put on her first bulletproof vest she had learned that they weren't for women either, and wearing one loose was not a good idea.

She supposed she was still feeling a bit traumatized. Last night she had been absolutely terrified, and being afraid was never a good experience for her. It weakened her and reminded her that she wasn't what she wanted to be. Being burned out of her house was also a great deal of work, and it all came at a time when she needed to be doing her job. Tanya had been in Portland last night, trying to kill her. This was Catherine's chance to get her.

As she reached her unmarked car, she realized that the loss of her house had been a good mental exercise for her. She had suddenly been deprived of all the papers that the average person collected over a lifetime, and it had reminded her of how important they were. She had been unable to get money from her own bank account, unable to buy anything to wear, unable to rent a room to sleep in. Technically, she had driven over to the mall illegally, because she was not carrying a driver's license.

Tanya Starling had been traveling the country for months under a half dozen different names. She had been buying and selling cars, opening and closing bank accounts, signing leases, and she had done all of it without raising much suspicion. Catherine had known since she had become a police officer that the average person didn't really take a close look at anyone else's identification. They just glanced at the photograph, at most read the name, and accepted it, as long as nothing else made them suspicious. Tanya seemed to be getting better and better at making people trust her. She seemed to be immune to the nervousness that made people sense that something was wrong.

She was learning quickly, and that was frightening. Learning was one of the things some of the worst serial killers did. They got more efficient and expert at committing their crimes – did the things that mattered, and stopped doing the things that were useless and could get them caught – and the chances of catching them declined. As that happened, they seemed to lose restraint.

Their cruelty to victims wasn't personal; it was detached, almost scientific. They studied their victims' reactions and their own, and as their studies progressed, the cruelty became more pronounced. A few months ago, Tanya had pulled a trigger and shot Dennis Poole in the back of the head. She had given him the easiest way to die – no fear, no time for the pain to reach the consciousness before the brain was obliterated. Last night she had tried to burn Catherine to death.

When Catherine arrived at the office, she saw that the first of the phone messages on her desk was from Joe Pitt, but she didn't have time to call him now. She had to work on Tanya's photographs. The one thing she had done that had shown any effect was to circulate Tanya's picture. Tanya had been recognized at least once in Flagstaff, and in Los Angeles before that. She needed to get the pictures out, and to be sure that the television stations that were running tapes of her house burning on the noon news would also show Tanya's photograph.

Catherine went to work preparing another set of circulars with the pictures of Tanya and the pictures of Rachel Sturbridge. This time, to the list of suspected crimes, she added arson and the shooting of Calvin Dunn. As she studied her computer screen, trying to make the pictures as large as possible, she became aware that someone was behind her. She turned, and saw the captain. 'Hi, Captain.'

'Hobbes. My office.'

She saved the image and followed him to the big office at the end of the hall, then sat on the couch across from his desk where his visitors sat. He said, 'I see you got some clothes with the emergency fund. Is there anything else you need?'

'I've ordered duplicates of all my papers. I've requested a new weapon and a new ID and badge. Nothing will come for a day or two.'

He picked up the phone, looked at a list of numbers taped to the desk beside it, and dialed an extension. 'This is Captain Farber in homicide. I have an officer here who had her house burn down last night in an attempt on her life. Right. Catherine Hobbes. I need to have her working cases, so I would like a new sidearm, badge, and identification card for her as of ten minutes ago. Can you possibly speed that up for me? Thanks. It's much appreciated.' He hung up. 'They'll bring it all to you in an hour. Who torched your house?'

'Tanya Starling.'

'Not the guy who stuffed his wife in the trunk of his car?'

'John Olson? No. He's been denied bail, and he's a solitary nut with no chance of getting any money to pay anyone else to kill me. This was Tanya Starling. She is – or was – in Portland.'

'Based on what?'

'I gave my business card to her landlady in San Francisco, and she gave my numbers to Tanya. She's used both my cell number and my home number to call me. I guess she converted the home number to an address. It's not hard. Anyone can do it on the Internet. Then there's the arson. The fire department investigators tell me it amounted to soaking the outside of my house with barbecue fire starter and lighting it up with a book of paper matches. She hasn't done any fires before. If it had been a professional there would be a timing device so he could have been a hundred miles away when the fire started, or it would have been set up to look like an accident.'

'Do I need to say that's inconclusive?'

'There will be more. I think Calvin Dunn is the best evidence for the moment.'

'What about him?'

'I was in the interrogation after he killed Tyler Gilman. Dunn said that he had been watching my hotel that night because he thought Tanya would show up to kill me. When somebody started firing at my car with a rifle, Dunn went after the shooter.'

'So?'

'He went after the shooter because he assumed it was Tanya. He was hired to get her, and not to save me, so he didn't try. He didn't do anything to help me get to cover, and he didn't return fire to keep the sniper's head down. He didn't call the police. He wanted the rifle shots to continue as long as possible, so he could spot where the sniper was and get to her. Last night, I'm pretty sure he did the same thing. He saw that my house was on fire, so he drove off trying to find her.'

'If that's true, then he should have succeeded. Have any idea how she killed him?'

'I might. It's possible that he saw the fire, then saw a woman running from it. He couldn't be sure it wasn't me. Maybe he hesitated to be sure he wasn't shooting the wrong woman, and she got him first. Or maybe he saw who she was but didn't know she had brought a gun on a trip to set a fire.'

'I'm not sure I'm buying this.'

'The point is, if anybody but Tanya – anybody at all – had burned me to death in my sleep, he would not have gone after them.'

'Are you sure about that?'

'Yes. He and I already lived through this once in Flagstaff. You notice that last night he didn't do anything else – didn't try to save me, didn't call the fire department, didn't wake the neighbors. If I had managed to die, he would have gone to the funeral to see if she showed up.'

He stared at her for a few seconds. 'Would you like to be removed from the case?'

'What? No, of course not.'

'Would you like to have someone assigned to work the case with you?'

'At the point where there's a fresh lead to follow, I'd like a task force. An army. But at the moment, all that can be done is to circulate her pictures to get people to recognize her while she's still in the area, or tell us where and when they saw her.'

'What do you think the chance is?'

'I don't know. People have recognized her before, but every time she turns up she makes fewer and fewer mistakes. I have her fingerprints, but having them doesn't help me find her, because they don't match any that are contained in the databases. She's never been arrested, served in the military, or applied for any professional license. I think that if I ask enough people and circulate her picture enough, somebody is going to remember seeing her, and tell me exactly where she is.' She stood up. 'I've got to get her soon, Mike. She's killing people faster now, and she's getting better at it.'

FORTY-SIX

Every day at eleven, when everyone else had gone to work and the halls were empty, Judith Nathan put on a sweatshirt and jeans and went to her mailbox in the lobby of her apartment building. Today there was an ad for a dating service, a sheet of coupons for local stores that carried things like lawn furniture and garden hoses, and one big brown manila envelope. She took it out, read the return address, and hurried back to her apartment to open it.

The envelope was full of mail forwarded from her Solara Estates mailbox in Denver. She quickly shuffled through the junk mail and bills, and found one white envelope that she had been hoping for. She held it and let her fingers tell her that the answer to her application had been positive. She tore it open. There it was – her new credit card. It was the one she had ordered as a second card on the account of the young woman she had met in a club in Denver. And there was her name, embossed along the bottom: Catherine Hobbes.

It was a wonderful thing to have. The billing address was the Solara Estates mailbox in Denver, so nobody but Judith would ever get a bill for it. Nobody else would ever know it existed. Judith held the card in her hand while she searched the desk under her printer. She found the driver's license she had made to go with the credit card, and looked at it. There were some good touches on this one that she had added in the last batch of ID cards.

This one had a little round sticker that said if she was killed she was willing to be an organ donor.

Judith had been preparing for this day for a long time. She had taken out a library card in the name Catherine Hobbes at the library in Lake Oswego, a couple of miles outside Portland, and opened a health club membership. She had made a social security card. Now she put all of the identification into a small wallet, so that the driver's license with her picture was behind the plastic window that was visible when she opened it. She practiced holding it open when she took out the credit card, so an observer could see several other cards with the name Catherine Hobbes embossed on them.

She went out during the afternoon to play with her new credit card. She considered the new name, repeated it to herself many times, and thought about the look she wanted. Judith drove to the mall and rode the department store escalator to the fourth floor, where the designer clothes were displayed, and was drawn to a tailored charcoal pantsuit because she had seen Catherine Hobbes on television wearing something similar. The only pantsuit she remembered ever owning was one she had bought to fly to New York once with Carl, and then never worn again. She had never worked in the sort of job where women wore suits. Most of her clothes had been dresses she had picked because they looked like they would be worn by someone she wanted to be – someone glamorous and feminine. During the day she had worn casual tops and pants. But as she stood in the dressing room looking at the four views of herself, she decided that she liked herself this way.

Catherine Hobbes was a cop, and she probably carried a gun on her somewhere. Would one of these suits have room for a gun? Where? She raised and lowered her arms, tried turning around to get a better view. Some male cops wore guns in shoulder holsters, but that would be an impossible look on a woman in a close-fitting, tailored coat. She supposed Catherine Hobbes wore a small pistol in a clip-on holster, probably at the spine, where the coat would cover it when she stood up, or maybe slightly to the right, where it was easy to reach. Judith looked down at the pants. She could even conceive of Catherine Hobbes with a gun in an ankle holster. There was room.

Judith kept trying on suits until she had found four that she liked. She selected the coats one size too large to give her extra room, then carried her purchases to the sales counter, where the girl at the cash register took her Catherine Hobbes credit card and asked, apologetically, to see her license. Judith opened her wallet and held it up so the girl could see it. The girl looked at it, said, 'Thanks,' and charged the purchases to the card.

Judith signed the slip, took the suits to her car, and went to lunch at La Mousse to celebrate her new card. Afterward she bought new shoes to go with the suits. She imagined that Catherine Hobbes would wear flats that were elegant but would allow her to run if she had to.

When Judith got back to her apartment, she turned on her television while she hung up her new clothes, and listened until the five o'clock news came on. Then she stood and watched. The news man said, 'For months Sergeant Catherine Hobbes, a homicide detective in the Portland Police Bureau, has been searching for a young woman who is suspected of killing local businessman Dennis Poole. Police now believe it was that young woman who set fire to Sergeant Hobbes's Adair Hill home last night and shot to death a Los Angeles private investigator. Here is the most recent photograph of her, taken a few months ago for a California driver's license.'

Judith looked at the picture of Rachel Sturbridge on

the television. The hair was long and looked almost black in the picture. The eyes were her original pale blue, and the face looked fat to her. The female half of the news couple said, 'She is described as five feet five, one hundred and twenty pounds, with brown hair and blue eyes. She is to be considered armed and dangerous. If you do see her, police say, do not attempt to detain her. Just call nine-one-one, and the police will do the rest.'

She watched with curiosity, but it was a detached curiosity. She had changed her hair color to match Ty's in Arizona, so it was a sandy blond, and she had been wearing the blue contacts, so her eyes were a deeper blue. She had lost some weight since then and changed the kind of clothes she wore. She walked into the bathroom, looked in the mirror, and felt safe. She turned off the television and went to the telephone to call Greg at work.

'Hey, Greg. Are you working late tonight?'

'Not anymore. At least not if this is who I hope it is.'

'Well, I hope it is too, because if it isn't, then you're hoping for somebody else,' she said. 'I'll tell you what. If you'll come right over here after work, I'll take you out tonight.'

'Take me out?' he said. 'You don't have to do that.'

'Not have to, want to. You've been taking me everywhere for weeks, so it's my turn to take you.'

'Well, okay,' he said uneasily. 'What do you want me to wear?'

'Whatever you have on now. I said I wanted you to come right from work.'

An hour later, when he rang the bell, she said to the intercom, 'Did you come straight from work?'

'Yes.'

She pushed the button to unlock the front door and waited for him in the hallway. When he came up the carpeted stairs, she saw that he was carrying flowers again. She let him in and closed the door. 'So, you raise flowers at work?'

'Well, no. They sell them on the way, though.'

'You're not very sure of yourself, are you?'

'I guess I'm not,' he said. 'I keep wondering if I'll wake up and you won't exist.'

'If you do, don't tell me. Come on. We're going to dinner.'

She drove him to a restaurant called Sybil's. She had chosen it because it was quiet and the lights were dim. While Greg was in the men's room, she moved the candle away from the center of the table so the light would be off their faces, and studied the place. She had gotten into the habit of looking at the faces of people around her to detect signs of recognition. She was comfortable tonight, because it was too early to be crowded, and the waiters sat the first customers to arrive in the dim private spaces along the walls, leaving the center tables empty and the aisles clear for serving. Later the dining room would fill up.

She knew that Greg always felt best when the light was dim. As they ate, she judged that he was happy because they were at this remote table, and thought how pathetic it was that such a good person should be so self-conscious about his scarred face. She knew that he was grateful to her for keeping him out of the light. He probably thought she was the most sensitive, considerate person he had ever met, because she arranged to protect him without ever alluding to it. It would never occur to him that she had done it because she didn't want people looking too closely at her face, either.

When the check came in its leather folder, Judith

palmed her Catherine Hobbes card, put it on the bill, and clapped the folder shut. The waiter snatched it up quickly and disappeared. A few minutes later he was back with it, she signed the slip, and she and Greg left.

After dinner they walked and she pretended to discover a club called the Mine, where promising music groups came to test new songs on a live audience. But tonight was a weeknight, so the band was an unenthusiastic, workmanlike group of middle-aged men who covered old rock hits. It didn't matter that they weren't inspired, only that Judith was out at night with a man who adored her, and she was paying for everything with a Catherine Hobbes credit card.

She ordered Greg a scotch and herself a martini. As they drank, she watched him, and decided she must get the maximum amount of pleasure out of him, even if she had to risk losing the use of him. As soon as they finished their drinks, she made Greg get up and dance with her. Like nearly all tall men, he was an awkward dancer, but at least his movements were only stiff and abbreviated. He was aware that his purpose was to provide a partner so she could dance, so he dutifully remained on his feet until she let him sit down and have another drink.

She drove Greg to her apartment, and then kept him for the night. She loved being out so much that she forced him to go out every night for the rest of the week. She insisted that every second time she be permitted to pay, and when she did, she paid with her Catherine Hobbes credit card.

The following Tuesday, Judith went out and bought a pile of magazines. She drove home and spent hours looking at pictures of women until she found the right one. Then she cut the page from the magazine and took it to a hair stylist's shop. She had the stylist copy the cut and strawberry-blond color in the picture exactly. It was a three-step process and she had to endure the stylist's lectures about the damage that frequent dyeing had done to her hair. When she came out, she drove back to her apartment and stared at herself in the mirror for a long time, holding up a hand mirror so she could see from every angle. 'Catherine,' she whispered.

FORTY-SEVEN

Catherine Hobbes's insurance company helped her rent an apartment not far from the police bureau. It was on Northeast Russell Street, about two blocks east of Legacy Emmanuel Hospital. The apartment building tenants all seemed to be young nurses, interns, and medical technicians. They used the place in shifts: no matter what time of the day or night she entered, there were people in medical uniforms coming in or out.

Catherine had not yet decided what she wanted to do about her burned house. The fire insurance would pay to rebuild it, but she was not sure if that was what she really wanted. At times she would awaken in the night and feel the same panic she had felt the night when she had seen flames glowing beyond the closed blinds. At those moments it felt good to her to be living in an apartment in a big building surrounded by people, and to hear the reassuring sounds of their footsteps in the hallway at all hours.

Catherine had been a cop for seven years now. She had seen traumatized people – witnesses and victims – suffer various kinds of aftereffects, and she recognized that hers was a very mild one. But she also knew that as long as Tanya Starling entertained some fantasy of killing her, it was not a great idea to rebuild the house and live in it alone.

When she had talked to Joe Pitt on the telephone about her burned house, she had started to cry. He had said, 'What's the matter? Are you hurt or something?'

'No. I guess I'm crying about my house.'

'What about it? Wasn't it insured?'

'Of course it was. I just miss it.'

'So you'll rebuild it, exactly the same, except maybe fireproof and with a great alarm system.'

'It won't be the same. And besides, I don't even know if I want to. It wasn't that great, objectively. I just loved it.'

'So while you're thinking about it, I'll come up there and rent a house for a while. You can live with me.'

That brought up even more complications. She had been holding Joe Pitt at bay. She had kept him from flying up to Portland the minute he'd learned that her house had burned. Every day he called, and every day he repeated the offers: they could rent a house or apartment together and he would protect her. She appreciated that instinct in men, that unfounded confidence that their sheer bulk and aggressiveness would prevent disasters.

Joe Pitt was the first man she'd had romantic feelings for in a long time, and she was cautious: she didn't want to suddenly collapse and become dependent on him, and she feared that artificial intimacy might be worse for the relationship than too much distance at this stage. She said, 'As soon as you finish the cases you've taken on and feel like coming up, I'd love to see you in Portland. If I get any time off, I'll use it to fly to L.A. But I won't live with you right now. And I don't plan to go anywhere until I've got Tanya.'

She had stopped calling the case 'the Dennis Poole murder.' It was now 'Tanya Starling' when she thought of it, and she thought about it all the time. Tanya was evolving. She killed more easily, and with increasing frequency, but she seemed to be able to disappear afterward. She was going to keep killing until somebody stopped her, and stopping her was becoming more difficult.

Catherine stayed at the office late for the next two evenings, backtracking, making telephone calls to the witnesses who had met Tanya Starling in any of her guises. She called neighbors, people who had bought Tanya's cars, clerks at hotels. She asked them everything she could think of that might help her find Tanya. She was looking for quirks, for compulsive behavior, preferences and habits that might limit the search area or give her an idea of where to look and what to look for.

She spoke with homicide detectives in Los Angeles, San Francisco, and Flagstaff to be sure that any new information from the crime scenes was being sent to her, and asked them for any new theories they might have, any leads they might be following. When there was spare time, she would send pictures of Tanya Starling to businesses that might find themselves dealing with Tanya Starling under some new name: banks, car rental agencies, hotels.

At night when she came back to her apartment there were telephone messages. Each night she had to spend time reassuring her parents that she was all right, that she would not be better off living with them than in a small dingy apartment with practically no furniture, and that she was eating and sleeping regularly. Always she had to fend off Joe Pitt's offers of help, protection, and various kinds of comfort. She was becoming increasingly devoted to finding Tanya Starling, and increasingly isolated. Comfort was distraction.

On the third night after the fire, Catherine had just returned to her new apartment when an unfamiliar buzz startled her. It seemed so loud that it made her stiffen, but even as her muscles tensed she realized that the buzz was only the intercom on the wall near her door. She pressed the talk button. 'Yes?'

The voice from the speaker said, 'Catherine? Is that you inside this box?'

She laughed. 'Joe?'

'I guess it is you in there,' he said. 'If this is a bad time I can come back at a worse one.'

She pressed the other button, which released the outer door lock. 'Get in here.'

Catherine waited inside her apartment for a few seconds, then flung open her door, walked to the door of the elevator, and waited there. She was angry at herself. She had said too much to Joe on the telephone, sounded weaker and needier than she was. She had made him drop everything to fly all the way to Portland to hold her hand when they both had important things to do. She had used up a call for help, wasted one of her chances to say, 'I'm in trouble and I need to be with you right now.'

The elevator door opened and Joe Pitt stepped out. He was grinning, holding a briefcase in one hand and a long white box in the other. He kissed her on the cheek and handed her the box.

'Thanks. I don't suppose these are roses?'

'I'm a bit ashamed of that, because I'm usually more original, so don't tell any of the other girls, okay?'

'I'll keep it to myself.' She led him to the door of her apartment and pushed it open. 'I'd hate to see your legend crumble.'

'I knew you'd understand.'

She closed the door and locked the bolt, then set the box on the dining table and opened it. There were a dozen long-stemmed roses with pink and orange petals. She said, 'They're gorgeous, Joe.' She put her arms around him and gave him a deep, lingering kiss. After a moment she pulled away to look down. 'Are you handcuffed to your briefcase?'

'I was being distracted by an erotic daydream and forgot.' He set the briefcase on the table, opened it, and pulled out a salt shaker and a small freshly baked loaf of bread. 'Somebody had to bring bread and salt to inaugurate your new place, so I got some on the way to the airport.'

'Thank you,' said Catherine. 'You think just like my grandmother.'

He turned in place and looked around at the sparse, utilitarian furniture and the bare walls. 'And quite a place it is too. It's a lot like the apartments in L.A. favored by hookers from the former Soviet bloc. They like the no-frills aesthetic. I've only seen them on a professional basis, of course.'

'Theirs?'

'Mine,' he said.

'That's good,' said Catherine. 'I think like my grandmother too, and we have an agreement.'

'I haven't forgotten,' he said. 'It's been kind of hard to be away from you.'

She could foresee that he was going to bring up the idea of living together again, so she diverted his attention back to the briefcase. 'Are you using that thing as an overnight bag?'

'No. I dropped my suitcase off at the hotel while I was waiting for you to get home from work.' He reached into the briefcase and pulled out a thick stack of manila file folders. 'These are just a few odds and ends I dug up for you. I stopped by Jim Spengler's office and picked up copies of interview transcripts from people who saw Nancy Mills in L.A. He also had some stills made up from security tapes at the Promenade Mall. One of them places her there at the same time as Rachel Sturbridge's bank manager from San Francisco, who got picked up there and killed. There's an analysis from a profiler, some reports from a blood-spatter expert and a ballistics expert.'

Catherine looked at the thick stack of files, then picked up the profiler's file and looked at the first page.

'This isn't from the LAPD. It says "Property of Pitt Investigations." You paid a profiler? This one says "Pitt" too. And this one.'

Joe waved his hand to dismiss it. 'I had a few people I've used on cases before take a look at what we had, that's all. There isn't much there that you haven't already figured out on your own, and there isn't anything to tell you where Tanya is, but sometimes one little item in a report can give you an idea.'

Catherine looked up at him. 'Flowers and case files? What could be more romantic?'

He shrugged. 'It's what we do, Cath. There's no use pretending you're somebody else, or that I am. We hunt down killers. I hope something here helps you get her.'

'You're worried about me.'

'Of course I am.'

'Joe, this is my fault, and I'm sorry. I've been whining to you about the case, and about my house, and I'm sure I've played the whole episode for all the sympathy I could get. I guess I've felt so close to you intellectually and so far from you in miles that I didn't remember to use restraint. You were too far away to do anything about my troubles except listen. I talked my head off, but not so you would come and solve my problems for me. I just wanted to talk about them. You understand?'

'Sure I do. I was reacting to what happened, not to what you said about it. She's tried to get you killed in two different ways. I want her caught now.'

'Me too.' Catherine picked up the roses, took them into the kitchen, and started searching the cupboards.

'What are you looking for?'

'I just realized I don't own a vase anymore.' She opened the refrigerator, took out a large jar that had a little Italian sauce in the bottom, rinsed it in the sink, filled it with fresh water, snipped the stems of the roses, and arranged them in it.

Joe watched her. 'Very beautiful.'

She looked at him for a moment. 'I really am glad to see you, Joe. I mean anytime. I just didn't want to drag you all the way up here to be my caretaker.'

'That wasn't why I came. I just grabbed any excuse I could get to see you.'

'How long do you plan to devote to that?'

'I have a return ticket for Monday. I've got to meet with a guy who knows something about a case I'm working on.'

'Three days. That's probably enough time.'

'For what?'

She took his hand. 'I'm going to your hotel with you now, and I'm going to do my best to make you really, really glad you brought those roses in person.'

Catherine and Joe spent the next three days in isolation. It was really Catherine's isolation, but she had opened herself to let Joe into it. During the sunlit hours they went over the outside experts' reports together, compiling and evaluating possible avenues of investigation. In the evenings they ate late dinners at restaurants along the river and talked about their families, beliefs about love, theories of witness behavior and forensic evidence. Then they walked back to Joe's hotel holding hands and made love until they could hear the footsteps of the hotel's early-morning staff in the hallways.

On the last morning, Catherine drove Joe to the airport. As they stood beside Catherine's small gray rental car outside the terminal, he said, 'Well? When is the next time going to be?'

'Whenever either one of us gets a chance,' she said. 'The second I can leave here, I'll be on your doorstep.'

While she was driving to her apartment to get ready for work, she found that she was crying. She drove around the block while she dried her eyes, then left her rental car on the street in front of her building, took her overnight bag inside, and opened her apartment door. The first thing she saw was the jar of roses. The weekend with Joe had begun and ended so quickly that the petals were still fresh and a few buds were not fully open. If it had not been for the roses, she might have thought she had imagined it.

Catherine spent the next few days working more intensely than before, following the most promising leads and theories that she and Joe had developed, and then, when those failed, moving to the less promising leads. All of them served to verify evidence she already had. None of them seemed to take her to the next step, finding the place where Tanya Starling was right now.

One night about two weeks after the fire, she called the number of her bank and listened to the long menu: 'For check orders, press four. For credit card billing inquiries, press five.' She supposed that what she wanted was probably closest to five. After a pause, a woman answered. 'This is Nan. How can I help you?'

'My house burned down about two weeks ago, and I called the next day and asked that my credit card be replaced. I haven't received it yet, and I thought I'd check to be sure that there's no problem.'

'Your name please?'

'Catherine Hobbes, H-O-B-B-E-S.'

'And your card was destroyed in the fire?'

'Yes. I ordered a new one right after the fire, and so it's been almost two weeks.'

'Two weeks? That doesn't sound right. Let me check. Do you have your account number?'

'No. When my house burned, so did all the old bills and records.'

'Social security number?'

Catherine recited the number, listened to the clicking of computer keys.

'I'm not sure what happened. It looks as though they tried to call you and verify your information before they mailed you a new card, and couldn't reach you. Do you have a new phone number and address to give me?'

'Yes.' Catherine gave it to her. Then she added, 'When I called before, I gave them my work number and address. I'm a police officer.'

'I suppose it's possible somebody there answered the phone and said, "Police," and our person figured it was a hoax. Let's try to get this expedited so your new card goes out as soon as possible. It will have a new number on it. We always do that when the other one isn't in your possession.'

'When should I expect it?'

'Tomorrow or the next day, if we can get it done without another glitch, and they're pretty rare. I'm very sorry about the mix-up. Have you ordered new checks and so on?'

'Yes, but if you have a way of verifying that that's being done, I'd appreciate it.'

'Happy to do it. And one more thing. If you're a police officer, you've probably already thought of this, but I usually advise people to order reports from the three credit services to be sure all your cards really were destroyed and nobody picked one up. I can tell you that nothing has been charged to your account at this bank during that time, but you should still run the credit check.'

'That's a good idea,' she said. 'I'll do that.'

She let a day go by, and then another. Her replacement card came, and she forgot about the credit reports. But at the end of the week she remembered while she was in the office and called the three phone numbers to order her credit reports.

When Catherine came home from work two days later, the reports were in her mailbox in the lobby of the apartment building. She took them to her apartment, sat at the kitchen table, and opened them warily. For the past eight years, she had always been uncomfortable when she thought about credit. That was something she had gotten as part of the settlement after her failed marriage.

Kevin had been an optimist. When the marriage had ended, the extent of Kevin's optimism had become apparent. He had been running up the balances on his credit card accounts for a long time, on the theory that his future salary increases would make the overruns seem tiny. After Catherine divorced him, the credit companies had been quick to inform her that the growing balances on debts he had incurred before the divorce were her responsibility as much as his. It had taken time for her to legally separate her portion of the debt from his, get a second mortgage on the house she had bought in Portland, and pay off the credit companies.

It had been a painful process for Catherine, and not only because it was a time when she'd needed money, but because she couldn't keep herself from thinking about where the debt had come from. Kevin had assured her that he had gone into debt only to spend money on her. He had not been very specific, so she looked at two years of old bills. The credit cards had been used for lunches and dinners at restaurants where she had never been, and hotels in Palo Alto, the town where they had lived. Cheating on Catherine had been expensive.

Today, when Catherine read the three credit reports, she was relieved to see that her credit was extremely good. She supposed that paying off her half of Kevin's debts must have healed whatever wounds her marriage to him had inflicted on her rating. Maybe she'd gotten a few extra points for being a sucker.

She went carefully down the list of open accounts. There were a couple of department store charge cards that she had forgotten. She had accepted them years ago because they had been offering large discounts to customers who opened charge accounts. They had approached her when she was buying her first bed after the marriage. It had cost eleven hundred dollars, and getting the card had saved her about two hundred. The other occasion was when she was still in the academy and making practically nothing, and was forced to agree to go out to dinner with a visiting couple from the days when she had been married to Kevin. She had known that they were still in touch with him, and she'd needed to have them tell him that she looked magnificent, so she had bought a dress, coat, and shoes that she couldn't really afford.

There was one account that she could not remember opening. It was a Visa. She looked for the issuing company. The issuer was the Bank of the Atlantic. Her stomach dropped: Kevin? How could he have done that to her? She had already paid for his girlfriends. She repeated the question to herself. How *could* he have done that to her? He couldn't. It would have come to her attention at some point in the past eight years. She looked at the date. It wasn't eight years ago. The account had been opened a month ago.

She kept staring at the entry. It wasn't right. The social security number wasn't hers. And it said, 'Additional card.' What did that mean? Could this be somebody else's credit card that had been added to her credit report by mistake?

She looked at the reports from the other two services. The card was listed on all of them. The one from Experion

403

said, 'Primary cardholder SSN' and listed a second social security number. That explained the 'additional card' business. The Catherine Hobbes Visa card was on someone else's account. Her eyes widened as all of the implications began to pass through her consciousness at once. A person on the run could get a credit card in her own name and an additional one in a false name. She could travel under the false name, and any business that ran the credit card would get the response that it was genuine.

Catherine reached for the telephone, then stopped, her hand in midair. It was too late to reach the captain anywhere but at home, and she wasn't sure what she believed, what she wanted to tell him. She decided what she was going to do, half-stood to go to her spare room to turn on the computer, then remembered that she wasn't in her house anymore, and the computer wasn't fifty steps away in that direction. She was in a small apartment, and the only computer was the laptop she had signed out from work. She went to the big briefcase she had brought in, unlocked it, and took out the laptop.

She plugged it into the telephone line, turned it on, and waited for the connection to the Internet. It took a very long time, then failed to connect, so she started the process over again. She was so impatient that she almost unplugged the computer to reconnect the telephone, but she forced herself to wait. It would not do to make a lot of fuss over what might amount to a relatively harmless credit reporting error.

She got connected, then found the Web site of the Bank of the Atlantic. She clicked on credit card accounts, then 'Access your account,' then gave the account number that was on her credit reports and the social security number of the primary cardholder. A box appeared that said, 'Password.' She swore under her breath, but then thought for a second. She typed in 'none.' A new page appeared, asking, 'Would you like to create a password?' She had been right: there had been no password entered before. She clicked on the 'yes' box. She typed in 'Steelhead,' the name of her first dog.

What appeared next was the current month's charges for the account. There were two women on the account, Laura Murray and Catherine Hobbes. Under 'Charges for Laura Murray' there was nothing. Under 'Charges for Catherine Hobbes' there was plenty: 'Stahlmeyer's Dept. Women's Wear, $2,436.91. Sybil's, $266.78. The Mine, $93.08. Tess's Shoes, $404.00. La Mousse, $56.88.' All of the charges had been made within the past couple of weeks. Catherine copied the bill into an e-mail and sent it to herself, then studied it one more time.

All of the stores were in Portland. They were all on the west side of the river, downtown. Catherine was sure she knew who this was. Tanya had made her mistake.

Catherine was operating now on an intuition. The part of it that was defensible was something that all cops were aware of and that the captain would understand: cops knew that coincidences existed, but not in the convenient numbers that people in trouble usually claimed. When coincidences turned up in the course of an investigation, they had to be viewed with skepticism. It was possible that even though there was no other Catherine Hobbes registered to vote in Oregon, and none besides her who had a telephone number, listed or unlisted, it didn't mean that one had not arrived in the past month. But that was unlikely.

The part of what she intuited that was not quite defensible would be difficult to explain to the captain, and it was the part that seemed most compelling. Catherine had a feeling about Tanya Starling. She had noticed that Tanya changed her identity more often than circumstances required. She seemed to change her name every time she arrived in a new city, every time anything happened that she considered unpleasant or unsuccessful. It reminded Catherine of the urge some people had to take a shower and change their clothes whenever they had a bad experience. Catherine was sure that she found it exciting, maybe even amusing. Tanya was getting very good at making or obtaining false identification.

Another thing that Tanya had done repeatedly was try to hurt Catherine Hobbes. Could a mysterious credit card in Catherine's name come up now and not be connected with Tanya Starling? It could, but it was unlikely. But how had Tanya done it? One possibility was that Tanya had been posing as the woman listed as the primary cardholder.

Catherine called the Denver Police Department and spoke with a woman who identified herself as Detective Yoon. The detective listened attentively to Catherine's story and agreed to find out whether there was a woman named Laura Murray living at 5619 LaRoche Avenue in Alameda. If there was, Detective Yoon would try to discover whether she had some knowledge of how her record and social security number had been used to get a credit card in the name Catherine Hobbes.

Detective Yoon called Catherine Hobbes the next afternoon at the police bureau. She said, 'There is a Laura Murray, and she's sitting in front of my desk right now.'

'She is?' said Catherine. 'Is she somebody who might have helped apply for the card, or just a victim?'

'She doesn't know anything about it. She's twenty-two, with no criminal record – no record of any kind except two old tickets, one for speeding and a parking violation. She's got a good job, and has lived here all her life.'

Catherine said, 'Let me fax you a set of pictures. See if she recognizes them.'

Five minutes later, they were on the telephone again. 'She remembers her,' said Detective Yoon. 'They met at a nightclub about two months ago in Denver, near Larimer Square. She says that when the girl in the picture danced with a man, she asked Laura to guard her purse. Then when Laura danced, the girl in the picture held Laura's purse.'

'Thank you,' said Catherine. 'This is a big help. Do you mind letting me speak with Laura?'

A moment later, a new voice came on the phone. It was young and nervous. 'Hello?'

'Hello, Laura. This is Detective Sergeant Catherine Hobbes, Portland Police Bureau. I want to thank you for your cooperation. It's very important to us. I need to ask you now for a little more help.'

'What do you need?'

'First, don't try to do anything about this credit card. Don't call the company or try to cancel or anything. For the moment we don't want to alert this woman to the fact that we know about the card. When the investigation is over the card will be canceled, and you won't be responsible for any debts. Can I count on you for that?'

'Sure.' Laura didn't sound sure.

'The other thing I need is to have you tell me everything you can remember about meeting this woman, everything she said to you, the way she looked, what she was wearing. There is no detail that's too small to be useful.'

FORTY-EIGHT

Judith opened her eyes and listened to the rain outside her apartment window. She liked it when the rain came down for two or three days at a time. It always seemed to her to be the world cleaning itself of the dirt and dead things, the unhappiness and mistakes. It rained almost half of the days of the year here.

Judith sat up in bed and looked at the window. The rain was running down past it from somewhere above, and she could hear it hitting below, splashing like a tiny waterfall. She got up, pushed the button on the coffee-maker, then padded out to the bottom of the carpeted stairs, where the manager left her newspaper every morning, and brought it back with her.

She sipped the coffee, sat cross-legged on the couch, and ignored the newspaper. Sitting here listening to the water outside made her feel very warm and safe. It was a feeling that she had not experienced until she had grown up. She had never liked rainy days when she was just Charlene.

In Wheatfield it sometimes rained for days like this in the spring and fall. Her mother hated the rain, hated ever being cold or wet, so she never went out. She hated being trapped in the house too, so she would wake up already irritated. Her blond hair would be in a network of ringlets that Charlene could hardly imagine having happened in the short time between last evening when she had gone out and the very next day. It looked like an unraveled rope.

Her mother's pretty, childlike face would be warm and pink from being pressed against her pillow, and it would carry impressions from the folds in the pillowcase. She would get up and stand beside the percolator and scowl at the sight of the coffee gurgling up into the little glass cap on top. She would find the green-and-white pack of menthol cigarettes on the counter, light one on the stove burner, and leave it in the corner of her mouth while she poured her coffee and went to the front window to stare out.

Years later, Charlene had realized that her mother behaved exactly like a cat. Even though she knew it was raining – had seen the water streaming down the outside of the bathroom window, had maybe even been awakened by it as it poured from the gutters out the downspout near her corner of the house, she still had to go to the front window to see if it was raining out there too.

After a few minutes of silence while she glowered at the rain and built her mood, Charlene's mother would begin. She would look at Charlene with frank curiosity. 'Have you rehearsed for the pageant next week?' Charlene would say she had spent most of the time doing homework, but she had rehearsed. Her mother would say, 'Let's hear the seashore song.'

Charlene would sing it, maybe not as well as she could, because she could see from the first seconds that her mother's expression was not admiring or pleasant. Singing for her was like pleading a case while walking up the steps of the gallows.

Her mother would hear the end of the song as a signal to respond. 'How could I have spent thousands of dollars and thousands of hours of my time on you? You sound like a trained parrot. You dance like a cow. How can you possibly be anything but embarrassing by next week? God, I should see if I can get my entry fee back.

And look at your skin. Have you ever thought of eating a vegetable instead of a candy bar? You look like the ghost of a ghost.'

When she had talked enough about the next pageant, which she had trained Charlene to believe was the last boat out of poverty, she would move on to a variety of new topics. 'Your room . . .' 'Your clothes . . .' 'Your . . .' As the morning got started, her voice would rise in pitch and volume until, during a pause for breath, Charlene would hear the current boyfriend creaking the springs in the bedroom, jingling his belt as he put on his pants. There would be a heavy thump as he put a toe in his shoe and stamped it to get his foot in.

A short time later he would appear, walking through on his way out, sometimes pausing to make some excuse, and sometimes just preferring the rain to the noise. Then her mother would blame her. 'You always make me look like I'm the big bitch. I wouldn't have to raise my voice if you'd just listen and do what you're supposed to. My God, look at that hair. I spend hundreds of dollars on cut-and-colors, shampoos and conditioners, and you have to look like the bride of Frankenstein. I'll tell you, if you don't do well on this pageant – either Miss Hennepin County or at least first runner-up – I'm through with you. You can be your own coach and man-ager and teacher and maid and chauffeur. Then where will you be? Miss Nothing. Miss Ugly Little Zero.' She would sit on the couch with her arms folded and put Charlene through a series of chores or a series of rehearsals, depending on her mood and the state of the little house.

Her mother would be distracted from her when the boyfriend returned, and there would be a fight. Usually the fight made it better for Charlene, but not always. She remembered one boyfriend named Donny, who was tall and thin and quiet, with long arms and legs. He was from somewhere in the South – was Tennessee right? – and he had an accent. He came in during one of her mother's tantrums on a Sunday, around one in the afternoon.

Her mother had heard the door and spun her head around to face Donny. She shrieked, 'And you too. You worthless—'

Donny's arm moved so fast that Charlene wasn't sure whether she saw it or only heard the slap and her imagination supplied the abrupt motion, the forearm bringing the backhand across her mother's mouth. Her mother went backward onto the kitchen floor, either because she had seen the movement at its start and tried to save herself, or was actually propelled by the force of the blow.

She could remember Donny's face while it was happening. When he heard what Charlene's mother was saying he might have narrowed his eyes slightly, but otherwise his face remained impassive. The long arm just swung, and there was something in it of the routine. It was like a horse twitching its tail to brush a fly away.

Charlene watched her mother. After a second or two, she raised herself on one elbow, staring, her nose and mouth bleeding. Her expression of anger and contempt was gone. She just lay there blinking, her mouth open, eyes empty and surprised, no more ready for thought than a person who had been hit by a truck.

Donny kept going toward the bedroom, and Charlene realized that the whole episode had not interrupted his progress for more than two seconds. He went in and closed the door. After a minute, her mother managed to sit up. Ten minutes later Charlene could hear Donny snoring.

Her mother had withdrawn to the couch, lying there and crying for an hour or so, feeling sorry for herself.

Charlene wanted to stand over her and ask, 'What did you expect? Are you blind and deaf? Did you live with him, sleep with him, drink yourself sick with him, and imagine that anything but this could possibly happen?' But she did not.

Charlene had liked Donny better than most of the others, because he had a kind of forthright simplicity. He had none of the willingness to struggle for advantage that made the others pathetic victims of her mother's manipulation. For most of her childhood, her mother's rainy-day scenes were acted out with a boyfriend of the other sort: Paul, or Mike. She would turn on the boyfriend, practically spitting venom, and he would respond. He would act exactly the way she did, as though he were not another person, really, but just her mirror and echo. Within a few minutes they would be simultaneously shouting different versions of what had caused the argument, then a list of bad things that each of them had done on other occasions, then bad qualities and habits, and, finally, there would just be an apportioning of ugly names.

It would go on all through the long, rainy day and into the evening, because her mother would not go out on a rainy night. If the weather didn't clear, Charlene would get two days of it. Between attacks on the boyfriend, Charlene's mother would deliver harangues against her for everything she was and everything she should be but wasn't.

It had taken changing herself into Tanya Starling and moving into the high-rise apartment in Chicago with Carl to teach her that there were pleasures to a rainy day. Carl had been an expert at enjoying himself. On a rainy day, if he wasn't involved in a legal case that had something urgent about it, he would sometimes stay home. They would lie around in bed and make love.

It was only when they were really hungry that Carl would jump out of bed, throw on some pants, shoes, and a rain jacket, and head for the elevator. He would be back in twenty minutes with croissants, Danish pastries, doughnuts filled with cream and jelly, and special coffee from the bakery around the corner.

She remembered how, as soon as she heard the apartment door close, she would be up, trying to use the twenty minutes as efficiently as she could. She would quickly bathe, running the water while she brushed her teeth. She would do her makeup, brush her hair, put on something that looked good on her but maintained the pretense that she wasn't bothering today. As she remembered, she felt a sharp sense of loss, not for Carl but for the days with Carl. What was lost was the way she had felt and been.

She picked up the telephone and called Greg's house. She heard his voice answer, 'Hello?'

'Hi,' she said. 'Are you planning to do anything important at work this morning?'

'Important, but not life-and-death important. Anything I can do for you on the way?'

'Yes. Come here instead of there, and spend a rainy morning with me. I'll make your dreams come true. One of them, anyway.' She hung up. Then she went into the bathroom and threw off her pajamas. She got ready with the same efficiency that she had used in the old days when Carl had gone out for pastries. She knew it would take Greg about twenty-five minutes to drive here at this time of the morning in the rain.

Today Judith was determined to live the life she had willed for herself. It was precarious, because some stupid piece of bad luck could throw her into the hands of her enemies at any second, but that didn't matter right now. Maybe perfection was always supposed to be brief, just a limited period when everything was in its prime. The life she had imagined existed only if she was at her most beautiful and energetic, not a girl any longer but a grown woman, someone who had been loved enough to take all of the man-woman maneuvering lightly, like a dance, and not be overwhelmed by it or scared. The rest was eternal: the nights of drinking martinis with their icy, oily shimmer, even the shape of the glasses unchanging; the man, purely appealing because he was the man of the moment only; the dim, romantic lighting and the music; a day of soft sun filtered through rain.

There had never been anything in the fantasy about having the perfect moment go on into some decrepit old age, and it couldn't. For now, for this series of heartbeats – whether now lasted for a couple of years or now was already ending – things had reached a perfect pitch.

Judith savored her rainy morning, and in the afternoon she and Greg dozed peacefully on her bed, listening half-consciously to the steady rain. She roused herself twice, once to lift Greg's sleep-heavy arm and drape it across herself so she could press her back against his chest and feel the skin warming her. The other time it was to crawl off the bed and pick up the newspaper she had never gotten around to reading.

She took a pen to the ads for the nightspots, then looked at the ones she had circled and made a plan for the evening. They would start at the Ringside for dinner, because on a rainy night she didn't feel in the mood to ruin a pair of heels and get a good dress splashed. A leather booth in a steak house with big, warm dinner plates and a coat rack behind her felt right. Then she picked out a cluster of four clubs within a couple of blocks of one another, so she and Greg could move easily from one to another.

She made fresh coffee, drank the first cup by herself, and let the smell of it drift into her bedroom to wake

Greg. When she heard him beginning to stir, she poured a cup and brought it to him. He sat up and took it, sipped it, and said, 'I'm trying to sort out what part of this day was real.'

'It's all real,' she said. 'The good parts have happened, or will happen, whatever they were.'

'What time is it?'

'Time to drink your coffee and wake up. After that it will be time to take a shower and get ready to go out to dinner with me. You can do it all slowly, because I intend to.'

'You sound as though it's all planned.'

'It is. I want to walk in the rain so I can see it and smell it, but without getting too wet. I want to eat, drink, and dance a little. Are you up to all that?'

'Of course.' He looked at her. 'Did I tell you I like your hair that way?'

'I did get the impression you had no complaints,' she said. 'I'll take the first shower, because it will take me longer.'

At nine they were in the Ringside, their umbrellas and raincoats hung on the coatrack beside their booth. Judith had not really eaten a meal today, just nibbled a few things from the refrigerator – a little cheese and fruit. She and Greg ate steaks and drank red wine, then sat and talked until they were ready for the rain again.

They walked to the Mine, listening to the drops popping on the fabric of their umbrellas. They stayed close to the storefronts, far from the curb, where a passing car might plow through a puddle and splash them. Once, Greg suddenly tugged her with him into an alcove outside a store entrance, and she thought he was saving her from a soaking. In a second she learned he had done it so he could kiss her in the alcove, where they were out of the lights and the rain.

The Mine was good tonight, the music all new work by a girl band called Danae. They had their own following, so the energy was all happy and appreciative, and the band tried to show itself at its best. Judith didn't mind that Greg's eyes lingered too long on the girls of the band. She might have resented the tight jeans on the bass guitarist, the ripped and abbreviated T-shirt on the drummer, but not tonight. It all helped to keep people's eyes on the stage, and not on her. She was enjoying a part of her perfect moment, and she didn't want to be disturbed.

FORTY-NINE

Catherine Hobbes knew exactly how she wanted to conduct her hunt. The only success she'd had so far was the result of circulating the pictures of Tanya Starling and Rachel Sturbridge. This time she had printed five hundred flyers with the two color pictures, the physical description, and the list of murders. The words 'armed and dangerous' were in larger, darker type.

During the early part of the afternoon, uniformed officers went to the businesses where the Catherine Hobbes credit card had been used, left flyers, and talked to salesclerks and waiters to find out what they could remember about the girl. Catherine had gone to Stahlmeyer's Department Store herself.

The women's-wear manager had checked the computerized record to find out exactly what purchases Tanya had made. As she walked Catherine to the right part of the fourth floor and began to show her the items Tanya had bought, Catherine felt the hairs on the back of her neck begin to stand.

Tanya had bought designer pantsuits. Two of them were almost exactly like the ones Catherine had bought at Stahlmeyer's a week before, tailored so the coats were not pinched inward to the waist but had a bit of drape. They were cut to hang from the shoulders, like a man's suit, so they allowed Catherine to carry a concealed weapon. Tanya was doing the same thing.

Catherine went outside to retrieve the digital camera

in the trunk of the unmarked car, then carried one sample of each of the four suits Tanya had bought into a dressing room and photographed them. The blouses Tanya had chosen to go with them were conservative, very like the ones that Catherine had bought.

Catherine knew that Tanya must have seen her on television in Arizona and probably in Portland. It wasn't difficult to find clothes like Catherine's in a big city. But why was she buying them? What did Tanya hope to accomplish by imitating Catherine Hobbes? Did it have something to do with getting the credit card accepted?

Maybe Tanya was working up to doing a killing and then taunting Catherine. She might rent a getaway car in Catherine's name, or leave a charge receipt with Catherine's name on it at a crime scene.

The idea that Tanya might be making her killings into a game was not a welcome one. The list of killers who had begun teasing the police and leaving riddles for them was long and ugly. From the time when they began to taunt the police until the time they were caught, they became more active and prolific. Catherine hoped that whatever Tanya was doing, she was not getting ready to kill somebody just to torment Catherine Hobbes.

Catherine drove back to the bureau, downloaded the photographs into her computer, and made copies for the evening-shift patrol officers in the downtown district. Then she went to the second floor, to the vice squad office, and found Rhonda Scucci.

Rhonda looked up from a file she was reading, and said, 'Hello, Cath. What's up?'

'Hi, Rhonda. I've got to go out tonight looking like somebody else.'

'What are we talking – whore? Drug mule?'

'This is a single woman, maybe five years younger than I am, if the light is dim enough. She works nine to five in an office. She might be out with a female friend or two. She hasn't got a date. You know the Mine? Metro? That's the kind of place. All I have to do is not stand out and not get recognized.'

'Yeah, there's a lot of that around this building. But don't worry. I know those places. You want what? A skirt and blouse? Shoes? Probably a raincoat tonight, just to protect our investment.'

'I can use anything you can get me. But the part I need most is the wig. The hair is really important.'

'So the suspect has seen your face?'

'Yes.'

'Jesus, Cath. A homicide suspect? Is that what they ask you to do these days?'

'Don't worry. I'm going to be backed up.'

'Just be sure it's close backup.' Rhonda led her down the hall to a storeroom and unlocked it. It looked as though it had been a broom closet originally, but now it held shelves full of electronic equipment for stings – microphones, tape recorders, video cameras – and a wide array of clothes for men and women on hangers. Rhonda picked a few things off the rack and held them up to Catherine until they agreed on an outfit. Then she helped Catherine try on wigs.

The third one looked right. Catherine could tell as soon as she looked in the mirror. The hair was dark brown, long, and straight, parted in the middle. It wasn't eye-catching, and if she ducked her head a bit, it would fall forward to hide her face if she wanted it to. 'What do you think?'

'What the hell do you care? It's to impress a killer. Want him to die excited?'

FIFTY

Catherine was on the street, walking the district where Tanya Starling had used the Catherine Hobbes credit card. Catherine had spent time in this neighborhood during vacations from college. Part of the attraction had been that the area had a bar scene full of young single people even then, and part of it had been that it had not been part of her father's precinct. She had been very careful to stay out of the parts of town where she might meet Lieutenant Frank Hobbes on business.

After that she had married Kevin and moved to Palo Alto. When that had fallen apart, and she had come home and become a cop too, she had not been assigned to fashionable places like this. She had spent her time as a patrol officer in the parts of town where people got robbed or killed, or bought ten-dollar bags of drugs.

The feel of the area had not changed, but it was much more crowded, much more expensive, and more stylish than it had been when she was in college. She supposed she could have said the same about all of Portland. It had spent the time filling up with the people who had ruined California.

Tonight was the third night of a persistent rain, and it was a weeknight, but it didn't matter. Men and women in their twenties and early thirties, some of them in suits and skirts from the office, were going into the restaurants and gathering at the bars, standing in knots while holding drinks in warm, wood-paneled taprooms.

Catherine needed to get used to the district again, and to develop a feeling for the spots where Tanya had used the credit card. She studied the entrances to the nightspots, picked out front windows where she might get a table to watch for Tanya, or where Tanya might be sitting right now.

All of Tanya's credit card charges had been between Eleventh Avenue and Fifteenth, as far north as Lovejoy Street and as far south as Glisan Street. The rain gave Catherine a chance to walk up each of the streets studying the buildings and the crowds, carrying an umbrella and wearing a hooded raincoat that hid her face. In Portland, rain didn't make anybody think of staying home, but Catherine's rain gear made it easy for her to study faces without much risk of being studied in return.

She patrolled systematically tonight, learning the traffic patterns. She began at the corner of Eleventh and Glisan and headed north to Lovejoy, then turned left and left again to go south on Twelfth. Each time she came to one of the places where Tanya had already been – the Mine, Sybil's, Metro, La Mousse – she lingered a few minutes, watching the doors, surveying the buildings.

One of the things she was trying to do was to evaluate the ambience and the customers. She needed to get a sense of whether the place would appeal to Tanya Starling or was somewhere she had gone once, had not liked, and would never revisit. Tanya seemed to like luxury – the bars in good hotels, nice restaurants – and the clothes she had bought in Portland were expensive. La Mousse and Sybil's were essentially the kind of restaurant that Tanya chose in every city, so Catherine was satisfied with them.

Catherine spent more time searching the parking lots

and the nearby streets looking for Tyler Gilman's car. By now, Tanya might have sold it or abandoned it, as she had done with other cars, but until it turned up, there was a chance that she had kept it and might drive it to this district on a rainy weeknight. The little blue Mazda was just the sort of car that Tanya might convince herself would not attract any attention, and Tanya would not want to show up at a restaurant or a club looking like a wet rat. She would want to look good to attract the next man.

Catherine had not been able to find any record of Tanya's having done anything for a living but accept gifts from men. She seemed to have lived in the high-rise apartment building in Chicago for an extended period of time. The building manager had said he didn't know how long she had been around, but he remembered seeing her occasionally for years. The apartment had been rented by a man named Carl Nelson, and her name had never appeared on the lease or the mailbox. About a year ago, Carl Nelson had died of a heart attack during a trip to Europe.

After Nelson had died, Tanya had gone to Aspen and found Dennis Poole. He had supported her and given her money and expensive gifts. She seemed always to be looking for a man to take care of her, and always finding that she had to move on.

Tanya should have left Portland. She had made an attempt on Catherine and killed Calvin Dunn, so Portland could hardly be considered a safe place to stay. She should be in the next city by now, but this time something was different. The charges on the Catherine Hobbes card had begun after Catherine's house had burned, not before. Catherine had to act on what Tanya was doing, not on what Tanya should be doing.

Catherine kept walking along the streets, her hood up,

staying in the shadows and moving quickly past the lighted windows, then pausing in the entranceways of closed businesses or under awnings near bus stops, where her presence would raise no questions.

Part of her consciousness was always devoted to watching for Tanya. Every time she came near a restaurant where a young couple was coming out, putting up umbrellas or trotting toward their parked car, she studied the woman. Whenever there was a woman visible through a front window, Catherine's eyes had to focus on her and find some disqualifying feature before she could release her from her gaze. When a car glided past her searching for a parking space, Catherine looked for Tanya inside.

She was also making mental notes about how to expand her search. The ideal way to do it would be to post a plainclothes officer at the bar in each of the district's clubs and restaurants for a few weeks, doing nothing but watching the door to see if Tanya entered. It was impossible, of course, but she thought maybe she could talk her captain into sparing one team. If there was one cop in Metro, Sybil's, the Mine, and La Mousse for a few nights, all of them connected by radio to a control van in the middle of the district, something good might happen. If Catherine drew the right male cops, Tanya might even try to pick up one of them.

She decided that the parking lot behind Sybil's, on Fourteenth near Irving, would be a good place for the van. The lot was used by a bank and about three smaller businesses during the day, but at night the only one that was open was Sybil's. When Sybil's was packed, there were still at least a few empty parking spaces. A plain white van parked in the far corner near the rear driveway would look as though it belonged to the restaurant or one of its suppliers.

She reached the Mine, at Fifteenth and Johnson, at eleven-twenty. There were no windows, but every time the door opened to admit more customers, she could see inside, where the crowd surged on the dance floor and the music blared and thumped briefly, and then was muffled as the door closed on it. The place was dimly lighted except for the stage, which she couldn't see from outside.

As she walked closer, Catherine had a subtle feeling that grew with each step: Don't walk past. Look inside. The Mine wasn't like a restaurant, where someone might make a second visit after a month or two. It was a night-club. Tanya could go there every night. The place was crowded, and the lights were low and wavering. Catherine should get a better look. As she walked toward the door, the rain picked up slightly, so three girls who had been smoking outside headed for the door. Catherine pushed back her hood, closed her umbrella, and moved in among them.

The music was loud, and she could feel the pounding of the bass in her stomach. She glanced involuntarily at the stage, a simple reflex of the brain because it needed to know where so much sound was coming from. She noted that it was a girl band, and returned her eyes to the crowd.

The patrons were of the right age and the right style for Tanya. There were at least two hundred people of both sexes in the big room, their faces sometimes illuminated by the glow of the spotlights on the stage, sometimes held in the dark for long periods. As she scanned the faces – smiling, laughing, trying to talk to each other over the music – she felt a shiver of fear for them. They looked like Tanya, clean-faced and alert, between twenty-one and thirty, all with good haircuts and dressed as though they were employed in some white-collar job. Tanya could slip in among them and be so like them that she would be unmemorable and invisible, until one of them was dead. It could happen any night that Tanya felt the urge. It could be happening now.

Catherine began to make her way through the crowd, squeezing into the border between the dance floor and the outer ring of patrons lined up for a turn at the bar. She would move sideways a few feet, then extend a hand between two people and let the arm and shoulder follow, repeating, 'Excuse me. Pardon. Excuse me' as she went, her voice just part of the mixture of voices to be heard trying to climb over the music but barely over it, so that she needed to be within a foot of the next person before he knew anyone was talking. Catherine slowly made it closer to the destination she had set for herself, the ladies' room.

She had known that in a crowd this size there would be a line of women waiting to use the ladies' room. No matter what else was true of Tanya, if she was here, she would have to wait in that line sometime. Catherine came within sight and began to move laterally in the crowd, studying the faces of the women in the line. Tanya was not among them.

Catherine devoted a few minutes to studying the layout of the Mine more closely. There were two fire exits at this end of the building, and probably another behind the stage. If there was a sighting of Tanya here, Catherine would have to remember to have those exits watched. She turned and began to inch her way through the mass of moving bodies toward the door. She was blocked suddenly as a tall man stepped into her path. 'Excuse me,' she said.

'Dance with me.' He was handsome, but he knew it.

'No, thanks. Got to go.'

'Come on,' he said. His confidence grew until he became repulsive. 'You know you want to.'

To his right Catherine saw something that didn't fit, the flash of a face and then a sudden movement that went against the beat of the music. She saw a couple moving off in the crowd ahead of her. 'Excuse me,' she said as she tried to go around him.

He held her arm. 'Please. I'm in love with you. The marriage is on.'

She looked at his arm clutching hers, then up into his eyes. 'Want a really nasty surprise?'

He let go, held up both hands, and stepped backward. She used the space that he opened between them to slip past him and make six feet of progress before the next obstacle formed.

'Excuse me,' she said to a group of young women who had just come in. The nearest of the women turned to look at her, just an aura of blond hair to frame an expression that was utterly empty.

Catherine said, 'You won't be able to get in unless you let people out.'

The woman reluctantly stepped aside six inches. Catherine brushed by her and the next two, and was out the door. She squinted into the rain, then down the street the other way, but she could not see the couple. She had lost them.

She tried to analyze the impression she'd had. It wasn't that the woman looked like Tanya – she had not been able to tell what she looked like in the dim light. It had just been the impression of furtiveness that had made her want to get a closer look.

She began to walk again, this time heading for Metro. She had noticed something, and it had not quite reached her consciousness until a moment ago. Every place where the Catherine Hobbes credit card had been used had one thing in common. They were all very dim. She hoped that when the officers had gone around this afternoon they had asked the owners of the businesses to post the circulars where people could see them.

FIFTY-ONE

Judith was sitting at her favorite table in Underground. This was the bar where she had met Greg, and the table was the one where they had sat and talked for so long on that first night. She was drinking her second martini of the evening, and it was probably going to be the last. This night was precious, and she didn't want to get sleepy. It felt to Judith as though she had finally managed to hold together all of the elements of the life she had always thought about when she was a child.

She had not realized when she was eight or ten that what she was imagining was only a single evening that was repeated endlessly. She had determined that she would grow up, get away from her mother, and stop having to be Charlene Buckner. She had known exactly who she would be: a woman who wore beautiful clothes and held drinks in a manicured hand adorned with jewels that sparkled. She would dance with a tall, strong man who adored her.

Now she was a success. Charlene had grown up, and right now she was Judith and she'd had that special evening a hundred times. She leaned close to Greg and said, 'I've wanted to go to the ladies' room since we were in the Mine, but I didn't want to wait in that line. I'm going now.' Since she was that close to him, she kissed his cheek before she stood.

Greg smiled at her and shrugged. 'I'll be here.'

Judith walked to the back of the room near the bar,

where there was a corridor. She passed the pay phone, then the door of the men's room, and then approached the ladies' room at the end. There was only one woman waiting ahead of her, so she waited too. She stood away from the wall, and pretended to look at the things that were written on it, glancing now and then in the direction of the telephone so she didn't have to make eye contact with the other woman.

She heard the door open and close, saw the girl who had been in the ladies' room move past, and heard the one ahead of her go inside. It was a relief to be alone. Judith waited, leaning against the wall. She hated being trapped anywhere with people who might have nothing to look at but her face. It had been about three weeks since the local television stations had shown the pictures of her old driver's licenses. People usually forgot everything quickly, but if just one person recognized her, Judith would be finished.

The door opened again, the woman edged past her, and Judith went inside. The room was small, like a half bathroom in a house, but it was clean and private. The walls were covered with copies of old movie posters, menus from forgotten restaurants, and travel ads, all pasted there like wallpaper. She flushed the toilet, went to the sink, and stopped.

Just to the left of the mirror, what she had thought was just another old poster wasn't. The pictures on it were the familiar ones of Tanya Starling and Rachel Sturbridge. But now there was a third one. Her face on the California license had been given a new hairstyle by computer.

Judith stared at herself in the mirror, then at the photograph. It had been doctored. The picture had hair like Judith's – hair like Catherine Hobbes's.

A dozen thoughts competed for her attention. Had

those two women a moment ago seen the picture and recognized Judith? They had been in here, and they must have looked at the mirror. Could they have missed the pictures? What did the poster say? She read the print under her face. 'Wanted for questioning . . .' That didn't sound like such a big deal. 'Homicide, arson, auto theft . . .' That was worse. Maybe the women hadn't read that far. 'Armed and dangerous.' Could anyone not see those words? Could they have seen this and not connected the pictures with Judith?

She tried to calm herself. Maybe she had been lucky. Her pictures had been all over the western half of the country, on and off, and almost nobody ever recognized her. She had not talked to either of those women, had not even made eye contact. A bathroom line was one of the places where people hardly looked at one another. Nobody wanted to get caught staring and then have to stand around with the person for five or ten minutes. And Judith had been careful.

She pulled the wanted poster off the wall, prepared to throw it into the wastebasket, but changed her mind. Whoever had put it up could be the one to empty the basket, and they might just stick it back up. She quickly folded it three times and put it in her purse. No, that was the wrong place. It was covering the handle of her gun, just when she might need to reach for it. She pulled the folded poster out again, put it into the side compartment of her purse, took a last look at herself in the mirror, and opened the door.

There was another girl waiting. Judith kept her head down and slipped past her, walking fast. She approached the next door, with its blue cutout symbol of a man. What if the poster was in there too? If it was in the ladies' room, why wouldn't they put another one in the men's room? Judith was alone in the corridor, but her solitude might last only a few more seconds. She quickly opened the men's-room door, glanced in to verify that it was empty, went inside, and locked the door.

There was the poster. She tore it off the wall, folded it, and put it in the side compartment of her purse with the other one. She went to the door, opened it an inch, and saw that the corridor was still empty. She slipped out and began to walk, then heard the door of the ladies' room open behind her. She should already be gone from this corridor, and the woman behind her knew it. Had the woman seen her coming out of the men's room?

She was filled with terrors, imagining possible disasters that demanded her attention right now. She was going to have to walk past the bar. Who had put the poster in the bathrooms? The bartender, or a waitress, or that creepy man at the end of the bar who was at least forty, too old to be anything but the owner. She couldn't let them see her face, but she couldn't look in the direction of the girl who had followed her up the corridor either. At least the girl had not seen the poster. No, that was too easy. Who was to say this was her first trip to the ladies' room? If she had been in there before she would have seen it, and now she would know it had been ripped down.

Judith came to the end of the corridor. She hurried past the bar and headed toward the table where Greg waited for her, looking pleased to see her. His happiness was an unwelcome reminder that she had been happy too, five minutes ago. Now his presence was jarring, something she had forgotten about but had to tolerate. As she approached she planned her words. It had to be better than 'Let's go.' She didn't want to open a discussion, and couldn't afford one. She would say something that had a finality. 'I need to go home right now.' Something like that should do it.

She saw that while she was gone he had ordered new drinks. He was sipping a scotch and water, and there was a fresh martini sitting next to the one she had not finished. It was irritating. How could he be so insensitive? A woman her size shouldn't try to drink that much at any time, and tonight it was dangerous.

She said, 'I need to go now.'

'What?' He put his drink down and moved his chair aside to make room for her to sit.

'I want to leave right now.' She picked up her coat from the empty chair, then the umbrella.

'Are you sick? Did something happen?'

He looked so pained, so stupid and slow, that she felt herself lose her feeling for him. He might be clever about business, but he had no instinct, no intuition. If he kept that concerned expression, he was going to be noticed. He looked like a big, foolish hoofed animal, ready to join a stampede, so she started one. She took a step toward the door.

'Wait. I've got to pay first.' He picked up the check, took out his wallet, selected a credit card, and tried to get the waitress's attention.

Judith snatched the check from his fingers, already reaching into the side pocket of her purse. She pulled out three twenties, set the bill and the money on the table, and kept going. At the door she slowed for a second and his long arm came over her shoulder to push the door open ahead of her. She was out.

'What is it, Judy?'

'I had to get out of there. I've had enough of that place.' She was calmer now that she was out in the night. The beautiful darkness made her feel anonymous again.

'Did something scare you?'

'Of course not.' She waited until he wasn't staring at her anymore, then glanced up at him.

He was gazing straight ahead up the sidewalk, his jaw muscles tightening and relaxing rhythmically. 'Then what was the hurry?'

'I just had a bad feeling in there.' She watched him. 'I wanted to go there in the first place because it was where I met you and it was a really happy memory for me. But after we were there, it wasn't the way I remembered it at all.'

His face turned down toward her, and she detected that his expression was false. Was it condescension, trying to pretend to take her seriously when he thought she was stupid? Maybe what he was feigning was any interest at all in what she said. Some men would patiently listen to all of the drivel a woman could say, biding their time until the woman seemed to wear herself out, free herself of nervous energy, and be receptive to sex. Was he hiding something worse?

Her heart stopped, then started again. How could she have forgotten? He had been in the men's room. He had gone in there right after they had arrived from the Mine. He had ordered their drinks, then gone into the men's room. He had come back quickly, before the drinks arrived. The waitress had accepted a tip, but begun to run a tab for the cost of the drinks. Judith tried to sort out the details, hoping to bring back a clear image of Greg's face when he had returned. Had he been concerned? Shocked? She tried to think clearly, but the two martinis were making her brain slow and unresponsive. Even the count was wrong, she thought. She had forgotten that at dinner she and Greg had both ordered wine. Damn.

She forced herself to concentrate. He had gone into the men's room. There was no absolute proof that he had seen the pictures near the mirror and read the things that Catherine Hobbes had written about her. It was possible that Greg had glanced at the reams of garish nonsense plastered over the walls and seen none of it. Men stood to pee, so he wasn't even facing the poster most of the time; he was looking at the other wall, or maybe down at what he was doing. But how could he not have seen the poster right next to the mirror? Maybe his pitted complexion made him behave differently. Maybe he was obsessed with staring at his own reflection and didn't see things like the poster, or maybe he hated the sight of his face so much that he avoided looking at mirrors.

She held him in the corner of her eye as she walked. 'I should have known not to go back to a place like that. It was a nice memory, and I shouldn't have tampered with it.'

'What was the problem?'

'It was just an impression. That creepy older guy at the bar kept staring at me. Then I went to the ladies' room, and there were these skanky girls ahead of me, waiting. And then I thought maybe I was kidding myself. The last time I had been in there, I was the one who picked up a guy. Then I had sex with him on the first date. I wanted to remember the place as romantic, but tonight the whole mess was – I don't know – depressing.'

'Then I guess it was a good time not to be there.' They reached his car, and he opened the door for her.

'Do you mind leaving?'

'Not at all,' he said. 'Where do you want to go next – home?'

She reacted quickly, instinctively, and said, 'Your place. I want to go with you,' and only then asked herself why. She realized it was because she had to stay with him, to watch him for signs. If he went off alone, she would lose control over him. She didn't know if he had seen the poster, but if he had, then leaving him alone to think about it would be a bad idea. She could imagine him spending some time trying to decide, then making the call: 'I think the person you're looking for might be my girlfriend.'

They got into the car and Greg pulled out onto the street. 'My place? That's great. Of course, if I'd known you were coming, I would have cleaned up a little. You'll have to be tolerant.'

'I'm reasonably tolerant. But if I find a girl in the bed eating potato chips and waiting for you to get home, we might have something to talk about.'

'Nope. No potato chips.'

'Then we're fine.' She had been watching him, and she was almost certain that they really were fine. He wasn't a good enough actor to lie to her about anything this important, and she didn't think he had the audacity to try. He seemed perfectly normal now that she had told him why she had wanted to leave Underground. He had not seen the poster in the men's room; if he had, he had simply let his eyes pass over it without having anything register in his mind. If he had actually recognized her and read the text, what he would have done was lead her outside the bar, and say something stupid very slowly. He would say it staring straight into her eyes, holding her shoulders so she couldn't look away, talking with that maddening ponderous slowness that dumb men used when they were being serious. He would make some promise to stand by her.

What he wouldn't know, because people like him never seemed to know it until it was too late, was that his standing by her now was worth nothing. It was holding her hand while a tidal wave approached, its frothy top rising to a crest a hundred feet above them, bearing things like the hulls of ships and the splintered timbers of wharfs aloft for an awful final second.

One of her mother's boyfriends had been like that. His name was Michael. He had watched Charlene endure her mother's shrieking fits and whimsical punishments, and had tried to befriend her. He had said, 'If you'd like to talk about it, I'm here for you.' Charlene had been about ten, so she had taken him seriously. No grown man had ever offered her anything before, so she had assumed he meant he would hear what her problem was and then solve it. But he had only meant what he had said. He would listen to her for a while, then shake his head and say, 'That's too bad.' He had never intended to imply that he would, or could, make her mother stop.

Greg would be like the rest. The way she would learn he had found out about her troubles was if he told her he was here for her. It would mean he was here to shake his head in sympathy while she got crushed and ground up by Catherine Hobbes and the cops.

She gave herself more time to make up her mind about Greg. He was a gentle, affectionate person, and he had not seen the pictures yet. It occurred to her that she should appreciate his plight, because he was living in the perfect, fragile moment, just as she was. But he was going to know eventually. He lived in Portland, went to an office every day, talked to people, shopped, watched television, read the papers. The only reason he didn't know already was that Judith had been taking up so much of his time. He and his friends all worked sixty hours a week, and every second that wasn't occupied with work, Judith had claimed. She had made him come to her straight from work, and today she had not let him go to work at all.

Judith had kept him in an artificial vacuum with her, where no information had reached him. But as each hour went by, the barrier that had kept out the news became more brittle. He would have to go to work. He would have to open his newspaper, turn on his television. She couldn't save him forever. How long, then? If she tried hard, she might be able to preserve him until tomorrow morning. That was all.

She stared out the window of the car, watching the people on the street through the streaks of water. She wondered about them. If her picture had been in Underground, it had probably been in other nearby places. These people had seen her picture, and a lot of them had read all of the things that horrible Catherine Hobbes had written about her. Were they thinking about her right now, or had they just acknowledged that there was a poster – what was it this time, a missing woman or a woman who had taken off with her own child? – and gone on with their lives? She couldn't know. They were all potentially dangerous, all threatening to Judith. If they saw her face now, their knowledge might kill her.

She watched Greg, saw his eyes moving in their sockets, focusing on cars slowing ahead, cars rushing past him, the mirrors, the road. He was going to see the poster. He was going to recognize the pictures. He was going to be a problem. 'You know, Greg, I think I haven't been as open with you as I should have been.'

'Yeah?' He looked at her in horror. It probably sounded to him like the preamble to a breakup speech.

She was beginning to hate him. 'I'm in love with you,' she said.

He glanced at the road, then turned toward her and said, 'I've been thinking that for a long time. I wanted to tell you.'

'Why didn't you?'

'I was afraid it would seem too pushy, and turn you off.'

Afraid, she thought. It was pathetic. He was so big and muscular. His flat, hard stomach and his thick hands and his success in business didn't seem to help him. He couldn't face the risk that if he dropped his protective timidity, he would find himself alone. 'I'm not turned off. I think it's sweet.'

'I should have said it first,' he said. 'I wanted to, but I thought I should wait a long time so you wouldn't think I was rushing you, or that it was too soon for me to love you.'

'It's okay,' said Judith. 'Maybe I said more than I should have because we had such a beautiful day, or because the martinis loosened my tongue. But I'm glad I did.'

'Me too.'

Of course he would say 'Me too.' It was absolutely inevitable. Imagining him not saying it was like imagining him drumming only three fingers and keeping the fourth from tapping.

Judith let him drive to his apartment. She had been there only twice before, both times late at night like this, when they had been out all evening and his place was closer than hers.

He lived on the top floor of a commercial building on Northwest Vaughn in a space like an artist's loft that had high ceilings with steel girders and big south-facing windows. Since he wasn't an artist, he was freed of the responsibility to be tasteful. He had a basketball backboard and hoop at one end of the room, and at the other a treadmill, weights, and exercise equipment. The pictures on the walls were mostly advertisements that relied on near-naked girls in odd places. Two that were astride motorcycles. One, wearing an open blouse with the sleeves rolled up and short cutoff jeans, held a chain saw. Several others draped themselves like cats on the hoods and roofs of shiny new cars. He had a work area set up on a twelve-foot table, divided between computer equipment and piles of papers, schematics, and mechanical drawings. Behind a partition was a king-sized bed with a bedspread made of the fake fur of a bearlike animal.

Tonight the loft was in the usual state of disarray. Magazines, books, socks, papers, sweatshirts all mingled in a circular pile around the overflowing laundry basket. In the part of the big room that was supposed to be the kitchen, the counter held two-day-old dirty dishes, a few beer cans, and a bowl half full of soggy popcorn.

She watched Greg go to the end of the apartment and disappear into the bathroom. She wandered in the empty space and looked at it in new ways. She had removed all but a tiny residue of uncertainty about Greg, but there was still that last layer, so she stepped close to put her ear to the door of the bathroom to be sure he wasn't talking on a cell phone. There was no voice, so she returned to her study of the apartment.

Greg came out, tossed his wallet and keys on the long counter near where she'd left her purse, and began to make drinks.

'Don't make one for me,' said Judith.

'Are you sure?'

'Yes. I'm tipsy enough already. Any worse and you won't be able to wake me up to take advantage of me.' She watched his face as she talked, and she could see that he was happy, amused, but also calm and contented. He assumed that she cared for him sincerely – that maybe she really did love him.

He came to her, held her hand and gave her a very soft, gentle kiss on the cheek, then kissed down to her neck, where it tickled. She liked it, and she knew that she was going to miss him. When she thought about Greg, she felt flattered, but she also felt the same surprised, distant curiosity she felt about dogs. He really seemed to love her in the same way dogs did, wildly out of proportion to the near indifference she felt for him. He always seemed to be quivering all over the way they did, wanting to dance around with joy. It must be wonderful to feel that joy.

Greg walked her toward the screened enclosure of his bedroom, and kissed her again. She glanced at the bed. 'My turn to use the bathroom. You see if you can make that mess look romantic, like someplace a girl would willingly go.' He released her and watched her walk off.

She stood in the bathroom, looking at her face in the mirror. There was a ringing in her ears from the alcohol in her system, and her brain felt sluggish. The remnants of the smile she had forced for Greg were still there, making her facial muscles feel tired. She regretted the martinis again. Was she thinking clearly enough for this? There were so many details to consider, and she had to think of all of them right now. She had no choice. Tonight was the only night.

So far tonight she had touched nothing but the door-knob. Had she ever left any prints in this loft? Maybe she had, weeks ago, and Greg certainly would not have cleaned anything. Did Greg have any photographs of her? No. He had once said he would like to have one for his desk, but she had made an excuse and he had forgotten to ask again. Was there anyone who had seen them together? Thousands of people probably had, but they were all strangers, just the undifferentiated mix of people sitting in restaurants or theaters and walking down streets where she and Greg had been. She had resisted meeting any of his friends from work.

Poor Greg. He had not known what he was getting into. If he had been stronger, smarter, maybe she could have taken a chance on him. But now, it was already after midnight. In a few hours he was sure to go to work, to read a newspaper, to turn on a television set, to talk to people. Judith had to stop him. She had to keep Greg in his current state forever – it was like a snapshot. There would be a flash and he would freeze – ignorant, trusting, and happy.

She looked into the mirror and fixed the smile on her face. She opened the door, walked out into the loft, picked up her purse. As she came around the partition she saw that Greg was already in bed, under the sheet, with the bedspread folded down to the foot of the bed. She set the purse on the floor by the near side of the bed, lowered the lights, took off her clothes, and laid them out neatly on the chair. It gave Greg a long time to watch her doing it, and she knew he enjoyed that.

She went to his coat rack, took a scarf, crawled onto the bed, and slipped it under his head.

'What's that? What are you doing?'

'It's a blindfold. I'm blindfolding you. Don't struggle.' She finished tying it and straddled his body.

'Is this an execution?'

She was taken aback for a half second. 'It's something nice. Don't peek or you'll spoil it.'

Judith reached into her purse and took out the gun. She drew the end of the soft, fake-fur bedspread toward her and wrapped it around the gun, held it there with her left hand, and pressed it gently to his head. When he felt the soft, smooth fur touch him, he smiled.

FIFTY-TWO

Catherine Hobbes examined the blood-spattered screen beside Gregory McDonald's bed. The coroner's crew had taken his body out earlier, but this space was going to be the property of the visiting blood-spatter expert for a day or two, so Catherine had to stay back and look in from the opening at the side. She didn't need to be any closer. Catherine Hobbes, or any other experienced homicide detective, could stand at the end of the screen and see what had happened.

Gregory McDonald had apparently been blindfolded with a scarf. The killer had wrapped the gun in the bedspread, held it to the left side of Gregory McDonald's head, and pulled the trigger. The blood had sprayed mostly from the exit wound on the right side of the head, and the blowback spatter had been taken mostly by the bedspread, but the killer had almost certainly been bloodied too. The upper end of the bed and the pillow under the victim's head had been soaked. Just from a glance at the bathroom, it looked to Catherine as though the killer had needed to clean up before leaving.

Catherine stepped away and surveyed the loft. What she could see made the murder seem even worse, more wasteful. Gregory McDonald had been a well-paid software designer with an engineering degree, but the loft was decorated in fraternity-boy baroque, complete with a basketball net and a few empty beer cans. He had not had time to reach anything she would have recognized as adulthood.

As Catherine thought about the simple, unembellished facts – a single man found naked in bed shot once through the head, but no gun at the scene, and a killer who had cleaned up afterward – she began to have a sinking feeling.

Her cell phone rang, and she took it out of her purse. 'Catherine Hobbes.'

'Hey, Cath.' It was the captain. 'I'm moving my knights around on the board. Where are you?'

'Gregory McDonald's loft. Where do you want me?'

'You may as well stay there. This one is going to be yours too. One of the prints the forensic people lifted off the tile in the shower belongs to your girl.'

'I was afraid of that.' Instantly she wished she hadn't said that. The captain didn't need to be reminded that she had predicted this. He had given her as many people as he could spare to canvass the area where Tanya had used the credit card. She had to think ahead, not back. 'Captain, I wonder if we could delay releasing the news about the fingerprint for a day or two.'

'Why? Do you think if she hears it, she'll take off again?'

'I'm not sure, but it's a distinct possibility. I'm sure that she watches the television news.'

'All right. Let's keep the print out of the press for the moment.'

'Thanks.'

She heard him disconnect, so she folded her phone and put it away. She raised her voice so all of the officers in the loft could hear her. 'Attention, everybody. One of the prints on the shower tile has turned out to be a match for Tanya Starling. That is not to be released to the press for the moment. We've got a female perpetrator who sometimes dyes her hair. The minute you find hairs that don't match the victim, please find me or call me. I need to know what color Tanya's hair is this week.'

She walked to the door of the bathroom and looked inside. The tiled walls, the sink, and the mirror were almost completely blackened with print dust. The crime scene people loved mirrors and tiles. Anything that got cleaned frequently and was smooth and glassy was made for preserving clear prints.

Catherine stood still and imagined the scene, putting herself in Tanya's place. Tanya had been in the bedroom area with Gregory McDonald. He had been naked, and so she had been too, probably. She had blindfolded him in some playful way. But she had done it because she had needed to have him lying still and not fighting her for the gun or ducking behind things. She had wrapped the bedspread around the gun to muffle the sound and then pulled the trigger.

The sound had not been as quiet as she had hoped. The gun must have sounded like a cannon in this loft. Catherine could almost hear the blast in her imagination.

Catherine imagined she felt the gun kick upward, heard the ringing in her ears. The bedspread had not muffled the sound. Tanya was afraid, and Gregory looked terrible now. She placed the pillow over what had been his face. She became conscious of her nakedness and felt vulnerable; the blood spattered on her was warm, almost hot, and the feel of it made her sick. She didn't know what to do. She wanted to put on her clothes and run, but she had Gregory McDonald's blood on her – on her face, in her hair, on her chest, her belly. She had been beside him, or maybe above him, straddling him, and now she rolled off the bed and crouched, the gun aimed at the door of the loft.

She stayed there for a long time, listening. Maybe it was ten minutes, maybe only five minutes, but it seemed to her to be much longer. She was waiting for a sound that would indicate that someone had heard. Cautiously she moved in the dark to the window and looked down at the street. Probably she knew that if a neighbor were coming to investigate, he would already have banged on the door. If the Portland Police Bureau had been called, their response time would not be this long. She reassured herself, because she knew the secret of shots fired in a city. When people heard one shot they told themselves it was a car backfiring or a firecracker. It was only when they heard multiple shots that they couldn't tell themselves that it was something harmless.

She went into the bathroom and looked at herself in the mirror. She was freckled with Gregory's blood, and she had to get it off. She turned on the shower, adjusted it to a bearable temperature, and stepped into it. She scrubbed herself, washing her hair and her skin, then stayed in the shower for a long time, being sure that the bright red blood was off her and the pink diluted remnant had long since washed off the tub. Maybe she was even aware that firing a pistol had left a residue of burned powder and heavy metals on her skin, so she scrubbed harder. She came out and dried herself with the cleanest towel she could find, then wiped the floor with it and the faucets and anything else she could remember touching. The one place that she missed was where she had touched one of the shower tiles and forgotten it: had she lost her balance for a second while she was getting out, or leaned against it to dry her foot? She took the towel back to his bedroom enclosure, stuffed it in the laundry basket beneath his clothes, or maybe tossed it in and then picked up some clothes from the floor and threw them in to cover the towel she had used.

Then she got dressed. If the gun was a revolver, she put it in her purse. If it was semiautomatic, she found the shell casing and put it in her purse with the gun. She went to the front windows again and looked outside to be sure the police were not visible in the streets below the building. Since they weren't, she explored the loft, probably with a flashlight. She was looking for money, or jewelry, or anything else that might be valuable. She took some time looking around, probably using something like one of Gregory's socks over her hand to open drawers. She bothered to do it not because she was desperate for money but because there was no reason not to, and the sound of a gun should not be followed by the sounds of someone leaving the building until a long time had passed.

Catherine knew that Tanya had learned that by now – that one reason people got caught was that they did not take time to think and prepare and act normally. They ran and they sweated and they looked suspicious. When she felt ready, she glanced outside once more, took Gregory McDonald's car keys, went down the stairs, and drove his car away. It had not turned up yet, but Catherine was sure it would later in the day, parked at a shopping mall or an airport or a public parking lot.

Catherine walked away from the bathroom and up to two of the forensic people who were dusting the long counter by the window. 'If nobody's done it yet, I'd like somebody to take out the trap in the shower drain to check for her hairs. I'm almost certain the reason she touched a tile was that she took a shower after she killed him. Another good place to look is in his laundry basket. There should be a damp towel about halfway down.'

Catherine walked down the stairs, not touching the

446

railings, and stepped outside the building to look up at the windows of Gregory McDonald's loft. Nobody could have seen anything from down here, and the buildings across the street were lower. They seemed to still be used for some industrial purpose, not yet part of the gentrification that was gripping the neighborhood, but she would find out who occupied them and ask.

She hesitated for a moment, then took out her cell phone and dialed a Los Angeles number.

A woman who sounded younger than she was answered, 'Pitt Investigations. May we help you?'

Catherine said, 'This is Catherine Hobbes. Is Joe in?'

'No, I'm sorry. He's out right now, but I'll transfer your call to his cell phone.'

'You don't have to do that,' said Catherine.

'Yes, I do,' said the young woman. Catherine thought she heard amusement in her voice. 'He told us all that if he misses a call from you, then whoever dropped it is in trouble. Please hold for a moment.'

After a few seconds she heard Joe's voice. 'Catherine?'

'Yes,' she said. 'It's only me. Do you really threaten your employees?'

'Sure. Don't you?'

'I don't have any. I just called to give you more bad news. Tanya has done it again. I don't know why I'm bothering you with it, but I felt as though you had earned a right to a share of the misery.'

'Who was it?'

'A young guy named Gregory McDonald. He was some kind of software engineer. He was shot in the head while he was in bed with her in his loft.'

'So it's like some of the others – Dennis Poole and the guy in the hotel down here.'

'That's what I've been thinking. I'm not sure yet if it

447

was a one-night thing or a bad end to a relationship. I just got word a few minutes ago that one of the prints in the loft belonged to Tanya, so I'm just getting started. Nobody has checked yet to find out whether they were seen together, and so on.'

'Would you mind if I flew up there tonight or tomorrow to take a look around?'

'Yes,' she said. 'I definitely would mind. This is my case, and my job, and you're the biggest distraction in the world. I've got to follow up the leads now, and then maybe later I'll talk to you about what it all means.'

'It means she's still there,' said Joe. 'Be thorough, and be careful. I love you.'

She said, 'Why do you do that?'

'What?'

'Say "I love you" when I'm just about to hang up. I could listen to you until my ears dropped off, but you never say it except at a crummy time like this.'

'I don't think that's true. Is it?'

'Yes, Joe. It's true. The first time, I thought it was a bad cell phone connection. Now, is it just a figure of speech, like "Take care," or are you actually telling me that you love me?'

'I'm actually saying that I love you. I'll say it again. I love you.'

'That's good,' she said. 'Because I love you too. Now I can hang up and have about a second of intense happiness before I go off to the coroner's and look at the young guy with the bullet hole in his head. Bye.' She pressed the end button, put her cell phone in her purse, and got into her car, thinking about Joe Pitt.

As she drove toward the coroner's office, she prepared herself for the sight that she knew awaited her. Head shots were horrible, but she had to look at everything that Tanya had done or touched or left. Maybe this time Tanya had acted carelessly. Maybe this time she had forgotten to eradicate some detail that would tell Catherine where to find her.

Judith had stayed in bed almost all day. She slept for nearly twelve hours during the first stretch, letting the exhaustion keep her unconscious and the time pass so the sights and sounds would not be so clear and sharp in her memory. When she awoke she lay in bed thinking and remembering, but what she thought about was not last night. Once an unpleasant decision had been made, there was no reason to go over and over it.

What she thought about was that nothing ever seemed to work out for her. It never had, and it was because there was always somebody who didn't want her to be happy. The very odd thing was that the people who really wanted to hurt her were always other women.

Judith didn't expect much of men. They were indifferent and thoughtless. They were insensitive and selfish. A few even had some sexual issue, some program running in their heads that made them behave a certain way, and want her to behave in a certain, exactly complementary way. In fact there was a little of that in all of them – they thought about sex all the time, and every dealing with them had that as a part of it. Even if it was wildly impractical or even impossible for them to have sex with a particular woman, they wondered about her. All of those things were part of the world that was known. Nobody was hiding any of it.

Women had a lot of reasons to be on the same side, but they never seemed to be. They always seemed to be competing. In her life, men had been difficult or disappointing, but the people who had been real tormentors had all been female. Her mother had been the first.

Sharon Buckner had never been able to pull herself together and move to Chicago or Milwaukee to get a serious job. Every night from the time when she was about sixteen, she had managed to get dressed up and transported to one of those same big cities to dance and drink and have fun, but the idea of going there to work was too far-fetched for her.

Charlene had been about ten before she had learned where the name Charlene had come from. By then Charles Kepler had married and left town – been shamed out of town, Sharon Buckner said – but the rest of the townspeople had not left. That day Charlene had realized that since her birth, all of the adults around her – the neighbors, her teachers – had been looking at her and knowing the most private aspects of her life.

When Charlene was little and first went on the pageant circuit, Charlene's cuteness drew attention to Sharon. She got to be the pretty young mother of the pretty little girl. But when Charlene was in junior high school, the situation changed. Now the girls in the pageant were thirteen to seventeen. Charlene won Miss Junior Hogan County and Miss Junior Carroway County, both on false addresses, and finally Miss Junior Central Illinois. But her mother's pleasure wore out.

They were both ten years older by then, and the years looked better on Charlene than on Sharon. She was the one who got the attention; she was Sharon's competition, her enemy. Her mother began to make disparaging remarks about Charlene's weight, her hair, her complexion, her performances. She began to mock the answers Charlene gave to the emcee's questions. Charlene knew they were good, because there were only about twenty-five questions that all emcees always asked, and she had memorized the best answers of the winners over the years.

Charlene had to drop out of the pageants at the age of fifteen because her mother refused to enter her anymore. She was glad that she would no longer be forced into hours of close proximity to her mother, but it made her feel more vulnerable to the horrible girls at school. She no longer had the secret life where she got to wear fancy formal dresses – and, most of the time, a crown. When that world was gone, she had nothing.

The girls at school had always been cold and unfriendly, but beginning in junior high they were actively cruel. Anytime she talked to a girl she was told she was obnoxious and pushy. When she talked to a boy she was a whore. When she didn't talk she was a stuck-up bitch. When she did well on a test she was showing off and sucking up to the teachers. She ate lunch alone, walked from class to class alone.

As she thought about it today, she decided that if she had the leisure sometime, she would take a drive up to Illinois and see if she could find a few of those girls. By now Gail Halpren would be married and have a couple of kids. Judith would walk up to the house and knock on the door. It would open. She would say, 'Remember me? I used to be Charlene Buckner. I thought you deserved to be thanked for the way you treated me in high school.' Then she would pull out the gun. Or she would find Terry Nugent. Terry would probably be in Chicago, working as a lawyer or a stockbroker. She would wait for her in a parking garage. 'Aren't you Terry Nugent, from Wheatfield? Yes, it's me. But let's not talk about those days now. We can talk about them forever in hell.' Pow.

After she moved in with Carl, the other women were

the wives and girlfriends of important men. None of them had liked her, but now the reasons were clearer. The parties in that social set had been beauty pageants too – women parading stiffly around with fake immovable smiles and wide, scared eyes. She had been more convincing at it than they were, and so they'd hated her.

Now the police were hunting for her, and the one who was causing it was another woman. She hated Catherine Hobbes, but she knew that part of her hatred was just outrage at the unevenness of the competition. Catherine Hobbes had the right look, very erect and tailored. She had a cool, imperturbable demeanor that made her seem wise and knowing. And behind her was all that power.

Judith got up from the bed, looked out the window at the clear day, went into the bathroom to shower, then came out and dressed. She wore a smart skirt and sweater as though she were going to work in an office somewhere, but she put Tyler Gilman's old baseball cap and his jacket into her backpack and took them with her to the car.

She wished she knew whether the police had found Greg by now. She supposed she could find out if they had by driving past his apartment and looking for their cars, but she didn't want to go there. She didn't know whether the police believed that old adage about killers returning to the scene of the crime. If they believed it, they would be watching for her.

She drove north and east across the Broadway Bridge, toward the police bureau on North Thompson Street. She found a parking space for her Acura on North Tillamook and walked around the block. As she approached the building, she tried to take in everything about it. She saw a number of cars, some of them police cars, coming and going from the lot beside the building. It was a busy place, and she was not the only pedestrian.

She had noticed other times that the people who came and went from police stations always looked hurried and preoccupied, never happy. This afternoon, none of them seemed to have much curiosity about anyone else.

Long before she reached the building, she saw what she had been looking for: beneath the building was an entrance ramp. She guessed that there must be some kind of underground garage where the police parked their personal cars. She walked past the entrance, looked inside, and made a decision.

She followed the ramp down into the lower level. The cars here had to be the ones that belonged to the cops, but as soon as she was there, she began to lose hope of figuring anything out. There were so many cars, and she'd begun with only a theory about Catherine Hobbes to help her.

She had believed that Catherine Hobbes was so sure of herself and of her tastes that she would have replaced the car she had lost in the fire with one exactly like it: the car would be a new teal blue Acura, paid for by her fire insurance.

Judith walked purposefully between two rows of cars, looking hard at them, but she saw no Acura, and no teal blue cars of any brand. She reminded herself that it was always possible that Catherine wasn't at work today, or that she had parked on some nearby street as Judith had, or that she was out right now using her own car instead of a police car. All of those things were possible, but possible wasn't the same as likely.

Judith kept looking, walked to the end of the aisle, then turned up the next aisle and headed back. She sensed that she had spent all the time she could down here. She heard a sound, and looked up to see a male driver in a Ford Explorer come down the ramp and turn into an empty space. He was obviously a cop – short-haired and beefy with a mustache – and he was in a hurry. He stepped down from the driver's seat, reached back into the vehicle to take out a hard-sided briefcase and a jacket, and looked at Judith.

'Can I help you find something?' He was like all cops. He was trying not to look suspicious, and he had no reason to be suspicious, but he couldn't help it. She could tell, however, that he had the wrong crime in mind. He didn't recognize her. Maybe he would recognize her later, when she was long gone.

She said, 'This is the police station, isn't it?'

'Yes, it is. But you can't park down here. You have to go up to the ground level and come in that way. There's visitor parking up there.'

'Thanks. I parked on the street,' she said. She kept walking, her heart beginning to beat hard only after the danger was over. She was nearly to the ramp before she realized that she might have seen the car while he was talking. There was a gray Dodge Neon with a license-plate holder from Enterprise Rent-a-Car on it. Catherine might not have replaced her car yet. She might still be driving a rental. Judith knew she couldn't go back and look at it more closely. She came up out of the parking area and headed for the front door of the station, then at the last moment went past it and walked quickly up the street.

She reached her car and drove off. She came back to North Thompson Street at five and parked where she could watch the driveway from a distance. She saw a steady stream of cars come out just after six, but Catherine's car was not among them. Judith judged that the shift had probably changed, but Catherine was Detective Sergeant Hobbes. She didn't have to keep the same hours as the traffic cops. She saw another group go at eight, and a third at ten, but she didn't see the small gray Dodge Neon.

She conceded that she could have guessed wrong. Maybe the rental car wasn't Catherine's. Some other cop could have his car in the shop for repairs and be driving the rental until it was ready. She might be wasting her evening. She was getting bored and hungry, and she needed to use a restroom. She started her car and angled the wheels away from the curb. As she prepared to move up the street, away from the police bureau, she glanced in the mirror to be sure the street was clear. The Dodge Neon was moving up the ramp and turning toward her.

Judith waited and let the Neon go by. She could see that the driver was a woman, and the woman seemed to have the right kind of hair, but the face was in darkness. Judith gave the Neon a head start, then pulled out after it. She followed at a distance, waiting for a few seconds before she made the right turn to follow it onto North Tillamook, then waited until two other cars had gone by before she made the second right up North Interstate Avenue.

Judith followed as the car made another right turn onto Northeast Russell Street. She managed to keep one of the two cars between her car and the Neon as they drove past the big hospital on the left side of Northeast Russell. Then the Neon signaled for a left turn. Judith went past on the right slowly, studying the driver, and saw that it was Catherine Hobbes. Judith went down the street for a block, and watched the car in the mirror as it turned into the driveway beside a modern brick apartment building.

As soon as the car was out of sight behind the building, Judith turned around, came back, and parked where she could watch the windows. But as she watched, Judith saw two women in scrubs walking from the direction of the hospital turn up the sidewalk toward the front steps. One of the women was fishing in her purse. She pulled out a set of keys. But before she could use them, a young man in a similar hospital uniform appeared in the lobby, came out, and held the door while they went in, then released it and headed for the hospital.

Judith saw Catherine come up from a set of stairs into the lighted hallway, apparently having come in from the back of the building. She walked past the elevator and stepped into the stairwell.

Judith got out of her car and walked closer, watching the side of the apartment building. After a few moments the lights in a row of third-floor windows came on.

FIFTY-FOUR

The next evening, Catherine drove up Adair Hill and parked her rental car across the street from her parents' house. She walked up the porch steps and tried the knob. It was locked. She had been hoping it would be, but she couldn't help feeling a cold, sad sensation as she took out her key and opened the door.

'Hello?' she called. 'Anybody home?'

'Where would we be?' It was her father. He came around the corner from the kitchen and let her kiss him on the cheek.

'I don't know,' she said. 'You're old enough to make your own decisions, and to live with the consequences.'

'Thank you, dear,' her mother called from the kitchen. 'Nice of you to come by. Did they close the police bureau and kick you out?'

'No, I left voluntarily.' She came into the kitchen, followed by her father. She kissed her mother, once again surprised by the incredible softness that her mother's cheek had developed in the past few years, and savoring the faint scent of gardenia soap she had smelled since childhood.

Catherine sat at the kitchen table and accepted the cup of coffee her father set in front of her. He sat down with a glass of water and eyed her as he would a suspect. 'Hard day, kid?'

She shrugged. 'I don't know anymore. Since we found that guy yesterday and Tanya's fingerprint in his shower, nothing much else has turned up. Maybe that's good. We're not up to our armpits in new bodies. But it doesn't feel like we're winning.'

'It never does until it's over,' said her father. 'I was betting she would be recognized by now, though.'

Catherine's mother seemed to be more and more agitated as her husband and daughter talked. She said, 'How about your life outside of work? Anything interesting happening?'

'Not that I've noticed. I seem to be the same bitter divorcée I've been for years.'

'We haven't seen you much. Has Joe Pitt been around?'

Catherine's father seemed to remember something else he had to do. He took his glass of water with him to another room.

'A couple of weeks ago. He's back in Los Angeles doing his own cases. We call each other a lot.'

'What do you talk about?'

'Meaning what?'

'Oh, I don't know. I think I mean, are you serious about him?'

'Or is he serious about me.'

'Both ways.'

'Headline: Mother Wants Daughter to Settle Down.'

'Or not,' said Martha Hobbes. 'Maybe you're getting too settled as it is. Is being a cop all you ever want to do?'

'Is that such an odd idea?'

'It's a big joke on me, I can tell you. I spent twenty-five years waiting for your father to get to retirement age without any holes in him. And now I worry about you. Marriage might not be so bad compared to having murderers burning your house down around your ears.'

'I was married, remember? That's how I realized I

should be a detective. I detected that my husband was screwing everybody he could reach.'

Her mother stared at her. 'Is that funny to you?'

'Funnier than it used to be,' said Catherine. 'Believe me, I've come a long way toward your way of thinking in the past few weeks.'

'You mean you really are serious about him?'

'Yes, I'm very serious. But I'm not making plans for any weddings. I wasn't going to go out with him at all until I purposely forgot everything my mother had told me about men.'

'He lives in Los Angeles, doesn't he? What would you do if he asked you to move there?'

'He hasn't.'

'That doesn't mean you have to put off thinking about it until he does.'

'I don't get it. Have you decided you want me to move to L.A., or that you don't want me to?'

'I want you to be happy.'

'Good. I'm happy.'

'I mean really happy.'

'Mother, make yourself happy. Make Daddy happy. I'm not in a position to be "really happy" right now. I have a reasonable facsimile of a boyfriend. We're seeing where it goes, but at the moment it's not going anywhere. Long-distance relationships are everything they're cracked up to be, which is horrible. We tell jokes and say "I miss you." Half the time when I talk to him I'm sure he's watching some game on television with the sound off.'

'There. Was that so hard?'

'What?'

'Telling me what I asked you in the first place.'

Catherine closed her eyes and took two deep breaths, then opened them again. 'No, I guess it wasn't.'

Her father came in, carrying a newspaper. 'Have you tried the emergency rooms?'

'Huh?'

'She killed this big fellow, right? Sometimes while they're killing somebody, they get hurt. Wood or glass chips fly, people you think are dead aren't. She could be hurt.'

'She's not. This one was blindfolded, lying naked in bed. All the blood in the apartment is his.'

'Oh,' he said. 'How about parking tickets? I picked up a few suspects by seeing what cars got ticketed near the scene. There's a description of the car and the license number on the summons.'

'Tried it.'

'How about security videotapes? That apartment is in a neighborhood that's mostly commercial.'

'Tried that too.'

'That's my girl.' He wandered off again.

Catherine's mother said quietly, 'Does he ever make any sense?'

'Always. He's trying to think of a way to shortcut this for me.'

'Well, that's a relief,' she muttered. 'It's hard to tell if you're just humoring him.'

'I'm not, but I would.'

Her mother put a piece of cherry pie on a plate and set it in front of Catherine. Catherine cut it in half and returned half to the pan without comment. Then she ate the other half and listened to her mother talk about the past few days in the neighborhood.

The stories were a peculiar comfort to Catherine. They calmed her and reassured her that the rhythms of the real world were intact. The sun dried the rain-soaked gardens, the roses bloomed, and Lydia Burns put a letter in a mailbox and accidentally dropped her car keys in with it.

At eleven Catherine went into the living room, where her father was watching the local news. He looked up. 'Have you had uniformed officers circulate her picture to the mom-and-pop stores?'

Catherine said, 'What am I missing?'

'She's got to buy food and toothpaste somewhere. Supermarkets are full of people standing in line staring at one another, and four or five assistant managers watching customers. Maybe instead, she shops at one of those little stores run by immigrant couples who can't tell one young American woman from another, or are afraid to cause trouble.'

'I'll give it a shot. Thanks, Daddy.' She kissed his cheek.

He said, 'Are you going?'

'Yeah. I've had my free slice of pie, so I guess I'll be on my way.'

'I drove by to check out your apartment building.'

'And you hated it?'

'I don't work for *Architectural Digest*. I like that it has a locked door with an intercom and a lot of people around. Looks like a lot of doctors.'

'They're all interns,' she said. 'The ones that are old enough to be keepers must all have houses.'

'When you park in that lot behind the building, look around before you get out of your car, and then watch your back.'

'I always do,' she said. 'Good night.'

'Good night, kid.'

She went out and stepped onto the porch. Her eyes took in the configuration of trees and houses that were so familiar to her they were the landscape of her dreams. She could see it was all as it had been for as long as she could remember, and there was no shadow that she had not memorized. She walked toward her car slowly, looking up and down the quiet street.

The day after Tanya had burned her house, Catherine had requested that a plain car be posted a hundred feet below here, on the curve of the road, so that an officer could get a close look at the face of anyone who drove or walked by. After a week there had been no adequate justification for keeping a car any longer. There had been no indication that Tanya had looked for Catherine's parents, but tonight something felt wrong.

She continued her walk to her car, stopped beside it, and reached into her purse, pretending to search for her keys while she watched and listened. There was no unfamiliar sound, no sign that anything was out of place. She stood there a bit longer, waiting, giving Tanya a chance to move. Nothing happened.

Catherine got into the car and started it, then turned on the lights and drove farther up the hill. She turned around in the spot where she would have hidden if she had been Tanya, just on the uphill side of the Tollivers' high hedges. Then she coasted down the road, turning the wheel slightly now and then to shine her headlights on the best hiding spots along the narrow street.

She kept encouraging her mind to feel its discomfort, trying to let it intensify so she could identify what it was. If she had seen something too subtle to interpret, it was gone: no troubling image formed in her memory. As she reached the bottom of the hill and turned left toward the bridge, she realized what it was: timing.

She had listened to the stories of her father and other old cops and had read files from hundreds of cases of serial killers. Serial killers were almost all male, and most of them seemed to be acting out some fantasy that was a mixture of violence and sex. Many appeared to search for a particular kind of victim. Others seemed to be trying to reproduce exactly some scene they had concocted in their imaginations. It was not clear to Catherine what

Tanya was doing when she killed someone. It seemed to Catherine that it had something to do with power. Maybe in some part of her past, Tanya had been powerless, and had been harmed or abused in some way. It seemed to Catherine that with the killings she had created a method of making herself safe.

Tanya seemed to be driven by fear. Every time she killed someone she had more to fear, so she had to kill again to feel safe. Whenever Tanya felt she might be losing control, she proved she wasn't by killing somebody. What was bothering Catherine tonight was that she had become accustomed to Tanya's rhythm, and it seemed to Catherine to be time.

She pulled her rental car into the parking lot behind the apartment building, and her father's advice came back to her. She turned the little car in a full circuit of the perimeter, letting the headlights shine on the low brush that came to the edge of the pavement. She selected a space in the middle and got out of her car, her left hand holding her purse and keys, and her right hand free to reach for her sidearm.

Catherine took a last look around her before she unlocked the back entrance of the building, stepped inside, and closed it behind her, listening for the click of the lock. She walked up the hall to the staircase at the front of the building instead of riding up in the elevator. When she was inside her apartment on the third floor she locked the door and flipped the latch across it. Then she headed for the shower.

FIFTY-FIVE

Judith lifted the package off her bed and worked at getting the heavy plastic wrapping off. She went to the kitchen and got a steak knife, then came back and made a slice along the top. The package said, 'Hospital Scrubs, size S, OSHA Compliant.' She held the pants up in front of the full-length mirror and looked at them critically. Were the legs going to be just a bit long? She had bought the scrubs this afternoon at a uniform store that specialized in medical clothes, and she had not wanted to spend much time shopping or ask any questions.

She had just picked up the package, paid cash for it, and gone. She took off her jeans and T-shirt and put on the scrubs, then stared in the mirror. They felt like starched pajamas, but she liked the way they looked on her. She turned halfway around to look over her shoulder, then kept turning until she was facing forward again. She was very pleased. The only essential part was that the fit be good: no nurse would have scrubs that weren't her size. Judith made a very attractive nurse.

She had chosen the maroon color because she didn't want to be too visible in the dark. Some of the men and women she had seen walking up Russell Street from the hospital wore bright white coats or pants, and when a car came around the corner they seemed to glow in the headlights. The ones who wore dark blue or maroon were almost invisible.

Judith put on the pair of walking shoes she had chosen and checked the pant length again. The pants came right to the top of the shoes and rested there with only a half inch or so of overlap. That was just right. She lifted the loose pullover top and looked at her bare stomach. That was the only place for a gun. The loose top would cover it.

She stared into the mirror. She made a serious face, as though she were a nurse hurrying down a hallway to a patient's room. Then she tried an empty face, and decided that was the right one. She wasn't going to be clapping a defibrillator on somebody's chest. She was just going to be a young woman coming off a long evening shift.

Judith used an elastic band that matched her scrubs to tie her hair in a ponytail, then put on the clear glasses she had bought in the hobby shop. They were for protecting people's eyes when they worked on crafts, but they looked just like regular glasses. She looked smart in them.

She took off her top and picked up the roll of adhesive tape she had bought. She wrapped it around her waist twice, then twice more to hold Mary Tilson's gun so it rode comfortably above the waistband without tugging on her pants. Then she put on her loose top and checked the effect. The gun was invisible.

She put on the hooded waterproof jacket she had bought when she had arrived in Portland, and decided the effect was right. It could rain in Portland at any time, and she had seen that the people she wanted to look like all wore jackets at night.

Judith examined the fabric purse with the long strap that she had carried in Denver, and tried it with her work outfit. She could fit the adhesive tape and the steak knife in it easily.

Judith looked around her small apartment to assess her preparations. She had already packed her suitcase. If she needed to run, she could. The place looked neat, nearly empty, and clean. She carefully folded her jeans and T-shirt, put them in a paper sack, and brought it with her suitcase.

She had a feeling of elation as she stepped out of her apartment and went down the back stairs to the outside. The night was clear and calm, a little like the late nights she had loved when she had been a little girl. There was a silent, private emptiness. There was nothing for a block or two that was moving, and the lights from the big busy streets to the south were blocked by apartment buildings.

She put the suitcase and the clothes in her trunk and started the car. She looked at the clock on the dashboard. It was eleven-fifteen, time to be moving. She let the car drift quietly down the alley behind the building, then accelerated gradually as she moved up the street.

Judith drove across the Broadway Bridge to North Interstate Avenue, then turned onto Northeast Russell. She could see the big shape of Legacy Emanuel Hospital as soon as she made the turn. She pulled over on the street near the east end of it and parked.

Judith looked at the car clock again. It was eleven forty-five. When she had followed Catherine up this street to her apartment building she had noticed that the activity picked up around midnight, which she assumed must be when the hospital shifts changed. She wanted to be ten minutes ahead of the change, so people would be leaving Catherine's building when she arrived. She got out of the car, put her keys into the pants pocket of her scrubs, and looped her purse strap over her shoulder.

She walked up to Catherine's apartment building just as a young man in green scrubs appeared in the lobby. She looked down into her purse as he hurried out of the building past her, but then she lunged ahead, caught the door before it could swing shut, and stepped inside. Her heart was pounding. She had made it past the first barrier.

But now Judith was in the lighted lobby, where people outside could see her, and anyone who came downstairs to leave would have to walk right past her. She stepped quickly to the row of mailboxes and read the Dymo labels stuck above them. There was one that said HOBBES. It was apartment 3F.

Judith opened the door to the stairwell and began to climb to the third floor. At least while she climbed, while she was in the deserted stairwell, nobody was looking at her. But when she reached the third-floor landing, she became tense again. She opened the door to the third-floor hallway a crack and listened. There were no voices, no footsteps, no sounds that indicated that anyone was awake. Judith moved cautiously into the hallway. She had never been in this building before, and so she had to think as she walked. She stepped along the hallway scanning, searching for any opportunity that would permit her to do what she wanted, and listening for someone who might stop her. As she came to 3D, she paused and listened for the sounds of people awake, then stopped at 3E and did the same, but there was nothing. She went on more slowly and quietly until she came to 3F.

When she had followed Catherine home last night, she had seen a whole row of windows light up. Catherine's apartment had to be big – at least three rooms along the side of the building, probably with the bedroom in the back, away from the noise of the street. But Judith couldn't know for sure. Catherine might be standing right on the other side of that door. Judith's hand went to her belly, and she felt the hard, reassuring shape of the gun under her shirt. She leaned close and pressed her ear to the door. Catherine's apartment was just as quiet as the others.

She prepared herself, then carefully touched the door handle at apartment 3F and tried to turn it, just in case Catherine had forgotten to lock it. The handle didn't budge. She looked closely at the lock on the door. She didn't need to try to slide a credit card between the door and the latch, or try to pry it open with the steak knife. She could see that the hardware was the heavy and expensive kind that was fitted tightly and would be sunk too deep into the receptacle to be opened.

She resumed her walk along the hallway. There was an unmarked door, so she tried it. The door opened. Inside were a set of circuit breakers and a supply of cleansers, carpet cleaners, mops, and rags. She stood with the door open and thought. She could pop the circuit breakers. People would come out of their apartments, and one of them would check the panel and flip the breakers back. But that wouldn't work unless the one who did it was Catherine. If she was asleep, she would never know it had happened. What would rouse her? Pulling a fire alarm would do it, but that would bring firemen and cops. She closed the door to the little room and moved on.

The only barrier that kept Judith away from Catherine was a single wooden apartment door. She had to think of a way to get past that door. Was there a way around it? Was there a way onto the roof? Maybe she could find a rope or make one, tie it to something solid – the central-air-conditioning unit, a pipe – and then lower herself down outside Catherine's window. She could look in and see her lying in her bed asleep. She could stay pressed against the window like a night creature. And then, when she was ready, she could fire through the glass. No. That was far too athletic for Judith – crazy.

She kept going, looking closely at everything she saw. The windows at the ends of the hallways opened, but that didn't seem to her to do any good. She studied the ceilings. They were made of plasterboard. If she'd had a ladder, she could go to the ceiling outside of Catherine's apartment, cut a hole in the plasterboard with her knife, climb up, and carve a hole into the ceiling on Catherine's side so she could climb down. It was crazier than the first idea: far too loud, and too likely to get her caught.

The doors were beginning to look less substantial. After all, they were made of wood. Maybe, in an hour or two, she could carve a hole through one of them with the knife, reach through it, and turn the handle.

If she had to, she could simply stay here – maybe in the third-floor storage closet across from Catherine's apartment – until dawn. She could wait and watch until Catherine came out. She recognized that as the first sensible strategy that had occurred to her. She had done the hard part, gotten in past the outer doors without being noticed. If she just stayed in the building, her chance would come. She decided to finish her tour of the building before she gave up and hid in the closet.

She reached the stairwell again, went back down to the lobby, and looked at the triple row of mailboxes. If the Dymo labels told her where people lived, then maybe an empty one would tell her which apartments were vacant. If she could find one, maybe she could break into it and wait in safety.

'Is something wrong?' It was a male voice from behind her.

She turned, her body instantly tense and ready to fight. He was in his fifties or sixties and he wore a uniform, but it wasn't medical like hers. He was balding and chubby. He looked like a janitor. She said, 'I forgot my keys.'

'Your apartment key?'

He didn't seem threatening now, but she knew it was an illusion. She couldn't make a mistake. 'Yes. I thought it was in my purse, but here I am, and it's not there. I'm hoping I didn't lose it permanently.'

'How did you get into the building at all?'

'As I was coming up the steps somebody else was going out. He held the door for me. I didn't know I didn't have my key until I got up there.'

'Do you have your ID?'

'Sure.' She was making a plan. It was just a series of pictures in her mind, a flash of images. She would fire, and step around him to go out the front door. She would dash back along Northeast Russell Street to the hospital. If she was being observed, she would go into the building as though she were late for the midnight shift, then come out of the hospital at the parking lot entrance with whatever stragglers were left, make her way to her car, and be gone.

She opened her wallet and held it up so he could see the Catherine Hobbes driver's license and the credit card. She pointed at the mailboxes. 'See? That's me – Catherine Hobbes.' She let her hand linger near the pistol she had taped to her body.

The man held out his hand. 'I'm Dewey. I do the handyman work for these apartments and three others that the company owns.'

'Pleased to meet you,' said Judith. She managed a sad smile as she shook his hand. 'We'll probably see each other a lot while I'm sleeping in the hall.'

'Don't worry,' said Dewey. 'I've got a grand master key for the building. I can let you in.'

'You can?' Her eyes widened, and her smile became real and grew. 'Oh, that's wonderful. You don't know how awful I felt. Thanks so much.'

'Don't mention it. What's the apartment again?'

'Three-F. But there are six or seven interns on my floor, and at least half of them will be trying to sleep off a forty-eight-hour shift. Do you think we'd be quieter if we took the stairs?'

'It's okay,' he said. 'I've had all kinds of calls to come here in the middle of the night, and the elevator never wakes anybody up. When it's a plumbing thing on an upper floor you've got to get up there quick, or it's going to start coming through the ceilings. You a nurse?'

'Hmm?'

'A nurse. Are you a nurse?'

She tried to think of something he would know nothing about. 'Yep. A surgical nurse.' She was fairly sure that anybody who'd had surgery would have been unconscious.

'You mean like when the surgeon says "Forceps," you're the one who says "Forceps" and hands them to him?'

'That's me. Only sometimes I hand him the monkey wrench or the pruning shears for fun.'

Dewey chuckled. He looked at the numbers lighting up above the elevator door: 2, then 3.

She had to get whatever talk there was going to be out of the way before the elevator door opened, and she needed to head off trouble. She reached into the pocket on the side of her purse and pulled out a twenty-dollar bill. 'I'd like to give you something for helping me out.'

He said, 'It's nothing.'

'Please,' she said. 'I insist.' She had to hold him off this way or he would expect to come in, have a soft drink, and be sure her faucets weren't leaking. She had to keep this under control and foreclose all chances of a mistake.

The elevator stopped and the doors slid open. She tiptoed to the door of apartment 3F, almost pantomiming the act of being quiet.

Dewey slipped his key ring off his belt and tried a key, but the lock on Catherine's door wouldn't accept it. As Judith waited, the noise of the keys on the ring seemed to her to be terribly loud. What if Catherine heard that jingling right outside her door? Even if he got the door open Judith might step inside and see Catherine standing there with a gun in her hand. Dewey held up his key ring again, picked another that looked like the first, and tried it. He pushed the door open, but Judith stepped forward and held it open only an inch. She leaned close, whispered, 'Thanks,' then slipped inside and closed the door.

It was dark. There seemed to be no sounds of movement in the apartment. Judith stood absolutely still, listening. She heard Dewey's heavy feet move off. After a few more seconds she heard the elevator doors open, then heard them slide shut. The last barrier was gone. She was in.

FIFTY-SIX

Judith felt relief, but it was only tentative. She was not yet sure that Catherine had not heard her enter. She listened and waited for a long time, and then began to orient herself in the darkness. This was a big open space, and ahead of her was the large window she had seen at the front of the building. She was standing in the tiled entry where Catherine had left a pair of shoes that must have been wet from yesterday's rain.

Judith stepped over them and onto the soft carpet, across the room to the window. She took her time, not rushing to the bedroom. It was only twelve-fifteen. There were probably day-shift people in the building who had not even gone to bed, and some of the night-shift people might leave late for the hospital.

She stood at the window and looked down at the street. She could see a white van down there that must belong to Dewey. It had steel screens in the back windows, probably to keep thieves from breaking in and taking Dewey's tools while he was inside some apartment building fixing a hot-water heater or something.

Judith knew that when this was over, Dewey's description of her would not be of much use to the police. It would make them lose a day finding all the female tenants Dewey didn't know and letting him see them, then showing him the identification photographs of the female employees of the hospital, and then probably interviewing the clerks at the stores where a person could buy hospital scrubs. It would all be a waste of time.

She wanted to wait until Dewey had left the building. She didn't see any need to harm him, and she knew that she would have to if he returned. She watched for several minutes, and then several more. Cars went by. The neighborhood had reached the hour of night when there were no pedestrians out, everyone's dog had been walked, and the hospital's visiting hours were long over.

Dewey's foreshortened, wide body appeared below the front window, coming down the front steps in a little dance. She watched him reach the bottom, walk down the sidewalk, step off the curb, and cross the street to his van. When he got inside she saw the van shake a little as though he were walking around in it, but then the tail-lights came on. The van slid forward, away from the curb, moved up the street, and disappeared. Dewey was gone.

She stared down at the street for another minute. Dewey did not return, and no one came to take his place. She looked at her watch. It was still well before one. She turned away from the window and studied the darker parts of the apartment.

It was sparsely furnished, just like the one Judith had rented on the west side, across the river. Catherine had not even added any pictures. She was treating her apartment like a hotel room, just a place where she came to sleep. Catherine was undoubtedly planning to rebuild her house very soon, and she would save her decorating ideas for that. Judith hated the thought of it – an insurance company paying to build Catherine a better, newer place. Judith had risked her life for that.

She walked slowly from the window across the room to a narrow hall. Her eyes were now accustomed to the dark. Every shape, every line was clear to her, but it had been cleaned of its color. Time had changed for her too: if she took a single step and did not take another for fifteen seconds, it made no difference. There was no need to risk making a succession of rapid sounds that did not fit with the slow current of the night. Soon enough she was standing in the doorway of Catherine's bedroom.

She could see Catherine curled up in the middle of a queen bed. She was smaller than Judith had thought from the television shots. Or maybe it had been the telephone conversations. She had always sounded big, authoritative, like a strict teacher. But Catherine was one of those people who looked like children when they were asleep, the closed eyes pressing the eyelashes against the cheeks, making them look longer, the skin on the forehead and around the eyes smooth and relaxed, the body curled on its side with the covers pulled to the chin.

Judith spotted Catherine's purse on the dresser. She drifted silently to it and reached inside. Her hands felt Catherine's wallet, a small leather case that seemed to be filled with business cards, a thin leather identification folder. She would go through all of that later. She didn't want to let her eyes stray from Catherine.

From this angle, she could tell that Catherine had left some things under the bed on the side where she slept, away from the door. She could see a long, black four-battery flashlight, a pair of slippers, and Catherine's gun, stuck in a tight little holster that barely covered the trigger guard and two inches of the barrel.

Judith drifted quietly to the bed, bent her knees, and picked up the gun and flashlight, then rose and stepped backward two paces. The pistol was a semiautomatic, and Judith had to get to know it by touch. There was a safety catch, so she clicked it off, then raised the pistol to aim at Catherine's head. 'Catherine,' she whispered.

She watched Catherine's face as the whisper reached her brain. Her body flinched involuntarily, her eyes snapped open, and her head gave a quick side-to-side motion that was like a shudder while she found the shadow near her bed. She started to sit up.

Judith turned on the powerful flashlight to blind her. 'Sit still, Catherine,' she said. 'Don't move.'

Catherine said, 'Hello, Tanya.' Her voice was a bit raspy from sleep, but she was making an effort to keep it artificially calm.

Judith knew Catherine was afraid. She could see Catherine's heart beating, making the thin pajama top quiver – *see* it. 'I'm not Tanya. I haven't been Tanya for a long time.'

'Who are you now?'

'Lie down again, this time on your stomach.'

'You don't really want to do this.'

'You really don't want to make me angry. You know that I wouldn't mind pulling the trigger.'

Catherine lay down again and rolled onto her stomach. 'You don't get anything for doing this. That's what I meant. I've been trying to help you come in safely for a long time. Breaking in here doesn't help your cause, and it's dangerous.'

'Hands behind your back. Cross your wrists.'

She watched Catherine do as she had ordered, then leaned over and pulled up the blankets, keeping Catherine's arms and hands on the outside. Catherine said, 'You came here to talk to me, didn't you? Well, I'm happy to listen, and I'll try to do what I can for you.'

There was silence. Catherine was beginning to feel heaviness coming on her. There had been a few seconds of hot panic, when she had heard the whisper in the dark, and then seen the shape that proved it had not been just a nightmare. But now the heat and the urgency were gone, and the cold fear had begun. Fear was bleeding her muscles of strength and making her nerves slow to transfer signals. Fear made her arms and legs weak and heavy. She concentrated on controlling her voice. She knew she had to keep talking. 'What can I call you?'

'Nothing.' The voice came from behind her now, beyond the foot of the bed. That was a very bad sign. Dennis Poole had been shot in the back of the head. The banker in Los Angeles had been shot in the back of the head. Gregory McDonald had been blindfolded in bed and shot in the head.

Catherine tried again. It was easy to kill someone who was lying facedown and silent. She had to keep talking to stay alive. 'If you were just planning to kill me, you wouldn't have needed to wake me up. You took a risk, so you must have wanted my help. That was a wise decision. Coming in to the bureau with me voluntarily to answer questions is the best thing you could do.'

'Answer questions?' The voice was bitter, angry. 'Are you still pretending that you just want me to answer a few questions?'

Catherine knew she had fallen into a way of speaking that could get her killed. She had to be extremely careful now not to offend her, and not to appear to be lying. She had to keep the same tone, not retreat. 'I'm a police officer. What I say and do have to reflect what the law says. You haven't been charged with anything. You're still wanted for questioning – here and in Arizona and California – so that's what I have to call it.'

'And when I'm done, I'll be able to walk out, right?'

Catherine spoke as carefully as possible. 'I think that you almost certainly won't. You're a suspect, and so you'll probably be detained. You can wait to answer questions until a lawyer is with you.'

'I'm not here for questions.'

'Why are you here, then?'

'I'm here for you. I'm what you asked for.'

'I asked you to come in to save yourself.'

There was a small, voiceless laugh, like a quiet cough that Catherine heard coming from the foot of the bed. She waited for the shot, the pain. But instead, it was only the voice. 'If I came in to the office with you tonight, the way you asked, you're saying you wouldn't get any benefit out of it?'

'Of course I would.'

'What kind of benefit?'

'Some people I respect would be proud of me.'

'Who?'

'Other cops. One in particular. He's retired, but he'd hear about it.'

'That's it?'

'Whenever a person in trouble can be persuaded to come in peacefully, it makes everybody safer. And no cop had to do anything that gives him nightmares.'

'God, you're such a liar,' said Judith. 'You'd be a hero. They'd promote you, and they'd show the mayor on television pinning a medal on you. That would be my life. You could pin my life on the front of your coat. Each time you wore it you could remember me.'

'That's what I've been trying to prevent – you losing your life.'

'Shut up, and don't move until I tell you.' Catherine heard her step in the direction of the closet. There were sounds of hangers scraping on the pole, then other sounds like the sliding and swishing of fabric. There were more sounds of hangers moving on the pole, a couple of dresser drawers opening and closing. Finally, after a very long time, she said, 'Very good, Catherine. You didn't move. Now listen carefully. Roll over to the center of the bed onto your back. Do not sit up.'

Catherine had been listening carefully to the sounds, but she had not been able to devise a way to take advantage of any possible lapse in Tanya's attention. Lying on her belly under the heavy blankets with her hands crossed behind her had prevented her from making any kind of quick move, and any move might be the wrong one. Now, as she rolled onto her back, she freed her arms, swept the blanket off her, and looked for Tanya. She was still standing at the foot of the bed, where Catherine could not hope to reach her before the gun went off. Tanya had learned a lot in a very short time.

Catherine saw the throw, and winced in advance, but what landed on her was an old white sweatshirt with the University of California seal on the front.

'Put it on.'

Catherine held it up with both hands, used the seal of the university to find the front, slipped it over her head and arms, and tugged it down in back. She knew she had to start talking again to keep herself human in Tanya's mind. 'Why do you want me to wear this?'

'For fun.'

That made Catherine feel the heavy, passive kind of fear again. Maybe Tanya had turned that corner too. Sociopaths talked that way. Things struck them as funny. Another bundle flew through the air. This one landed on Catherine's stomach, and she flinched. She touched it and felt denim. It was a pair of blue jeans. As she slipped them on, still lying on her back, she decided that Tanya had made a mistake. Clothes made her feel stronger, less vulnerable and helpless.

'All right. Sit up.'

Catherine sat up. The light came on, and she saw

Tanya. She felt her breathing stop for a second, as though her chest wouldn't expand to take in the air. Tanya was standing at the foot of the bed, holding her gun. She had taken off whatever she had been wearing, and now she was in one of Catherine's suits.

Tanya smiled. She opened the coat. Catherine's badge was pinned on the belt, where Catherine wore it sometimes. 'I'm Catherine,' she said. 'Maybe Cathy. I think I'll be Cathy.'

Catherine knew that she should have anticipated this. All this time, Tanya had been lost, trying to invent a person to be. Each time she had tried it she had succeeded for a time, been discovered, been chased. Of course this was what would happen. At last she had decided to stop being the runner. Now she wanted to be the pursuer, the one with the power and authority. 'Don't,' said Catherine. 'Don't do this.'

'You don't think I make a good Cathy?'

'It's not a name you can take, because it will get you caught, and maybe killed. People would know that something had happened to me.'

'Then what? They would search for me? They're searching now.'

'You've got to start thinking clearly about how to end this.'

'I have.' She was Cathy now. There was nothing that she needed to decide. 'All right, Catherine. Listen carefully. You and I are going out. We're going to walk together about a block to the west, and get into my car. There will be no talking along the way, and no noises. If I think you've made a noise that might wake people up, I'll wake them the rest of the way by killing you.'

'Where are we going?'

'I told you. My car.'

'After that.'

'We're going to go for a ride. Or I'd like to. Obviously, if at any point you cause me trouble, I won't be able to bring you any farther. You'll stop there.'

'Why are you doing this? Do you think I'm the only one who's been looking for you? I'm one little cop in one town. Police forces everywhere are searching for you right now.'

Cathy raised her gun and aimed it at Catherine Hobbes's head. Her expression was cold impatience. Catherine waited for the shot. From this distance Cathy could hardly miss her forehead.

Catherine wanted to close her eyes, but she knew instinctively that closing her eyes would be a bad idea, a signal of resignation and readiness. She forced herself to keep her eyes unblinking and focused on the eyes of – she had to accept the new reality – not Tanya, but Cathy. She tried to keep the fear and anger out of her eyes, and show only calm. The two women stayed that way for several seconds, an age, while Cathy decided.

Cathy lowered the gun a few inches. 'You're right,' she said. 'I did come to talk. I need to make a decision about how I want this to end. It will take time to make a decision and time to come to an agreement, and we can't do it in this apartment. Being here is too dangerous for me. We're going to my car now. Remember what I said. No talk, no noise.' She gestured toward the door. 'Stand up. Put on those slippers and walk to the door.'

Catherine looked at the closet. 'My sneakers are right there. Do you mind if I wear those?'

'Yes. Do what I said. Quiet.'

Catherine stepped into the slippers and began to walk, the slippers flapping at each step. Cathy was lying. She wanted Catherine to wear the slippers so she couldn't run or fight. Cathy had no interest in talking. She had become so much more sophisticated at killing that she now knew how to make the victim help her. She had learned that anyone she held at gunpoint would help her fool him. The victim might detect the false tone, but he would choose to believe it because it bought a few more minutes of hope, a few minutes when he could still be a person who was going to live and not a person who was about to die. It occurred to her that Cathy might be trying the lie for the first time. Everything a killer like Cathy did was a kind of experiment. She was learning now, preparing for the next person.

Catherine walked to the apartment door and stopped in front of it. From this moment on, she had to force herself to stay calm, to see every spot of the world around her with immediacy and accuracy – with her eyes and not her mind – and try to construct an advantage. Accepting this woman as 'Cathy' had been a first attempt to acknowledge the fluidity of events. Each second from now on, she would need to do it again.

Things were not as they had been, and not as they should be. They were what they had become. Catherine stood still and let Cathy open the apartment door. Catherine was thinking like a police officer again, and not like a scared young woman who had been dragged from her bed. She wanted to make sure that if she died tonight, there would be fingerprints here to tell the forensic team who had killed her.

She watched Cathy's left hand clasp the doorknob and open it. Then Catherine stepped out into the hallway. As Cathy pulled the door shut, Catherine watched surreptitiously. Cathy had taken a tissue with her from the box in the bedroom, and now she wiped the doorknob clean.

Catherine walked toward the elevator, but Cathy touched her arm and shook her head. They walked to the stairwell. Once again, Cathy used her left hand to open the door, and kept her right hand on the gun. Catherine had to step into the stairwell, then stand in silence while Cathy closed the door with her left hand and wiped off the knob. There was no reason to wipe off the fingerprints unless Catherine was going to die.

The two women walked down the two flights of stairs to the ground floor, and Catherine stopped. She considered the possibility that this was the place to make her stand. It was a lighted, closed vertical space with only cinder-block walls and a set of steel steps, so no bullet would go through a wall and kill a sleeping neighbor. She took too long to think about it, and the moment passed. Cathy had the door open, and she was waiting with the gun aimed.

For a second Catherine felt anger at herself, but that passed too: the opportunity had to feel right before she took it. An intuition was not magical; it was a conclusion that came from a hundred small calculations made at once – distance between her body and Cathy's, momentum and balance, eye motion and focus. If the conditions had been right, she had not detected it. The moment had not yet come. Catherine stepped out into the lobby.

She walked to the front door and waited. Cathy pushed on the crash bar and guided her out. They walked down the steps to the sidewalk. 'Keep going,' Cathy whispered. 'Cross the street.'

Catherine's eyes swept the route ahead, still trying to find a feature she could turn into an advantage. Could she use something ahead as a weapon? A distraction? Was there a dark place where she might be able to slip away and outrun Cathy? On this side of the street she saw only a broad sidewalk, a few young trees too thin to hide behind, a few parked cars. She longed for the comfort of a plan. When she realized that her desire was for the comfort, she abandoned it. She had to keep this difficult, not comforting. She had to keep searching, identifying, and evaluating, second by second. The moment would come, and she simply had to recognize it and act instantly.

She slowed her walk and turned her head slightly to get a view of Cathy, then immediately turned her head forward again to keep from alarming her. She felt a panicky shortness of breath. The sight she had glimpsed was unsettling. Cathy was not only wearing one of Catherine's new suits, with the coat unbuttoned, so that Catherine could catch a glint of her own badge at the belt; she was also carrying Catherine's purse, and her hair had been redone to resemble Catherine's style.

Cathy was walking along, planning to kill Catherine and take her name, identification, weapon, look – her place. The sight of it in the light of a streetlamp made it seem worse than just dying. This was a total obliteration, not like being killed but like being devoured.

She looked ahead to see if she could spot which of the cars parked at the curb would be the one, and her breath caught in her throat. It was a new, teal blue Acura. It was exactly the same as Catherine's car, the one that had been burned in the fire.

Catherine knew now that Cathy had stepped off solid ground, and then kicked reality to pieces behind her. There was nothing holding her to the world anymore except some perverse interest in playing in the spaces between things – moving, fooling people, hiding, changing herself.

Catherine could see where this was going, as though simple foresight were clairvoyance. Cathy had made herself look enough like Catherine so she could flash the driver's license or the police ID and get most people to think it was a match. She had probably become good enough at manipulating strangers to convince them that she was a police officer: people who met a cop weren't suspicious of the cop's identity; they were defensive about their own, anxious to get the cop's approval.

What was coming was handcuffs. The handcuffs were in the purse, and Cathy had been using the purse to shield her gun from sight. She must have seen or felt the leather case with the handcuffs. She couldn't hope to drive Catherine anywhere without them.

The handcuffs introduced a time limit. Cathy would walk her up to the car, and only then take out the cuffs. She would restrain Catherine's wrists behind her, and put her in the seat. Catherine had to make a move before that happened, before they even got near the car. Cathy was smart enough to know that rather than being restrained and put in a car, Catherine would take the chance of dying in a fight.

Catherine stared ahead to detect an advantage, but it wasn't there. It was still the broad, flat sidewalk, a few widely spaced saplings, a few parked cars. There were no garbage cans, no pieces of loose metal or wood, nothing she could snatch up and swing. The teal blue Acura was only forty feet away.

Catherine pivoted and swung hard. Her fist grazed Cathy's chin, slid off, hit her neck and collarbone. Cathy staggered back, and the gun fired. There was a ricochet sound as the bullet chipped the pavement at their feet and flew off into the night.

The gun came up fast. Catherine had no time to strike it away, so she charged under it and plowed into Cathy's midsection. Cathy's left hand tangled in Catherine's hair, tugging at it to pull her off, but Catherine kept pushing, digging in hard with her feet, and Cathy fell backward. Her back slammed into the door of a parked car, and the gun fired again. She couldn't get the barrel of it around to aim it, so she pounded it down on Catherine's head.

The pain exploded into a red flash in front of

Catherine's eyes, and she could feel it growing, blossoming. She punched at Cathy's belly, and her hand hit something hard. She knew the feel – a gun. Cathy had taped a gun to her waist under her clothes. Catherine hit at Cathy's face with her left hand and used her right to snatch the gun out of the tape, bring it upward, and pull the trigger.

Catherine Hobbes stepped off the airplane at Los Angeles International, hurried along the concourse carrying her overnight bag, and joined the gaggle of people stepping one by one onto the crowded escalator. She could hardly wait for it to take her down to the baggage area, where Joe Pitt would be waiting for her.

There was a tall man on the step ahead of her, so she had to look over his shoulder to see down through the glass wall below the escalator into the waiting area. She smiled when she spotted Pitt standing a distance away beneath the television sets that displayed flight arrival times. She could see him in profile, talking to someone. Catherine craned her neck to see the other person.

Beside him was a young blond woman clutching the extended handle of a small suitcase. She was clearly charmed with Joe Pitt. She reached up to touch her hair twice, her eyes widened as she looked at him, and she leaned forward to laugh at something he said. She gracefully reached into her purse, took out what seemed to be a business card, and held it out to Pitt. He took it.

Catherine's stomach felt hollow, and her mouth was dry. She sensed that she was watching her time with him ending, just as she had watched the end of her marriage – Catherine was once again on the outside, looking into a room, seeing what she was not supposed to see. She knew that Joe had probably not even intended anything like this. He had come to the airport to pick her up, and while he was waiting, he had found himself in a conversation. He was simply being Joe Pitt. One of the reasons he was fun to be with was that he liked women. He had a cheerful, mildly cynical view of things that made them laugh. She was sure he had not searched for that young woman. He had simply found her – probably looked at her appreciatively, or said something friendly – and she had liked him.

There would always be women like that, and they would always like Joe Pitt. If Catherine was with him, moments like this would always be part of her life. They would happen over and over, and she would always catch herself wondering. She had known enough to understand this from the beginning, and she had decided she could live with the feeling. But this was more than a feeling. How could she have picked another man who would not be faithful to her? Somewhere there was a man who would be satisfied with just Catherine Hobbes, but Joe Pitt wasn't the one.

Catherine looked over her shoulder, up the escalator. Maybe she could slip between the other passengers, make her way back up to the concourse, and exchange her return ticket for the next flight to Portland. She could call him on his cell phone. She would say, 'Joe? You know, I've decided not to fly down to Los Angeles after all. Something's come up and I can't get away.' What was she thinking? A woman – an armed woman, at that – scrambling the wrong way up the escalator would be a breach of security, and they'd probably close down the whole terminal while they arrested her.

Already it was too late to do anything. She reached the foot of the escalator, looked down, and stepped off. She could not even pause, or she would cause other passengers to pile up behind her. She looked up and spotted him again, now standing alone. She walked directly toward him, and watched him recognize her. He grinned happily and bounded forward as though he was going to hug her.

She veered to stay an arm's length from him, walking beside him toward the door to the street, and said, 'Hi, Joe. Sorry if I'm late. I hope you didn't get too lonely waiting for me.'

'No,' he said. 'I happened to run into a woman I knew from the days in the DA's office. She's a crime reporter for the L.A. *Times,* the one who covered Tanya's killings here.' He reached into his pocket, produced the business card that Catherine had seen him take a moment ago, and held it out to her. 'She asked me to give you her card. She wants to interview you about the case.'

Catherine glanced down at it, then stopped and faced him. She said, 'Aren't you going to kiss me or anything?'